# The MAGIC JOURNEY

# The MAGIC JOURNEY

## JOHN NICHOLS

Illustrations by the Author

BALLANTINE BOOKS • NEW YORK

Library of Congress Catalog Card Number: 77-13670

ISBN 0-345-31049-7

This edition published by arrangement with
Holt, Rinehart and Winston

Printed in Canada

First Ballantine Books Edition: May 1983

For Stephanie, with love

*Your theater is courageous and beautiful.*
*Fiestas await their orders.*
*In your wake, imaginations unfold.*
*Soaring is always the answer.*

*Juventud, divino tesoro,*
*ya te vas para no volver. . . .*
*Cuando quiero llorar, no lloro,*
*y a veces lloro sin querer. . . .*

**Rubén Darío**

# THE DYNAMITE SHRINE

# I

# Home Free

FORTY YEARS BEFORE the Pueblo electricity scam rocked Chamisaville a year after April Delaney had returned home to resurrect an embarrassingly radical newspaper called the *El Clarín,* April's father, Dale Rodey McQueen, a sometime prizefighter, medicine-oil hustler, cowpuncher, flesh peddler, and general all-around energetic ne'er-do-well from Muleshoe, Texas, entered Chamisaville seated behind the wheel of a rattletrap school bus riddled with bullet holes.

Almost immediately, this archaic vehicle, which was loaded to the ceiling with pirated dynamite bound for a black-market bonanza compliments of a fly-by-night mining operation near Leadville, Colorado, blew two tires and lost an axle in one of those famous Chamisaville potholes which abounded on the brink of the Great Depression when the North-South Highway was but an unsightly dirt path betwixt Here and There.

In those days, Chamisaville, a soporific little town of relatively forgotten people, would just as soon have stayed forgotten. Sheep and cattle outnumbered human beings by a hundred to one, several dozen big old horses were always tethered to hitching rails around the dirt plaza, and the ten automobiles usually parked between those horses were already nearly twenty years old. A stagecoach rattled irregularly into town from a railhead at La Piedra across the gorge. And a lone hostelry, the seedy Plaza Hotel, catered to any prospectors, missionaries, or presidential candidates happening to employ a wrong turn somewhere between St. Louis and San Diego.

Rodey McQueen took one look at the place, belched, and wondered how to get himself and his dynamite out of that godforsaken pastoral burg. After a while, in a cave-like but animated thieves' den called the El Gaucho Bar, he happened onto a loquacious young lout named Cipriano García, a boozer by trade speculating in some idle smithing on the side. And after six white workhorses had hauled his bus to Cipriano's spread two miles north of town, in a battered little community called Vallecitos, McQueen retired to the Plaza Hotel. There, having stoked up on enchiladas and warm beer, he settled into a poker game with the young hotel owner, Miss Loretta Wellington Shimkus, and a gaunt, sloe-eyed lawyer from Old Mexico, Virgil Leyba. As they played, Virgil launched into the mournful story of his tragic career up until that precise moment, which happened to be the evening of his thirtieth birthday.

Born at the century's turn in the small Morelos town of Cuachitlán, Virgil was, by age thirteen, a confirmed Zapatista, the only survivor in a large peasant family, half of whom had been executed by Juvencio Robles's federal troops while the other half were being deported to Quintana Roo. During the revolution, Virgil was first a courier, then a soldier, finally a lawyer. He had seen half the Morelos small towns and almost all its arable land burned over, and he had helped bury a thousand comrades. Eventually, exhausted by the killing, he had traveled to Mexico City during that lull when the official carnage ceased, obtained a degree, and returned home determined to legally assert the Plan de Ayala, securing for his people their permanent rights to long-held and oft-lost ejido lands.

"When I arrived at my hometown," he told Rodey McQueen, "there was nothing but graves, char, ruins. The trees, splintered and leafless, cast gruesome reflections in river water that ran black. As for the plaza fountain—it was blown to bits. A dead quiet weighed down the air; ashes fluttered in every stirring of rotten breezes. I rode into the plaza and dismounted. A group of crippled old folks limped around a corner and approached me, carrying a tin-plated wooden box caked with dirt, warped from water, burnt by fire. Five old men, several women, all that remained of our town. We squatted together in the plaza; they opened their box. Inside were all our town's papers to every ejido, the legal lifeblood of each person who had ever inhabited our village. The papers had been protected all during the revolution—hidden, buried, guarded with lives. Blood discolored the wood, it stained the legal papers, which were also burnt and splotched from rain water, in many places illegible. But the old people spread out these documents on the plaza dust, and, adjusting a pair of glasses missing one stem and a lens, the leader of that inconsequential group, Emiliano Tafoya, began reading to me about the land, where it lay, and what he knew of the fate of those who owned it. 'With these papers,' he swore bitterly, 'we will begin again.' "

For six years Virgil was engaged in the legal and emotional struggle to recapture the correct destiny of his hometown. Before the revolution, Cuachitlán had been controlled by a huge sugar hacienda. During the terrible decade that hacienda had been abandoned; its owners fled to the capital or to the United States. But with Carranza, and then Obregón in power, the planters decided to return and retake their empire. And Virgil commenced a seesaw existence between Cuachitlán and Mexico City, where he filed papers, badgered the law courts, and bargained with the central government, seeking the rights and the land guaranteed by those legal papers. But Zapata was dead; many other chiefs had retired; and the new government—the "Revolutionary Government"—had decided to face reality. Cuachitlán's fight became a losing battle.

To make the town viable and strong again, Virgil and Emiliano Tafoya searched throughout Mexico for refugees from their village. Sometimes they brought back a single man, occasionally an entire family, more often than not only gunnysacks carrying bones for reburial in home soil. Meanwhile, the hacendados rebuilt their mansions and reclaimed their land. Clashes between the peasants and the owners occurred. Compromises were enacted, rescinded—the government vacillated. The farmers, eased by false hopes, suffered little nibbles to be taken from their ejido land, and won that land back in the state courts, only to have a federal court restore the land and the neighboring acreage to the cane planters.

One night, finally, Emiliano Tafoya removed his broken glasses and, leaning back in his chair, closed his eyes and tipped his head until blindly facing the smoky ceiling. He declared: "Everything that we fought for we are losing. In two years the hacienda will control all the land it cost us ten years of bloodshed to win back after they robbed it from us in the first place. We will again be a miserable town of jornaleros, stumbling along on the brink of starvation, slaves to those plump bastards."

Virgil, a tired, pale young man wearing an ill-fitting gray suit, an uncomfortably starched shirt, and a necktie, gazed morosely at the old man.

4

"All the old chiefs are dead or compromised," Emiliano continued. "I don't think the revolution can begin again."

Leaning forward and placing his hands on the table, he opened his eyes. "Still, I know where there are rifles and some ammunition, and I think we must go to war. I am tired from trying to capture with paper and words what it is only possible to win successfully from the barrel of a gun."

Two nights later the thirty-six-hour revolution of Cuachitlán occurred. Eleven men, among them Virgil and Emiliano, assaulted and occupied the hacienda. A half-dozen foremen were immediately executed by firing squad; forty laborers imported from other states were ordered to stand and join the uprising or leave immediately. Other Cuachitlán citizens, among them many women and children, set fire to the cane fields, and entire families recaptured small huts they had owned before the hacendados returned.

Government retaliation was swift and predictable. Two hundred federal troops, some of them revolutionaries only a few years earlier, marched from the nearest railhead. After shelling the hacienda for an hour with a half-dozen cannons, they attacked. Against them stood eleven men with rifles and a hundred other men, women, and children throwing stones and sticks and brandishing shovels, pitchforks, machetes—anything they could get their hands on. In twelve minutes, fifty-three Cuachitlán peasants died; two federal soldiers were killed. Thirteen prisoners were immediately shot or clubbed to death.

"Me, I had five bullet holes in myself," Virgil said with a sudden wry grin as he spread out two pair, aces and eights, and reached for the pot. "But I had lost most of my blood over the past fifteen years, so there wasn't much remaining to lose. They left me for dead, and when a detachment of federales appeared next morning to help bury the dead, I had escaped. It took nearly three months, but I made it out of Mexico to Chamisaville. I have relatives in this town."

At that stage of their poker game, Chamisaville was rocked by a stupendous explosion which instantly denuded fifty pigeons roosting in the cupola atop the Plaza Hotel: their feathers rained into the plaza, alighting upon a mangled heap of horseflesh, splintered wagons, and a crumpled Packard touring car. Every window within a three-mile radius was shattered by shock waves; every cottonwood and chinese elm in town was uprooted and

5

stripped of its foliage, providing easy firewood pickings for the next three years. Yet, being squat and thick-walled, most adobe houses in town and the surrounding area withstood the explosion, thus saving a great many lives, including those of Rodey McQueen, Virgil Leyba, and Miss Loretta Shimkus, who disentangled herself with astonishing aplomb from the twisted branches of a coat rack, staggered rather drunkenly over to the poker table—which had not budged an inch—and, after carefully fanning three kings across the green baize tablecloth and copping the pot, she demanded to know, "What in tarnation was that?"

At the time, nobody would have thought to reply: "That was the explosion heralding the Betterment of Chamisaville."

But it was.

Bootless and hatless (though otherwise unscathed), Rodey McQueen lumbered outside and hightailed it up the north-south artery to the edge of a steaming crater commencing about a half-mile from Cipriano García's Vallecitos smithy.

McQueen groaned—all was lost!

But then, utterly dumbfounded, he rubbed his eyes, pinched himself, and gasped incredulously. For as the smoke cleared, and as tiny particles of his atomized school bus no larger than pollen flakes settled like a fine, golden gauze onto the crater floor, he spied, standing at the heart of this preposterous holocaust, a man, clad only in boots, and holding, in one hand, a single rose—Cipi García himself, minus every personal possession he owned except the boots, that rose, and his life, unscratched by a dynamite blast, which detonated four feet from his head, had leveled everything else within a half-mile radius from where he stood.

At first, McQueen figured his Leadville trip was a total bust. But then, as a smattering of local farmers began to arrive and hesitantly poke about in the smoking ashes with their canes, shovels, and rifle butts, cautiously circling by oblique and disinterested routes ever closer to Cipi García, ideas began to form in the Muleshoe ne'er-do-well's larcenous noggin.

"A miracle," one hunched old crone, dressed in black, whispered, reverently blowing her nose on a hand-embroidered handkerchief as she pointed, not only at Cipi García, but at the large steaming hot springs uncovered by the blast.

6

Another tottering ancient, outfitted in baggy Levi's, sporting a Villa moustache and a cheap straw cowboy hat with the steam-bent brim tucked over in front, responded in kind:

"Yes. I don't believe it. Most certainly a miracle!"

EIGHT DAYS LATER, Rodey McQueen, Cipi García, and a taciturn young Chamisaville Pueblo man, Icarus Suazo, added some finishing touches to the Holy Chapel of the Dynamite Virgin and stepped back to admire their handiwork.

Located at the exact center of the still faintly sizzling crater and garnished on either side by the large pools of recently discovered mineral waters casting a theatrical mist across the scene, the chapel was a tiny, whitewashed adobe structure, so humble it was pretentious, with clear natural-glass windows and a small bell tower. Narrow wooden pews flanked an aisle that terminated at a single, lovely rosebush framed by two sawed-off concrete pillars, painted red and lettered in black (DANGER—DYNAMITE), dangling heavy rope imitation wicks from their tops. Several hastily commissioned retablos gracing the wall behind the rosebush depicted the Our Lady of the Dynamite Virgin blessing a kneeling, naked, and downright contrite Cipi García.

Before the retablos' paint was dry, Rodey McQueen had located a telephone, using it to transmit a Cipi García Miracle scoop to the foreign editor of the *Capital City Reporter,* a paper whose hometown lay eighty miles to the south. One day later, a steaming Ford motorcar lugging a dozen local and wire-service reporters, photographers, and well-dressed female hangers-on chugged into the valley. As the women, daintily wielding pastel parasols, tiptoed sweetly through the ashes as if posing for a Sunday afternoon pointillist, the photographers snapped pictures of Rodey McQueen with his arm around Cipi García, and the reporters interviewed the former blacksmith, who expounded at great and flowery length upon the cosmic aspects of this incredible occurrence.

Hearing this colorful bombast, and observing the effect it had upon the reporters, photographers, and parasol ladies, Chamisaville's young sheriff, R. J. García, suddenly found an idea-whose-time-has-come dawning on him. Sidling over to McQueen, he politely queried the fast-talking medicine man about the exact nature of the license pertaining to the combustible materials responsible for the pit obliterating no small amount of acreage under his law-enforcement tutelage.

Within minutes, R. J. García began turning up in the photographs of Cipi García and Rodey McQueen. And later on—as the Ford motorcar timidly crept along a narrow dirt path descending through the precipitous Rio Grande Gorge—the reporters, scanning their notes, discovered that one R. J. García had mysteriously materialized into a downright chummy partnership with García and McQueen Enterprises, Inc. "Yes, *we* plan to maintain this as a permanent shrine," one reporter had him saying. And: "No, nothing illegal was implied by the blast," he had assured them confidently. "A purely accidental explosion."

Four days after Cipi García feature articles and photographs appeared in the *Capital City Reporter* and in a thousand papers across the nation subscribing to one wire service or another, the first pilgrims began trickling into Chamisaville. Some were crippled; many flaunted health, youth, vitality; a few dropped to their knees at the crater's edge and humbly crawled to the shrine. Upon arrival, they found it refreshing to roll up pantlegs or demurely hoist skirts so as to bathe their aching feet in the soothing mineral waters. Inside the chapel, they encountered Cipi García himself, unctuous and humble, his eyes already glazed by dollar signs, a man only too willing, for those pilgrims clinking donations into the silver bowl at the door, to bless, kiss, and even autograph a passel of pamphlets (on which the ink had not yet dried) describing his life story and the miraculous annihilation of Vallecitos through which he had unaccountably lived.

About this time, a grandiose yellow vehicle emerged from a dustball which had been rolling steadily southward down the straight dirt highway for half an hour. Out of this car stepped a crusty old deus ex machina named Philpot Eggington, accompanied by his radiant teen-age daughter, Cynthia, both residents of Denver, Colorado. Eggington, whose fortune had been bullying these parts for quite a spell, bankrolling various major sheep operations and other commercial endeavors, could call most financial shots long before the trigger of pecuniary fate sent the proverbial economic hammer of marginal speculation into the rimfire cartridge of a potential killing; hence he immediately buttonholed Rodey McQueen, introduced himself, and said, "Son, you've got a problem."

"Problem?" McQueen exclaimed, thoroughly astonished. "I made thirty-eight dollars in pennies, nickles, and dimes today, and I ain't even scratched the surface. I'm sitting on a veritable gold mine and you're teling me I've got a *problem?* Hogwash, mister! Picking these pilgrim chickens is easier than hogging catfish! Go back where you came from and don't distract me from counting my money."

"Listen you two-bit, randy, unwashed son of a bitch," Eggington explained. "I control three large mercantile and outfitting stores in this part of this state and I'm the biggest goddam sheepman in New Mexico, Colorado, Utah, and Arizona. I'm on what's left of the stock exchange in New York City and I own three Colorado banks the Crash has literally bypassed. One year later I'm twice as wealthy as I was twelve months ago. I've got oil and cotton interests in the South, and mining in the North. Now, as perhaps you may already have noticed, this miraculous dynamite shrine—hot-springs crater you've got going here is worth its weight in gold, but I don't think I need tell you it ain't worth penguin dung without the capital to develop it. I'm talking about another hotel, maybe several in town, and that takes labor, which I can control if I want to, and that takes financing of the most powerful kind, which means credit to get it. In one month those hot springs could be enclosed, concretized, glamorized with a little landscaping, and then you're going to need bathhouses, exercise rooms, a restaurant. Pilgrims in this town means hay for their horses if they're riding, or, better yet, gas for their automobiles if they've got them, and they'll have them. And right now I pump the only gas in town right out front of my company store, and if you think I'll let you compete with me, you're crazy. I'll call up whoever's the head of whatever gas company you contact and tell them who I am and what I'll do to them if ever they dare send you even one single keg of uncut crude, so help me God. Not to mention the impossible time you'll have trying to convince the state they should finally pave this North-South Highway in order to facilitate the rush to your bonanza, if I'm against you. Furthermore, have you been watching these pilgrims? The pamphlet was a good idea, the bowl at the door is fine, but my God man, where's your vision? You'll need a shop that manufactures those wax stomachs, eyeballs, arms, legs, whatchamacallits, to

9

hang on that rosebush in there, plus candles to light for this, that, and the other thing. And how long do you think that rosebush will last? Watch these people, they're religious thieves. Every last one cops a petal—that bush will be naked in a week at this rate, in an hour if business picks up like it should. Around Easter time it wouldn't surprise me if you lost a bush every fifteen minutes, so we're talking here about a big, *big* nursery operation—greenhouses! And maybe you noticed, maybe you didn't, but across from the Plaza Hotel, next door to the county courthouse, there's a Chamisaville First State Bank, and believe it or not, mister, that's more than half my institution and it's the only bank in town."

"You're right," McQueen murmured contritely, his eyes laying more than a little sugar on Cynthia Eggington, who smiled provocatively in return. "I do have a problem."

Philpot Eggington wheeled, said "Come along, Cynthia," and, with his daughter safely ensconced on the plush leather seat beside him, he told the Muleshoe conman: "We'll sit down and start hashing out the details by phone in the morning."

Then, laying a finger beside his enormous vehicle's gas tank, up the highway he rose.


VIRGIL LEYBA had overheard their conversation. Addressing Loretta Shimkus, he said, "I'm tired. Let's go for a moment to Nobody Mountain."

They rode horses back down the dusty highway to town, turned east at the plaza, and trotted quietly along the Plains Road, another dirt track, only recently enlarged for automobiles, that funneled traffic up through Chamisaville Canyon and over the Midnight Mountains at Bad Arrow Pass, descending the eastern slope of that southern Rockies chain onto the Great Plains. The short stretch Virgil and his woman traveled bisected La Ciénega, a rich bottomland community of small farms nourished by the Rio Chiquito, a tiny stream with origins eight miles up the canyon in a high, meadowy basin known as the Mosquito Valley.

The riders had only gone two miles when they pulled off the road at the base of a soft mountain foothill and climbed for five minutes up a narrow path winding through piñon pines and juniper trees to the bald top of the hill, from where they could view the entire valley.

Virgil produced a tobacco pouch and paper, rolling a

cigarette for himself and Loretta, and they smoked quietly, gazing pensively down at the valley. Most immediately at their feet lay the La Ciénega community—damp, green, pastoral. Casual bunches of sheep, cattle, and horses grazed; some fields glittered silver where men and boys were irrigating; other lands had recently been mowed by horsedrawn sickle bars. La Ciénega had a bar, also a tiny church, and a graveyard—the camposanto. Too, there was a small schoolhouse with swings and a basketball area in the dirt yard. For groceries and mercantile needs, the people shopped in Chamisaville.

Between La Ciénega and Cañoncito to the south stretched five miles of unused sagebrush land. Beyond it, the Rio Puerco and Magpie Creek met in another small valley bordered on its northern edge by Cañoncito, on its southern edge by Mota Llano, communities similar to La Ciénega, each with its own small church, camposanto, bar, and schoolhouse. Immediately west, the sightly larger community of La Lomita boasted a big church, a general store, a bar and dance hall, a miniature post office, and a community center.

Farther west along the Rio Puerco still more communities blossomed—Los Valerios, Borregas Negras, Ranchitos Abajo—each highlighted by ancient housing clusters beside the river, always featuring a church, a camposanto, and a school. At Ranchitos Abajo, the Rio Puerco joined the Midnight River, a stream descending through the Indian Pueblo north of Chamisaville and meandering past Vallecitos, then curving westerly into García and Alamito and Ranchitos Arriba, arriving eventually at the valley's southwestern outpost, Ranchitos Abajo.

At this juncture, the Midnight River dived into a small gorge, some of whose boulders were decorated with ancient petroglyphs; six miles later, it emptied into the Rio Grande. The green vega land within the villages of Ranchitos Arriba and Abajo, García, and Alamito halted abruptly at a sagebrush mesa that continued uninterruptedly for five miles to the Rio Grande Gorge. Beyond the gorge, on this quiet evening, Virgil and Loretta could dimly perceive the smoke trail of a narrow-gauge train heading for La Piedra, twenty-five miles due west of their lookout.

Chamisaville itself, located at the center of all these communities, was the hub of a rough wheel. At the heart of this hub stood the plaza, featuring the most important buildings in Chamisa County: the First State Bank, the

11

Plaza Hotel, the county courthouse and jail, one company store and feed bin with a gas pump owned and operated for the special benefit of sheepmen, a Woolworth's five-and-dime, a drugstore, the El Sol movie theater, three liquor stores and two bars—the Cucaracha and the El Gaucho—Don Jefe's Indian Curio Trading Post, Chamisaville Boot and Saddle, the Prince of Whales Café, Jeantete's Furniture and Hardware, Romero's Bakeshop, the regional Forest Service headquarters, and the *Chamisaville News* office, complete with a printshop in back. Dominating the plaza's central, park area was a small wooden bandstand; nearby loomed a concrete monument and flagpole honoring the town's World War I dead.

Directly west, a cluster of impressive buildings featured the Catholic church, its parochial school, and the Chamisaville elementary and high schools. Next door, a football field, where a few bedraggled dandelions and some fuzzy yellow foxtail tried to pass for grass, petered off into a bare dirt baseball diamond. North, east, and south of the plaza, a few impressive adobe houses demanded attention. Some, reeking of flowering lilacs, hollyhocks, hummingbirds, and butterflies, even flaunted quasi-manicured yards. They belonged mostly to a few merchants and company-store employees, to the druggist, to some theater, five-and-dime, newspaper, bank, and hotel people, and to several successful farmers. Nearby, Chamisaville's modern wonder, a brand-new sewage treament plant, which to date had fifteen hookups, sparkled in the evening dew. Beyond, Chamisaville was simply a larger version of all its satellite communities, the patchwork fields and small orchards sustained by a complex pattern of silvery irrigation ditches, as numerous and as necessary to life as the veins and arteries nourishing a human body.

In all, among the dozen farming communities, including the Pueblo, there lived approximately four thousand people, Spanish- and native-speaking for the most part, with a smattering of Anglos who already controlled just about every business in town necessitating a cash flow except the Catholic church.

That the valley's small farmers and Pueblo dwellers were impoverished went without saying. That many of them, in particular the sheepherders, had been mercilessly exploited for years by absentee-landlord sheep companies, was also a given. Yet for centuries these people had been developing the suffering of subsistence survival to a fine

12

art, and they had already lasted longer than many civilizations. And although, since the end of the Mexican-American War, the United States government had systematically managed to channel much communal land-grant and Indian territory into national forest and Bureau of Land Management coffers, there remained still, in 1930, land and water enough to go around. Meaning the valley yet remained a place where human beings with roots into land and the indigenous cultures could survive with some dignity. A rhythm existed here; the people were relatively self-reliant; and, if it offered no less than a truly difficult life, the valley also, truly, was home.

Virgil Leyba rolled and lit another cigarette and turned his attention to the sore spot on the landscape below, that crater, the hot springs, Rodey McQueen's preposterous shrine. Ridiculous and lurid as it might seem—nothing that tacky or openly exploitive could expand beyond its own distasteful vision—Virgil nevertheless murmured unhappily: "God dammit all anyway." And Loretta nodded her head in agreement.

Churches began ringing the Angelus. A fine beige mist, stirred up during the day by the wind, by horses on dirt roads, by wagons and the few automobiles in town, now hung low over the fields and houses; it seeped dreamily through puffy, twisted cottonwoods. An evening chill glided off the mountain slopes. A few fires started, and ax blows resounded faintly. Kids, who had been catching fish with their hands along the riverbanks and in irrigation ditches, were walking home carrying stringers heavy with brown trout, cutthroat, a few rainbows. Sheep bells tinkled. And a stagecoach barreled along the western mesa in a great dusty cloud, bringing a new batch of pilgrims over from the railhead at La Piedra.

WORD WAS OUT. The shrine had become world-famous overnight, thanks to a deluge of shrewd publicity bombast initially financed by Philpot Eggington, and then copiously promulgated by Rodey McQueen when the enterprise almost immediately feathered him in riches. Exactly one year after Cipi García pulled his phoenix act minus everything except a rose and his boots, McQueen took out a million-dollar life insurance policy on his main attraction. Cipi was worth that much, if not a lot more. Thus equitized, come wintertime, when both the North-South Highway and the La Piedra stagecoach road dissolved into impassable trenches of muck, McQueen felt able to take his pious humbuggery on the road. Shaking down southwestern tank towns at first, they soon graduated to St. Louis and San Francisco. And, within two years, the Cipi García Dynamite Miracle Show was cracking New York, London, and Paris.

It was a curious entourage that traipsed around the world from November through March, pitching a humble white tent lacquered with rose tattoos on the floor of the Cow Palace, the Rose Bowl, Madison Square Garden, and the Gare St.-Lazare. Inside the tent, Cipi García, R. J. García, Rodey McQueen, and Icarus Suazo received a million pilgrims, hawking pamphlets and sacred miniature wooden dynamite sticks (for which the Pueblo, thanks to Icarus, had the production contract) while allowing the gullible gathered multitudes to hear about the miracle from Cipi García's own mouth. This done, the pilgrims kissed Cipi's symbolic boots. Their ardent lips wore out five pair each winter.

As the road haul skyrocketed, and as the shrine itself became ever more popular, Rodey McQueen began to curse the day he had allowed R. J. García and Icarus Suazo—and even Cipi García—in on the play. For in his eagerness to get the ball rolling during those first reckless moments of inspiration while crater ashes were still settling, McQueen had hastily drawn up a document allocating to all involved an equal piece of the cake if they would only help construct the shrine and initiate the ballyhoo. The Muleshoe magnate especially resented Icarus Suazo's participation, having discovered early in the game that the imperturbable little man planned to invest his profits in a legal battle, on behalf of the Pueblo, seeking reclamation of all that land upon which the hot springs and the shrine stood, terrain formerly owned by the tribe.

In fact, Icarus Suazo had recently been appointed by his tribe to deal with all manifestations of the outside world pertaining to, or affecting, the Pueblo. At Chamisaville town meetings, or during official caucuses relating to one sort of election or another, Icarus was always present. He was inevitably called upon to state "how the Indians feel." He also acted as intermediary between the Pueblo governor's council and the mayor-domos and ditch commissioners representing Spanish-speaking communities irrigating off the Midnight River during any water squabbles arising between the two cultures.

14

Upon occasion, visitors utilizing the La Piedra stage-coach might pass a solitary horseman en route, none other than Icarus Suazo—mute, steady, dignified, with an old cavalry rifle in his saddle scabbard and a spanking new leather suitcase tied behind him where a bedroll should have been. Next day, passengers on the narrow-gauge train screeching nervously down toward the capital might find themselves facing this stern little man, perched stiffly beside his spiffy suitcase, that ancient rifle rigidly fixed in an upright position by his right hand. There followed long train and airplane excursions across the United States, then weeks of mysterious and convoluted meetings in sweltering Capitol offices dominated by cigar smoke and the American flag, during which time Icarus pleaded, threatened, and bargained with the government, asking for a return of fifty thousand sacred Pueblo acres harboring the legendary Albino Pine Tree (at the base of which arose the maiden springs of the Midnight River), which the federal government had appropriated as national forest land in 1906. Along similar lines, this diminutive, rigid man had recently filed some thirty-seven different lawsuits in county, state, and federal courts reclaiming Chamisaville terrain that only yesterday had belonged to the Pueblo.

In fact, Icarus had one suit brewing that, if successful, would eradicate Vallecitos, García, La Ciénega, Chamisaville proper, and Ranchitos Arriba in one fell swoop.

Upon first hearing of the Indians' hot-springs suit, McQueen and Eggington screamed so loudly Icarus backtracked, intimating that in return for the dynamite-fetish contract the Pueblo would cancel court proceedings against the Vallecitos land. "Done," growled McQueen. After all, at that point in time, the dynamite fetishes, brainchild of Sheriff R. J. García, seemed like a dull-witted endeavor at best. But before two years were up, the simplistic fetish had turned into a veritable gold mine, their hottest-selling item. By the mid-thirties, thanks to a WPA grant, nearly half the Pueblo was employed fabricating them in Mc-Queen's plant. And, while almost all the native earnings were channeled into the Albino Pine Defense Fund, at least half the Eggington-McQueen profits went to lawyers tangling with the Pueblo's battery of shysters.

The other half of their profits was invested in a slew of speculative Cipi García Miracle projects: underwriting the winter jaunts and the dynamite-fetish industry; erecting an honest-to-God service station on the North-South

Highway near the plaza; constructing the Dynamite Shrine Motor Court one block north; and wresting the La Piedra stagecoach concession from Loretta Shimkus, replacing the archaic wooden vehicle with up-to-date buses and limousines. Several additional endeavors, revolving around the shrine proper and having to do with bathhouses, tiling the hot-springs swimming pools, and building a new restaurant, golf course, and new tennis courts, called for a major injection of capital. But as none of the other partners had enough experience with money to believe it could grow when reinvested, responsibility for the bulk of these subsidiary projects had devolved on McQueen and Eggington.

Amid all these manipulations, the Denver tycoon and his Muleshoe apprentice were approached by a lean and hungry lunatic newly graduated from an Omaha undertaker's college. In honor of the Cipi García Miracle, Claude Parker wanted to embalm a whale and put it on display in Chamisaville for a year or two, charging admission to see it, more money to walk around inside, additional fees for being photographed at ease beside it—and the young man almost had them convinced. "Listen," Claude begged: "I know I can do it, just give me the chance."

"You can't embalm an entire whale," Philpot Eggington scoffed.

"Sir, please, don't you understand? I *can* do it, I know I can, it would be simple. I'll fly to San Diego, hire a crew, it'll take us—who knows?—maybe a week to harpoon the whale. I'll drain it on the beach, pump it full of juice, we'll load it onto railroad flatcars, unload it in the Capital City, lash it to several specially constructed rafts, haul it halfway up the Rio Grande using a narrow-gauge engine, and, where the train tracks leave the riverside, we'll switch to mules. When we reach the old La Piedra Junction road we'll only have to haul it—what?—another eight miles overland—"

In light of all this activity, the developers and their legal team, led by a dour young Dracula named Moe Stryzpk, had been striving to seize copartnerships in the rapidly expanding enterprises from the various local dupes involved, who could do nothing, in the long run, except be a drag on the industry. The heavies were not, however, enjoying as much luck effectuating this sellout as they had originally anticipated. Counting on primitive greed and a lack of sophisticated vision to make their cohorts easy pickings, the Eggington-McQueen cabal had decided to offer the natives, in return for a generalized quitclaim, a prodigious cash settlement, which R. J. and Cipi García and Icarus Suazo, never having seen such loot before, would be unable to reject. Rather than make the offer in a verbal or written form, Moe Stryzpk actually clanged cast-iron knockers at the homes of García, García, and Suazo, and, while proferring the legal papers for signature, he shoveled thick packets containing crisp new bills onto their respective tabletops from out a slim, pigskin briefcase.

Icarus Suazo sniffed a packet while his quick eyes flicked through the quitclaim clauses and propositions, then gave a tiny, disgusted little smile and said, "I'm not interested."

R. J. García also thoughtfully sniffed the greenbacks, as if wondering were they ripe enough or dry enough to bale, and finally said: "Mister, you should take your money and roll it up and kill flies with it."

At the sight of all those crackling dollars, Cipi García protested vehemently. "Oh, hey man, oh no, that's too much, man. Gee whiz. Pues, entonces, allí, ahora. All that for me? Who you kidding, man, I can't even get half of it into my bolsillos. Not all that, sir, really, that's too much, I don't need such riches, I'm just a humble peasant chaval, you know that, here, take this back, and this, this, and this, here, take all of it except just this one little packet, this is so much and my needs are so simple it could last a lifetime. I mean, I'm so humble, man, I can't even read or write. So what am I gonna do with all that mazuma? Here, if this is what Mr. McQueen wants, well, by gosh, he sure been good to me, you just give me that papelito and I'll sign my X wherever you want me to." But when the attorney, pointing to where Cipi should make his X, daintily pushed over the contract, the ex-smith turned carnival huckster wrote: *Shame on you, Mr. McQueen, for trying to take advantage of a pestiferous analphabetic little country bumpkin like me!*

Following these glum results, the Eggington-McQueen axis considered challenging the original contract in court, figuring superior contacts and cash could buy the system up to and through the Supreme Court, if necessary. But, taking the precautionary measure of running a financial profile on their partners-enemies, they learned everybody was raking in so much dough a court showdown might be suicide. Their fears were confirmed when, on behalf of

17

Cipi García, Virgil Leyba negotiated an audience in Kansas City with Clarence Darrow, who agreed to take the case. Even as Darrow threw in his hat, Icarus Suazo threatened to strike the Dynamite Fetish plant, plunging McQueen into a manic depression. And when a few errant shivers even tickled Philpot Eggington's spine, McQueen and Company pulled out of the courts, and immediately tranquility reigned supreme.

Though not for long.

Curious accidents began to happen. During a Sunday race at the Pueblo, the cinch binding a saddle occupied by Icarus Suazo to a quarter horse named Pueblo Boy snapped, spinning the saddle under the galloping animal. But Icarus popped slightly aloft so that he did not revolve with his gear, and when, in the next split second, the horse broke three legs in the saddle trappings, his rider merely gave another slight twist which had him tiptoeing on the stallion's flanks for a brief instant before hopping deftly to the ground, completely clear of the carnage.

One week later all four wheels on R. J. García's Ford patrol car fell off at once—while the car was parked in his driveway. Apparently, however, the sheriff had been cruising around town minus his wheel-lug nuts for the previous eight days—without incident.

But when Cipi García slammed his front door, causing the entire roof to fall in, it didn't take a college diploma to figure out that the Anglo Axis was still eager to become an uncontested monopoly. Fortunately for Cipi, he had banged shut the door on his way out of the building instead of into it. Nevertheless, the time had come to resolve this situation, which had begun to exhibit the earmarks of going off a deep end.

So Cipi asked his copartner, R. J. García, to ask his first cousin Fasho García, then a state representative, to ask *his* first cousin Primitivo García, to locate for them all the cleverest lawbooks in the Capital City. And four days later a tall, blond young Anglo with wide effeminate hips, a bulbous pink nose, and an aloof bourgeois gleam in his eye, disembarked from a splendiferous Reo and proceeded to found, or rather extend, one of the state's more merciless dynasties.

This legal button-man's name was Bob Moose, scion of awe-inspiring potentate Harold "Bull" Moose, the Capital City DA and capo of the most heralded (and pitiless) law, banking, and real-estate operation in the state. Always chary of sharing his own immediate territory, and with five sons eagerly snapping at his heels, it seemed to the Bull like a good time for expansion. Hence, when opportunity knocked, Harold sent son Bob north, not only to vivisect the natives, but also to get him out of his hair.

Discreetly shutting the door of his dusty motorcar, young Bob brushed himself off thoroughly, adjusted both the shoulderpads glorifying his double-breasted pinstripe suit and the front brim of his gray fedora, and headed at a no-nonsense clip through the large crowd gathered on the courthouse portal and straight for the First State Bank boardroom, a plush second-floor box that L'd off the bank building onto the minuscule county jail. Already gathered in this room by the time Bob arrived were Philpot Eggington, Moe Stryzpk, and Rodey McQueen. Also present were Icarus Suazo and his retinue, including two icy, long-haired thugs wearing sunglasses and VISIT ANADARKO lapel buttons, an enormous, grave-faced Pueblo teen-ager named Marshall Kickingbird (whom the tribe had elected to groom as its first homegrown legal counselor) and a brace of clean-cut Denver mouthpieces, Joe Brady and Win Potter.

R. J. García was on hand, of course, accompanied by his sullen cousin and bodyguard, Onofre García, in whose belt resided an enormous handgun of erudite lineage. Beside Onofre sat a fellow recently hired on to R. J.'s team, Wolf Hobart, a jolly, heavyset financial hatchet man based in Dallas; his pudge jiggled irritatingly whenever he laughed.

Last but not least, Cipi García was framed by his newest friend and mentor, an egocentric Hupmobile dealer from the Capital City, Randolph Bonney, plus his newly acquired accountant, a young, plump lambe lawyer and financial magician called Damacio Mares—gracious young thieves both—who'd been more than happy to motor up from the capital for this momentous confab.

Instinctively, Chamisaville's population understood the meeting was of great historical importance. Though many could not understand how, they felt that a mammoth re-distribution of territory, power, and wealth was about to occur. Among those swelling the portal and courthouse crowd were several Capital City and wire-service reporters; Chamisaville Mayor Rudy LeDoux and one of his sons, Jaime Bernardo; three town council members; three county

19

commissioners; the brisk, young Forest Service regional director, Denzil Spivey; and most pastors, priests, prelates, and poseurs representing the satellite communities' religious organizations, including dynamic young Father Molé from the central Catholic church.

Across the plaza, in Patrocinio Godoy y Godoy's bucket of blood, the El Gaucho Bar, numerous less-than-upstanding locals had tied their horses to the hitching post outside and gathered to consume vast quantities of cheap beer and wine while awaiting the boardroom meeting's outcome. Most notable among the boozers ensconced there was Jesus Dolores Martínez Vigil, a short, pudgy man of indeterminate old age sporting an old-fashioned greasy sombrero, a Villa moustache, and a heavy bulletproof vest made of thick hemp wrapped around his torso. Once the leader of an 1880s revolutionary outlaw group known as the Gorras Blancas, a contingent which had waged a guerrilla war against the cattle barons and government sharpies illegally taking over locally owned land grants, Jesus Etcetera was now pushing a hundred, or even more, nobody knew for certain. Some Chamisa Valley amateur historians, who claimed he had died years ago, actually suggested that the robust feisty little man who persisted in haunting the valley was merely Jesus Etcetera's soul wandering through purgatory. Others believed that Jesus was very much alive and would one day spark a White Cap army renaissance that would banish all the outsiders, newcomers, thieves, cattle barons, land hustlers, and tourist hucksters like Rodey McQueen from the picturesque Midnight Mountain area once and for all.

A *Chamisaville News* reporter, Juan Ortega, a bright young Cañoncito iconoclast, had gotten himself arrested the night before while staggering drunkenly around the plaza wielding a stepladder that kept knocking down evening strollers. Juan had vociferously refused to give up his ladder; hence it had been impounded with him. And at this very moment, Juan, the lone (and completely ignored) Chamisa county jail prisoner, was perched atop his ladder with an ear glued to the bottom of a soda glass pressed against the ceiling, a glass smuggled to him that morning by his lawyer, Virgil Leyba, in a large chocolate cake. The ceiling was fairly thin, and, as providence would have it, the thick rug usually carpeting the First State boardroom had been removed for cleaning only the previous afternoon by a chambermaid employed by Loretta

20

Shimkus, in the rear of whose premises was located the only cleaning establishment in town. Hence, through his glass, Juan could hear every word being spoken above his head.

Bob Moose hung up his hat, thumped his pigskin briefcase onto the mahogany table and unfastened the belt tabs, removed a sheaf of cream-colored papers as thick as a good sirloin, and said, "Gentlemen, I take it we are all gathered here in order to avoid, if possible, the sort of internecine warfare that most often destroys empires. Since time is valuable, then, I'm sure you'll all forgive me if I suggest we commence."

And so they began.

Moe Stryzpk Damacio Mares, and Wolf Hobart sized each other up while Bob Moose outlined the original contract, the current assets and structure of various Dynamite Shrine enterprises, and what future expansion might encompass in the form of personal commitment, capital outlay, income and other benefits to be reaped. Then he suggested several possible restructurings of the loosely formed association.

For the next few hours they haggled and quibbled, fought and thundered, bickered and bitched, exploded and driveled, glared dully, threatened, whined, laughed, plotted, swore, and whispered. In love with flowery rhetoric, Wolf Hobart talked too much; Icarus Suazo and Marshall Kickingbird were more conspicuous because they said nothing. Moe Stryzpk interrupted his imaginative doodling every eight minutes to rattle off an informed flood of facts, figures, and propositions with a deadly self-assurance that quashed conversation for a few seconds. Philpot Eggington blustered and sputtered, calling Bob Moose the "son of a philandering mugwump!" He was immediately ordered by his own attorney to apologize. Everyone took turns saying, "Gentlemen, *please*—" Having no idea what was going on, Randolph Bonney giggled a lot and chain-smoked Fatima cigarettes. Everybody else also smoked, except the Pueblo contingent and Onofre García, who was too busy scowling to light up. Rodey McQueen speechified elegantly about the necessity for harmony. And a very dour Damacio Mares threatened to snatch control of the Dynamite Shrine organization from the Anglo Axis if that axis didn't shape up. At that, Rodey McQueen bit clear through his cigar and pounded the table, then started climbing across

21

the table intending to keelhaul Mares; he had to be restrained by Moe Stryzpk.

Cool as an autumn cucumber throughout, Bob Moose rattled off an additional dozen alternate plans; they were promptly ridiculed by Philpot Eggington. Rodey McQueen suddenly agreed, however, that compromise was possible, if not probable. The VISIT ANADARKO thugs were sent to the Prince of Whales for midmorning sandwiches and coffee; Randolph Bonney volunteered to pick up the tab. Shedding suitcoats, ties, and shirt collars, they rolled up their sleeves. Bob Moose unveiled another plan, but Moe Stryzpk shot that profit-sharing outline full of holes. And Cipi García simply shot off his mouth.

"My investment brokers here are ashamed," Cipi howled dramatically. " 'You bumpkin!' they sob. 'Qué plebe más desgraciado!' they wail. 'You are being taken for a ride, fed to the sharks, plucked naked like a chicken, hacked apart with no feeling like a snake, stabbed like a sheep full of bloat. Green they are giving you,' my accountants advise. 'Green like in green alfalfa, and it's making this big gassy foam in your financial picture, and in minutes, if you allow it to go on, you will swell like a balloon and croak!' Del árbol caído, todos hacen leña," Cipi continued hysterically. "From a fallen tree, everybody makes wood. That's me, the fallen tree. I started it all, but where am I now? They want to push me out. They want to throw me to the dogs. Here, Cipi, here's a little bone, now, you go lie in the corner like a good little doggie and keep your fat yap shut. Well, to hell with that! Without me there ain't no miracle, and I want my equal share!"

They fulminated, cogitated, ranted and raved. Cipi García strutted, Randolph Bonney giggled, Bob Moose methodically laid out more alternatives, Wolf Hobart sweated a lot and wished he were on the Eggington-McQueen team because he could tell the lay of the land by now, Onofre García glowered, and R. J. García, undecided whether to fish or cut bait, instead pretended to be bemused by it all in a worldly fashion. Moe Stryzpk diddled on yellow legal pads while his big eyes behind Coke-bottle glasses perceptively quartered the room; and the Pueblo contingent sat there—solid, unbending, dead-quiet.

Rodey McQueen thumped the table, screaming at Cipi García and at the sheriff: "What'll you biggity, lit-up, doddering fools take to get the hell out of my business? Go ahead, name a price, try me! There's work to be done and

22

you fops are harvesting an outsize cut for cluttering up the scene! Hellfire and damnation! Intelligence around here is almost as scarce as bird dung in a cuckoo clock!"

"Don't be crude," Bob Moose cautioned.

They flailed, flapped, dickered, cajoled, harrumphed, and scratched their testicles. Copies of the one-page original handwritten contract made the rounds and everyone studied it ponderously with furrowed brows. It was so simple. And this thing was getting so complex.

Cipi García shouted, "I swear, on my mother's grave, that no two-bit Tejano like you, Mr. McQueen, is gonna con me out of my just deserts."

Cipi and the Eggington-McQueen machine traded insults for twenty minutes; everybody else burrowed heads into their hands. The room had grown heavy with smoke, sweat, and flies. Down below, people began drifting off for lunch; several bored horses whinnied; Denzil Spivey settled into a chair on the Forest Service headquarters portal and lit a pipe; pigeons cooed. In the El Gaucho Bar, Juan Bautista Godoy y Godoy, a Mota Llano sheepman and brother of the bar's dueño, Pat, threw his arm around Jesus Dolores Martínez Vigil's shoulders, clinked beer glasses with his La Ciénega friend, Espeedie Cisneros, and drank a toast to the memory of the Gorras Blancas. Five Cañoncito Arrellano brothers noted for their horse-racing prowess—Vidal, Genovivo, Telesforo, Cenobio, and Albino—joined in.

Then Espeedie Cisneros, a short, plump, mischievous buffoon, held up his hands for silence. "My friends," he cried happily, "I am now gonna tell you all the story of the Mejicano magpie and the gabacho flea!" And, while his drunken buddies applauded or groaned or cursed at the appropriate moments, Espeedie enthusiastically recounted his fable.

"It seems one day a Mejicano magpie felt a tickle on his rump. But as he went to peck the itch, he heard a tiny voice cry out, 'Please, please, Sr. Magpie. Don't hurt me. Don't eat me. I'm just a poor little gabacho flea, and I don't mean you no harm. Winter's coming and I'll die if you don't let me stay here under your feathers, up against your warm skin.' Well, the magpie was a compassionate (and also a very stupid) fellow, and, respecting the flea's plea, he left the poor little gabacho bug in peace. But then one day, while the magpie was picking corn kernels out of some barnyard pigshit, a gabacha flea hopped off a

23

nearby sow onto the magpie, and immediately engaged in some conjugal shenanigans with the gabacho flea. When the magpie went to peck this newcomer, she cried, 'Please, please, Mr. Magpie. I'm just a poor little gabacha flea, and I just married the gabacho bicho on your rump, and I don't mean you no harm. I'm pregnant, winter's coming on, and my children and I will freeze to death if you don't let me stay under your feathers, up against your warm skin.' Well, the Mejicano magpie was a sucker for any clemency petition based on motherhood and la familia, and so he didn't peck the gabacha flea, and let her and her novio cohabit on his rump to their hearts' content. That night the magpie went to bed resisting an urge to snap at the gabacho fleas whenever they took a little nip out of his fanny. By the time he woke up next morning, the gabacha flea had had a thousand babies, and they were all over his body driving him loco with their nibbling. Too late, the Mejicano magpie commenced pecking at those gabacho fleas, but already brothers and sisters were fornicating and having babies, and each time they bit the magpie they took out a drop of blood. Frantically, the urraca pecked and slashed and jabbed. But as fast as he could eat one, five more were born. Pretty soon he was pecking out his own feathers trying to get at them, going crazy from all the itching, and growing weak from loss of blood. Finally, he had no more feathers. Then a blast of icy winter air hit the weakened magpie, and he keeled over, frozen to death.

"With that," Espeedie concluded, "all the gabacho fleas went running off in different directions, each one looking for a tenderhearted lame-brained Mejicano magpie to exploit."

The bar exploded into applause and bitter cursing. Church bells rang the noon hour.

Taking a break, the boardroom gang caucused. Nothing had been accomplished, and yet something had been accomplished. They visited each other's groups informally, chatted about other matters, patted backs. All except for Icarus Suazo and Marshall Kickingbird, who remained seated waiting for the meeting to continue. Philpot Eggington uncorked a bottle of Tennessee sour mash, and the VISIT ANADARKO thugs were dispatched for glasses. Upon their return, Eggington toasted a "new Chamisaville." All except Icarus Suazo drank to that. More Prince

24

of Whales sandwiches arrived, and everybody except the tribal contingent chowed down.

During this lunch break, Juan Ortega descended the stepladder and sat on a cell bunk, riffling through his steno pad, making margin notations explaining his shorthand or elaborating on some complexity wherever he felt necessary. While he was thus occupied, Virgil Leyba located the cell key in a desk drawer, brought Juan some food, and, as the newspaperman hungrily wolfed down a burrito, Virgil quizzed him about the meeting.

"Oh, they all got plans and high hopes," the scribe replied. "My feeling right now is Cipi and R. J., they don't know it but they are already axed. Moose is negotiating an alliance with the Anglo Axis. Mares and Hobart will probably remain with their respective employers just long enough to hand them over, ruined, to the Eggington-McQueen people. And nobody knows how to chill Icarus Suazo, although I figure his own lawyers are gonna make an offer to the Anglo Axis, a move I doubt they can effectuate before Suazo fires them."

"They're talking about all this up there?"

"Obviously not in so many words. They're discussing partnerships, shares, profits, corporate structure, dividends, projects, pilgrims, tourism, paving the highway—all that sort of thing. But the other, clandestine maneuvering you can read between every line."

Come afternoon, summer storm clouds gathered over the Midnight Mountains and over the First State Bank's sweltering boardroom. Hot and tired, the men were feeling petulant and harassed, their heads ached from the cigar smoke weighing down the stagnant atmosphere. Despite open windows, the air inside refused to circulate. Cicadas in plaza elms buzzed noxiously. Banking off a flowering lilac near the World War I monument, a large yellow butterfly flapped lazily through an open southern window, zigzagged over the cluttered table, and exited by a northern window. Perfecto Torres and Celestino Lucero (two young rabble-rousers who ran a Ranchitos Abajo dairy), one bleeding from the nose, the other with an eye rapidly puffing shut, stumbled raucously out of the El Gaucho, and, laughing uproariously, vomited in the dusty gutter while fly-beleaguered horses at the El Gaucho hitching rack eyed them glumly.

Lunch over, nobody was talking. Grumpily, the boardroom crowd leafed through reams of legalese, proposals and counterproposals, plans and payoffs, dreams and schemes. A mute, leaden apoplexy riddled them all. Eyes had grown pouchy and dull. They had reached a standoff, an impasse. Cipi García paced nervously, pretending to read a brief, tearing at his rambunctious curly hair. The air was heavy and melodramatic with things left unsaid. Bob Moose folded his arms, calmly waiting. Across from him Icarus Suazo closed his eyes, catnapping. What to do next? Where did they go from here?

Moe Stryzpk went to a plaza-side window, cleaned his Coke bottles on a shirttail, refitted the stems behind his rumpled ears, and hawked at a pigeon. A lone native, wrapped in a cheap blanket, ruminated atop the adobe wall at the plaza's north corner, waiting for the Indian taxi to ferry him home. Teresa Lujan, a bittersweet young waitress planted laconically behind the Prince of Whales screen door, gazed sleepily out at the park. In alleyway shadows between the hotel and Vigil's Liquors, a few drunks were snoring. From the El Gaucho came the garbled strains of "Cielito Lindo." The American flag stirred once, limply, then succumbed to breezelessness. And Moe Stryzpk thoughtfully tapped his teeth with a pencil eraser.

The only sound accenting the stale, uncomfortable boardroom was the faint rubbery tapping of that pencil eraser against Moe Stryzpk's ivory. For a moment the muffled summery tension became so acute it seemed all were holding their breath. And at the apex of this tense, befuddling pause, Onofre García cracked. His chair popping over backward with a clatter that almost knocked young Juan Ortega off his ladder in the cell below, Onofre scrambled erect, fumbling for his enormous revolver of erudite lineage. Spellbound, nobody cried foul until Onofre swung the weapon on Moe Stryzpk, ending the pencil-tapping with an explosion that knocked Moe over backward half out the window, and also sprung the room to life. Turning wildly, screaming obscenities in Spanish, Onofre fired again as men scrambled, dived, and lunged, either for safety or for that gun, which discharged again as the table cracked, tipping sideways, and a hundred sheaves of legal paper, pens, pencils, briefcases, whiskey glasses, and Prince of Whales plates commotioned into the air, the room deafened by gunshots now as R. J. García managed to find his own piece and started slinging lead at his crazed cousin.

Hands fumbled; bodies flopped and thudded; a sound comparable to the thunder of a hundred big guns rocked the universe for three seconds as the only two weapons aboard were emptied. A climax of sorts occurred as Onofre, his forehead blasted open, a bead-handled hunting knife lodged in his chest, broke two table legs sliding sideways into the Denver lawyers' laps, even as R. J. García, backed up against the wall and plugged once in the groin, twice in the chest, slithered to a sitting position from where he stared at a snowfall of legal papers while life departed his eyes. Wolf Hobart, his jugular nailed by a jagged ricochet, coughed out, "No . . . Christ . . . Jesus," and also expired.

Paper fluttered back to earth for ages. The survivors remained crouched, entangled, incredulous, even after all the documents had settled and all the overturned furniture had ceased quivering. Broken glass, splashes of ink and blood, drenched the room.

Confronting his crimson hands, Rodey McQueen suddenly realized it wasn't his blood, this; it belonged, rather, to Cipi García. Cipi had taken a slug in his shoulder; and another bullet had clipped off the back of his head as neatly as if it had been the top of a soft-boiled egg, splashing Philpot Eggington, already dying of a heart attack, with so much gooey brain matter it seemed the old man's face had been creamed broadside with a meringue pie.

Icarus Suazo deftly traversed the carnage, and, mumbling under his breath in his own tongue, with an abrupt, brutal twist, he yanked the hunting knife from Onofre García's chest, wiped it clean on the dead man's thigh, and tucked it into a scabbard on his belt, out of sight beneath the jacket he had not removed.

Rodey McQueen cast about, dazedly at first, then with a certain realization flickering in his eyes as he toted up the score.

Abruptly, with a startled, almost mirthful expression on his face, the Muleshoe conman exclaimed, "Well, I guess that settles that. We're home free!"

ON THE MORNING of the Cipi García burial, three large black motorcars purred along the Plains Road and parked at the foot of Nobody Mountain, disgorging a dozen prosperous-looking men and one woman and a boy, all garbed in funereal pomp. First to appear was Rodey McQueen: the last, wheelchair-bound and manipulated awkwardly

27

down a ramp by the valley's ambitious young doctor, Alfred Gracie Lamont, was Moe Stryzpk, now paralyzed from the waist down for life. Taking turns behind the wheelchair, the mourners puffed up the narrow path leading to the bald crest of Nobody Mountain, where all turned to admire the view.

A line of bumper-to-bumper cars stretched out along the North-South Highway, beginning several miles below the La Lomita–Cañoncito communities. A thousand mourners plodded dustily along on foot. West of the plaza, cars were strung out along the La Piedra Gorge road, flanked by pilgrims afoot and a great many devoted and curious visitors on horseback. The Plains Road was deserted, the Midnight Mountains an effective check on populations immediately eastward. But another five thousand dusty automobiles and assorted vehicles and people were creeping down from the north, some hailing from towns as distant as Colorado Springs and Denver. Already, an area around the shrine had become a vast parking lot. The mineral springs were engorged with bathers; the restaurant had been staggering meals around the clock for two days; the Plaza Hotel was creaking at the seams, about to burst; and pitched among the gleaming cars occupying the crater were a hundred tents, from which arose the smoky curlicues of a thousand cook-fires burning. A bandstand had been erected near the shrine; from the summit of Nobody Mountain, strains of poignant, melancholy music could be heard. And, thousands deep in the immediate quarter-mile area before the Dynamite Chapel, spectators camped on rough benches, in deck chairs, on blankets, waiting for the Cipi García services to begin.

The man responsible for programming this event, young Claude Parker of potential whale-embalming fame, was perched on the mountain, overlooking the scene. By his side, passing around binoculars, were Bob Moose, Moe Stryzpk, Dr. Alfred Garcie Lamont, Denzil Spivey, Damacio Mares, and the Capital City Hupmobile dealer, Randolph Bonney. Nearby stood Rodey McQueen and his new girl, Cynthia Eggington, wearing black in mourning for her father, whose fortune she would inherit. Next to them were Chamisaville Mayor Rudy LeDoux and his young son Jaime Bernardo. And, of course, the event's official photographer, Karl Mudd. Immediately setting up his view camera, Mudd tucked himself under the black cloth and began taking photographs destined to circulate around the

28

world, pictures which would still be, forty years later, a standard hot-selling item in every Chamisaville store containing a postcard rack.

Several men doffed their top hats, allowing slight summer breezes to riffle their curly locks. And an abundance of hair characterized this group, for it was, by and large, a young crowd. Some, like Rodey McQueen and Randolph Bonney were in their mid-twenties; others, such as Bob Moose, Karl Mudd, and Moe Stryzpk had barely entered their thirties.

"What did you say the average income, cash, per family was down there?" McQueen asked for the umpteenth time. He already knew the answer, but in his excitement drew comfort from any litany affirming his understanding of the situation.

"This valley's full of people that barely earn two-fifty cash a year," said the mayor. "Ranching, farming, you don't need many dollars. Taxes are nonexistent, people grow their own feed and seed. You want flour ground at the Rio Puerco mill, you can have it done in exchange for goods—I guess just about everything happens that way. Been a subsistence valley for centuries; there's not much cash flow at all."

"And everybody owns their own land, their own house, their own animals—is that right?"

"For the past four hundred years," Bob Moose affirmed lazily. "You could count the mortgages in this valley on one hand."

Moe Stryzpk squinted through his Coke bottles at the picturesque patchwork landscape below, the arable portion so limited and enclosed. "To develop means shaking it loose, getting a turnover started."

"These people won't mortgage," Rudy LeDoux said quietly. "You might as well pray for rain in April."

"The new hotel can provide eight, ten new cash jobs," McQueen said. "Already I've got twelve of them who were farmers yesterday working as carpenters for me today. With cash, they'll be able to buy cars, electricity, indoor plumbing, radios. That's a beginning. They ain't no different from anybody else, they'll take to hard cash like honeysuckle to a front porch. We'll lure them in. Mechanics at the new gas station, waiters at the Dynamite Shrine Dining Salon, attendants at the baths. And when the highway is paved over, that's jobs which will get them off the farm, especially the young ones. They'll come piling out of those dirt houses like red ants out of a burning log."

"We can't just pull a paved highway out of our rear ends," Damacio Mares said.

McQueen turned on him, his ruddy face aflame. "Look down there, confound it, man! There's people thicker'n cloves on a Christmas ham! Twenty thousand attending a single event! And they had to perform the seven labors of Hercules to arrive here! We get pavement on that lousy dirt path and there'll be twenty times that number a year pouncing onto this little burg like rats onto a fat cheese!"

"You can't go and shoot a bona fide saint once every month, Dale, can you?" asked his bride-to-be.

"Enough of this pessimism!" McQueen barked. "You people know what's in the works, let's not be coy. Thanks to Denzil here and the Forest Service, we've already got special-use permits to develop the Mosquito Valley, and I can predict twenty-five, thirty summer homes up there in five years, no problem. Look at that sagebrush land between La Ciénega and Cañoncito, six miles wide—you know what I paid Atiliano Montoya for that last month? Two dollars an acre, because it's worthless, it has no water. But we get that highway paved, and the land sextuples in value overnight. This county's due for a land reassessment anyway, and with the industry and people we've already brought in around the shrine and the baths, property taxes are going to zoom. And when folks don't have enough cash to pay those taxes, they'll have to sell pieces of what they do own in order to meet the debt on the rest. Moe here is a real-estate wizard, he'll have half the county on the auction block inside ten years, you mark my words. That's all it takes, just an initial boost, and once you've got it moving, once you create that little bit of instability, once you get these people out of subsistence farming into a cash economy, land will start changing hands like bad news at a church social. This will be a new ballgame overnight. You know what I see here? I see a middle-class retirement city of twenty thousand people. Give me twenty years and I'll have all land out of agricultural production and onto the market, onto *our* kind of market—it'll be like shooting ducks on a pond."

"What about the Pueblo?" somebody asked.

"Five hundred bedraggled Indians don't scare me."

Randolph Bonney complained, "But if I set up a dealership down there today, I'll be broke tomorrow."

"Not if there's a paved highway, you won't. All we need now is for people to be able to get here; the rest is as easy as picking chickadees."

"Yessir, this lovely little valley is going to grow," Bob Moose said confidently. "Rest assured."

Already loosely allied in a grand plan, the men shared a mutual vision. They were slightly nervous, having made commitments—most of them lifetime promises—to remain in Chamisaville; and they were excited. Youth dominated their dreams; no job was too difficult. Quite firmly, they believed themselves able to move mountains, changing the course of their times.

Nobody realized that on a hillside behind and slightly above their group, Icarus Suazo had them fixed in his binoculars. After a while, the Pueblo secretary slipped his rifle from its saddle scabbard and aimed at Rodey McQueen. And for a moment he held the gun that way, impressed by what he could do, and perhaps even prevent, simply by pulling the trigger. Then, lowering the gun, he spat bitterly and resheathed the weapon.

Ever afterward, that slight, tense little man was to wonder why in hell he had not planted something fatal between the shoulder blades of that obnoxious Texan.

# THE
# MAGIC
# JOURNEY

# II

# The Betterment
# of Chamisaville

CONTRARY TO the general historical drift through anguish, despair, and bitter hard times, the first glum years of the Great Depression constituted a relatively prosperous era for the founders of the Betterment of Chamisaville.

Joined in matrimony to the beautiful Cynthia Eggington less than a month after Cipi García's immortality had been exposed for the humbuggery it was, and almost immediately the father of an eleven-pound two-ounce daughter they named April, Rodey McQueen felt more than able to launch his fantastic dream—in earnest. Aided by the Anglo Axis of Moe Stryzpk, Bob Moose, Claude Parker, Al Lamont, and Randolph Bonney (not to mention by the substantial inheritance brought him by his young bride), McQueen went at the Chamisa Valley like Red Grange heading for a touchdown. Payoffs occurred, Claude Parker's dream was financed, trips were made to the capital, where important members of the legislature caucused in private. Soon, in places of influence and power, a consensus developed that Chamisaville and its fabulous Dynamite Shrine complex might grow to become the "playground of the heart of the Land of Enchantment." In fact, to that end, the first significant event to occur after Cynthia Eggington McQueen became publisher of the *Chamisaville News* was the addition of just that slogan to the masthead of her little weekly newspaper.

And the first momentous headline to grace the newly sloganed front page of that timorous blat announced the arrival of Claude Parker's whale.

Embalmed in San Diego and accompanied on its overland railroad journey by Claude Parker himself, the whale arrived in the Capital City covered by flies but otherwise fresh as a daisy. It was promptly propelled on a raft up the Rio Grande to the La Piedra road crossing; and from there, employing a horse-drawn rig invented especially for the occasion, Claude maneuvered the whale a final ten miles into Chamisaville and parked it a hundred yards north of the plaza in a grassy meadow formerly belonging to Atiliano Montoya, the questionable spokesman—for communal landholders of the La Ciénega Grant—who had not long ago unloaded a third of that grant to Rodey McQueen for not even half a verse of the proverbial song.

"But I didn't sell you no acreage *north* of town," Atiliano protested to McQueen's Spanish interpreter, Mayor Rudy LeDoux, shortly after he had wandered into his meadow one morning to brand some calves and discovered the enormous bloated mammal blighting his fertile holdings. "You can't park no dead whales on my property!"

"The hell I can't," McQueen laughed. "Read our agreement."

"What are you talking about, man? I would have to be crazy to of sold you my irrigated land, even for twenty dollars an acre, let alone two pesos apiece."

McQueen handed him a contract of their La Ciénega Grant negotiation, asking the mayor to say: "Read the description of the land you sold me, Mr. Montoya. It's all there in angles and degrees, and that's your X on the bottom, witnessed by myself, Moe Stryzpk, and Bob Moose."

"I can't even speak English, let alone sign my own name, Rudy. So you tell this horse-thieving Tejano faggot how am I gonna read his fucking contract?" Atiliano protested.

"What did he say?" McQueen asked.

"He said, 'Excuse him very much, sir, but if he can't speak English or even sign his own name, how was he to interpret the effeminate slyness of the agreement you two made?' "

" 'Effeminate slyness'?"

Rudy LeDoux allowed his eyes to go vague, arched an eyebrow inspecting the clouds, then shrugged, letting his gaze wander toward the whale. Finally, nodding noncommitally, he released a vapid grin.

McQueen said, "Ask him this, Rudy. To sell that land he collected a hundred and fifty signatures of the grant members, didn't he? And didn't they all read the agreement? Surely somebody could have explained."

"Who among my friends, neighbors, enemies, compadres, cuates, vecinos, and primos reads English?" Atiliano sputtered feverishly. "We're all farmers, not lawyers."

"If a bullfrog had wings, he wouldn't bump his fanny. Ask him so how did he convince them to sell in the first place, then?"

"You tell Mr. McVenom here that I lied through my teeth. I told them the sale papers were necessary to protect their land and their water rights."

"So the fox kills a weasel," McQueen laughed, throwing an expansive arm around Atiliano's shoulders. "All's fair in love and war, amigo—qué no?"

Atiliano Montoya's misfortune was promptly forgotten in the hoopla stirred up by Claude Parker's whale. Never had the arrival of anyone or anything so captured the plodding imaginations of the Chamisa Valley. High-country inland bumpkins, in whom the term *ocean* inspired awe, flocked in droves to view the beast. They came from Milagro in the north, from La Piedra in the west, from tiny superstition-shrouded villages like Chamisal and Piñoncito and Los Ojos high in the Midnight Mountains. Curious hordes were disgorged daily from Cañoncito, Mota Llano, and Ranchitos Abajo. Farmers who should have been plowing, irrigating, or haying saddled up their horses instead, or hitched teams to their ancient buckboards, and for a day, sometimes for an entire week, they deserted their farms in order to ogle the monstrous animal from the sea. Grouped around it, deaf and dumb with amazement, they gawked. Timidly, they shuffled over to the thing and gingerly tapped its sandpapery hide. They circled around the mammoth hulk, philosophically kicking it the way they may have occasionally booted the curious tire of a stray modern car that wandered into the plaza. Some speculated on its edibility. "That's a lot of meat on the hoof, so to speak," Amaranta Godoy y Godoy, a pretty Mota Llano woman, murmured nonchalantly.

Her husband, Juan Bautista Godoy y Godoy, otherwise known as Juan GeeGee, the pintsized, gregarious Mota Llano sheepman, assumed a heroic stance before the whale, gesticulating wildly as he invented a song-poem—corrido—on the spur of the moment, reciting it enthusiastically to the gathered multitudes.

> *Into the valley of Chamisa*
> *In Nineteen Thirty-One,*
> *A cajonero called Parker*
> *Brought a huge leviathan!*
>
> *Bigger than a brave bull bucking,*
> *Higher than a Midnight hill,*

36

*This great big stinking carcass*
*Gives me a great big stinking thrill!*

*I wish it was stuffed with money,*
*With pennies and nickels and dimes,*
*Then there wouldn't be no more poverty,*
*And there wouldn't be no more crimes!*

*All the hicks came in from the valley,*
*All the hicks came in from the cerros;*
*Mamas and papas and chavalitos,*
*Vacas and muertos and perros!*

*Not the Virgin of Guadalupe,*
*Not even Jesus Christ himself,*
*Could lift up this ten-ton hunk of carne,*
*And place it on a shelf!*

*Cause it's bigger than a football field,*
*It's wider than a big hay bale,*
*It's taller than the Catholic bell tower,*
*And much deader than a dead doornail!*

Immediately, Juan's good friend Espeedie Cisneros joined
the Mota Llano bard in his efforts.

*The reason it isn't putrid,*
*The reason it hardly stinks,*
*Is they filled it full of alcohol:*
*The kind you shouldn't drink!*

*But I wish we had a little faucet*
*To stick into its hide,*
*So's to drain off all that pickling booze,*
*'Til the creature's empty inside!*

*Just thinking about the ocean beast*
*Gets my imagination tipsy;*
*I think I'll go to the El Gaucho*
*And have a couple of nipsies!*

And, while their sheep and their farms rotted, these
two engaged in an epic-poem duel and boozing spree in
front of the whale, a debauch, lasting the better part of

two weeks, that caused much livestock and precious cash to be wagered on who might emerge triumphant.

Inspired by Juan and Espeedie's antics, the two Ranchitos Abajo dairy farmers, Celestino Lucero and Perfecto Torres, drove their 1912 Buffalo Fire Engine (converted into a milk-delivery wagon) to town, unsheathed long cap-and-ball pistols, and enthusiastically punctuated the rhetoric by shooting homemade bullets into the whale, a practice soon discouraged by Claude Parker, who frantically reconnoitered his impressive leviathan with a pocket full of corks, plugging up the holes.

A pale, taciturn youth named Ralphito García walked eighteen miles into town one day, gingerly placed his palm against the whale, then left without a word, a beatific smile lighting up his bewitched features: he promptly hitchhiked to the West Coast and drowned himself in the Pacific Ocean.

The newspaper scribe, Juan Ortega, pulled up a chair, lit a cigar, and, his eyes sparkling brightly from the enthusiasm being generated all around him, he read to the people excerpts from a Spanish translation of *Moby Dick*.

Thus, as the Great Depression worsened, Chamisaville was ensnared in a magic time. For a moment, the daily doldrums and implacable toiling of subsistence survival were suspended. The valley skidded into a whacky celebration, a vacation, a fiesta. People accustomed to a slow pace reared back and frankly embraced the sudden good fortune flooding their valley. First a Cipi García miracle, then a Dynamite Shrine that enticed exotic tourists and pilgrims from as far away as Xanadu and Never-Never Land. There was construction everywhere, a brand-new highway on the boards, an automobile dealership slated for town. And now a whale! Excitement permeated every nook, hayloft, and Penitente morada; the formerly plodding definition of hopes and dreams was topsy-turveyed; sexual mores headed for a dunking. An outside world not only existed, but now it beckoned. And for the lucky few it might actually become a possibility, because the Don Quixote in every slow-witted, long-distance runner had been awakened. Folks whose most risqué dreams had dared hope for no adventure beside their final trip to heaven now began to fantasize about gold in Califas, gambling in St. Louis, and skyscrapers in New York City—or floating on an ocean!

The valley was perched on the brink of a magic journey.

Cash appeared everywhere, easy pickings: it could be gathered up as effortlessly as people collected sheep turds or ancient Pueblo pottery shards down on the Mota Llano mesa.

Karl Mudd set up his camera and started taking pictures of people standing beside the whale. The Arrellano brothers—Vidal, Genovivo, Telesforo, Cenobio, and Albino—sat for a portrait astride their race horses flanking the carcass. Presently, Rudy LeDoux thought of leaning a ladder against the whale, and his son J. B., a solemn and hefty teen-ager, became the first to stand atop the leviathan, frowning down into Karl Mudd's enormous Graflex as relentlessly as Zapata himself used to double-dare a lens. Eloy Romo, a young La Ciénega boxer, posed wearing his gloves, his shorts, his raggedy sneakers and a black-and-silver cape, delivering a haymaker to the corpse's jaw. Not long afterward, Rodey McQueen's volatile little daughter, April, crawled through a slight opening into the whale's mouth, and when they propped open the jaws in order to grab her before she wriggled into the stomach, a new—and this time definitive—pose was born. The initial Chamisa Valleyites to be immortalized in the mouth of the whale were little April McQueen and Georgie Parker, Claude's and Rachel's first kid, holding hands and shining brightly in coy booties and sailor costumes, April's face squinched up merrily and her tongue stuck out as she delivered a nasty Bronx cheer.

THE DYNAMITE SHRINE, the sudden onslaught of economic development, and Rodey McQueen's promises of "a tourist boom for every man, woman, child, and borrega in this valley," unleashed several unparalleled lunacies.

The Godoy y Godoy brothers, long noted for streaks of practical jokesterism and a flair for the unorthodox, laid the original foundations of many future tall tales and exaggerated recollections. First Juan drove a thousand sheep north to Colorado for auction, journeyed south to the capital with his pockets full of money, and spent every last cent on a large Ford automobile. Too broke, then, to buy fuel, he had friends tow the car back home and up Chamisaville Canyon to the Mosquito Valley, where the wonderful Horse Without Shit was born. Thanks to gravity instead of gasoline, that Ford barreled down the steep, twisting dirt road loaded to the gunnels with a ribald crew composed of Juan GeeGee, Celestino Lucero, Perfecto Torres,

Espeedie Cisneros, Bernardo C. de Baca, and Pancho Ortiz y Pino and his oversexed, mute little brother everyone jokingly called Pedro Cabrón y Puto. And it was the first automobile ever owned by a longtime local farmer.

Selling his sheep to buy that car made Juan a destitute man. It also gained him much notoriety, and inspired the newspaperman Juan Ortega to invent a corrido:

> Juan Bautista Godoy y Godoy,
> We'll never fail to remember—
> He traded his sheep for a Model T,
> 'Twas in the month of September.
>
> He hauled his car to our canyon top
> And aimed it toward the valley.
> It didn't need any gas in the tank,
> To speed down that treacherous alley.
>
> Faster than lightning the tires hummed,
> Juan jerked the brakes instead of a bit,
> But once rollicking crazily down toward town,
> Who could stop the Horse Without Shit?
>
> It was filled to the brim with drunken bums
> Named Tranky, Jacobal, Canuto,
> Juan and Bernardo, Eloy and Joe,
> And Pedro Cabrón y Puto.
>
> They screamed and shouted, they ranted and raved,
> They weren't afraid of flying;
> They laughed and cheered and drank warm beer,
> They weren't terrified of dying.
>
> Down in La Ciénega children squealed,
> Old brujas gathered by the road,
> And when the Horse Without Shit appeared,
> They pelted it with toads!
>
> Hail! hail! that loco gang,
> Those boys with hearts in their throats,
> Plummeting heedlessly down that road,
> Running over kids, and puppies, and goats!
>
> For never a man breathed air so pure
> Nor exposed a more sparkling wit,
> Than the devil-may-care insane assholes
> That rode in the Horse Without Shit!

Juan GeeGee's car also fired the imagination of his elder brother, Pat, who had deserted the sheep business many years earlier to open the El Gaucho Bar. By catering mostly to a few Chamisaville drunks and out-of-town valley-dwellers on their once-a-month supply runs, Pat had barely broken even. But with the Dynamite Shrine, the pilgrims, the whale, the highway construction, the Dynamite Shrine Motor Court and gas stations and other growth related to the Rodey McQueenification of Chamisaville, business had picked up considerably. Farm boys and girls, quitting the land to work on the highway and in town as waiters, pool attendants, busboys, and chambermaids, had money to burn, and burn it they did, handing their glossy new dollars over to Karl Mudd for whale photographs, to Randolph Bonney for down payments on automobiles, to Damacio Mares in Cynthia McQueen's Eggington Mercantile Store for newfangled appliances such as refrigerators and electric heaters and even radios, and to Pat GeeGee for what his establishment offered. And before he knew it, Pat had become a momentarily rich man.

"Put it in the bank, this can't last, when the construction on the highway and the motels and hotels is finished everyone will be broke again," warned Pat's wife, Lucinda. But he couldn't listen.

After all, a universal thrill trembled the air. Only last week, the famous Cañoncito racing Arrellano brothers (Vidal, Genovivo, Telesforo, Cenobio, and Albino) had challenged the famous García racing Casados brothers (Elvirio, Avelino, Tuburcio, Nicanor, Elfego, Conferino, and Candido) to a run up the Chamisaville Canyon from La Ciénega to the Mosquito Valley. And what a race that had been! Six horses died, four brothers suffered concussions, eight animal and five human legs were broken, and Nicanor Casados beat out Genovivo Arrellano by a nose! The race had hogged the entire front page of the *Chamisaville News!*

Competing with the dramatic doings, Celestino Lucero had recently captured the valley's imagination by accidentally killing a man over a woman down in the capital, and then escaping into the Midnight Mountains. He walked home on foot in less than a week, catching trout by hand for food, and killing a mountain lion that pounced upon him in his sleep by biting through its juglar. He arrived home with a big scar on his cheek and, on his shoulder, a pet magpie he called Tierra o Muerte.

So Pat GeeGee wanted to make a grand gesture that would be remembered for all time. He wanted to outdo the Arrellanos, the Casados, Celestino Lucero, and his own brother. He wanted to outshine the wonderful Horse Without Shit by making a bigger, brighter, and more imaginative fool of himself. Stuffing all his excess profits into a large cowhide bag, Pat hiked into the Rio Grande Gorge, roped a wild burro, rode the bucking burro over to the La Piedra rail station, released the cantankerous animal, got on a train, and traveled to Dainger Field, Texas, where he bought a small single-engine Piper airplane from one Carlito Epstein, a daredevil air stuntman, who flew the plane, with Pat aboard, back to Chamisaville.

As soon as they landed on a piece of flat mesa Pat owned halfway between Cañoncito and Ranchitos Abajo, the commotion around the whale, the Dynamite Shrine, and the Horse Without Shit shifted to Pat's aircraft. Most local folks had never seen winged machines. Many farmers and their wives and children who had mustered enough courage to slap the whale, or perhaps even have themselves photographed in its mouth, dared not touch the slick skin of Pat GeeGee's amazing Piper Cub. For a price, Carlito Epstein hung around Chamisaville for six months, taking less timorous souls up into the air. Pat GeeGee, for one, flew almost every day, investing all his El Gaucho profits in fuel and maintenance and Carlito's salary. Gleefully, he ordered the amenable pilot to buzz the mouth of Chamisaville Canyon just as the wonderful Horse Without Shit, half empty because most local hayseeds with suicidal penchants were camped around the Patrocinio Godoy y Godoy Airfield, barreled noisily out of the canyon into La Ciénega proper.

Virgil Leyba and Loretta Shimkus and their baby, Junior, went aloft more than once. Rudy LeDoux's nervous son J. B. saved up money earned building adobes for the nine-foot wall rising around the McQueen mansion grounds to buy a ride in the sky for himself and the lovely but morose Prince of Whales waitress Teresa Lujan. "The valley looks so beautiful from up here," she crooned. "The land and the horses are so pretty. There's no visible poverty or bad luck at all. I wish I could spend the rest of my life in the sky." And she was crying uncontrollably when the wheels touched earth again.

Others who paid heavily to fly were Celestino Lucero and Perfecto Torres, Espeedie Cisneros and the rest of that gang. However, miffed by his brother's pretentious arrogance, and also ashamed that he could not even buy gas for the Horse Without Shit, Juan GeeGee pompously refused to go aloft. Naturally, he regretted his shallow-brained pride for the rest of his life, as the opportunity to canvass the sky and the ground below like a bird never came his way again.

Even Icarus Suazo appeared one day to try out the airplane with his new wife, Juanita, a frail and mysterious Pueblo woman pregnant with their first—and destined to be only—child. Once airborne, the Pueblo secretary produced a Brownie camera, and asked Carlito Epstein to patrol the valley in an orderly pattern while he used up several dozen rolls of film shooting sequential pictures of the land below. His wife unrolled a government geological survey map and began furiously marking it up with various colored pencils according to directions Icarus kept mumbling at her in their native language.

These two had just disembarked from the tiny plane, when Jesus Dolores Martínez Vigil appeared mysteriously from out of the darkening sagebrush, reined in his horse, and suspiciously eyeballed the shimmering aircraft as it cooled. Eventually, dismounting and waddling over to Carlito Epstein with his numerous firearms and cartridge belts squeaking and clanking loudly, he fished up ten old-fashioned silver dollars from a deerskin drawstring pouch and handed them over.

Carlito handed them back. "I'm sorry, sir, but you'll have to shed all those guns," he said politely.

"Qué va!" Jesus Etcetera replied, hawking in the sand barely a millimeter from the pilot's boot. "Pa'onde me voy yo, me van mis pistolas."

"Then you can't go up," Carlito insisted, blushing because this man was definitely descended from the type of person known in the gringo vernacular as "one mean hombre."

Jesus Etcetera drew a pistol, tossed up a silver dollar, laconically shot a hole through the middle of it, holstered his weapon, laid a gob of spit between Carlito's flight boots, adjusted his sombrero, waddled back to his horse, struggled for three minutes to catch his toe in a stirrup, lugged himself with much puffing and grunting up into the saddle, and disappeared onto the mesa.

At the age of three, one week after she had learned to swim when Rodey McQueen chucked her into the mansion's just-completed pool, April McQueen had a ride in Pat GeeGee's folly. Carlito Epstein had never encountered such a beautiful child: her startling radiance both chilled and fired his blood. Leaning over, he kissed April and she returned the bussing in no uncertain terms. Even her pigtails' bright ribbons glittered as if riddled with a magic pixie dust. April chattered a mile a minute and sensuously caressed the controls. "Let me drive the airplane," she cooed, grabbing the stick with her chubby fingers. "I wanna do a somersault and a nosedive. I wanna do a cartwheel and a loop-the-loop."

Carlito tumbled them about like an autumn leaf buffeted by rude October winds. April giggled and laughed and cried for more. They dipsied and doodled and, beside that animated infant urging him on, Carlito experienced an air borne euphoria he had never known before. He wanted to fly to the moon, dress that pugnacious kid in diamonds, marry April and live with her for the rest of his clumsy days. I'll settle in Chamisaville and wait for her to grow up, he thought. When we land I'll ask the old man if I can marry April right now—I'll promise not to screw her till she's fifteen. No female had ever even remotely so scrambled his heart and his daredevil guts. The plane pirouetted insanely like a punch-drunk clown celebrating the Fourth of July. Whenever Carlito glimpsed her spendiferous blue eyes, they sparkled with a vitality and sexuality that yanked a string in his chest and made him want to howl. Exhausted, he landed the plane, received his final salary from Pat GeeGee, and fled Chamisaville in the dead of night, though his departure was too late to avoid a broken heart. And Pat's airplane never left the ground again.

Often Rodey McQueen himself gazed enrapturedly at his daughter, mystified by her radiant beauty. How had somebody that precious emerged from his loins and the womb of his lovely, but regular wife? April had an unearthly attractiveness that scared him sometimes. Then again, she also made him inordinately proud.

"Now I know how Joseph and Mary must have felt," he once joked to his wife. Cynthia, however, could not respond in kind. Jealousy, an inarticulate fear, clouded the relationship between mother and daughter: April was her father's child.

One evening, while perusing the *Capital City Reporter* on the side lawn by the pool shortly after men building the adobe wall around his mansion had quit for the day,

McQueen heard a faint noise. Looking up, he was startled to discover his daughter airborne, her arms outstretched like wings, her exquisite face beaming from among fluttering folds of transparent pink taffeta as she sailed off the roof. Before the danger registered, April hit the ground on her stomach, bounced onto her back, stood up, brushed herself off, shouted "Ha ha, Daddy—see? . . . *I can fly!*" and cheerfully pranced away. McQueen reached out a hand to stop her, to make a comment, to gasp—but she was gone.

So April pranced beyond the fingertips of everybody, always poised to take dangerous flight. At four she could ride a horse better than most men: before school began she had learned to read: and while in kindergarten she plowed through *Gone with the Wind* in a week. No doubt about this one, then: she was the quickest kid in town. And pretty as a speckled pup.

"Yessir, that sprite was champing at the bit from the second she left her mother's tummy," McQueen proudly told his friends and neighbors and confederates, hooking thumbs through his fireman's suspenders and taking care not to let the worry he felt deep down affect his braggadocio. "She's smart enough to track bees in a blizzard. The rest of this doggone valley is gonna spend a lifetime eating her dust!"

A MAGIC TIME transfigured Chamisaville. Inspired by Claude Parker's whale and the flamboyant shenanigans of the Godoy y Godoy brothers, Espeedie Cisneros bought fifteen cans of paint, hard-plastered his adobe farmhouse, and, aided by his brother-in-law, Canuto Tafoya, he proceeded to cover the dwelling with gaudy murals. Between bright flowers, corn, cattle, magpies, eagles, moons, sunshine, and stars, he alternated religious scenes: Joseph in his coat of many colors, the Virgin of Guadalupe in her snowy rose-bedizened robe congratulating Juan the Indio, Jesus with a fishing pole and a stringer of rainbow trout. Saluting more modern times, airplanes, a few dirigibles, and motorcars also drifted spectacularly across his outside walls.

The idea caught on immediately. Much loose cash was circulating the valley to pay for these dreamy artistic endeavors, and for a year or two Espeedie and Canuto hustled around the valley in a horse-drawn wagon, painting murals to order on old adobe farmhouses. On both sides of Juan and Amaranta GeeGee's long narrow dwelling blossomed an intricate jungle of cottonwood trees and sagebrush among which Adam and Eve, the Virgin Mary, and a wingèd and haloed Cipi García shared space with opulent sheep, fiery white ponies, effeminate pink bulls, glistening yellow cows, and, of course, the wonderful Horse Without Shit. On Virgil Leyba's and Loretta Shimkus's small Alamito house he painted likenesses of Zapata and Pancho Villa and dozens of dark-skinned armed Indians in white pajamas and sandals, engulfed by enormous cacti, symbolic rattlesnakes, colorful eagles, puffy white clouds, and soaring gulls. Eloy Romo had a number of famous boxers from Jack Johnson to Max Baer posturing among flocks of chimerical sheep; Pat and Lucinda GeeGee surrounded themselves with flying birds of paradise and airplanes; Joe Archuleta decorated his house with tambourines and blissfully fatted pigs; the Arrellano and Casados brothers put Christ and the Virgin Mary on horseback racing around their adobe walls; and on his enormous dairy barn, Celestino Lucero had Espeedie and Canuto paint scenes from his mountain odyssey after killing that Capital City man over a woman—Celestino wrestling a mountain lion, catching trout with his bare hands, capturing and training his pet magpie Tierra o Muerte, and shielding his eyes from golden rays bursting off the Virgin perched on a snowy mountaintop.

When her parents refused to decorate the protective wall around their estate, April McQueen filched several paint cans from a tool shed and went at the hard-plastered adobes beside the front gate herself, splashing on several dozen crude and colorful mandalas, sunflowers, butterflies, and assorted childish monsters before her mother discovered the vandalism and paddled her lovely bottom.

On warm Sundays, it seemed as if all the Chamisa Valley gathered in Balena Park to have their pictures taken in the mouth of Claude Parker's whale and to stroll about the fields wielding parasols, drinking lemonade, and listening to the sabbath concerts on the Balena Park skating pond's floating bandstand. Women lounged demurely on the grass, their wide dresses fluffed out. Men in their Sunday finest leaned dapperly on canes as they picked their teeth and sniffed snuff. And little children in Communion outfits and sailor suits gathered around the pond, loving every minute of Espeedie Cisneros on violin, Juan GeeGee plucking his guitar, Juan Ortega squeezing his wheezy accordion, and

46

Loretta Shimkus pounding the piano. They played such favorites as "Au Clair de la Lune" and "My Bonnie," "La Golondrina" and "The Handkerchief Waltz." It wasn't long before toe-tapping onlookers paired off and began to dance: polkas and waltzes and quadrilles. The child April McQueen would never forget the sight of Ursula and Perfecto Torres happily doing the varsoviana, or the waltz of Gorgonio. Lips pursed at a white dandelion halo, for hours she would refrain from blowing the seed apart, completely enthralled by the graceful antics of Rudy and Marina LeDoux dancing an indita, la raspa, or a schottische, a popular Scottish import. And whether it was "Carmen Carmela" or "Lupita Divina," a wonderful sentimental animation engulfed that Sunday crowd, and people were convinced that good fortune for everybody might last forever.

Yet even at the height of the valley's halcyon days, a nefarious groundwork was being laid. The Anglo Axis had a plan for Chamisaville and the surrounding land and communities; and the implementation of the so-called Betterment of Chamisaville was the heart and soul of that plan.

RODEY McQUEEN, Bob Moose, and Moe Stryzpk met in the spacious office-and-den complex of the Stryzpks' rambling home. And, while Miranda Stryzpk, a sarcastic and sexy woman pregnant with her second child, catered their gastronomical needs, Moe screwed up his dark and embittered features, and, chain-smoking while he nervously fingered his wheelchair's brake handle, he analyzed the situation, pointing, as he talked, to maps and illustrations that papered his walls: composite Bureau of Land Management photographs of the valley, Forest Service special-use permit areas, government geological study drawings, the state engineer's hydrographic survey maps, and Moe Stryzpk's own demographic choreography, showing every house and shed and goat corral within a twenty-square-mile area.

Moe knew where each man, woman, child, and animal was located; he knew the size, type, and value of their dwellings, their outbuildings, their corrals. He knew the extent of everyone's land and stockholdings and what they claimed for water rights. He had at his fingertips copies of all the tax records on file in the old plaza courthouse; and he knew approximately how much cash each family made and controlled. He had copies of most deeds, proclamations, titles, and quitclaims connected to the local com-

47

munal land-grant territories; and he knew which men and women were most intricately involved with grant activities. He had records and rosters of each acequia within the valley and could trace every family and every acre that every ditch served. He could count exactly how many old people lived in the valley, and how many middle-aged and young people there were. He knew exactly which families and individuals were the weakest links in the landholding chain, and he also knew who would battle the Anglo Axis right to the end. Given such information, Moe had programmed initial strike points based on financial, community, and personality profiles of the local residents involved. And he was ready, willing, and able to commence legally marching through their Georgia.

Moe said: "We've got some of them off the farms already, working for cash in the shrine complex, in the new motel, the greenhouses, the two new gas stations and garages, and on paving the highway—that's good. People like old Vidal Mondragón in Borregas Negras—Black Sheep we'll begin calling that community, the English will give us a psychological edge. Old Vidal has lost three out of four sons, who used to help him on the farm, to highway construction crews. And he's a sick man, he can't take that. So he hired two of Juan GeeGee's sons to work on his farm, and that means Juan is short of help. To hire Juan's kids, in order to get cash to pay for help on his place, Vidal sold five acres to me. And I sold the land to that new chef from San Francisco we just hired for the Dynamite Shrine restaurant, Vito Rosselini, which effectively removes that land from agricultural production—all the wop wants to do, outside of making a mint at the shrine, is grow peonies and letch after the local Mexican girls. Vito is also hiring, for hard cash, four more La Ciénega farm boys to build his house on that land, which weakens the noncash agricultural structure those boys were in before, and gives them the money to get themselves in debt, adding another weakened link to the growing general insecurity caused by an economically competitive society.

"Meanwhile, Vidal Mondragón is furious with his sons currently working on the highway not only for deserting the farm, but also for forcing him to sell that five acres to buy the labor to work the rest of his farm, weakening not only the Mondragón family structure and the Black Sheep community structure, but also Vidal's shaky heart. And that's what we want. Vidal will die sooner than he should have, and the sons won't be around to take care of the farm. In fact, Vidal may be so angry at them for their disloyalty that he'll refuse to will them the land and we can get it clean, on the open market, without a struggle.

"Too, there is now a feud between Vidal and Juan Gee-Gee, who resents the fact that his own boys, whom he can't pay in cash to work at home, have gone to work for Vidal, leaving him—Juan—strapped for farm labor, which *he* must now pay for, since his sons aren't at home. Juan is in the same boat as Vidal, but can't bear selling a piece of land to raise cash to work the rest of his farm. So he has sent his wife, Amaranta, into town looking for work to acquire the necessary cash, and, as we all know, she has hired on at your place, Dale, as a governess and a maid. And, because they are so poor and so desperate for that cash to keep their farm and sheep operation going, and because many others in similar straits already are seeking like employment, the going price for labor is at a minimum, and people like Amaranta can be had for a song. With her meager cash income they can buy labor to help Juan run the farm, but with Amaranta out of the home, a stabilizing influence on their other children is gone. They have less supervision. Juan himself must cook his own meals half the time and that leaves him full of gas and cranky. And so the family begins to drift, it is no longer securely anchored, they become ripe for some kind of plucking.

"Naturally, the feud that exists between Vidal Mondragón and Juan GeeGee helps us in many ways. For example, in previous years Vidal used to graze a bunch of his cattle on Juan's lowland pasture in exchange for giving the GeeGees apples from their orchard and plenty of cheese from the Mondragón goats. But because Vidal used cash to entice Juan's boys away from the GeeGee farm, Juan won't speak to Vidal anymore, let alone allow him to use the GeeGee pasture, hence Vidal just recently had to rent a pasture, for cash, from Cipi García's uncle, Tito García, to graze the cattle allotment he used to run for free on Juan's land, and also to graze the cattle he used to run for free on the five acres he had to sell to hire Juan's boys to help run his farm. And Juan GeeGee, it goes without saying, is looking elsewhere for his apples and his goat cheese, which he'll have trouble locating as barterable commodities because, now that his sons are no longer helping him run the farm, he doesn't have as much access to labor or goods that he can exchange in trade. Hence, if we can continue to break down the system of subsistence interdependence that has held this valley and these people together for over four hundred years, then we are well on our way to controlling the land and economic situation completely, and can pretty much dictate the type of middle-class, retirement, and tourist-oriented profit-making (at least for us) community we're aiming for. And it all begins with a little thing, like enticing Vidal's sons off the farm to work on the highway for more cash than they have ever seen in their lives."

Moe paused, wiping his Coke bottles clean, refitted them, and wheeled himself across the room to a file cabinet. Locating a manila folder, he thumbed through it and removed several papers.

"So it begins by enticing them off the farm," he said quietly. "And within five minutes, already, we've got them on the hook. Let's take Eduardo Mondragón, Vidal's eldest, here's his file. Already he's in hock for a radio, and he had the Custer Electric Co-op run a line down to the new house he just finished building on the land his father gave to him two years ago. Because he was working on the highway, Eduardo had to hire neighbors to work on the house. A few years ago those neighbors would have built his house for him free, because he would have helped them build their houses. But now he's too busy earning money to help them, so of course they want cash for helping him, on the grounds that if they didn't work for him they could also earn cash for their time by working on the highway, or at the shrine complex, or elsewhere. So Eduardo got a mortgage at First State to pay them for building his house, and that was the *first* recorded mortgage for a Spanish house in this valley! Eduardo also got caught up in the automobile excitement and put a down payment on a roadster at Randolph Bonney's. Like Juan GeeGee, he can't afford to buy gas for it. Soon, no doubt, he'll sell a couple acres— to us because we'll pay higher than local folks, who won't have the cash—to buy gas for his car. Thus already he's paying off a lot of people, and when the highway construction ends next year, cutting off his cash income, we'll have him in our trap and there will be no way out. To protect his house, paying the monthly bills for his mortgage, appliances, and his car, he'll have to sell some more of his land —the only security he really possesses, the only true stability in his life—for cash, and we can grab it up for a song because he'll be so desperate. And when he unloads

50

that land, that's less pasturage for himself and his family to run their cows on for free, or to barter grazing rights on for other goods. So they'll have to sell some of their cows —which means less meat in the smokehouse—to eat themselves or to exchange for potatoes or hay-baling services from somebody with a baler. And sooner or later, if this cycle keeps up, they'll no longer be self-sufficient. They'll have to start buying groceries from the local markets, in particular the Your Own Food Store our group has set up that Randolph here's younger brother Jerry just came up to manage. The reason they'll have to buy there is that we'll extend them infinite credit and, given that, once the gravy projects end, their cash will be tight, they'll have to charge their groceries. Ultimately we'll get plenty of people deeply enough and desperately enough in debt that they'll have to start exchanging land for victuals—a half acre here, a full acre there, paying off their charge accounts. Believe me, very quickly it adds up. When people are deeply in debt like that, of course, we'll sue them for our money, and, since they'll have no cash, we'll ask for land, which is what we want in the first place. We'll try to get twice as much land as their charge tickets are worth—no problem, I would surmise, as we control the legal system; the laws will always back up our point of view. Obviously, they'll hire lawyers to fight us, but Virgil Leyba won't be able to handle a tenth of the cases that we should be able to generate in the next few years, and all the rest of the legal expertise is on our side. So I imagine that you, Bob, and Damacio Mares, and all the rest of the attorneys in this county can get rich demanding land as payment for services rendered to people who have no cash to defend that very land. Win a case or lose it, we come out ahead: it's perfectly legal to defend somebody's land successfully in a court case and then to claim that same land from the people you defended when they have no cash to pay your fees. Once on the hook, gentlemen, they can't get off; it's a downhill battle for them all the way."

McQueen said, "These people are more stubborn than a hungry jackass tugging a broken Gee Whiz. It might take a while."

"God is on our side, Dale. Don't give me a hernia with your reservations. We'll employ certain surefire catalysts, of course: they've never failed anywhere before. I'm talking about the Cañoncito Dam and the formation of a conservancy district to implement it. Conservancies north of the capital right now are forbidden by law because our populace is too poor to support such powerful taxation districts. But we are going to elect Rudy LeDoux to the state senate this autumn, and he'll introduce a bill to change that law, it's as simple as that—we've already got the votes lined up to pass it. You wouldn't believe how many outside senators and representatives and other business people already have investments in the Dynamite Shrine complex, the Mosquito Valley, and so forth.

"Next, the development of the Mosquito Valley should enable us, legally, to just about cut off the river into La Ciénega and make irrigation farming over there insecure at best, and probably impossible over the long run. Then we'll take over the Magpie Creek Lumber Mill. . . ."

Moe paused, brushing ashes off his chest. Bob Moose said, "All right, Moe. Not to throw you a curve, but what is your thinking on the Indians?"

Moe fished yet another cigarette from a rumpled pack and lit it, his hand shaking. Waving out the match and dropping it onto the polished stone floor, he backed away from them and over to a window, where he could look past a delicate Japanese garden, a low adobe wall, and beautiful sagebrush land to the soft brown monolith of the southern Pueblo structure silhouetted against the base of the sacred mountain.

"To be frank with you, Bob, I really don't know. My instincts are to hang fire on them until we've got the valley kind of where we want it. Ed Lange, the BIA flunky out there, is on our side: you all know Ed. He'd like to terminate the whole bunch and relocate them in Los Angeles and Chicago. Barring that eventuality, because we've already cut him in on the Magpie Creek Lumber Mill operation, Ed will work for us to realize some kind of timbering contract on that sacred Albino Pine land Denzil Spivey and his boys have been managing ever since Teddy Roosevelt robbed it from the Pueblo in 1906. Unlike the Magpie Creek García Grant land, there's apparently still a whole lot of restrictions on the Pueblo's sacred trees—even if the Forest Service does control them—so long as Icarus Suazo can keep a suit for its return alive in one district or federal court or another. Once he exhausts his resources, however, we're home free. But so far that little man has exhibited a nimblefootedness that defies understanding—for an Indian, that is. And right now, ridiculous as it may seem, we are sort of in contention for the entire valley with that man.

52

And, incidentally, with his people. We have a pipeline into his every move, of course, thanks to Brady and Potter, who, for a relatively modest sum have been passing us information in advance on all of Suazo's moves. My understanding, however, is that Suazo knows exactly what they are doing and is camouflaging his every action in accordance with that knowledge. And as soon as Marshall Kickingbird passes the bar exam, he'll fire Brady and Potter, who, frankly, will be lucky to escape with their lives. But until Kickingbird is a full-fledged lawyer, Suazo needs those two Denver-based Benedict Arnolds to front for him in court. And we'll have a before-the-fact record of his, and their, every move."

McQueen said, "What the hell, Bob. Your daddy's head of the state bar. Marshall Kickingbird hasn't got a chance of passing the bar exam. He can study from here to Hades and all those brains won't do him any more good than tits on a boar hog."

"Not so, Dale, I'm afraid. The word coming down from above is that Washington wants at least one Indian lawyer in this state, and Marshall is going to be that lawyer."

"I don't understand."

Moe Stryzpk turned away from the window. "Some idiot back there says it's time to throw the redskins a bone, and he has the influence to pull that string. Apparently, Bull can't quash it because the feds have threatened to get us all disbarred if he does."

"Well, that's democracy for you," Bob Moose chided lightly.

"It's a free country," Rodey McQueen guffawed, slapping his thigh like a good old boy.

"There's a couple of ways of looking at the Pueblo." Moe returned to his file cabinet, extricating yet another manila folder, and wheeled over to his desk, riffling quickly through its contents. "First of all, it's costing the Pueblo a royal mint to keep all its court suits alive, which means we have an automatic wedge in the door. Chances are that they're going to have to open the Pueblo to tourism on a paying basis in order to raise funds to fight for the return of that land. When they do that, we already have the state highway department lined up to pave the four miles of road from the North-South Highway to their church, and a clause in the contract will stipulate that the local crews will have to be Indian laborers. Which gets some of their people off the farm and into our cash-and-carry economy.

Suazo knows—hell, they all know—that a bunch of crippled pilgrims and nosy tourists poking around the Pueblo compounds every day are going to raise havoc with those private people, a havoc which works in our favor, as the more unbalanced they are, the easier it will be to pick them off when the economic war begins in earnest. Suazo has court suits now claiming that the entire town of Chamisaville rests on Pueblo land, that the Dynamite Shrine complex is on Pueblo land, that the Rio Grande river is flowing through Pueblo land, and that he has a right to set up highway tollbooths north and south of town because the road is desecrating Pueblo land. His insistence is a nuisance, but it's not costing us prohibitively to keep him at bay. And, as soon as we have the conservancy district, I see no problem in diverting conservancy taxes to fight Suazo, since most of his cases involve land that falls within the proposed district boundaries."

"Including the Pueblo? And the Albino Pine land?"

"Nope. Being under federal protection, their land is immune to that sort of thing." And then, glancing up suddenly, Moe said, "But I have a dream."

McQueen and Moose looked at him questioningly.

"First, we concentrate on the valley," Moe explained. "And we'll suck those Indians into our cash society right along with all the Mexicans. It'll take them longer, but after a while they'll want to go modern, they'll want tractors instead of plow teams to cultivate their fields, they'll want automobiles instead of horses to get around in, they'll want electricity out there to run pumps so they don't have to draw all their water by hand—and when the time is ripe we should be able to force them to vote in favor of installing electricity out there. And then—"

Moe stopped, and, wheeling himself over to the window again, he peered for a long time in silence at the stolid bulk of the Pueblo across the mesaland several pristine miles away.

"And when they have electricity out there?" McQueen prompted.

"I just have a dream . . ." Moe said lingeringly, mysteriously. And then, abruptly wheeling over to his desk: "But first things first, gentlemen. Let's field the ball before we throw it."

THE FORMER CHAMISAVILLE MAYOR, Rudy LeDoux, was elected state senator from Chamisa County. He traveled to the capital for a three-week legislative session, and when he returned to oversee construction of several vacation homes and a golf course in the Mosquito Valley, conservancy districts north of the capital were legal, whether the local citizenry could pay for them or not.

One week later, down in the capital, a practically secret district court hearing on the formation of a Chamisa County conservancy district was held, attended by Rodey McQueen, Moe Stryzpk, and Bob Moose. The judge formed a district, appointed five of the present Chamisaville cabalists to its board of directors, and, as quietly as that, the deed was accomplished, the legal tenets of democracy upheld, the native population of the Chamisa Valley placed upon a rack for the stretching.

The first inkling anyone had that something was up occurred in the predawn hours of an overcast autumn Saturday when Juan GeeGee hitched up a plowing team to the wonderful Horse Without Shit parked in his enormous hay barn and proceeded to almost trample a government surveyor glued to a sextant set up on the shiny dirt yard eleven feet beyond that barn's creaking weathered doors.

"What the hell are you doing here, cousin?" Juan asked amiably. "You take a wrong turn someplace? You lost or something?"

"No sir, Mr. Godoydidoy," the surveyor replied politely. "I'm just laying down a preliminary track for the cement-lined Juan GeeGee Canal that'll be running through here from the dam we're going to build up there just south of the lumber mill."

"Hijo de la gran puta que me parió!"

The honeymoon was over.

Farmers and ranchers on every main acequia and ditch-lateral drawing water off Magpie Creek, the Rio Puerco, and the Rio Chiquito joined together in an anticonservancy coalition called the Four Rivers Association, taxing themselves fifty cents an acre to pay court costs and Virgil Leyba. And the lawyer from Cuachitlán told Rodey McQueen and the rest of the conservancy board that if they did not dissolve themselves immediately he would have them in the state penitentiary before the year was up for half a dozen violations of the conservancy act and the state lands purchasing act, and other assorted peccadillos. And if, somehow, he failed either to quash the district or to incarcerate the honorable gentlemen involved, he could

55

promise them that every member of the anticonservancy coalition would take up guns, sickle bars, machetes, axes, and meat cleavers and start cutting off testicles and severing heads much as had the Pueblo natives and assorted local Spanish-speakers back in 1858 when the first territorial governor and his wife and children had met a similar fate worse than death at the hands of locals incensed by unfair taxation.

In reply to this tirade, Moe Stryzpk arranged a meeting with Virgil in the King Cole Exective Room of the recently completed Dynamite Shrine Dining Salon. Alone in the lavishly brocaded private eating den whose picture window overlooked a small hot spring beyond which stretched 150 miles of sagebrush terrain, gorge, and rolling hills and mesaland, Moe frowned at Virgil, opened a file folder, and, without once glancing up at the lawyer, read him a riot act.

"According to my information, Virgil, you're still a Mexican national. In fact, as far as I can figure out you're not only a Mexican national, but if they could get ahold of you down there, they'd stick you in front of one of Señor Whatshisname's firing squads and blow a hole the size of a prize-winning county-fair pumpkin in your chest before you could even ask for a cigarette or one last kiss from a Juárez puta."

Moe paused for effect, brushing ashes off the papers before him, and squinted his bruised, exhausted-looking eyes that were blown up all out of proportion by his thick lenses.

"Now as I understand it, Virgil, in going over your record, you must have had a lot of friends in this state to get yourself set up as a lawyer in the first place, because if the bar had known anything about your criminal record, not to mention lack of citizenship—who forged these naturalization papers anyway? If they had known that, well, Lord God Almighty, we sure wouldn't have to be sitting here today having this little tête-à-tête, would we? And Chamisaville would still be a peaceful little town with its heart dead set on progress, while your bones jangled from a piece of hemp tied to a big old cactus way down south in Oaxaca County, Old Mexico, isn't that right, sir?"

Impassively, Virgil waited, amused by Moe's linguistic act, his chillingly jocular attempt to intimidate with a folksy redneck tone.

"What I'm saying, Virgil, is if somebody up here decides

to blow a whistle, you're in a heap of trouble. If they decide not to return you to Cuachitlán for burial, we can probably put you away up here for the rest of your life."

His eyes focused on the distant panorama, Virgil smoked an icy cigarette and waited.

"Naturally, I hate to bring this up, Virgil, but here's another thing. You know as well as I do that Uncle Sam is deporting you people just as fast as he can round you up and ship you south of the border. After all, we've got a depression going in this country and most of the unemployment in the Southwest is due to all you illegal aliens taking jobs from genuine, bona fide, destitute American citizens like me. Stryzpk—now that's a fine Yankee moniker. So I don't imagine that fact is going to help you very much, Virgil . . . *if* somebody blows a whistle. You understand what I'm saying?"

Brushing aside one flap of his suit jacket, Virgil removed a moderately large-sized Colt revolver, cocked it, and laconically touched the chilly snout of that pistol to the cold tip of Moe Stryzpk's nose. And, aiming his jet black eyes along the shiny route of the dark blue barrel into Moe's enormous goggle eyes, Virgil said quietly:

"In Mexico, Mr. Stryzpk, for ten years I was a revolutionary soldier in the peoples' army of Emiliano Zapata. As a revolutionary soldier I killed many men. I shot them to death from ambush, I killed them in pitched battles using rifles, pistols, machetes. I have beaten several men to death with rocks. I have garroted sentries at night with pieces of rope and wire. I once split open a traitor's chest with an ax. And I cold-bloodedly slit the throat of a woman who caused the death of three revolutionary comrades by informing on them to General Huerta's flunkies. I probably am not going to blow your brains out right here, because such a move would inevitably expose me and send me into hiding and make it impossible to work for the people of our town. But let me explain something so that we understand each other with perfect clarity. If you expose me, if I am arrested, if I am jailed, if I am deported, you are a dead man. If I can neither bail myself out before trial, nor escape, nor in some other fashion obtain the few minutes of freedom I would need to murder you, somebody else in this valley will do the job for me within one hour of hearing that whistle you plan to blow. When you arranged this meeting, I understood what you would say, and believe me, the whole valley knows what is going on between us here today. If my official secrets stay officially secret, you will live longer, Mr. Stryzpk. If you blow the whistle, I guarantee that before nightfall you will be as cold as last year's horseshit."

Moe could not move his head; nor could he take his gaze off Virgil's terrifyingly steadfast eyes, which seemed to merge with the ugly lead noses of the deadly chambered slugs on either side of the gun barrel. And Virgil held him like that for a moment after he had finished speaking, already murdering the cripple with eyes so fierce they congealed the blood in Moe's temples; he grew faint and breathless, totally incapacitated by fear. No threat he had ever received had even remotely approached the certain horror of Virgil's promise.

Virgil said, "Then it's understood?"

Moe gulped.

"If it isn't understood, then, with apologies to the people of this valley, I will kill you right now."

"It's . . . understood. Believe me."

Virgil put away the gun; his gaze drifted out the window again. After a pause, Moe also allowed his eyes to shift away from the blurred sheets cluttering his file folder to the landscape beyond the faintly steaming hot pool.

"It's going to be a long winter," Virgil mused. "You bastards want too much blood."

# Paradise
# On Earth

DESPITE MOE STRYZPK'S indefatigable drive and diabolical grasp of the situation, three hundred years of insane bad weather, poverty, sectarian mumbo jumbo, rotten luck, disease, and general all-around hardship had created a rugged breed in the Chamisa Valley, and it was not as easy to displace the native population as the Anglo Axis and its vendido henchmen had at first surmised.

All the same, forces of progress, a.k.a. Betterment, were in motion. Enough legal work cropped up, suddenly, to support a pack of lawyers. And four hundred years of traditional subsistence survival could no longer be taken for granted. The mierda, as the saying in bastardized local lingo went, had really hit the abanico.

Virgil Leyba tried to have the conservancy dissolved on a dozen different counts. But while he talked and argued, prepared briefs, and sought expert witnesses to counteract Bureau of Reclamation testimony, exhuming every pertinent piece of information he could locate on land and water laws and priority rights, the conservancy district plowed ahead. A plague of public and private surveyors, demographers, and hydrologists infested the valley. They hailed from the Bureau of Reclamation, the Bureau of Land Management, the state engineer's office, the Interstate Streams Commission, the Dynamite Shrine Miracle Development Corporation, the Mosquito Valley Ski Company, the Bureau of Indian Affairs, the Four Rivers Association, and the Albino Pine Defense Fund. Gardens were trampled, cows frightened while calving; horses bolted through fences, and cattle strayed. A hundred peeping toms were reported to the police, No Trespassing signs went up everywhere, angry shots were fired at the official strangers in puttees and knickers and pith helmets drawing imaginary lines through the locals' sacred property.

Pretty soon Virgil Leyba was defending dozens of penniless small farmers against manslaughter, assault and battery, aggravated injury, even a couple of murder charges, as farmers and ranchers defended their private property against the invasion of menacing officialdom bent on enslaving their land and their water rights in a merciless web of inefficient porkbarrel projects and unfair taxation.

Stirred up, off-balance, the valley trembled and a hundred ghosts emerged from the uneasy, tingling woodwork. Despite the odds stacked in their favor, it wouldn't be that easy, the Anglo Axis discovered, to encourage middle-class outsiders to come in and contend with the old ways of life.

When Randolph Bonney's younger brother Jerry first entered town to manage the Your Own Food Store, he had lived with his elder brother; now, desirous of his own home, he purchased Atiliano Montoya's fine old adobe. The aging double-crossed double-crosser was destitute and had to sell. For, after tricking the La Ciénega grantees into a sellout, and subsequently losing his own rich pastureland to the Balena Park moguls displaying Claude Parker's whale, Atiliano had fallen on even harder times. Acting on behalf of the Four Rivers Association, Virgil Leyba had sued him, hoping to discredit the grant sale and thereby void the conservancy district. The grant heirs had also hired Virgil to nullify the sale and seek restitution from Atiliano. To defend himself, Atiliano had hired Bob Moose; and Bob had enough pull, in the end, to defeat both Virgil and the La Ciénega Grant heirs. However, while Bob and his cocounselors, Damacio Mares and Tucker Moose, and Atiliano Montoya were in the King Cole Executive Room of the Dynamite Shrine Dining Salon celebrating their victory with champagne, Bob presented Atiliano with a bill for six thousand dollars.

"But I'm on *your* side!" Atiliano protested.

"You can't expect me to work for free," Bob Moose replied.

Meaning that at a fifty-dollar evaluation per acre, Bob Moose now owned all the rest of Atiliano's wealth except his small, picture-book-perfect farmhouse so recently decorated with lambs, bears, and guitar-playing angels by Espeedie Cisneros and Canuto Tafoya.

Before moving out so that Jerry Bonney could move in, Atiliano sought revenge on his ruinators. Digging through the hardpacked dirt floor, he retrieved a turquoise chunk some Pueblo friends helping to build the house had buried there long ago, its purpose being to keep the walls steady and the roof from caving in. Pocketing the turquoise, Atiliano then painted both doorway frames and all window lintels white: previously they had been robin's egg blue to keep the devil from entering his house. Finally, Atiliano asked a brother-in-law, Malaquias C. de Baca, to approach his sister, Genoveva Bachicha, a witch, about putting a curse on the house. And for a slight fee—Atiliano's good-luck silver dollar—Genoveva tucked a tiny bundle of rabbit's teeth, bear hair, and Bayer aspirin into a wall chink, plastering it over with a mud paste taken from a spot where Atiliano had urinated in the driveway.

On his first night in the house Jerry Bonney was slumbering peacefully when a nearby windowpane, for no discernable reason, shattered, sprinkling him with glass. After cleaning up the mess, he found sleep difficult because somebody, a woman, was sobbing in the kitchen. But each time Jerry got up and lit a kerosene lamp to investigate, he discovered nothing. The autumn night outside grew chilly and snow began to fall. As soon as Jerry lay back down, the kitchen ghost started moaning again. Some dirt landed in his eyes, and shortly thereafter, as the miserable woman took a breather, he could hear a different sound, difficult to place at first, a kind of sibilant sprinkle, as of sand or dust trickling from the cracks in his ceiling. After turning into that for a while, Jerry realized that the sound *was* being caused by sand and dirt sprinkling down from the ceiling. In point of fact, he remarked, sitting up and growing alarmed, the whole house seemed to be faintly trembling. Still, what could he do before morning? Jerry adjusted his pillow, left the kerosene lamp burning, arranged cotton wads in his ears to counteract the kitchen poltergeist, and had almost conked out when a hairy arm emerged from underneath his bed and heavy, clammy fingers gripped his thigh. Screeching, he bolted upright; the arm retreated under his bed. But when Jerry mustered enough courage to peep fearfully beneath his mattress, nothing was there. Still bent over, searching the shadows for something, he heard a knock on the door. It grew light outside; snow was still falling; the lady at the kitchen wake shut up.

Wrapping himself in a bright red woolen robe, Jerry opened the front door. Six toothless neighborhood crones dressed in black stood on the portal: two were holding a tiny, ornate coffin in which a pale child dressed in a white Communion outfit lay on satin pillows. The others, gripping tall burning tapers, did not even flinch when hot wax dripped onto their wrinkled skin.

"She drowned in the ditch," the women muttered fatalistically. "The angels have her now."

Jerry slammed the door in their faces, opened a bottle of Chamisaville white lightning sold to him only that afternoon by Pat GeeGee in the El Gaucho Bar, and camped rigidly on his bed waiting for dawn to get rid of all these nightmares.

Instead, another bizarre vision appeared in his broken window. A group of men, all members of the local Penitente brotherhood, were crawling on hands and knees through the snow, heading toward their nearby place of worship, a small, windowless morada. Some moaned and groaned; a couple flagellated each other with soft whips; another pulled a rickety wooden cart in which a skeleton sat, brandishing a large hazelwood bow, gaily shooting arrows in all directions. One feathered shaft sailed through Jerry's broken window and tunked into the floor, quivering

61

threateningly. But by then the future head of the Chamisa-ville Sierra Bell Telephone office was so drunk he didn't give a damn. Already he had determined to rent a semi-permanent room at the Plaza Hotel and wait until the valley settled down.

So when a magpie—actually Celestino Lucero's pet bird, Tierra o Muerte the Second—came through the window, landed on a lampshade, and, in Spanish, said "Go screw yourself!" he paid no attention.

Next day, the walls of Atiliano Montoya's beautiful little house shifted significantly; and before nightfall the roof had collapsed.

THE SAME WEEK that Atiliano Montoya's old house collapsed, a band of angry local residents, made furious by formation of the conservancy district and by the all-around lethal arrogance of the Anglo Axis, moved on Claude Parker's wonderful whale in the dead of night. They carved off all the blubber, meat, flesh, and organs they could reach, leaving little behind except baleen and bones, and galloped home to chew on whale fat for a while. Rodey McQueen, Claude Parker, and the rest of that oily crew immediately launched a relentless investigation. Within two weeks seventeen members of the raiding party were apprehended, tried in a court of law, and fined outrage-ously. If unwilling to sell land for the cash to pay their fines, the men spent six months in the pokey, during which time their wives or children sold a few acres for cash to hire hands to work the farms, frantically genera-ting produce and animals they could peddle for cash to meet the initial conservancy assessments and inflating property taxes.

While those poor men did time, paying dearly for Claude Parker's loss of income, another scruffy midnight band sidled into the park and dismantled the whale skele-ton until not even a whitened fiber or cartilaginous chunk remained on the musty yellowed ground where that em-balmed carcass had rested.

Shortly thereafter, the bones reappeared, scattered around the county and in use as fence posts, more durable and economical than the best cedar—especially as Rodey Mc-Queen and his lumber mill cohorts now had permits monopolizing the Magpie Creek García Grant cedar quo-tas. In fact, that enormous stretch of national forest had been declared off limits to all locals who had formerly gathered piñon firewood, cedar posts, and ponderosa lumber trees up there. Likewise, cattle and sheep people, among them Juan GeeGee, Celestino Lucero, and Bernardo C. de Baca, men who for years had been grazing animals on the García Grant, lost their permits when McQueen and Company moved in and began clear-cutting like crazy in order to meet the lumber demand for all the expanding Anglo Axis enterprises and developments. In the process they deliberately planned to unsettle the ecology so that when the Cañoncito Dam was built, silting problems would immediately skyrocket its costs. Local resentment over the commercial collusion between the hell-bent developers and the Forest Service soon reached crisis intensity. For months, war seemed imminent. And then one day, as the Floresta chief, Denzil Spivey, paused during a tree-marking operation to take a leak, a hidden rifleman, with destined-to-be-legendary expertise, shot off his testicles!

While the conservancy and dam battle focused on the Magpie Creek and Rio Puerco watershed, the Anglo Axis moved ahead on other fronts, the foremost being the Mosquito Valley. For his good work in the capital, State Senator Rudy LeDoux had obtained rich jobs constructing a hunting lodge and a dozen posh summer cabins for wealthy Chicago and Dallas sportsmen Rodey McQueen knew he could attract to the Midnight Mountains. Permanently leaving the care of his farm to his young sons, Chavo and J. B., Rudy commenced redecorating the Mosquito Valley. After the main lodge and four cabins were finished, McQueen ordered him to bulldoze several ponds in the rich meadowland, diverting water from the Rio Chiquito so that he could stock the ponds with rainbow trout for his summer or autumn visitors.

"I think that's illegal," Rudy said politely. "I'm afraid you can't build ponds and divert the river; barely enough water reaches La Ciénega during the summer as it is without further tapping the watercourse up here."

"Listen to me," Moe Stryzpk told the flustered construction foreman when Rudy arrived at his home office. "State laws say we can build any pond we want so long as the dam for it is no higher than ten feet, and the water impounded is no more than ten acre-feet."

"Well, I guess one little pond wouldn't hurt the stream much," Rudy allowed. "I thought Mr. McQueen wanted me to dig something real big that would adversely affect the water flowing down to La Ciénega in the dry months."

"He wants you to bulldoze eight little ponds," Moe said. "These people coming out here to hunt and hike and re-create, we want to be sure they can catch fish for breakfast before heading into the mountains."

"But if you build eight small ponds up there, Mr. Stryzpk, that'll kill the river at its source."

"We're not asking you to do anything illegal, Rudy."

"Listen, Mr. Stryzpk. You folks have done a lot for me and I appreciate it. But I'm not gonna do that to my own people. Lo siento mucho."

"Well, all right, Rudy. I can certainly understand your point of view. I'm a sentimental man myself. But you might ponder what we're asking you to do for a spell before making your decision final. You might chew on this, too. You took a pretty substantial cash hit to change that conservancy law in the legislature, and if the authorities were to find that out you might be in serious trouble. Who knows, an investigation could develop—"

"But you people *gave* me that money, free and clear. Expenses, you said. It wasn't a bribe. It wasn't extortion. Or a kickback."

Moe shrugged understandingly. "Sure, sure. You know and I know it wasn't a bribe, Rudy, but what do *they* know? You get some stranger, say, some half-assed government accountant or investigator or member of the FBI in here nosing around, and how is he going to know the difference?"

"If I get in trouble, you get in trouble," Rudy said.

Moe tinkered absentmindedly with a letter opener, jabbing the sharp point against the tip of a nicotined finger. "That might not be exactly the way things would fall into place, Rudy. Think about it. First think about your position, then think about our position. Think about who has got the power, and who these government investigators work for, and what the general attitude about you Mexicans in non-Mexican circles is, and weigh carefully what it is that you decide to do, and who it is that you decide to squeal on. You might also reflect that *you* received that cash from Atiliano Montoya, not me, not Rodey McQueen, not Bob Moose, not anybody indispensable. And Atiliano Montoya is already so far up shit creek that we don't even have to wind him up anymore to get him started kissing backsides. Another thing; you cross us, pal, and we'll fire you and hire Eduardo Mondragón to be crew chief in the Mosquito Valley."

"That son of a bitch would bulldoze a pit to bury his mother alive if you asked him to!"

Moe raised his eyebrows and smiled: "It's your choice."

Rudy LeDoux slumped home, got drunk, beat up on his wife and kids, and next morning he directed Mosquito Valley bulldozers to gouge out eight legal-sized trout and recreation ponds, each hole located either slightly below or directly atop various crucial springs feeding the Rio Chiquito.

Eight miles downstream the water-flow reduction was noticeable almost immediately.

That night, fifteen La Ciénega men entered the Mosquito Valley. No night watchmen were present; keys had been left in both bulldozers. The men started the machines, spent two hours knocking down every dam, and disappeared into the night.

On the following day McQueen ordered the dams rebuilt. After Rudy LeDoux had carried out his orders, McQueen further commissioned the state senator to select a few friends to stand armed guard that night in case the saboteurs returned.

The shootout which occurred around 1:00 A.M. went down in history as the Mosquito Valley Bulldozer Skirmish. Though no lives were taken, several volleys shattered the moonless night; Rudy LeDoux himself sustained the lone wound. The first bullet struck an eye, circled halfway around the skull, and exited from his ear, taking most of that appendage with it. A second slug splintered the ex-mayor's right leg. Most raiders scattered as soon as Rudy's vigilantes opened up on them: only their leader stood fast, the pudgy, ancient White Cap, Jesus Dolores Martínez Vigil. Mounted on a rearing stallion, this fierce little man emptied the magazine of a short-barreled saddle rifle at Rudy and his boys, shooting with remarkable accuracy from his dancing steed, his white teeth glistening from an excited and savage grin providing the only light by which he aimed.

The ponds remained, however. In fact, over the years, many more—cleverly financed by conservancy assessments paid in part by the poor farmers whom the ponds robbed of water—sprang up. The state engineer even granted the Mosquito Valley Development board permits to drill irrigation wells, further depleting Rio Chiquito headwaters. As for Rudy LeDoux, blind in one eye and crippled for life, he went into a swift decline. Out of construction for good and a bit dull-witted and gun-shy after the bullet clipped his eye, Rudy was abandoned by the Anglo Axis, defeated for state senator by Damacio Mares, and became incapable of working his acreage. Some farmland paid Al Lamont for maltreating his wounds; the rest of his land dissolved in similar bits and pieces. Neighbors, angry about his former alliance with the Anglo Axis, refused to offer condolences, let alone neighborly aid. Ashamed of her husband's weaknesses and his downfall, teased by riches only to gain a ludicrous poverty instead, Marina LeDoux created a scandal of her own by running off with a gambling man. The young sons, Chavo and J. B., closed out of jobs on the Cañoncito Dam, which had commenced abuilding, labored instead for the Civilian Conservation Corps, building national forest trails, earning a pittance to pay conservancy taxes and protect their dwindling farmland. Then the state informed Rudy LeDoux it was going to sell his farm for back taxes anyway.

"I always paid my taxes," the half-blind old man shrieked. "Just look at the courthouse records!"

"That's the problem," the stateys told him. "There's no record of any payments from you for the past ten years. Naturally, you could clear up the problem by letting us see your receipts."

"Nobody ever gave me a receipt. I always trusted—"

They moved to impound the farm. Rudy LeDoux begged Virgil Leyba to save it. Although already working eighteen hours a day trying to save the rest of the Chamisa Valley, how could Virgil refuse? Only a few years ago Rudy LeDoux had been a successful cattle rancher, a respected mayor, a conservative, level-headed leader who had always started the summer Cipi García fiestas by playing corridos on his mandolin from the plaza's quaint bandstand. The bastards were merciless! So Virgil took the case, one more legal headache and spiritual heartache, compliments of a reamed citizen with nothing to offer in return. The Morelos lawyer managed to stay the sale, but not the evaporated back taxes, which the state demanded right away. To obtain money for taxes already paid, Rudy refinanced the farm. Grimly, he put his signature on the loan papers, walked outside, took a last gander at the Indians' sacred mountains, the lush green valley, and a sparrow hawk perched on a recently installed telephone wire and, after singing gently, tears violating his weathered cheeks, he dropped dead.

After their father's lonely funeral, the hardened teen-agers, Chavo and J. B. LeDoux, sold their home, paid off the mortgage, and, with the little remaining cash, purchased a fifth-hand backhoe, using the machine to build adobes for valley newcomers constructing their modern, middle-class mud homes. The first client to purchase an allotment of bricks was a noted American artist formerly of New York and Kansas City, suffering from asthma, emphysema, gout, pleurisy, TB, and other assorted ailments. Sent by his doctor to the Southwest, Judson Babbitt was a famous painter, paramour, roué, and moneybags. Wanting to live within a half-mile of the plaza, he purchased the Atiliano Montoya land from Jerry Bonney, hired Pueblo Indians to clear away the haunted-house debris, purchased ten thousand adobes from Chavo and J. B. LeDoux at enormously inflated prices, and hired the brothers to build an ornate adobe mansion, expansively paying quadruple the going construction wages.

Tremendously excited by his newfound wealth, J. B. LeDoux determined to buy back the land he had just lost, recapturing his roots while the memory of them still quivered. But with people like Judson Babbitt paying huge-ly inflated prices for land and adobes and labor, the value and prices of those three commodities had every-where risen correspondingly. A pasture J. B. had sold for a hundred dollars an acre last year, was five hundred an acre today. And when J. B. queried other local workers about constructing a house for himself, he discovered they wanted as much for their labor from him as he was getting from Judson Babbitt.

J. B. scratched his head, and, lying on cool sand in the shadow of Pat GeeGee's rotting airplane, with Teresa Lujan in his arms, he felt tentacles of debilitating despair reaching through his veins and arteries to strangle his sickened heart.

Teresa snuggled her plumply tapered body into his con-fused, powerful bulk, whispering, "It's all right, querido. You're earning money; you're going to be one of *them*. In a couple more years we can be married and buy land and build our own beautiful house. And neither of us will ever be poor again."

A brilliant shooting star erased constellations crowding the sky. Although only midnight, a rooster crowed. Old men, middle-aged women, and little children vented a muffled crying in their sleep. Up late, Judson Babbitt scribbled letters to his famous painter friends, singing the praises of Chamisaville, urging them to come and settle. After all, there was a mint to be made off Indian portraits alone: "I never saw a race with such a marketable pathos and dignity. And they are so poor that they're willing to pose almost for free!"

While Babbitt agitated for a commercial, if not aesthetic, artistic gold rush, April McQueen, the most vivacious, also the naughtiest little girl in town, slid down a rope outside the nine-foot adobe walls protecting the McQueen estate, and prowled the deserted town.

In an alleyway between Vigil's Liquors and the Plaza Hotel, she came across a sprawled human lump wrapped in a blanket—Atiliano Montoya, already Chamisaville's first homeless public drunk. Going through his pockets for money, she found none, tiptoed away, and pressed her nose against the window of Virgil Leyba's office. A light was on; the rangy, overworked lawyer slept at his desk, much too exhausted for dreaming.

The imprint of her sensual child's lips shaping a kiss remained on the windowpane, and later on the lawyer's heart, forever.

BOOM DAYS, DEPRESSION DAYS, poverty, riches. After Atiliano Montoya, Rudy LeDoux, Vidal Mondragón and a few others of their unfortunate ilk had bitten the dust, it was not as easy to exploit their peers.

The whale was gone. The Horse Without Shit had twelve rattlesnakes hibernating in its gas tank and a bluebird nest blocking the carburetor. Pat GeeGee's airplane would never fly again. And any religious significance of the Cipi García miracle had been lost amid the commercial hoopla surrounding the little shrine and hot-springs area. Construction on the Cañoncito Dam was halted unexpectedly (according to plan) because tests had revealed a possible fault in the dam bed rock-layer. Many local workers (according to plan) were caught once again overextended financially, having invested, during flush construction times, in automobiles, radios, a telephone or two, and even electric stoves. During the layoff, a frantic scramble to save cars, appliances, and even houses occurred. Thieves

68

sprouted like mushrooms after a rain, stealing vehicles, tools, Celestino Lucero's milk bottles off back stoops— anything that might be fenced at home or abroad for cash to save the things that everybody else in a similar predicament was stealing in order to pay off their creditors.

The general situation backfired briefly on the Anglo Axis when a few desperadoes about to lose everything they owned kidnapped April McQueen, holding her prisoner in a deserted gold-mine shaft behind Hija Negrita Mountain for a $100,000 ransom.

Rodey McQueen almost had a breakdown. Offering the full amount immediately in cash, he promised to double the sum if the kidnappers wished, no questions asked. Never again would he exploit anybody in the valley— scout's honor! Ownership of all his Dynamite Shrine ventures would be transferred to a ruling junta of local folks, whoever the kidnappers named, if only they'd return his darling daughter unharmed. "Hell," he pleaded, "I'll move on back to Texas and never set hide nor hair in Chamisaville again, if only you'll just give me my daughter!"

"Aparentemente, usted es una persona que tiene mucho valor en los ojos de su padre," the chief abductor, Jesus Dolores Martínez Vigil, told April as the two warmed themselves by a fire, sipping coffee laced with white lightning out of porcelain-coated tin cups. Strictly monolingual, the dumpy and dangerous little man, wrapped in cartridge belts and a filthy rope vest and weighed down ridiculously by a half-dozen holstered revolvers hanging like smoke-room sausages and hams about his body, had no problem communicating with the Muleshoe tyrant's daughter. For, unlike the rest of her culturally chauvinistic family, April spoke a fluent Spanish learned from Amaranta GeeGee, who worked fourteen hours a day in the McQueen mansion for the piddling cash that kept her family and little farm afloat. Aware of Amaranta's plight, and embarrassed at an early age by her family's position, April had been passing on most of her weekly allowance—triple Amaranta's salary—to the wonderful lady, who in return had taught April Spanish and much local lore. Amaranta had prepped her on herb curing and witchcraft, had helped her learn to play local songs and corridos on the guitar, had given her lessons in reading the cards and making hexes, and had taught her colcha embroidery, exorcism, and how to ferment chokecherry wine. Amaranta had also fingered the little girl for the snatch.

"Of course, do not worry," Jesus Etcetera reassured her. "If he refuses to cough up, we won't kill you. We'll set you loose in the sagebrush and let you wander home. But you must promise to tell everybody that you escaped, so that they will think we might have killed you if they hadn't produced the loot."

"If he says you can take over the Dynamite Shrine enterprises and the Mosquito Valley Development Corporation, make sure you get it in writing," April advised. "Also, you better be certain that everybody from the local coppers to the state gangbusters sign a paper that they won't prosecute any of you if I'm returned safe and sound."

"That's a good idea," Jesus Etcetera said. "I never thought of that."

All alone at night, Rodey McQueen rode onto the mysterious western mesa as instructed, his saddlebags stuffed with cash and several pounds of cream-colored legal documents absolving the kidnappers of all blame and turning over control of his enterprises to the bandits. Although McQueen was unable to see even ten feet ahead, his horse knew the way. Clouds covered the moon and stars; no night bichos made noises. As McQueen neared the gorge an errie echo stirred the air without making any sound his ears could define. And, alone in the ghostly void, for a moment the successful conman really believed he could give up everything for April's safe return.

Jesus Dolores Martínez Vigil said, "Buenas noches, McReina."

An exchange of money and documents occurred.

The plump outlaw said, "These documents are written in English instead of Spanish. How can I determine if you have given us what we want unless you write it all down in Spanish?"

Unable to understand his words, McQueen nevertheless got the drift. Next evening he returned with contracts translated into Spanish. The illiterate pirate pretended to read through the convoluted verbiage, made his mark, and disappeared into the night. Two hours later April was safe at home in her weeping mother's arms.

Naturally, the contracts were never honored, no immunity from prosecution had been granted. Although April refused to squeal, one by one, four of the organizers and perpetrators of the plot—Fecundo Lavadie, Max Jaramillo,

70

Bonifacio Herrera, and Ikie Trujillo—were rounded up, jailed, and tried for a capital crime. Their families suffered spiritual, psychological, and economic deprivations: other valley locals were ashamed of their actions: the case received statewide attention. Yet on page one, the *Chamisaville News* covered a donkey softball game, a sewing bee, and two grass fires—the kidnapping got a one-line blurb in the police blotter. As if life wasn't tough enough, Virgil Leyba had to defend this bunch of uncoordinated country bumpkins who were so stupid they had written their names in the blank spaces McQueen had provided on the contract relinquishing his assets and his enterprises to the kidnappers.

Ultimately, Virgil saved their lives by insisting that the power structure had to honor its nonprosecution promises at least a little: and in a magnanimous concession favoring leniency, the court agreed not to hang the kidnappers. In return for their lives, the four men gave back the ransom money, which had been hidden in an unused well. Case closed, Fecundo, Max, Bonifacio, and Ikie were sent off forever, leaving their ashamed and shattered families behind.

WITH THE ADVENT of the Anglo Axis and its Betterment policies, a decision was made to bring Chamisaville education "into the twentieth century." The proper amount of money and influence was floated among enough of the electorate to vote Rodey McQueen, Moe Stryzpk, Bob Moose, Randolph Bonney, and Al Lamont onto the local school board, and from that point on the American Way of Education was home free. Teachers who could not or would not converse in English with their students were fired, or they were not hired. Suddenly Anglos were running most grades, and children of the burgeoning white population had catapulted to the head of their class. United States history that commenced with Columbus, the Pilgrims, and the Thirteen Colonies became mandatory fare; the story of native tribes on the North American continent long before the birth of Christ was squelched; the settling of Mexico became a footnote. Indians, dubbed "bloodthirsty savages," were only mentioned in passing as the dull-witted victims of heroes like Kit Carson: once castigated and reservationized they were forgotten. And human beings of Mexican descent, called lazy and shiftless, pictured always under a fat hat and snoozing, existed only

71

as the butt of a few crude jokes before they were totally buried.

"Find 'em, fuck 'em, assimilate 'em, forget 'em," Juan Ortega said bitterly to Virgil Leyba one evening in the El Gaucho Bar. "What are we going to do about this mess, primo?"

"We could strike back with our own cultural organ," the lawyer said gloomily.

Already Virgil was so tired he couldn't think straight. Fighting the conservancy district, trying to stop the dam, going to bat for the delinquent individuals on the verge of losing their land for failing to pay assessments for dam water they weren't even receiving kept him occupied eighteen hours a day. Representing local hotheads who assaulted government surveyors further encroached upon his time. Defending outright bandits like the Mosquito Valley raiders and the kidnappers of April McQueen gave him headaches even while he slept. Struggling to secure valid titles for all the valley natives whose shaky property claims had descended by word of mouth or from vague communal land-grant papers kept him busy—and dizzy—for whatever hours remained. Although he had a wife and a young son, Virgil rarely saw them. Loretta ran the Plaza Hotel, pouring their small profits into his legal practice. But after a few years, run-down, shabby, and subject to an effective Anglo Axis boycott, the hotel could barely pay for itself, let alone keep Virgil in court fees.

During the lawyer's rare moments at home, little Junior stretched pudgy arms toward his melancholy papa, asking for love, but Virgil was usually too preoccupied or fatigued to notice. In a dream, he hugged the child without feeling him, his head pondering a thousand desperate legal moves. "If you don't learn to relax, you're going to kill yourself," Loretta warned. Beyond repair, Virgil failed to realize she had spoken. Doomed to be a victim of the poor, how could his superhuman efforts stem the tide, or even successfully stall for time?

Yet who else was there?

Virgil and Juan Ortega met with Espeedie Cisneros, Juan and Pat GeeGee, Celestino Lucero and Perfecto Torres, and Flakey Jake Martínez and Marshall Kickingbird from the Pueblo. They decided to publish a newspaper called the *El Clarín*. It would tell the real valley news in Spanish and English and Tewa, and also publish poetry, stories, and essays by local talents, keeping the real culture alive. A column would deal with Chamisaville history as it truly happened. An entire page would feature dichos and recipes and old-timers recollecting the past. A people's tribune, open to everybody, it would print interviews with men and women from all walks of Chamisa County life. Whenever possible, the *El Clarín* would publish photographs of valley citizens and of artwork by the people.

"How could we possibly finance such a dream?" Espeedie Cisneros asked. "Who can find that much money?"

"I can find the money," Virgil said.

"Where?"

"Hotel profits, the legal practice, I don't know. Where there's a will . . ."

Because the *Chamisaville News* refused to rent its presses, the paper had to be printed in the capital. This meant somebody had to escort the *El Clarín* down south, nurture it through paste-up and the presses, and lug it home for distribution. But who, among all these involved, could squander the time and the money? In the end, Virgil morosely agreed to squeeze the trip into his schedule and he bought a small roadster to facilitate the process.

"Where did you find the money for that car?" Loretta complained. "We have enough debts, how could you add this on top of them all?"

"It's a thing that should be done. . . ."

On the eve of World War II, the *El Clarín* survived erratically for a while: it never even remotely flourished. No merchant would buy an ad. Few impoverished locals could contribute more than their lore, their talk, their goodwill, and a bit of their time come evening. The paper's mainstay was Juan Ortega, a young man already hobbled with eight children and a wife almost continuously pregnant. He drove around the valley in Virgil's motorcar, or canvassed the small communities on horseback, collecting information, stories, old ferrotypes, dichos, news items, interviews. He photographed neighbors, relatives, and friends irrigating, chopping wood, harvesting chile, building houses, slaughtering kids and hogs, embroidering, grooming horses, making chicos. He sat in courtrooms reporting the other side of every drama, explaining the "guilt" of the "guilty" from a different point of view. He listened to musicians until his ears ached and published their long love songs, their ballads, their protest corridos.

One issue had an illustrated feature on the house murals Espeedie Cisneros and Canuto Tafoya had painted; another issue ran side-by-side biographies of Jesus Etcetera and Rodey McQueen. Special conservancy district and Mosquito Valley editions lambasted the Anglo Axis with no holds barred. The history of the Albino Pine sacred-land suit made page one. Page two featured Perfecto Torres and Celestino Lucero talking about their dairy farm and the 1912 Buffalo Fire Engine that delivered milk twice weekly to some seventy families in the Chamisa Valley. The Arrellano and Casados brothers engaged in another showdown, this one a benefit—all proceeds went to the paper. In another charity event for the *El Clarín*, Eloy Romo donned his raggedy sneakers, high-school track shorts, black-and-silver cape, and four-ounce gloves and agreed to spend six hours in a plaza ring taking on all comers for a buck a throw. By the end of that grueling afternoon, Eloy had been knocked out sixteen times, and he had KO'd eleven men. The twenty-seven dollars Eloy earned for his questionable pugilistic talents promptly ended up in Al Lamont's pocket, though, as the valiant doctor trepanned into the boxer's head to relieve pressure from a blood clot, did an entire restoration of his flattened nose, and surgically removed the stumps of half of Eloy's teeth.

When Icarus Suazo fired Joe Brady and Win Potter as soon as Marshall Kickingbird passed the bar exam, the *El Clarín* detailed in full the Denver lawyers' treachery. Marshall planned to sue, but the two attorneys disappeared on the day of their release, leaving barely a ripple behind them.

When conservancy assessments jumped in order to build a Cipi García Miracle Memorial Museum in Balena Park, the *El Clarín* editorialized against it, almost literally issuing a call to arms. Every issue belabored such unfair "TAXATION WITHOUT REPRESENTATION!" The scare headlines were invariably accompanied by photographs of the half-constructed dam for which all Chamiseños were paying, even though no supplemental irrigation water was being delivered enabling them to grow fabulous crops to sell for the cash needed to pay off their conservancy assessments incurred by construction of the dam.

Often the newspaper articles were not written and handed in until late at night. And then, frantically rushing to meet publishing deadlines, Virgil and Juan would drive south to the capital at midnight, a dangerous trip on that narrow highway twisting for thirty miles down between the sheer walls of the Rio Grande Gorge. They sang songs to keep each other conscious and babbled giddily about themselves, or about life in general. Juan had always had a dream of going to college and becoming a wise man; of traveling the globe to discover people, places, things. Instead, he had not survived school beyond the fifth grade. Married at seventeen to Mari-Elena, he had fathered a child almost every other year since. But Juan had learned to read early, and always wanted to write. He had loved the *Chamisaville News* even though it suppressed many unpleasant facts; now he prayed that the *El Clarín* could last forever. "I'm gonna win me a Pulitzer," he joked sleepily, bleary-eyes barely focused as they rattled over unpainted macadam, a five-hundred-foot dive into icy water only inches from their right-hand tires. "And after that I want to write novels, short stories, all kinds of fiction. I want to be a great American writer, no kidding."

Virgil could barely keep awake as their automobile careened through starlit darkness. His body, all bones, felt hollow. I'm so gaunt and angular if I swallowed a cherry whole an observer could trace its progress down my throat and esophagus into my shrunken belly, he thought.

"A strange pair."

"What?"

"A strange pair we make, you and me," Virgil groaned.

Juan laughed. Young, hard working, involved in the whole social scene—what matter if he was trapped in Chamisa V. forever? "It's okay," he laughed. "Life is worth it."

In the middle of nowhere they would stop the car, pissing onto hard sand or onto some cholla skeltons, side by side, heads tilted back, gazing at stars while goosebumps rippled around their shoulders. Virgil never commented on the dark, bizarre galaxies; he muttered and grunted for punctuation while Juan rejoiced and rambled on, seething with piss and vinegar.

In the capital, they babied the *El Clarín* through typesetting and lingered at the printer's long after all others had retired, proofreading copy far into the early morning hours. Their mission accomplished, Juan collapsed into a chair, instantly snoring. But Virgil could never rest. Outside, on the prowl, he visited barrio bars, rarely talking with fellow boozers, drinking hard, and inevitably chasing down a woman: if she was not a gratis pickup, he paid at a whorehouse, experiencing no shame, calming his need.

Occasionally, Virgil made these rounds with a close Capital City friend, Abe Gallegos, an uninhibited young doctor who knew everybody they might bump into, a compassionate and skillful man, rabid leftist, brash womanizer. Chubby and rumpled, absentminded and volatile, he waddled along beside Virgil singing, arguing, on tiptoes trying to get an arm around the somber lawyer he loved and admired.

Back at the printer's after his rounds, Virgil slumped restlessly into his car, drowsing fitfully behind the wheel until dawn, lonesome and beaten badly, his head teeming with frightening phantasmagorical memories of yesterday, today, and tomorrow, his passionate sensibilities enveloped by the pleading of downtrodden people, his mysterious wife, and antagonizing little boy. Though the child was already pitted against him, perhaps for life, Virgil dared hope that one day Junior would join his law practice, seduced by Virgil's cynical idealism into throwing away a shot at lucre by dedicating his heart and his talent to the floundering peasant class. But son and father could hardly inhabit the same room together for minutes at a time; and, without understanding why exactly, Virgil already mourned his offspring's soul.

Finally, they carted the finished paper north. Through many a violent snowstorm they traveled, bringing the real news to Chamisaville. Virgil tilted sideways in the passenger seat, his face ghastly pale, his jaw dropped wide open, snoring as Juan guided the sluggish automobile up the steep road, singing songs to keep awake and fantasizing always that *this* issue of the paper would turn society upside down, waking up the slumbering masses who would arise and tell Rodey McQueen and his indefatigable henchmen to cut out all their crap.

Then war was declared and the *El Clarín* died. Juan Ortega was snatched up, trained to be a rifleman, and deported, arm in arm with Virgil and Icarus Suazo and Marshall Kickingbird. Joined by a dozen other boys from the valley, the protectors of the Chamisa Valley were gathered up and trained to become the protectors of empire abroad. In fact, almost all Chamisaville's gadflies were rounded up, trained in the manly arts of extermination, and shipped to Armageddon. Espeedie Cisneros, Celestino Lucero and his pet magpie, Tierra o Muerte the

Third, Perfecto Torres. The draft also nailed Eduardo Mondragón—and with that his shaky empire collapsed. Wounded in Guadalcanal, again on Iwo Jima, and weighed down by medals, Eduardo eventually returned home with only one leg and an aggregate of four fingers . . . to discover he had no home to return to.

WITH MOST OF THE radicals gone, peace and well-being permeated the gorgeous valley peppered with quaint villages and handsome brown-skinned people. The artist Judson Babbitt awoke each morning tingling with expectation. Toting a bag of bread crusts and grain, he ambled through high-country sunshine to the plaza and camped on a bench, lazily feeding the pigeons that swooped off the First State Bank, the *Chamisaville News* building, the old courthouse and the Eggington Mercantile Store. Other artists from the expanding colony of aesthetes sprinkled throughout the valley often met this patriarch of American art, whose noble mane, at forty-five, had already gone gray. They held bull-sessions on the plaza, or at the Prince of Whales Café, or in the Courthouse Bar and Restaurant, another McQueen enterprise. On other occasions, Babbitt, the partner in his art school, Staughton van Peebles, and lesser luminaries piloted their automobiles over to the Dynamite Shrine complex, bathed to their dreamy hearts' content, and later indulged in profound or merry or silly coffee klatches in the King Cole Executive Room of the Dynamite Shrine Dining Salon. From time to time, they entertained a reporter or two—at the baths, on the plaza, in private adobe palaces: the newspapermen returned to the capital or to farther reaches of the nation and wrote enthusiastically of the growing art colony hatched by the sleepy little Dynamite Miracle village. A nationwide mystique began developing about the beautiful town nestled high in the southern Rockies where the deer and the antelope played. And the artists built galleries and renovated old homes for commercial purposes; then they sat in canvas deck chairs painting the vivid landscape, or journeyed to the Pueblo and immortalized Indians willing to pose for fifty cents an hour. They sported like Etonians, these gentle colonialists in their abstract foreign nation, where the poverty was belied by beautiful landscapes, and the people were "dignified and happy and simple folks rich in wonderful native lore."

"Quel paradise on earth!" Judson Babbitt sighed as pigeons floated gracefully off buildings and down from the foliage, landing hungrily at his feet.

Local inhabitants viewed Judson Babbitt and his fellow artists with trepidation; their bohemian ways constituted a puzzling addition to the valley. Their social habits teased the people, making them curious, often defensive, sometimes envious. Their effervescent, noisy women flounced around in outrageous clothing with plunging necklines and no bras, revealing too much of themselves through almost transparent chiffon blouses, nearly knee-high skirts, and slacks that were too tight for comfort. They wore exotic makeup, smoked cigarettes in ivory holders, and entered the bars, drinking beside their noisy men, even kissing in public. At the Coronado Hot Springs, located in foothills east of Mota Llano, they shed their gaudy plumage, bathing naked beside their bearded husbands and lovers. Ensconced among junipers and sage bushes above the hot springs, sons and daughters of Juan and Amaranta Gee-Gee and Espeedie and Pancha Cisneros gawked at the plump sensuous bodies cavorting in the nude. Entirely naked except for a wide-brimmed straw hat sporting a pink ostrich plume, Felicia Babbitt, a large-breasted woman with waist-length red hair, sat cross-legged on a blanket dreamily reading Plato while noisily sucking on a juicy peach. Huggable green eyes and ruby lips sparkled from the shady dapple half obscuring her features. Almost touching one of her thighs, a red wine bottle, half wrapped in almond-colored wicker, glittered.

The peeping toms ached for her body, her life-style, her "freedom." Everyone knew about her glamorous, heart-rending affair with Staughton van Peebles, whose mistress, slinky high-school music teacher and fabulous pianist Ruby Starvitsky, had often been observed sneaking across the fields late at night to visit another noted painter—and poet—Earl Moses, even as Mrs. Moses, an alluring former dance-hall follies girl known as Amanda Santana, cavorted illicitly with several newly arrived bohemians and a pueblo man named Gabe Suazo, no relation to Icarus, whose wife and family were unalterably shamed by Gabe's faithless behavior.

Mystified Chamisaville citizens didn't know what to make of the new mores. Brazenly, the artists flaunted their freedom, apparently unaware that their behavior might offend, or tantalize, the locals. The artists were resented, feared, envied. Some local yokels nursed crippling sexual hungers for those loose floozies. Others cultivated dreams of falling in love with the Anglos—they had money. A few women admired Felicia Babbitt's seductive clothes, nail polish, makeup and hairdos, bewitching sophistication, cigarette smoking, and ability to drink in the bars with her man. Yearning for that independence, they were ashamed of their lust, yet gave in to their own men more easily and dreamed of romantic liaisons instead of the hard life under a macho yoke they had endured forever.

A deep uneasiness pecked at the weakening social structure of the valley. Evaluating the artists, disliking them, resenting their lack of dignity, hating their influence on good little Catholic children, many Spanish-speaking locals nevertheless felt, in their tough worker bodies, an uncomfortable dissatisfaction aborning.

Dreams of empire, conquest, and romance unsettled Chamisaville citizens. And although they ostracized Gabe Suazo for destroying his family by screwing Amanda Santana, many people also envied that son of a bitch, and would have jumped into the Rio Grande Gorge headfirst just for a piece of his provocative piece of ass.


# Lesser Skilled
# Than Birds

BUT FOR HIS DAUGHTER, Rodey McQueen would have been on top of the world, no strings attached. Yet April, his most precious possession, also caused him frightening pain. Beautiful beyond almost any man's ability to describe her, April seemed possessed by devil-inspired energies. Volatile, criminally attractive, all-American, and healthy—almost any superlative might describe that wild and moody child. By April's sixth birthday, McQueen had realized they were in for trouble. April was wilder than a peach-orchard shoat, cocky as the king of spades. On her eighth birthday, Karl Mudd photographed April in a demure taffeta party dress . . . with a two-sixgun holster cinched around her waist. April's mischievous blue eyes and mouth-watering golden hair were intoxicating in ways McQueen did not understand. Often, staring at her, the financier felt his groin prickle, an erection on the way. And at a terribly early age April understood exactly the power she had over men. Right from the start, boyfriends clustered. And April played the coquette, tormenting them for fun; it amused the child to break their hearts in two.

Oh, she was brighter, smarter than any other little girl or boy in the valley. Gregarious, athletic, in love with parties and dancing, April also spent long hours alone locked in her room, reading books, anything and everything—novels, encyclopedias, tracts on geography and art.

Watching her on horseback, pigtails flying, winning barrel races at the local rodeo, or, outfitted in black cap, red coat, and jodhpurs, winning ribbons at Capital City horse shows, McQueen understood they could never hold her. April played baseball, also tennis at the country club; no one swam a better crawl, or could execute a lovelier swan dive. On her thirteenth birthday, April emerged from the country-club pool in a skintight ecru bathing suit that caused the Mooses, the Bonneys, and the Lamonts to gasp. By that time, her wide shoulders, large womanly breasts, tiny high waist, classically feminine hips, and Betty Grable legs assaulted any eye. She knew it and played her body for all it was worth, onstage every minute, the queen of pizzazz and glamour. April wiggled her pinkie and doors fell over, sycophants leaped to attend her train, boys howled at the moon, pretty girls shrank into wallflowers, grown men cursed and broke their knuckles hitting tree trunks.

A sadness had lodged in the Muleshoe conman almost as soon as his daughter could walk. Her vitality was too much for any single—even if powerful—family to control. And although she was gifted with an enviably quick mind, he foresaw for her a destiny of unparalleled anguish. McQueen understood that nobody she captured would ever be able to even-steven his undisciplined daughter. He worried that April would burn out early, tragically. He guessed that she would impetuously waste her exhilarating vigor on half-wits. And her rosy cheeks and beckoning wild blue eyes, her luxuriant hair and hourglass body, and all her electric, soft, sickeningly intoxicating moves and rhythms rode with McQueen wherever he strode, jabbing at his solar plexus, causing a sorrowful turbulence in his mind.

Bewildered by April's beauty and mercurial personality,

Cynthia had lost her daughter years ago. Now they teetered on the brink of debilitating antagonisms. April had always felt uncomfortable in the family's opulence, in their echoing mansion. A teen-ager now, she insisted on driving second-hand jeeps, dilapidated station wagons, or decrepit battered convertibles instead of the Cadillacs her father wanted to give her. Her beautiful clothes she had always given away to school chums, daughters of the impoverished local folks who were also her constant guests at the tiny country club, much to everybody's incessant consternation. Cynthia McQueen tried hard to love her child: instead, she hated April for being a walking reprimand, a relentless indictment of her values and aspirations.

Insatiably curious, April forced everybody to teach her something. She absorbed and easily perfected their skills, robbing their limelights and demanding more until they had nothing left to give, then raced on to somebody better or different or just plain new.

April studied art in a school founded by Judson Babbitt and Staughton van Peebles. Both men agreed she was the most gifted youngster they had ever tutored. Jonathan Moose, Bob's youngest brother and member of the Moose firm, regularly entered the McQueen mansion, teaching April classical piano, even as his conservative composure was bruised against her shoreline of dangerous boulders. Within two years April could outplay Jonathan on the keyboard. And, despite her parents' objections, she mastered boogie-woogie and blues, learning from Amanda Santana, from old records belonging to Staughton van Peebles, from sheet music ordered from lascivious New York Tin Pan Alley connections. She knew all about Billie Holiday and Josh White, Huddie Ledbetter and Bessie Smith, Champion Jack Dupree, Ma Rainey, and Ardella Bragg. And when guests gathered at the mansion, April was as likely to flop down at the piano and render "Pig-meat Blues" or "Chocolate to the Bone" as she was to make everybody safely happy with the "Moonlight Sonata."

In a valley where half the population knew at least a few songs on the guitar, she soon could play that instrument like a virtuoso, squeezing a real disquieting funk out of it, be it blues or Jimmie Rodgers, Hank Williams or Bob Wills and the Texas Playboys. From Amaranta GeeGee she learned the valley corridos, rancheras, popular Mexican songs—the best of Pedro Infante, flamenco tunes, and religious canting.

No man, having spent time with her, could avoid making a grab for April's body. Judson Babbitt sidled up behind her while April painted in his studio and slipped his hands gently under her arms, cupping her ample breasts. The insouciant girl continued applying her brush as he pressed his groin against her buttocks. He had expected a reaction—feverish, confused, sexual: instead, April was so unimpressed that the famous artist fell apart. Like a jerk, he found himself muttering, "I love you . . . would you marry me?" Ice cold, her head tilted slightly, inspecting her painting, April said, "Do you like it? Is the sky too blue?" Babbitt relinquished her tits, backing away, feeling ashamed, angry, stupid—he had made a terrible fool of himself with this heartless nymphet. "Please don't tell your father," he babbled, suddenly viewing her as jailbait. "He knows," April said vaguely, frowning at her painting. "Everybody wants to fuck me." And, abruptly spinning around, she grinned at him with a merry, false innocence, a devilish glitter in her piquant daffodil-blue eyes. Babbitt wanted to grab, rape, murder this unbearably healthy and buxom temptress. If he could not have her, he would destroy her. If he could not destroy her, he would make her pregnant, ground the high-flying blond bombshell, give her a taste of "real life."

April tittered and twitched her beautiful head, enjoying every minute of his pathetic anguish. And while J. B. LeDoux, Icarus Suazo, Juan Ortega, and Virgil Leyba were doing time in prison camps after having been captured by the Japanese and surviving the death march of Bataan, April McQueen was swimming, riding horses, driving automobiles (without a license) too fast, smoking cigarettes and drinking her first booze (at fourteen), and painting lush Fauvelike canvases. Too, she took ballet lessons from Amanda Santana, who one day captured the young girl in her wiry, brown arms and, with a miserable groan, wrestled April gently onto the floor of the sunlit music room, touching fingers between her thighs, and soaking the fabric covering April's magic bosom with passionate spittle.

Nothing fazed April. She wore tight skirts and peasant blouses, soft pink cashmere sweaters and dramatic short-shorts, silk stockings and high heels, men's work shirts and baggy dungarees, white tennis shoes, cowboy boots. Sometimes her hair tumbled in undisciplined folds around her face and shoulders; or again, she wore it in double ponytails; or suddenly, tucking it up in a bun, she became sophisticated, remote, otherworldly, and, attending a junior-high-school dance with Junior Leyba, she resembled a woman of thirty-five.

Yet the very next morning, joining her fellow cheerleaders, April spent four hours on the high-school football field wearing an old sweatshirt, cutoff jeans, and sneakers, practicing innocent, peppy routines.

As a pillar of Chamisaville, McQueen, feeling the need to become a socially religious man, had imported a young Episcopal minister named Dagwood Whipple. North of town, he had built a mighty church for that inauspicious creature, an edifice grand enough to compete with Father Molé's Catholic castle. But April wanted nothing to do with religion. For a while, the family insisted she attend; Cynthia McQueen dressed her daughter in demure, throat-high ruffles, hoping to lower her profile. Yet April's husky voice made heads turn during every hymn; a torch singer for God among the humble congregation! By her teen-age years, April was arriving at church dressed to kill, her mature bosom mocking the disconcerted preacher through chartreuse jersey fabrics, her hips laughing above the ripple of pleats on knee-high skirts. Gratefully, her parents finally allowed her to withdraw from Sunday rituals. April amused herself elsewhere on the sabbath, racing horses for money at the Pueblo, skinny-dipping with artists at the Coronado Hot Springs, playing golf with best pals Junior Leyba, George Parker, and Rebecca Valerio up in the Mosquito Valley.

Or, alone in her shabby convertible parked on the deserted mesa halfway between town and the Rio Grande Gorge, she sat atop the back seat strumming her guitar and singing the blues, show tunes, pop and country songs. Or sometimes April merely rested out there on Sunday mornings, listening to the faint clanging of town church bells, fingering her crotch, which seemed always greasy, masturbating and yearning for the sexual experience, for men, for women, for friends, for horses, for mountains and foreign countries and new music, wondering what it would be like to be a Pigalle prostitute, a New York fashion model, a Hollywood starlet, a big-band—Dorsey, Miller, Goodman—torch singer. Or a comedienne. I'd like to act with the Marx brothers, she mused. And attended every El Sol picture show, avidly learning by heart all the gush in the film magazines that came her way. The

El Sol was owned and operated by Clarence Moore, a devil-may-care, swaggering, potbellied soldier of fortune and alcoholic longtime buddy of her dad's. He adored April, and booked any film she desired, hoping to take her just once some day, knowing he'd lose her the second he scored, because April was meant for bigger things, for the movies, fame, recognition, magazine covers, Europe, Persia, Babylon—

She was one of the exceptional few destined for a truly magic journey through life.

On Sunday mornings in her battered convertible on the mesa, April listened to church bells and the sweltering sunshiny murmur of the sageland. Grasshoppers buzzed, far dogs barked, the enormous mountains gave off soft rumbling twinges. Stripping to the buff, April stretched over the hot front hood, loving the warm sun that melted into her cinnamon skin and formed sweat bubbles on her lips, between her breasts, and in the sweet creases of her nubile tummy. Ay, such impatience colored her days, such a longing for things unknown! Sex—a lust for, and a fear of, it : and a scornful pity for all the men who had grabbed at her, made impotent by their overwrought desire. An intolerance of everyone's imperfections gave a cold cast to her heart and muted her compassion. She had a desire to rule everybody cruelly, because they were so stupid, incompetent, and unlovely compared to April McQueen. Who, in this life, was good enough for her? And she worried that her enormous talent, positive energy, and accidental beauty had forged her into an irrevocably spoiled brat. April baked in empty desert sunshine with her almost sickening lust for life framed by an idealism and capacity for hope that often made her nauseous.

On other Sundays April rode a horse to the Pat Gee-Gee airfield, where the bar owner's old airplane was rotting. Windows had been shot to pieces, the control panel stripped bare, the engine boosted. Its wings dripped metal and canvas shreds; broken wires ensnarled the body; tires had been robbed, wheel stays broken. Losing its shape, the plane sagged into the sand. Spiders, lizards, and bluebirds occupied the tumbleweed-infested crannies of its crumpled skeleton.

"Already ten years have passed since Carlito Epstein took me up in this poor plane." April was almost moved to bitter tears by the wreck. The wonderful memory of that flight was mitigated by this utterly destroyed machine.

Despair cracked a whip; her head ached. Life was unfair, everybody—the blessed as well as the wretched—held untenable cards.

April snarled at the plane: "They'll take the silver spoon out of my mouth and shove it right up my privileged ass."

Everything happened at once with April. It had always been that way. A mass confusion—of needs, skills, ideas, plans, hopes, fears—threatened her sanity. She protected herself by being glib, heartless, jazzy. Hopping dementedly halfway between laughter and tears, she flapped her arms, trying to will her body aloft. And one of the biggest disappointments of her brief childhood was being grounded, unfeathered, lesser skilled than the birds.

ONE DAY APRIL BEGAN receiving love letters from a stranger named Charley. "You don't know me," he wrote, "but we met long ago. If you will have me in a few years, I want to marry you, make you pregnant. . . ." At least once a month a letter came, postmarked St. Louis, Anadarko, Jersey City; Oakland, Boise, Sheboygan. Charley revealed nothing about himself except his lust for her. "Darling, I think of your bright blue eyes, the dimples when you smile, the innocent creamy blush of your skin, your firm and swollen breasts. So long ago! How can I explain why I love and wish to plunder your treasures? Words are not sufficient! I dream your body into my arms every night. Send me a photograph, darling—how long is your hair? How much do you weigh, how wide are your hips? Do you play tennis dressed in T-shirts and white shorts? How many men in your life—?"

For fun, April wrote him back: no last name, just "Charley." Usually care of some grand, dilapidated hotel. Was he a salesman, a circus cat man, a triple-A ballplayer, a machine-gun-toting gangster, a colorless stray pilgrim who may have spied her at a Dynamite Shrine hot pool, learned her name from an attendant, and familyless, unloved, decided to quest her from lonesome distances? Who knew? What did it matter? His postcards, depicting the Mississippi River, Grauman's Chinese Theater, the Black Hills, and the Empire State Building fired her imagination, increasing her itch to run away.

April replied: "Sweet Charley, big hunk, brave man." Giggling, she poured it on, daring to be obscene. "I want to lie with you, my man, hold you tenderly, nibble on your flesh, draw my ripe red velvet tongue down along your thighs—" And wrote SWAK on the envelope flaps; and soaked the epistles in pink perfume.

He retaliated: "Jesus, my gorgeous April! From where did you sprout, the devil's loins? Are you really only thirteen—or actually going on thirty-five? Send me some photographs, please, so that I can hold your lovely wicked image before me, lay you on my pillow when I go to sleep—"

April bought a do-it-yourself photograph manual, transformed a downstairs closet into a darkroom, and purchased all the necessary supplies: a camera, an enlarger, chemicals, developing pans, paper. She photographed her friends, the mountains, camposantos, horses, the Pueblo—and herself. April arranged floodlights downstairs, donned a bikini, set the camera's timing device, and assumed silver-screen poses. Eventually, her heart beating excitedly, April shed the bikini and photographed herself in the nude.

She developed the film, made up prints. Her mirrored image on the glossy sheets startled April: her one-dimensional body captured in phony glamour poses was lascivious and dangerously provocative. And something else: her eyes, revealed by the black-and-white photographs, transformed the hopeful vitality of her teen-age flesh into a perverted womanly sadness that should have been impossible. A soft, tragic quality shone from her coy, sexpot poses; her eyes echoed painful, sentimental wisdom; mortality riddled her wonderful body, death was inevitable. Her nakedness, the fraudulent poses on black-and-white gloss, exposed her silly, flighty soul.

The photographs disturbed April as her nude body fed back to her by mirrors never had. All the same, she mailed the pictures to Charley, a disembodied letter writer a thousand miles away in Grand Rapids this week, in Toledo next week, always on the go—and she anxiously awaited his reaction. Some day they were going to meet; in a year, in ten years—it was preordained. And they would make love. And it would be one of the saddest and happiest adventures of her life.

MEANWHILE, APRIL TOOK HER early teen-age years by storm, garnishing—with wild vocabulary, exaggerated enthusiasm, and hyperbolic imagination—any adventure that dared a lackluster moment. She slapped on the lipstick and the makeup, fabricated stories, told outright lies. Every experience, no matter how outlandish, could always be enhanced by her nimble tongue. She led her gang of pals out of a hectic childhood into a spirited juvenile delinquency. When McQueen forbade her to drink, April siphoned his vodka into empty Coke bottles, added cola-tinted food coloring, recapped the containers, and walked past her parents with six-packs of potent hard liquor under each arm. At fifteen, April was one of the few Chamisaville kids with her own automobile: she taxied her buddies around town, laid down scratch, dragged with the guys along the North-South Highway. Junior Leyba loved her; so did a dozen other boys. They wrestled her into positions April laughingly escaped, knowing she wanted to be loved, but not by them, not her first time around. Damned if some inept, milky-eyed moron spouting cracked-voice soprano endearments would bust her cherry. April envisioned somebody special for her initial lover. And she could wait until she knew exactly who was destined to be the lucky man.

Together, during the war, their band comprised the valley's chosen few. Jolene Popper, vivacious but not too bright, might have been Chamisaville's Anglo queen had not April been around. George Parker was the all-American athletic son of Claude and Rachel Parker. Rebecca GeeGee, the quick daughter of Juan and Amaranta, was a dark, sexy child who spoke mostly Spanish with April. Other pals included Juan Ortega's wisecracking twin boys, Juanito and Panky; Karl Mudd's bookish daughter, Mary; and Junior Leyba, a withdrawn, fiercely handsome teen-ager with the best academic brain in the Chamisa Valley school system, an inarticulate and intense kid who rarely smiled. Miserably in love with April, Junior was a hunter, a hawk, a cynical, sharp-tongued disquieting person. His eyes rarely lifted or lit up. Mororse and brooding, Junior had emotional roots into a dark heritage. He carried around a profound chip on his shoulder and moved with the others like a distraught ghost, sharing their pranks from afar, attending mesa picnics or horseback excursions without really tagging along, drinking heavily but never getting drunk. An inaccessible boy, nobody really called Junior their friend. And yet April was intrigued. That opague son of a man she had always admired from a distance interested her more than the rest of her friends combined.

They shoplifted from the Eggington Mercantile and from the new five-and-dime. Late one Fourth of July night, they deposited a rotten cow on the plaza at the base of the World War I monument, an American flag planted in its putrid belly. They soaped *Denzil Spivey is a eunuch* on the front window of Forest Service headquarters. One night the county sheriff, retired lumber-mill operator Filiberto García, shined a flashlight on the whole gang crowded into the alleyway between the Plaza Hotel and Vigil's Liquors. Dressed in tuxedos and strapless gowns, seated by candlelight around a card table covered by an old Irish linen tablecloth and set with a feast of roast beef, scalloped potatoes, artichokes, chutney, caviar, lemon meringue pie, and champagne, they were enjoying a meal with that drunken bum Atiliano Montoya and two leprous pilgrims from Panama.

Often they climbed fences into the darkened Dynamite Shrine complex and skinny-dipped—only Junior Leyba never took off his clothes. Instead, he slouched in a deck chair beneath an umbrella April had opened so he wouldn't be burned by the full moon, and watched them cavort in the misty hot pools, seldom taking his eyes off April's fluorescent yellow hair and bouncing breasts. Inspired by April, the gang—excluding Junior—broke into the Dynamite Shrine, shat on the altar, and hung dollar bills and inflated condoms on the sacred rosebush. "What's the matter, Junior?" April joked. "You're too good for this sort of nonsense?" "It's childish," he scowled. "You act like a bunch of five-year-olds."

And yet he stuck around, eyeing them and providing a caustic commentary when they stole a victim of one of Al Lamont's less successful operations from Claude Parker's funeral home, lipsticked *BOO!* across its forehead, propped the stiff against the good doctor's door and rang the bell. They were halfway back to the plaza when Abigail Teyter Lamont opened the door and collapsed backward with a corpse in her arms!

Junior inhabited their periphery, aloof, above it all, never taking his eyes off April, hunting her with an already twisted heart, waiting for something to happen.

The war ended. Virgil Leyba, Juan Ortega, Icarus Suazo, J. B. LeDoux and others came home and were greeted accordingly. A dozen names, including J. B. LeDoux's brother, Chavo, were appended to the plaza's World War I monument. While Mayor Max Ortega spoke on the crowded plaza after a veterans' parade from the Dynamite Shrine complex to the courthouse, Virgil Leyba was already back at work in his ground-floor Plaza Hotel office. Looking up once, he saw April McQueen, wearing white satin, a crimson ribbon in her hair, present an enormous bouquet of roses to J. B. LeDoux, representing all the valley's ex-GIs: he limped now, and had grown more surly.

Two hours later, Virgil was still at work. The band had quit playing, the crowd had dispersed—only Judson Babbitt, his hands stained by rainbow paint, remained in the park sleepily feeding pigeons. With an enticing rustle of expensive material, April whooshed eagerly into Virgil's office and secretively closed the door. Tiptoeing to his desk, she curtsied, and offered a single red rose. Virgil twirled the flower in his bony fingers, thinking its color offensive. April whirled, her skirt rising, fanning out, so that he caught a glimpse of pink panties above strong brown thighs. Her head cocked, she smiled bemusedly into his sorrowful eyes.

"I brought you a rose, Virgil: the war's all over." Her ruby lips complemented the crimson rose. "I'm glad you're back, love. The people of the valley need you more now than ever before."

"What else is new?" he replied with a wry grin, puzzled by the awkward feeling she caused. "Everything is a mess."

"It's because my father is such a son of a bitch, qué no?"

The lawyer nodded: yes.

April stood there, swishing her hips a little, tapping a foot, touching her hair, adjusting an earring, unable to be still. Virgil's eyes tarried at the hem of her satin skirt, on her dimpled knees.

"I love you," April said breathlessly, heart thundering, almost frightened—for once—by her own audacity.

Virgil closed his eyes.

"That's not a joke. I'm telling you the real McCoy."

After a while he looked up, they faced each other. His heavy-lidded, sad black eyes scared her; his scrawny neck in a too-wide collar touched mothering chords. The lack of presumption indicated by his faded unfashionable suit and soiled tie promised that he was no phony. For his part, her beautiful slightly plump face was like erotic apple pie. Virgil thought her eyes had already misted with a kind of bedroom emotion belonging to a peasant revolutionary or a tired whore.

Virgil murmured, "Te agradezco for the compliment."

April waited, plucking at the ruffles around her bosom.

"What do you want, then?" Virgil asked. "I have a wife, a son your age. I don't trust you. Go play games with gente of you own ilk."

Tears dribbled over her cheeks, slick as silken sperm. Virgil set the rose among his papers and continued staring into her face the way a general, or a lover, might probe the attitude of a man, or woman, about to be shot or indifferently abandoned.

"Go home, child. Many thanks for the rose."

April left, cantering, her brazen laughter chilling his heart.

That night, badly drunk and alone, April lost control of her convertible at seventy miles an hour and rolled off the highway down an embankment into a cattailed bog, breaking an arm and losing two teeth, but otherwise escaping unscathed.

Two months later on a warm autumn night, she and Virgil made love in the back of his car. Neither gentle, nor too rough, Virgil kept his mouth shut. When April asked for more, he gave it quietly, holding her hard but not brutally in his arms. When she cried he made no move to wipe her tears, soothe, or sympathize. For April, it was at first a frightening, then an almost comforting, lay. Temporarily, he answered her need but did not satiate it. Nobody would ever satisfy her yearnings. Love, life—it was all so beautiful and unfair.

Drying her eyes, then overcome by sadness, April leaned against a window; they smoked. She touched herself and sniffed the blood on her fingertips. Virgil got out and peed, returned, located a pint bottle of whiskey in the glove compartment and took a quiet tug, then offered the liquor to April, but she refused. He said, "Someday you'll be a fine woman: we all have so much to learn."

A month later, much to Teresa Lujan's chagrin, April was going steady with J. B. LeDoux. And when, after a traumatic confab with Rodey McQueen, J. B. abruptly terminated the affair, April turned right around, and, bypassing a natural like George Parker, she sashayed into Junior Leyba's arms, got pregnant, sneaked up to Wyoming for an abortion, and returned with a slightly frantic glitter to her mien.

"I feel constricted in this town," she told her longtime confidante, Amaranta GeeGee, as the two were drying dishes one night in the mansion kitchen. "I want to run away before I explode or wreck myself and my future! In a place like this, you make the wrong move and suddenly you're trapped for life!"

Amaranta sighed wearily. "You're such a beautiful child —I'm sorry for you. Physically, God played an ugly trick on you—he should have plied a more cautious hand. No good can come of it. I'll always be on your side."

April hugged the woman, crying, laughing, grateful "Te adoro tía! Bruja! Amiga! You're the best!"

Amaranta pressed her face into the girl's eager bosom, allowing April's undisciplined and dangerous wings to flutter against her frowning brow. The only reveries and passionate fantasies that middle-aged descendent of ancient tribes and conquistadors entertained were dreams about the return of three sons killed in the Pacific and buried anonymously on sandy foreign isles; and to be left in peace on her own land in the Chamisa Valley, surrounded by naturally growing things, unthreatened by an outside world. A continuance of roots, the lifeblood of her family and her community for centuries, was all Amaranta ever asked for.

She embraced April, trying to breathe courage and good luck into the child's body because she loved her.

ICARUS SUAZO RETURNED from the war unscratched despite the Bataan death march and his years as a Japanese POW. While he was away, however, his wife Juanita had died of malaria; his child, Nicolas, was killed by bubonic plague. Icarus returned to an empty Pueblo apartment, whitened bones, mysterious memories. The news he took stoically, without dilating a nostril or flickering an eyelash. At the cemetery he stood still for an hour, staring at the grave until Juanita and little Nicolas appeared, assuring him they were okay. Icarus gave them a small package containing gifts for various ancestors, kissed them gently, and then, as they dissolved, lifted his eyes to the mountains streaked with veins of yellowing aspens. Magpies glided laxly through the air, jackrabbits rustled in the sagebrush. A bright blue lizard clung to a polished rock. An orange jittering butterfly suddenly died of old age and spun drunkenly down to the ground. Icarus squatted and carefully lifted the insect, taking it for a sign; its color was bleached away, most of its powder worn off. Pursing his lips, he tasted the autumn air; aspens and mauve sage and chill winter snowflakes mingled with the sunny currents. Crushing the butterfly in his hand, Icarus narrowed his eyes a little, then doubled over, releasing several pained grunts. Breathless, hollow from sadness and rage, he retreated from the burial ground, climbed ladders to his home, and opened the Albino Pine Defense Fund files.

At night, the Pueblo secretary dreamed neither of war nor of his wife and child. Instead, the two Denver-based lawyers he had fired a decade ago, suave remote little men who had double-crossed the Pueblo for years and then melted into obscurity, fidgeted around the edge of his subconscious activities. Their presence made him uncomfortable; often he awoke with a bitter taste in his dehydrated mouth. A scent of illegitimate smoke clung to the thick mud walls. After their departure, the uneasiness they had created was not easily dispelled.

"I must not forget them, then," he concluded. "No matter what. For some reason, they remain a factor."

ON THE SAME DAY in 1947 that a "mysterious fire" of "unknown origin" destroyed many of the crucial old records, deeds, titles, and surveys pertaining to local water and property rights in the county assessor's and treasurer's office, Rodey McQueen had it out with his daughter.

The fight occurred in the second-floor billiard room of the mansion's north wing. April had not attended school in four days: instead, she had been on horseback prowling Pueblo land, fishing in the Magpie Creek García Grant, skinny-dipping over at the Coronado Hot Springs, or out on the mesa. On this day, a truant officer had grabbed April and brought her home: McQueen was furious.

She said, "I don't care. School is ridiculous, it's irrelevant. I don't give a damn about Rudyard Kipling, and nobody else does either. All my friends are being destroyed by their classes, made to feel ashamed of their heritage, their culture, their language. If that's education, screw it!"

"Watch your language with me, young lady!"

"That's something else I can't stand. All this asinine hypocrisy from you and your kind. You can sit around destroying the little people in this valley, driving them to suicide, pulling every legal trick in the book to steal their land, but if somebody dares to use a cuss word—oh lordy, lordy, you'd like to burn them at the stake!"

McQueen said, "Button your lip, little daughter. You're making more goddam noise than a jackass in a tin barn!"

Poised to fly at each other, the father leaned over one end of the pool table, the daughter leaned over the other. In a soft aluminum-pink jersey and tennis shorts, April was so alluring McQueen wanted to burst his shell and spank, rape, murder his own daughter. Nobody, ever, came away neutral from April McQueen.

"I'm going to send you down to the capital," he said.

"What for—to attend a boarding school? You wouldn't dare."

"To see a psychiatrist."

"A *what*—?"

Cynthia drove her down: April kept her mouth shut all the way. The shrink, a limp, intelligent mystic with Freudian hang-ups and Jungian pretensions, raised his eyebrows when April entered his lair and decided to seduce her.

"Sit down, please, Miss McQueen."

"Call me April, Dr. Morgan." Chewing gum, she cracked it defiantly.

"We won't get anywhere if you don't cooperate," he said, reassuringly touching her thigh.

"Cop another feel," April sassed, "and I'll tell my big old rich politically powerful daddy on you."

They got nowhere. McQueen threw up his hands in anguish. He wasn't alone. Junior Leyba wished that he could be a butcher knife, sliding himself through her belly, nailing April up against a wall and holding her there— pinned and whimpering—forever. When J. B. LeDoux occasionally saw April on the plaza, he thought his heart must surely burst like a bitterly thrown egg. If George Parker happened to sit next to her in class, he couldn't keep his eyes off her chest and wouldn't ever speak—big football hero that he was—for fear of stuttering. Virgil Leyba alone never changed his demeanor in April's presence; he had judged that they shouldn't make love again. But he held her hand, offering compassion, a sympathetic ear. And chewed her out upon occasion, too.

"You don't know anything about love or loving or lovers. You are young, beautiful, unskilled. I have known women your age who carried rifles and ammunition belts, who loved me sexually even as killing was on both our minds. You are soft, privileged, spoiled rotten. Your talent scatters like badly thrown seed and seldom takes root. Although one of the special people in this valley, I don't consider you half as worthwhile, yet, as Juan Ortega or his wife, Mari-Elena, or Pat and Juan GeeGee, Celestino Lucero, Espeedie Cisneros, Perfecto Torres—I could continue, there are many others. Right now you are coy, cute, sexy, intelligent, undisciplined, flighty, shameless—"

"God damn you, Virgil Leyba!"

"Listen, I'm not trying to hurt you. But most people you meet will flatter you unashamedly in order to rob your body and your positive energy. They'll tell any lie simply to own you for a minute, or for a lifetime. Ninety-nine percent of the compliments you receive you won't deserve—remember that. Men will fall in love with you, automatically, instinctively, the way lemmings fall into the ocean, because you are very beautiful—but it won't mean much. I feel sorry for you and your too-attractive surface. If you can make it through the mess life is going to serve up in the next twenty years, you'll be one of the best human beings I have ever known."

"That's all?" she coughed, managing a sardonic smile despite her tears.

"I like you. You have no more faults than the rest of us. And you got a plethora of raw material to start out with. I'm curious about how you will grow."

"You think I'm a really shallow person, don't you?"

"I think you have only a snowball's chance in hell of outrunning yourself alive."

"Christ, you're a pompous, self-righteous, hypocritical, lecherous, cliché-ridden stuffed shirt!" April sputtered angrily.

"I know."

And they hugged each other—a heartfelt abrazo—cast as special friends until the end.

PEACE RESTORED THE PILGRIM and tourist trades to Chamisaville. For the power elite, cash registers chimed and bulged. For every six inches of reporting space, the *Chamisaville News* published eight pages of ads. But longtime local folks were more disoriented than ever before. Many young people, who might have inherited the land-based culture, had been killed defending the right of Rodey McQueen to eradicate those land-based cultures. Many war survivors were shell-shocked, or incapacitated by bitterness or a debilitating wanderlust. According to the state, much land they returned to, unirrigated for four continuous years during the war, no longer had water rights. Back from the martial nightmare, then, they barely had time to thank God and Father Molé before they were in court again, and desperate for menial jobs to earn the cash to defend their right to water their land. Others, who had deserted Chamisaville for work in war industries, earning cash to save their lands and houses, also found themselves, upon their return, spending their war bucks in court defending titles and water rights, exhausting in legal battles what they should have used to pay skyrocketing conservancy assessments, to buy supermarket groceries now that the law practically claimed they could no longer grow gardens, to buy the automobiles they now depended upon to ferry them over to the rejuvenated Cañoncito Dam or into town for low-paying service jobs that gave them cash to buy gas for their cars that were needed to drive back and forth each day to their jobs.

Teresa Lujan married J. B. LeDoux. He was back in the Mosquito Valley and out by the dam, strawbossing McQueen and Moose and Stryzpk construction activities. But Juan Ortega, slightly stupefied by the killing and the death march and his years of deprivation as a Japanese POW, had trouble getting started. No *El Clarín* offered him a literary outlet; the *Chamisaville News* wouldn't touch him with a ten-foot pole. No businesses or projects controlled by the Anglo Axis would hire him on. And Pueblo residents monopolized the Dynamite Fetish factory. Juan grew vegetables and grazed a few cows, but a family could no longer exist solely off the land. The subsistence infrastructure had crumbled; the dependency of people on each other's skills and labor and goods and resources had broken down significantly during the past fifteen years.

Virgil hired Juan on but could pay him little. The former reporter did paralegal jobs and unofficial legwork. He was an errand boy, he tracked down the gente and brought them in. But Juan tired easily. His mind wandered and he gathered sloppy or incomplete information. He couldn't hold his liquor, angered easily, and got into almost nightly fights in the El Gaucho with Nicanor Casados and Cenobio Arrellano, similarly shell-shocked souls. Occasionally, he even passed the night in the alleyway between Vigil's Liquors and the Plaza Hotel, crying on Atiliano Montoya's shoulder.

Communication between the old friends suffered: Virgil could not trust Juan in a courtroom. Their relationship became strained. Back at home, too often, Juan remained seated at the table after dinner, immobile, palms flat on the wooden surface before him, Mari-Elena perched fearfully on the edge of her chair across the way. For perhaps a half-hour he would say nothing. Mari-Elena feared he was going insane. Suddenly, he would start to cry, silently, the most awful thing his wife could have imagined. After crying without comment for a while he would lift his eyes, causing Mari-Elena to gasp: all the fierce and playful prewar light had been replaced by a deadened sullen gleam. She feared him; he rarely touched her, they never made love. "Go fuck Denzil Spivey," he once snarled when she begged him weepily for sex. Absent-minded, maniacally silent, Juan was strangely absorbed in inner thoughts, like somebody contemplating murder. At night he couldn't sleep: during the day he kept nodding off. Heading for Cañoncito or Ranchitos Abajo to fetch legal papers for Virgil he would simply pull off the road and pass out. His dreams made no sense, he could never recall their content, but they ensured that he got no rest. Town and county police cited him regularly for being a dangerous nuisance beside the road. Instead of getting better as the horrible war experience receded, Juan grew worse. All night every night he lay with his eyes wide open: Mari-Elena had no clue to his thoughts. Come morning, Juan ate listlessly, trudged off to work for Virgil, and repeatedly fell asleep behind the wheel of his battered pickup truck. Too many tortillas and too much beer bloated his belly and his brain—he became lethargic and fat.

Virgil refrained from commenting at first. After all, who was he to talk? In every man there dwelled a self-destructive devil, and Virgil had problems of his own. Loretta and Junior were living in the hotel again after a brief run at the Alamito house: she had asked him to work out details of their divorce.

But Virgil finally blamed Juan for botching his para-legal job: "You can't let personal troubles sabotage our work for the people," he explained, and sent Juan out to do it all over again.

One evening, in the El Gaucho Bar, the rapidly sinking newspaperman wearily referred to his dying interest in life. "I don't really care anymore," he moaned. "It's all hopeless. This earth is a gruesome place."

"It was always hopeless, it was always gruesome."

"I don't pity myself," Juan said. "I got in my licks, I had my fun. I just don't give a shit. Three of my sons died in that war."

"Maybe you need a little more time to purge the war from your blood. But you can't mourn forever, primo. Life goes on."

"What keeps you going, Virgil?"

"Instincts. And I became used to the carnage early. And I want the dignity of going down fighting. And I don't want to give them the satisfaction of ever seeing me give up."

" 'Dignity,' " Juan said miserably. "Jesus, Maria, and José!"

Virgil's dark eyes drilled into his pal's softening head: Juan stared back cheerlessly.

"I love you with all my heart, but I don't admire you for giving up," Virgil said.

"Qué sabes tu? I don't understand it myself. There's nothing I can do to stop the process. I made a boo-boo in the prison camp, I guess, after I learned that José and Billy and Timothy had died, and I shit out my soul by mistake."

Rearing back and making a fist, Virgil slugged Juan on the chin as hard as he could. With a sound like muffled balloons popping, the knuckles of his right hand broke, and Virgil howled. Juan tipped over backward off his El Gaucho stool, landing relatively unhurt on the greasy, sawdusted floor.

"Basta ya!" Virgil cried. "Despiertate, pendejo! Wake up, I've had enough! Bury your dead and move on!"

Rubbing his jaw, astonished by the whole performance, Juan's dead soul suddenly blossomed, causing him to unlease a dilapidated, yet joyous guffaw as he blurted: "I'm awake, you son of a bitch! Touch me again, Virgil Leyba, and *I'll bang your teeth so hard they'll come popping out your asshole like albino goat turds!*"

# In Search of
# Magic Gangsters

GEORGE PARKER was a high-school junior, a football, basketball, and track hero, excited by the literature of Hemingway and Thomas Wolfe, and going steady with Susan Bonney, when April McQueen went out on a date one night and called home at 4:00 A.M. from a Texas border town to announce that she was never coming back to Chamisaville. Sixteen years old and living with his mother in a Plaza Hotel apartment, Junior Leyba was absorbed in his own inexplicable doom: he cried when April deserted the valley. So did Rodey McQueen—in private. Cynthia said, "We'll hire a detective, track her down, bring her home. We can send her away to school. Back East, or to San Francisco."

"Hunting for her'd be like looking for a horse thief in heaven. To hell with all that. Let her go."

"All right. That's fine by me."

"She's like yours truly when I was a kid. We won't interfere. Our job is just to pick her up when she's down. And we'll pray a lot for her safe return."

"You pray, Dale." Cynthia moved to their second-floor bedroom window, which commanded a view of the pool. "I've got other things to do." Down there, her white poodles romped across the lawn.

"Too bad you hate her." McQueen carefully prepared a cigar and lit it while sitting on the edge of their bed. "She's barely turned sixteen."

"I don't hate her." Cynthia placed fingertips against the cool pane. "But April is no woman's woman, and I'm certainly not an exception. Maybe she can take care of herself, though I doubt it. If you say let her go, fine: let her go. I can take the unspoken 'I told you so's, the smug behind-the-back satisfied sneers if you can, Dale. Nobody will say anything out loud, and that's good enough for me. Let her make some other town miserable."

But April left a hole in Chamisaville. She seemed to

98

take with her a vital portion of the town's romantic memory and aspiration. Her sudden vanishing act seriously compromised its capacity for wonder. Hooking the collective imagination the way a skillful fly-fisherman hooks a trout, April reeled it away with her. Some tinsel, almost Hollywood aura that had elevated the awkward, brooding valley traveled with her. The hopeful, outlandish, provocative spirit she had personified for nearly a decade, the best and the most raucous of everybody's yearnings—it was now a casual, rip-roaring gleam propelling her dilapidated convertible through a lazy west Texas night with Patsy Cline and Kitty Wells and Bob Wills riding for fair on her hot-to-trot tail, weaving the coarse honky-tonk fingers of their voices through her air-battered starlet hair.

An emptiness caught at Chamisaville's throat. When, walking toward school next morning hugging books to her hillbilly chest, Jolene Popper passed by the McQueen estate's high walls, she almost burst into tears. George Parker trotted onto the football field late that afternoon feeling cheated, because deep down April had been the only person he had ever truly hoped to star for.

Junior Leyba entered the plaza after school, halting for a moment on his way to the hotel, his face twisted into an ugly grimace as his anguish delivered blows. Hating her, loving her, whichever—now his life had been robbed of hope. And although buried as usual in the obscene paperwork of his trade, Virgil Leyba happened to look up and out his window through an invisible lip-print six years old, catching his alien boy's contorted face: and his heart jumped, he wished to extend a hand.

That afternoon, Loretta Shimkus prepared a thermos of tea and sherry, and sat on a Balena Park graveyard bench among dying hollyhocks and a few leftover hummingbirds, more wistful than a mere autumn day could induce. She had a longing for things to long for. Remembering her own twenty-five-year-old exodus from a small New Jersey town, Loretta envied April McQueen, felt sorry for the little bitch, and already mourned the scars that rambunctious child's impetuosity would carve across her own soul.

His battered guitar under one arm, a bottle of Dos Equis beer in his other hand, Juan GeeGee lumbered onto his portal, where Amaranta, weary after a long day mopping up the McQueen mansion, sat in a wicker armchair, tiredly enjoying an exquisite ripple of cottonwood leaves nudged off a towering nearby tree. The leaves puttered lazily down onto stiff beige poppy pods and brown curling sweet peas and dying hollyhocks. Juan dimmed in the fading light, plucking a few chords but not singing, while Amaranta sternly challenged the Angelus beauty to fulfill some intricate personal meaning. Both Amaranta and Juan understood that the valley was no longer bewitched in the special way it had been when April flounced noisily at the core of its marvelous chingazos.

And Amaranta remembered April asking her about Juan the Indio and the Virgin of Guadalupe: those red rose petals on the snow.

"Do you really believe in miracles?" April had asked.

"I believe in what happens," Amaranta had replied.

Over the Texas flatlands and through the hill country April zoomed, her worn tires squishing unfortunate rattle-snakes who had waited too late to go denning. She pulled into an all-night, one-pump, one-bulb gas station, bought a Coke for a nickel from the vending machine, and left the attendant—who else but a Homer, an Elmer, or maybe a just plain, chicken-fried country-bumpkin Joe Don?—lean-ing over the pump long after she had peeled away, wishing himself down the deserted road far into that blackness where she had evaporated, so fired up with fantastic dreams of the outer world that he'd be sleepless and un-happy for a week.

Outside Lubbock, April traded her car to a cross-eyed mechanic on his way from Rome Air Force Base in the Mohawk Valley of upstate New York to Santa Barbara, California, where his girlfriend ran a rooster supply ranch for Tijuana cockfights—she traded her car for his big Harley motorcycle. And by the time she hit Brownsville her hair was almost white from the sun, it frothed like ocean foam around her brown-speckled windblasted face. Her lips were cracked and bloody, her blouse was filthy, the seat of her too-tight dungarees had split, and her kid-neys hurt like hell. And when he opened the door of his enormous broken-down hotel room, Carlito Epstein—booze-hound, stunt flyer at traveling carnivals, forty-four-year-old vagabond and insanely lonely good old boy, other-wise known to April as Charley—dropped back apace, astonished by the mirage with a torn-open blouse backing him onto the sagging double bed.

"Holy mackerel!" he exclaimed.

"I love you," April crooned, settling atop him slowly,

her eyes squirring out of focus and clouding with erotic mist. "Will you plank me for fair, please, Mr. Epstein?"

"If I don't die tomorrow," Charley promised, giggling over this inexplicable good luck.

"Let's do us a real loop-the-loop" smacked like a ripe wet plum into his flushed and buzzing ear.

POSTWAR BOOM LANDED on Chamisaville like heavy January snow. Some had fun playing in the powder of a new economic order: many more were inconvenienced, locked in, even suffocated by it.

New buildings popped up overnight on land released for development thanks largely to Moe Stryzpk's solitary machinations in his domestic operations room. Moe's knowledge of the area's economic and psychological composition was vast and overpowering. Working carefully with Bob Moose, Rodey McQueen, Randolph Bonney, Denzil Spivey, Al Lamont and the expanding legal and business fraternity, Moe plotted moves, deciding who to lend to and for how long and at what interest—he had it gauged to the last decimal point, the economic pulse and character and personality of the overall Chamisaville scene. If a larcenous newcomer entered town, Moe learned about it instantly— his spies were out touching everybody; he controlled competition among the real estate and insurance businesses, among the banks and the county offices. And he had the Forest Service headquarters in his pocket. Moe not only had a listing of all special-use permits granted by the Floresta, but he was also an important factor in deciding who received them. He knew the exact permit head count of every rancher's herd, and he had caucused with Denzil Spivey on many occasions, thinking up ways to reduce the permits, slowly but surely closing off national forest land to local sheepmen and cattle ranchers, managing the rich mountains toward wilderness areas, campgrounds, fishing, out-of-state big-game hunters, and mining and timbering interests.

Moe Stryzpk could set the financial pulse of Chamisaville as precisely as he could set a watch. He could manipulate all parties concerned into a disaster or a killing, depending, because the valley's character was on his walls, totally exposed on the ever-changing maps detailing productive land, development land, fallow land, choice lots, bad lots, land with uncertain title. It was in his file cabinets, in planning reports, and economic and demographic profiles, in family alliance profiles, in the composition of the Republican and Democratic parties and the precinct setup. He had the whole picture under his thumb; he owned a little black book on everybody; he had a more complete knowledge of the score—the factual, and even, perhaps, the spiritual score—than anyone might ever have again. Chain-smoking, his shirts dirtied by a constant waterfall of ashes, Moe wheeled around his plush home-based bunker working figures, chewing on pencil erasers or tapping them against his teeth, punching buttons on his telephone and calling out constantly, taking incoming calls every five minutes, keeping abreast of the wheeling and dealing, psyching it out, selling information, giving orders, helping the five percent of the town that owned ninety percent of its business empire to continue rolling over the weakening locals.

Moe projected his own maps, hired surveyors, penciled in new buildings, new people, new subdivisions. As the fifties opened, a hundred outsiders wanted to build motels, hotels, art galleries, curio shops, gift stores, jewelry emporiums, diners and restaurants and cafés, ski lodges and ski tows and summer music camps, religious retreats, hardware stores, a lumber supply outlet house, used-car dealerships and auto-parts stores and gas stations, and a bowling alley and another insurance agency and an airport.

Eventually, all these projects were realized; but only by the Anglo Axis or under the auspices of the Anglo Axis. Dude ranches appeared up in the Chamisa Canyon, Woolworth's and Wacker's joined J. C. Penney's and Safeway. The General Custer Electric Co-op was growing. Sierra Bell built a Chamisaville office to service the eight hundred homes that now had telephones. South of town, on McQueen's Atiliano Montoya La Ciénega Grant land, the General Custer Drive-In Movie was born. An office-supply store touched down on the north end of the plaza. Another drugstore opened; a shop that sold records appeared; a nationwide shoe chain came in. County offices expanded; town and county police departments got bigger; the state cops built a tiny district bungalow south of town. Several tour services sprang up; their raunchy, gaudily painted double-decker buses (owned by McQueen and Moose, managed by Damacio Mares) ran between the Dynamite Shrine complex, the open Pueblo, and the several dozen art galleries proliferating like gnats after a summer rainstorm. A Capital City chain-dairy began delivering milk to the valley: government inspectors appeared regularly at the Lucero-Torres farm, citing them for health infractions, ordering them to invest heavily in modernized equipment and sanitation methods or else get out of the milk business altogether.

Moe Stryzpk had it all plotted, he knew exactly what was going to happen, who would profit, and by how much. The key was to create a carefully manipulated anarchy, throwing the valley into an apparently chaotic turmoil of "progress, American-style," disarming the natives with muddle, confusion, complexity, always moving faster than they could handle, keeping them off-balance, giving no respite, breaking down the solidarity of their old ways by creating a town that didn't know its ass from a hole in the ground, fabricating false uproars and fraudulent conflicts, separating society into individuals so perplexed they lost their communal instincts and wound up divided, every person competing against his neighbor, every man looking out for himself. Then the tightly knit Anglo Axis, a small group acting together like a well-oiled and synchronized machine, could rake in the profits with ease.

Impoverished local farmers hated Rodey McQueen and others like him because they were public figures and visibly growing richer by the minute. But Moe Stryzpk was the most feared person in Chamisaville, a mysterious and deadly recluse confined to a wheelchair in his enormous den, like some strange telephone operator completely hidden from view, plugging in all the circuits, making all the crucial connections, giving all the orders, supplying the juice for every flagrant shenanigan. An underground, inaccessible being, Moe's existence played on the superstitious valley. A grotesque little wizard was he, guiding the darkest aspects of destiny, the king under the bridge over Chamisaville's golden river.

But Moe was almost an embittered, powerless man, his fanatical lust to control a substitute for more earthly skills he lacked. Barred to him since the providential and catastrophic First State boardroom meeting about twenty years ago was the simple ability to walk, feel ground underfoot, hike into the purple hills, or meander downtown—tipping his hat effortlessly to passersby—for a Sunday cherry Coke after buying the paper at Lamont's drugstore. Moe was sick of feeling numb. Miranda, his healthy, attractive wife, couldn't stomach sex with a cripple: she dabbled perfume on her wrists and between her breasts, pulled on tight sweaters, brightened her lips and licked them to raise the shine, penciled in thin eyebrows, smoothed out skirt wrinkles over her temptingly swollen tummy, and, long hair mockingly swishing, drew on gloves and pecked him an adiós. Her girdled ass chugging voluptuously as she clacked outside, Miranda drove off, leaving him alone day after day.

And well into many a night.

Moe Stryzpk was the first Chamiseño to own a television set. Nevertheless, wheeling around his paper empire of land and water and mapped-out human lives, hatching plans, Moe carried with him always thoughts of a weedy grave.

ELSEWHERE, WRAPPED SNUGLY in her dissipated lover's bomber jacket, April McQueen stood on the edge of west Texas high-school football fields surrounded by dusty sunflowers, or she wandered across Mississippi country hoedown carnival grounds; or she sat atop rickety buses, drinking beer and licking her carefully lacquered fingernails after a mess of Tennessee fried chicken, and waved a pink scarf while the assembled hick spectators cheered and oh'd and ah'd her daredevil man. She and Charley danced in Georgia honky-tonks crawling with drawling crackers and shelled peanuts, chasing their malts with sour mash, tequila, or rum. April wore a formal gown to a sleek outdoor night club buffeted by the deep-sea rumbles and palm-frond rustles of the Florida Keys. They collected shells on a pristine beach, ate fried calms and king crabs, and pointed impolitely at imperial flamingos. April stared sullen-eyed at her red-faced flyboy hovering, hung over, near a bowl of chili and saltines in a South Dakota allnight diner; and split a case of champagne during a three-day high jinks on the cross-country train. April saw him crash—miraculously unhurt ("I got *you* to live for, baby,") —in Bangor, Maine. Then April left him alone to do Hartford while she hitchhiked to New York City where everything—except Carlito Epstein, the small-time stunt pilot son of a Brooklyn dock hustler and a Puerto Rican migrant worker—was happening.

When she telephoned that night, April screamed in his ear so hard it hurt: "This is *it*, god dammit, Charley! New York is like a fucking Hieronymus Bosch! It's like jumping into a bushel of overripe peaches! You could commit murder here and nobody'd know the difference! The coppers all ride horses and the whores are stacked up on every midtown corner like Minnesota flapjacks! I saw six Jesus Christs on Forty-Second Street. I wanna learn how to be a stripper! I'm gonna go see Joltin' Joe DiMaggio and take a boat to Staten Island, give a bird to the Statue of Liberty and find out how much it costs to sail to Paris!"

Already he had lost her.

But that night April dreamed about her funny obsessed little man with the wan eyes and saggy pale chest, plump buttocks and rough proletarian hands, and a half-pint flask always in his pocket. He had taught her to fly, gotten her a license, given her all his fumbling loving, and pro-testingly paid for her second abortion even though he desperately wanted the kid—she owed him for many things.

Next day, April called again and, barely masking her dismay, tears in her Irish mourning eyes, said gently, "Charley, let's us go home and let my daddy give us a real big old Chamisaville wedding."

He was overjoyed; also grateful—Charley knew their days were numbered. "What is it," April wrote in a plain-tive note to Virgil Leyba, the first of many she mailed to him over the years, "that makes us do what we don't want to do? Commit ourselves to stupid futures? Love people we got no business loving? Do folks really *marry* other folks just because they feel sorry for them? What kind of nonsense is *that?*"

Her notes—and later her long rambling letters—Virgil filed away, and rarely, if ever, answered.

On the way across country, April decided they couldn't wait any longer. She tackled a J.P. in one little Missouri town or another; he agreed to tie their knot. "But we'll pretend we aren't hitched," she laughed feverishly. "Just so we can get a big feast and all the appropriate goodies from my old man."

Ten minutes after they arrived, a fight broke out be-tween April and her mother. "But we've been shacking up for almost a year!" the daughter shouted angrily. "We're *together!* And this is my *home!*"

"Not in my house, April. Not until you are legally mar-ried will you or any other gullible lout that follows you home sleep together in the same room!"

"You'd throw me out of the house the week of my own wedding?"

"Nobody's throwing anybody out of the house. You are just not sleeping together, that is all, and that's final."

"What kind of hypocrisy reigns in this moldy castle?" April ranted.

McQueen was blunter. "What the hell is my daughter doing with a Jew?" he raved. "You can't marry a Jew, god dammit!"

"I'll divorce him in a week and come back next month with a nigger!" April wailed.

"April Epstein!" McQueen groaned. "April *Epstein!*"

"She's just doing it to make us suffer," Cynthia said icily. "We should pay no attention."

McQueen laughed, albeit a touch hysterically, throwing up his hands, loving his daughter, hating her convoluted guts. "Ignore her?" he coughed. "Ignore World War Two in pigtails and thirty-eight-inch tits?"

"Don't talk like that, Dale, it's unbecoming."

"Aw hell, Mother: let 'em sleep together. Unless I miss my bet she already lost her cherry when she was ten. You ain't keeping anything Bible-sacred by holding those two apart."

"I'm just going to ignore you, Dale, because you are being a very unpleasant person. To tell the truth, I'm shocked."

"Hey, *hey!*" McQueen railed, scrambling his hands in his hair. "Can't we just call a truce and have fun at the party?"

"You do whatever you want, but those two just are not going to cohabit sinfully in this house, not until they are legally married, and that's all there is to it."

"Stow the palaver, folks." April sauntered into their argument. "We're going to the Dynamite Shrine Motor Court."

McQueen balked: "Don't be ridiculous—"

April rolled her eyes, jerking a thumb at her mother, and strolled out of the room.

"Why didn't you tell them we were already married?" Charley asked glumly, hunched on the motel bed, shoulders pressed against the papered adobe walls.

"What, and ruin our act?"

"Well, this whole thing is stupid. I wish we had never come. I don't believe your mother, I really don't—"

"What's the matter with my mother?"

"What do you mean? You yourself—well, her attitude makes no sense."

106

"Hold on a second." April jutted her chin at him angrily. "Who gave you a license to denigrate my mother?"

" 'Denigrate' already. Listen to all them fancy words."

"Wait a minute, dammit. Just because I happen to have a little tête-à-tête with my mother, that doesn't give you any carte-blanche right to start making ugly remarks about people you don't know from Adam and Eve."

"I didn't claim I knew anybody from Adam and Eve. I just know this whole thing makes no sense. If we're already married, why can't we sleep together in your house? And whether we're married or not, we been together and he knows that and she knows it, so why all the fuss? And if it's gonna be such a problem for them, why didn't we just sleep in separate rooms and make everybody happy? Why do you always have to make everything that's dog-gone simple turn into something that's so complicated isn't any way anybody can get out of it without catching their cock in the zipper?"

"*Your* cock in *your* zipper, maybe. Does it give you a thrill, Charley, to be so gross, to talk so insultingly around me? I mean, it's as if I wasn't a woman or anything—"

"*Piss on it!*" he suddenly screamed at her. "Hogwash! Go fuck yourself!" he sputtered, tears flying. " 'Woman' no less, she calls herself. How can you be so conceited?"

April snatched the Gideon Bible, whacking him over the head with it. He grabbed for her chest, catching the jersey fabric, and yanked his wife into him so hard her mouth banged the top of his head, knocking out her bridge and a third beautiful, absolutely perfect front tooth.

Charley groaned. "Oh no, I didn't mean it, I didn't think—"

April kneeled over him, astonished by the tooth in her palm, while blood filled her mouth. With a giddy whoosh, she sprayed the red into his face. Charley rolled out from under her, and, standing in the middle of the room, help-lessly waving his head, he whimpered, "You're a crazy little girl—you know that, don't you? You're a plumb crazy little girl, you really are."

April cleaned up, used a penknife to excavate a small hole in the dirt wall, then borrowed a rubber from her husband, and fitted the tooth, her diamond engagement ring, and a strand of golden hair into the condom. She poked the tiny package into the hole, answering his silent question with a shrug, saying: "Time capsule; hex; for good luck—don't ask me." Outside, April gathered some dirt, dampened it at the sink, and carefully mortared over the little hole, pasting back the wet white paper she had peeled off at the start.

Collecting her things, April headed for the door. "Where you going now?" Charley muttered anxiously.

"Mexico."

"What the hell for?"

"What the hell do you think for? For a goddam divorce, that's what for."

"Good luck."

"You mean good riddance. Oh, I forgot—here's your lousy bomber jacket."

"Keep it."

"Okay, don't mind if I do, Lash La Rue—"

April looked so good, leaving him forever, that misery collected in his guts like a punch to the solar plexus, and Charley doubled over. The screen door banged shut; April bowled over Eduardo Mondragón, now a one-eyed peg-legged *Capital City Reporter* newsboy who lived in a Dynamite Shrine cubicle; the car started up and roared away. Stupefied, wondering what next, Charley sat there. A few minutes later the automobile returned and April came in, kneeling contritely before her man. Unbuttoning his fly, she held his limp penis cupped tenderly between her palms while she spoke: "I'm sorry, flyboy, I really am. I didn't mean to be such a bitch. We had a good time together, but it made no sense. I'm too young to settle down. It was just an escapade, though a darn good one at that, it really was. But Jesus, sweet lover, I could never spend the rest of my life, or even the rest of this month, in your shivering, awkward arms. You're a dear person, but you're not tough enough, or scary enough, or macho enough, or dangerous enough for me. I'm searching for magic gangsters to play with, can you understand? I love you, Charley; fly well, don't drink so hard, find yourself a carnival gal with less ambition and a more desperate need to keep you warm. Let's make love for old time's sake, then call it quits, okay?"

He nodded.

On her way out at 1:00 A.M. April passed by Virgil Leyba's small house in Alamito. Shirtsleeves rolled up but still wearing a loosened tie, he was seated at the kitchen table, typing. When he answered the door, April impetuously leaped into his arms, excited and radiant, impatient to tell him all her news. Virgil held her with a strong but cautious warning. April stepped backward, and they regarded each other—quizzical, slightly puzzled. "Hey, Virgil, I'm back. But already I'm going away again." April unzipped the bomber's jacket with a flourish.

In only a year's time Virgil seemed to have aged a decade. Pouches weighed down his eyes; facial bones had become more prominent; his neck had grown thinner. Operated on by Abe Gallegos for a tumor that turned out benign, Virgil told her: "If ever your body breaks down, remember—Abe Gallegos is the only man to see." But his overall appearance shocked her. He was too gaunt and drawn, made sadly vulnerable, at last, from dealing exclusively with beautiful losers. And Virgil was surprised by the womanly attitude of her flesh, a vague pathos around her eyes, and a posture wearier than he would have imagined.

From April everyone had expected an ebullience lasting forever; from Virgil, a compassionate revolutionary hardness that could never falter, weaken, or wear out.

"Pobre macho." April touched his cold cheek.

"A tough year for everybody," Virgil replied.

April sat down. "So—tell me about it, please. Who is winning, who is losing? How are Pat and Lucinda GeeGee and Juan and Amaranta? George Parker and Jonathan Moose and Rebecca Valerio, Juan and Mari-Elena Ortega? Half the century's gone."

They talked through the night. Before dawn April kissed him sadly and drove away, beeping her horn goodbye and causing a thousand dogs to bark, heading east again toward a resilient dawn.

Midway into his small back field, Virgil peed into the irrigation ditch, rolling a cigarette while he pissed, facing the sacred mountain, its dim hulk like a lost boat slowly inching through fog. April occupied his thoughts for a minute: he reflected on the characteristics of a universal fate that allowed nature's special children to be killed too easily, stripped of their gifted exuberance as cavalierly as dandelions are ruptured by the wind. Virgil recalled a lost comrade-in-arms, a robust peasant lover. Stumbling across her sloppy body, foreshortened by death and jellied in rainy-season mud, he had lifted a gunbelt off the corpse, unbuttoned her blouse, and sleepily confronted the clean bluish holes pocking her chest. Ants and other bichos crawled between her bloodless lips, cameo teeth; her black hair had turned gray from life's draining, a seventeen-year-

old become meat rotting into placid earth. Her last—
April's last—words echoed among older memories already
forging the foundation of a later cacophony that would
dominate his brain:

"Hey, Virgil: I don't want to waste myself. I know I'm
beautiful, not just on the outside. But sometimes, right in
the middle of my happiest moments, everything falls apart
and I get killing cold and have this premonition that I'm
gonna throw myself away; that somehow I won't be able
to escape—it's in the stars. What's that Masefield line? 'A
beauty chased by tragic laughter.' But Jesus Christ, man,
I'm so good, you know? I'm so alive! And I just don't
want to waste myself, don't let me do that—*please?*"

But what could he do about it?

Virgil stood in his little back field, smoking a hand-
rolled cigarette, laying down his angular darkness on the
silver tips of brome.

IN NEW YORK, determined to be a painter, a poet, an
actress, April became involved with that crowd. Everyone agreed she had a marvelous, if undisciplined, talent.
Her first tiny apartment, in Chelsea, lacked hot water and
had a toilet down the hall. Furiously, she read books,
went to museums, sketched and painted, developing her
art, widening her intellectual range. Men clustered—painters, poets, novelists, critics, gallery dealers. Every night she
had a choice of parties, happenings, ribald drunks. Many
friends were political; they took her to rallies. Several
lovers claimed they were Communists, and April liked the
glamour in that until the McCarthy period gathered steam
and people, some of them good friends, started getting
truly hurt. During one period in her early New York days,
April did not lift a brush for months because her boyfriend, an enormous, bushy-haired poet named Tim Lanahan, had talked her into working full-time on a dozen
defense committees.

What a marvelous, two-fisted time! Disoriented by the
speed and scale of New York, April alternated between
euphoric optimism and hideous depressions. Out of control,
she catapulted through the scene, determined to experience
everything, touch everybody, intimately get to know all
women and all men. Too desperately, she wished to be admired and considered sophisticated. April bought clothes
and attended parties to be seen and admired, self-consciously developing a personal theater nobody could ignore.

She had the ability to walk into a party and stop it cold. On the other hand, April despised herself for choosing the cheapest way to admiration. Abhorring her superficiality, she nevertheless continued faking too much, speed-reading books thoughtlessly, absorbing catchphrases instead of ideas, and spitting them out eagerly to prove she was no provincial cowgirl. Why had she become such a fast-quipping smart-aleck clotheshorse? The drinking bothered her after a while—it never let up. Friends congregated in bars, had epic fights, hyped each other, shared tender moments, played politics. After poetry readings and strange plays, heated discussions followed in crowded lofts and noisy bars. Heady stuff, inundated with tragedy and triumph and the sense of being at the heart of an important historical moment.

Her poet wanted to get married, so they went to city hall. His most recent book of poems had a triumph. Tim was drafted for Korea; he refused to serve. And was subpoenaed before a congressional committee for being a Communist. Their friends rallied; the *National Guardian* published editorials. Such madness! Maybe the world would end, the Russians might drop their bomb. Close friends were sent to Korea; others, fearing McCarthy, did cowardly things. Much art was suppressed by people running scared. Once up in the morning, her friends started drinking wine and trying to work: the work was always interrupted by meetings, spontaneous demonstrations, parties. April functioned for years on a memory of adrenaline. She and Tim quarreled daily, had scary fights, and hurt each other by announcing affairs on the side. Long discussions were apt to terminate in tearful, whimpering displays over loss of political integrity. And everybody grew half suspicious of everyone else.

In the back of her mind, April felt guilty about Charley Epstein, J. B. LeDoux, Junior—and even Virgil—Leyba. This marriage with her frightened (and frightening) bear of a poet must work out, even if obviously wrong. How had she managed to do it again, leaping before she looked? Her beauty had made him dangerously bitter, he couldn't stand the way people flocked and praised at parties. Terrified of losing April, Tim drove her into the arms of others. He wanted children—she balked; and, without telling him, got another abortion. April suffocated in his jealousy; he suffocated in her movie-star attractiveness and positive energy. Their work fell apart. Embroiled to the hilt in emotional battles, they had little energy left over for creativity. Too often their daily routine went down a drain, wasted in screaming and accusing, making up, making love, getting drunk, carousing through Village bars, hobnobbing with friends, parrying sadistic conversations, worrying about America.

Nothing ever stopped long enough for April to inspect it closely. Caught in a whirlwind, she couldn't think straight. Tim pinwheeled into the night and collided from bar to bar, quoting his own poetry as he killed himself (and his talent) with liquor and bragged about Dylan Thomas as if the Welshman's gift had somehow rubbed off on himself. They loved the theater. April designed sets for local storefront productions. One night, for a happening, she painted her body silver and danced nude while jazz musicians and beatnik poets provided an impromptu score. She screwed a famous artist whose work she despised, and went to bed with a shy homosexual whose fingers had been lovely on the guitar. At parties April occasionally played her own guitar, singing Spanish songs; or read the cards, or fiddled dramatically with a Ouija board. Alcohol, marijuana: April tried cocaine, but stayed afraid of heroin. Nothing damaged her body. She ate like a pig, drank like a fish, never gained weight, and always seemed to look more gorgeous than she had the day before.

Propositions came at the rate of three, four a week, even with Tim by her side. When they got home, blubbering childishly, he knocked her around: she grabbed chairs to ward him off. "Oh God I love you!" he howled. "But I can't stand you!" he added. And went through a period of bringing home women and screwing them on the living-room rug, April the lone spectator in a drunken stupor. Their loft was a shambles. Each apologized profusely to the other; they were going to hell on a handcart. April sometimes confronted a canvas for hours, weeping, unable to make a stroke. Friends snapped up the few paintings she finished and praised her lavishly. She kept setting schedules for work, but then the telephone rang or somebody needing a transfusion of pep or of love dropped by.

Tim went into hiding. In East Hampton, April passed a useless month with a well-known writer. Her closest friend was a gay musician destined to be one of America's best-known composers. His politics jibed with hers, his suicidal tendencies bored her to tears. It seemed one of the criteria for talent was to be an unreal asshole into the bargain.

112

"Get rid of Tim, get out of New York," the gay composer warned. "They don't love you for what you are, none of them do. They're all jealous, they'd like to kill the one thing in you, darling, that makes you better than anyone any of them have ever known."

"I'm not afraid of anybody," April bragged. To prove it, she prowled New York streets at all hours, a flask in her back pocket, daring muggers to mug her, rapists to rape her, cops to cop a feel. But nothing ever happened. She had that gift of being immune, eternally young, invulnerable.

"I'm a long-distance runner," April wrote to Virgil. And she added:

I'm still so young, love, I feel so full of spunk. Sometimes I think it's really awful here; other times I'm happy as a big old clam. People say I'm like sunshine whenever I enter a room. They cluster like moths to a light bulb. I'm a winner, Virgil, and all of New York knows it. I'm as strong as Babe the blue ox! It may be a mess around here, but there's a togetherness too that you wouldn't believe. It's like one great big creative lunatic asylum of music, art, poetry, affairs and laughter! We're going to get divorced, Tim and me, it's inevitable. The whole thing is crazy. People hurt each other deliberately all the time, and they die for each other, too. So much bravery, so much cowardice. And when it all seems too much, I go up to Central Park and rent a horse, or go SRO to the opera. I love jazz—Charlie Parker, Thelonius Monk, Miles Davis—and the theater. I play tennis a lot and I ride in the park hansoms sometimes, just for fun. Course, you can always swim in the ocean. I don't understand my stamina, love, but believe me, I'm not going to look *that* gift horse in the mouth! Always I'm horny: sometimes I wonder, am I a nymphomaniac? Sex is so strange—I want it so much, but I never feel satisfied. It's impossible to love just one person, I love everybody. But I don't feel bad, I feel rich and powerful and complicated. I'm reading Marx and Trotsky and Ouspensky and Engels. I'm surrounded by Communists, anarchists, veterans of Spain. There's been lots of paranoia: people have gone to jail. This berserk government has destroyed the art of half my friends: others have fled to Mexico and Europe. Right now, forces are pushing me into everything that happens, I don't seem able to control where I land. But once I get the pacing figured out I'll be able to call my shots, I know. When it gets too cold I just snuggle into Charley's bomber jacket and think about you in your ground-floor office on the plaza, or Amaranta GeeGee telling the cards, or Juan GeeGee singing a corrido and playing his guitar, or the way we all used to trick or treat on Christmas morning, and my folks couldn't believe that I'd rather do that than open all their dumb presents. I get phone calls from Charley, when he's in Albuquerque or Dallas or Texarkana—like half the people in the world, he's drinking himself to death. I love him still —*but my God!* I outgrew him in minutes! He's such a sad little almost-fifty-year-old boy with nothing left to do except stunts in the sky. Occasionally I feel locked in a web of such sweet agony. And maybe I'll come home some day, Virgil, and help you save Chamisaville. A postcard from George Parker the other day said he's a college football hero now—is that true? Amaranta writes from time to time, but never says anything *personal*. I want to know all the gossip and all the skullduggery! What's *really* happening back there in the playground of the heart of the land of enchantment? How's my favorite eunuch, Denzil Spivey? Will Icarus Suazo ever win back that Albino Pine Land? Do Perfecto Torres and Celestino Lucero still deliver milk twice a week in that 1912 Buffalo Fire Engine? Has Jesus Etcetera shot anybody lately? Gosh, speaking of him, I had a bizarre dream the other night! Jesus Etc. as the Angel of Death entered the alley between the hotel and Vigil's Liquors and, after gathering up poor old Atiliano Montoya in his arms, he carried him back to his horse at the El Gaucho hitching rack and together they rode out of town, both of them shining weirdly as if dipped in phosphorescence, with halos bobbing merrily above their heads. Now and then, of course, I worry about the lack of mountains and sagebrush in my life, about the lack of cottonwoods and nighthawks and posole. But the ocean is like mountains. And skyscrapers make my nipples go hard, they really do. This city is a match for my imagination, I walk around with goosebumps (literally!) all the time! I'm not at all focused, as you can tell. But I really don't need to be yet. I'm not going to fall into that trap, have babies, stick with one stifling scene, label myself this or that. I just don't need to yet. *God I love life!*

WHILE APRIL JAMMED in New York, pressures mounted against the longtime landholders and native people of the Chamisa Valley, and their communal society continued to disintegrate.

Construction on the Cañoncito Dam was finally completed twenty years after taxes had been increased to pay for the additional irrigation water promised by the reservoir. With inflation, operation and maintenance costs had skyrocketed; assessments rose accordingly. Now a series of unforseen events conspired to push conservancy assessments even higher. Because of a dry winter, the reservoir only accumulated 2,400 acre-feet of water, none of which could be released for irrigation the following spring because a "permanent trout pool" had to be maintained for summer tourists. Without these fish, according to Bureau of Reclamation twenty-year-old cost-benefit analyses, the project wasn't feasible.

The bureau had further decreed that local farmers must convert their land to truck gardens when they "owned" "assured" Cañoncito Reservoir water, because the "profits" they made selling vegetables would enable them to "meet" damn and conservancy taxes. Unfortunately, it cost about a hundred dollars an acre to convert pastureland into truck gardens. Yet, given no alternatives, many local farmers negotiated loans or mortgages on homes that had had no lien on them for two hundred years and turned their pastureland into truck farms, forgetting that they were gardening at seven thousand feet, where the growing season lasted barely over ninety days.

And sure enough, that first year, when only enough water for trout accumulated in the reservoir, a last freeze occurred on June 15, wiping out every marginal farmer's beans, corn, and pumpkins. Frantically, they replanted, and new shoots had just surfaced on June 27 when the latest freeze an old-timer could remember hit the valley, and almost everyone was ruined. A few who survived were partially wiped out in mid-July by a three-day hailstorm. Finally, on September 6, an early frost killed any vegetables that had made it until then.

The court-appointed conservancy board, which still con-

115

sisted of Rodey McQueen, Moe Stryzpk, Randolph Bonney, Al Lamont, and J. B. LeDoux, shook its collective head sadly and continued taxing anyway.

Next, Judson and Felicia Babbitt's six-year-old son Justin wandered away from his family during a picnic, commandeered an unattended rowboat on the Cañoncito Reservoir shore, paddled himself onto the lake, and, falling overboard, promptly drowned. The Babbitts wailed, tore their hair, sued the conservancy district for a million dollars, and collected a hundred thousand in cold cash, an assessment that was distributed among all the poor farmers located within the district. And impoverished men and women like Juan and Amaranta GeeGee and Perfecto Torres were not only taxed exorbitantly for that disaster, but they also had to pay enormous legal fees to the conservancy attorneys protecting their so-called interests in the case, the firm of Bob Moose, Damacio Mares, and Sonny Stryzpk.

Although he challenged the right of the conservancy to commit the sinking agricultural population within its boundaries to such enormous financial commitments, Virgil Leyba was defeated at every turn. The laws governing such districts made no allowances for human frailty. The point was to separate the weak from the strong, rubbing out subsistence economies in favor of a competitive system dealing in cash on the barrelhead and controlled by the affluent few.

Still, a part of Chamisaville was prospering. The art colony had expanded, the Mosquito Valley Ski Area, boasting a half-dozen new condominiums, had become famous nationwide; a steady traffic of private airplanes justified the paved airfield north of town. Some of Chamisaville's artists were well known in New York, Los Angeles, and Dallas. The Dynamite Shrine complex expanded its recreation facilities—tennis courts, a golf course, an indoor swimming pool. Several major resort hotels were built to handle an ever more privileged clientele—the Shalako Lodge, the Chamisaville Inn, and the Saint Cipriano House. Two stores on reservation land, owned by the Pueblo council, sold curios, pots, jewelry. A molybdenum mine situated in Doña Luz, twenty minutes north of town, employed over a hundred valley workers, taking them off the farms, putting much cash in their pockets, further weakening the agricultural structure that had protected communities for centuries. The cold war, the arms race, and hints of outer-

116

space development might keep that mine in business forever.

Because defense industries flourished to the south around the capital and in Albuquerque and Los Alamos, New Mexico, Chamisaville experienced a brief bomb-shelter scare: the local power structure immediately forged a number of concrete holes in the ground. J. B. LeDoux built shelters for Randolph and Flora Bonney, Bob and Letitia Moose, Rodey and Cynthia McQueen, Judson and Felicia Babbitt, Al and Abigail Lamont, Moe and Miranda Stryzpk, and Damacio Mares. Teresa wanted one for themselves. J. B. replied, "Cut the crap, it's only a rich man's fad." But she insisted, making life miserable for him until he acquiesced. After her childhood, Teresa could never again be too secure. When J. B. finished the work, she tastefully decorated the bomb shelter, stocking it with food, drink, and a thousand books she would never read. Often, whenever feeling especially insecure, Teresa descended into the shelter with their child, Benny, and sat there, while the kid played with blocks or assembled a Cootie, allowing that underground concrete pillbox to soothe her worried mind.

The LeDouxs were getting rich. J. B. was closely allied with Rodey McQueen, Moe Stryzpk, Bob Moose. He was their liaison, the Spanish-speaker, the Hispano front man for many Axis enterprises. J. B. made projects legitimate, hired and fired, mollycoddled and persuaded. For his loyalty, he received choice contracts, was elected to the county commission, amassed enormous power.

Always, in the back of his mind, J. B. remembered his father, remembered how they had built up Rudy LeDoux and then pulled the plug. The precious land had been lost, his father had died impoverished, disillusioned, double-crossed. And J. B. remembered that he and Chavo had been drafted by men metaphorically the henchmen of Rodey McQueen. J. B. also remembered his days as a prisoner of the Japanese, in the same boat as people like Icarus Suazo, Juan Ortega, and Virgil Leyba. And, understanding himself to be both victim and pawn of a racist society, J. B. knew precisely where his power came from, of what it consisted, and just how fickle its grantors might be if he slipped up.

When the Anglo Axis proposed that Chamisaville's Bataan veterans make a highly publicized annual pilgrimage to the Dynamite Shrine, thanking God for their salva-

117

tion by walking the last half-mile on their knees (and incidentally drawing many tourists and much lucre to town for the gala affair), only J. B. agreed to do it. Rodey McQueen offered Juan GeeGee, Espeedie Cisneros and others a hundred dollars apiece to make the trek, but they refused. A picture of J. B. on torn and bloody knees, progressing painfully toward the shrine down a corridor formed by thousands of tourists and newspaper and newsreel people appeared on the front pages of the *Chamisaville News* and the *Capital City Reporter,* and on page three of the *New York Times*. Pat GeeGee clipped the photograph, tacking it to the El Gaucho bulletin board, and bar patrons used it for a dart board now and then.

J. B. obeyed his bosses and dreamed of somehow caching enough power so that one day he might kick their asses. He lived with the illusion of revenge, every hour, every day. He might be a solid-gold patsy and supervendido today, but they had better watch out tomorrow. He would shamelessly brown-nose, feathering his own nest and co-opting his people right and left, building a position from which he could deal a fatal blow. Virgil Leyba and his self-righteous clients would have long since been muscled into oblivion by the time J. B. flared.

Obsessed by his brief love for April McQueen, or Epstein—what was it now? he wondered grimly: hard to keep up with that nymphomaniac! Obsessed with her and permanently scarred by the way McQueen had ordered their affair terminated, had ordered J. B. to end it because the powerful Texan could not push April around, J. B. also wanted retaliation for that shameful episode in his life. He wanted revenge on both the Muleshoe tyrant and his daughter for having been privy to his cowardice and his confusion about what he really was and truly desired.

Was it to be rich and successful, American-style? Or to be a rebel, an avenger and defender of his people? Perhaps it was already too late for salvation. J. B. had only scorn for Virgil Leyba, who lost most of his battles because he refused to compromise his integrity. And he despised the way Teresa fawned around powerful ladies, unctuously flattering Cynthia McQueen, Letitia Moose, Abigail Lamont, and Flora Bonney. He knew they laughed behind their backs, calling them all "lazy Mexicans," mocking their Spanish accents and "primitive" culture, deriding the "rustic simplicity" of their sheepmen, pig farmers, toothless old crones, curanderas, quaint little farming communities, and beautiful dark-skinned children. Already they had convinced Teresa that Benny should speak only English. And J. B. wanted to strangle his wife when she happily told him: "Benny's not too brown, querido, isn't that wonderful? He's so light, he could almost pass for white."

White, J. B. thought, his eyes narrowed as Teresa undressed for bed. White, he mused, comparing her dark breasts, almost ebony nipples, and pitch-black groin to a memory of April McQueen's white bosom, sweet pink teats, and golden crotch. The difference tore him apart: J. B. hated his twisted lust. That damnable dynamite blast years ago had opened the way for untenable emotional positions, needs, and desires. His passions had been maimed by Anglification, distorted by April McQueen's energy and fearlessness compared to his wife's subservient flesh. Teresa's sensual muscles were cramped by racism; her loving had been muted and made tentative by dishonesty and fear. Her mulatto beauty had been shamed and subjugated by his fixation on white pussy. Maybe after all he would cripple them irreparably by the betrayals, infidelities, and misrepresentations lining his route to revenge.

"The old days are over, thank God!" Teresa repeatedly exclaimed, brainwashing herself to believe it. "The old ways are finished. It's stupid to hang on. We're all Americans. The stubborn people will just be ruined in the end and they won't share any of the wealth. And there's plenty of wealth for everybody," she insisted brightly, that fear of her troubled past never leaving her eyes for a second as they laughed jovially at a McQueen cocktail party, sang hymns in the Episcopal church, and played golf with the Bonneys on Saturday morning. "There's plenty of money and happiness for all us Americans," she litanized. "Anybody can succeed if they want to and aren't lazy. No need to rock the boat."

Teresa even gave teas down in their bomb shelter: that was the rage for a while. She cruised around town in their new Cadillac and made certain English was the only language little Benny ever heard. All his carefully selected playmates were sons and daughters of parents like Jonathan and Kathy Moose.

J. B. seldom entered their bomb shelter; he hated that Cadillac, driving instead a pickup with a rifle on the rear window rack. Whenever he bumped into the filthy, crippled

119

newsboy, Eduardo Mondragón, hawking *Reporters* on the plaza, J. B. was so embarrassed he wanted to throttle that failed bigshot on the spot.

And occasionally, alone, overlooking Chamisaville from the top of Nobody Mountain, J. B. actually wept real tears. How long he could play his tormenting role remained to be seen. But he couldn't hold on forever, that was certain.

## Communists!

IN HIS OLD AGE, Flakey Jake Martínez, devil's advocate to Icarus Suazo, fathered a child he and his wife, Gloria, called Anthony. They had numerous other children, grown, married, gone: their previous youngest had volunteered for Korea and was killed three days after landing at Pusan.

Other families, still in mourning from World War II, ponied up their surviving sons to Korea's carnage. Juan and Amaranta GeeGee's Alfredo lost an arm and a leg; another son, Alberto, was killed outright. Andrés Ortega, Juan and Mari-Elena's sixth boy, was sent screaming to the angels by a land mine. But the children of the Anglo Axis rarely got near the war. They were officers stationed stateside, or busy going to college, or politely deferred for one reason or another. Bad knees saved George Parker. A second-string all-American and starting halfback on the state university's football team, a great basketball and track man besides, the most renowned athlete by far ever to come from Chamisaville, he suffered torn ligaments in both knees on a routine off-tackle slant play in the Colorado game. And, with a year and a half of eligibility remaining, his athletic career had ended. While others died, then, George finished school, came home, and married Susan Bonney. Accepting a coaching and teaching job at the high school, George felt terribly helpless, as if his life had somehow been nipped in the bud.

Junior Leyba arrived in Korea a silent, frightening officer who seemed bent on a foolhardy heroism bound to endanger all his men while he himself committed suicide.

Wounded four times, Junior always rebounded quickly, back on the line in record time. He moved through a darkness not even war could mitigate or fathom, yet despite his desire for death, Junior survived, finding himself all too soon back in Chamisaville, a highly decorated veteran praised to the skies by everyone. The Jaycees raised money to help defray his college expenses; the *News* ran a series of articles recounting his brilliant war experiences. Two weeks after his return, Chamisaville sponsored a Junior Leyba Day. A parade, featuring high-school cheerleaders, majorettes, and the band, began at the Dynamite Shrine, circled down around the plaza, and continued south, terminating at a new shopping center where a laundromat, a Wacker's, a Piggly Wiggly, and one more liquor store had recently been constructed. After the parade, Junior was honored on the bandstand that sat atop the town police concrete pillbox in the plaza. Mayor Damacio Mares gave a short speech. Loretta Shimkus joined the dignitaries, including the state's lieutenant governor, on the podium. Virgil Leyba watched from the back of the happy crowd.

When asked to say a few words, Junior panicked. Awkwardly fingering the microphone, his fierce eyes burning uncomfortably, he was unable to speak for long, embarrassing seconds. Finally, dropping his eyes and toeing stupidly at the floor, Junior mumbled what everyone had come to hear: "I only did what any man would have done. I was proud to serve my country. I'm very thankful to God that I came out of it alive. . . ." When he left the platform, ashamed of his cowardice, his inability to articulate his hatred of them all, Junior was almost in tears. The Medal of Honor, a Bronze Star with oak-leaf clusters, and several Purple Hearts meant nothing. Encapsulated at the center of an official beaming crowd, Junior hurried past Virgil and did not even catch his father's eye.

Junior finished college in record time, studying around the clock, valedictorian of his class. And, without telling Virgil good-bye, he entered law school in Cambridge, Massachusetts—at Harvard.

WITH JUNIOR GONE, he thought for good, Virgil felt old, sad, unrequited. For too long he had despised his own son, been separated from his wife, and had had no time for emotional, loving amenities.

Virgil was lonely. Too often, these days, the recollection of April McQueen's teen-age contours nestled against his bony skeleton teased hungers which had rarely been sated, arousing lusts that had never died. All his life Virgil had wrestled with ample women. And even now, every night, their longed-for shapes needled his dreams. Riveraesque, Lachaisian, Rodin-like, they snuggled against his aging ardor that literally steamed with regret because he had failed to love a hundred others similar to the first ninety-nine with whom he had shared a night, a year, a portion of his lifetime. Without ever tempering his loneliness.

A desire for loving had carried Virgil—guilt free or guilt ridden, it didn't matter—into the arms of peasant women, schoolteachers, and summer visitors alike. It was a cold-blooded lusting he had never learned to curb nor cared to quash. It had given him pleasure to let his wants and curiosity—albeit in a somehow strong and if possible dig-nified manner—run rampant.

For decades Virgil had displayed the powerful, melan-choly mien of a man on the verge of death who understood dying. "You remind me of Manolete," a woman once whis-pered, hypnotized by his cool sorrowful eyes and narrow muscled body. Fingertips touched his old bullet-wound scars with passionate awe. Women pressed damp lips to his skin, clinging for dear life while he loved them, an insatiable and silent, yet somehow thoughtful lover capable of giving to his partners the real gift of themselves, minus banalities, leaving them drained, feeling important and skillful, and, above all, cherished. And Lord how he ached now, remembering, wondering why his sex life of late had become imprisoned in the exhaustion of his daily routine, his energy—which he had not the skill to apportion sen-sibly—clobbered by the demands of his legal trade.

Virgil's loneliness, a cold fever, chilled his body—a per-petual, icy ache. Jumbled remembrances of things past burned like an acrid smoke in his nostrils, ever present and confusing, often detracting from his work, which had become, during the accelerating drive toward the Better-ment of Chamisaville, literally overwhelming.

Consciously, Virgil was sacrificing himself to the people, a logical action, given his convictions. Yet he still could not believe age had so withered his vitality that he was forced to make a choice.

His marriage to Loretta Shimkus had been the most in-comprehensible love of his life. As neither he nor Loretta had been much on words, Virgil looked back on that time now as an unpardonably silent holocaust, featuring an almost underwater confusion and hatred-plagued loving.

Neither he nor Loretta ever discussed the attraction uniting them in the first place, that mystifying alchemy of arrogant curiosity which had created intense erotic battlefields where they bruised each other during a thousand consecutive nights without once commenting on their affair, both frightened and made ebullient by the intensity of their sensational mating. To this day Virgil had freckle-sized scars sprinkled across his tight skin, tiny slash marks where she had worked him over. And on areas of his body—around the shoulders, buttocks, and calves—faintly lavender hues glowing beneath his pale skin were echoes of bruises that had endured for years, soft permanent blemishes, subdued monuments to their passion.

Unable to penetrate the silence, they had always been mistrustful, suspicious, off-balance. True, Virgil had never —as a youth, as a young man—been comfortable with women. And although fired in a revolutionary epoch that cast aside a thousand barriers between sexes, Virgil had emerged with that inability to converse intact, and a tenderness he often felt for women, for all humankind, locked severely behind his heart. Tempered by atrocity and great loss, Virgil had moved through his new world with quiet dignity, submerged passion and violence, and a fervent, uncalculated despair.

They cracked against each other, Virgil and Loretta. Afraid to touch except by clashing, they had circled each other warily, looking for an opening, not to kill, but rather to love each other.

Each had tremendous yearnings for an emotional stability which never came. Their only child had been raised traumatically in an atmosphere of smoky tenterhooks. That unrelieved tension eventually had become unbearable. Never understanding it, Junior had felt his parents hated each other. He always believed that what was actually an inarticulate ardor unaided by an ability to communicate on more banal levels was, rather, a personal feud steeped in a hatred so volatile it must have come from a terrifying experience he found impossible to imagine as anything other than his own unwanted birth.

Given luck, they might have enjoyed a rare marriage. Instead, too proud to grovel, and trusting time to unlock their stalemate, Virgil and Loretta immersed themselves in work, leading separate lives while strangling in the gap between them.

Only haltingly could they discuss practical matters: money, schooling, menus. All else was the most bitter mystery either had ever confronted. Even after the divorce, however, they had remained civil, and these days Virgil often slipped into the hotel late at night to make love as before—they battered each other ruthlessly, trapped in uncomprehended emotions.

With other women, loving was so easy. His tensions flowed into their bodies; they swayed in his wind—subtle, brazen, deferential. Virgil sprawled against them like a man asleep on a haystack, perfectly satisfied with a woman he had not known yesterday and would forget about tomorrow, blissfully happy as long as his thoughts did not blunder into a memory of Loretta. If they did, he bolted up, cold and strung-out again, nervous, and scornful of the woman beside him and of himself, wanting to ridicule the petty sexual affairs of men and women together.

All his life, Virgil had dreamed of discovering Loretta. But he had never solved the riddle of their relationship. She had become a hard businesswoman who wore her stately loneliness as a woman might wear a severe but beautiful shawl.

They met several times a week for drinks, sometimes sharing a meal together in the La Tortuga. And what most characterized their frequent get-togethers was the silence, the air of lost expectation, the feeling of tensions about to burst.

THERE WAS NO LETUP. Each year La Ciénega farmers had less irrigation water because Mosquito Valley Ski Area development was seriously depleting the Rio Chiquito. When water did manage to arrive in their pastoral community, it was seriously polluted because of the inadequate sewage plant servicing the hunting lodge, pro shop, restaurants, shop, summer vacation homes, condominiums, and ski dorms propagating like rabbits there. By now, twenty-one small trout ponds dotted the Mosquito Valley, all legal because no dam was higher than three-plus yards, no pond impounded more than ten acre-feet of water. But they badly reduced the river at its various spring-fed sources. Adding insult to injury, the ponds were considered part of a public park area—including the golf course and tennis courts—that was being developed by conservancy district funds.

"Which means," Espeedie Cisneros told an angry group of La Ciénega farmers, "that our taxes we are paying down here are being used to build ponds up there that are keeping us from having the water we need down here to grow the vegetables we're supposed to sell to pay our conservancy assessments."

"What can we do about it?" the people asked.

"We can look up Jesus Dolores Martínez Vigil, if he's still alive, and hire him to lead another band of us up there to kick out some of those trout ponds so that we can irrigate our goddam gardens!"

"What are you turning into," half the audience mumbled fitfully, "a lousy Communist?"

"Listen to me, you ignorant baboons!" Espeedie shouted angrily. "I'm gonna tell you the story about the Mejicana puta and the gabacho prairie dog!

"It seems there was once a young and beautiful Mejicana girl who lived across the border from El Chuco in Juárez. Her daddy was a cripple and her mamá was blind. So the little girl went to a whorehouse and sold her body to gabacho soldados from Texas in order to support the family. Her dream was to earn enough money so they could buy a little piece of land and have a garden to feed themselves: then she could quit being a puta and become a farmer. So every night for ten years the puta opened her legs for gabacho college boys and Mejicano soccer players and rich turistas, and finally, having saved up the money, she bought a piece of land with a little house on it, and immediately planted a big garden. She and her mamá and papá had never been so happy in their lives. But then one morning the beautiful little puta spied a hole in the ground in her field made by a gabacho prairie dog that had been run out of Texas by the heartless farmers over there. Immediately, the little girl borrowed a pistol and aimed at the gabacho tusa. 'Wait, don't shoot, please, have mercy!' sobbed the varmint in English. 'They beat me in Dallas and they poisoned me in Brownsville, they shot at me in Austin and tried to drown me in Big Bend National Park. I got no place else to go, I've run out of running room. Let me stay in your field, I won't hurt nothing, I'll be a good little prairie dog.' Well, the puta had a soft spot in her heart for animals, so she didn't kill him. But, when she cut irrigation water into her field, incredibly, all the water disappeared into that single hole made by the gabacho prairie dog. Then, while she looked on in disbelief, a hundred more holes, made by the large family of the gabacho prairie dog, appeared everywhere in her precious field. In no time flat, they turned her land into a desert. When she borrowed a tractor to replow the land, its big wheels broke through the crust of the honeycombed field and it got stuck. The little puta spent the last of her savings having it pulled out. By then, the land was worthless, it belonged to the gabacho tusas, and so she went back to banging huero teen-agers in order to support her folks. The beautiful little Mejicana puta died at an early age of gabacho venereal disease.

"So don't you people accuse me of being a lefty!" Espeedie said, incensed by their stupidity. "You better praise me, instead, for being aware of the state of the world!"

THE LA CIÉNEGA FARMERS weren't the only ones in trouble. Five miles south, in Cañoncito and Mota Llano, the natural flow irrigation water was being withheld by Magpie Creek Lumber Mill wash ponds. The problem became so acute that Juan GeeGee and the nearly destroyed farmer Vidal Mondragón called for a community meeting.

"I say we just load our guns, attack the lumber mill, burn it to the ground, and shoot any gabacho, gringo, lambe, or vendido connected with the operation!" Juan GeeGee said. "I've had enough of this bullshit. I gave my sons to World War Two and Korea, while boys like Jonathan Moose and Georgie Parker sat around going to college, dating pretty coeds, and growing fat off the hog. We always been a patient people, but while my boys were dying, Denzil Spivey, that de-penised Floresta maricón, was cheating me out of a third of my sheep permits. And his creepy draft-age kid Roger was playing Legion baseball and visiting New York and having a grand old time eating hamburgers and milkshakes out at the Chamisaville Country Club. I bet that money from the sale of the three acres I had to give Claude Parker for burying my boy Alberto was used to buy his kid a medical deferment and a new Chevy convertible!"

"Careful, you're beginning to sound like a Communist," Vidal Mondragón cautioned. "Don't raise your voice so loud when you say those things, somebody might be listening. Now, I'm sure we can find a more reasonable solution to this problem of the wash ponds."

"For example?"

"Well, we're all residents of the conservancy district. And those wash ponds are retaining our conservancy water. If we don't get that water, we can't grow the crops to sell on the local market to earn the cash to pay our assessments so we won't lose our homes and our land. Therefore, the board of the conservancy should order the conservancy's legal team to go to court, enjoining McQueen and his lumber-mill associates from withholding our water by having those wash ponds up there."

"You're ignoring one important fact at the heart of all your reasoning, cousin," Juan GeeGee said politely.

"What's that?"

"Our conservancy board and our conservancy legal team also happen to be the owners and operators of the Magpie Creek Lumber Mill."

"Then if they refuse our suggestion, we'll bag them for conflict of interest," Vidal said unhappily.

As elected representatives of the Mota Llano–Cañoncito farmers, Juan and Vidal arranged a meeting with conservancy board members Moe Stryzpk, Rodey McQueen, and Bob Moose, all three of whom were developers of the Magpie Creek Lumber Mill. Bob Moose was also the conservancy district's chief legal counselor. As politely as possible, Vidal explained the situation, suggesting that the conservancy board was obligated to protect the district citizens it governed by forcing the lumbermill owners to knock out their wash ponds.

Moe Stryzpk explained that the wash ponds did not fall within conservancy jurisdiction. He rattled off facts and figures about priority water rights, national forest reservation clauses, and other complex precedents until his listeners were completely befuddled. Bob Moose, however, opined that the conservancy might have a case. And he agreed to file for an injunction against the lumber mill and its wash ponds. A costly legal battle ensued. Bob Moose and the conservancy suffered a defeat, the wash ponds remained, and Juan GeeGee, Vidal Mondragón, and all other poor farmers and ranchers within the district boundaries received even higher conservancy assessments in order to pay off Bob Moose for being their lawyer.

Vidal Mondragón gloomily called the whole thing an act of God. But not Juan GeeGee. Storming past a startled secretary without so much as a "buenos dias," he banged open Rodey McQueen's office door, and, withdrawing a six-inch hunting knife from his belt, he stabbed it down through four inches of contracts, legal papers, and letters into the hardwood top of the tyrant's desk, saying, "Excuse me, Mr. McQueen, for acting like a brute, but I need a moment of your attention."

McQueen removed a .38 pistol from his drawer, settled it in front of him, looked at his watch, and said, "Certainly, Johnny. You've got exactly three minutes."

"All right. Now, the way I see it, this conservancy board can't represent us in the matter of the wash ponds because there is a clear conflict of interest on your parts. Therefore, it's my impression this whole court case to test the validity of them wash ponds was rigged. It was an illegal farce, and maybe people like you and Moe Stryzpk and Randolph Bonney, Bob Moose and Al Lamont ought to be impeached for illegal actions detrimental to the rights of all of us small farmers."

"I hate to say this, Johnny," McQueen replied, heaving up out of his chair until he had both enormous palms on the desk, supporting his great weight as he leaned forward, casting an imposing shadow across the tiny sheepherder, "but you are knocking around the conservancy laws like a goddam blind dog in a butcher shop. Not only that, but you are beginning to sound just a little bit like a Communist."

Reaching over, Juan grabbed his knife and resheathed it. "Then maybe we'll get Virgil Leyba to impeach you bastards for us. And furthermore, if I was you I wouldn't bet no money on the longevity of your precious wash ponds either!"

Juan thundered across the plaza and convinced Virgil to sue the conservancy board and the lumber-mill board on behalf of the Mota Llano–Cañoncito residents. But at 5:00 A.M. the next morning, while he was bottlefeeding some motherless lambs, Juan was collared by the new county sheriff, Big Bill Baca. Assault and battery of Rodey McQueen with a dangerous weapon, willful destruction of private property, and trespassing were the charges. Instead of suing the conservancy board, Virgil wound up spending most of his time raising bail for Juan. Then, during a series of long and costly court maneuvers, he labored just to keep his client free. Eventually, Juan got off. But his defense had cost time and energy. And the case frightened other locals away from protesting the wash ponds. Better to suffer in quiet than to risk losing everything by challenging the situation as Juan GeeGee had.

The controversy flared again, however. A small group of shadowy delinquents, reputedly led by a diminutive roly-poly outlaw wrapped in rope, gunbelts, arrow quivers, and ancient weapons of all makes and sizes, infiltrated national forest land above the Magpie Creek Lumber Mill and dynamited the dams of all three wash ponds.

This experiment in democratic problem-solving backfired on its perpetrators, however. A great wall of water crashed down Magpie Creek, joined with the Rio Puerco, and unfurled a minor tidal wave across the reservoir, thumping brutally against the dam, causing that earthen structure to shiver and crack a bit on one side. Into that fissure turbulent water swirled. By morning, a substantial leak had developed. All residents of Cañoncito, Mota Llano, La Lomita, Borregas Negras, and Ranchitos Abajo were ordered to higher ground.

"But if we go we'll desert our animals and our gardens at the most crucial time of summer!"

"If you don't evacuate," the board replied, "maybe all of you will drown."

They scrambled for higher ground. Gardens withered in their absence. A crew of men driving mammoth earthmoving machines repaired the wounded dam. Working around the clock for a week, they built forms, poured cement, then abruptly drained half the reservoir to relieve pressure on the earth-fill structure. Water cascaded uselessly past the abandoned farms and tumbled into the Rio Grande.

Ultimately, at an enormous cost, they saved the dam. When the emergency assessments for that arrived, farmers tore their hair, wailed, sold off more acreage to meet the taxation, and cursed Juan GeeGee and Jesus Etcetera and anybody else who'd favored annihilating those wash ponds.

Juan Ortega and Virgil got drunk in the El Gaucho Bar. "What I would like to do," Juan said dazedly, "is I would like to organize the people into a small army, and I would like to attack the Cañoncito Reservoir and dynamite all the fish in its permanent trout pool. Then I would like to march on each house belonging to each member of our wonderful conservancy board, and I would like to tie up all the inhabitants of those houses, steal their jewelry and silverware and TV sets and anything else of value, and sell all that stuff down in the capital, using the proceeds to arm every longtime Spanish- and Indian-speaking citizen of our valley. Then I would declare war on the United States of North America, and especially on our own Anglo Axis!"

"What are you turning into," Virgil groaned humorously, "a lousy Communist?"

"Well," Juan said, "at least we got rid of those wash ponds. Next year the reservoir will fill up and provide plenty of irrigation water for any farmer who has survived that long."

Pat GeeGee shook his head. "It doesn't matter how much water everybody has, and I'll tell you why. If everybody gets sufficient water, everybody will grow plenty of vegetables to sell around here, earning the cash to pay for the water, qué no?"

"Claro que sí."

"Well, if everybody in the valley is selling vegetables, two things will happen. First of all, I doubt anybody can undersell the chain stores like Safeway and Piggly Wiggly, because they are enormous monopolies and deal in tremendous volume and can undersell anybody—that's how they make a profit. But they won't even need to do that because with such a glut of vegetables on the market here, the bottom will fall out. You won't even be able to give away the food because everybody will have vegetables."

Juan said, "So we'll sell them in the capital. We'll sell them way down south in Albuquerque, or way up north in Denver."

"Where will you store them while they are awaiting transportation? And who's gonna raise the cash to hire the trucks for distribution? Who in this valley can afford that?"

"I guess nobody."

"Precisely."

Virgil smashed his beer glass on the floor, muttering, "Go fuck yourselves, all you lousy Communists!"

J. B. LeDoux HAD CLOSELY followed conservancy developments, the Mosquito Valley story, the wash pond controversy. And sometimes the insidious nature of the process undermining his people jolted the construction boss. The Chamisa Valley's demise made him sick to his stomach and guilty. How could his pathetic wife embed herself so gratefully into the warm muff of their economic expansion? J. B. felt a need to perform some feat that might restore a little dignity, allowing him a moment of pride. His growing security and accumulating creature comforts had no meaning. At the McQueen mansion for cocktails one evening, he nervously broached the subject.

"As it stands now, Mr. McQueen, I think the conservancy is doing more harm than good. Realistically, if no effort is made to revamp the district's structures and priorities, it could end up eradicating the very people it was supposed to save."

"What are you suggesting?" McQueen asked. "Sounds like you're just running off at the mouth to hear your head rattle, J. B. Conservancy laws were created by lawmakers elected for and by the people. That's the way our democratic institutions function."

"Aw, cut it out, sir. Everybody knows how our so-called lawmakers are elected and how our so-called democratic institutions function. Particularly when it comes down to the little man versus big business."

"What the hell are you talking about?" McQueen roared. *"You're beginning to sound like a goddam Communist!"*

"A Communist?" J. B. froze. Then he backpedaled so fast his tongue tripped all over itself rattling off a mollifying babble. "I didn't mean . . . I wasn't suggesting . . . you know me, Mr. McQueen . . . it's just that . . . well, after, you know, that wash pond affair . . . not that the courts didn't decide fairly, of course, I wouldn't suggest that. . . . *Communist—?*" he asked again, growing positively white: "I really think you misunderstood, sir. I suppose you were joking. . . ."

That night, on top of Nobody Mountain, J. B. stuck the barrel of a revolver into his mouth. For a long time he contemplated death while overlooking the twinkling town —his expanding home. New lights shone everywhere, bright baubles marching south from Chamisaville and La Ciénega and Upper Ranchitos toward another grouping of lights, originating in Cañoncito, Mota Llano, La Lomita, and Borregas Negras, marching north to meet them. And J. B. grew lazy and sleepy and almost sensual inside. All that remained, after he thumbed back the hammer, was to touch the trigger, ending his life. But even as the darkness lulled him into a perfect, peacefully relieved acceptance of the suicide that would erase the anguish of his paranoid

131

existence, some clammy thing slipped into the core of his resolve and sabotaged his intentions.

J. B. lowered the gun, opened the chamber, and poked out the heavy bullets: they plopped into the dirt at his feet.

Perhaps he needed revenge more than he needed to die.

"What are you turning into, J. B. LeDoux . . ." he whispered tearfully, "a stupid Communist?"

WHILE THE CONSERVANCY'S unforeseen difficulties multiplied, Icarus Suazo forged ahead with his grand plan for recapturing fifty thousand acres of sacred Albino Pine land from the Forest Service. He also intended to reclaim for the Pueblo any and all valley land that he possibly could.

It was a long and frustrating process. Many times Icarus and Marshall Kickingbird left the valley, journeying to Albuquerque and Phoenix, to Denver and Washington, D.C. They conferred with federal and state officials and historians, with representatives of other Indian tribes seeking restitution for stolen land and genocidal crimes committed against their nations. They stockpiled information, tracked down legal precedents, rubbed their weary eyes after plodding through endlessly vague records in federal archives. Their various court suits, petitioning a return of the Albino Pine land, asking for restitution of the acreage upon which Chamisaville and its surrounding environs now sat, crawled through the courts like a nearly frozen snake. Marshall Kickingbird grew numb from collecting information regarding Indian land and water rights and treaty commitments. Often, he and Icarus discussed self-determination. They quarreled with the BIA, which apparently defined "termination" of the Indians' federally protected status in the same way the late Adolf Hitler had defined his "Final Solution."

"You're supposed to be *for* us," Marshall wearily told the Pueblo BIA administrator, Ed Lange. "Instead, you poison our culture, actively lobby against our best interests, lobotomize our children in your boarding schools, negotiate contracts with outside developers to come in and exploit reservation resources to their hearts' content, and siphon off half the funds slated for native peoples in order to feather your own corrupt nests."

"What are you turning into, Mr. Kickingbird," Ed asked suspiciously, "a goddam red?"

During the Second World War, Rodey McQueen's Magpie Creek Lumber Mill had obtained exclusive rights from the Forest Service to cut timber on Albino Pine land. For almost a decade, Icarus Suazo and Marshall Kickingbird had been laboring unsuccessfully to reverse that decision, terminating McQueen's contract. Now the Pueblo dwellers were getting fed up. Icarus Suazo visited Flakey Jake Martínez, asking for advice, and Jake replied:

"Close the Pueblo to tourists, shoot any gringo who steps across the reservation boundary, occupy the Albino Pine land with every native capable of toting a gun, and lynch any Florestista, federal dick, state chota, or National Guardsman that lays even half a tootsie on our sacred property. And if Rodey McQueen won't raise Pueblo salaries to six bucks an hour at the Dynamite Fetish factory and throw in some health insurance and retirement benefits to boot, kidnap the son of a bitch like they did his daughter, hold him for a million-dollar ransom, and if his family or the power structure pussyfoots around longer than twenty-fours refusing to cough up the boodle, cut the old bastard's head off and mail it back to them bookrate!"

Instead, Marshall Kickingbird chose to be moderate when he addressed a meeting attended by Floresta nabob Denzil Spivey, Rodey McQueen, Moe Stryzpk, and Randolph Bonney.

"The clear-cutting of those timbering gorillas has destroyed our hunting, ruined the game, and cast bad spirits onto our homes," he said. "The river is always cloudy from erosion, and our ancestors cannot sleep because of the constant rumbling of big machines and trucks and falling trees. Each day you rape our land and our religion, you trespass on the very spirit of our existence. We have been patient for many years, but the people have had enough. I cannot vouch for them in the future."

McQueen said, "It's all legal, Marshall. You know that as well as I do, and as well as everybody else in this room does. We wouldn't be up there barging around like an oversexed moose in a wigwam if it wasn't all legal."

Eyes trained on the ceiling instead of on their faces, Icarus Suazo spoke:

"Of course, there is always the law, that goes without saying. There are laws, however, and there are other laws. And there are always conflicting interpretations of the laws by various interested parties depending on which side of the fence they are standing. Almost fifty years ago an American president issued a decree which took from us our sacred land, making it a part of the national forest. Ever since that time we have labored to win back our land by legal means, even though we believe that a simple presidential decree did not constitute fair play in the matter. Now we have arrived at a point where we see our sacred land being chopped apart mercilessly by the forces of progress and profit with no consideration for the well-being of mother nature, or for a people who have long held that the Albino Pine land gives religious impetus and true meaning to their current lives, past history, and future aspirations. A general dissatisfaction exists among my people. Their grumbling reaches from the depths of the darkest kiva to the top of Hija Negrita, as you people call the sacred mountain. Who knows what will happen, or how much longer Marshall and me are gonna be able to vouch for our people?"

"Come on Icarus, what the heck are you saying?" Denzil Spivey asked irritatedly.

"Aren't I talking English?"

"Sure—but . . . What are you saying?" the Forest Service head reiterated.

"He is saying that when the deer has no more wild pasture, it is likely to begin foraging in the garden," Marshall explained.

"Cut the crap!" Rodey McQueen exploded. "Who are you two pretending to be with your goddam 'mystical allusions' speeches? You went to college, you're both more sophisticated than a dandy in a Dodge City saloon in these matters. So spare the hominy, boys, and let's hack out this thing around the pertinent points!"

Icarus bowed his head sadly. "It would be apropos, Mr. McQueen, if you would suspend your operations on Pueblo land."

"That ain't Pueblo land, and you know it!"

The Pueblo secretary finally looked the Muleshoe tycoon straight in the eye: "Excuse me if I was impolite, gentlemen. I hope nobody has been made uncomfortable by this exchange. Good day."

And the two of them politely left the room.

In subsequent weeks, Magpie Creek Lumber Mill bulldozers were shot at, set afire at night, dynamited. Enormous logging trucks rumbling down narrow mountain roads were fired upon, their tires punctured, their operators driven to hiding in the forest. Armed guards, hired by McQueen, joined the crews, protecting the loggers. Shot at and deliberately missed, these bodyguards could only retaliate by pumping lead willy-nilly into impregnable lifeless foliage. Nobody ever saw an enemy. McQueen and Denzil Spivey called for another powwow, but Icarus and Marshall were occupied by other pursuits. The FBI and the National Guard entered the reservation, searching for clues: native people gathered wood, broke horses, and harvested beans without looking up. Lumbering operations continued for a spell in a hail of hot lead which began zeroing in on the loggers. Government helicopters quartered the Albino Pine sacred forest, searching in vain for the guerrillas perpetrating such pesky hit-and-run tactics. For a week the woods crawled with federal and state police personnel, and with members of the same National Guard unit that had participated in the death march of Bataan.

Pretty soon so many various military personnel crowded the forest that soldiers couldn't move without surprising, and occasionally shooting at, each other. After five men on the same side were wounded by their buddies, all police maneuvers were canceled. And Denzil Spivey informed Rodey McQueen that due to circumstances beyond their control the Forest Service had decided to revoke the lumber mill's permit to clear-cut Albino Pine land.

So the lumbering scars were left to be healed by the wind and the rain. Denzil Spivey received a restrained letter of appreciation from Marshall Kickingbird, thanking him for his "humanitarian approach to a difficult situation." And the next time they met, Icarus Suazo shook hands with Rodey McQueen and never alluded to the logging war at all.

To settle his nerves, McQueen booked passage on a boat for Africa and went on safari. He shot a few koodoo, water buffalo, elephants, and so forth. Back home, he built a large trophy room onto the mansion and in it displayed a rhino head or two for all Chamisaville to admire.

Shortly after McQueen finished his trophy room, a medium-sized package from an anonymous sender arrived in the mail. It contained a stuffed field mouse, two stuffed prairie dogs, one stuffed kangaroo rat, a bundle of chicken feathers, a skunk pelt and a stuffed hamster, two gerbil skins, and an amateurly taxidermized guinea pig.

The enclosed typewritten note said: *Please hang these in your trophy room, señor.*

Chamisaville was riddled with Communists!

BEFORE EMBARKING FOR Europe in the middle of Ike's second administration, April Epstein Lanahan née Mc-Queen returned home for a short visit.

Behind the wheel of a battered Ford convertible, she drove into Chamisa County with little fanfare. A lime-green scarf protected her short hair; no wedding or en-gagement rings hampered her fingers; she was feeling right snug inside Charley Epstein's carefully tended bomber jacket. Nobody, not even her family, had known of her visit. For two straight days and nights she had driven with-out sleep. But as she topped the gorge and the sage brush plain stretched away before her, leading to the jagged Rio Grande Gorge on her right and the Chamisaville com-munities clustered beneath the Midnight Mountains on her left, April released a huge nostalgic sigh and began weep-ing. In a sense, memory of this sight had sustained her for years in New York. She had a Camel between her lips, a bottle of cream sherry in the glove compartment. Slimmer than before, her provocative teen-age plumpness was gone. Beautiful blue eyes were surrounded by bruised-looking skin. April was tired, fatigued clear through to her bones.

She didn't stay long, only about a week. Subdued, not very talkative, a sadness encompassed all her movements. Gentle, reflective, and considerate—April's parents hardly knew her. She imparted to them little information about her life and future plans. At the Dynamite Shrine Dining Salon she had shared a neutral lunch with Cynthia. And one night killed a six-pack with her father while they shot straight pool together. Early on the October mornings she donned a black tank suit and swam slow laps in their pool. Dreamily, she walked around the shallow end, languorous-ly scooping up yellow aspen leaves that had drifted off nearby trees. Hours of unnatural quiet ensued, April on a towel in crisp sunshine reading novels, books about art, beatnik poets, philosophy.

At the new record store she made her only purchase of the week: a dozen albums including Elvis Presley, Stan Getz, Dave Brubeck. Seated on her old bed, legs tucked beneath a wide peasant skirt, chain-smoking cigarettes and sipping little glasses of cream sherry, she listened to her records while writing in a diary. "Are you all right?"

Cynthia asked her one day. April smiled: "Oh sure, Mother, I'm fine. I'm just thinking . . ."

Cameras hanging around her neck, April drove about the valley taking photographs of the rustic Chamisa County scene. All too soon, she guessed, it would be irrevocably changed. At the Espeedie Cisneros ranch, April photographed his house, corrals, a horse-drawn plow rig and sickle bar. She took pictures of Espeedie and his wife, Pancha, branding, plastering their mud outbuildings, and on horseback among their few sheep. From Nobody Mountain she did several portraits of the valley—at dawn, at sunset. All her friends she coaxed before the lens—Pat and Lucinda GeeGee, Perfecto Torres and Celestino Lucero, Virgil Leyba and Jake Martínez. April also made certain to document—in both black and white and in color—all the old houses painted during the thirties by Espeedie Cisneros and Canuto Tafoya, adobe homes which still carried those faded murals of Jesus toting a fishing pole and a stringer of trout, motorcars with wings, Zapata and the Virgin and bucking ponies.

And she took some photographs of the incredible Cañoncito Dam site. The reservoir was empty. It had been filled after the wash pond controversy, but all the water had leaked out. Finally, the entire project had been abandoned. Now, bulldozers were busily at work grading the reservoir floor to make a public golf course for "the people" that "the people" would never be rich enough to use, even though their taxes were paying for the useless development.

April walked into Virgil Leyba's office one day and embraced him quietly. Over a shot and a beer in the El Gaucho, April pumped Virgil and Pat and Juan Ortega about the state of Chamisaville.

Next morning, she settled beside Judson Babbitt on a plaza bench and talked about art. He was astounded by her knowledge of New York: "I left that unholy place," he confided tritely, "because I knew it would kill me in five years if I didn't escape." When she had cocktails with Felicia Babbitt and Amanda Santana in the La Tortuga, two women now middle-aged and dumpy, though dressed in chic gypsy regalia, they pumped April for details of the Eastern scene. And everybody exclaimed, "My God, April, how you've grown!" Actually, they were surprised by the changes New York had wrought, puzzled by her modulated voice and remote and gentle demeanor.

April saddled up a horse and galloped across the western mesa to the gorge. Walking the horse north along the rim of that deep crevasse, chain-smoking as she sipped from a small silver flask, April sang melancholy songs to herself, apparently lost and a little lonely. But gathering strength—every minute of every day—absorbing landscape, mood, architecture, the personalities of people she loved, recharging her batteries for the next run.

Another morning she rode up the Midnight River accompanied by Flakey Jake Martínez and Jake's lovely September child, Anthony, a seven-year-old by then. Jake synopsized Pueblo politics, the nefarious (or glorious, depending) deeds and misdeeds of Icarus Suazo and his lawbooks, Marshall Kickingbird. He gave her a hilarious blow-by-blow of the Magpie Creek Lumber Mill logging war. Halting for lunch beside the stream, they ate cold beans wrapped in tortillas. Little Anthony caught trout by hand in the shallow waters of the icy river. "I got lucky late in life," Jake said, a twinkle riding strong in his ancient eyes. "That kid is gonna return my investment tenfold."

April ran into George Parker on the Plaza portal. They embraced, crossed into the park, and occupied speckled sunshine for a moment, reminiscing. Mostly, George talked about himself: about playing varsity football, basketball, and track at the state university until his ligaments were ruined. He had gotten a degree in English, was teaching at the high school and coaching athletics, and had married Susan Bonney, Randolph's daughter. So far they had a daughter, a son—"and Susan has a pumpkin belly again." A moment later, he said, "Boy, have you changed!" Assessing his short-cropped hair, healthy muscled body etched by a white T-shirt, and something sad and tense behind his all-American features, April replied: "So have you, George. We all do. It's only natural."

"Occasionally I hear fantastic rumors about you," he said shyly, made a little nervous by this sophisticated woman he barely recognized, a stranger he might never have run with. "It's always second-, third-, fifth-hand. Away from us all, you're still incredibly romantic. Nobody will let the legend die. I've heard that you dated Mickey Mantle, were Marlon Brando's mistress, that you were gonna be in a Broadway play and star in a movie. Most of the stories are terribly apocryphal: that you were off in Paris, in Morocco, in Marrakech: that you've already been married six times; that you played your guitar in the White House."

April laughed. The clear air smelled like autumn piñon smoke; little kids, as numerous as hop-toads on September creeks, hawked the *Chamisaville News.* The glowering cripple, Eduardo Mondragón, waved a *Capital City Reporter* held in a two-fingered hand, growling, "Extra, read all about it," under his breath. Vito Rosselini, grown hideously fat in the past few years, clumped up, gave April a jovial abrazo, shouted at her in fractured Italo-English for a moment, then waddled down the plaza waving his arms and blaring out snippets of opera in a basso-profundo voice. No sooner had Vito turned into the courthouse, than Eloy Romo, wrapped in his old boxing cape and smoking a cigar, limped up and gave April an emotional hug. These days, after a stretch in the pen for draft-dodging during World War II, he sold *Playboy, True Detective,* and *True Romance* magazines in Lalo Chavez's Magazine Emporium, located next to the La Tortuga Bar and Restaurant three doors up from the Prince of Whales Café. "Where did you go?" he cried. "Carai, hermana, we have missed you! Genoveva Bachicha told me you were up in heaven playing strip poker with God! How come you never said good-bye? What did you think of Floyd Patterson? Do you ever go to Madison Square Garden? Did you hear that Rocky Marciano came to Chamisaville and ate an enchilada with green chile in the King Cole Executive Room of the Dynamite Shrine Dining Salon? They say Vidal Mondragón pisses red everyday and that Ralphito García walked into the El Gaucho two months ago with seaweed dripping from his ears and ordered a beer! They also say Pancho Lucero, Celestino's son, joined Jesus Etcetera and Atiliano Montoya in the mountains— they are starting another Gorras Blancas. Me?—I'm gonna be a special attraction in next summer's Cipi García fiestas, re-creating that boxing benefit I did for the *El Clarín,* re-member? Adiós, beautiful sister, go with God, knock 'em dead!" And, giving her a soft looping uppercut to the jaw, Eloy limped off, cigar smoke swirling, his black-and-silver cape fluttering ridiculously.

"Are you happy?" George asked.

"Happy?" April shrugged. "I don't know, George—is that what it's supposed to be all about? I don't think I've ever worried too much about being happy. That's not really the point, is it?"

"I don't know, maybe not. But sometimes I feel pretty good, you know?" Suddenly he was expansive. "I wish I could explain to you how I feel. I mean, I haven't had all your experience or all your adventures, but I guess I don't really need all that. It's fun to dream. But there's also something neat about being alive in a place you've known all your life, about being in love and having children in a real hometown. Surrounded by familiar people and buildings and roads and mountains. It's the rhythm, you know. I guess I really like it. I'm in shape. I play basketball, I drive up Magpie Creek and run dozens of miles on autumn afternoons in the hills. I've got two beautiful kids—"

He stopped, grimacing embarrassedly. To her, his enthusiasm sounded off-balance, hollow.

"Hey, listen to me, would you? Jack Armstrong, All-American Boy. I sound like I'm trying to sell you a Fuller brush!"

April laughed. "You're okay, George. You're sweet and innocent. Strong and good. I bet there's even a dimple in the middle of your cheerful soul!"

"Uh, what are you gonna do in Europe?"

"Fuck, write, paint, photograph, explore, expand, grow up."

"Maybe after all I do envy you."

"Don't. It's not worth it. Believe me."

"If you ever want to come home for a husband, I'd like to marry you," he said lightheartedly, kidding her.

"You're already blissfully married," she teased, stubbing out a cigarette, coughing a little.

"I'd get divorced at the drop of your hat. I'd sell my soul for just one night in the passionate arms of April Mc-Queen!"

Spontaneously, April hugged him hard. "Thanks, old pal. You're a good joe, George; you're one of the most gentle, most decent characters I've ever met."

"Which shows how much you know," he laughed, and, kissing cheeks, they parted.

TV aerials were proliferating: the plaza circle had been paved; vague rumors had electricity entering the Pueblo. Amaranta GeeGee embraced April, shoved her down at the oilcloth-covered kitchen table, slapped a beer in her hands, and commenced shoveling food from the refrigerator onto the table. "Look at you!" the aging lady cried in dismay. "Hija—qué te pasó allí? You're a skeleton! Don't they have food in New York? Here, let me introduce you to Mr. Tortilla; take a bite out of Chiquita Banana! What do you want, a fried egg, french fried

140

potatoes, a bowl of frijoles, a tamale, an empanadita? Nibble on this biscochito while I prepare——!"

A moment later, April's head framed in her hands, she said, "Are you happy, hija, back there in the big city? How is life in New York?"

"Why does everybody always ask if I'm happy? What does that have to do with it?"

"You embodied all our aspirations," Amaranta said without reflection. "If you succeed—in whatever—that's a reflection on us all."

Still later, as April opened a third beer, Amaranta said, "You look lonely. 'Jita, you smoke too much. You're very subdued."

"I'm okay. I'm not lonely, God knows, that's never been my problem. I'm just resting up, that's all. Right now I'm between husbands, revolutions, and continents. So I felt like snoozing for a few weeks, barely thinking at all, listening to people talk, but not talking back. I'm getting myself a transfusion of clean Chamisaville air and innocence and mountains and sagebrush and absolutely aqua sky."

Amaranta said, "Mira tú, you're an old woman. When are you gonna have babies and settle down?"

April threw up her arms as she shrieked, "Qué no te burlas de mí, vieja!"

One evening, while April was still in town, J. B. LeDoux picked up his home phone and dialed her number. But when April herself answered, he froze, unable to speak. Hanging up, J. B. stumbled to the den and, pouring himself a long bourbon from the porta-bar, downed it in a single blistering gulp.

April visited several camposantos where buddies who had died in Korea were buried: Andrés Ortega, Alejandro and Bucabir Valerio, and others. She laid blue cornflowers on the graves. In one camposanto she sat very quietly for almost an hour as chickadees, recently down from the mountains, cavorted on the wooden crosses, stony mounds, and white metal cribs. For a moment, April longed to return home and settle into a predictable security, giving up whatever it was that made her such a questing animal. I'll lay down my weary tune in Chamisaville, she thought, allowing some man to fill me with children. My unarticulated dreams will settle to earth like October leaves— what the hell. Her life had refused to jell in the heroic manner to which April knew she must have been born.

Stooping, April selected a smooth, elliptical stone and popped it into her mouth, shifting it around on her tongue while gently massaging her groin until she was wet. Then she slipped the stone into her vagina. With that solid form inside, she sat quietly smelling her own funky scent and the odor of sunbaked camposanto pebbles, powdery pungent sagebrush, juniper trees and piñon.

A tarantula appeared. April kneeled, poked down the body, forcing the legs up into a pyramid and pinched hold of the pyramid, lifting the large spider. For a second, she gazed at the sharp little jaws, then set the spider back on the ground and watched it hurry off.

Juices were coming back. Within minutes they occupied her body like the roiling waters of a flash flood. That night, at dinner in the mansion, an enormous argument developed concerning the right of the United States to have dropped that bomb on Japan way back when. Halfway through the meal McQueen and April were clawing at each other like two bobcats in a gunnysack, while Cynthia buried her head in her hands. And when April claimed that the Western nations had deliberately appeased Hitler, allowing Germany to develop a powerful war machine on the understanding he would attack and wipe out only Communist Russia, McQueen suddenly slammed the table so hard he dislocated his thumb, and bellowed at his wayward daughter: "What have they turned you into, all those goddam fairies and perverts back there—a fucking Communist?"

Aching with laughter, April fell out of her chair.

# The City of Juaja

IN BOSTON, Junior Leyba raced effortlessly through law school. A flawless memory served him well. The law excited him more than anything ever had. It made so much sense, giving a rational structure to an ordered universe. Sometimes after a long session with various lawbooks, he surfaced for air, literally weeping for joy. Junior had discovered a thing in which he not only excelled, but tremendously enjoyed. Dominating it so easily, he knew the law would make him powerful as well. For the first time he was flexing intellectual muscles for the sheer fun of it! Junior grew absurdly cocky, blissfully strong.

Being in love with a Wellesley student helped. Her name was Charlotte Pierce, a Salem native descended from an old Yankee family with roots extending deeply into the history of the sea. It had been love at first sight. Now, recently engaged, they had their sights on marriage. Dark-haired and large-eyed, Charlotte was an entirely feminine, fragile girl, with small shoulders, perfect breasts, pale creamy skin. Junior had never held such an ethereal, exciting woman. Her flesh, textured like rare soft marble, was as cool as rainwater to his touch. Her tiny wrists and exquisite fingers left him dazed.

Despite her beauty, Charlotte was a simple woman. Not especially bright, either, she had tumbled for Junior the way a rabbit might fall in love with a hawk. His abrupt, almost cruel approach to loving frightened Charlotte: she was mystified by the range of his shifting moods. His exciting complexity swallowed her personality whole.

Junior was animated, excited by life. Two thousand miles from Chamisaville, he could laugh and play tricks; he loved to drink and sing Spanish songs, attend football and hockey contests. In Charlotte's car they visited Plymouth Rock and Hyannis Port, Truro and Provincetown, and skied in New Hampshire and Vermont. Younger than ever before in his life, Junior did all the college things, frequented cafés, joined a club. Junior had shed a thousand skins. A deft lover, he was also loved. Tops in his class, he was way ahead of the students battling over second place. Dark genes of a revolutionary father and outcast mother locked in a tragic play couldn't touch him here. People knew nothing of his background but what he chose to tell. His acceptance came on exactly the terms he dictated. He was the most attractive young man Charlotte Pierce or any of her kinfolk had ever met . . . even if obviously of Mexican origin.

Junior graduated; they got married; he passed the Massachusetts bar exam with the highest grades recorded in twenty years. A law firm intimately connected with the Kennedys welcomed him into its fold. Almost at once, the partners invited him to be on a team of advisers for the young senator John F. Kennedy.

Bob Moose, Damacio Mares, and a half-dozen other big-shots all sent Junior letters, asking him to practice law with them at home. Their glowing terms depicted the situation in Chamisaville: unlimited opportunities existed for making money and knocking down other benefits. They hinted it was almost his civic duty—having starred both in Korea and at Harvard—to indulge his tremendous talent helping lifelong friends and neighbors realize the good aspects of American life.

Politely, Junior declined their invitation. Next thing he knew, Bob Moose was in Boston. During a luncheon downtown, Bob touted the influence and prestige enjoyed by their firm in Chamisaville and the northern portion of the state. Junior could expect a highly lucrative practice under their wing.

At that, Junior made a decision he would regret forever, and never understand. Convinced it was wrong, perhaps even fatal, at the end of dining with a powerful racist son of a bitch he had despised all his life, Junior nevertheless bewilderedly promised to fly home and "bless Chamisaville with his talent, his dignity, and his integrity" (as Bob Moose put it, actually calling Junior "amígo," one of two words he knew in Spanish, the other being "cabrón"). The deal sealed, Bob gave him an abrazo to prove he was just folks, and the younger man almost vomited.

Dazed, Junior nevertheless stuck by his decision. Wrapping up his work in Boston, he made plans for moving out West. Charlotte was pregnant, but lost the child. Perhaps the thought of heading into that barbarous territory frightened her. In any case, she suffered a miscarriage and spent a week in the hospital recovering. Then, in a brand-new Chrysler hauling a trailer, they drove across country, visiting all the tourist attractions. All too soon, as Chamisaville neared, the darkness inside Junior began to expand. His face changed, his mood grew mellow, then silent, and finally foreboding. Despite the obviously wrong nature of his decision, he had no strength for turning back. By the time they entered Oklahoma, his chest was constricted and he could barely breathe. "What's the matter?" Charlotte whispered, giving him a slow massage. "What's happening, my love?" But Junior couldn't talk to her. Avoiding her eyes, he hoped she would not catch the gathering of his tears. Why am I doing this? he asked himself a million

144

times. And however magnificent or monotonous, he paid no attention to the landscape zipping by.

This time no band, no drum majorettes or cheerleaders, no mayor or lieutenant governor welcomed him back to the fold. But four men smoking genuine Havana cigars in Moe Stryzpk's situations room effusively welcomed him to the firm. They offered a cigar, good cognac, and explained that his bar exam was already arranged. He would be a practicing attorney by the end of the month.

Surrounded by Randolph Bonney, Moe Stryzpk, Bob Moose, and Rodey McQueen, Junior understood exactly why they wanted his bilingual ability and native roots in their firm. But it was too late to leave the room. He smoked the cigar, drank a little too much, and tolerated their patronizing tones. The worst in them was kin to the evil in himself. But among them, using them, Junior might also achieve revenge for being brown in a racist nation; for losing April McQueen; for being drafted to die in Korea while boys like George Parker obtained questionable deferments; for having roots into a history of poverty, madness, and stupid peasant endurance. If he adored his father, and had always prayed for that man's love, Junior also could use the Anglo Axis as a forum for destroying the old revolutionary. Junior had only scorn for anybody who could dedicate himself with such hopeless idealism to defending a bunch of illiterate peasants who ought to be culled from the face of the earth. Survival of the fittest being the name of the game. And Junior had plans, however unconscious, to gain some kind of salvation, maybe, by eradicating his own traces.

Like a man driving at night, hypnotized by bright headlights into veering toward an approaching vehicle, Junior joined all the lawyers, real estate dealers, and hustlers effectuating the Betterment of Chamisaville. Right away he proved himself good at it, playing the game grimly, with no sense of humor—and no holds barred. It became immediately evident that Junior Leyba gave no quarter.

Rodey McQueen whistled as they all watched him go to it. Even Moe Stryzpk raised an eyebrow. Randolph Bonney said, "Look at that frigging greaser go after his own kind."

"Set a Mexican to kill a Mexican," Rodey McQueen chuckled, but relatively few of his cohorts, bastards in their own right, could take it lightheartedly. Junior Leyba just wasn't that funny.

Almost a year to the day after his return, Junior was driving home around 6:00 P.M. when a horseman trotted into the open a hundred yards ahead, and halted in the middle of the road. Angered by anyone who got in his way, Junior accelerated, honking his horn impatiently. When he realized the rider had no intention of backing down, Junior slammed on the brakes and screeched noisily to a stop several feet away from a grotesque apparition.

The man was squat, roly-poly. His face, shadowy under a floppy wide-brimmed sombrero, was further obscured by filthy, reddish-brown whiskers. His upper torso, almost completely covered by an array of old-fashioned weaponry lodged in tattered holsters, was additionally festooned by two cracked leather bandoliers holding enormous rifle cartridges. His plump appearance was further accentuated by strands of blackened hemp wrapped protectively around his upper body.

The lawyer reached forward, clicking off his radio. As he did so, the man raised a Colt Dragoon cavalry pistol, aimed it directly at Junior, and grimaced triumphantly as he pulled the trigger. Junior flopped sideways; a horrible explosion initiated a ringing in his ears that would last a week; bits of glass sprinkled all over his back; and a big, soft-lead slug whumped into the driverside seatback at approximately the spot where his heart would have been.

Enraged, Junior bolted out the driverside door determined to strangle that horseman with his bare hands, no matter how many slugs from the pistol entered his body before he dragged that farce off his mount and battered his bewhiskered face to a pulp against the concrete roadbed.

But Jesus Dolores Martínez Vigil was nowhere at all to be seen.

Nor was Junior's windshield broken.

SOMEWHERE ALONG THE WAY, April McQueen had decided to write a novel. And, on a luxury liner steadfastly chugging across the autumn Atlantic, she began mapping out the story. Although she had an address book filled with names in London, Amsterdam, Brussels, and especially Paris, after landing in Europe April made no stops elsewhere, and spent little time in the French capital, looking up but one person, a former lover, now an expatriate writer living far from the action in Auteuil.

Rainy and sad, Paris was all wrong for her mood. April

took a train south, and was caught briefly in wintertime St.-Tropez. The novel nagged at her, though, and she soon traveled westward, her destination Collioure, drawn there by Matisse's bright Fauve paintings of window and harbor scenes in that picturesque fishing village, paintings April had profoundly adored for years.

A rented room, a jug of sherry, a carton of Gitanes, and April went to work, determined to succeed. That winter France was a chill country; it rained excessively. April had imagined blue skies, hearty sunshine, and cicadas all day from the dry pines. Fishing boats were lined along the rocky beach, in dry dock for winter, cafés were deserted, dimly yellow, out of season.

April had never been so alone, and rather liked the solitude. In Charley's old bomber jacket, chain-smoking Gitanes and sipping sherry, she pecked at a portable typewriter, edging slowly toward a first draft. Few clothes hung in her closet: Levi's and quiet slacks, jerseys and T-shirts, coarse bulky sweaters, a pair of sneakers, loafers. Little mail arrived, for almost nobody knew her address. The *Paris Herald-Tribune* came each day; a New York friend forwarded care packages of the latest books from America.

In the springtime she met a rough-hewn peasant man. Enrique Arnus was the son of Spanish refugees: they had lived in a camp near Collioure since 1939. Almost thirty, a fisherman, he spoke French badly, English not at all. Powerful physically, full of easy laughter, he was the most gorgeous man April had ever seen. One day he would return to Spain. Passionately anti-Fascist, Enrique was also politically unsophisticated. April translated a chapter of her book, and read it to him—he was illiterate. The fisherman shrugged, laughed, embraced her, and called it bullshit. He could play the guitar, and sang for April many of the wonderful songs she had loved all her life. Enrique had never heard of Matisse or García Lorca, or even of Picasso. He had no interest in learning to read or in going to movies. His first love was the sea, his second his own extended family. Dominoes were a passion. He told tall tales, lied to her a lot, and chattered endlessly about bullfights and soccer. He was the purest innocent April had ever met; his straightforward ignorance and simplicity delighted her. She agreed to live with him. But he wanted to get married. So they had a ceremony and moved into a tiny house on a rocky hill surrounded by terraced vineyards, overlooking the harbor. Their sex was routine, his Latin machismo unimaginative and uneventful—but April had long since tired of complex erotic scenes. A life lived close to the basics with this man promised a balm she had never known.

It was a disaster from the start. Enrique wanted her to have children—April refused. He got drunk and threatened to kill her for wearing a diaphragm. Twice she escaped to Paris for abortions; he threw maniacal tantrums on her return, knocking her unmercifully about their claustrophobic home. April screamed back at him and demanded an even say in their relationship. She was told to go to hell—by Enrique, by his family, by the entire exiled Spanish community. If Enrique caroused at night, he ordered April to stay at home. Incredulously, she told him to fuck off, and insisted on tagging along. Other men in the bars and cafés refused to speak with her and offered condolences to Enrique. April was completely ostracized. Comments people made openly in front of her, as if she didn't exist, were malicious, ugly, threatening. Enrique drank so hard he became a buffoon. The man had a violent love of life, a destructive abandon. Some moments April loved him so dearly that she begged herself to become a different person, a fatalistic peasant woman, obedient, willing to crawl, scrub, stay at home behind whitewashed walls, immersed in the petty subsistence boredom of fisherpeople around picturesque and aesthetically famous Collioure.

Impossible, of course, to write or paint; or even to think straight. She had done it again, somehow forging an emotional quagmire within which it was impossible to function creatively. Enrique went to sea, barely earning a living. He despised her easy access to income so greatly that she had to disguise any money that came into her hands, dispensing it in secret, and never buying much for fear of enraging her volatile man. His drinking accelerated; they both drank, trapped in an untenable situation. His family was afraid to approach April: they hated as well as admired her. Enrique's pals, who envied his good fortune, goaded him into bragging about his wife. All of them coveted April. They also measured her in a way she had never been measured by men before, making no effort to camouflage their lust or dreams of murder. How such a simple, bucolic existence could be so fraught with trauma,

even outright danger, had never entered April's mind.
Now she stumbled through her latest amorous disaster appalled by her naïveté and impetuousness, even while fascinated by the magnitude of her mistake. Intensifying the complicated situation was the fact that she had powerful yearnings to love him, making it work. As did Enrique. He would hit her, then grab stones from their yard and bang them against his own head until he was a bloody mess. Once, after they had made love, Enrique sat down at the kitchen table and stabbed a knife blade straight through his hand, uttering no sound. As blood bubbled from his palm, he said quietly, "That's how much I love you, April. I can withstand any pain for you, amor. I would kill myself before letting anybody say bad things about your name."

That their marriage was absurd made it no less painful or poignant. "You should have stuck with your own kind!" she cried out. "And so should I!" He shrugged, a helpless man. It wasn't his fault, April knew. But the more she tried to discover a solution, saving them both, the worse it became. Finally, the only answer was leaving. When she understood that, April packed a few clothes and caught a train, so low that she left her manuscript behind. And her departure killed him. Enrique's body, the wrists slashed, washed ashore a week later; they never found his boat. April got the news in Paris from Enrique's sister; her letter arrived in a packet containing the death certificate and a desperate love letter (begging forgiveness, swearing eternal love) that a literate friend had penned in Enrique's name between the time April left and the day her fisherman died.

All right. A year and a half after she had come to Europe, swollen with grief, dizzy from mourning, April made the Paris scene. She went to parties, easily became well known and highly desirable, and lived with an American painter, doing some painting herself. Plunging haphazardly, a little deliriously into intellectual pursuits, she swore never again to trap herself, or anyone else, in an alien rhythm.

Often, during a rare pause, April wondered about the "choices" she had made in her life. Buffeted by apparently random decisions, she had often felt out of control even when most creatively involved in love and work. Deep down a panic stirred: when would the pieces fit into place?

"You're an old woman," Amaranta GeeGee had said. "When are you gonna have babies and settle down?"

Sometimes April feared she was botching existence, losing her best years by somehow catering to bitched commitments, inadvertently reinforcing a lack of control in her relationships and her work, making escape clauses not only possible, but inevitable.

Yet April had a morbid fear of being tied down. Grounded, she could not help but rebel. Committed to narrow visions, she could not help but flee the thing that held her. If her various talents—drawing, painting, writing, acting—had never matured, it was because she feared specialization . . . and hated boredom. I'm not ready, she thought. I'm not yet ready to make *those* decisions.

All the same, April had a sensation that time (and luck) might be running out. No regrets, of course: at heart she adamantly believed in, and admired, herself. Nobody was ever going to rob her particular headstrong energy or make her ashamed of her complicated existence. Nobody was going to pigeonhole April McQueen, giving her a child before she wanted one, forcing her into a corner when corners weren't her stock in trade.

"You're terribly self-destructive," a French girlfriend said matter-of-factly. "You shouldn't hurt yourself so much. One day you'll wake up not very young anymore, and your body will be unable to stand the shock. You'd better get a grip before that happens, learn how to shift gears, find a good man and start to train him."

April nodded stupidly, and accompanied a lover to Spain. Disguised as a man, she raced with the bulls in Pamplona. After caping lessons in Barcelona, they followed the corridas for a summer, partying with Ordóñez, Dominguín, Ava Gardner—that crowd. In a private ring on the Domecq finca in Jerez, April caped a fighting calf, was knocked down, jumped up, passed it to loud hurrahs and drunken olés, was knocked down and trampled again, staggered up and executed three half-assed veronicas, was tossed, cracking a rib, and then knocked into the barrera, breaking her arm.

Six weeks later, in Madrid, running with an American and Spanish film crowd, April posed naked for a painting to be hung over a bar in a film. She also hired on to be a stunt rider, and did several scenes with falling horses. A postcard, mailed three months earlier, arrived from George Parker:

I dreamed of you last night. On a white horse, naked of course, galloping across the mesa! Your head was shaved! Swallows burst up around the horse's hooves! I fired at you with an old-fashioned pistol—the bullet made a big hole between your shoulderblades, but you just looked around, glaring at me! We beat the St. Michael's Tigers, down in the capital, 14–6 last weekend! There are parking meters all around the plaza now. I hope your reach continues to exceed your grasp, else what's a heaven for? An abrazo and love—

George

After a winter in Málaga, Marbella, and Torremolinos, April moved north to Alicante, then lived for a while on Formentera. Tanned almost black, April passed her languorous days in a skimpy white bikini. Her nearly white hair extended halfway to her waist. She kept her hardening eyes inscrutable behind Lolita sunglasses. No woman was more admired or coveted. Sometimes she wrote in a diary; occasionally she typed fragments for a new novel. And executed some pastel drawings and pen-and-ink sketches, but few paintings.

For a year, April lived with a serious painter taking a break from his work while he still had the energy of middle age. After that, she spent about eight months with a sculptor who had decided to live it up after years preparing for successful shows, recently completed, in Rome, Berlin, and Paris. Thus, "by accident," she hooked up with hardworking people momentarily on a toot. Barred to her was any banal day-to-day rhythm that could have helped resolve her own artistic problems. But I'm stockpiling learning and experience, so it doesn't matter, April thought. There'll be plenty of time for work when I begin slowing down.

But one misty morning on a Santander beach, she awoke beside an Italian Communist who designed sets at La Scala, and the European experience had gone sour. The day before they had traveled by motorcycle up through Basque country. Tomorrow they were heading along the northern coast of Spain out to La Coruña. But today April awoke with a vision of New York harbor in her head. Superimposed over it was her own hometown nestled under the Midnight Mountains. And she knew it was time to go home. April filched money from her friend's wallet, slipped into town, wired her father for help, boarded a Paris-bound train, signed for McQueen's money order at American Express, and got on a boat—first stop, America!

The second morning out, while every other passenger was down below suffering from the choppy weather, April met Matthew Delaney. On the rear deck, tourist class, wrapped snugly in a camel's-hair coat and 1920-ish motoring scarf, he was cheerfully probing the ugly whitecapped sea with binoculars, searching for whales.

"Whales!" she exclaimed. "What are you—crazy? In *this* kind of weather?"

Slowly he turned and stared at her, wondering where this obnoxious beautiful broad had come from. Medium-sized, yet almost delicate, Matthew was the son of a New York City college professor: he was returning to America after a sojourn at the Sorbonne. A French and classics scholar, with pretensions toward poetry, he held both a master's and a Ph.D.

"If I want to *see* a fucking whale," he explained carefully, "I got to *look* for a fucking whale, no matter *what* the fucking weather. N'est-ce pas?"

They were in love, and in bed, three hours later.

On the day President Kennedy died in Dallas, Cynthia and Rodey McQueen threw an enormous birthday bash for their wayward daughter.

In honor of her first visit home in five years, there were preparations to do the thing up really brown. Over 250 guests were slated to quaff unlimited gallons of beer, hard booze, and champagne at an open bar beneath a red-and-white tent awning on the lawn beside the pool. A thousand pounds of quartered beef and several barbecued pigs awaited the onslaught. Three bands, one mariachi, another Anglo old favorites, a third rock and roll, had been hired to play until dawn. A bevy of discreet heaters surrounded the pool, protecting bathers from the crisp November weather. An underpaid army of Juan and Amaranta Gee-Gees had refined the preparations for a week, even though few of April's impoverished valley friends had been invited. But anyone else who was anybody had received an invitation: J. B. and Teresa LeDoux, Junior and Charlotte Leyba, George and Susan Parker, three generations of Mooses, Stryzpks, Bonneys, and Lamonts would be present at the social event of the season.

Two days before the shindig, April traveled around the

valley inviting all her left-out friends, from Virgil Leyba to Juan and Pat GeeGee and their families and Flakey Jake and Gloria Martínez and their son Anthony . . . and hundreds of others related to that whole indigenous crew.

The night before her party, April casually mentioned her personal invitations. As she always did, Cynthia clammed up, eyes going hard: arms folded, she looked to her husband.

McQueen, predictably, exploded. "No, god dammit!" he bellowed. "A thousand times—*no!* If I want to throw a party for those people I'll let you know! Giving these local Mexicans good liquor is like trying to play harp with a hammer! Now you get on the telephone and call up every last person and you tell them there has been a mistake! You do that, god dammit, or I am going to call off the party!"

"Call it off."

"What?"

"You'll have to call it off," April said.

"You're kidding!"

"You know me better than that, Father."

McQueen stomped, tore at his hair, banged his fist into the door, kicked a throw rug across the room, and repeatedly smacked his palm. "You're lying like a dead hound! You didn't do it. You're not that irresponsible!"

"The hell I'm not."

"Then screw it! Cynthia, call off the hootenanny!"

"How do you propose I do that? We've already got two cows and three pigs simmering. The bands are committed and we'll have to pay them anyway because they can't obtain other bookings on such late notice."

"I don't care! I'm not gonna be pushed around by my smirking little spoiled brat of a daughter! Cancel everything! Take the meat out to the Pueblo! Give it to the people for nothing! Return the booze to Vigil's! Hire somebody to do the calling for you!"

April said, "I invited my friends to a party. If you cancel, Father, I'll buy my own cows and my own pigs and I'll rehire those bands to play and I'll buy my own booze."

"Aw shit!" McQueen collapsed into a zebraskin armchair, bit off a cigar end, spitting it into an elephant-foot wastebasket, and, sweat streaming down his bewhiskered face, he exclaimed, "Trying to communicate with you, daughter, is like talking Chinese to a pack mule!" And, conceding defeat, he laughed in spite of himself.

"You win, damn your slick spittle hide and go to hell! Jesus Christ! Whatever did we do to deserve such a belligerent daughter?"

When news of the president's death reached Chamisaville, the telephone at the McQueen mansion started ringing: guests wanted to know if the party had been canceled. When Cynthia telephoned McQueen at the country club, he blurted, "Hell no, it ain't canceled! I just ordered another side of beef from the slaughter plant!"

"Don't you think it might be in poor taste to have an enormous celebration while the rest of the nation is in mourning?"

"What are you," McQueen blustered angrily, "a closet Democrat? We're Republicans, and we have been Republicans all our lives, and we don't owe that Communist in the White House a damn thing!"

Cynthia was in tears. "I don't want to be known in this town as the woman who celebrated the president's assassination by throwing the biggest party Chamisaville ever saw, I really don't."

McQueen took a different tack. "Listen, sweetheart. It's what President Kennedy himself would have wanted. Good lord, if anybody in this country knew that life must go on no matter what, it was that old egg-sucking dog in the White House. He wouldn't have wanted us to call off this party. Hey, we haven't seen our pretty little April in years!"

A pause followed; a loaded silence.

"By the way," McQueen said warily. "Where *is* our darling daughter?"

"She's upstairs in her room watching it on television, getting drunk."

"What do you mean, 'getting drunk'?"

"When the news came she fetched a bottle of cream sherry from the fireplace cabinet and said, 'If you want me for anything, Mother, I'll be up in my room watching the carnival and getting drunk.' "

McQueen exhaled in a faint whistle. "What did she say about the party?"

"She didn't say anything about it."

"Go ask her."

"Right now?"

"Not tomorrow, dammit! What do I have to do around here all the time, draw everybody a picture? I swear to

154

Christ you couldn't hit the ground with your hat even if I gave you three throws!"

When Cynthia returned to the phone she informed her husband, "She says we might as well."

"Might as well what?"

"Might as well have the party."

"On what grounds?"

"On the grounds that we've got three cows and three pigs simmering, fifteen crates of liquor ready to swill over three hundred people into a stupor, and on the grounds that President Kennedy would have wanted us to have a gay old time in his honor."

"Don't you start poking a stick into my wasp nest, Cynthia."

"Those were her words, Dale, not mine."

"Well, we'll just have to make sure everybody gets looped right away, that's all."

The Mooses, Bonneys, Stryzpks, and Lamonts all came early and stayed late. April's friends, from Juan and Amaranta GeeGee to Espeedie Cisneros, their families and all the clans in between, showed up in energetic Spanish-babbling clusters. Junior and Charlotte Leyba appeared, as did Virgil Leyba. Loretta Shimkus arrived. J. B. and Teresa LeDoux weren't far behind. Judson and Felicia Babbitt, Staughton van Peebles and his new femme fatale, and his old femme fatale, Amanda Santana, squired by her two beaus, Gabe Suazo and the new Art Association prexy, Wilfred Muncie, marched noisily into the tipsy throng. The driveway, the parking lot, and the street beyond the high adobe walls were jammed with Cadillacs, new Fords, big Chryslers, rattletrap pickups, rusted Oldsmobiles and Studebakers with cracked windshields, and at least a dozen horses. Children belonging to Mooses, Lamonts, and Stryzpks had stayed home with baby-sitters: chavalitos pertaining to GeeGee, Flakey Jake and Gloria Martínez, and other longtime locals fanned out everywhere, crawling among the dancers and drinkers, sleeping under Levi jackets on the lawn or on basement couches. Guests mingled, separated, flowed, argued about politics, wept for Kennedy, lost their shoes, wives, and children, gobbled deviled eggs and Guaymas shrimp, ate pig with their fingers and wiped their fingers on their bluejeans or on their tuxedo pants, checked out Jackie's hysteria, LBJ's swearing-in, and joined arms, forming brash drunken huddles, singing, "Ay-yi-yi-yi, canta y no *llores!*" A servant battalion served, hustling among the people, making sure everyone stayed well loaded. Nevertheless, a few independent souls kept returning to the mansion's five TV sets, guzzling the best alcohol money could buy as they giddily insisted on witnessing the tragedy. An overcast sky without stars hovered in a hostile manner.

Dressed in almost miniskirted white, wearing stockings but no shoes, her only jewelry simple gold hoop earrings, and protected from the chill air by her old bomber jacket, April threaded between revelers, smiling politely at familiar faces. J. B. LeDoux wished to approach her, but could not bring himself to travel the last few yards. So April took the initiative, giving him an abrazo. "Hello there, J. B. You sure look great." His powerful hands wanted to linger, but instead fluttered off her shoulders as he backed self-consciously away. "Oh, I can't complain," J. B. laughed stupidly. "I guess the years have been good to me." Naturally, he mistrusted April, just as he eyed askance any person with a pipeline to McQueen or other members of the Chamisaville power structure, fearing they might tattle if he made a false step. Who knew if some unnoticed on-looker had already misinterpreted their abrazo?

Bluntly, April said, "Actually, you don't look so hot, J. B. You look like a man, torn between this and that, who does a lot of suffering."

He frowned, fumbled, fumfered, his jittery eyes everywhere except on her face. A thin, sleepy-eyed kid approached, asking: "Oyé, Papá, has visto mi mamá?" Grabbing his boy by the shoulders, J. B. presented him to April: "This is our son." "Mucho gusto," Benny said, extending his hand. "He always speaks Spanish," J. B. apologized after the boy left. "I don't know where he learned it, not in our house, that's for certain, dammit. And not in the fucking schools. . . ."

April said, "What's wrong with speaking Spanish? I don't understand."

Checking to make sure Teresa wasn't in range, J. B. said, "Believe me, I don't understand it either. The boy hates us, I know. For giving him the American way of life. Two years ago he couldn't speak a word of local lingo. Now, it's almost impossible to keep him in school."

"Sounds like there's hope for him yet."

"He'll just be squashed, used, exploited," J. B. said vehemently. Then, to take the onus off his bitterness, he giggled, making a flip gesture. "I don't really mean it. What the hell. Life is a bowl of cherries."

Junior Leyba and his fragile wife blocked her escape: "April, welcome home. Meet my lady, Charlotte. Charlotte, this is the famous April Epstein Lanahan Arnus Etcetera, formerly known as McQueen."

Charlotte smiled, wanting to be friendly. "I've heard so much about you."

"Oh, I'll bet you have. I'll bet Junior really filled you in."

They hemmed, locked in confusion and hostility—ther hawed.

Junior said, "It's been a long time."

Charlotte asked, "How . . . how long are you going to be in Chamisaville?"

"Chamisaville?" April stared straight at Junior. "Thanks to folks like the Mexican-American whiz kid here, Chamisaville is becoming just a memory."

"I earn a living."

"Oh, I'll bet you do."

Charlotte whimpered, "What's the *matter* with you two?"

Grabbing his wife's arm, Junior jerked her into the crowd.

April tarried a moment, disoriented and angry. John F. Kennedy, a man she had never liked, believing him to be dishonest, ineffectual, conservative, and entirely manipulated by the CIA and the military-industrial complex, was dead. The Bay of Pigs; the October missile crisis. A description of Jackie with his brains splashed on her lap (and among the bouquet of red roses) buzzed in April's head. Virgil Leyba landed beside her, putting one skinny arm around her shoulder. "Hola nena—lo siento mucho."

"I'm all right, Virgil. Thank God you came."

"It isn't every day we celebrate the assassination of a president of the United States."

"Don't you be cruel, too. Te ruego."

Virgil swished the liquid in his glass. It seemed to her he wore the same suit he'd been wearing ever since she was a little girl: baggy, knees and elbows shiny, no creases. An overstarched, yellowy shirt collar was too big around his scrawny neck: his once-dark tie was grubby, faded. In his sixties now—had it been that long ago?— Virgil was a weather-beaten, tall and mystifying man, his skin dark and tough, eyes bitter and penetrating, features strong. Virgil moved with a deliberate, dangerous dignity that still carried the menace of a man who had once killed for impeccable principles. The persistence of this lonely, beleaguered man touched April profoundly. In recent years the memory of Virgil in his rumpled suit, half collapsed at the desk in his paper-strewn office smoking a cigarette nub, had kept her strong, giving reasons for getting up off the floor when life seemed to be pure shit. The image of Virgil had forced her time and again to ridicule her own self-pity and forge ahead. Of all the people who'd touched her life, April most wanted to be liked or esteemed or loved by this plodding, fanatical man.

Virgil kissed her cheek. "I came to say hello, honor you on your birthday, and ask you to come home and help me save what's left of this valley from the Betterment of Chamisaville."

"I'm in love with a man who lives in New York."

He shrugged, nodded, drank.

"How's Juan? I know he's here, but I haven't talked to him yet."

"Ortega? He's okay. He had an auto accident and they took away his license: now he can only ride a bicycle. But he says that has gotten him back into shape and he feels better than ever before. Mari-Elena has been down in the dumps ever since they moved into a trailer. Juan helps me all the time, but I have little money to spare. Still, he knows almost as much about the public and private construction of this valley as Moe Stryzpk. He gets along on welfare, some social security—there are programs. He is writing a novel, sends an outraged letter to the editor of the *Chamisaville News* almost every week, and has put together reams of local folklore, stories—he travels everywhere with a tape recorder. He always tells me, 'I want to get it all down before it's over.' "

Marshall Kickingbird bumped through, almost flattening April and Virgil. Catching himself, he swayed, squinting down at them, frowning, trying to place them both. But it was hopeless—he shrugged and teetered off, looking for more alcohol.

"I didn't know he drank," April said, really disturbed.

"For a couple of years now it's been like that."

"Why?"

"Because what he must do is hopeless, but he must do it anyway."

"That's no reason to commit suicide."

"Perhaps not. But it's a good enough reason to drink."

Wheelchair-bound Moe Stryzpk, hidden behind thick dark glasses as he drank from a paper cup, was parked beside a boxwood bush, apart from the general milling. April ambled over and plunked down in the damp grass nearby. As they both observed the party from this removed vantage point, April said, "Well, Moe, long time no see. How is everything?"

"About as could be expected."

"I see."

"I doubt that."

April looked up, but he wouldn't glance down at her. His eyes were fixed on the party; she followed his gaze. Miranda Stryzpk, vivacious and sleazy in a revealing yellow knit dress, was laughing too loudly. Not quite accidentally, she bumped into McQueen; his arm fell familiarly about her shoulders, her hand tucked lovingly around his waist. They swayed, laughing.

April said, "It's not something you haven't known about for years."

Moe dropped his head back, gazing blankly at the sky. He licked his lips, preparing a reply, thought better of it, and said nothing.

Espeedie and Pancha Cisneros were growing really fat; Canuto Tafoya was going blind. Celestino Lucero—murderer, barehanded killer of mountain lions—seemed feather-light, his taciturn nature hardening to stone. Even his pet magpie, Tierra o Muerte the Eighth, looked sickly perched on his shoulder and had nothing to say. Perfecto Torres explained: "They have got us up against the wall—who knows how much longer we can hang on. The town council is trying to place a new sewage plant on our land, condemning the dairy. The Anglo Axis is putting pressure on us in other quarters—every week some kind of government inspector goes over our barns, checks out the cows, inspects and tests the milk. Time and again they order us to dump thousands of gallons; they are forcing us to buy sterilizing equipment we can't afford. Holiday Hill Dairies down in the capital are taking over, wiping us out. They have all the chain contracts; they even supply the Your Own Food Store now. It's a monopoly. We only have a fifth of our former customers, but we work five times harder to supply them—"

Nobody was swimming. Upstairs, April donned a red terrycloth bikini. A minute later she stepped into the shal-

159

low end of the pool and progressed slowly toward the deep end. Few people watched her—there was too much noise and confusion. Mariachis whined, barbershop singers drunkenly cawed around the living-room piano, younger kids howled rock and roll at the trophy room's upright. Children raced between legs, shouting and crying, searching for their parents. In a cacophony of English and Spanish and Tewa, exclamations, drunken laughter and shouting, macho cries, threats, arguments, hysterical storytelling abounded. And steam from barbecued animals boiled through the crowd.

But J. B. LeDoux and George Parker had their eyes on April. So did Junior Leyba.

The water rose over her breasts. At the side of the pool April discovered a half-full champagne glass, raised it to her lips, laconically drained the contents. As she did so, her eyes lifted and she noticed a man she had never seen before, a middle-aged Mediterranean type with sallow skin, small fat-surrounded eyes and bushy eyebrows, thick lips, and a double chin, a plump, lethargic-looking body bulky and awkward in a shiny blue-silk suit. On one stubby finger he wore a pinky ring, a tiny sapphire set in the hood of a golden cobra.

He had been gazing at her, expressionless, all this time. When their eyes met, his features did not change. April smiled sweetly: "Hello, there. This party is in my honor. But I don't believe we've ever had the pleasure."

"Bonatelli," the plump man said.

"That's your name?"

"It ain't my address."

"Nice to meet you, Bonatelli. You don't look like you're from around this neck of the prairie."

"Just visiting." Bonatelli spoke without emotion.

"Well now." April lazed away from him, pushing softly through the tepid water across the pool. "It's been great having this conversation. You all have a nice visit, hear?" she called over one shoulder.

George Parker, his shoes and socks removed, his pant-legs rolled up, sat down on the edge of the pool, dangling his legs in the water. April arrived beside him, standing in water up to her armpits. She rested her head dreamily against her arms folded on the tile border.

"Hello, George Parker. How are they hanging?"

"Okay, I reckon."

"I mean, how's the old log, George—getting any lately?"

"Sure. Of course. You know me."

April poked his knee with a long, painted fingernail; she drew squiggly circles on his skin. "Are you happy as a big old clam?" she asked.

"You kidding? It's nip and tuck every day. Sometimes I just want to give up, tell her to go to hell, dump the kids, screw the school, run away. If I do, can I look you up in New York?"

Startled, April assessed him for a moment, probing. He was pretty drunk. "You still look like the happy-go-lucky all-American shit-eating-grin boy to me."

"Well, what the hell—everybody has problems. Angst these days comes in little packages, a dime a dozen. Forty percent off for the large economy despair."

"That's funny . . ."

"Are *you* okay?" he asked. "How's your life, April Etcetera?"

"Well, right now, contrary to the usual flow of events in my placid existence, it all seems to be fraught with lackluster turmoil," she joked groggily. "I'm in love, of course, getting laid with brutalizing regularity, *comme d'habitude,* and my man, as usual, is a semigorgeous bastard. And he's black, and of course he's very beautiful. Naturally, there's talk of marriage, and of course that scares me to death. I've been to the amorous well so many times I'm beginning to feel like I'm in a horse race with Zsa Zsa Gabor and George Sand. Put another way, I've already been around the block so many times I've got all the cracks in the pavement memorized. My life is turning into a game of musical names. But that's neither here nor there, is it? Don't pay me no mind, kid: self-pity gives me the unholy blues, it really does. So anyway, I'm in love with this fella —name of Matthew Delaney—and when we started out he was gonna be a college professor and we planned to live in Brooklyn Heights. Finally, everything was going to be steady, I'd have a studio and I'd paint pictures, get me a gallery, write books, find me a publisher—you know, the whole bloody schmeer. So then, guess what happens?"

"He found another woman? He got fired for being a Communist? It turned out he hates sex?"

April laughed wearily. "Almost, almost. What happened is it turns out my beautiful man has this core of burning steel, and a lust to avenge his race's past through political

161

organizations like SNCC. I haven't painted in a year. I've been down South in Alabama, Mississippi, Arkansas staging sit-ins, riding buses, getting knocked down by fire hoses, running away from police dogs, going sleepless for weeks on end, attending the funerals of little children."

George placed his hand gently atop her head. "You sure are a funny person, April."

"Ha ha."

"No, I mean it makes me feel strange and unhappy to hear you talk like this. I think of you a lot. See, it always comforted me to know that you got out and that you're leading this incredibly adventurous life and that you hang out with many famous people, and that you have exciting affairs, and on top of it all you are going to be a famous artist, or musician, or writer some day."

They sat quietly for a moment, feeling close, outside of the party, far away from the hue and cry.

". . . But the funny thing is," she blurted suddenly, "I think I'm just about ready to take the big plunge. I think I'm just about ready to have a kid. With this cultured, erudite, intellectual, soft-spoken raving lunatic."

"So—?"

"So two years ago when it all started I wouldn't hear of it. He wanted to marry me, I told him to bug off. He wanted to have a child, I told him to go to hell. Now—" She stopped, belched, rubbed one eye.

"Now?"

"He's ashamed of being a black man in a black movement with a white girlfriend, let alone a white wife. And he doesn't even want to joke about having little mulatto children half full of redneck honky Texas blood."

George said, "Say what you will, I still love you, April McQueen."

April giggled, pinching his calf affectionately. Pursing her lips, she sent him a soporific kiss through the air, then proceeded into the shallow end of the pool. She got out, disappeared into the mansion, put on an old white shirt Junior Leyba had given her ages ago, tight Levi's, and her bomber jacket, and rejoined the party. She bumped into George again, tears in his eyes.

"What's the matter, George? Hey man, don't cry."

"I dunno. Our president got killed today, that's all. I mean, doesn't anybody give a damn? Look at us all here. Look at this *party!*"

April cupped his cheek. "Don't take it too hard, love. He was just another Fascist in disguise."

George pulled away. "You don't mean it."

"I don't wanna talk politics. Not now. Please? Not tonight."

"But you said . . . I mean, well—Kennedy was beautiful."

April grinned stupidly, brushing her damp hair back. " 'Scuse me for being dumb, sweet, but JFK was just another beautiful son of a bitch."

At four o'clock, while Espeedie Cisneros (on violin) and Juan GeeGee (on guitar) and Juan Ortega (on accordion) were playing the "Chiquiao Waltz" for their friends Pat and Lucinda GeeGee and Canuto and Maria Tafoya to dance to, it began snowing. The dancers cried, "Más música!" And, laughing, the musicians gleefully provided it, sawing out spirited, completely off-key and practically atonal renditions of "La Cuna" and "La Varsoviana." And April, seated in a chaise longue near the pool thoughtfully smoking a cigarette, almost in tears from old-fashioned music and the old-fashioned dancing, did not look up when the first snowflakes quietly drifted to earth. Nor did she move to shelter when the snowfall thickened, becoming a curiously placid autumn storm.

The doorbell rang; only April heard it. She waited until it rang again, then arose painfully, staggered slightly off-balance around the two madcap waltzing couples and through the living room and the hallway, and opened the front door.

Jesus Dolores Martínez Vigil, as ferocious and filthy as ever, smelling like campfire smoke, juniper trees, and bear grease, stood on the welcome mat grinning at her. He reached out, taking her hand between his leathery arthritic palms, and gave a little squeeze. "Feliz cumpleaños," he said, pronouncing the Z in an old-fashioned Castilian way, like a th. Then he turned and walked off, melting mysteriously into the storm.

A ghost? A figment of her imagination? Or some real protoplasmic being, beyond age, destined to save her life during some traumatic future encounter?

Snow made the nocturnal landscape even more beautiful. The old musicians had stopped playing, and, alone, his voice booming, Espeedie Cisneros was standing in the snow by the swimming pool, arms joyfully upraised, drunkenly singing "La Ciudad de Juaja":

163

*Let's go to the city of Juaja,*
*Where everything is frilly:*
*And ducks and geese fall out of the sky,*
*Already baked in chili.*

*There are two streams of milk and honey,*
*And three mountains made of tea,*
*And instead of water in the river,*
*There's champagne for you and me!*

# Coming Apart
# at the Seams

AS THE BETTERMENT of Chamisaville gathered steam for its final run toward mainstream America, endless strange characters slouched into town, taking up residence wherever possible. A host of human non sequiturs moved in and planted their spiritual flags, staking a claim to the befuddled turf, bringing to the valley, as it had never been brought before, Progress, American-style.

Irving Newkirk arrived in Chamisaville one day wearing a gray bowler, a camel's-hair coat with a carnation boutonniere, and as pretty and pretentious a pair of five-hundred-dollar spats as had ever been seen west of the Pecos River. In no time at all, scorning amenities such as building permits, Irv had constructed the Irving Newkirk Motel (out of condemned plywood salvaged from a Capital City lumberyard fire) and the Irving Newkirk Café. Next, he established a trailer court and began raising Irving Newkirk racehorses on Vallecitos land he bought for a song for back taxes, even going so far as to outbid Rodey McQueen at auction in order to possess it. His racehorses were champion hayburners that rarely if ever showed, let alone broke a tape, but no matter: many broke their legs stepping into the holes of prairie dogs Irv imported onto his land and had to be destroyed. Meaning Irv made a small fortune combining tax losses with insurance settlements and using the horsemeat in his plump, 110-percent Pure Beef Hamburgers, which were an instant Chamisaville hit, weighing in at a pound or more, and costing but a quarter.

To boot, in front of his motel six enormous Irving Newkirk signs in impeccably poor taste announced UNIQUE INDIAN DANCES NIGHTLY—*free with room key.* Many rich transients registered at his place primarily to view these exhibitions. And sure enough, on the dot at nine o'clock a bell rang, a wizened little troll squirted lighter fluid at a forlorn piñon log blocking the motel driveway and dropped a match onto it, and Irv's eleven-year-old grandson Tommy, decked out in enough feathers, rouge, and greasepaint to sink a theatrical battleship, hopped forward and circled the log, chanting "Ish biddley oaten doaten, sis boom bah; boomalaka, boomalaka, rah rah rah!" Hardly had his act commenced than the brazen kid passed a tambourine among the startled grandmothers from Quinter, Kansas, and the balding claim adjusters from Roanoke, Virginia, catching them so by surprise they usually coughed up nickels, dollars, and dimes.

The old and venerated artists of Judson Babbitt's and Staughton van Peebles's generation had been traditional painters and sculptors. But the newcomers arrived equipped with gobs of polyurethane and other strange, poisonous plastics; they concocted mobiles out of jockstraps, golf balls, tennis shoes and eagle feathers; skunk pelts and tin cans hung from their "canvases"; their papier-mâché mannikins screwed each other, and they painted pictures of drunken Indians instead of noble ones. In other works God, dressed in drag and wearing lipstick, poured Coca-Cola from a traditional green bottle all over the sacred mountain.

A young New York woman named Hilda Nicety, who wore leather motorcycle jackets and mauve turbans, painted an enormous picture of a white-maned old fart, very much resembling Judson Babbitt, seated in the plaza feeding pigeons. Birds were defecating on his knees and on his lap. Pigeons perched on his shoulders and atop his head, their feet submerged in their own droppings, which covered the old boy like a cake icing. Stalagmites of pigeon dung teetered on the tops of his big hairy ears and on the tip of his bulbous, booze-red nose. A one-hundred-dollar bill peeped from his partially unbuttoned fly. The Living Legend was painting a picture of an Indian. The canvas likeness was noble, haughty, beautiful: wearing an eagle-feather headdress, ornate buckskin, and porcupine quill necklaces, he held an exquisite clay peace pipe. But the real native, crouched on an inverted tom-tom nearby, posing, had scraggly, bushwacked hair, a runny nose, puffy and red-rimmed eyes, a Band-Aid on one cheek. He wore a white shirt soiled with pigeon droppings, vomit, and God knows what else, and cradled a half-empty Old Granddad bottle on his lap. Facsimiles of other longtime Chamisaville artists populated the plaza background. Partially hidden in lilac foliage, Staughton van Peebles, a bewhiskered potbellied old satyr, was humping a plump, cosmeticized Felicia Babbitt. The picture created a terrible scandal. Old-time artists bemoaned the ruination of Chamisaville, collected rent off their land- and house-holdings from the more recent immigrants, and, having invested in additional galleries to peddle the new avant-garde shlock, they pissed and moaned all the way to the bank.

The Dynamite Shrine Motor Court fell into disrepair, becoming a symbol of the deliberate helter-skelter decay infiltrating the little burg as the Anglo Axis stoked the fires of a final commercial kill. Once a posh hangout, catering not only to bedraggled pilgrims but to the idle rich as well, now it had gone to the dogs. Rodey McQueen had bankrolled bigger and better facilities: the Chamisaville Inn, the Don Quijote Motel, the Shalako Lodge, the Bluebird Cabins, and the enormous baroque Saint Cipriano House. Plus a dozen other modern, auto-oriented tourist traps flanking the North-South Highway below and above town, and along the Plains Road leading up Chamisaville Canyon to the condominium-infested Mosquito Valley. So eventually he had unloaded the old-fashioned court to Moe Stryzpk, who'd presented it to his eldest kid, Harvey, for Christmas one year. Harvey lost the Dynamite Shrine to Junior Leyba in a poker game. When Junior hired Solomon Teel to manage it, Solomon subcontracted the managing job out to Izzy Stryzpk the Third, a ne'er-do-well cousin of the Stryzpk family, fatally drawn to Las Vegas, Nevada. He left the motor court in care of Sue Ellan Beaubien, daughter of the PDQ manager, Juan Beaubien. And her philosophy of minimum investment for maximum feasible profits had allowed the cabin complex to become the most ramshackle dump in town, where the pilot of recently instituted regular marijuana flights, Skeezix McHorse, and other similarly suspect and downtrodden characters such as Eduardo Mondragón and Eloy Romo passed their luckless days and nights.

On the advice of Eloy Romo, Eduardo Mondragón had changed his name to Little Kid Lujan. And often Little Kid lay on an old straw-filled mattress in his nine-by-twelve cubicle in the Dynamite Shrine Motor Court, staring through the heavy summer nighttime gloom at his cracked and sagging ceiling, tuning into his fellow inmates at the dilapidated motor court. He could do this because his dimming eyesight was offset by amazing ears. For as usual, with sight impairment had come a terrific intensification of his ability to hear. In fact, he had become so sensitized to noise that even the most minimal emotional and physical vibration hurt. He could hear distant mountains glowering with a quiet but audible rumbling. Velvet cloth draped over a hardwood table gave off a fuzzy, muffled heartbeat. Little Kid could accurately judge the distance between himself and a hummingbird at a plaza hollyhock by the sound of its wings. He could hear butterflies sucking at plaza lilacs; and he deciphered the cloudiness or clarity of a night from the volume of noise stars made sparkling. A hawk's shadow gliding over Balena Park grass rattled in his eardrums; as did the heartbeats of the trembling rabbits those hawks were hunting. On hot afternoons in the park, Little Kid could hear flowers wilting. And sometimes, quietly at repose in the lush Little League outfield after a morning of hawking the news, he could hear things growing, roots probing sluggishly another millimeter into the earth, grass groaning as it advanced an additional tenth of a green centimeter skyward. If a single breast-feather popped from a passing finch, he heard it. If an autumn leaf fell he traced its gay zigzag crackle down to the ground. And the crisp confusing clatter of snowflakes falling enthralled the aging newsboy; he giggled at the soft booms they made, crashing against the planet.

Hence, it was little problem to eavesdrop on the queer doings at the Dynamite Shrine. And a diverse bunch had come to occupy the sixteen seedy units. Little Kid knew the intimate details of their lives by heart.

Immediately next door lived Ursula and Perfecto Torres, a proud and embittered couple who, having lost it all in the recent dairy wars, had taken up residence in the Dynamite Shrine while their widowed partner, Celestino Lucero, wound up in a tiny, second-hand trailer parked in Irving Newkirk's mobile home barrio. To make ends meet, Ursula and Perfecto worked as caretakers and bulldozer operators at the town dump north of Chamisaville, a huge landfill pit, lined with hungry ravens and a few bewildered sea gulls, out in the heart of the desolate sagebrush mesaland. All night long Little Kid listened to strange happenings in their spare, spic-and-span little den. Jesus Etcetera's pistols and leather cartridge-holding accoutrements clanked and squeaked; Atiliano Montoya unleashed melancholy plaintive moans; Melchior and Moises GeeGee, Juan and Amaranta's dead sons, sat in front of the TV pensively smoking cigarettes. Seditions were afoot: or maybe Ursula and Perfecto—finally beaten after all these years of struggle and ashamed at depending on food stamps and welfare while surrounded by bums, criminals, junkies, and other assorted grotesques—maybe they had gone crazy.

Nearby dwelled the onetime Magpie Creek Lumber Mill boss and former county sheriff, Filiberto García. Currently a bank dick at the El Conquistador Peoples' Jug, he shared his disintegrating apartment with Atiliano Montoya's ancient brother-in-law, Malaquias C. de Baca, now a professional courthouse loafer, and the Pueblo pariah, Gabe Suazo, Amanda Santana's onetime lover, now dying of tuberculosis. Gabe wore black gloves to bed and disgorged vivid disquieting dreams that Little Kid could easily fathom because they resounded with desperate erotic grunting, sounds of a longing to be amorously fulfilled just once more . . . cottony, tearshaped, muffled, and as tense as murder, slithering sinisterly around the motel compound like a cheap, nickel-plated revolver looking for a game of Russian roulette. Then a silence, as solid as four-feet-deep in quicksand, would be punctuated occasionally by brief frightening noises such as a mouse might make suffocating in the slimy folds of belligerent liver.

Almost every night Little Kid begged those ludicrous disillusioned refugees to succumb to an exhausted slumber so that he might bank some shut-eye himself.

All over Chamisaville, with accelerating rapidity and brutality, the lives of old-timers were coming apart at the seams.

ABOUT FOUR YEARS AFTER JFK's assassination, April Delaney wrote to Virgil Leyba:

> You wouldn't believe New York, querido. Everything is so much more crazy than it was during the fifties. I don't have much truck anymore with the old arts community: I've turned into a raving radical welfare

mama, no fooling! The scene is heavy. I go to MDS meetings, SDS, SCLC, I work for the Moratorium Committee, for SANE. I've met Coffin and Spock, Herlihey and Mailer. Matthew is doing liaison for the Panthers: he's spending a lot of time in Harlem, getting hassled, harassed. Do you like Phil Ochs? Do you even know who Phil Ochs is? Sometimes I walk in the evening pushing Duane in his stroller along 8th Street, over to Sixth Avenue. Every few steps people are on soap boxes, decrying the war: the Spartacists, Arabs against Israel—suddenly I've learned the other side of *that* story. What's your opinion of the PLO? What do you think of *Soul on Ice*? Have you read *The Fire Next Time?* It seems as if every Saturday there's a demonstration up in the Sheep's Meadow, in Central Park. Did you ever hear of the Bread and Puppet Theater? That's street theater, guerrilla theater—I've done sets and costumes for them: we drive around New York giving anti-Vietnam shows wherever the neighborhood seems receptive. Did you read about the march on the Pentagon? —we were there. I was pushing Duane in his stroller up the ramp of the Pentagon when all that shit began to come down! They were clubbing people with guns, pregnant mothers—the works! There's something so terrifying, so exciting in that kind of confrontation. I never thought of fascism in America, but it's really possible, isn't it? I do draft counseling too—for the Quakers. They are beautiful people, but sometimes I wonder about their peace trip. After watching the violence at the Pentagon, or just daily on the streets of this city, on the tube in Vietnam, the Quakers seem old-fashioned, innocent, irresponsible—nonviolence, I mean. *You* should know—Sooner or later all political power comes from the barrel of a gun, qué no? Sometimes a savagery to this whole business really freaks me out. I went up to Hunter, got my teaching certificate, and now I can teach in the public schools. Instead, I'm working in an alternative school for kids. I teach one course at night, too, in a free university on 14th Street—I teach about the Mexican Revolution and about Chicano activism in the Southwest. Ever since Tijerina's courthouse raid in New Mexico last June, people want to know where he came from and why. They are interested in the land-grant problem in

169

Arizona and New Mexico, southern Colorado and Texas. If you have any literature, send it on, would you please? Write me a letter, too, tell me all the stuff you've done—I'll read it to my class.

I'm pregnant again: for good or for bad? I'm not sure. I love this man, Virgil—I really do. But he's away too much. This white-black thing is getting harder to pull off. Such tension between us! But I feel very strong, very solid. I'm devouring books, mostly nonfiction, a half-dozen a week. Tom Hayden, George Jackson, *The Arrogance of Power, The Rise of American Civilization, The Rise and Fall of the Third Reich,* Gerassi on Latin America—all hail United Fruit! I'm into the poetry of people like Pablo Neruda. I'm also plowing through Miguel Angel Asturias—pobrecito Guatemala! Duane walks, he talks, he wets his pants, he laughs, he screams. He looks about as black as me, god dammit—but he's got this beautiful foot-wide curly auburn Afro that knocks everybody dead on the street. We practically live in Washington Square Park among the bums, the chess players, and the golden sycamore trees, the jive kids on skateboards, the volleyball players, and the NYU students. I don't know if I'm happy, love—what the hell is that all about anyway? Chamisaville seems eons of miles away—in another country, in another century. I bet all the generals have harvested a good crop of impoverished minority boys from my Old Home Town, though, haven't they? Sent 'em over to Vietnam to kill their impoverished Asian counterparts! Sometimes I'd like to come home and talk to the local kids—"kids," listen to me yet! I'm beginning to sound so *grown-up!* And explain to them why they are just American gooks, dinks, slants, greasers, spics, niggers. Is there any hope, Virgil? I can't decide. When I arrived at the steps of the Pentagon with my child in my arms and saw those teen-age American boy-soldiers with fixed bayonets aiming guns at us, I wanted to weep. Out of anguish, out of joy. *I pray that we can force this moment to its crisis!*

I'm so fat and sassy, my cheeks are rosy. *This* kid will weigh fifteen pounds! I love you more than time can tell. Sometimes I miss the mountains, the nighthawks beeping in the evening, the frothy smell of hot horses and powdery sagebrush. Write me a letter, huh? You never do, you know: you're a solid gold pendejo, Virgil Leyba. I hope your bullet holes ache from guilty feelings! Toma a cold one in my honor with Juan Ortega and Pat and Amaranta and Juan GeeGee and Espeedie and all the rest of the courageous old SOBs who refuse to go under.

Qué te quiero mucho, querido. Ay te watcho, caramacho!

April

Virgil never wrote back to April: he was much too preoccupied. Things were coming to a head in Chamisaville proper: all the stops were out. Any old-timers who had survived the Betterment plot up until now finally had their backs irrevocably up against the wall. Call it "assimilation," call it "termination," call it "the melting-pot theory" of Progress, American-style—what it amounted to was cultural genocide. What it amounted to was the displacement of a people who had nowhere else to go. What it amounted to was the gratuitous economic and spiritual destruction of a race—or more importantly, a class (a lower class, a working class, a peasant class) of people—who demanded nothing greater than the simple right to survive on land they had owned free and clear for centuries.

Chugging wearily home after a disastrous twelve hours at the office, Virgil thought he spied something up ahead hogging the middle of the road. He regarded the object curiously while approaching it at about twenty-five miles an hour, but his brain was so fuddled after a bitter day spent toting up the score against his floundering clients, that he never thought to brake or swerve. And only at the very last moment did he realize he was about to run over an old and rather smallish man bent intently over a surveying instrument set up on the center line.

A loud *thump!* sounded as truck, surveyor, and instrument collided, at which point Virgil finally swerved, doing a slow nosedive into the roadside ditch. Sliding down the seat and out the passengerside door, he landed in a soggy clump of browbeaten cattails.

Appalled by his mistake, the old lawyer scrambled to his feet and raced awkwardly around the pickup to see if he had actually killed the man, or only crippled him for life.

Down on one knee, Icarus Suazo was shaking his head

and spitting out blood and bits of teeth, although he did not otherwise seem fatally impaired.

Bewildered by the whole surreal action, Virgil leaned against his tailgate, saying, "What the hell are you doing, Suazo, surveying from the middle of the goddam road at twelve o'clock at night?"

The Pueblo secretary glanced up at Virgil with inscrutable concern, asking politely, "Is your truck damaged? I certainly hope not. I never saw you coming. I'll pay, of course."

"You'll pay *me?*"

"You didn't hit me deliberately, did you?"

"I saw a thing in the road that looked like a man looking through a surveying instrument. But I didn't believe it until I hit it."

Standing, the Pueblo secretary almost fell down: he regained his balance and shook his head, clearing it. "I was concentrating so hard I never saw you coming. I'm glad you weren't traveling any faster. Good night, my friend."

"Where are you going?"

"Home."

"On foot?"

"How else?"

Icarus gathered up his ruined sextant, ducked between barbed-wire strands into the nearby field, and began striding north, disappearing almost immediately, leaving Virgil behind, lodged against his sizzling truck, a very long mile from home.

The lawyer fetched a fifteen-dollar plumber's wrench, his deer rifle, and a box of ammunition from the truck, squeezed through barbed-wire strands, and began heading west across the fields toward his own house. Sullen cows, morosely chewing tasteless cuds, quit working their sluggish jaws as he lumbered by, one hand shielding his eyes from the blinding glare of distant security lamps, whose garish glitter wiped out the ground directly in front of him.

Horses, so demoralized by the festering early autumn weather they had lost all curiosity, paid no attention to Virgil as he passed. Then a prickly rotten smell warned him he was about to go from vega land into a truly boggy patch. Breathing heavily, suit drenched with sweat, Virgil halted to get his bearings. Security lamps by the Ranchitos Arriba church made it almost impossible to

172

discern a path through the leached-out grass and shadowy, spongy hummocks.

Virgil essayed a few steps, but, unable to shield his eyes sufficiently to eliminate the lamp glare, the way became a total mystery. He knew a board walkway traversed the bog—but how to find it? Blindly probing off to the right, he promptly sank to his knees in tepid muck.

Losing a shoe in the process, Virgil extricated himself, backtracked a few yards, and stood very still for a minute, wondering how to solve this pickle. Though slow in coming, once Virgil had the answer, he swung into action. Loading his rifle, he took careful aim at a security lamp over the Ranchitos Arriba church, and pictured himself squeezing off a dazzling two-hundred-and-fifty-yard shot, eliminating the blinding object in a magnificent phosphorescent burst. The echo would scarcely have died, than Virgil would fire again, exploding another lamp in a similarly spectacular fashion. With that, the way lying clear before him, he would immediately spot that narrow plank walkway traversing the bog.

Such a simple solution. Though idiotic even to contemplate so petulant a gesture. But Virgil hated security lamps. And, given his attitude toward these glittering abominations that severely dislocated the natural nocturnal order of things, Virgil decided it would be downright blissful to go on a criminal rampage.

Starting near the Ranchitos Arriba church, he would pot the lamp in Randolph Bonney's yard, then move over several fields, shooting out the lamp over his brother Jerry Bonney's abode. Traveling a northeasterly curve through García, Alamito, and Vallecitos, he would next blast out the glare surrounding Damacio Mares's opulent split-level ranch, then execute a host of mercury obscenities surrounding the Dynamite Shrine and Baths complex. After that, what joy to drop down the North-South Highway, clobbering lamps at the Art Association's new theater, the electric co-op, the post office, the National Guard Armory, the phone company, and the brand-new community swimming pool. His final shells would be used up trying to plunge the heart of town, the plaza itself, into darkness. Ears ringing after his prodigious feat, Virgil would stand there, basking in the glow of unadulterated darkness, congratulating himself.

Of course, it would be a childish thing to do: counter-revolutionary, downright idiotic.

But it would *feel* so good!

Suddenly ashamed of an inebriated mind almost as wobbly as his old legs, Virgil lowered the rifle and lay down, flat on his back, hands under his head, facing the sullen sky. Stars barely twinkled, their shine cut to dull bare bones by a vapor of human anguish polluting the air, a sort of clumsy noosphere with the IQ of a moron. If you subscribed to the big-bang theory, the universe was still exploding: a new Chamisaville was emerging in a similar slow-motion explosion. Even on a heavy night like this Virgil could feel the valley trembling.

"I'll sleep outdoors tonight," he said to an inessential form lying beside him. "That's what I'll do, just lay me down where I am, I'm tired."

And the ground felt good. Ever since that slaughter-filled decade of his youth, Virgil's body had automatically accommodated itself to terrain. His muscles assumed irregular shapes, cushioning bones; it was almost as if the bones themselves became supple and pliant, bending with earthly contours.

Virgil was never more comfortable than when sleeping against the globe.

In olden times, he could go to sleep on a dime. But nowadays Virgil almost never slept soundly. When his eyelids closed, the racket tossing his brain rose in volume, growing more distinct. A lifetime of echoes pertaining to friends and enemies sounded off. Many voices and images belonged to acquaintances he had never met in person, great men and nobodies who had entered his life through the radio, the newspapers, TV. Lyndon B. Johnson's portentous whining, Villa's staccato arrogance, Zapata's firm, sincere mumble, FDR's oratory. Wild noises, promises, cries for blood. Flakey Jake Martínez's fiery tones mingled with galloping horse hooves, weapons reports, bomb blasts, howitzers, police sirens, Japanese voices, and static. Women making love, razors being sharpened. The *thwack* of cutting cane, a rattle in falling fields. Bulldozers chugging across the floor of the Cañoncito Reservoir, building a golf course where irrigation water should have been. Juan Ortega's sad eyes and bitter chatter; April Delaney's voluptuous teen-age body. Coyotes—and vultures grunting. The weather-beaten impoverished faces of his clients Ikie Trujillo, Fecundo Lavadie, Max Jaramillo, and Bonifacio Herrera as they were sentenced to life in prison for kidnapping April McQueen. Rodey McQueen and Bob Moose and Moe Stryzpk, all those people explaining, insisting, cool and persuasive, evil as Dracula—in control. Chubby little Abe Gallegos laughing, shouting songs, grabbing pussy. It was all in there, profane, haggling and swearing, whispering love words, shouting, accusing, growing clearer and more confusing yearly. His memory, instead of fading, seemed to focus sharply as he approached the grave, demanding to clarify the experience of his lifetime, squaring accounts. Each day additional voices appeared, accompanied by more incidents, sights and smells. An intricate expansion of personality and phenomena crowded his mental carnival, jockeying for position, a fiesta of the living and of the dead.

Often Virgil ignored it for hours; other times he could barely work, and worried that smoke wisps, a stench of burning horses, or a Guernican perfume was trickling out his ears, visible to passersby. Lately, if people looked at his eyes, Virgil blinked or turned away, afraid they could see his tumultuous life reflected on those tiny screens.

"I know I'm crazy, but so what?"

On this night, Virgil's interior menagerie emptied into the fields, where all hell broke loose. Unconfined, the generals, peasants, sheepherders, women, friends, foes, and famous people went crazy. Real horses reared back rolling their eyeballs, pawing the air in fright, then galloped in panic-stricken zigzag patterns, kicking dirt clods onto Virgil's face, their hooves missing him by fractions. Blinded by security lamps, they crashed into the bog and floundered, whinnying loudly—yet Virgil, dog tired, never, stirred.

Phantoms poured from the slumbering lawyer, dancing off into unaccustomed freedom: startled cows lumbered heavily erect and fled, battering through fence posts and barbed wire, snorting in dismay as, tangled in loose wire and broken cedar posts, they crashed to earth. Calves, separated from their mothers, bawled as they frenziedly ran and dodged and crashed into each other. A few horses that escaped the bog plowed into enormous heaps of sprawled animals hogtied by a great snaggle of fence posts and barbed wire.

An endless cornucopia of ectoplasmic human drama emptied from Virgil's head, ladening the fields with profane and sickening spirits, some whose clothes had been blood-spattered for a century, others with hands so pristine and fingernails so carefully manicured you could tell immediately they were butchers. Animated Hieronymus Bosch, Palmer Cox, Brueghel, Rivera, Orozco, they pranced above the bog or knifed through dazed, struggling horses, clanking, kissing, and stabbing each other, howling for justice, generating true pandemonium. And more than anybody else, a hundred Virgil Leybas scrambled about, tackling lovers, strangers, Fascists, leaping Hollywood-style into combat with Huerta, Robles, and Carranza, McQueen, Moose, and Stryzpk—a savage and playful young man wearing a sombrero, white peasant outfit, an elaborate charro costume, bleeding profusely from bullet holes, steeped in this hurricane of apparitions gone berserk.

Much later, come the first peach-aqua tints of dawn, Virgil awoke and was astonished by the mayhem which had taken place while he slept. An unbelievable snarl of exhausted livestock lay around him, entrapped in what seemed like acres of accordion wire, covered with bloody slashes from struggling, too pooped now for anything more melodramatic than a few pathetic, animal whimpers.

"Hijo madre!" Virgil exclaimed. Jumping up, he grabbed his gun, his ammo, his plumber's wrench, and hustled away before the chotas arrived to nail him at the scene of the crime!

# Emotional Kamikazes

APRIL DELANEY RETURNED to Chamisaville in the spring of 1968. Accompanied by both her kids, she flew out to the capital from New York, rented a VW Beetle from an Econo-Car outfit at the airport, and drove north. Her first-born, Duane, was three and a half; Tina was six months old. And her marriage to Matthew Delaney was effectively over.

It had failed for political, emotional, unfathomable reasons. April had never worked harder to make anything succeed: she had never (even remotely) lost as much in a breakup. Fifteen pounds overweight, and in rotten shape, she was drinking steadily, chain-smoked, coughed often, did a lot of pot. For the first time April was truly frightened, wondering if this time she had really blown it for good.

The state of America hadn't helped at all. Their relationship collapsed during paralyzing garbage strikes and the traumatic Tet Offensive in Vietnam when they had shared the crazy belief that not only had the Vietcong finally won, but racist, capitalist, imperialist America might come tumbling down. On all counts, they had been dead wrong. Three days before April left the city, Martin Luther King was assassinated. His death triggered a fight between April and Matthew that was beyond belief. They were both exhausted from four years of political struggle from trying to make a black-white marriage work despite nationalist rhetoric, the early Panthers, African identity crises, white guilt. At its best they had exulted; at its worst they had gone almost berserk from paranoid guilt trips. In the end, April lost track of herself, winding up confused, subservient, apologetic, defensive, resentful. When Martin Luther King died, despite his supposed political sophistication, Delaney went into a blind rage and accused her of pulling the trigger. And April didn't understand: Matthew had always sneered at King, labeling him an Uncle Tom, a dangerous pacifier, a liberal.

But the eruptions between them had come to make no sense. The problem was personal, historical, political, evangelical. For too long Delaney had been queasy about his identity, his color, his bourgeois background. For the first time in her life, loving this man and their family unit, April had effaced her own personality, accepting much of his shit without protest, giving him the benefit of too many doubts, refusing to battle on equal terms. Above all, she wanted their marriage to succeed. Instead, a million lousy structures constricted reason. How else could it have ended but in a blaze of irrational fury?

When he accused her of pulling the trigger on King, that did it. April erupted, blasting him with every foul resentment she had harbored for years or could invent on the spur of the moment. Before Delaney could threaten to kill her, she had threatened to murder him. April actually went at him with a knife in a great flood of bitterness, grief—and relief. He disarmed her: a pot-throwing, glass-breaking, chair-wielding frenzy ensued. The children screamed throughout; neighbors called the cops. April hit him, hurt

177

him, bit him; Delaney kicked her, banged her head with a flashlight, slugged her in the stomach. They fell out of the apartment and downstairs. Grabbing her, Delaney shoved his wife into the trunk of their car and locked it. April beat on the door until she passed out. An hour later, cops finally pried open the trunk—Delaney had chucked the keys into a vacant lot and retreated to his parents' Westchester enclave. Badly bruised, on the verge of a breakdown, April decided to get out of New York. The hell with him, the hell with it, the hell with everything. Her world had collapsed again.

Cynthia and Rodey McQueen welcomed her in disbelief. Of course, they had never seen the kids because it had been impossible, before this moment, to accept the fact that she could actually cohabit with, and even bear the children of, a nigger.

April tarried at the mansion exactly ten minutes. "I can't stay," she told Cynthia, avoiding her mother's eyes, unable to look at anyone these days. "I just need for you to take care of the kids for a week or two, I think I'm gonna drive around a little, down to the desert, I need to be on the move in completely neutral territory. I'm sorry—"

"But you're sick, April, you look terrible. Please, darling, stay here, let me put you to bed. We'll get you a private room at the hospital—"

"You don't understand, Mother, you really don't. Please, just be sweet to the kids, they've had a rough time of it. Call up George Parker or Rebecca GeeGee or somebody and invite their children over to play. Spoil them rotten, I don't care, I really don't, not this time. Take them out for sodas and ice cream, please, buy them bicycles and tricycles, baseball mitts or electric trains. The taboos are off. But I can't stick around, I don't want anybody in town to see me like this, I just want to be by myself and moving. I'm going down to the desert. I have to think and try and pull my act together, and I can't do it around this house, you know that. But please be nice to the children," she pleaded, breaking into tears. "Don't give them any moralistic speechifying for a little while and don't call them niggers. Hug them and read them bedtime stories and forget if you can all the garbage that's come down between us, just for now, just for this time, I *need* you to do this, I'm *begging* you for that help. . . ."

Virgil Leyba was at his kitchen table when her rented

Bug jolted frenziedly up his potholed driveway. He had a suicide letter from Loretta Shimkus in his hands: when it rains it pours. Only a week ago Marshall Kickingbird had blown his brains out, dealing the Pueblo's legal strategy a terrible blow at a time when electricity was apparently slated to enter the Pueblo. And now this. He had not known of Loretta's fatal cancer: two days earlier she had shot herself, leaving the hotel and a few properties for Junior to dispose of, protecting Virgil by granting him a permanent free-of-charge lease on that first-floor office, and otherwise bequeathing him only this brief note:

For Virgil Leyba, revolutionary, lawyer, distinguished man of principle, impossible womanizer. You were the only man I ever loved or cared about. Bless you for whatever times we shared. And God damn our loneliness.

Loretta Shimkus Leyba

April hugged Virgil, moaning softly, rocking in his arms, then sat down at the table unable to face him.

"Ay diós," he sympathized. "What happened?"

April shook her head. "I don't know. I mean yes I *do* know, but it's too complicated. I'm so tired, Virgil, I don't know what's the matter with me. It's like everything has fallen apart once more, nothing new, but I just don't have the reserves to pick up the pieces and start over again this time around. It feels like my whole life has been this goddam self-indulgent jigsaw puzzle and everytime I get it halfway put together, either myself or some other son of a bitch comes along and kicks it apart, and I spend forever picking up the pieces. The kids are over at the mansion, I've got two thousand dollars in traveler's checks, and I don't know what to do this time around, I really don't. I mean, I've had husbands die on me, and I've been punched around more than once, and I've had everything collapse before, God knows, a dozen times, but this experience is different. Definitive. I feel like I've hit bottom and there's no bounce. Nothing. Just splat. Boom. *Fini.* I can't think of anything to do except drive, just drive around, keep moving, just zoom along at sixty. I'm gonna head for the desert. . . ."

"Do you want a drink? Please calm down."

"I'd like to make love with you, Virgil. I know, it's crazy, I'm sorry. I'm so confused. But it would just be so good to be naked and in your arms. I want you to hold me like I was a sixteen-year-old girl, Virgil, would you? Hold me like all these years hadn't gone by. Oh Lord, love, I apologize, don't pay any attention. I just want some relief. I just want somebody who's wise and compassionate to hold me and soothe me and tell me it's okay. I really need that tonight, that's all. Then I can take care of myself, I promise, I've always taken care of myself, there was never a time that I couldn't and didn't go it alone. But tonight I can't hold on, Virgil. I need somebody like you to just hold me and love me and listen to me babble, and I'm sorry. I heard about Loretta from Mother, but I can't even think about anybody else's problems right now. I want to be able to give up and be protected, just for this one night, Virgil love, beautiful man, longtime friend, protector of the pathetic. Excuse me, forgive me for being so selfish and maudlin, but I can't hold on anymore, I really can't. I can't stand the responsibility. I just have to let it loose right now. . . ."

Virgil provided a drink: actually, they shared a bottle. He held April while she sobbed, leaning awkwardly across the corner of his table. Later they stood up and in the middle of his small kitchen Virgil embraced her, soothed her, and April could not stop crying. It had been light when she arrived, and now it grew dark while Virgil comforted her. April made fists, the unpainted fingernails bitten down to where her fingertip skin was split, and pressed the fists together against his chest, sobbing. She cried all through dusk, until it was dark. Virgil simply held on, protecting her in a gentle embrace. Although his legs ached he did not move. The telephone rang and he did not answer. When it quit ringing, he took it off the hook so that it wouldn't jangle again. April cried, beginning to get dry heaves, and finally bolted into the bathroom and threw up. Virgil stood over her while she kneeled, vomiting into the toilet bowl. He touched her head, saying nothing. April pulled down the lid, resting her cheek against the cool white-painted wood, and continued crying, more quietly now, exhausted. Seated on the edge of the tub, Virgil held a rolled cigarette in one hand. His other hand lay protectively on her shoulder. Eventually, her sobs died away. Virgil said, "I'll draw you a hot bath." April undressed while he cleaned the tub, put in the stopper. As it filled with steaming water, April sat on the toilet lid, hands in her lap, eyes on the floor. Although her body had thickened, and her breasts were spreading, starting to droop, she remained one of the more alluring women Virgil had ever seen.

The aging lawyer cut off the water. April slipped into the bath, slumped down; it felt so good she closed her eyes and seemed about to sleep. But when Virgil started to leave, she whispered huskily, "Stay, love, please. Let's keep talking. That is, if you can."

Virgil mixed them both drinks and rolled two cigarettes. April felt numb, all played out. But as soon as he settled onto the toilet lid, she began talking, quietly, relatively controlled now, though unable to stop.

"I been married how many times now, four, five? See, I can't even remember. Everything blurs. What's the matter with me? Why can't I stick things out, why do relationships always end so traumatically? I'm a good person, Virgil—I really think I am, I've always believed I'm special. But maybe there's something horribly wrong with me. Talk about your fatal flaws. I've had so many wonderful adventures and good relationships, but so much that I'm involved with seems plagued by the kiss of death. Yet I tried so hard with this one, I really did. I actually thought that this could be it. I wanted those kids so badly. And I loved this man so deeply. I needed him sorely, I really did, and he needed me. And we shared a growth, and hard times and insights into ourselves, into this country, into politics, art, intimacy, you name it—it was the best, Virgil, it really was. But I blew it. He blew it. *We* blew it, I guess. Maybe America blew it for us, who knows anymore? Oh Lord, God help me. Fuck God. Oh Lord, God help us all."

Virgil drank and smoked, taking care not to interrupt. Eyes closed, her face wreathed in steam, April talked on, calming down.

"I want to be an artist, Virgil; I also want to be a political being. That's become terribly important to me. But if I can't get my heart straight, if my private life just resembles an emotional kamikaze, how the hell am I gonna focus my politics? Everybody trusts me, but nobody wants me on their committees anymore. I got a talent for blundering because I work too fanatically, I lose patience, I become intolerant. It's all not happening *fast* enough for me. Meanwhile, I haven't painted a picture in three years. I took my sketchbook into Washington Square Park one morning last week and just sat there for three hours—I couldn't make a line. The only drawings I've done in the past five years are of nude lovers. Silly little erotic pictures. I get so sick of my physical needs, my emotional hang-ups. Yet I still want more, I still want better, I still get hungrier every day. Nothing ever leaves me satisfied. And somehow that keeps me from concentrating like I should. I can never simplify, taking one thing at a time. I'm always overextended. And then I blow it. In my love life. In my art. In my politics. I don't play the guitar any more, there's not time. I've got no paintings to show for fifteen years of sloppy work. No poems. The only copy of the novel I wrote I left in Collioure. I have trouble focusing on problems because my brain is always racing ahead. I think of things—drawings let's say—and have them halfway completed when I get a newer, better idea and throw this sloppy finish on the last idea in order to start the new one I'm excited about right away. And it's been like that with people in the past, with countries. . . ."

April cupped her breasts, pursed her lips, and let escape a soft whistle.

"Why can't I be totally rational, down to earth, steady, a pillar of strength? Why didn't anybody ever teach me discipline? That's the trouble with having so much bread you don't have to earn a living. Everyone was always so enamored of my risqué, raucous rebelliousness that instead of teaching me where it was at, they catered to it, spoiled me rotten, urged me on. They adored my undisciplined self-indulgence and made me bend over backward to meet their fantasies of how outrageous and glamorous and independent I ought to be. Chamisaville's, New York's, Paris's living legend! Jesus Christ Almighty! So I never learned to control it, me, anything. Oh gosh. I only sleep four hours a night but I never seem to get enough done. I'm so sick of worrying. Can art and politics exist side by side? Is art worth it in this country? Maybe I'm just a whore. But I'm also a beautiful creature, I really am, I *am* special, everybody's still always telling me that. But I sure as hell ain't seventeen anymore. I'm almost forty. I'm beginning to feel maimed, twisted, crippled. I couldn't count with a computer all the people who have loved me in my time: all gone."

April opened her eyes.

"My body doesn't feel right lately, I don't know what's the matter. I hardly eat but I'm gaining weight: I feel stuffed all the time. Sometimes I get prickles in the tips of my fingers. I get this sharp ache occasionally in my hip. I cough too much. I'm a fucking low-key alcoholic, I really am. Am I growing old, Virgil? I'm only—what?—I seem to have lost track. Thirty-six? Thirty-seven? Jesus, the time goes so quickly. I feel puffy inside. Despite all this trauma, I've gained, like, ten, twelve, fourteen pounds. Maybe that's just what happens when you get older. Compliments of corporate America. I'm so tired. I don't have all that natural energy anymore. I have to actually *force* myself to be energetic, now. It's like those people who don't breathe automatically, you know? And have to consciously think their way through each breath? That's the way it's become with me and my energy now. I'm so tired, Virgil. I drink too much. I smoke too much. I don't know what's the matter. . . ."

April talked. And Virgil—an aging man who had done this all his life—listened.

The water grew cold. April got out of the tub and put on Virgil's bathrobe. They sat at his kitchen table slowly killing the bottle while April talked on, running herself down so that they could both sleep.

Finally, she said, "What is happening to Chamisaville? I see trailer parks all over the place. Four, five, six housing developments. I read articles in *Playboy* magazine about how the Mosquito Valley Ski Area is better than Aspen or Vail. I read another article in *Art News*, no less, saying that this was the third-largest art capital in the world, after New York and Paris, in terms of volume of business done—is it true there's over forty galleries in town? Back in the city the underground papers, even the *Village Voice*, are writing articles on how this area has become a mecca for hippies and religious refugees from Tibet. 'Little Lhasa' somebody called Chamisa County. 'Tiny Tibet.' What the hell is happening? What kind of stupid diversions are these? Did my father start it to keep all the local people from heeding Tijerina? How did J. B. LeDoux get to be mayor? Does Juan GeeGee have any more sheep? Is it true that Ursula and Perfecto Torres are living at the Dynamite Shrine Motor Court and taking care of the town dump? Is my dad still balling Miranda Stryzpk? What's this rumor I hear about electrifying the Pueblo? Is there any hope at all, Virgil? Is there any hope at all for some kind of compassionate and humanistic outlook on life to prevail in Chamisaville, let alone the fucking Big Apple, in the end?"

Gently, he said, "Who knows? But that's one assumption that keeps me breathing."

"I don't know what I'm going to do now, Virgil. I really don't know. I'll have to tie up a thousand loose ends in the city. But I just don't know. It's weird. I seem to have run out of options and energy and belief in myself for the time being. Half the wonderful people—the artists and Communists and hustlers and actors and entrepreneurs and poets and good-time Charleys that I knew when I first hit New York are dead; or they're retired and being alcoholic in Connecticut and Vermont. Not too often, but often enough to scare me, I have this great desire to let everybody else take care of business. I did my share."

Virgil looked at his glass, and then out the window into the darkness.

"I don't really mean that, love. Guess I just feel like griping—"

"Come home, why don't you?"

"Somehow that feels like the most enormous defeat I could imagine. And anyway, there's too much past here. There's no privacy. Everybody in the valley charts everybody else's course. I would get roasted alive in this town, branded with a dozen scarlet *A*'s Who needs it?"

"We could use you here. We need you here."

"Nobody needs me anywhere."

"Please don't talk nonsense. Juan Ortega always mentions starting up the *El Clarín* again. If possible, it would be wonderful to try and establish a legal-aid office in the valley. There are still people like Espeedie Cisneros and Perfecto Torres and Celestino Lucero trying to fight the Mosquito Valley expansion. There is much valuable here that ought to be saved. You could come home, teach in the school system, help this town, struggle for our friends."

April rested her hand on his. "Thanks, old Virgil. Thanks, sweet, you're the best. I love you for that."

"If you come back we could give them more of a run for their money."

"Moe Stryzpk? My dad? Randolph Bonney?"

Virgil nodded. "Them. And there are others involved in this town, now. There's more to electrifying the Pueblo than meets the eye. Outsiders, men with strong—and I think even gangland—connections. Perhaps one day in the not too distant future Chamisaville's destiny will even pass out of the hands of folks like your father and Moe Stryzpk and Icarus Suazo."

"Icarus Suazo," April mused forlornly. "Is that quiet little man still trying to figure out how to finagle his people into possession of their sacred Albino Pine land?"

Virgil nodded. "He never rests. But I'm afraid they will kill him one of these days. Tensions have never been higher."

EVEN AS VIRGIL WAS SPEAKING, Icarus Suazo parried the first serious attempt on his life.

The Pueblo secretary lived in the northern Pueblo compound, in a two-room third-floor apartment, all alone since his return from the war. In the kitchen there was a wooden table, two large filing cabinets, and a wood cook-stove, no windows, and only a small skylight above the table. In a single wall niche he kept a kerosene lamp which he used at night when poring over papers at the kitchen table. In one corner, beside a firewood basket, stood a water bucket: in another corner sat a small footlocker for edibles —dry cereals, powdered milk, sugar, instant coffee.

In the living room a narrow bed doubled as a couch, and several trunks harbored the mementos of a lifetime. In a shallow fireplace two charred cedar logs rested. Pegs driven into the adobe wall held an old-fashioned carbine; and one large, framed photograph hung on the wall, of Icarus himself, cradling that carbine in his arms, standing in the mouth of Claude Parker's embalmed whale. He displayed no pictures of his dead wife, Juanita, or their child, Nicolas. The living-room floor was hard, well-oiled dirt. No windows and no skylight brightened up the space. During the day light entered through the single doorway opening into the tiny apartment. At night, the inner door open and the screen door locked, Icarus lay in his bed able to see the stars.

He reached the apartment by ladder, hauling up his wood, his water, and his food.

But these chores he had performed all his life were difficult now. Too often the Pueblo secretary returned home tired, disgruntled, and peculiarly lazy. The workings of Anglo character constantly amazed the wiry little man who dwelled in a legal, political, and sociological mare's nest that defied understanding.

Still a copartner in the Dynamite Shrine Corporation, he had repeatedly refused, over the years, to be bought out. With a regularity that had infuriated the Anglo Axis over four decades, Icarus had garnered his outsized cut for

185

doing little besides committing his stoic presence to annual board meetings, and auditing the books whenever he sensed himself being set up for a patsy. Naturally, Icarus plowed all his revenues from the enormous Dynamite Shrine profits back into a hundred court suits, many of which challenged the right of the Shrine and Baths complex and other connected tourist endeavors to exist. It was a hole card the sly native had used to advantage over the years; it was a power that he had played off against the Powers-That-Be, buying and selling time, and retarding the Better-ment of Chamisaville just enough so that he could still deal for Pueblo land and spiritual survival against a struc-ture that might have gobbled up the native population years ago had it not been for the careful conniving of this quiet, ascetic little man.

Icarus was sitting alone in his kitchen on the same eve-ning April Delaney rattled off her desperate story to Virgil Leyba. A dim ray of evening light extended down through the small skylight. Icarus carefully rolled a cigarette, lit it, and smoked quietly, thinking over a recent unsuccessful Albino Pine meeting he'd had with Denzil Spivey. Icarus missed Marshall Kickingbird, but avoided thinking about his late attorney. The man had chosen to move on for per-sonal reasons that had classical roots into a mania of despair. Born with a flaw, that brilliant pal had been swal-lowed alive by his flaw. Someday, when they met, Icarus might broach the subject. But right now he had double the work to do.

When it got dark, Icarus selected small sticks from the corner basket and, dropping them into his cook-stove, splashed in a few drops of kerosene, then flicked down a wooden match. Ladling water into a cheap aluminum pot, he placed that pot on the stove, and, when the water boiled, fixed himself a cup of coffee, which he sipped thoughtfully, smoking another cigarette.

That done, Icarus stepped outside, approached the edge of his roof, and assessed the night. Just topping the Mid-night Mountains, the moon was mellowy-orange and huge, heavily distorted. The sacred mountain loomed gigantically overhead, dark and comfortably foreboding. Icarus gave a quirky nod of his head, aimed at something mysterious and cynical and amorphous in the darkness, and returned to his apartment. Quickly, he stripped off his clothes, fold-ing them neatly onto a wicker chair, locked his screen door, and slipped under the thin blanket—no sheets, no pillow —on his bed.

Closing his eyes, he was asleep. After a while he dreamed. The two Denver lawyers he had fired without pay years ago floated into his head on moats of summer sunshine, smiling disarmingly, as innocent as dandelion seeds. Their disembodied faces bobbed around cheerfully, speechless. Yet an aspect of their features was so evil Icarus wished to murder them. They hovered directly overhead, well within reach. But when he lifted one hand to gauge their reality, his fingers passed through senseless gossamer material, touching nothing. Something was terribly wrong—

Icarus opened his eyes, instantly awake, completely alert. A soft squeak overhead suggested a foot shifting; the wall just barely shivered. Soot splashed faintly into his fireplace: a soft thud followed. And a barely audible recoil on the floor indicated that a snake had landed in his room —large, thick, and heavy . . . a rattler.

He waited, listening. No noise followed. Terrified, completely disoriented, sluggish in the chill summer night, the snake refused to move. Only a change of electricity in the air, a dry, almost motionless quiver indicated another living presence occupied the apartment.

Icarus lay still about five minutes, waiting for the snake to commit itself. When it would not, he peeled back the blanket and swung his feet onto the floor, pausing again, expecting a reaction from the reptile.

But it held still.

The old man cursed disgruntledly, took several steps and squatted, once more tuning into the snake's presence, determining its size and position. Extending his hand through the dark, he slipped his fingers around behind the coiled rattler's head, and with that the hypnotized serpent struck, buzzing, and tried to loop a coil around the secretary's skinny wrist for leverage to pull free its head, but Icarus darted in his other hand, grabbing the tail, and pulled the body out straight between his extended arms, immobilizing three feet of heavy, blacktail rattler.

Grasping the tail just above the rattles in his teeth, Icarus used his free hand to unlock the screen door, and emerged onto the roof. The moon had disappeared into the pitch-black sky, a heavy morning pall hung over the mountains and the sagebrush plains. The Pueblo compounds rested, nothing afoot, nobody stirring. While he stood on his neighbor's roof, alert for a telltale sound, the old man quietly strangled the snake. A minute later he flung it over the parapet for dogs to eat.

My people move too naturally through the darkness, Icarus Suazo thought. "Well: a couple of security lamps around here would change all that," he grumbled petulantly.

Was it because of those lamps that they had sent the snake? Or had the assassins been in the employ of Joseph Bonatelli or Rodey McQueen? And if so, why? The electricity negotiations had barely started.

The Pueblo secretary returned to his apartment, locked the screen door and arranged himself rigidly on his back under the single blanket, lying like that for about five minutes with his eyes open, sniffling toward various logical and illogical conclusions.

Then he closed his eyes, immediately asleep again.

SHORTLY AFTER RETURNING to New York, April Delaney realized she was in serious trouble. Although she ate little, her body continued to puff up: her blood seemed permeated with concrete, barely able to flow. Old energies had fled; increasingly, she was unable to fake it.

Up early each morning, April dressed and fed the kids, then dropped off Tina at the baby-sitter's. Duane accompanied her to an alternative storefront school, not far from Cooper Union, where April taught art and social studies. Exhausted by 2:00 P.M., often she could barely make it back home. A town which had always bolstered her own vitality and imagination, now the city clobbered her sensibilities, its traffic was demoralizing, its tension debilitating, its noise insupportable. I can't stand this filth, she thought about everything her eyes touched upon.

Nineteen sixty-eight was a bad year all around. April had no special affinity for Bobby Kennedy's presidential candidacy, but his assassination was a terribly traumatic blow. Old friends invited her to another East Hampton summer, but she declined, afraid of the scene, ashamed of her fat body. In three months she had gained twenty-five pounds. Her thighs and ankles were swollen; her once-slim waist protruded past her breasts. What had happened to the tendons in her beautiful neck? Creases were buried in her face, lost in pudge. If friends commented, she shrugged them off. Their concern, or curiosity, echoed at night, however. Even Duane had begun asking, "What's the matter, Mom? Why do you look like an elephant?"

Why was action so impossible? Maybe I just want to die, she thought. April had never been this tired in her life. In bed at eight, she could barely rouse herself ten hours later. Throughout the summer she moved sluggishly, winding down, giving up. Two funny lumps developed in her neck. Maybe it will go away, she thought. Probably I'm just demoralized. Friends rationalized how this sort of thing could happen: because of guilt, because of sorrow—after breaking up with, after the death of, a loved person. If it's fatal, I don't want to know about it, April told herself. Yet I've always been strong, I can overcome anything.

On a September day when misty rain pattered eerily onto sidewalks polka-dotted with yellow ginkgo leaves, April finally checked into a clinic. For tests, a biopsy: they told her it was cancer.

"What kind of cancer?"

"Of the lymphatic system. Lymphoma. Lymphosarcoma."

"Well . . . I guess that figures."

April sat there, waiting for tears, hysteria, recriminations. But nothing happened. Tired, and dull, and ugly, she felt the hell with it all anyway.

"If you've got to have cancer, at least this is the best kind to have," the doctor said. "We can probably control it. You should have an operation because there are several concentrations of the disease—in your neck, with tentacles going down into your back—that need to be removed. Then we can control the thing with chemotherapy."

April grinned weakly. "Boy, if it ain't one thing it's another."

"I guess so."

"What are my chances? I mean honestly—no bullshit."

"I don't know. We'll do the operation. You may have other operations depending on how the disease develops. The chemotherapy should hold it at bay—I'd estimate about thirty percent of our patients recover completely, at least for a while."

"Then there's no problem. No doubt I'm in that thirty percent already, which means I'm practically home free."

"I hope so."

Above all, nobody must discover her problem. April had seen it happen—the sympathy trips, the way fatal diseases co-opted, and eventually destroyed, relationships. Ready to give up before the diagnosis, now that she had the sickness confirmed April knew for certain she could lick it. Nothing could kill April McQueen Epstein Lanahan Arnus Delaney before her time. No way, she thought, almost jubilantly accepting the fight. Cards were on the table again—she could deal with this. Outside of a tonsillectomy at five, she had never had an operation. No matter, though: "I'll show the bastards!"

Hard as nails—that's how April suddenly felt. Depositing the kids with a friend, she entered the hospital alone. In her suitcase were the chicest nightgowns, silk robes, silver slippers, hand creams, face creams, and the best fingernail polishes that money could buy. Uncompromising flair, chutzpah, and arrogance were the passwords of the day. No condescension to any disease. They had said five days?—she would be out of that grisly semimorgue in two.

Alone, convinced of her own invincibility, caught in a belligerent, almost happy posturing, she let them prepare, gas, chop. Awaking groggy in a ward room, however, all her oomph and positive resolve had evaporated. Nothing could be more horrible, more gloomy. Her head ached, nausea was all-encompassing, even her heart hurt. Surrounded by doomed people covered with bloody bandages (missing eyes, all their hair, limbs twisted, dying, clinging pathetically to hope), April the blimp sank into fresh despair. Her other life—gay, vital, questing—was over. This kind of morbid scene would frame the rest of her days.

Immobile, depressed, April lay still, despising herself. Go to it, kid, let's have a big cheer for those metastasized lymphocytes and leukocytes! Crying might have helped, but fuck that. Her mouth, minus its three false teeth, felt puckered—but so what? Might as well look just as grotesque as she felt!

April lay there alone, toughing it out. No tears, no phony-baloney sympathy and flowers. She lay there numb, aching, swathed in bandages, looking like some grisly *before* snapshot in a *True Romance* reducing ad. The whole sick schtick must have developed because of the irresponsible way she had lived her life. All the people she had made suffer by being such a gorgeous, flighty, self-indulgent, self-seeking, spoiled-rotten, whimsical, cruel person had purchased shares in her diseased cells. The poison in her blood was fair punishment, justly deserved.

No question about *that*.

April lay there in drab hospital garb—to hell with her

pretty robes! I don't care how I look anymore; I never will again. Beauty is only skin-deep, folks, qué no? An obsession with surfaces, with personality, with her body had preordained all the bust-ups, misguided romances, unhappiness, lost opportunities, bad work in her life. Reckon I overdrew that account in spades. Maybe if she stayed fat, pampering her ugliness, a more worthwhile focus on living, loving, and working would infuse her daily existence. Just possibly she might meet a man who'd love her for deeper, more human and humane qualities than her lovely hair, sexy tits, and a wardrobe to sink the Bismarck.

Crippled and dying patients circulated in the background like phantoms from a poison dream, their heads shaved, faces black and blue from surgery, eyes frightened —their pimpled shapeless buttocks were always visible through sloppy openings in their cheap, wrinkled hospital gowns. A thing lived on her ward floor, a three-quarter torso, male, with two powerful arms, a beautiful curly blond-haired head, and whimsical, innocently beautiful blue eyes. He pulled himself up and down the hall in a canvas wheelchair apparatus. At first April avoided looking. Later, whenever the sqeak of that apparatus sounded, she made it a point to see. He always lifted one powerful hand and waved cheerfully from the hall, winking at her. Later, he came over to the bed and introduced himself— "My name is Bob"—just Bob. No mention of his lack of hips, legs, feet, genitals—they didn't talk about themselves. Bob was a sports fan, so they discussed the Mets, the Knicks, the World Series. And pushed on to weather, politics: the disastrous Democratic convention; would the U.S.A. land on the moon next year? And New York. But nothing personal. Bob had some background in art: he knew a little about writers and writing. When he left her, April wondered: How does he shit and piss? Are there any sexual feelings left? Would he ever escape the hospital? Was he married before this happened and if so, how did she take it? What horrible life had he led to deserve such a fate? Could he ever earn a living in the outside world? Or was he stuck here forever, alive so long as they kept whittling pieces, bit by bit, hacking away, chopping him down, until finally he became a lump with no arms, just a ball of scar tissue enveloping a mechanical heart and plastic veins topped by his beautiful head and vibrant, cheerful eyes, loved by a perverse lady somewhere—like the operatic Salome—lying nude on her back holding that head above her. They could whisper sweet nothings, and, tightly grabbing his ears, she would manipulate his gorgeous head, helping him to ball her with his nose.

Eyes squeezed shut, April drifted painfully through her cancer-ward days. Perhaps she was dying. Her past life buzzed around like bees trying to enter a blocked hive, a mass of faint voices, uncomfortable dreams—people, places, faces. Charley Epstein, hangdog, apologetic, dipping his wings at her from the sky. The abortionist in Wyoming—disinterested, nervous, uncaring. Tim Lanahan smooching with a naked lady, deliberately hoping to hurt April. Enrique up to his waist in Mediterranean water, his head bloody from having bashed it himself with rocks, beckoning her—leering, laughing, making muscles and obscene gestures: "Come on over to the other side!" Virgil Leyba, a gaunt skeleton, a mute Abraham Lincoln, wandered through the misty background, smoking one cigarette after another, condemning her with his sad eyes. Juan GeeGee stroked a guitar from which no sound issued; Amaranta GeeGee held those nude photographs in her hand, and, frowning, glanced suspiciously up at April with evil eyes. Oh why had she sent them to Charley? And how could she have given them to Junior Leyba? "I want them back," she whispered, half-awake. She really wanted those photographs back.

A chill permeated the ward. Outside weather was gray and drizzly. Charley's bomber jacket kept her warm. And, snug in that ancient sheepskin, she let the past enter, a habit April had almost never indulged in before.

Ghosts, skeletons, memories. Charley's airplane again, flitting fragilely through clouds—their American odyssey, the honky-tonk music and cheap booze that accompanied a fantastic, melancholy adventure through a boondocks carnival existence. New York openings and art parties, April at the center of a hundred important people, a diamond tiara in her silver hair, her voluptuous figure revealed through the tight jersey fabric of a creamy white formal, a woman literally Too Good To Be True. Junior Leyba returned, mistrustful and brokenhearted, suffocating through this thick honey. J. B. LeDoux was the most physically powerful man who had ever been awed by her. His thick chest, enormous arms, heavy thighs—none of it loved correctly: the marvelous flesh was color struck, culture

fucked, too deferential, constrained. And Tim Lanahan—
dead already, liquored out stupidly, a fair talent in a half-
assed human being enamored of the romantic, self-destructive ritual. He gave her fumbled, apologetic bear hugs.
Delaney hauled off and slugged her, trying to smash her
beautiful white face. Who had she truly loved? Everybody,
nobody; probably there was no accurate answer. Delaney
more than anyone: she had let him own it all. But politics
seemed to give the only real focus. Although so far April
had spent too much time doing what she felt she should
do, rather than what she wanted to do. No real beliefs
had as yet hardened in her, making everything else easier—

April healed and shook hands with Bob the lump: her
stay in the hospital ended.

WHILE CANCER THREATENED April Delaney in New York,
a different disease was working on J. B. LeDoux, recently
elected mayor of Chamisaville. One day he almost killed
his son, Benny, shortly after the boy had returned—shell-
shocked and a junkie—from Vietnam.

J. B. did this because, with electricity rumored about to
enter the Pueblo, and with Joseph Bonatelli and his retinue
creeping around town beginning to negotiate deals, J. B.
sensed he was perched on the edge of a dream-killing that
could land him on an easy street for life. But he didn't
know for sure, because crucial information was being
withheld from him, pending—pending God knew what.
Hence, J. B. was so uptight he couldn't see straight.

Naturally, J. B. and Teresa had given Benny everything
under the sun: a bathroom with a pink sunken tub, a
twenty-dollar Spalding baseball mitt for Little League,
piano lessons and a real piano to practice on, the best
bicycles, motorcycles, and finally automobiles money could
buy. And, naturally, they had looked on in stunned cliché
disbelief as Benny metamorphosed into a long-haired,
sullen teen-ager who hated their guts and their life-style,
called them pimps to their faces, and painfully taught himself Spanish, speaking nothing but that language with
them even though they angrily answered in English. Finally
he dropped out of high school, left home to join the army,
did Vietnam, and on his return started living among all
the disgraceful bums at the Dynamite Shrine Motor Court,
with no other interests in life, apparently, except scoring
and dealing and pulling off a kinky sex life when not on
the nod or driving aimlessly around with his pal Alfredo

GeeGee in a souped-up Camaro with the tape deck blasting and his sleepy eyes inspecting Chamisaville the way a dying shark, its guts slowly unraveling out a long belly wound, might canvass the feathery gams of a meal that might have been.

An American story: very banal.

Increasingly, J. B. had taken to drink. And on this tense evening, when a thousand schemes and obligations pertaining to the Betterment of Chamisaville and his fawning, sold-out role in it weighed heavily on his mind, he dropped into Vigil's Liquors after work for some gin, went home, and, while awaiting Teresa's return from her stint in the plaza's chamber of commerce information booth, knocked off about six martinis, retrieved a .38 police special from a bureau drawer, and went out to end his own life and career by killing his errant son.

A rosy dusk, such as occurred every other day in Chamisaville, gilded the Midnight Mountains with a bloody light. And the horizon, punctuated by clouds from which cotton-candy wisps of pink rain fell, was so lovely, and created such an ache, that J. B. wanted to close his eyes, disbelieving the beauty because it would be gone so quickly, accenting, too much, precarious mortality.

The mayor found his spaced son behind the wheel of the Camaro, parked outside the Dynamite Shrine cabin, slouched halfway into death, listening to a Rolling Stones cassette, alternating dreamy sucks on a warm beer with a few last tokes from a damp roach. J. B. reached in through the driverside window, touched the .38 snout to Benny's head, and said, "You ungrateful son of a bitch, I'm gonna blow your brains out!"

The kid exhaled smoke. "Far out, Pop. Do it."

J. B. thumbed back the hammer. "Don't you have anything to say?"

Benny shrugged and twitched one hand draped on the steering wheel. "What's to say? The longer we live the sooner we're going to die. So long, Pop. It's been real."

Enraged, J. B. suddenly saw white, something whirred in his head, he clenched his teeth so hard a muscle in his jaw snapped and a tooth filling cracked, and he pulled the trigger, horrified eyes wide open, fully expecting to see Benny's brains erupt across the front seat, impacting gorily against the closed passengerside window.

But he had forgotten to load the gun. A cutworm moth emerged from the barrel, shivered, and flew off.

"Very funny, Pop. Great sense of humor." Benny shrugged again, indifferently snuffing out the roach. Lying back, his hands plopped without tension into his lap, he aimed glazed eyes straight ahead through the windshield.

The mayor yanked open the door, shouting, "Move over, dammit!"

"Try the other door. It ain't locked."

J. B. hit his son's shoulder with the gun, slapped and punched at him with the other hand, tried to get his leg in there for a kick, and bapped the gun barrel across Benny's cheek, tearing open his lips. But it was like striking a dead weight, like flailing into weird Jell-O. The boy offered no resistance, he just lethargically allowed his old man's attack, joggling and lurching passively whichever way the blows drove him, eyes half closed, a silly radiant smile on his bloody lips. J. B. knocked him onto the passengerside floor, fell in behind the wheel, smashed the tape deck into silence with his gun butt, and chucked the weapon at Benny, hitting his chest. Then he gripped the wheel with both hands, wheezing and gasping, so full of hate and rage for a second that he flashed they were heading at eighty toward the cabin where he hoped Benny's girlfriend and his one-legged pal Alfredo GeeGee would be lying zonked out of their skulls directly in the Camaro's path.

Benny fumbled with his father's gun, sticking the barrel in his mouth—he sucked on it contemplatively. The mayor settled his forehead against the wheel, and, too exhausted to move, he just held the position, drooling from his mouth.

"You should rejoin the army," Benny said. "Get away from town for a while, work out some of those poison juices, reduce those venomous frustrations by killing gooks."

"Callate la boca, for crissakes."

"Man, that's a high, killing gooks. Chicanos and gooks, niggers and Indians and poor white trash doing the off-each-other mambo while the Man gets a grin on his chinny-chin-chin. Dig it. After a while we'd just be in the truck, driving over to Cam Ranh or someplace to pick up some ordnance or Bob Hope or somebody, and the rice paddies, they'd be full of gooks and buffaloes, and the riding shotgun you'd just swing down and pop some little dink bent over his rice plants, chug-a-lug, and wasn't nobody knew the difference."

"Come home, Benny. You're sick."

"How does it feel, Pop, when some gringo Tejano like Rodey McQueen has got you by the balls?"

"We'll get a doctor, we'll take care of you."

"They're laughing at you, Pop. They'll use you, and when they cap off all the shit that's been coming down for years by getting electricity into the Pueblo they'll toss you a couple of bones, and then they'll drop you like a bad habit."

"I want to help you, Benny, I really do."

"The Northland Grazing Association is gonna fry your butt, Daddy. Joe Bonatelli is gonna shove a poker up your ass."

"Son, you keep on like this and you'll be dead before the year is out."

"I've always wanted to help you, too. But your head is stuck so far up their ass you never heard me."

"What's the matter with you?" the mayor groaned.

"Nothing's the matter, man. Life is a bowl of cherries. I drove seventeen miles on a flat tire last week. Don't ever take pieces of tabs, Pop, you just get ragged. Whole hog or nothing. Twenty-five hits is where it's at because when you flash it's the old white light and you stay there. Dig it. And fuck the Betterment of Chamisaville, Pueblo electricity, the whole bit. Back to basics, Pop. There's no such thing as a rose garden."

"You're sick. You're crazy."

"La vida es a toda madre."

"Estás enfermo, Benny. I don't know what happened."

"I dunno what happened to you either, Pop." He poked the gun barrel back in his mouth.

"Just because you experienced a war doesn't mean you have to turn into this," the mayor said weakly.

"Tell me about Rodey McQueen, Pop. Tell me about what it feels like when Moe Stryzpk orders you to dance. Tell me about that."

The mayor opened his door, walked over to the cabin, and peered inside, swaying. Dark, musty, it smelled of incense. He had expected a holocaust, dishes piled high, clothes and garbage scattered all over, pages from torn magazines everywhere: a regular dump. Instead, the dimly lit place was spare and tidy. Everything was in place, silent. Several moths battered against one window, otherwise the only motion was the measured breathing of a nude woman lying on a bed, staring at the ceiling. A cigarette burned between the fingers of one hand held loosely against her thigh, the smoke twining quietly toward the ceiling. "Who is Joseph Bonatelli?" the mayor whimpered desperately to himself. "What is the Northland Grazing Association?" Then the woman trembled slightly and became a skeleton of burnished gold lying atop enormous fluffy white wings.

Benny touched a gun against his father's head, just behind the ear, saying softly, "Now I'm going to kill you, Pop. But with a loaded gun."

The mayor thought of spinning around, ducking, anything to save his own life, but he failed to act on that immediate urge, and froze, then relaxed, giving up—grateful.

"Now," said Benny, pulling back the hammer, the sound it made locking like a gunshot itself in J. B.'s ear.

"Oh—" was all the mayor had time to say before the kid pulled the trigger and the hammer sped forward . . . with another click.

Staggering backward, doubled over, Benny howled with laughter. His father turned, incredulous. The boy floundered against his car, laid his old man's gun on the hood and then crumpled softly earthward, screeching in an awkward, hiccuping voice:

"One to one . . . Pop. Score's tied. And it's the last . . . of the fucking . . . *ninth!*"

ELSEWHERE IN CHAMISAVILLE, a sweet twilight had descended, lazy and sad. Football practice was over, and, from his seat in the empty grandstand, George Parker watched the boys leave, walking slowly, dusty and tired in the dimming light, helmets carried laxly at their sides.

Unabashedly, George ached for youth, to be young again; for his heroic athletic days. He was tired and would have felt grim, perhaps, had it not been such a lovely evening. The school grounds were largely deserted; a car started in the parking lot, idled for a moment, the radio clicked on. A savage music, muted by the autumn cocktail-hour quiet, sallied over the football field. In his high-school days it had been Perry Como, Frank Sinatra, Patti Page. The groundskeeper, old Filiberto García (who had once run the Magpie Creek Lumber Mill), was setting down fresh stripes for tomorrow's game, and the lime powder glowed fluorescently in the gathering dark. George could have wept. Wrapped in this suave autumn dusk, he didn't want to move, he just wanted to sit there and savor. Winter should have arrived a month ago. Instead, they were locked in the kind of Indian summer that Chamisaville experienced only once every decade. Each morning, people in the valley expected it to end. But one sunny crisp day followed another. Students twitched nervously, gazing forlornly out the windows. George's blood refused to slow down. He wanted to be out, in the hills, on the streams, moving through the buttery texture of this best season he had ever known. Today might be the last beautiful day of autumn, he woke up thinking at each dawn—tomorrow, for sure, the sky would be overcast, no doubt it would snow.

George felt he had made a genteel mess of his life. Not that anything was "wrong" according to all the barometers, thermometers, and other instruments measuring such things. He had a faithful wife, socially and economically competent. He had decent kids and a respectable job, also a powerful father (and father-in-law) who had given him/them the wherewithal to own plenty of land, a large house, some stocks and bonds. In short, he was a modest pillar of this society.

Yet George lived surrounded by imaginative might-have-beens, by wishes that he could have been different, escaped, seen the world, not settled down quite so quickly. A sadness inside bulged up at the slightest provocation—in the bathtub, over a Sunday meal, and at a moment like this when athletic echoes still hovered over the lush green field, and he could smell grass, the faint odor of his own sweat, and fresh lime. A juniper scent drifted off the nearby foothills. Beyond, the Midnight Mountains, as yet unsnowed upon, towered. A fine dusty smog hung over Chamisaville several miles north. Headlights winked through the soft haze, a line of them trickling down the highway toward the high school.

His children—Tommy, Billy, Sarah—were gone although they still lived at home. But they seemed terribly far away; somehow he'd lost interest in them. They were rich kids, snobbish, selfish. They related to the Beatles, the Grateful Dead, Alice Cooper. George didn't really like them that much anymore. And Susan was settled in for the long haul. She got her kicks from the hospital auxiliary, the PTA, from working the Used-A-Bit Shop every Wednesday with Charlotte Leyba. Her friends were his parents, her parents—the power structure and their kids . . . Stryzpks, Bonneys, Lamonts, and Mooses. But George couldn't stand those people. His crowd, granted—but they bored him stiff. He wanted poetry, emotional adventures, the romanticism of a Lord Byron, a Dylan Thomas, a Coleridge, a Thomas Wolfe, an Ernest Hemingway. He subscribed to *Ramparts, Rolling Stone, The New York Review of Books, The Sunday New York Times*. Yet all the excitement had drained from his life; he was sick of vicarious thrills—football, baseball, hockey on TV; other people's novels, travelogues, derring-do.

Inside the gym, George donned a tank suit and entered the swimming pool. Pausing for a moment on the one-meter diving board, hands placed laxly against his stomach, touching a slight ridge of soft flab, he thought, At least I've remained in shape. The pool was empty, the atmosphere mufflingly warm. George let his eyes unfocus, too tired for diving. Instead he should take a hot shower and go have a vodka and tonic at the Chamisaville Inn before heading home. But he was drinking too much lately. The soft layer of flab made him self-conscious. I wonder if I'll ever get fat? he mused.

George measured his distance, forced himself alert, and executed a graceful forward one-and-a-half. Breaking it too late, however, he slapped the back of his thighs against the water. Grimacing, he breaststroked slowly to a ladder. The diving wasn't much fun, but he continued anyway, practicing for fifteen minutes until he miscalculated a full gainer, striking both legs and a hip against the board, banging his hand, and scraping his stomach. His head struck water inches away from the tiled edge of the pool.

"Jesus Christ, George, do yourself a favor, cut out this kid's crap and go home!"

Bruised, aching, he let the shower pound him. The water was heavy, soothingly hot. It drummed against his stomach, crotch, chest, and battered his face, feeling good. Back at his locker, he toweled down slowly, savoring the rough cotton against his weary muscled flesh. A few tarrying football players cracked jokes among the lockers. Liniment, wintergreen, athletic tape, soap. George sat on the bench, slumped over, in his underwear, contemplating his hands.

The locker room was silent: he loved its odor. Overchlorinated water had left his eyes red. One hand hurt, his scraped stomach burned, his left knee throbbed. "For the love of Christ, man, you could have broken something," he muttered incredulously. "Grow up, become an alcoholic, learn to play golf with Randolph Bonney, Al Lamont, and Rodey McQueen."

His Chevy Blazer was almost alone in the parking lot. They had two other cars—Susan's Chrysler Imperial and his Mustang. Slightly scared, George also felt wonderful—athletically tired. Where it wasn't bruised, his skin glowed. But he had not hit the board like that, miscalculating that badly, ever.

Hands draped over the steering wheel, George waited. It was dark now, very peaceful. He did not want to turn on the motor or the lights. The head of the state cops, Gray von Brockdorff, made a turn through the lot and cruised away. Maybe next summer, instead of taking the family on a float down the Colorado River, or on a camping trip to Glacier National Park, George would rent some old sheepherder's shack outside of town and try to do something different, something even quasi-useful and exciting—like writing a novel. A drowsiness filtered into the bus; closing his eyes, George sighed, fearing his own loneliness, hating the idea of going home. He had heard rumors of April McQueen's imminent return. That thought dwelled in him for a moment. Ridiculous as it might seem, he found the idea exciting. For years George had fantasized an affair between them, their impassioned lovemaking right out of *The Pearl*, *The Story of O*, the *Kama Sutra*.

"Ah, let it be," he whispered morosely. "Do yourself a favor, pal, just let it be."

A rich orange moon cleared the mountains. They said that by next summer Americans would land up there. Its light touched his face, ruffled his hair with feminine fingers, and George opened his eyes, geared up once more. Turning the ignition key, he headed for his happy home.

HER OPERATION, doctors told April Delaney, was a success: chemotherapy followed.

She dropped the kids off with a friend on Friday afternoons and entered the clinic. They placed her alone in a small windowless room with an IV of creatively poisonous stuff draining icily into her arm. Eyes closed, grimacing, she wondered which was worse—cancer, or destructive chemicals entering her veins, spreading slowly until even her heart, circulating the medicine, felt clammy, downright polar. In some ways, she thought morbidly, it's like being embalmed.

Afterward, April usually just made it from the subway to her apartment before vomiting. And she was sick all weekend, upchucking until even her hair seemed cramped and almost paralyzed. During those three days, she could barely focus her eyes, and moved only with great pain. Every weekend was like that, spent alone in her tiny East Side apartment, collapsed on the bed or crouched over the toilet, unable to read or otherwise function, wanting to die. By Sunday evening the reaction had almost completely abated. She went outside, greedily inhaling the city air, so relieved that she often collected Duane and Tina with tears in her eyes. On Monday morning she headed back to work again.

All winter April received weekend treatments. By March her skin had turned gray; her eyes were dull, resigned. She had lost much weight. Advised to quit smoking and drinking, April could not abstain. Friends, shocked by the transformation, were repulsed when they asked questions. Everybody thought her troubles derived from the breakup with Delaney. April had kept mum about the cancer. And she hadn't missed a day of work.

Her periods stopped and did not resume. Premature menopause, thanks to the therapy. She had been forewarned, but all the same, the appearance of that blood had always made her feel good, womanly, totally alive. She had never had cramps or the moody blues. And had always especially loved men who liked balling in her blood.

Treatments were suspended for a while; the doctors wanted to see how things developed. "That's certainly okay with me," April moaned listlessly: she had been functioning on a faint echo of past energy. Yet springtime entered her heart early, giving a lift. Fluffy cherry blossoms added color to Washington Square. Millions of people broke winter cocoons and hit the streets all dolled up in colorful clothes. Such a world of breasts, thighs, biceps, and joggers' powerful calves! Facing a mirror, April frowned at her new gray hairs, streaked them, and fiddled with makeup. Suddenly, bright costumes she hadn't worn in months made her feel better: museums beckoned, sidewalk tables appeared, Bergman and Truffaut had new movies: the baseball season began. The regeneration caught her by surprise. No time in April's life had been as sordid as last winter. But she had survived it, gaining added courage from her ability to withstand that trauma.

A friend was heading for Cuba to cut sugarcane on a Venceremos Brigade. April applied for the trip, was accepted, farmed out her chidren, took a bus up to New Brunswick, and boarded a rickety, crowded ship for Havana.

For two months she swung a machete, lived in a tent camp, and met Cubans, North Koreans, and Vietnamese peasants all working in the cane harvest. A Vietcong woman gave her a metal ring made from an American bomber shot down over North Vietnam. Up at four each morning, April worked so hard she had little time for thinking; only on a rare evening could she stay awake past nine o'clock. During the last two weeks of her stay, she traveled by bus around the island, viewing the revolution, talking with people. In late May she arrived back in New York, brown as a berry, her hair as bleached as it had been fifteen years earlier after Hampton summers, her body back to normal—tough, shapely, big and beautiful. April was exhausted in a way that felt like a million dollars. When friends asked her impressions of Cuba, she most often remarked: "The thing that's incredible is you get the feeling, from everyone, that they are all united in a single purpose. Everybody believes they have a role in the revolution, in the future of the country, in the future of humankind. They all feel that they, personally, count: that they, personally, have a say in history. They are so united and unalienated, it's almost completely the opposite of the feeling in North America."

Going on five, Duane would be entering school come fall; and April had tired of New York. All during the winter of chemotherapy and her Cuban experience, she had thought of returning home. Around Chamisaville's mountains, rivers, and mesaland, the children would flourish. Suddenly, April felt a need for the small-town atmosphere, a less frenetic existence, life on a smaller scale.

One night she excitedly telephoned Virgil Leyba to test what was on her mind. "You should return," he said simply. "We need all the horses we can get."

"What about starting up the *El Clarín* again? I could do that. And I think if maybe I finagled a gig at the high school I could begin a special social-studies class, teaching a more relevant culture and history to the local kids."

"That would be good. Anything you might do would be very valuable."

"I wish I had kept a low profile long ago, though. I'm terrified of carrying my reputation back into that little town."

"It's not so small any longer, tu sabes. There must be ten thousand people in all the communities together. Every day I see faces I never knew before. In the past two years the process has accelerated; your dad and the rest of the Axis can smell roses. Even since your visit a year ago there have been a thousand changes. They built a new court-house south of town on the highway, a new shopping center with a Piggly Wiggly, a TG&Y. There's a Seven-Eleven on the highway, and another one in Cañoncito. The new post office just completed north of town is double the size of the old one. The First State Bank has a drive-in branch four blocks north of the plaza on Fiesta Street, and an-other branch, open from June to September, up in the Mosquito Valley."

"And so how's by you, Virgil?"

"I work—what can I say? As always, I have hope. You could help. People of conscience still exist here. All our friends are determined to go down fighting. A stubborn-ness and a will to survive still pervades the valley. So they don't gain an inch but what we make them pay for it."

"Can you find me a house to rent? I really think I'm coming home."

"I'll look around."

Toward the latter part of July, driving a U-Haul van, April left New York City. Her Manhattan doctors had referred her to Virgil Leyba's old carousing friend, Abe Gallegos, who had become one of the better-known cancer specialists in the Southwest. She had few posses-sions: many books, a lot of records, a stereo set, and a nest of drawings and paintings given her by lovers and by good friends. Her only furniture was a few mattresses on which the kids slept and played. In the old days April had crossed the country a dozen times, driving straight through, nonstop, forty and fifty sleepless hours of drink-ing coffee and Cokes, popping raisins and No Doz, and yelling out every rock-and-roll song written between 1954 and 1957 to stay awake. But this voyage was different; the old stamina no longer existed. And besides, what was the hurry? On their first night out they slept in an Ohio motel; the second night passed in a Missouri rest area. And as they crossed Kansas during the third day, April

203

suddenly realized—from the radio, and from newspapers bought along the way—that Americans were about to land on the moon.

Around 9:00 P.M., while a mellow light still colored the corn and wheat fields, April pulled off the highway, simply driving onto a vague dirt track leading into tall corn. She penetrated the opulent stalks until far removed from the highway, completely hidden from view. The kids were asleep. April maneuvered a sponge-rubber pad and a pillow onto the roof, tuned the radio to the moon shot, and sat on the roof while light died, drinking thermos coffee and eating a sandwich.

The moon adventure crackled over her radio: she was both dismayed and awed by the whole thing. April resented the shot, she begrudged America the moon-program billions that could have gone for people, housing, medical research, environment. The jingoistic propaganda circus surrounding the event, especially when viewed in light of the Vietnam war, had to be one of the most vulgar phenomena she had ever observed. After Southeast Asia, the moon landing made her most ashamed to be a U.S. citizen. It was irrelevant for most peoples, especially Third World citizens; April felt that—on a grand scale— it lacked imagination. And the men involved, the all-American sanitized automatons scheduled to make man's first track in that gray powder, bored her to tears.

A sensation of tragic sadness acutely manipulated her focus on the moment. Lost in an enormous field of Kansas corn, sipping sherry now and smoking dope, April faced the pale high globe while voices of the men puttering around up there crackled eerily over the radio. Similar sadness she had on occasion experienced reviewing her own adventures. The need to flee Chamisaville and experience everything, chalk up lovers, travel to the ends of the earth, be a great writer, poet, painter— All that.

Lying atop the van, drowsy from her meal, the long drive, the booze and the pot, April wondered what now? What next in her checkered career? "What is my corn-ball destiny to be after all?" Confused, sad, happy— everything was hopeless, but so what? "Hey," she said to the moon. "I got this lascivious, overpowering desire for a macho man."

A six-month drought of loving should end. Part of her abstention related to the chemotherapy. The rest of it hinged on a decision made to control her emotional life, consciously guiding herself toward what she needed instead of into what happened to come along. Never again —*never!*—would she fall into bed with the first beautiful human being that came strutting down the pike. From here on in all her sexual moves would be deliberate moves. That way she could protect her weakened body, conserving her strength . . . and her mental well-being. *Half cocked* and *thoughtlessly* had been relegated to the cluttered junk bins of her volatile past.

April killed the radio after Neil Armstrong's great step forward for mankind, and climbed back onto the roof. Warm in Charley's old bomber jacket, April stayed awake a few minutes longer, eyes fixed on the serene sky, lazily picking through thoughts of returning home. Then, closing her eyes, she dreamed. Of floating off the mansion's roof, of Claude Parker's whale, of Pat GeeGee's airplane and her first trip aloft, of the wonderful Horse Without Shit. In her dreams she remembered a first swim in the mansion pool, and the discomfort at being served breakfast in bed by a servant who was the mother of a little girl in her own elementary class. And April dreamed of Amaranta GeeGee on a Magpie Creek picnic, teaching the teen-age April McQueen about edible wild herbs.

A few tears sneaked out the corners of her eyes and trickled into her hair, under the wide and wonderful Kansas sky.

EARLY ON THE DUSTY MORNING after North Americans achieved the moon, a Trailways bus ground into the Chamisaville depot beside Bob's Auto Parts and the cheap tin and Plexiglas "simulated adobe" Kentucky Fried Chicken barn. Four old men got out. Shiny, old-fashioned pinstriped suits hung loosely on their frames; cheap, state-issue sneakers protected their feet. Under an arm, each man carried a small, twine-bound cardboard box. Smoke from their Camel cigarettes gathered beneath the brims of their battered straw cowboy hats. They had sparse white hair (neatly clipped), sad eyes, aquiline noses, tight lips, tobacco-stained teeth, and slight beard-stubbles. Pausing for a moment on damp macadam recently hosed down by the station agent, they blinked their eyes against the matinal mountain sunshine. The top of Hija Negrita was just visible above telephone wires, gas-station signs, the Colonel Sanders billboard, and other commercial accoutrements. Bumper-to-bumper traffic on the North-South

Highway amazed them: they gaped at it, almost ashamed to be home.

Other debarking passengers bumped into them, their suitcases knocking against the old-timers' legs. Shambling aside, they turned, and, in a tight protective clump, watched other passengers descend, load up on Fritos and soda at station vending machines, and scramble back to the bus. A new driver nodded at the four men and leaped enthusiastically aboard, trailing a parting shot: "You all be good old boys, now—hear?"

The uncertain old men closed their eyes as gray-green monoxide billows engulfed them: the bus headed uneventfully north.

No band, no bigwigs, no family, no nothing. The men gawked a moment longer, amazed and perturbed. Then one of them nodded brusquely and they traipsed single-file across the parking lot, hopped over a muddy ditch, climbed a slight embankment, and limped through the deserted Kentucky Fried Chicken lot, entering the garish cubicle, where they ordered a fingerlickin breakfast.

One grizzled man laid a wrinkled five-dollar bill on their table. And, after each old galoot had licked his thumb and tamped up every last crumb, they gathered their cardboard boxes, and, single-file again, walked north, crossing the street and circling the PDQ, heading behind Aaronson's Brothers into the notorious alley that emptied onto the plaza between the hotel and Vigil's Liquors. In the gloom, a half-dozen lost souls wrapped in tattered blankets and old overcoats were hunched against flaky walls or sprawled among beer cans, cardboard boxes, and Popsicle wrappers. Among them lay Amanda Santana's long-ago paramour, Gabe Suazo, one of Juan and Mari-Elena Ortega's twin sons, Panky, Nicanor Casados, and Cenobio Arrellano. A cloud of mist, rising off Gabe Suazo's damp jacket, seemed for a second to assume a human shape—Marshall Kickingbird, with a half-pint of ethereal Golden Glo at his lips?—and then dispersed as the men ambled through. Irritating flakes of an inquiet nostalgia settled onto their shoulders like dandruff—but they didn't notice.

On the plaza, the men paused again, surprised by the transformation, by all the early morning cars and the total absence of horses. Judson Babbitt, that enormous white-haired man, resplendent in his leather vest, love beads, turquoise rings, and fabulous concho belt, was seated on a bench surrounded by pigeons and his prizewinning basset hound, Michelangelo. In a moment he would enter the Prince of Whales for breakfast with men like Rodey McQueen, Bob Moose, and J. B. LeDoux.

While the four strangers watched, Little Kid Lujan (a.k.a. Eduardo Mondragón) shuffled onto the plaza with two dozen *Capital City Reporter*s under one arm and his World War II medals pinned haphazardly across the chest of a Snoopy sweatshirt. Rebecca Valerio, secretary for the DA, Damacio Mares, bought a paper from Little Kid and clacked into the Prince of Whales for a coffee-to-go. Smoking a big cigar, Eloy Romo, the punchy boxer, was seated on the concrete base of the war monument absorbed in news accounts of the moon landing, taking his own sweet time about opening Lalo Chavez's Magazine Emporium. Ancient Malaquias C. de Baca, the late Atiliano Montoya's brother-in-law, had already taken up his stand before the old courthouse, now an art gallery complex and English tea garden called Picadilly Circus, owned and operated by Junior Leyba and Damacio Mares. Filiberto García, the plaza caretaker as well as high-school groundskeeper, was running an American flag up the tilting flagpole . . . upside down (deliberately) as usual. In vain, decrepit old Father Molé berated the totally deaf descendant of Onofre and R. J. García.

Nearby, Malaquias C. de Baca's angry sister, Genoveva Bachicha, a welfare witch now residing in Karl Mudd's Trailer Towne, was putting curses on Texans, trying to make them disappear, have car accidents, drown at the hot springs, or catch hepatitis from polluted trout.

Murmuring indistinctly, the four old men turned right and peered into Virgil Leyba's uninhabited, disheveled office: he was at the Prince of Whales breakfasting with Pat GeeGee, Juan Ortega, and Flakey Jake Martínez. The men then shuffled down to the El Gaucho, but nobody was behind the bar. Since the door was open, they entered, climbed onto stools, and waited for service. When nothing happened, one of the men muttered a profanity, circled the bar, and served up four cans of Bud. They popped tops, and, while thoughtfully sipping on the brew, each man reconnoitered the El Gaucho bulletin board with its articles about the old days, its photographs of Claude Parker's whale, Pat's airplane, the wonderful Horse Without Shit, Eloy Romo posing in his plaza ring. Inevitably, their eyes came to rest on several yellowed newspaper pictures, of themselves in their early thirties, almost forty years ago, when accused of kidnapping April McQueen.

Released from the state pen only that morning, Fecundo Lavadie, Max Jaramillo, Bonifacio Herrera, and Ikie Trujillo had finally come home.

Beers emptied, and payment left on the bar, they ambled next door to Vigil's Liquors, where each man bought a pint of his particular poison. After that, they crossed the plaza, their shadows making pigeons scatter: Judson Babbitt looked up, irritated, but the men strode by without giving him even a scornful glance. Minutes later, two blocks north on the highway, the ragtag pandilla of ancient farmers who had spent more than half their lives in prison entered Midnight Sporting Goods and approached Billy Moose, teen-age grandson of Bob Senior, about buying guns. Billy kept up a cheerful patter as he laid various pistols and rifles on the counter for them to inspect. Ikie Trujillo peered solemnly into the business end of a Colt revolver, then casually fingered six bullets from his pocket and slipped them into the chamber. Bonifacio Herrera sighted along the barrel of a .270 hunting rifle, swinging it around the store, drawing a bead on fishing poles, salmon-egg jars, baseball gloves, and Coleman stoves. Max Jaramillo morosely checked the lever action on a .30-.30 repeater. And Fecundo Lavadie strapped on an elaborate leather holster, fitted a long-barreled .38 into it, and adjusted the squeaky gunbelt until it rode comfortably around his skinny hips.

Pointing his loaded revolver directly at Billy Moose, Ikie Trujillo clicked out the chamber, saying, "You see this, kid? I put real bullets in it." Snapping the chamber closed, he added, "We're gonna take these guns. We also need ammunition. So fork it over, little gabacho."

While Max Jaramillo held open a blue and white athletic tote bag, Billy obligingly shoveled in cartons of ammunition until Fecundo Lavadie said, "Bueno, basta, le agradezco mucho, nene—let's go."

Outside, the men stepped into the street. Ikie Trujillo leveled his pistol at the first car that came along. Braking his wine-colored Continental, Randolph Bonney banged on the horn, shouting out his window, "Hey, you old sheepfuckin horse thieves, get the heck out of my way— go sleep it off in the alley beside Vigil's!"

Ikie poked his gun barrel into the electric co-op executive's ear, while his pals entered the car—two in back, and Max Jaramillo beside the driver: he clicked off the radio.

Bonney exclaimed, "You don't mean this is actually for *real—?*"

Ikie got into the car behind him, saying, "Pos, bueno—adelante."

Bonney asked nervously, "Now what? What do you want me to do?"

"Just keep driving." Ikie encouraged him with a nudge from the pistol.

Randolph Bonney steered his luxury automobile north, up past the park, the National Guard Armory, the new post office, a half-dozen motels and art galleries, hardware stores and drugstores, a new lumber supply company, the Kit Carson Gas Works, a bunch of service stations, and the Dynamite Shrine complex—out of town. Irrigated farmland suddenly came up to the highway shoulders. Several more bars went by, then a truck stop and a gravel pit. After that, deserted mesaland dominated the landscape.

"Stop here," Fecundo said.

The co-op chief braked, lurching nervously onto a shoulder. Sagebrush carpeting stretched east into Midnight foothills above the Pueblo; it extended westward toward the Rio Grande Gorge. The four kidnappers got out and assembled in front of the Lincoln, waiting until a caravan of Winnebago Braves, Chiefs, and Indians rumbled by. Then they crossed the road at a deliberate, unhurried clip, their weapons in hand, cardboard boxes tucked under one arm. Walking into the waist-high sagebrush, they headed due west.

Outraged by this outrage, Randolph Bonney grabbed a .22 Ruger pistol from his glove compartment, banged outside, and was almost run down by a family from Georgia pulling an Airstream trailer decorated with ten-speed bicycles and Honda trail bikes. Unfazed, Bonney leaped across the road and started blasting away at the four old devils.

Fifty yards from the infuriated co-op executive, the kidnappers halted and turned around, fixing Bonney with doleful glares as he attempted to gun them down. His nine shots wreaked no apparent damage on the outlaws, but they had little interest in revenging his foolhardy play. Instead, while the powerful old man stood there paralyzed, the smoking pistol held uselessly at his side, Ikie, Fecundo, Max, and Bonifacio fixed him with their baleful features a few seconds longer, then about-faced again, and continued marching onto the mesa.

Randolph Bonney blinked stupidly. Heat waves made the kidnappers' bodies quiver; they went out of focus, losing shape. Bonney rubbed his eyes, and when he took his fists away, the men had evaporated into the bristling clarion atmosphere.

Dazed by the experience, Bonney stumbled back across the highway, narrowly missing death as a chartered Greyhound toting Baptists from Hollyhock, Nebraska, veered to avoid him. The co-op chief dropped behind the wheel of his big automobile, wondering if the experience had actually happened. By the time he executed a U-turn, almost colliding with a pickup truck carrying nuns from Muskogee, Oklahoma, Bonney had convinced himself he was crazy. Nobody would believe his story; he had no evidence; he would let the matter rest. No point in making a fool of himself by tattling on a group of demoniac old ghosts who had dissolved before his very eyes.

# A
# GHOST
# IN THE
# MUSIC

# III

# The Mexican Burro
# and the
# Gabacho Butterfly

ALMOST EXACTLY FOUR DECADES after the arrival of her father in Chamisaville, April Delaney came home hoping to help people like Virgil Leyba, Juan Ortega, Espeedie Cisneros, and Perfecto Torres throw a wrench into the Betterment of Chamisaville.

Times had changed significantly since Rodey McQueen first spied gold in the form of a pugnacious naked blacksmith wearing boots and a single rose grinning from out the center of that Vallecitos holocaust. A lawyer now decorated every Chamisaville street corner, a mouthpiece held court in every café. Bob Moose had married, multiplied fruitfully, and helped railroad McQueen and Moose and Sons into the largest game in town, controlling the First State Bank, Moose Insurance and Real Estate, McQueen and Moose Construction, the conservancy district board, the ski valley, and a half-dozen interrelated enterprises scattered throughout the county. Little Stryzpks galore, decked out in Coke bottles if not wheelchairs, shuffled land like cards from several prosperous real estate and entrepreneurial offices, banking bundles off quiet title suits alone. Aside from his car dealership, real-estate office, wrecking yard, conservancy-board position, and other legal endeavors, Randolph Bonney was president of the General Custer Rural Electric Co-op. He also had connections to Futz and Company, the first brokerage firm in town, on the tips of whose financial tentacles dangled a bunch of little Bonneys who had recently graduated from Harvard Law School. Dr. Alfred Gracie Lamont had contributed a shingle of his own, Melissa. DA Damacio Mares also copartnered the firm of Moose (Bob, Jr.), Mares, and Leyba, the latter Virgil's son who had broken his father's heart long ago by joining the cabal now moving in, after forty years' maneuvering, to slash Chamisaville's jugular.

212

Some said that Junior, town attorney and cofounder of the El Conquistador Peoples' Jug, was the cleverest lawbooks around. Others knowingly called him the richest Chicano in Chamisa County. And yet others predicted that one day his old man would barge into the Prince of Whales Café, shove aside the happy-go-lucky waitress, Gloria Armijo, stagger back to the rearmost shadowy booth where Junior would no doubt be conferring clandestinely with a cigar-smoking criminal from Detroit, and plant a bullet in his kid's sternum for going so far astray.

Which is more than likely a solution both Rodey McQueen and his wife might gladly have visited upon their own daughter. For as soon as April returned home several months prior to the Big Freeze, she commenced raising all kinds of hell.

For starters, April gave a series of slide shows on her Cuban experience, commandeering for this purpose not only several private homes, but also managing to insinuate her bald-faced revolutionary rhetoric into both the basement community room of the First State Bank and the Cipi García Meeting Room of the State University's Rodey McQueen Library, an imposing structure built, stocked, and funded in perpetuity by the benevolent despot himself shortly after a 1956 gallbladder operation had emphasized his personal mortality.

Next, April began a local moratorium committee against the Vietnam war, recruiting such diverse locals as George Parker, Espeedie Cisneros, Celestino Lucero, and Pat Gee-Gee. They circulated petitions advocating the impeachment of President Richard Nixon.

As if this weren't enough, April refounded the *El Clarín*. And, principally aided by Virgil, Juan Ortega, and Flakey Jake Martínez and his son Anthony (who had survived Vietnam and recently become a prominent spokesman for the Pueblo Anti-Electricity Coalition), April had so far managed to publish the *El Clarín* twice a month. It was as vituperative a rag as ever enraged a power structure, a newspaper that specialized in lambasting the shenanigans of the Mooses, McQueens, Lamonts, Stryzpks, Bonneys, and little Leybas in no uncertain terms.

On many fronts, during the year of the Big Freeze and other disasters, the *El Clarín* was not only vocal, but downright obnoxious and embarrassing as well. When January's ice gave way to a glorious February sunshine, threatening ski-valley operations, Rodey McQueen stuck a needle into

213

Mayor J. B. LeDoux's town council, which abruptly pillaged four thousand dollars from Chamisaville's general operating fund to hire an itinerant Texas snowmaker named Homer Glasgow. Even as Glasgow and an assistant commenced burning silver iodide–saturated coal in oil drums transported about by two coelacanthine pickups, McQueen was convincing the county commissioners to go halves with the state weather control and cloud modification commission in seeding anything resembling a vaporous entity that floated within ten miles of his elaborate ski basin.

SNOWJOB! OUR TAXES HELP MCQUEEN GROW FATTER! the *El Clarín* hollered, as eight feet of new white powder fell from raped clouds covering the Mosquito Valley.

"What the hell is town General Fund money and county property taxes doing in the pockets of a private enterprise that pays our local people slave wages to scrub toilets and wash dishes for fat cats from Chicago, New York, and L.A. in those lodges up there?" April wrote. She added that the town council had decided to allocate snowmaking funds in a closed meeting, thus violating newly enacted state open meetings laws. Calling for an attorney general's investigation, she then published a full Mosquito Valley stockholder's report, printing the profits and dividends figures in bold type, and further accenting them with an in-depth analysis of the ski valley's wage scale, where top locals considered themselves lucky to knock down $2.10 an hour. Anthony Martínez's cartoon, depicting an obese pop-eyed Rodey McQueen on skis eating a drumstick-shaped small farmer à la Goya, amplified the general picture. And Juan Ortega completed the rout by interviewing retired schoolteacher, and La Ciénega farmer, Espeedie Cisneros, who cried:

"They've taken almost all our water, and now they're taking our taxes, which should be used to feed our poor children in a school lunch program or something. What good is that snow gonna do us local people anyway? I don't own no skis or no boots, I can't afford that crap. I can't even afford to rent that crap. And if I could somehow squeeze that much dinero out of the twenty-seven hundred I earn a year, how the hell am I gonna pay for a tow ticket just to get myself onto the mountain? Or for an instructor so that me and my kids won't break our legs and wind up getting crippled for life by that inept carnicero over in the county morgue, Dr. Lamont, who

214

owns a big piece of the valley himself, I heard tell? I bet Lamont even gets out there every morning, before the tow starts, to build up those whatchamacallits, those 'mugglies' on the beginner's slope, so he can make another million pesos off all the poor jerks up there that break their legs."

On page two, Virgil Leyba's rambling dissertation dissected the financial empire of the town attorney, who had assured the council they possessed a legal right to allocate funds for the creation of Mosquito Valley snow. *I.e.*, Virgil stuck it to his own son, detailing Junior's credits, which began with legal counselor to the Catholic Church and board director of the El Conquistador Peoples' Jug, and ended in a summary of Junior's various land parcels within Chamisaville, Cañoncito, Mota Llano, La Lomita, La Ciénega, and Ranchitos Abajo and Arriba that totaled 3,812 acres.

"Which, for a thirty-nine-year-old Spanish-speaking lawyer in this neck of the woods, where the average small farmer's landholding is three acres, ain't bad," Virgil commented acidly.

Lest McQueen himself suspect he was getting off easy, page three, written and photographed by the Pueblo teenager, Anthony Martínez, contrasted McQueen and Moose Construction Company's handling of a Mutual Help–Turnkey HUD poverty housing development, for which they had the contract, with their construction of Mosquito Valley summer and winter vacation homes. The Valley houses were handsome, custom-built chalets catering to every whim of the idle rich occupying them for no more than several weeks every year. But the sixteen little Mutual Help rush-jobs plopped into a La Lomita dust bowl were unadulterated garbage. Six months after completion their foundations cracked, houses tilted, heating insulation disintegrated, stone facings collapsed, and roofs leaked like sieves. *El Clarín* editors urged the impoverished Mutual Help dwellers to desert the houses and file suit against McQueen and Moose, HUD, the Turnkey board, and anybody else with fingers even remotely stuck into the pie.

Shortly after this *El Clarín*, warm weather arrived with a vengeance. The snowmelt provided by Rodey McQueen's cloud-seeding operations promised to be the best in history. Forgiving the tyrant his winter trespasses, a few surviving native farmers like Espeedie Cisneros and Celestino Lucero, men who had all but given up the struggle for

215

land and water, unearthed their hoes and shovels, deliriously clearing irrigation ditches, digging them deeper, appending new laterals. They leveled land and prepared it to receive wheat, corn, and beans. And for several weeks feverish activity occurred on that portion of the valley land remaining in stubborn agricultural hands—until too much of a good thing proved bad.

For of late, given subsistence farming's decline during conservancy district scamming and the general Betterment of Chamisaville, most old-timers had grown somewhat rusty at their bucolic trades. Hence, when the old boys responded to the wonderful cloud-seeding runoff of liquid gold by leaping whole hog into heavily expanded agricultural endeavors, they soon discovered their ancient bodies couldn't take the strain. And wise old men, who for centuries had quietly survived utilizing a lean and hungry style while awaiting deliverance, were abruptly executed by abundance. Their tattered hearts fibrillated, going haywire as they tottered lustily from one soggy field to the next, growing the most bounteous crop in three decades. And for a grisly moment, during this richest of all possible springtimes, Claude Parker was stacking the bodies of hoary octogenarians like cordwood upon his embalming tables. Almost all the old folks arrived at the funeral home with their irrigation boots on, a few still clutching shovels, a pained expression of puzzled joy lighting up their toothless fizzogs. In this manner, another handful of important dynasties died, and many more important land tracts were "shaken loose," as Moe Stryzpk had so aptly put it years before. Placed mournfully on the market, they were immediately gobbled up by the buyers and sellers of modern progressive dreams.

POISON SNOWMELT! wailed the *El Clarín*, the only news organ making a connection. And although the Mooses and McQueens scoffed publicly, they bridled in private, wondering how to stifle old Rodey's daughter. And as for April, she launched troops of newsboys each time her disquieting paper surfaced, selling every copy by hand so it couldn't be suppressed at a newsstand or bought up by her old man.

In fact, April often quartered the town herself, a curious dynamic gringa sometimes accompanied by her two children, all three of them hawking the rag.

And observing her, watching April Delaney in action,

nobody would have guessed that her body harbored a fatal disease.

On a Sunday shortly after the fourth *El Clarín* hit the streets, Rodey McQueen and his wayward daughter had a virulent discussion. Gathered at the dinner table were Cynthia McQueen, close friends Bob (the elder) Moose and his wife Letitia, April's kids, and Junior and Charlotte Leyba.

The last time McQueen had asked his daughter to say grace, over ten years ago, she had replied: "Good food, good meat, good God, let's eat." Today, when he inadvertently again entrusted her with the benediction, she responded:

"Let us give thanks to the Rockefellers, Mellons, Carnegies, and Morgans who made it possible for us Americans to wallow in all this scrumptious gluttony, consuming a goodly sixty percent of the planet's resources each year while two-thirds of the world is starving to death— amen."

McQueen banged his fist so hard against the table the pot roast jumped half off its platter, a wine bottle tipped over, and glasses and silverware clinked, rattled, and danced.

"God dammit, April, you're going too far!" the tycoon roared, scrambling to right the wine bottle. "Every time you open your mouth, you stir up everybody like a goddam rattlesnake entering a dog town!"

"Now, now, *now*," Cynthia cried. "Please, let's not begin, this is Sunday. This is the Lord's day, we're not going to have a fight. We simply just are not going to have a fight, I won't allow it."

"Well, I am not going to have my daughter, under *my* roof, taking this table in vain!" McQueen sputtered, shaking the carving knife in April's direction. "If you don't want to eat our food, you don't have to attend our table. If you want to shit on God, go shit on Him someplace else! Make fun of me in your home, not in my home."

"Oh dear, please let it ride," said Letitia Moose. "She's just being funny to get our goat."

"I am *not* doing it to get anybody's goat," April said. "I'm just doing it so that perhaps one little fact of life might insinuate itself into your parboiled atrophied brains, that's all. God has nothing to do with it, and nobody's making fun of anybody."

217

"I said we are not going to have a fight, not at this table, not on such a beautiful Sunday afternoon, I simply will not tolerate it," Cynthia said.

"You never tolerate anything, Mother." April grabbed a toothpick, angrily stabbing at her teeth. "Everytime anybody threatens to wake up at this table, you've got to slip them another Mickey Finn. God forbid there should be controversy around here. God forbid there should be a little life and agitation!"

"Do you hear how she's talking to me?" Cynthia complained to the financier. "Dale, do you hear how our daughter is talking to me in the presence of these our guests and our friends?"

"Of course I hear it. What am I, deaf?"

Letitia Moose tried to change the subject. "I hear the opera guild is planning to raffle a calf so that some deserving little Indian child can attend *The Magic Flute* in the capital this August."

"I might as well tell you," the rubicund tyrant snapped at April as he butchered the roast, "that we are thinking seriously of suing you and your *El Clarín* crowd for libel."

"Dale, not at the table! You promised."

"This is *my* table and I'll goddam well say what I please at it!"

"Maybe me and my *El Clarín* will sue you and your Fascist crowd for genocide!" April snapped.

Bob Moose, a pale flabby man whose large nose had gotten crimson with age, launched another diversionary tactic. "If there's going to be fighting here, why not postpone it for the moment? After dinner you can put the gloves on and have it out on the lawn. Politics and digestion make terrible bedfellows."

"What's so fucking awful about fighting?" April cried. There was a shocked silence.

"Mommy, is Grandpa going to hit you?" Tina asked.

"Grandpa never hit anybody in his life," Cynthia said coldly.

"Yes, dear, Grandpa is going to hit me. He's going to punch me in the stomach and stab me with the carving knife, and cut off my ears. After that he'll gouge out my eyeballs with his thumbs. And then he's gonna throw me into the driveway and run over me with his great big Lincoln Continental until I'm flat as a pancake."

"No he's not really, is he for reals?" the big-eyed little girl asked her brother. Duane rolled his eyes sarcastically, pretending to know it all: "Of course he isn't—is he, Mom?"

Charlotte Leyba asked, "Why are you saying those things, April? Why do you put such terrible ideas into their heads?"

"I'm joking, Charlotte. I'm being humorous, get it? Doesn't anybody around here have a sense of humor?"

Junior looked up darkly. "What's so funny about getting sued for libel?"

"I dunno, Junior. What's so funny about being the biggest vendido in Chamisa County?"

"April, I'm sorry to say this, but you are truly making an ass of yourself." Bob Moose scraped a blob of mint jelly off his thigh. "With apologies to your family, but you have become a rather unseemly spectacle in this town. Whether you know it or not, people are laughing at you behind your back."

"Oh come on, Bob. Stop wearing a girdle, let your stomach hang out, learn to relax a little."

"We aren't going to say these things at my Sunday table!—" Cynthia groaned, even as her husband banged his fist down again, striking the rim of a butter dish and flipping a yellow pad up at his face: it stuck against his forehead.

With that, Letitia Moose caught a broccoli chunk in her windpipe and began choking: Bob slammed her back.

Ignoring the butter pad, McQueen said, "April, for a great many years I have been diligently trying to help this town raise itself by its bootstraps by bolstering its economy. I have initiated projects creating literally thousands of jobs. When I first came here all this town had was fleas and empty pockets, right, Bob?"

"Right, Dale."

"Why doggone it," McQueen added, daring to be folksy, "the North-South Highway was just a little itty-bitty dirt path. And we've got an airport now and a bridge over the Rio Grande Gorge and—and I don't like to brag, but when we kissed this ugly toad-frog of a two-bit tank town, it went and turned into a prince, it really did. And we like the way it's progressing. And pretty soon this is going to be as prosperous a little town as ever—"

"You've run this pathetic dog-eared valley like it was your own personal satrapy," April interrupted. "You initiated projects like the Cañoncito Reservoir—knowing they would never hold water—in order to tax poor people

219

off their land and into oblivion! Now you're going to put electricity into the Pueblo so that people who barely earn enough bread to buy groceries can dangle even more desperately from the time-payment, all-American hook!"

"Satrapies yet," McQueen barked gruffly. "What's a satrapy?"

"Just can the hominy, will you, Father? You wanted to talk about suing for libel?—let's talk about suing for libel. You drop a suit on us, gentlemen, and I'll roll that suit into a conical shape and shove it right up your collective you-know-whats."

*"Go to your room!"* Cynthia exclaimed.

"God, we spoiled you rotten!" McQueen struggled mightily to control his temper. "Oh but did we ever spoil you rotten. Looking for humility in you, or even a little bit of common human politeness, is like looking for hair on a goddam newt! Boy, I wish I had taken off my belt when you were a little tacker, I really wish I had done that."

"So go ahead and take off your belt now," April grinned cockily.

"Who'll protect you if I sue?"

"I'll hire Junior here because he's such a liberal and conscientious and compassionate person."

Junior stared at her icily.

"Be serious. You might actually be in some kind of trouble."

"So who else, Father? Virgil will do it. Or perhaps I'll call somebody down at the capital ACLU, although those delicate birds wouldn't know a civil right from a dead magpie if one fell in their laps. I don't know. First you have to sue."

"Virgil can't fight his way free of the El Gaucho Bar anymore, let alone out of a paper bag." Bob Moose surreptitiously brushed a scalloped potato off his thigh onto the floor. "Uh, with apologies to you, Junior, of course."

Junior shrugged and dabbled his fingers in a fingerbowl.

"Is Grandpa really gonna take off his belt?" Tina asked.

"Of course not, stupid," Duane assured her.

"Grandpa only takes off his belt and beats up poor people," April told Tina. As she said this, her eyes flicked across Junior's face: he was gazing at her darkly, threatening in a way she did not completely understand. And as their eyes locked for a second, he gave her the sort of chill nobody else at that table could have raised. Their long-ago affair was an adventure April very much regretted today, largely because of how Junior had turned out—she did not trust him, despised his cynical, grasping politics and world view, and was ashamed of having granted so much of herself to him, a gift she half expected Junior to use against her in a terribly ugly way some day.

April said, "Oh, the hell with it. What's the use? Father, I don't know how you tick, really I don't. I don't know why any of you function the way you do, I don't understand the motivations or what makes the Betterment of Chamisaville fun. I try to picture it, really I do. I try to picture you in your youth perched atop Nobody Mountain looking down into the valley and having a dream, maybe even a good dream including milk and honey for everybody, I don't know. And suddenly you and Bob Moose here and Moe Stryzpk and all the other men running this town awakened, saying, 'We're seventy years old, and it's almost over, and it's not complete yet, we haven't achieved the dream.' Causing a panic that immediately generated a frantic chorus of 'now or never!' Explaining why some button got pushed—"

McQueen said, "Don't you pity me, April. I have done it all. I have *dominated* the big old crap game of life! And I feel goddam good about it."

"Who would like coffee?" Cynthia asked gaily.

"Don't you *ever* pity me," McQueen reiterated. "Don't you ever use that patronizing tone with your father." Pushing back his chair, he stood up, and, placing both hands on the table, leaned forward, an enormous, enraged specter facing his daughter.

"Because if I want to, April, I can snap you in two, just like that, so's you won't know if you're afoot or on horseback! I can say, 'The game's over, go play with your little dolls now, I'm not amused anymore.' So don't you *ever* use that tone with me again!"

Abruptly, McQueen left the dining room. Passing through the kitchen and a utility room, he stormed downstairs into a basement game room, fixed himself a straight gin on the rocks at the bar, and racked some balls on the pool table. Then he stood there, a drink in one hand, the cue stick in his other hand, gazing for a moment with watering eyes at nicely framed photographs on the walls. Of his daughter April McQueen, the spunkiest kid around, gleaming in riding outfits on golden roans, in bathing suits, in clean white tennis clothes, framed by untold blue ribbons and tiny bronze plaques; always a winner.

He had loved her then. And McQueen loved her now more than he would ever dare admit. April, the most precious thing he had ever touched or birthed, had been his single most truthful piece of luck. McQueen adored her, and was uncommonly grateful for her return. April also frightened him, because she alone in his life had moved him to feel a tremendous compassion, she alone had hurt him to the point of tears. Cynthia did not know the extent of his feeling, for he had never let it show. McQueen had always been ashamed of April's ability to make him emotionally vulnerable. He hated her for placing him in a position not on her side. Hence, April was the biggest heartache of his life, the only person that he had truly, *viscerally* cared about. She did not know this and would never learn his secret: the old man was not one to reveal an Achilles' heel. Yet he would have given anything to make peace, holding her in his arms. Nowadays they shook hands—formally, forlornly—while McQueen had dreams of holding his daughter tenderly, protecting her from the world, enfolding April in the security of his wealth and his narrow, all-encompassing love.

The old man knocked off his liquor in a single gulp. Then, leaning over, he carefully lined up the break shot, fired his cue ball into the rack, and the balls broke apart on impact, spraying as if by magic into each pocket on the table—he had sunk every one!

McQueen confronted the cue ball, alone against the smooth green nap, shining mysteriously . . . like his daughter.

Banging his forehead in anguish, the puzzled tyrant plastered the heel of his palm with butter.

BY THE MIDDLE OF MAY, to electrify or not to electrify the Pueblo had became the hot issue. The *El Clarín*'s resident cartoonist, foreign correspondent, and delegate to the Pueblo's Anti-Electricity Coalition, Anthony Martínez, assumed electricity would garrote his people.

"The average cash income for a family of four in my Pueblo is $836 a year," he wrote passionately. "So how can we afford telephones, freezers, TVs, Water Piks, electric can openers, humidifiers, movie projectors, stoves, and well pumps? It's crazy. We don't need the debtor's society of the white man, we got enough trouble to hone our ulcers on without this. Randolph Bonney and his Custer Electric Co-op want to sink their revolting meathooks into our tribal chest and shock out the surviving pieces of Pueblo heart. For a thousand years we survived minus electricity; this current plot will destroy us!"

The name of that mysterious new organization called the Northland Grazing Association, perhaps connected in lethal ways to Pueblo electrification, kept cropping up in various suspect contexts. And although some people had heard about it, nobody knew where it came from, what and who it was comprised of, and where it was going.

Icarus Suazo, enigmatic as always, kept mum on that subject, also on most other subjects. And he continued juggling court suits and Pueblo finances in hopes of recapturing Pueblo land within Chamisaville, at the same time that he sought to win the sixty-year-old battle for those fifty thousand national forest acres and the sacred Albino Pine Tree guarding the Midnight River's headquarters.

Rumors implied Icarus would allow Pueblo electrification as part of a complex kickback-bribery scheme successfully terminating the Albino Pine struggle, robbing Pedro to pay Polito, extorting the land exchange payoff and myriad related gifts from Randolph Bonney's electric co-op crowd (and their political mentors) in return for an open season on the gullible, ill-informed, totally defenseless Pueblo electrical market bonanza.

Tempers flared. Imaginations scampered. For her part in opposing Pueblo electrification, April Delaney received an obscene telephone call that ended with a threat on her life. And at 2:00 A.M. one night, members of the Pueblo's Anti-Electricity Coalition entered the plaza and burned effigies of Randolph Bonney, Icarus Suazo, and Rodey McQueen.

Next day, two Forest Service signs adjacent to Pueblo land were burned. In a rage, McQueen telephoned his daughter.

"It's your goddam rag!" he shouted. "You're baiting these people, trying to foment trouble! You got everybody in this pretty little town hotter than a fucking fox in a pepper patch! I wouldn't be at all surprised if it was actually your crew over there, you and that brash juvenile delinquent, what's his name—Anthony Martínez! And I bet Virgil has something to do with it also. That sneaky Mexican was a criminal in the Mexican revolution!"

"Father, grab hold of yourself and start reasoning like a human being! And take your racist attitudes about Virgil and shove them up your puritanical Texas asshole!"

She slammed down the telephone. Almost immediately it rang again: *"April—!"*

"Don't start again, Father! Not on me, not on Anthony, not on Virgil, not on the *El Clarín!* You have something to say to me, you say it like a civilized human being!"

"Look who's talking about civilized human beings! *Puritanical Texas assholes!*"

"If the shoe fits, wear it!" And then, because their shouting match was so ridiculous, she burst out laughing.

Incensed, McQueen stammered, "What are you doing, are you laughing? Are you laughing at *me?*"

"At us, Father. Believe it or not, at us. Are you listening to the things we're saying?"

"I don't see what's so goddam funny. They burned down two Forest Service signs last night, and that amounts to treason. People are running around here like a bear in a hog pen, and all you can think to do is blasphemize your own father?"

"You quit blasphemizing my friends, and I'll start treating you decent, not until."

And she hung up on him once more.

To further clarify their position on Pueblo electricity, the *El Clarín* published a long editorial by Flakey Jake Martínez:

. . . Not that electricity in the Pueblo, per se, need be unmitigated evil personified. Times are tough, native people could use pumps to deliver their water instead of lugging it in pails from the river. Refrigerators are an honorable way to keep food from spoiling. And as much as anyone else we want radios, record players, and TVs to brighten up our lives a little. Good lighting at night would aid the more studious among us who enjoy reading and studying after sunset. Telephones are wonderful inventions which not only tighten communication between peoples, but also save many persons during emergencies. And humidifiers and vaporizers could probably salvage some lives annually lost to croup and pneumonia. No question but that electricity could be a benevolent servant, helping maintain, rather than destroy, our culture.

The problem, of course, is the framework in which

it will arrive, gliding into our Pueblo not as a servant of the people so much as just another aspect of maximum-feasible-profits America overjoyed at having yet another market to exploit and subdue. Like a tidal wave, electricity will overpower the lives of our subsistence culture where the average cash income, per family of four, is $836 a year. I can picture it already. The *Chamisaville News* will run ebullient full-page co-op ads touting electricity's virtues, without once mentioning the expense. And, no different from the rest of Yanqui America, natives will line up a hundred deep to ask that telephones be installed. Just like housewives and husbands in Paramus and Possom Trot, they'll line up for hours purchasing mixmasters, blenders, waffle irons, and washing machines. And when the dust has settled, even before initial electric bills are issued, the entire Pueblo will be so deeply in debt simply from purchasing various electrically served appliances, that it will never get off the hook.

To meet their payments, people will auction off entire cattle herds, selling cheap in their desperation to hang onto what they have barely been able to use. In no time at all, the reservation will become a community of frantic individuals fighting like mad to avoid repossessions, robbing each other's radios and TVs and selling them at Irving Newkirk's pawnshop or on the black market to people with money outside the Pueblo, in order to meet payments on their own freezers, refrigerators, and telephones.

In this way a fabric woven over ten centuries will start to come apart, simply because we native people can't afford the fulfillment of market-created desires.

Even me, I'll probably be sucked in, I'm only human. My wife Gloria will beg me for a phone, force me to give in, wring her hands delightedly as it's installed, immediately grab it off the hook and call up relatives in Fort Thompson, South Dakota, Anadarko, Oklahoma, and Needles, California, and nearly faint when a bill for $120 arrives. That sum being her entire budget for food, medicine, clothing, laundry, and amusement during the upcoming eight weeks. I'll howl, and rip the phone cord out of the wall. But Gloria will throw such a tantrum I'll wind

225

up paying a telephone lineman an extra $26 the following month to reinstall the pernicious instrument.

"After all, what if somebody needs us in an emergency?" Gloria will reason. And me? I'll scream "For eight hundred years we lived without it!" and tie into her like a windmill going berserk. And it won't be just me. All over the Pueblo similar scenes will be enacted, families capsizing over the added tension of insoluble financial burdens.

Immediately, you'll be able to buy native labor even cheaper than before, because we Pueblo dwellers will be even more desperate for some cash, any cash, to meet some part, any part, of our new obligations.

Crime will leap, instability will grow. The timeless character of our land-based culture will become less timeless, even as our land-based culture becomes less land-based. Farmers will no longer be able to survive at a subsistence level—they'll need cash on the barrelhead.

With a television in every home spouting English twenty-four hours a day, the Pueblo language will suffer. Children, who previously spent all day listening to their grandparents' stories and advice, passing history on from generation to generation, now—incapacitated by this spellbinding gadget—will spend their daylight hours gooning at the boob tube. And worn-out mothers will let them watch. "TV is a good babysitter," they'll rationalize. Maybe so, but it will rub out our ways, injecting a gabacho culture.

Naturally, the Pueblo divorce rate will triple. The suicide rate, among a population with a high suicide rate to begin with, will quadruple. Murder and robbery will take great leaps forward. Kids will quit school earlier for jobs to help their families meet time payments. Illiteracy will surge. Bombarded by advertisements touting the virtues of a great consumer culture out there, many natives will soon decide they can no longer survive, look good, or be sexually attractive without this hair spray, those clothes, that Mustang. And they'll wriggle more securely onto the hook obtaining these life-style accoutrements.

Not only that. But how can men and women and boys and girls go to the kiva for weeks on end during our time-honored traditional rituals when they have to hold down nine-to-five jobs six days a week earning the pittance that pays the interest on the loans for their refrigerators, electric coffee pots, and vacuum cleaners? Self-sufficient for countless generations, smoking our own meat, drying or canning fruits and vegetables, now we'll chuck everything we shoot, butcher, or grow into freezers. But many of us won't be able to afford new freezers. So we'll stack supplies in ancient, fifth-hand models, which will promptly go on the blink. And, before we owners, completely unknowledgeable in electric matters, can repair the freezers, a year's supply of homegrown nourishment will rot and we'll go deeper into hock buying replacement goods from the local supermarkets. Or, on the verge of starvation, we'll bicker among each other, have knock-down drag-out battles, and our families will split up. It'll be everybody for themselves in a cash economy.

Sometimes when a freezer breaks down, the owner will frantically ask somebody to fix it, and that somebody will no doubt charge an arm and a leg, being the most valuable person around, salvaging entire yearly food supplies. Naturally, Chamisaville freezer repairmen will soon become almost as filthy rich as Chamisaville lawyers.

Of course, when my wife demands a freezer, I'll decide to beat the odds by learning repair and maintenance beforehand. I'll locate a library book, and bone up but good. With a real sense of security, then, we will load the thing to the brim. But no sooner have all our earthly goods been iced, than a series of widespread electrical brownouts will burn out the motor. And no sooner have I paid exorbitantly for another motor, than the electric co-op will start suffering mysterious blackouts. These blackouts are a matter of commercial course in a freely competitive consumer society. Discouraging self-sufficiency, they assure a constant trade at the town supermarkets, which have auxiliary generators that keep *their* food from rotting. Given the sort of commercial margin *we* live on, however, native Americans won't be able to accept these blackouts philosophically, because, once ruined, we have no resources for reestablishing a food supply.

The blackouts will grow so frequent that I'll take to staying up all night, every night, staring at a light bulb, waiting for it to flicker and die. When it dies,

I'll jump out of bed, race into town, buy ice at the PDQ, roar home, and dump the cubes into the freezer, keeping our food until the electricity returns.

One night, racing for ice during a blackout, and exhausted from a thousand sleepless vigils, I'll catch a tire on a soft shoulder, overturning our pickup. I'll emerge from the vehicle unharmed, but the truck will be a total wreck.

So I'll go even more deeply into debt buying a small freezer for making ice that I can dump into my large freezer during the blackouts.

Pretty soon this idea will catch on, and everybody in the Pueblo who owns a freezer will also keep another freezer handy making ice to dump into the food freezer during the blackouts.

But as soon as everybody has hocked their souls acquiring auxiliary ice-making freezers, the blackouts will cease, leaving all us idiotic folks with useless electrical appendages on our porches. And after the blackout moratorium has been in effect for a while, people will sell their standby freezers for a song in order to meet payments on a car or an electric organ. But as soon as the last auxiliary ice-making machine has been sold, at a tremendous loss, to the salesperson it was bought from initially, the blackout plague will commence again, sending everybody running townward to buy back, at tremendously inflated prices, the auxiliary freezers they just unloaded for next to nothing. After that, having learned the bitter concept of "insurance," we Pueblo people with freezers will always keep an auxiliary freezer full of ice handy, even though—so long as we have those backup freezers around—no blackouts will occur.

"That's it?" my son Anthony asked me the other day.

"In a nutshell," I replied.

"Still and all. If Icarus Suazo successfully works the trade-off he wants to, once electricity hits the Pueblo the sacred Albino Pine land will belong entirely to our people, all fifty thousand acres—lock, stock, and barrel."

"I wouldn't bet on it, my son," I said.

MAYOR J. B. LeDoux sat in the gloom of his office, practically tarred and feathered with quivering cutworm moths whose wings were pasted to his sweaty brow and cheeks. He listened to Chamisaville's noises: taped church bells playing "God Bless America"; jackhammers ripping up sections of the plaza to get at a broken water main; the incessant new ski run blasting in the Mosquito Valley, an activity sending ripples of violent noise down through the canyon and over the dusty, steaming town like ocean breakers, eight hours a day, a rhythm which never ceased.

Almost as regular was the belligerent honking of some ten thousand tourists and local folks half smothered in dust and cutworm moths, caught in a traffic jam that had been unrelieved now (despite the erstwhile efforts of the police chief, Fernando Popper) for eight days, simply because Chamisaville's lone traffic light was on the blink.

While some idiot from Randolph Bonney's electric co-op tried to determine which of the sophisticated traffic control device's twenty-seven thousand wires had been shorted out by the two thousand cutworm moths somehow squeezed into the airtight, hermetically sealed control cabinet, J. B. suddenly snarled, lumbered out to his car, and peeled away from the curb in a screech of slick rubber, almost sideswiping the aging newsboy, Little Kid Lujan.

Damacio Mares was locking up his law office for the day when J. B. LeDoux's car wheeled into the parking lot, and the mayor gave him a short beep. Fearing the worst, Damacio pocketed his keys and walked over to the mayor, whose face looked drawn even though he wore dark eyeglasses. J. B. made Damacio nervous, largely because the instability crippling the mayor was all too visible on the surface. J. B. rarely smiled these days, he had no sense of humor. In fact, he looked like somebody who might go berserk one day soon.

The DA said, "Hello, J. B. What's up?"

"I need some information. I thought maybe you could help."

"You know me, J. B. Any way I can, I like to help. So shoot."

"Well, what I'm basically concerned about is the Northland Grazing Association. What is it, who is it, what is it doing to my town, and why?"

Damacio said, "The Northland Grazing Association?"

"You heard me. What is its connection to Pueblo electrification?"

"I never heard of it."

229

"Listen, Damacio. I have been your friend in the past. You owe me some favors. Who is Joseph Bonatelli?"

"We all owe each other favors."

"Oh sure, I know that." J. B., confronted, backed down a little: he had no spine anymore. "I would just like to know what is going on under my nose in my own town —you know what I mean? Everybody and his brother seems to have heard of the Northland Grazing Association, except myself. How come?"

"Lord knows, J. B. Why pick on me? I know about my cases, and after that I know what I hear. We're all together in this town."

"My own kid, he's a junkie lives in the Dynamite Shrine Motor Court blasted out of his skull twenty-eight hours a day, *he's* heard of the Northland Grazing Association!" J. B. said angrily. "For all I know him and that one-legged Alfredo GeeGee are members of the board!"

"Hey, take it easy." Damacio was embarrassed by the mayor's lack of cool. "Please."

Closing his eyes, J. B. pinched the bridge of his nose with the thumb and middle finger of his left hand. Taking in a deep breath, he let it out slowly in a noisy fatigued sigh.

"Oh yeah," he said shakily. "Oh yeah."

"Well . . ." the DA said nervously, wanting to head for his car, but unable to leave because he was uncertain if the tête-à-tête had ended.

"There's something wrong," J. B. said vaguely. "Can you feel it?"

"Wrong? In what way?"

"There's just something wrong. Something unusual in the air. A different force in this town, doing something to it. This has always been a rough place, I suppose, but it's changed now. People were never frightened before, and now they are frightened. A thing is happening. You know who I thought I saw yesterday? A kid named Ralphito García, Remember him? He left town maybe forty years ago and drowned himself in the Pacific Ocean. Well, just last night, around I guess nine P.M., I went into the PDQ for a quart of milk, and while I'm paying Johnny Beaubien at the counter I glanced out the corner of my eye and I swear there was Ralphito García, half hidden by the magazine rack, with strands of seaweed dangling from his ears, reading a *Penthouse* magazine. Would you believe that the dead could be infiltrating back into town? All the old men and women and boys and girls who got screwed and up and died over these past handful of decades?"

"I don't get what you're driving at." J. B. was giving Damacio the creeps. The man had lost control, he ought not to speak of his son like that, in public. The DA felt a little queasy, because of course he did sort of understand what J. B. was talking about. Lately, the mood had changed in town: something ugly hovered; outsiders were poised to make mincemeat of them all. Men like the mayor and Junior Leyba were losing their grip. Even old Rodey McQueen, a generally good-natured and supremely confident tyrant, was irritable, abstracted, off-balance. Those burned Forest Service signs, the secret Pueblo electrification scam, had everybody on edge.

"Sometimes I'm just driving down the street," J. B. said, "and the air looks different. It looks clammy, as if filtered through a sinister fog. The town is jumpy. Even the sidewalks are quivering. The people are perturbed, they all seem to have presentiments of ghosts. And their noses look too big."

"Uh, J. B.—"

"You know what I heard?—I think it was over six months ago. I heard that they paroled Ikie Trujillo, Bonifacio Herrera, Fecundo Lavadie, and Max Jaramillo, and they came home without any fanfare, robbed Midnight Sporting Goods of a half-dozen guns and enough ammunition to wage war in Vietnam for ten years, and then disappeared. But I never read anything about it in the paper. And when I asked Bob Moose about the robbery he looked at me like I was *crazy*—"

"Uh, J. B.—"

"When it gets quiet—have you noticed that?" the mayor asked abruptly, changing his tone. "Suddenly it gets quiet, at very odd times, like a heart stopping for a beat, like that moment just before a thunderclap. And there's nothing. There's even no air just for a second. And Chamisaville is crouched like a little field mouse, frozen and scared stiff, waiting for the talons of Betterment, like a divebombing hawk, to strike. Remember how in the old days people used to bury a chunk of turquoise under a house they were building to protect it from collapse and bad luck and evil spirits? Well, it's as if somebody recently stole the chunk of turquoise we had buried under this entire town—"

"Uh, J. B.—"

"And then . . . and . . ."

He faltered. Damacio wanted to leave this floundering man, probably on the brink of a nervous breakdown. But as long as it seemed J. B. had something to say, Damacio could not leave him. The DA had always been extremely self-conscious about being impolite, he had always been unable to cut people off, fending for himself in social scenes. He listened when there was no point to listening, hooked by politeness. He listened when he really was not listening at all.

Nothing happened. J. B., staring through his windshield, seemed barely to breathe. And Damacio waited, sweating, slightly nauseous. They could hear dynamite blasts, muffled by the summer heat, rolling down the canyon from the Mosquito Valley: J. B.'s dynamite, his construction crew.

"And then—" the DA prompted.

"Nothing, Damacio. I guess nothing. This heat bothers me, that's all. Give my regards to the wife."

"Then I'll see you," the DA said tentatively.

J. B. turned his head, facing Damacio directly, his features yellowy and damp, and he gave the easily flustered DA a bright, skull-like, truly terrifying grin as he joked: "Not if I see you first."

His tires spitting chunks of gravel, J. B. spun out of there and careened back into traffic, almost clipping a couple of bumpers. Downtown, stewing in the snarl around the nonfunctioning traffic light, he beckoned Little Kid Lujan—or was his name Eduardo Mondragón?—over from the curb and handed him a dollar bill for a *Capital City Reporter,* saying, "Keep the change." But Little Kid fumbled his two-fingered hands among the nickels and dimes in his newsbag, the late sun—glinting off his Purple Hearts and Silver Stars—hurting J. B.'s eyes as the crippled vet came up with the correct amount in coins.

"I said keep the change," J. B. hissed, casting about to see if anybody was looking. "I don't need it, man."

"Go fuck yourself," Little Kid croaked, dropping the coins into J. B.'s lap.

Fernando Popper waved him on.

South of town, J. B. coasted into Irving Newkirk's trailer park. Threading uncomfortably between the garish modular houses, he arrived at a small green and white mobile home belonging to Celestino Lucero. Leaving the car running, J. B. got out and circled around to Celestino's backyard where the former Ranchitos Abajo dairyman had a tiny corral and a fifteen-foot-by-fifteen-foot vegetable garden. Inside the small corral lived a milk cow —Daisy—and her calf, two goats, a ewe and her lamb, a dozen chickens, two geese, several turkeys, and a rabbit hutch containing one female and seven little bunnies. Every day Celestino spent at least an hour shoveling manure over the fence into his pickup: he was engaged in this activity when J. B. appeared. His pet magpie —Tierra o Muerte the Twelfth—was perched on one shoulder strawbossing the job.

"Hola, primo," J. B. said, a pained friendly smile breaking from his sallow features. "Cómo le ha ido? Mucha mierda, qué no?"

"Lots of shit, that's right," Celestino replied in English, pitching another shovelful into his truck.

"Well, it's sure been a while since I've seen you," the mayor continued in Spanish, maintaining his painful grin. "I'm working hard these days. Too much work, in fact. Never do have the time to visit anybody—"

"What did you come for, eggs or tomatoes—or both?" Celestino asked gruffly, still speaking English.

J. B.'s smile withered. He could have killed this arrogant son of a bitch. But what the hell. He gave in, speaking English. "A dozen eggs Teresa said she needed. And three tomatoes." J. B. handed over an empty egg carton.

Celestino cast aside the shovel and entered his miniature hen coop. A moment later he came out, surrendering the filled egg carton without a word. The mayor noticed he hadn't bothered to polish the eggs; several displayed little smears of pullet shit.

Back in the garden, Celestino picked three ripe tomatoes. J. B. gave him two dollars, saying quickly, as he headed for his large automobile: "Keep the change."

"Just a minute, J. B., you only owe me a buck fifteen." Celestino dug among jingling coins, removed his hand, and counted eighty-five cents into one palm.

"I said it's okay, man. Keep the change, all right?"

Ignoring him, Celestino stuck his hand through the window, letting the coins slide onto J. B.'s lap. As he did so, Tierra o Muerte the Twelfth suddenly scrawked, "Chinga tu madre, mama tu padre, chupa tu hermana, *cabrón!*"

"You should wash that bird's beak with soap—"

J. B. LeDoux wheeled out of there, bitter tears in his eyes. Light like milk made crimson by droplets of human blood flowed slowly over the sacred mountain. The mayor waved at Randolph Bonney heading south in the other lane, but—preoccupied, no doubt, with business thoughts —the co-op chief failed to notice J. B., and did not return the salutation.

A THICKENING SPRINGTIME brought little victories, and bigger losses. Randolph Bonney, the Mooses, and Rodey McQueen, accompanied by their guest, Joseph Bonatelli, and other various and sundry members of the Kiwanis– chamber of commerce–Anglo Axis gang, nosed their enormous wine-colored automobiles onto Pueblo land, disappearing into Ed Lange's pink BIA school-building where Icarus Suazo, Denzil Spivey and the Forest Service mafia, and a shadowy huddle of Pueblo elders waited to hash out the electricity agreement. When the wine-colored automobiles left the reservation land at dusk their oc-cupants' pale faces wore perplexed, concerned expressions. Icarus was stalling. Rumors decreed the Pueblo might close itself off from tourists. Chamisaville merchants snarled, threatening to close down the Dynamite Fetish factory in retaliation.

SO CLOSE, ALREADY! Anthony Martínez suggested in the *El Clarín.*

There are no Pueblo people in supervisory positions. Safety conditions stink. The machines are never re-paired or replaced. The people can't earn more than $2.00 an hour, and every time they try organizing a union the organizers are fired. There are no workers' benefits. Rodey McQueen is leasing the building free from the Town of Chamisaville, yet the Pueblo is responsible for repairs. On top of everything else, the Federal Government's Indian Vocational Train-ing Act is subsidizing half the salaries of Pueblo workers while they learn; then, their training over, McQueen fires the trainees and hires a new batch in order to keep the federal handouts flowing.

The newspaper also printed an Espeedie Cisneros fable entitled "The Mexican Burro and the Gabacho Butterfly." To wit:

It seems that one day a downtrodden, bitter, starving Mejicano burro was plodding listlessly through a field of lovely indigo asters when his jaundiced eye was attracted by a beautiful rainbow-colored gabacho butterfly fluttering just above the smiling heads of the pretty flowers. "Follow me, burro desgraciado," said the butterfly in a husky provocative voice. "Keep your eyes fixed on my exquisite wings and I promise to lead you to the City of Juaja, where everything is frilly—and ducks and geese fall out of the sky, already baked in chili!" So the burro trotted after the butterfly, his gaze fixed on the gorgeous insect . . . and immediately tripped over a log, breaking one leg. Still, the poor burro had had so much misfortune in life, he couldn't reject the promise of that gabacho butterfly, and hurried after the dancing insect on three legs. But a moment later, with his eyes still glued to the pretty gabacho bug, the burro tumbled into a pit and broke two more limbs. "Get up, get up!" cried the gabacho butterfly. "We're almost there. Follow me and I'll lead you to the City of Juaja, where there are two streams of milk and honey, and three mountains made of tea!" So the crippled Mejicano burro struggled onto his one good leg, and was hopping across a highway on that pogo-stick appendage desperately chasing after the tantalizing gabacho mariposa, when he was hit and killed by a Cadillac car carrying four gabachos—a banker, a real estate developer, an agribusinessman, and a state chota.

Apparently a stalemate existed. The Albino Pine sacred land suit, tied up in sixteen district and federal courts, slouched toward an undetermined conclusion and had the Pueblo very much on edge. Icarus Suazo's yellow pickup could be seen parked beside Randolph Bonney's wine-colored Continental for several hours a day in the Custer Electric Co-op parking lot on Fiesta Street. Complex and hairy deals hung in abeyance. The Anti-Electricity Coalition leafleted Chamisaville with an Anthony Martínez cartoon depicting an old Indian farmer in the electric chair: the flyer claimed electricity costs would bankrupt the impoverished Pueblo dwellers and insinuated that Randolph Bonney, Rodey McQueen, and other locals, in cahoots with "outside" money, were negotiating toward enormous illegal gains connected to Pueblo electrification.

Then one morning around 6:00 A.M., Chamisaville's spanking-new street cleaner, piloted by city road crew chief Rumaldo Ortiz y Pino, rumbled off the North-South Highway into the plaza and ground to a halt with a great hissing of air brakes, stopping six inches shy of a brand-new Norelco refrigerator (robbed from Moose Furniture and Hardware barely an hour earlier) literally pincushioned by beautiful homemade eagle-feather arrows, with *Fuck the Northland Grazing Association!* scrawled across its door.

And a black, bulletproof limousine with a bar, a color TV, and a telephone in back appeared to further serve the taciturn Joseph Bonatelli.

IN NEED OF A ONE-NIGHT VACATION from the hysteria of putting out a newspaper, April Delaney left Duane and Tina with her parents, ordered the *El Clarín* staff to keep away from her house, and had just settled down with a bottle of cream sherry and Frederick Keisler's *Inside the Endless House*, when a car jounced up her potholed driveway, and George Parker tumbled out, already drunk, hugging a jug of wine, a Safeway steak, and a loaf of french bread.

Facing each other across a corner of the kitchen table, they ate the steak, drank the entire bottle of wine, and talked for four hours. After a while April realized that she was consuming most of the alcohol, while George did most of the talking. One minute they had been licking steak grease off their fingers and somberly discussing the socioeconomic showdown in Chamisa County; next minute Life in General became the topic, soon to be supplanted by their own lives in particular. Finally, April simply quit participating and sat there listening to her old high-school chum, prankster, all-American boy and star athlete compulsively rattle off his loneliness, impossible marital situation, and bleakened soul.

"I don't know what it is, or how to handle it, April, I really don't. I go out to that old Martínez shack I've rented on the mesa south of La Lomita, remember? I think I told you about it once. That's where I'm writing my so-called novel. It's amazingly peaceful there. No Winnebagos, no pilgrims, no crew-cut tattooed freaks in Day-Glo muscle shirts peddling genuine heishi necklaces, no traffic jams, no art schlock, no drunks, no pathetic old Genoveva Bachichas trying to make Texans disappear by

236

blowing powdered yarrow into their gas tanks, no nothing. No sir, there's just a couple of juniper trees down there, and I've hung up a wind chime that tinkles in the hot summer breezes. A thousand old bones—I reckon the former owner gave them to his dog—they surround the front of the house. Then there's nothing but sagebrush, a dusty purple expanse stretching for about two miles down to the edge of the gorge. With the door open during the day it's so quiet I can almost hear sand sprinkling against those bleached bones when little lizards scamper by. Sometimes trees rustle, the sagebrush audibly sizzles, magpie wings flutter, mice feet patter in hollow roof places over my head. . . ."

George sucked in air, blew it out hard and noisily, and kept going.

"But I can't work. It's too quiet or it's the wrong kind of quiet. The solitude scares me. As does the task of writing. Hours pass while I sit at my table in front of a big picture window, staring out at the sage, smoking cigarettes, sometimes drinking a warm beer. There's no refrigerator or anything, no hums, no technology. I always arrive excited; but then everything drains out of my body. I feel lazy, I grow sleepy. I want to cry, it's so beautiful and uncomplicated. Just me and my table, my bookcase, a hot plate for making coffee or cooking soup for lunch, and a mattress, a blanket. If the mood hits, I spend hours in the outhouse. It faces west, away from the shack, and has no door. I sit there hypnotized by the sagebrush, the gorge, those delicate hills beyond. God, what a dreamy silence! Buzzards float over the mesa as gracefully as cottonwood fluff, never beating their wings. . . ."

George ran a hand through hair only recently allowed to grow long. He twisted strands into little knots, pulled out the knots, and immediately tied others.

"I sit there wanting to leave my home, my job, this town. I'm tired of almost running over half-blind Eduardo Mondragón at least twice a week; I can't stand the sight of all those tiny corrals harboring one cow, two lambs, a Shetland pony, eighteen chickens, and a rabbit hutch appended to trailers in Irving Newkirk's park, while enormous pastures, surrounding houses owned by people like your dad and mine and *me* support no livestock at all. I want to be unmarried; I don't want to hassle kids anymore. I'm sick of all our conspicuous consumption while half the county is on welfare and food stamps. I hate screw responsibilities. I'd like to give my land to Espeedie Cisneros or somebody else who would *use* it! Lust, and fantasies about sexual perversions are killing me! I'd like to be an unconscionable madman, I really would—"

"Who wouldn't?"

"Huh?"

April smiled winningly. His anguish moved and excited her and she was drunk, dizzy, high. It was wonderful to be this drunk, listening to a passionate asshole wail the blues!

George said, "I want to leave this town, I really do. I'm tired of feeling guilty for being an Anglo, for having a father and a father-in-law who've been a part of the ruling cabal for four decades. I want to go places, have affairs with a dozen different women! I want to meet completely different people! I'm getting old, and I'm sick of being steadfast! I'm sick of security, I'm sick of my lawn and my goddam cars and my goddam students!"

April touched his face, shaking her head sadly, sympathetically.

"April, sometimes I stay out in that little house until after dark. I lie on the mattress with the door and the windows open and listen to coyotes hunting on the mesa. I lie out there in the dark in a practically catatonic state, listening to the coyotes, and it seems there is no way out. I mean, there's no *honorable* way out, there's no decent way out. And I think about you and your good politics and your compassion and your courage and your experience with different places, with different people—"

Her fingertips brushed his lips. Reaching up blindly, George grabbed her hand and raced on.

"I'm, like, trying to write a novel, right? With all these characters in it—men, women, children, people like you, me, Susan. Rebecca Valerio, Denzil and Lurleen Spivey, Gloria Armijo, and Juan GeeGee. But what do I know about people in any intimate ways? Susan's the only woman I ever slept with in my life! Can you imagine that? How many men have you been with in your life?"

"That's not the point, love, it really isn't. Different strokes for different folks. You know that. One man's meat—"

"Bullshit."

Neither spoke for almost ten seconds. Then George began again.

"I want to be free. . . . I also hate self-pity. I know this our three cars and our credit cards. And our four acres of lovely pasture Susan won't rent out or bale for neighbors because she thinks the hay is so 'pretty'! I'm tired of sleepless nights, and bitching over petty details."

George looked up, not that drunk, his eyes blank, then wild.

"I feel so trapped. I'm bored—horribly, horrendously bored. Sex has been dull since our second year together. I feel a rage, and I just want to bust out of my situation. We hardly talk. Actually, I don't think we could talk, ever. My dialogue never blossoms, I feel like such a moronic failure. A pathetic high-school English teacher; a moronic track coach. Every beautiful runner I ever had dropped out and joined the army, got killed, became a lush, a pachuco, a junkie. I'll never get to Paris or New York. I'll never—"

April clasped his hand, whispering, "Hey," her husky voice and her smile mischievous, sexy, compassionate. Time for him to end this diatribe.

He brushed her hand away; April replaced it.

"I really don't know what happened to sex," George blurted. "It never seems spontaneous or playful or erotic. I want it to be more romantic, I want it to be more prurient. We're never at *ease* together; we don't joke or kid each other enough. I'm so dissatisfied, I can't tell you how dissatisfied. I want life to be some kind of adventure again. To hell with a routine existence, a banal and ordinary life. I think I want to leave my family, I really do, but I can't muster the courage. I'm so confused."

April gave his hand a friendly, encouraging squeeze.

"Every day we talk about separating, Susan and me. About getting divorced, about staying together, about how a split would affect the kids. . . ."

George stalled. Then cried out, *"Christ, I hate that daily litany!"*

"Hey old friend, old amigo, it's okay, you know? No te preocupes tanto. You're not alone. We're all in the same boat. It's not that terrible—"

"But I can't stand *hurting* each other! Jesus, it's so dumb! All my life I wanted to be a fine husband, a wonderful father, a conscientious teacher! I always wanted to be decent, but I never *really* wanted to be decent, you know? All my life I've been hypocritical. I'm so sick of being 'square' and 'good.' I've always wanted to commit adultery! I'd like to tell everybody to bug off, go to hell, doesn't sound like it, but I do. . . . I'm terrified of losing the kids . . . if we got divorced she might move . . . *I* might move. I lust for a new life. I'd like to get rip-roaring blotto and spend a night among the drunks like Nicanor Casados and Canuto Tafoya in the alleyway between the hotel and Vigil's Liquors! All those houses Canuto helped Espeedie Cisneros paint murals on back in the thirties—where are they now? The only two surviving that I know of are Virgil Leyba's and Juan and Amaranta GeeGee's. But I can't seem to force anything to a climax. Do I dare to eat a peach? Should I wear my trousers rolled—?"

"George . . ."

"What's the matter with me anyway? I'm sorry I'm so clumsy. This is ridiculous. I wish I knew how to have your kind of wings."

"George . . ."

"I wish—"

"Hey! God *dammit!*"

"What?"

"Why don't we make love?"

"What?"

"I want to make love. Right now."

He blinked. "You and me?"

"Well who the fuck else? My God, how many other people are there in this kitchen to choose from?"

"You don't mean it. You're joking."

April unbuttoned two buttons on his blue work shirt and slipped her hand across his chest, pressing her palm against his wild heart. "George, if I didn't mean it, I wouldn't have brought it up, believe me. That's not my style."

"But . . . but . . ." His face exploded into panic.

Leaning, April kissed him, cupping her hand behind his head, crushing their lips together, prying her tongue into his mouth, giving an urgent groan. It had been so long, so miserably long! Hunching half off the chair, she dropped her other hand into his crotch. So *damn*ably long! He pulled back slightly, lifting one arm, fluttering his hand indecisively against her shoulder.

"George, a lightning bolt isn't going to strike you dead, I promise."

"I don't know. I never thought—"

"You just finished telling me how much you wanted to know other people. You just finished—"

"I know. But I—"

"Every time I have seen you for the past twenty years you've made jokes, you've told me that you envy me, that I'm glamorous, desirable, sexy."

"I know all that. But I never dreamed—"

"Sometimes you have to take what you want, love. If you don't, the aftermath torment is unbearable. You have to accept what is being offered, just to know it, satisfy curiosity if nothing else, force a conclusion. Doesn't that make sense?"

"I guess so. I don't know. Everything is so complicated."

"Don't you want me? I may be a scarred veteran, but I'm still attractive. This is no strings attached, no commitment, no nothing—just for fun."

"Of course you're attractive. Good Lord, April, you're beautiful. You're the most beautiful—"

"Then what's the problem? You don't have to worry about being good in bed, or about being macho, or about being a great lay with me. That's not what sex is all about. You don't have to be a superman, it doesn't matter if we're awkward. I just want to hold you, be close, feel your body against mine. You don't have to worry about me getting pregnant—I'm all taken care of inside. I won't run screaming to Susan, either. I want a close, physical loving—but no commitments, sweet. No guilt trips. Let's try each other once and see what happens. I'm not asking you to be my man, nobody's after your wife and family. We can do it easy, I know. Let's just ball and have fun, roll with the physical punches."

George shook his head. "I can't."

"Why can't you?"

"I don't know why. I just can't. I'm afraid. There's Susan and the kids—"

"After what you just told me tonight about the state of your marriage, your sex life, your mind?"

"I know, I know." His head swayed stupidly. "I can't explain it. I must be the world's greatest idiot. I've fantasized about this moment since I was a teen-ager scoring touchdowns just for you even though you didn't know it. I'll leave here tonight and kick myself over the next twenty years for not accepting what you offer. I'll hate you for not convincing me we should have screwed. I'll torture myself dreaming about how it would have been. I'll hate Susan for being such a drag on my life I can't fall into the hay with you. I'll hate my children for forging the kind of guilt that makes it impossible to leave or betray the family, even when I'm sick and tired of the family. But . . . but. Period, I guess. Just plain *but*."

April poured a fresh glass of wine and chug-a-lugged it. She hadn't been this drunk in years.

"All right, George. What the hell. I understand, I'm sorry. Got carried away for a minute. Apologies to the Pope."

"I don't know what's the matter with me, I really don't."

"You're okay, friend. I mean that. You're a good person. I shouldn't have imposed. Booze, I reckon. That ol' debbil booze."

"You're not imposing. I can't tell you how much I'm flattered that you would even want—"

"Let's not get maudlin, okay? I'm terribly drunk. Maybe you better go on home now. Susan will be wondering—"

*"Forget about her for crissakes!"*

"George, I really wish you'd leave now. Can you drive home all right?"

"Of course. That's one of my qualities—I never get so drunk that I lose control of my reason. I'll hop behind that wheel and *bingo!*—I'm sober as a judge. I've never been able to just cut loose, get rip-roaring drunk, go bananas, have a ball."

"Good night, love. Thanks for the dinner, for all the soul talk." They both got up. Silently, George pleaded with her to understand, his hand ineffectually fluttering again, brushing against her neck, falling across her breasts. With a sigh April settled into his arms, letting him hold her. He embraced her with apologetic, embarrassed strength; his erection was pressed into her groin. The apology accepted, April felt sorry for his confusion and lust. She also wanted to knee him in the groin for being such an exasperating dope!

George broke away, banging out the screen door, and plunged over to his car, emitting strangled sounds. Recklessly, gunning the motor, he jounced out her hideously potholed driveway.

Seated on the concrete portal steps, April lit a cigarette. Oh Lord, she thought, am I ever going to be hung over tomorrow! Only yesterday she had discovered a tiny bump under her right sideburn; now she pinched it experimentally, then dropped her hand, forcing the presence of that growth out of her mind.

Later on, in the bathroom, standing before her mirror with a cigarette stuck toughly between her lips, April shed her blouse and her bra, and, eyes squinted against the smoke, she assessed her naked body. Lovely, full, heavy; her nipples were hard, surrounded by prickled pap. A three-pronged scar, beginning halfway down the left side of her neck, branched at the collarbone into separate rivers extending over her shoulder, around to her back, and down across her throat.

Holding her breasts, she felt like a defenseless five-year-old: tears gathered and fell. For several weeks now there had been a dull, persistent pain in her left hip—it wouldn't go away.

"You're old, you're ugly, you're crippled. You're still acting like a flighty teen-ager," she accused. "Look at your hair, who do you thing you're fooling?" Gathered at either side of her head in ponytails, it was tied with bright orange yarn. "Grow up, April Etcetera," she threatened scornfully.

The telephone rang.

"April, this is George. Listen, I don't know why I rejected you just now, I really don't."

"I don't either, but let's not start flogging dead horses, okay?"

"It has nothing to do with you."

"I know, believe me, I understand. I've been around."

"You're really angry with me, aren't you?"

"George, I'm very drunk, I'm very weary, I'm very alone. Yes, I'm bitter because I didn't get my rocks off, but no, I'm not holding it against you personally—I promise."

"The trouble is, you're . . . you're too beautiful, you're too wonderful," he said. "I—"

"Don't hand me that cornball bullshit!"

"I never expected that you would fall into my lap like that. I mean, I can't tell you all the fantasies I've had, ever since you and me and Rebecca and Junior and Panky used to run together, fantasies of just that sort of thing happening. But I always knew you were completely unattainable. And then when it happened—"

"George, please. It's okay, you know? I'm not offended, honest to God. You must forgive me for broaching the subject. It was unfair, I should have known better than to lay that on you when you were so emotional, confused, vulnerable. I'm always goofing by being impetuous. I never seem to learn that the road of excess usually winds up at the shithouse."

"Oh hell!" he shouted. *"I don't know what to say?"*

"Don't say anthing, love. Just go to sleep, dream off the liquor, rise up early in the morning and drive down to your bungalow and write a good chapter—you can do it. That's what I'm going to do."

"Can we still be friends?"

"Of course! These things happen all the time between people. It's a part of life. We handled it like mature adults, like real troupers. Nobody got hurt, nothing irrevocable was done—"

"Are you sure?"

"Absolutely positive."

"I love you, April Delaney."

She rolled her eyes to the ceiling. "Same here, George. Buona sera."

"Goodnight—"

April hung up, collapsed at the kitchen table, dropped back her head and, shot through with a debilitating sorrow, she unleashed a series of sarcastic, profoundly bitter howls.

They were interrupted by the phone again. Angrily, she snatched off the receiver and growled, "George, enough is enough for one night. Be a sweetheart and don't belabor the point, okay?"

A calm voice said, "April, if you don't quit your opposition to Pueblo electrification, we'll kill you. *We'll cut off your tits, shove them into your mouth, and you'll choke to death.* Understand—?"

IN RESPONSE TO THE TWO Forest Service signs that had gone up in smoke, a pair of FBI agents named Chet Fulton and Len Goodwin appeared in town and took up residence in the Shalako Lodge. The next day, legs belonging to one of the few solvent Chamisa County sheepherders, Mota Llano's own Juan Bautista Godoy y Godoy, were blown off by a dud howitzer shell Mosquito Valley ski personnel had fired last winter during their avalanche-control program.

"Our people are very careful," Wednesday's *Chamisaville News* quoted Rodey McQueen as saying. "They always chart the position of every dud shell fired and send a man around in the springtime, after the snow has melted, to detonate or defuse the faulty ordnance. It was a one in a billion chance that a freak accident like this could happen, and of course it would not have happened if this man, illegally, and under cover of darkest night, had not been poaching grass on the private property of my ski runs."

Virgil Leyba cried, "What kind of a community has this become where sheep are so desperate for food they'll graze at night?" And he immediately filed a million-dollar suit on behalf of the victim.

April Delaney visited Juan in the hospital. He was bald now, half toothless, shriveled up, but with long powerful arms, enormous hands, and sweet, steel-blue eyes.

Before she could talk he said cheerfully:

"Did I ever show you a picture of me and Amaranta when we were young and so full of beans I limped around with a salute in my trousers all day long?"

"No you never did."

Fumbling in a back pocket of some jeans hung on his bedpost, the sheepherder withdrew a cracked leather wallet, and from it extracted a plastic-coated snapshot in which a skinny grinning young dervish with wild, bushy hair, wearing bib overalls and irrigation boots, had one arm around a shyly smiling Amaranta exuding health, hope, and vitality. They were standing in the mouth of Claude Parker's embalmed whale, so many years ago.

"The air had a whiskey zing back then," Juan recalled with a shy smile. "We all knew for certain that the mood could never be plundered, that it would last forever. That whale," he added, a bright twinkle in his eyes. "We loved it like little children. And if the motive was to murder us, still the event gave us much joy. Imagine having the opportunity to actually see and touch a whale: for centuries that was beyond the wildest expectations and dreams of all our valley's people. And even though Karl Mudd became rich taking snapshots, those snapshots have been an important part of a generation's spiritual nourishment. Yessir," he rambled on, "even though Karl Mudd was out to pluck all our feathers, sometimes charging an entire cow for a little picture it cost him a nickel to produce, still, he preserved some crucial moments which would have grown hazy and shapeless if left only to the memories of tottering old folks like me."

Poking in his wallet again, Juan removed another yellowed snapshot. In it a group of young hayseeds practically inundated a Model T Ford speeding toward the camera at the mouth of Chamisaville Canyon.

"That was the first automobile any of us locals around here owned," Juan said lovingly, talking to the ceiling, to the heavy air, to himself. "I guess I must have driven three hundred borregas to auction in Colorado, earning the dollars for that Model T. It was a stupid thing to do, because what use had I for a car? But it was one of those inexplicable things that occurred around the time of the Dynamite Shrine and Claude Parker's whale. You know, that embalmed monster had so fired my imagination I was feeling more oats than I had ever felt before. I wanted to do something big and outrageous and immortal. So I drove the borregas north and sold them at auction. Then, attired in my Sunday finest, I hiked into the gorge, roped a wild burro, rode it to La Piedra and caught a train for the capital—my first trip to the big city. That night I spent in the La Fonda Hotel; next morning, after purchasing the car, I had no money left over to buy gas. Fortunately, some capital cousins wanted to journey north; we hitched up their four-horse team to the car and towed it eighty miles home. Still, I didn't have cash for fuel. So what we did, me and Bernardo C. de Baca and the Martínez twins and Tootie Valerio and Pancho Ortiz y Pino and his little brother, the oversexed mute we used to call Pedro Cabrón y Puto—all of us there, we would hitch a team to the Model T, haul it up the canyon to the Mosquito Valley, eat a picnic lunch, and after that draw straws for who must return with the team. The others shoved the car around, pushed it to get started, turned on the key so we could honk the horn, piled aboard, and guided that rampaging auto down eight miles of dirt road at a hundred miles an hour. . . ."

Wearing a beatific smile, he suddenly eulogized that machine:

"Oh, that Horse Without Shit, that wonderful Horse Without Shit! My God, I remember it so clearly. The people who lived in La Ciénega, right next to the Plains Road, whenever their children heard that honking far up in the canyon they rushed inside crying, 'Mamá, Mamá, here come all the crazy boys in the Horse Without Shit!' And the mamá would drop whatever she was doing and race outside with the kids to the road. They hopped up and down, growing ever more excited as the honking grew louder, until finally we came barreling into sight swaddled in a huge dust ball going a hundred miles an hour. They

246

screamed 'Horse Without Shit! Horse Without Shit!' and threw flowers or little stones or biscochitos at us as we went noisily careening by. Oh yes indeed, I certainly remember the Horse Without Shit. Often even now, in my dreams, I can hear that horn tooting, very faintly, far away high in the dark canyon of my younger days. And I get just as excited all over again. I wake up tingling, and I want to rush out of the hospital at midnight for a last glimpse of myself and my friends in that fabulous Horse Without Shit!"

After a long silence, April said, "I'm sorry about your legs, Juan. There's nothing I can think to say. It's just horrible and unfair, period."

"Things end whether we like them to or not. We'll probably lose the farm now, because I put it up as collateral for a loan after I lost so many lambs in that early blizzard last year. But don't cry. It's only the Betterment of Chamisaville—ha ha ha. Please draw the shade."

Later, after April had left, Juan wrote a poem:

My name is Juanito Bautista—
GeeGee stands for Godoy y Godoy.
I spent all my life in the mountains,
Ever since I was just a boy.

I used to climb to the tops of peaks,
I used to kick my stubborn mule,
In school I whopped an old football—
My toes were my best tool.

All my life I drove a truck,
A tractor, and a car;
My wife she used to scream at me,
When I tracked in highway tar.

My feet they got me into trouble,
They got me out of it, too;
My feet they took me courting,
And they carried me to booze.

My feet fit into stirrups,
They kicked dust in a drouth,
They fit into my cowboy boots,
And they fit into my mouth.

It was sometime close to summer,
In a month real full of heat,
That Yours Truly stepped on a big land mine,
And etherized both feet.

Off to heaven my puppies flew,
Qué va?—that's how it goes.
Yet how much I wish I had that itch
Back between my toes!

Juan entitled it "The Corrido of the Missing Tootsies," folded the sheet of paper, slipped it into an envelope, and addressed the envelope to the *El Clarín*. After that he fell asleep and dreamed.

In a rainstorm he was chopping wood. It had been dry for a long time, and a piñon scent tingled in his nostrils; sap-tinged dust prickled his sinuses. Then the storm broke, a summer afternoon rain with thunder and much lightning, and he continued chopping as the rain soaked his hat and his shoulders, his chopping block, and the six inches of wood chips surrounding the block. It felt wonderful to work and sweat in the driving rain. After a spell he paused, testing his ax blade to see if it needed sharpening, and, ascertaining that it did, the old sheepherder sat down on the block with a file and began working on the damp blade. Chickens in a nearby pen stood in a doorway, waiting for the rain to end. In another field, shirtless children unafraid of the thunder and lightning galloped a Shetland pony around in circles. Sheepskins flapped quietly on the walls of Juan's sheds; bleached-out deer and elk racks tacked to the sheds pulsed phosphorescently. The smell of old damp manure and rotting leather and mildewed hay bales rose up in the rain, a musty fecund odor. Juan thumbed the cork from a bottle of homemade chokecherry wine, stopped sharpening, and treated himself to a slug. The wine, dry and sweet, slid down his gullet like quicksilver, landing in his stomach the way morning dew alights on a lamb.

Opening one eye, Juan discovered the Angel of Death at the foot of his bed aiming an arrow at his heart. With a short cry, the old man raised one hand for protection, but the arrow zipped straight through his palm, feathers and all, skewering him expertly in the exact center of his fragile chest.

\* \* \*

How THE HELL DID I let *this* happen? April Delaney wondered over a cigarette and coffee at her kitchen table shortly after her kids were in bed. On the table was a letter from George Parker: she had received it that morning.

Dear April,

I don't know how to explain what happened last night. After I got home I sat downstairs in the dark living room and thought about you, wondering what it would have been like to make love. And I couldn't believe my cowardice, my hypocrisy. I know it would have been wonderful and important to have been with you. I'm terrified that I insulted you beyond repair. How *did* I refuse? I don't understand that at all! A thousand apologies for being so clumsy! Why can't I articulate the peculiar agony in my soul? Too often, during this married life of mine, I've refused what I really wanted—to break away, have affairs, begin anew, satisfy my curiosity. At the same time, I have failed miserably to provide what others close to me —Susan, the kids—really need. Struggling to work out or give up on a marriage, I find myself desperate from loneliness and from a desire for magic moments. Yet I can't act, I defeat myself at every turn, nip fantasies before they can even bud. "Action," quoth Conrad, "the first thought or perhaps the first impulse, on earth! The barbed hook, baited with the illusion of progress, to bring out of the lightless void, the shoals of unnumbered generations!"

I'm a regular J. Alfred Prufrock. Will I ever again feel truly content with any aspect of life? For so long I have been dissatisfied. I feel like a tight end who dropped a touchdown pass in a championship game. Do you know that poem of Neruda's, "We Are Many"?

> . . . and when I summon my courageous self,
> a coward completely unknown to me
> swaddles my poor skeleton
> in a thousand tiny reservations.

It goes on, but you know it and no doubt get the point. I go to movies like *Shoot the Piano Player* and *Zorba the Greek,* and I weep. I read *Death in*

*Venice* and *Tonio Kröger*, and those things frighten
me so much: am I destined/doomed to be like that—
to watch always instead of participating? I'm so tired
of being mundane, everyday. I don't want to be a
"good person" anymore, but I can't help myself! Babbitt creeps into my blood displacing Icarus: I feel
cornered and savage and often very nasty. All my
life, believe me, I have been like that enormous and
costly boondoggle and victimizer of our almost extinct small farmers, the Cañoncito Dam—waiting to
hold acres of water! *Fill me up!* I want desperately
to sleep with you, crushing your breasts against my
chest, I want to kiss you while I'm inside you, learning how your butt fits into my hands, somehow having
overcome my fears of being a lousy lover— I really
want to fuck you silly, April! Screw all the grave
consequences human beings seem so intent to shackle
themselves with! *I want what I want!* But I don't
know what to do. Why am I so ineffective?

George

Several times she reread the letter. It evoked anger; and
also caused a heat to rise. A sexy letter, for sure. April
could have him yet if she desired—that was within her
power. But in retrospect, of course, the proposition had
been a horrible mistake. Thank the wine for that. "His
reaction is what I deserve for getting so drunk." No matter how hungry that was no way to begin an affair. And
George Parker was in no shape to be an affairee. "Affairee,
for God's sake!"

Naturally (however), she was touched by his passion
and confusion, by his innocence, by his obviously overawed admiration and envy of her. If he envisioned a
glamour and romance she could not provide, it would be
criminal to lead him on. And yet—and yet how in hell did
one even *begin* in this town? Especially a woman like
herself. No discreetness could prevent eventual discovery.
If nothing else, two thousand dogs would start barking
the minute either of them tired creeping anywhere at
night! If April and George lay down together, the whole
town would know by morning. A car parked in a driveway might blow the whistle; perhaps the FBI, observing
her movements, would be the first to know. The FBI?—
*Jota, Eme, Jota!* "I'll kill it, apologize, write him back

a tender but firm no-nonsense letter, and get on with the *El Clarín*."

Yet bodily aches cried for release; her heart was no stone. A good lay right about now could do wonders for the spirit. And George was so ripe he sizzled.

But what above love? "Love, for God's sake! Listen to me *now*, will you?" Like the Russians and the Chinese who would worry about intellectual and artistic freedom *after* the people had food, medical care, and roofs over their heads, April would worry about love *after* she had gotten her rocks off!

Making a fist, she laid it against the letter. An obvious, honorable solution was available. Cut him off gently and lovingly, explaining her philosophy of life, easing them back down into the friendship that had existed before they got drunk two nights ago.

The phone clanged at her ear—*him*, she knew, even before lifting the receiver.

"April, do you have a minute? This is George. Can we talk?"

"George who?"

"What? *Who?* George *Parker*. What do you mean, 'George who'?"

"A joke, lover. I'm sorry. I'm feeling a little light-headed, is all. What's up?"

"Well, I don't know. Did you get my letter?"

"Sure did."

"You sound awfully blasé about it. . . ."

"I got it, I read it, and I thought about it. I had plans to write you back."

"What were you going to say? No, never mind, I don't think I want to hear it. I can't *believe* I told you to back off that other night when we got drunk!"

"George, please, enough of the hair shirt, already. It's not a disaster, believe me. That nothing happened between us is the best thing that could have happened between us. Count your blessings."

"I want you. I want you very badly. I know I love you now. You just took me by surprise, that's all. Because it had never occurred to me that I might be able to have you. That's why I acted so stupidly. I was stunned. I didn't know if you were joking or what."

"What the hell did you *think* was going to happen when you somehow figured I'd be alone and showed up with a steak and a bottle of wine?"

251

"I know what you're thinking. But that's simply not true."

"Hey, love, excuse me for shouting. But you have a family, you're struggling to hold it together. That is one of the world's most admirable endeavors. Believe it or not, I've been there. It's so precious, what you have and are trying to keep alive, that I would hate to see myself as the catalyst that finally enabled you to jump ship. I came back here to try and salvage what was left of these good familial things in a valley going to hell because of a careless and disloyal attitude toward the value of human togetherness. It's not worth it, sweet, really it isn't. An affair between us right now would be just plain wrong."

"No it wouldn't. I've thought it over and I'm ready."

"Then you will forgive me if I say that you are too innocent."

"What?"

"Please don't be insulted, love. But there are many things you don't understand. My God, George, I've been married four times, I have been with a hundred different men!"

"So what?"

"I don't want to talk about it anymore, all right? I'm sorry, I'm very tired."

"Can I call back? Can I write more letters, trying to convince you I was wrong, and you were right? I have so much I want to say. I'm going crazy! While I'm driving around town, doing errands, I wind up scribbling answers to you, replies, wails, cool and calm calculations, love poems, on envelopes, on scraps of paper, on the backs of checks. I keep stuffing my pockets with all these scraps. I'm even writing things to you on the backs of the sales slips that come out of cash registers! There's so many words, it's like the Bible on the head of a pin!"

"George, really, not now, not tonight."

"When, then?"

"Tomorrow, the next day, next year, who knows? Now leave me alone, would you please?"

"All right. I'm sorry—"

"Stop apologizing. I hate it."

"Well what am I supposed to do?"

"I dunno. Act your age. Go home, sweet. Play with your children. Watch TV. Calm down. Go out to the Martínez shack and write. Sit quietly at your window and watch magpies in the junipers."

252

"Goodnight," he said, hurt, suddenly curt.

"Goodnight—"

April grabbed her typewriter and started writing:

Dear George,

I apologize for cutting you short just now. That seems to be our litany, already, isn't it? "I'm sorry," "I apologize," "excuse me!" "pardon me"—for being clumsy, arrogant, stupid, forward, backward, indecisive. No matter. Let's analyze the thing, talk it out, settle down, and continue without all this indeterminate anguish. George, you say you love me— in return I might even say that I love you. Fair enough. Certainly, you're physically attractive. And I feel a warmth, a sort of brotherly love for you that has been in my bones since we were kids dropping corpses on Al Lamont and having champagne dinners with Atiliano Montoya and those lepers from Panama. But right now when I think to myself that I love you, I must also say that so much of it comes from *loneliness* and *lust*. Got that? I repeat—*loneliness* and *lust*. Real biggies in the so-called romantic lexicon, my friend. My body and my blood pulses and I can't deny that the urges are pretty strong. But you must understand that that is why I propositioned you in the first place. Nobody was on the make for complicated commitments and *love*. I just really and truly wanted to get laid, have myself screwed, blued, and tatooed for fair, without any traumatic postscripts! You dig? I'm *horny*, pal. It's been a long time. Yet too often I have landed in emotional mares' nests by asking just that sort of thing from people who couldn't handle the simplicity. And before I knew it I was being crucified by ardor, love, passions, commitments, wants, and needs I had never intended to unleash. Believe me, I understand my own powers. I hate seeming stuck-up, but I hit men hard, George. Rare is the male who doesn't want to own me, cherish me, idolize me, use me, show me off, beg me to mother him, suck him, save him, fuck him—you get the point. Somehow I project something that convinces men I can be all things to them—when actually I'm merely mortal, George—that's the truth. Poke me a little, you'll discover I'm as screwed up as the next guy, and no more precious a human being than any other girl next door.

But I have traded on my beauty and sexuality and my fickle heart more times than I care to tell. Admittedly, I've enjoyed doing it for the most part, but that epoch in my life must end. For both personal *and* political reasons. I don't want to break any more hearts nor have my own heart crippled any more than it already is. I would hate for you to understand just how battered a lady you are dealing with—

The telephone gave her a start. Another obscene threat? Tempted not to answer, April snatched it on the seventh ring anyway: Juan Ortega said, "Hello, April. Did you hear about Juan GeeGee?"

"No—yes—I mean, what about him? I saw Juan in the hospital yesterday. Tomorrow I'll go over there right after I drop Tina off in the morning—"

"You can't. I don't know how to say it any other way —he's dead. I'm sorry to be the one, hija. I hate like hell being the son of a bitch who brings bad news."

"He *what*?"

"He's dead, and Amaranta is in the hospital."

"Come on, Juan! Don't you do this to me, dammit! *Not right now!*"

"He died last night. A blood clot or something reached his heart. Amaranta's grief was so terrible she tried killing herself by jumping into the well. She's over at the hospital right now—"

"Hey Juan," April whispered. "Tell me it isn't true, please? Come on, hombre, you *must* be kidding!"

On the other end Juan choked, let out a sob, and then shouted angrily: "One of these days, little sister, we are gonna get revenge for all the Juan GeeGees who have died!"

254

# Resisting
# Temptation

APRIL WORE A PASTEL apricot-colored dress, and a single white daisy in her hair. Her kids were decked out in their Sunday finest—clean jeans, new sneakers, Lacoste tennis shirts. It was a sunny, windy day. While Father González muttered his litany over Juan GeeGee's grave, mourners gathered in the small Cañoncito camposanto could hear the muffled booms from dynamite blasting on new Mosquito Valley ski runs. Otherwise, a peculiar stillness characterized the moment. Swallows flitted through the dry air; turquoise-colored mountain bluebirds zipped around the eaves of a windowless, sagging Penitente morada at the edge of the cemetery. A meadowlark landed on the pile of stones over a nearby grave and unleashed several poignant notes.

Nobody blinked; no one was weeping or too sad. Their faces held a kind of stoic, almost peaceful sorrow, April thought. She envied their calmness, their roots that were complexly intertwined with life and dying. They had intimate knowledge of this earth, and no fear of whitening bones, old age, or vengeful archangels.

Taking off, the meadowlark set its wings, gliding into a greening alfalfa patch next door: an old man was irrigating the field. He had not stopped busily shifting clumps of mud when they drove in, but now he leaned on his shovel, hat in hand, gazing at them. Around him, magpies and blackbirds waded through the water, busily hunting tidbits. Farther away, some killdeer were screeching.

Slowly, April inspected the mourners' faces. Eyes squinted, Espeedie Cisneros stared beyond the preacher at the western view. A short, fat little man with an enormous potbelly hanging over a turquoise belt buckle, he wore faded bluejeans, cowboy boots, a tweed winter sportcoat, a denim shirt, and bolo tie. A stubble of snow-white whiskers covered his cheeks and chin. Pensively, he

255

sucked on a toothpick. His wife, Pancha, almost as rotund, held onto his arm, and did not compromise her dignity one whit by moving to brush away a lovely purple dragonfly when it became entagled in her veil and frantically whirred its iridescent wings, trying to escape.

Beside them stood Perfecto Torres. His olive face and sagging jowls cast a demeanor as sad as a basset hound's. Uncomfortable in a double-breasted blue suit with a lapel carnation, Perfecto lazily licked his lips, staring straight into the hole, and held against his chest a rolled cigarette he would light as soon as the ceremony ended. He would have lit it earlier, but his wife, Ursula, a broad-beamed no-nonsense tyrant, would have slapped it out of his lips. She was a fierce-eyed woman with an enormous Aztec nose and thick lips; pride emanated from her posture and attitude like boulders exploding from a damp cliff.

Next to them, Celestino Lucero's face was so weathered it seemed almost black. His moustache was neatly trimmed; his scarred cheek and jowls were carefully shaved. He seemed to be lazily smiling. Cut all wrong, an old-fashioned gray suit accented his arthritic bones; they poked out all over. His Adam's apple protruded painfully far, making him resemble a leathery old rooster. A magpie tail-feather (from the late Tierra o Muerte the Eighth) arose at a jaunty angle from the band of his old straw cowboy hat.

Virgil Leyba's puffy white eyebrows boiled angrily off of his spare, morose features. Recent widowers Juan Ortega and Pat GeeGee squinted as they had all their lives against the harsh midday brightness, Juan jutting his chin, looking stern and perplexed, Pat with a contemplative, melancholy air, lips pursed as if to whistle, faintly blowing into the hot, playful wind, twitching his head occasionally when struck by the twittering shadows of swallows.

Everything about Vidal Mondragón had gone white and shriveled up—his skin, hair, eyes, and faded clothes. Trembling, his underlip was always damp, his head nodded constantly as if to some jazzy heavenly rhythm; his hand quivered against the handle of a cane.

And many others had come. Juan and Amaranta's crippled tecato son, Alfredo, and a schoolteacher friend, Rafaela Maestas. Anthony Martínez and Eloy Romo and the bruja Genoveva Bachicha and her brother, Malaquias C. de Baca. Plaza caretaker Filiberto García and a bunch of the Arrellano and Casados brothers and sisters. Amaranta GeeGee's sisters, tiny and birdlike in simple baggy dresses, were there: Josefita, Maria Estafana, Dorothy, Eulogia, and Neargarita. Also the Prince of Whales waitress, Gloria Armijo, and her husband, Johnny, and their children.

Perhaps fifty people had gathered on this sunny windy day, paying last respects to Juan GeeGee, a man—like many of them—privy to little luck for a long time.

After the coffin was lowered on ropes, Father González released a handful of dust over the stony excavation. The dust puffed out of his hand, sprinkling into the mourners. Tiny bits of symbolic earth pinged against Virgil Leyba, Espeedie Cisneros, and Juan Ortega. The brief mist of dirt glanced off April Delaney's soft cheeks, laid nearly invisible flecks of powder across her bosom, and deposited dry specks in the veil half covering Gloria Armijo's plump, friendly features.

Celestino Lucero and Espeedie Cisneros, both members of the Penitente brotherhood, stepped forward. Placing a small, hand-carved wooden flute to his lips, Espeedie began playing a solitary mournful tune. Celestino dropped his head back slightly, closed his eyes, and sang an alabado:

> Buenos días, paloma blanca,
> Hoy te vengo de saludar,
> Saludando tu belleza,
> En tu reino celestial. . . .

As they finished, a dozen men on horseback appeared from behind the morada and approached them. On the outskirts of the crowd, they halted. Ikie Trujillo, Fecundo Lavadie, Max Jaramillo, Bonifacio Herrera, and the ghosts of Atiliano Montoya and Rudy LeDoux remained in the saddle while their leader dismounted. A few old-timers stepped back, making an aisle through which he passed. A chunky filthy little man who might have been only a memory or an apparition caused by the summery heat striking ancient addled brains, Jesus Dolores Martínez Vigil approached the grave in a bowlegged gait, his face darkened under the wide brim of an old-fashioned sombrero, his features all but lost behind his bushy walrus moustache. It was hard to determine if his head was flesh or simply skull, a calavera straight out of some graphic revolutionary Mexican broadside. His rope vest squeaked as he progressed: the various pistols and bandoliers and other armaments decorating his body like Christmas ornaments clanked and rattled; the tip of his cavalry sword scabbard chinked against the flinty earth and banged off his ancient leather botas.

At the grave, Jesus Etcetera dug his bony hand into a vest pocket, removed an ancient silver dollar, and spun it laconically from his dirt-blackened fingers down atop the coffin, where it rattled and settled. Then he plucked a single rose from the snakeskin band of his sombrero, held it dramatically over the excavation for a second, and let it fall.

"This dumb kid was my very good friend," he rasped in barely audible Spanish. "Like us all, he had a tough life. They cut off pieces of his fingers, his heart, his land, and his soul, little by little, bit by bit. They smuggled an angel of death—La Sebastiana—into his body when he wasn't looking. Right now, Juanito's widow is lying in the hospital with her bones all broken and her mind impaired by grief and old age and fatigue. The fat cats get fatter, and you and me and our little kiddies spend too much time digging holes in the camposanto. Well, me too —I'm tired: it's been a long life. But lest anybody here forget, keep in mind always that I'm ready whenever you are."

So saying, the fierce little man unholstered an old cap-and-ball pistol, pointed it at the sky, poked a finger in one ear, and discharged the weapon. An enormous puff of acrid smoke burst from the old iron mechanism, almost totally engulfing Jesus Etcetera. Then the wind carried the thick pungent cloud into the mourners. For a second the black powder smoke seeped among Virgil and Juan and Pancha and Espeedie Cisneros, Gloria Armijo and April Delaney, Ursula and Perfecto Torres and Celestino Lucero and all the others, twining around them, sinuously caressing their bodies. Then it dissolved into the wind.

Jesus Etcetera holstered his gun, tipped his sombrero to the coffin, nodded at all those present, and rattled and squeaked back to his big, gangly horse. On tiptoes, he grabbed the saddle horn and struggled mightily to raise one plump foot into the stirrup. With a series of painful grunts, he tugged himself awkwardly up into the saddle, turned his horse around, and led his band at a slow walk away through the graveyard. Almost immediately, they began shimmering in the heat like a mirage; and slowly, tantalizingly, they melted from view . . . disappeared.

Mourners stirred, murmured, broke up, retreated to their cars, drove away. Quickly, two old brothers, Anselmo and Roberto Vigil, filled in the grave, then they shuffled into their ancient pickup and rattled off toward the La Lomita Bar for cold beers.

That left only the old man irrigating the field next door. Settling his hat on his head, he sloshed down along the ditch a ways and commenced digging again, letting water into new rows. Magpies, blackbirds, grackles, and killdeer followed the flow. And swallows twittered over the camposanto, their lively shadows dancing among the old wooden crosses, plastic no-fade flowers, and rocky mounds.

The odor of black powder dissipated completely. And worms began ingesting the blood-red velvet petals of that symbolically tendered rose.

THREE MILES SOUTH of Juan GeeGee's funeral, Dr. Alfred Gracie Lamont, already the victim of three heart attacks, shut off his intake valve, fiddled with several snobblecocks, raised his rose-tinted oxygen mask, adjusted the fluorescent orange tank on his back, stooped and sank a white wooden tee and his golfball into the grass on the third tee of the Cañoncito Reservoir Golf Course, selected a driver from the bag held for him by Rodey McQueen, and took forever lining up his shot. While he puttered and futzed with his stance, getting it just right, McQueen dumped the bag back into their golf cart and addressed Joseph Bonatelli, who was standing beside the cart, awaiting his turn.

"Al Lamont there, he may not look it in that outfit, but he's one of the most intrepid athletes in this valley. I never knew a man to do better with a hunting bow. From a hundred yards he could send a shaft up a frog's fanny without touching its balls. I'll wager he's killed an elk with an arrow every autumn for the past twenty years. At tennis, I can rarely beat him, unless his oxygen tank runs low and he gets a little whiskey-headed. Four coronaries already, and look at that son of a bitch swing!"

Lamont's ball soared in a high arc directly along the parched brown fairway, landing on the fringe of a pasty-looking green surrounded by brown furze which was surrounded by sagebrush.

"As a surgeon he's a bit notorious for his propensity to light into a body utilizing everything from a machete to a size-fourteen X-acto knife at the slightest provocation. And yet—"

"None of us should need a surgeon," Bonatelli interrupted, his fat face turned painfully away from the driving summer sun. "Not if we play our cards right."

"Of course," McQueen said quickly. "Sorry I brought it up."

"Does he fuck with that claptrap on?" Bonatelli asked crudely.

"I don't know, you'll have to ask him." McQueen smiled, even though he found the question in poor taste.

Icarus Suazo teed up his ball, spent a few seconds settling his feet, and swung quickly, effortlessly. His ball seemed to float with little power at all, sliding in a low, soft line drive through the high desert air, barely spinning. Yet after it struck the fairway twenty feet shy of the green, his ball continued rolling at an unconscionably dawdling rate, and, at the end of the final inch of its forward motion, plopped dramatically into the cup.

Bonatelli said, "Hrmph."

"Oh hell, that's nothing," Randolph Bonney said. "Mr. Suazo here, it's news when he *doesn't* get a hole in one on this hole, isn't it, Mr. Suazo?"

The expressionless Pueblo secretary tipped his white golf hat in their direction, shouldered his red-and-green bag, and began walking along the side of the brown fairway.

Randolph Bonney hit next, slicing the ball badly: it soared off into the sagebrush mesa. The co-op chief giggled, teed up another ball, and sliced it into the same location.

"*Damn!*" he growled under his breath, embarrassed, his elbows—in fact all his joints—aching. He needed a Joe Bonatelli in his life like he needed a hole in his head; consequently the negotiations had him much more than on edge. Maybe McQueen's plan was sound, but a town like this could only take so much trauma, and Bonney feared their proposal would backfire, hurting them all. Allow the mob into a town, and chances were they'd lose the town. And, despite his lust for progress, there were things he loved in the valley: cocktails on his lawn during

260

the brilliant sunsets, crisp autumn days on this golf course, and trout fishing along the county's many streams. Sentimental old bastard that he was, Randolph Bonney wanted *something* to remain inviolate.

When his third ball stayed on the fairway, the co-op executive retreated apologetically to the golf cart. Having adjusted his oxygen mask, reactivating the flow, Al Lamont joined Icarus Suazo—those two always hiked together. Bonatelli teed a ball, hit immediately, a straightaway shot, then plopped sluggishly into the cart piloted by McQueen and also carrying Randolph Bonney.

"It sure is a hot day," McQueen said, smiling lazily, his eyes fixed on the upcoming green. "I reckon it's hot enough to scorch a nun's twat."

"I've seen hotter," Bonatelli replied.

"I would imagine." McQueen glanced at him significantly, accenting the double entendre.

Bonatelli said, "I never let it bother me. I like the heat. I like action. I like to sweat. But if a bunch of red-skinned assholes start slinging lead around out there, I'll move my operation to Timbuktu, unnerstand, McQueen?"

"Does a coyote fart at night?"

McQueen braked the cart close to a sandtrap where Bonatelli's ball had landed. A rattlesnake curled around the ball stared blindly at them, its tail quiet for the moment. McQueen reached to the floor of the cart, located a .38 pistol, and fired once at the snake, blowing off its head.

Bonatelli said, "Are there a lot of snakes around here?"

"Not around town. You get onto the mesa though, out in the sagebrush or down in the gorge, and there's enough rattlers to make a preacher squirm. Don't know what attracts them to this golf course, but I kill three or four a month out here—during the season."

Bonatelli said, "Down in Arizona, they also got snakes."

Icarus Suazo came over and, picking up the snake McQueen had shot, he dropped it into his golf bag.

"What did he do that for?" Bonatelli asked.

"He eats them," Randolph Bonney explained.

Bonatelli adjusted his crotch with a pinkie. "That prick is our only problem," he said. "I wish he was on our side."

"But he is," McQueen and Randolph Bonney said in unison.

Bonatelli gave each of them a disconcertingly limp and

sarcastic fisheye. Then he said: "You people are jerking me off so regular, I won't have to get laid for a year."

FROM JUAN GEEGEE's funeral, April drove directly to the hospital. Amaranta was snoring, her head aslant on the pillow, great whistling exhalations issuing from her drooling mouth. April seated herself in the chair beside the bed and sighed loudly. What a day! On their best behavior during the funeral (under threat of extermination, withheld allowances, and no desserts for a week), Duane and Tina had collapsed as soon as it ended, and were outside bickering in the car. She could use an injection of the peace and quiet in here.

April rummaged in her purse for matches, lit a cigarette, and smoked, enjoying the lull, watching Amaranta sleep. The old woman's face, softened by pain, by drugs, by the deep hospital languor, cast a lovely mood. Without her fierce open eyes, a calm transposed Amaranta's features, imparting a glow of great wisdom. It was relaxed, not at all strained: April found her visage profoundly moving.

One arm lay outside the blankets, exposed, extended limply. April let her eyes meander along those aged but muscular contours, the dark leathery flesh, the powerful battered hand at the end. And the picture of that isolated strength at rest was more powerful to her almost than Amaranta, awake, had ever been.

April found herself thinking about George again—as a lover. And she let the thought grow; a sudden upsurge of energy excited her body; it soothed April to let the sexual yearning loose, allowing it to run a course. The sensation lasted as long as her cigarette. Then she stubbed out the butt, bent over, and gently rendered a smoky kiss. Amaranta stirred: a tiny muscle in one wrinkled cheek twitched. Leaving, April ran her index finger over the old woman's biceps, curved it through the crotch of her elbow, and let it trickle down along the inside of Amaranta's forearm.

In the hospital parking lot, George Parker stood beside April's dented Bug, jawing with the kids; his car was parked nearby. He looked young, gentle, and strong in a black T-shirt, powder-blue flared denims, and striped sneakers. April cocked her head slightly, grinning, and made light of their encounter. "Hello, George Parker, you look ravishing. Like somebody straight out of a *New*

262

*Yorker* ad. 'Visit Bimini: come catch our trout in New Zealand—' "

"From the highway I saw your car parked here, I figured I'd better stop." He had bent his head down as he spoke. April reached out and lifted it, tilting up his chin with her index finger. George could not see her eyes through the dark glasses, but her lips were smiling.

"You figured you *had* to stop?"

He shrugged. "I've said it all before. Because I love you. I want us to get together now. I don't care how, really I don't. If you only want to make love once a month, once a year, even, that's okay. I can accept that. If you want to be secret, we can be secret. I can pick you up late at night, take you out to my writing studio—nobody will ever spot us. I won't tell Susan. I'll be grown-up and very cool. I'll do whatever it takes to get even a very tiny little piece of you. I'm just not going to let the opportunity pass, that's all."

"Are you finished?" There was a twinkle in her voice, in her eye.

"No. In fact, I haven't yet begun to fight."

"George, I'm sorry, but I can't look around and see just how fucked-up everybody and everything is, all the people I care about, from the Vietnamese to the inhabitants of this valley, and then decide to lead you on into something I know from the start is wrong."

"Why is it so wrong?"

"You don't really want me, love. You want what you think I am. You want some essence of my experience that you think is so romantic—you want it to rub off on you. And I suspect that you want to use me to forge a break with Susan and the kids that you can't make by yourself. But I don't want to be used that way, it's no good. I know Virgil wouldn't approve, and neither would Juan or Anthony Martínez, or Amaranta GeeGee, or Celestino Lucero —they wouldn't say anything, but they would be disappointed. And those are the people I care about, I can't risk their censure. Society is fragile enough."

"I won't break with Susan. I'll set it up any way you want it. I'll stay with my family. I'll do anything—"

"Hey, shh." She touched his lips. "Can you hear what you're saying?"

"Christ," he muttered painfully, "I had you in my hand and I let you get away."

"I have to be responsible, George. Believe me, it isn't

263

that easy. I haven't been noted for being overly responsible in my life. I want you now, I don't deny it. We're talking ourselves into a regular froth—"

George pulled her against him, holding her head against his shoulder. Eyes closed, April thought, It's all hopeless, he'll win in the end if he persists, and we'll blow it—but good.

"Jesus, George, I dunno. Where you are at, with Susan and the kids—it's not cowardly, believe me. Resisting this temptation isn't cowardly at all. Most people can't and don't resist it, and they destroy everything because of their weakness and lack of courage. Does that surprise you? I came home to make a stand against the careless destruction of precious human values."

"You keep saying that."

"Where you are, believe it or not, is at the very center of life. It is precious beyond your recognition. Cherish it. Be more careful than you have these past days. Really."

"April, you are the most fulfilled, most exciting person I've ever met. You're the most glamorous, and you're the most courageous politically. I've never met anyone with even half your compassion and sensitivity. You're probably the most honest person, the most straightforward person I've ever run into—"

"Oh Jesus Christ man! Cool it, will you? I am so battered, deformed, desperate, that I don't know whether to laugh or cry at the character you evoke. God, I'm ashamed of intruding on you when you're locked in such a crucial time!"

"No. Don't say that. You give me such hope."

"What else *can* I say?"

He held her. Hot sun burned her eyelids, her hair. Hundreds of cars passed on the North-South Highway—how many of their friends or acquaintances had already seen them like this? If she stayed in his arms another minute, it wouldn't matter if they ever made love or not, the damage would be done, the rumor machine would be operating full tilt. By nightfall Susan would know.

Miserably, George said, "How do children survive their parents? How do human beings successfully drive cars, run countries, make revolutions, develop a polio vaccine, feed eight hundred thousand people, land on the moon?"

April didn't respond.

"Everything I say to you sounds like such melodrama.

Forgive my clichés! When I talk I must sound so damn phony."

April squeezed him. "No, you don't sound phony. I would never mock the sincerity of your passion. I find that most traumatic and romantic emotional bullshit like this usually sounds as if it came straight out of a *True Romance* magazine no matter how articulate or intelligent the participants."

"So—?"

April pushed out of his arms. His intensity had her unsettled and frustrated. She yearned to give in, let fleshly desires have their go-round. His body felt good, strong; April very much wanted—needed!—a man. To hell with her resolve, this abstention was getting ridiculous! Maybe it was impossible, after all, to choose a lover rationally.

"George, I don't have the strength right now to deal with you."

"Can I come over sometime again?"

"I don't think so. Not right now. I'm busy with the paper, the kids—"

"All right." He backed away, then turned and dived into his car, started it up, and pulled swiftly out of the lot. April slumped into her Bug, clicked the radio on, clicked it off, removed her sunglasses and angrily cleaned them, and replaced them on her nose, and—surprise, surprise!—discovered she was almost crying. Fingering the lump at her ear, she wondered how much it had grown in a week . . . or since yesterday. Maybe this time it would kill her. The hip joint ached, so did one shoulder a little. She wished it was arthritis, bursitis, but knew it wasn't. Well, maybe it would all go away. She simply had to be in that thirty percent who recovered fully. Any other outcome was unthinkable.

But if it's going to return, if I'm going to go through all that shit again, April thought, then I should at least give in to George, screw my principles, take that befuddled son of a bitch and give him a lesson in loving!

She had forgotten about the kids. Suddenly Duane asked, "Is George in love with you, Mom?"

"What?" April looked at him, startled.

"Is he in love with you?"

"For God's sake, I don't know. Why? Good Lord, darling, whatever made you ask a dumb question like that?"

Hurt by her sharp reaction, Duane shrugged, and, mum-

265

bling "I dunno," he fell back against the rear seat and sulked.

Almost running over Felicia Babbitt as she pulled angrily out of the parking lot, April turned onto a bumpy back road, taking a shortcut home. Duane frowned grouchily, and Tina started chanting: "Duane's a stupid *sour*puss! Duane's a stupid *sour*puss!"

"I am not, Tina. You shut up!"

"I'd just as soon you kids didn't say 'shut up' to each other, do you mind?"

"You shut up yourself," Duane growled.

"Hey!" April slammed on the brakes, skidding to a halt, and, swinging around dramatically, she grabbed his arm. "Just what the hell was that all about, young man? What kind of a bug have you got up your ass today, anyway?"

"Leggo of me!" Tears starting, Duane attempted unsuccessfully to wrench his arm free of her too-tight grasp. *"You motherfucker!"*

Releasing his arm, April sighed, banged one fist against the steering wheel, and admitted, "All right, okay, I blew it. I'm sorry, Duane, love, I really am. I'm too tense, that's all—I'm not mad at you, I'm mad at myself. So what's the problem?"

"Just leave me alone, I don't want to talk with anybody. I *hate* you." Duane slouched as far into the corner as he could manage.

"Darling, I apologize for snapping at you, but I won't leave you alone, not when you obviously feel so terrible." A panic arose inside April, triggered by all the time she had not spent with her children during their turmoiled existence. "Please tell me—what's the matter? I blew it, I know, I'm really sorry." Christ, all these *apologies!* "Now—"

Duane opened the door. Sliding quickly to earth, he stormed off angrily along the road.

"Come back!" April shouted, bundling out her own door. "God dammit, Duane: *you come back here!*"

"Yeah," Tina echoed self-righteously. "You better come back, Duane, or Mommy's gonna kick your butt!"

"Oh shut up!" April snapped. "Nobody's going to kick any butts around here. *Duane!*"

Outraged by the injustice of her mother's reprimand, Tina started to bawl. "You said not to say 'shut up,' Mommy! You said not to say 'shut up'!"

"Hijo madre!" April started sprinting down the road,

266

but a sharp twinge in her hip almost made her jackknife over in pain—she let out a startled squawk, caught herself immediately, and, forcing herself not to limp, grimacing from the hurt, she loped around in front of Duane, blocking his path, and settled her hands on her hips, legs spread defiantly. The boy halted, biting his lip. He kept his red eyes locked on the ground.

"Hey, Duane, lover—come on, have a heart," April coaxed. Kneeling, flinching from the intense fire in her hip joint, she took his chin between thumb and forefinger and tilted up his head. "Hey, sweet, please. I said I'm sorry. Now knock it off. I didn't mean to be brusque back there, honest. It's just hot, and I'm a little pooped, that's all. I told you I'm sorry. I really mean it."

"You're *always* a little tired," Duane complained unhappily.

"Okay, I'm guilty as charged, I'll admit that. Now come on, love, back to the car. Let's go home, have a soda— we'll make a black cow, okay? Please—"

"We don't have any ice cream," Duane said cagily.

"So we'll buy some on the way home, all right?"

"Sure. . . ."

He followed her to the car, and they turned around, heading back toward town. April zoomed into the Foodway lot, almost hitting Miranda Stryzpk this time, parked the car, and everything would have been all right if, just as they were getting out, Duane had not mustered the courage to insist: "Well, I still think he loves you."

"Who?" April asked abstractedly; her mind had already been on more pressing considerations.

"George Parker."

"Jesus Christ, honey, are we back *there* again?"

Once more bursting into tears, Duane jumped from the car and ran away. "Oh no!" April cried. "I don't believe I did it two times in a row!" And the chase was on again.

"I want a daddy!" Tina shrieked, incensed at being left behind, alone and abandoned. *"Won't somebody please find me a fucking daddy?"*

ON THE EVENING OF Juan GeeGee's funeral, Charlotte Leyba parked a late-model car outside her father-in-law's small house and banged on Virgil's door. Her knock woke him up. Arriving home from work only a few minutes before, he had fallen asleep at his kitchen table. A pot on the stove, its coffee water boiled off, was burning. Virgil let her in. Charlotte sniffed the air and rushed to the stove.

"Good Lord, Dad, you'll burn the house down!"

"Let it burn. Let it burn."

"Oh come on, things can't be that bad."

She plunked her purse down and sat in his other kitchen chair. Dark hair was fluffy around her shoulders; beautiful black eyes floated sadly in her pale face. She wore a lime-green jersey and a cream-colored skirt, stockings, and a pair of green suede shoes. Her subtle perfume touched Virgil enormously. And, gazing at her sleepily, he wondered how Junior had won her, and why he treated her with such disdain.

Any other visitor would have automatically fashioned a drink without asking permission. Charlotte awaited his offer, asked for a gin and tonic, accepted some white wine on ice instead, and stirred the drink once with her finger, licking the finger. And Virgil continued gazing at her. A woman that feminine awed him—fragile, provocative, smooth. Her fingernails were done so perfectly; no blemishes marred her exquisite face. Sensually, Virgil enjoyed her immensely, always looking forward to her visits. She rarely came, however; Junior forbade it. And when she did appear, it usually meant trouble.

"How are you feeling, Dad? Is that cough any better?"

"Oh, I'm in tip-top shape," Virgil said vaguely. "How's everything between you and the human piranha fish?"

She surprised him by being abrupt. "If I could leave him I would, Dad. It's no better, it's much worse."

"I'm sorry to hear that."

"You don't know what goes on between us," she said.

"That I'll certainly admit."

"I don't know what's wrong with Junior. I don't know what's wrong with me."

"I haven't known what's wrong with Junior since he was a little kid," Virgil said bitterly, rolling a cigarette.

"He loves you, Dad."

"Bullshit."

Easily intimidated, Charlotte stirred her drink again, sipped from it, and set it down. Then she blurted:

"We're so unhappy. Junior never talks anymore. We avoid each other, we can't raise our eyes when we do talk. We eat so many silent dinners. Sometimes I glance up and he's looking at me like he put poison in my food, and it scares me so I burst out crying. I don't know what's happening to him, I don't know what's happening to us. The phone is always ringing, it's always for him. Most nights he leaves the house after dinner and comes home late, and sometimes he never comes home at all. I suppose he's having an affair, and I don't even care. In fact, if he's having a relationship that offers some gratification, all I can do is wish him well. It's horrible being so alone even though you're together. A man, a Mr. Bonatelli, visits the house sometimes, and they talk in the den, and then I feed them and we all eat silently. It's driving me crazy because I don't know what's happening, but I do know that something is going on. I ask Junior, and he won't tell me. Once when I insisted, he slapped me and said, 'The fucking Betterment of fucking Chamisaville is none of your fucking business.' Those were his exact words. There are so many deals going on, and he's so nervous, and I know he's afraid of going to jail because he talks in his sleep. Electricity in the Pueblo has a lot to do with it. Once he tore an *El Clarín* to shreds and literally screamed that if Anthony Martínez did one more anti-electricity cartoon, he'd go out to the Pueblo and personally strangle him with his bare hands. But he won't tell me what's going on, and it doesn't make him happy, not at all. He hates himself, and he can't stop himself, and I can't stop him. And sometimes I think he's going to shoot me with that pistol of his, and sometimes I wish he would. And sometimes I think he's going to shoot himself with it."

Virgil expected her to cry. Instead, Charlotte sipped from her drink, then held it quietly in both hands.

Virgil said. "He's no good. You ought to leave him."

"Where would I go? What would I do?"

"You're a beautiful woman," Virgil said.

"As if that had anything to do with it."

"You should not stay any longer. He's no good, he'll kill you."

"How can you say that, being his father?"

"I *was* his father."

"Sometimes I wonder if you know anything at all about Junior," she said defiantly.

"At this late date, that's immaterial. He chose to rape people with his skills. There's no justification."

"I told you he loves you. That's a fact."

"He hates my guts. He poisons my life."

"He idolizes you," she said courageously.

Virgil squinted, inspecting the tip of his cigarette. He didn't wish to be rough or cruel with this gentle woman.

"He is a human being who has no love."

"When we first met, he was full of love. I don't know what happened. For almost a year we were so happy it was insane. He had so much energy, such good energy. He often told me it was because he was two thousand miles from home, and nothing bleak could touch him back East. We used to make love three, four, five times a night. He was a wonderful lover, and he used to smile a lot back then, and laugh sometimes, and he was a terribly handsome man, and very strong. I believed in him. I believed in him totally. Then we returned, and it all went wrong. And I don't even know why. It was already here, waiting for him. For us. He was sullen right away, and then he turned into a monster, and then he disappeared, leaving this shell behind."

"Drop him before he kills you."

"Dad, you're so gentle, you're so strong. You work yourself to death for people, you don't make them pay if they can't, you're a beautiful and compassionate man. Why is it that all you can muster for Junior is hatred?"

"I've told you before. He is a false man. He would sell out anybody for a price."

Fumbling in her purse for cigarettes, Charlotte lit up a filtered brand. A cat hopped silently onto the table and sniffed through old dirty dishes and half-filled glasses, then curled up among the newspapers and legal papers, making a nest, and fell asleep.

"You must understand what's wrong," Charlotte said. "You must have the key, Dad, why won't you tell me?"

Virgil opened his hands, palms up. He wondered how to express it to her, how to convince her of his position.

"Junior is a mystery," he said at last. "I have never understood him, you should believe that. Between us, from a very early age, there has always been an antagonism. We were never able to talk about it. I tried to love him, I think, although I have always been an aloof man. But I couldn't love him because he was coming from somewhere and headed toward someplace that I did not understand. I could never figure our problem out, I'm sorry. But it was always there. Both before and after he broke my heart by becoming a thief, an opportunist, a viper."

"Didn't you ever try to think it out?"

"I couldn't," Virgil said. "I don't know why. I couldn't help him."

Charlotte stubbed out her cigarette on a plate and used the butt to push around the ashes. Virgil sat very still, feeling sympathy for her, wishing he could do or say something to lessen hurt.

Finally, she said, "This place is a mess," and began clearing the table. Virgil said nothing. She made him coffee, then stacked all his dishes, filled a tub with suds, turned on the radio to pop music, and washed everything she could gather. Virgil made no move to stop her. He simply sat at the table, sipping his coffee, letting her clean and organize the kitchen as they listened to sappy music. Charlotte, crying very quietly, could not look at him, although he followed her every move around the kitchen. She neatened the newspapers, stacked his legal papers in a pile, emptied ashtrays, cleaned the stove, and junked the old cat box Kitty Litter, pouring in a fresh sack.

When everything was properly arranged, she put her arms around his neck and rested her damp cheek against the top of his head for a moment. It had gotten dark outside, almost nighttime. Charlotte gave Virgil a little kiss, walked out the door, and got in her car, but did not start it up. From his place at the kitchen table Virgil could see her, seated behind the wheel, not moving. It grew darker in his kitchen. A last meadowlark called; nighthawks were overhead, chasing evening insects. Virgil heard a trickle of music from her car. Still, Charlotte did not start up or move. Virgil could feel a faint cool sensation as dew stirred through the screen door. He began drifting, and as he did so her car started dissolving, until several minutes—or perhaps an hour—later, she was gone.

At the table Virgil slept. His unquiet dreams commenced their restless prowling. But before they could take shape, he was awakened by a change in his body chemistry, a chill sprinting through his bones, causing his flesh to spring cold sweat, making his scalp prickle with fear—and he awoke.

A skeleton, its bones shiny gold, was sitting in the chair across from Virgil, framed by its own enormous white wings, which rose considerably above the sardonic, grinning skull—Cipi García, believe it or not, back from the dead to torment any and all of the lost souls involved with the climax of his violent legacy.

"Go away," Virgil said grumpily. "Don't bother me. Life is tough enough."

And the ghoulish thing melted through his wall into the night.

ON A SINGLE MORNING, two days after their brief confrontation in the hospital parking lot, April received three letters from George Parker: jumbled, passionate, single-spaced . . . three, four, six pages long.

> . . . I want you now more than anything I have ever wanted before. I want to lie down with you, holding you close, getting to know you. I want to lie down with you out of curiosity; I want to know all the mystery of you. What happened in New York, in Paris, in Collioure, in Spain? I want to lie down with everything I don't know about you and don't want to know about you. Tell me about lovers, famous artists, movie stars, matadors! I want to lie down with all the things that have become old and tired to the woman I lay down with before, but which can be fresh again in new arms, new limbs, a new face, new ears! *Escape!* Take me away from the Mosquito Valley, the trailer parks, the Judson Babbitt kitsch and the Denzil Spivey fascism and the pathos of those drunks in the alley beside Vigil's! I am so excited by all the nameless and the well-known dangers! I know you have been battered and I'm willing to batter you some more! I'm willing to insult you by asking you to be a part-time lover, to be my "mistress" I guess is the term, even as I know you must have needs I probably can't fulfill. And I'm scared stiff you don't really like me at all, scared stiff that if you gave in to me it would be some kind of charity lay because you feel responsible for opening a Pandora's box. But you *are* terribly lonely, aren't you? You *are* terribly hungry, aren't you? You don't have to answer, I already know.
>
> . . . Christ, I feel guilty, hosing you down with so much passion when it's been years since I treated Susan to some kind of sincere ardor! But I can't help it—you feel what you feel what you feel!
>
> . . . I've been crying so much lately. Tears surge up out of nowhere at the drop of a hat. I'm so confused and full of yearning! It feels miserable; it also

272

feels *good*. At least I'm *alive!* I'm trying hard to write somehow half-assedly honest and lovely letters to you. Then again, sometimes all this seems too much like a kind of verbal masturbation; and I've had too much truck with all kinds of masturbation in my life. Lord, how I envy you your *experience!* I envy you the number of people you may have known who sing, or have sung, your tunes! I'm so hungry to have truck with men and women like you, with your frame of reference, your attitudes about life! Wouldn't it be good, couldn't it be simple, just the two of us out at the Martínez shack? With a bottle of wine, and the door open, listening to the coyotes howl? How can I convince you? I'm ashamed at what I'm doing, but I can't stop. I can't believe I'm so pushy, obnoxious, intrusive. But if you get away I feel that there'll never again be any magic in my life. I *need* this adventure for my own survival, it's as simple and as selfish as that!

April groaned, blew strands of hair from her eyes, and replied:

George, for Christ's sake! You're running too fast, do me a favor, stop and think for a minute. There's too much room, in a liaison between us, for hurting other people, for hurting each other. Whether you like it or not you are still a married man in a small southwestern town. I have a thousand friends in this valley who would be offended if they discovered that we were into some so-called hanky-panky. If that sounds like I'm coming on mighty square for this day and age, let alone my personal story, perhaps that's so. Not that the scandal could shock anybody: but it could lessen the *trust* of people I really care about and came back to work for. But of course you cannot know the kind of investment I now consider that I have in this valley. I came home last year desperately hoping to focus a life that has for too long been unfocused and tawdry at times, and seriously weighed down by waste and carelessness and impetuous decisions. I came back determined to eradicate the self-indulgent streak in myself and to conquer the spoiled brat that has led me astray, made me arrogant when I should have been humble, sabotaged my efforts to achieve some kind of dignity in this old Crap Game, as my father says. I'm tired, and I don't want to blow it again. We need each other like we need holes in the head. Figure out where you are at *by yourself, please. Don't use me to make decisions about your life!* Perhaps a day will come when we may get together in some kind of more legitimate manner. You still have a decent life, George, and I believe that I have established myself in a good realm, and I am determined to work harder than ever to preserve this hard-won position. I'd survive our affair, and you'd survive it—we all would, I know, but why encourage the trauma in the first place? Why more shit? Why diminish ourselves in a world that is basically, to begin with, a fucking slaughterhouse? Look, what makes this whole thing so damned difficult is the undeniable *goodness* of straight-out, knock-down, funky passion . . . yet I think I understand it a little more than you do, and I think it is inevitably co-opted by some very destructive contradictions. So I can even say "I love you, George." I love you, *but*— Still, I wish I could tell you truly emphatically to fuck off, but I can't. I can't seem to close the door entirely. I keep thinking in the back of my mind that there's a way something could work out. It's possible. I can't maintain my celibacy forever. I was never that kind of woman. But I think that anything with you is much too fraught with danger. I picture you, if we once began, suddenly slamming down on me, outraged because the glamour you thought you saw in me didn't exist the way you wanted it to, because the adventurous sexuality you sensed from afar turned out to be ordinary and everyday, only special in a way that the mundane can become special and precious when it is good. I have had too much experience with men who, overcome with my surfaces, became enraged when I turned out different and couldn't meet their chauvinistic expectations. I feel only danger in your awe of me, in what it might touch off in myself, even though I have changed a lot, in how it might enchain or detonate things in you that I don't want to deal with.

Yet I love you. Or anyway, right now I love the idea of fucking with you. The more I think about you, the more I stoke my personal lusts, and I wish

274

for a time with you. If only to use you to satisfy those base and beautiful needs that have always rocked my world, keeping me off-balance. But Juan GeeGee's legs were blown off, and he died; there's murder in Vietnam! Something terrible is going to happen if electricity enters the Pueblo, and we've got to learn *what* before it's too late. In the next issue of the *El Clarín* we're going to publish a suppressed hydrologist's report, done in the early 1930s by somebody named Wayne Tupalo, claiming that the Cañoncito Dam *never would hold water!* They went ahead and built it anyway in order to tax the marginal people off the land. That's what's important for me now.

Yet sometimes, George, I read your letters, and shiver. It's a trick, isn't it, the way desire is increased —artificially—by all this ranting and raving about abstinence and constraint. It is so bourgeois it's humiliating! Jesus our programming runs deep! Yet the more adamantly I press for us to drop the subject and go back to our old friendship, the more I want to fuck you. I should have cut you off cold, but I didn't. That must mean I can't. Maybe we should give up and try each other out, see what happens, if only for a single evening—but I know that couldn't happen. If we begin, who knows where the hell it will end? There's almost no such thing in life as a quickie! Lord, but life is a raucous dance!

He called her up, his voice trembling. "April, I'm not sure I understand your last letter."

"I'm not sure I understand it either."

"We have to get together."

"I know."

"Oh wow," he whispered, "then we can." And stopped himself from asking: Do you *really* mean it?

AS HE DID REGULARLY AT THAT TIME, one day each week, Rodey McQueen parked his automobile in front of the Chamisaville Inn and entered the main lobby and bar area where nearly two hundred locals, tourists, and a nasal folksinger held sway. McQueen nodded to the nattily attired bartender, an Anglo anthropology Ph.D. from Massachusetts named Ben Updike, greeted Jonathan and Tucker Moose with a quick howdy and a shoulder-squeeze, and never stopped moving between the front desk and the hallway leading back to the rooms and cabins of this splendid hotel.

In that short stretch, however, McQueen took in the entire room, making notations on who was there, and who was with whom and why. Joseph Bonatelli was seated at a table with Junior Leyba—McQueen had known of the meeting, had approved it, in fact. Elsewhere, Virgil Leyba sat with a young and rather attractive Anglo woman whom McQueen had never seen before: perhaps some lawyer connected with downstate Legal Aid or the ACLU. Long-haired young toughs like Benny LeDoux and one-legged Alfredo GeeGee and their crowd leaned on the bar, numb from drugs or drink, talking little, and eyeing the folksinger with lethargic hostility. Close by, a lovely, dark-skinned girl was engaged in an animated conversation with that obstreperous Anti-Electricity Coalition and *El Clarín* youngster, Anthony Martínez. At one table, the two FBI agents, Len Goodwin and Chet Fulton, chatted with town police chief Fernando Baca, in plain clothes, and the county sheriff, Big Bill Baca. Ralphito García was standing in a corner, nursing a beer. And members of a summer softball team, wearing Moose and McQueen T-shirts, had jammed together several tables, lifting beer steins, being noisy—no doubt they had won a game that afternoon. Though they were mostly Anglos, McQueen only recognized a few of the ball players. So many newcomers were flooding town . . . business had never been better.

McQueen nodded at some people, shook a couple of hands, and then passed into the hallway, heading outside again. Turning left onto a weathered wooden staircase, he climbed toward a third-floor "tower," the most select accommodation his hotel offered, a square room bordered on all four sides by windows offering a 360-degree panorama of the Chamisa Valley.

Miranda Stryzpk was seated in a deep, deerhide armchair with a martini at her elbow, reading the latest *Vogue*. The coy, frosty smile she gave him matched her icy lipstick. A fiftyish sleek woman of enduring sexuality, Miranda kept in good shape with a careful diet, yoga, plenty of swimming and horseback riding, two Geritols a day, and all the proper civic activities. An after-five alcoholic with strawberry blond hair, wide-set eyes, cool full lips and unwrinkled features partially the result of several face-lift operations, she had wide shoulders, a high slim waist, an attractively plump belly, ample hips, and long, shapely legs. The hem of her one-piece jersey dress was slightly above the knee; her suede slingbacks had skinny two-inch heels. But no jewelry; McQueen didn't like jewelry.

The boss took off his sportjacket, loosened his bolo tie, and quickly rolled up his sleeves. Moving to an ice bucket holding the martini pitcher, he poured a short drink and sat down on the bed, facing her. Miranda turned the *Vogue* toward him, opened; her calculating eyes watched him coolly over the edge of the magazine as he reacted to an ad her long, well-tanned finger indicated. A voluptuous young woman in a crimson tanksuit cut to her navel was emerging happily from a frothy turquoise ocean. Her breasts were wholly etched against the damp nylon fabric; even the pattern of her pubic hair and the shape of her vagina could be seen through the tight, soaked elastic.

McQueen said, "Big deal. She's got nice jugs, but I bet she couldn't sell hacksaws in a hoosegow."

"I thought you might like her."

"I might. But I'm old enough for my wants not to hurt me anymore. Besides, I've got all the poontang I can handle."

"What you were supposed to say, darling, was that she might be nice, but nobody could ever take my place."

McQueen tossed off his drink, stood up, and went to a window. On the highway traffic was thick, the parking lot directly below was filling up with cars—he recognized many of them. Arm in arm, Claude and Rachel Parker walked away from their aqua Buick, heading toward the entrance. Up north, all kinds of construction bordered the highway. McQueen knew most of the jobs, the crews employed, the financing, the subcontracting, how the materials breakdown added up, what payoffs had been necessary. Dust hanging in a low layer farther north partially obliterated Chamisaville itself. A turn to the west brought a more rustic plain. Fertile fields dotted with grazing animals stretched into Ranchitos Abajo, ending at a sharp cliff rising a hundred feet to mesa level.

"Dale," she mocked, "I don't think we can go on meeting like this."

Frowning, he glanced down at her legs, nicely stockinged in a nylon not quite sheer; a hint of snow opaqued it. Right now he desired her sexually, but had no inclination for talk or arguments. In fact, despite all the years of their trysting, McQueen had never really gotten used to her sharp tongue. Miranda always made him a bit uneasy, he had never been certain that she wouldn't turn on him one day. Occasionally, he wondered how much Moe knew about their affair. And although such dramatic thoughts rarely bothered a man of his blunt and shortsighted arrogance, there flickered in his unconscious self a tiny flame of catastrophe that always left him feeling a tad unsettled after a meeting with his attractive woman, the frustrated wife of a brilliant paralytic who suffered—even McQueen knew this—through a weather of the heart so dark nobody would ever even halfway correctly gauge it.

Kneeling between McQueen's legs, Miranda puttered with his fly. While she busied herself, he gazed out the window at the steady stream of automobiles—vacation vehicles, hippie vans, Cadillacs, VW buses filing by. A staccato hammering carried from a dozen frames of cheap houses rising out of the mesa on his subdeveloped land. Grinding gears signaled that cement trucks were tipping their big beehives to pour foundations, working overtime. Dynamite booms carried down from the new ski runs at the Mosquito Valley. Lately, the commercial agitation of the valley might suddenly thrust against McQueen, making him feel slightly out of kilter in a manner he did not understand. And he had dreams of the whole scheme melting through his fingers, escaping his control, running away from himself and Bob Moose and Moe Stryzpk and Randolph Bonney. Certain aspects of the growth confusion, and all the newcomers intimately related to Anglo Axis concerns, were beginning to make him feel old-fashioned. A new ruthlessness had seeped into the Old Crap Game. Juan GeeGee's death weighed on his conscience. Granted, to get this far they had all been unmitigated bastards: "You can't make an omelet," McQueen had been fond of saying, "without breaking some eggs."

But these days, with the biggest deal of all hanging in abeyance, waiting for Pueblo electrification, there was a new kind of evil afloat that made his skin crawl. Just the other day, J. B. LeDoux had approached him with a wild look in his eyes. "When it gets quiet—have you noticed that lately?" the mayor had asked abruptly. "And there's nothing. The air stands still. The whole town is like a deer frozen in fear, sniffing for the scent of a hunter it knows is around, but can't quite yet locate."

J. B. had said that. And then he had whispered, *"There's a ghost in the music!"* And even though McQueen

278

had no idea what J. B. meant, that statement had caused his neck hairs to quiver!

April's return, and her role as gadfly to their reactionary scheming, had focused the discomfort nudging his guts. I'm growing old, he often thought, and somehow not everything is adding up. All his accomplishments had begun to give him but restricted satisfaction. If only this final scam—and he thought of it that way often, as "final" —if only it could less sluggishly approach fruition. Icarus Suazo had at least three council members out there lined up in favor of the electricity, one other was undecided, two still opposed it. According to Suazo. But he was convinced he could win them over—yet why was it taking so much time? Whenever McQueen asked that question, Icarus merely shrugged, and a twinkle seemed to enter his eyes as he murmured, "That is the Indian way, McQueen."

All his life, Rodey McQueen had expected "something special to happen" as a result of his grand-scale finagling, his hotels and his ski valley, his motels and his banking interests and the Dynamite Shrine complex. But a mystical, magical rapport with his realized dreams had failed to materialize. Instead, the rhythms of his work grew more pressing, he felt a more urgent drive to expand, grow, accumulate. It had never been, and was not now, possible to stop, reflect, or really enjoy. The result was an insinuation of frantic feelings, even panic, into his daily labor. Yet McQueen had an honest longing for rest and retirement. He had a longing to cast his arms around a complete experience—his life's work—and be able to judge it and enjoy it and inspect it much as he might judge and enjoy and inspect a fabulous painting. But he had chosen a métier which allowed no summing up. Capitalism had no limitations: Progress, American-style would sit still for no photographs: the Betterment of Chamisaville condoned no reflection in tranquility upon the meaning and origin of things.

McQueen said, "I don't know what's happening with people, I really don't. Everybody's running around so helter-skelter; when they stop for a breath it takes their shadows five minutes to catch up. Old age should allow for dignity, instead we're all becoming too shrill. This should be a time for enjoying the fruits of our labor. Instead, the pace quickens, there is no end to it. I'm taking too many Alka-Seltzers these days. There's not room enough in Chamisaville anymore to skin a cat without getting hair in your mouth. Sometimes I wake up in the middle of the night shivering like a lizard looking for a hot rock."

A splash of magenta in the air by Magpie Creek, east of Cañoncito, caught his eye. Startled for a second, amazed at the size of such a bird, he then realized it was only a hang-glider. Two years ago some newcomers had started floating in gaily colored kites off the rocky slopes of a perfect foothill down there. McQueen had driven over with Cynthia one Saturday for a look-see. Footloose long-haired boys and a lanky, brown-skinned California girl glided into updrafts and sailed happily through the air like splashy molecules from a futuristic dream. Instead of delighting McQueen, their daring, free-form soaring and hawklike antics had made him angry. As if they were stealing his thunder, mocking his generation by their cavalier attitude toward gravity, their fey drifting somehow a threat to his flights of plotting, wheeling, dealing, and stealing. The danger they ignored had roots in a purposeless wanderlust antithetical to the purpose he thought he had had all his life. Scornful of all work ethics themselves, the kids were wealthy worthless bums, living on Daddy's dole. Now, as he watched the hang-glider float over Cañoncito and the highway, heading toward the gorge, McQueen felt bitter and betrayed: Miranda gurgled quietly in his lap.

"So many things that make no sense are happening. Did you hear that Fecundo Lavadie, Max Jaramillo, Bonifacio Herrera, and Ikie Trujillo were paroled? I'm told they came home completely unnoticed, robbed Midnight Sporting Goods, and made off with a virtual arsenal. It was kept quiet so as not to alarm folks. But rumor has it they joined up with Jesus Etcetera—even though we all know Jesus Etcetera has been no more than a figment of everybody's imagination for over fifty years. Still, I don't understand how people manage to cling to him—symbolically, metaphorically, or however the hell it is they cling. I don't know. Every now and then I just feel like there's a weevil in the boll. Never lasts for long, of course—I don't believe in doom. But after all these years . . ."

And then McQueen caught his breath. Jackhammers stopped, hammers ceased banging, gears quit grinding. Traffic, in a five-mile jam, came to a complete halt. The brightly colored hang-glider above the mesa beyond Borregas Negras slowed down as if entering invisible molasses and then it actually stalled, suspended in a colorless amber. McQueen gasped, sucking for air in a vacuum, his entire body wreathed in panic as sperm swelled up through his penis and halted at the tip, refusing to explode. In agony he waited, and Miranda waited, and the automobiles waited; and the hang-glider quivered motionlessly, captured in secret historical forces McQueen knew nothing about.

Not even a cry could break from his throat. Feeling dizzy, he begged for an orgasm that never matured. Sluggishly, the hang-glider quivered and commenced a slow descent . . . a car-horn beeped . . . church bells pealed . . . automobiles began again to move. *Ralphito García . . . ? In a corner . . . ? Nursing a beer . . . ?*

Miranda lifted her head, eyeing him with bemused, and prurient, and superior disdain.

# I Wish
# I Could Stay
# on This Earth
# Forever

WITH FILM TO DEVELOP and several *El Clarín* articles in the typewriter, Juan Ortega had agreed to stay over, babysitting Duane and Tina. April's alibi was the movies, a double feature, and afterward a few drinks, perhaps, at the Chamisaville Inn. She clicked beer cans with Juan and polished off the last of her Bud, the third she had downed in half an hour. Smiling gaily at the old man, April gave a little clenched-fist salute, said, "Hasta la victoria siempre," and tripped lightly out to her car, giddy, already on fire, as nervous as a bucktoothed teen-ager heading for her first prom.

In town, she hit Vigil's Liquors for a half-pint bottle of blackberry brandy. A dusty, summer dusk settled over Chamisaville as she headed south past the Wacker's and Foodway shopping center, the new courthouse complex, the Piggly Wiggly and TG&Y shopping center, the Tastee-

Freez, A&W, Our Lady of the Sorrows Hospital, and Irving Newkirk's motel, pawnshop, café, and trailer-park development. April could remember when all the highway land between La Ciénega and Cañoncito had been wild sage—desolate and beautiful. Back in the forties dead jackrabbits and prairie dogs often lined the highway shoulders. But no more; and never again. The honky-tonk strip was here to stay.

April slowed down for cars turning into the General Custer Drive-In: a Wednesday-night double feature in Spanish—Cantinflas and Antonio Aguilar. April recalled regularly attending that same Wednesday double feature twenty-five years ago, with Junior Leyba, George Parker, and all the rest of her pals; Jolene Popper, Rebecca Valerio, the Ortega twins. Instead of rising clear, however, the memory of those days created a nostalgic clot in her throat, and she gasped slightly, hurt by the mortality of all experience, her life rhythm betrayed by a sudden urge toward remorse. Ever since her cancer had been diagnosed, the past would occasionally intrude, catching her off-guard, belittling her style. For April had never lamented the past nor pined for better than she had received. She had never been haunted by what might have been, nor had she ever been homesick for what had occurred.

But sometimes memories of "the old days" generated a brief guilt and disappointment that perturbed her. She likened the sensations to early stirrings of self-pity and forcefully cut them off. A real horror that she had was of somehow ending up in a bitter middle age. To that end she must always review the past without active pain; and keep it from becoming too real.

April unscrewed the top of the blackberry brandy and took a swig. Cool wind swooping through the sunroof buffeted her free-flowing hair: thick strands battered her face softly. She was in no great hurry; the car drifted past gas stations, trailer rentals, Bonney's Ford dealership, the Chevrolet showroom, Moose's Used Cars, the new Seven-Eleven, a package store, a bar, some real-estate housing mockups, a Pizza Hut, the KOA Kampground, and her father's enormous complex, the Chamisaville Inn. In Cañoncito, the general store was closed, fluorescent lights illuminated the tiny post office, beer signs blinked and sizzled outside the La Lomita Dance Hall—jukebox music blared through the door. As the road dipped, April geared down, veering to avoid several cows stupidly arrayed along the highway. Accelerating up past the Mota Llano turnoff, she climbed onto the level mesa again; all development fell behind. Maintaining a speed of forty, April sucked more juice from her bottle, and the pain in her hip joint receded, died away completely. She removed her sunglasses and grooved on the Turneresque twilight—cottony crimson swirls, mellow jaundice, layered rainbow pastels. Sagebrush swooped away from the highway in a creamy lavender drift; the gorge was a dusky crack in the earth; soft hills and chubby mountains beyond had a pointillist purple tinge, and seemed weightless, floating against the horizon whorls like calm breasts and limbs after heated loving. As usual, the smell of the dissolving daytime was almost poignant enough to make April weep.

Out in the middle of nowhere she turned right onto an unmarked dirt path and followed it for about a half-mile through relentless, shoulder-high sage to the old Martínez shack, where her lover waited. Parking in front of the simple structure, she cut the engine and sat still with the bottle in her lap, the taste of sweet sticky liquor fresh on her tongue. A hundred wind-blistered, sun-brightened bones fanned out from the front stoop. Many, half buried in sand, twinkled phosphorescently. The door was open; a kerosene-colored light showed within. Wind chimes tinkled as a puff whispered through. April waited a moment longer for George to emerge, and then realized he was looking down at her from the roof.

"Hello, George. Fancy meeting you here."

"Hi. Come on up. I was just sitting here, getting pickled, watching the sunset."

"You don't have to get drunk, you know."

"It's a lovely evening, I feel good. Come on."

April climbed the handmade ladder up to the dirt roof, and touched his face with her hand; his lips formed a kiss in her palm. She settled beside him, cross-legged, facing west. He had a six-pack in his lap: he was wearing a white T-shirt, faded dungarees, no shoes.

They drank, without talking, while the sun merged with the burnished horizon. The western hills quivered in an apricot sheen; the sagebrush glowed eerily; stars came out. April pressed fingertips against his chest, urging him over onto his back. George joined his hands behind his head, facing the sky. Kneeling over him, blond hair splashing around his face, she barely brushed his lips with a kiss. George closed his eyes and murmured; he was trembling.

"Don't be scared, love."

"I'm not. I just can't stop trembling."

April shifted, unbuttoning his jeans, and held his penis between her palms. With her tongue she dabbed spittle on his tip and used her thumb and forefinger to rub it around a moment, then lowered her head, giving a slow blowjob, sucking gently—"It's all right . . . you can come in my mouth if you want."

Fearfully, George slipped his fingers into her thick hair and held her lightly, afraid to exert any pressure. April ceased all motion, held him in her mouth just barely squeezing with her tongue every few seconds, both of them absolutely stilled. Then she could feel an intensification of heat, a sudden swollen expansion preceding ejaculation that made an exciting pressure slam down through her own body—half pain, half orgasm—she gagged as his come clogged her throat, swallowed some, and let the rest drool between her lips down his erection into the curly pubic hair. Backing off, she gasped for air, happy but wishing the relief had been greater.

"Oh Jesus, April! I don't know where that came from! I don't know how to explain how good that felt—"

"This is nice," she said, lips pressed against his T-shirt, the hard muscles beneath. "This will be so lovely, George. I promise. . . ."

His body shivered in a different way: he was crying, gripping her head tightly, silently wailing.

"No no, love, please. Don't do anything to this. It's all right, it's going to be a perfect night."

"I'm okay. I just never thought it could happen. I still don't believe— I didn't want to come that quickly. I'm terrified of not being good enough for you."

"Don't worry about any of that, darling. It doesn't matter at all. I told you before. . . ." Hey, what *joy* to be engulfed in the arms of a man, his still-hard cock slimy against one ear, the taste of his come in her mouth! How did I go so long without it? April wondered dazedly. I mustn't ever do that again. Sex is too much a good part of the good things in life.

"I don't believe this is happening," he said, still crying. "I love you so much."

"You have to promise me one thing." April cupped his softening penis and balls.

"What is it? I'll promise anything."

284

"If you want this to end, if you want the affair to stop, you must say so and it will stop. I promise."

"It isn't an 'affair'—Lord, how I hate that word! It's so fucking tawdry. I don't want it to stop. I love you."

"Listen to me carefully, George. You have no obligation, understand? Neither do I. If I feel it should end, I'll say so, and that's it. If you want to cut it off, all you have to do is say so and it's over."

"Don't *say* that, dammit. I don't want to think about that."

"You just need to understand, that's all."

"Are you saying you don't love me?"

"No sweet. I love you in certain ways. It's just very important that you understand I'm making no demands. That I'm very grateful for whatever loving we can share. But you have to know that if you ever feel trapped, or if you begin to feel guilty because of Susan and the kids, that I'll cut it off, just like that, at a single word from you. I don't want to accept anything from you George, except whatever you're willing to give."

"Shh. What are you saying? We haven't even begun and already you're talking about endings."

"I'm saying these things because I think I have some experience that you don't have, love. I know what the future can be, the many ways it might develop. And I don't want to be a drag on you. I want this to be clear and clean and good."

"It is. It has to be. You don't know— Oh man, you understand so much, April Delaney! You are so wise!" His hands came, fondling her breasts. "You have the most beautiful tits in the world!" While his fingers manipulated her nipples, playing them hard, she kneeled again, tossing her heavy hair, and drowsily smiled at the stars. Barely visible, bats stuttered around the shack; their wings whooshed close by. Far away, up north toward Borregas Negras and Mota Llano, where the irrigated pastures began, killdeers were screeching. Chamisaville twinkled at the foot of Hija Negrita, a looming silhouette of ponderous calm. Magical, peaceful, perfect. George unbuttoned her blouse, her breasts tumbled into his grasp. She straddled his waist, bent over, while he gently munched her tits. Erotic prickles traveled down her spine, claiming her buttocks, her groin, her thighs. A deep and easy pleasure formed. Maybe this man will turn out to be a real love, she thought hazily. Or my last, my only true love. Hope greased her limbs, saddled her soul. I still have so many years left to mature in, she thought. Roots, leaves, laughter branched throughout the superstitious soil of a strange country, and now this loving with George would clinch it—"I'm finally home."

An apparition gathered in her languid imagination, thick as woodsmoke, pungent as ovarian foam gradually accumulating in the drowning bodies of Chamisaville's beautiful slumbering brown women. A vivid menstrual stink mingled with the complicated nighttime smells. A kaleidoscope of odor slanted through the crystal darkness. Of skunks and damp roses, dust and horse manure, piñon and cedar, sagebrush and juniper, beehive honey and thigh-high fields of irrigated brome.

Sucking her breasts half into his mouth now, he grew urgent. April moaned gratefully, wanting him badly, but she was still only slightly lubricated, had been dry ever since the chemotherapy. Quietly drenching her fingertips with saliva, she massaged the lips of her vagina with the slime, then took him in easily with a happy sigh.

Shivering, April licked her lips, laughed, mussed his hair, chewed on his mouth, shined his teeth with her tongue, whispered, "Ay amor, I absolutely *love* it," and then rested blissfully, her body slackened with endless waves of orgasm, listening to coyotes barking in the sage.

A shot rang out a mile downwind on the mesa. Immediately the coyotes ceased their racket, bats quit flying—the night air emptied. Only a trembling of stars and of Chamisaville security lamps against the black cushioning skulk of Midnight Mountains defined the aftermath.

"What was that?" George asked.

"Probably just Jesus Etcetera and the four kidnappers, riding the western range, biding their time."

He scoffed, "Jesus Etcetera is dead."

April directly confronted his eyes and, bemusedly, teasing George with her tender affection, she sang:

> I dreamed I saw Joe Hill last night,
> Alive as you and me.
> Says I, "But Joe you're ten years dead,"
> "I never died," says he—

"You're beautiful, April. . . ."

A silence, composed of the mesa, the profound and mysterious gorge, a silky membrane of darkness, and the

286

looming Midnight Mountains, engulfed them in pitying arms. April dreamed she could hear pins scratching in three hardware and two sporting goods keyholes fifteen miles north of them, thieves attempting to pick the locks. And a particular splashing framed by an aged sigh indicated that Virgil Leyba, perched on the bank of his back field irrigation ditch, was relieving himself before bed. His zipper went up; a crickle of cigarette paper carried downwind as Virgil fashioned a final smoke. April smiled as Virgil's thumbnail struck a kitchen match. Then it was quiet but for a faint curly swirl each time the lawyer thoughtfully released smoke, gazing morosely aloft at the radiant, insolent universe that had sold out Mexico, and was making an incoherent salad of Chamisaville.

Farther north, at the Pueblo, the abrupt silence was as if a hole existed where the native people have been. Even the Midnight River dislodged no pebbles trickling through the main compounds. That eerie black emptiness almost chilled her. Each night the Pueblo dwellers temporarily died, freeing their souls to steal into the mountains where they kept prisoner a past century, hidden in a deep canyon somewhere on sacred Albino Pine land. That old century dwelled in a big cage up there; the souls of living people gathered each night to recharge themselves at the prison bars restraining their ancestors. But what could anybody ever really know? When April hearkened to the unelectrified Pueblo at night, it was like listening to an absence of thunder where thunder should have been.

FAGGED OUT, PLUMB TUCKERED, Benny LeDoux was going down fast. His life, a blur lived at half-speed, held few surprises. No longer ravaged by his own restless heart and confounded mind, he had drooped into a nihilistic conclusion. Total cynicism manipulated the controls of his body like a premeditating murderer. Alienation diseases of the North American continent, jelled by his Vietnam stint, dominated his aching flesh. Nothing mattered. "Live fast, die young, have a good-looking corpse" was a quotation, from a book he had once read, that repetitiously hammered on his mind. A listlessly aggressive junkie, his hapless days unraveled in a tense banality. Benny scored and cruised, listened to music, shot up, snorted, got high on whatever, dug summer snowstorms, balled a few lame chicks, got down on anybody who stepped on his shit or burned him in a deal, and slept only when exhaustion dropped him in his tracks. Pushing himself to fuzzy narcotic limits, he toyed with death, tinkering with the ultimate high, a sandman playfully teetering at the brink of hell among angels and archangels. He could be found, on his comatose middays, slouched halfway into midnight torpors, always doing dope, copping acid, fed up with dreary existence, no longer tormented by memories of better days or by dreams of an innocent ambition his parents, his school, his society had cynically murdered in childhood. And he was almost twenty-one.

Oh sometimes, very occasionally, the curtains parted, and Benny faced a long-haired strung-out Jesus in his mirror, surprised by the absolute beauty of his suffering black eyes, the enigmatic set of his powerful lips, and he dared wonder if a miracle would reach him in time. Then he shuddered as his face stiffened, growing callous, his pupils dilated, and a careless smile transformed his bloodless lips into an affectation of cruel stupor. Fuck it, he could dig it, this life that had chosen to dull all racist conflicts by vaccinating him against his parents' shamefulness, obliterating the anguish of alternatives, making him invulnerable because he had nothing to lose.

The ultimate high—Nothing To Lose. It had solved all his problems, answered all his prayers. Freedom was just another word—

At first, in Vietnam, dead bodies had been a real freakout. He had worried about souls—the souls of the dead, the souls of their killers. Awash in guilt all during his childhood, infuriated by the injustices that had castrated his old man and disemboweled his lovely mother, transforming them into pimp and prostitute, sycophant and whore, Benny had almost lost it in Vietnam. The war had threatened to tip the scales, driving him insane. Volunteering with an eye toward committing suicide, instead Benny had joined a murdering machine of almost faultless execution—an easier absolution, it turned out. And after a while he'd sauntered through Indochina like all relentless mercenaries of yore, repeatedly annihilating himself by slaughtering a racially stereotyped enemy he could despise as much as he despised his parents, himself, and everyone and everything else that a careful American minority upbringing had created, blowing them gooks to smithereens by day with the same unflagging determination he used blowing himself to smithereens at night in his dreams, in his marijuana fantasies, in his heroin reveries. Benny had castigated himself unmercifully by jigging dehumanized dinks with his M-16, cleansing the invisible earth of his own soul with their demise, purging his worthless culture, language, and Chicano hide by becoming an exterminating angel, the killing hand of a mighty and manifestly destined nation.

Benny LeDoux had had his day. If the Dynamite Shrine expanded, if electricity entered the Pueblo, if Joe Bonatelli planted a business associate in a shallow Nevada grave, if Miranda Stryzpk cheated on her tortured husband, if April Delaney died of cancer, if George Parker left his commonplace wife, if Virgil Leyba alcoholed himself beyond legitimate sorrows—it was so much rotten cotton to Benny LeDoux. The overall plan held his interest no better: how history turned out couldn't claim a footnote in his curiosity. Benny hunted money because it was the bullets to bring down his high-flying high, keeping him loose and goosey so that he could drift along the edge and be amused by the echo rebounding at him from the gorge.

More than once, in fact, Benny had driven north of town and west to the suspension bridge over the real gorge. Parking at a rest area, he walked to the center of the span and gazed with morbid fascination at the tiny Rio Grande a thousand feet below his Wellington boots. He made paper airplanes, decorated them with absurd mandalas, elaborately colored the mandalas with dime-store crayons, and sailed them off the bridge. They twirled endlessly, taking minutes to hit the water, no bigger than snowflakes by then. He drew sticklike pictures of himself on the paper airplanes, and flicked them over the railing. In his dreams he tumbled off that bridge, soaring lazily down toward the cream-green ribbon. The exhilaration generated by that fantasy flight toward death was so real that sometimes he awoke full of a miraculous pep he had not felt since early childhood.

Sometimes, Benny slumbered south to Cañoncito, halted his automobile on a mesa path near the foothills, and watched suntanned hang-gliding enthusiasts soar into the sky, sluicing their graceful shadows over his car where the tape deck blasted and the motor was always idling—Benny felt uneasy if his pistons weren't pumping and growling, he drew comfort from the constant mechanical consumption of gas, that motor involved somehow in a symbiotic alliance with his heart, keeping him vicariously alive.

Out on a secluded mesa drop-point quite early one morn-

289

ing, waiting for the first of the day's three regularly scheduled marijuana planes up from Chihuahua to drop him a
parcel free and clear of the taxation demanded on all their
bush when it was okayed through Big Bill Baca and his
county law enforcement crew at the airport, Benny was
doing a joint while listening wearily for the small plane's
drone, when he heard a snort behind his back. And, after
waiting an appropriate moment for some greedier *carnal* to
split his head open or plink a teeny bullet into his heart,
he turned around.

Several feet away a strange bunch of old horsemen regarded him somberly. Benny recognized the legendary
Jesus Etcetera, Fecundo Lavadie, Max Jaramillo, Bonifacio
Herrera, and Ikie Trujillo. Although the kidnappers still
wore their thin suits, jail-issue tennis shoes, and cheap
straw cowboy hats, now old-fashioned cartridge bandoliers
crisscrossed their chests and gunbelts circled their waists.
Bushy moustaches puffed from under their noses, and
grizzled beards would keep them warm come January.
Their eyes, vague and milky when they had arrived on the
Trailways bus a year ago, were hard and clear now, sizing
up Benny with unconditional severity.

"Hijo la madre!" Benny exclaimed matter-of-factly. "The
Cisco Kid, Emiliano Zapata, Pancho Villa, Tony Aguilar,
Tonto, and Gabino Barrera ride again."

Jesus Etcetera said, "I knew your great-grandfather, little
boy. We rode together against the cattle barons who fenced
the eastern land grants. We cut their barbed wire and
recruited the people into a militia. We invented the saying
'Cuando vino el alambre, vino el hambre.' We raided their
corrals and took back the horses they had stolen from us,
burned their shacks and broke into jail to free our own
people when they were taken prisoner. I also knew your
grandfather, and I watched them cut off his balls, fork his
tongue, rob his land, and set him against his own people,
making him so compromise his own soul that he finally
ended the disaster by forcing himself to drop dead. I have
watched them suck your own daddy into the vortex of
their relentless whirlpool, luring him ever farther into their
style of conquest until he is only a shell of a human being,
drenched in irreparable shame. Now I'm looking at you—
talk about pathetic!—continuing in what has become a
family tradition. Giving up, laying down between the
shameless thighs of their civilization, allowing them to
romp home, free of charge. But you have martial skills and

290

perhaps a corpuscle or two of pride left in your dissipated frame. We are forming an army to cut them off at the pass, so to speak, and need all the bodies we can get. Ride with us, young LeDoux, save yourself as a man."

Benny laughed sarcastically. "Get off my case, man. Who you trying to kid? Army, for crissakes! You old farts ride against them with those antique popguns and they'll blow you out of the saddle, paint your faces, throw you in a circus, charge admission to watch you jump around when they crack the whip, and knock those silly hats off your heads with popcorn shot from jockstraps!"

Jesus Etcetera said, "Benny LeDoux, I pity you."

"Save your pity for somebody with feelings."

Back home in his Dynamite Shrine room, Benny lay on his bed, puzzling not over Jesus Etcetera and his ragged-ass bandidos, but over why the pot drop hadn't materialized —for the plane had never showed. A double cross? Stopped at the border? Shot down over Alamogordo? Benny tapped his feet against the wall, wondering what to do for bread this week. His toes dislodged a piece of paper, a clod of dirt fell from a chink between adobes, and he thought he spied something funny jammed into the crack. He raised himself with an effort, and, using a toothpick, pried out an old condom, unraveled it, and fished clear a little bundle containing an old tooth, a lock of yellow hair, and a diamond engagement ring.

No longer susceptible to superstition, Benny whistled wryly over his good luck, hustled the ring on down to Irving Newkirk's pawnshop, received a hundred dollars, and on a whim decided to buy a piece—"just in case." So Irving recouped forty of his bucks in exchange for a palm-sized .25 automatic.

"No way a well-heeled vato like me is gonna receive any lip when he's got his rod at hand," Benny chuckled, sauntering gaily back to his idling automobile and blasting tape deck, happy as a clam and hungry as a jungle panther to score.

EVERYBODY IN THE Chamisa Valley was uneasy or agitated by some resolute anguish or agony. J. B. LeDoux teetered on the same brink he had patronized for years; Junior and Charlotte Leyba groveled sluggishly through a truly doomed love; Amaranta GeeGee lay in a hospital bed dreaming of the past, frightened of a future that now seemed to hold no hope; Celestino Lucero, romantic murderer, barehanded killer of mountain lions, shoveled shit and sold eggs for pennies to people like J. B. LeDoux; out at the town garbage pit, fast-sinking Ursula and Perfecto Torres passed their dreary hours among the flies, ravens, and putrefactions, running the bulldozers, collecting dumping fees, and—whenever either the town truck or a pickup hauling certain private trash appeared—picking through the refuse, searching for documents that might come in handy to the El Clarín; Virgil Leyba accumulated a dozen defeats each day and battled the cacophonous rattle of ancient sabers and historical vaudevillains in his brain; Juan Ortega struggled with anger, sanity, and sorrow, controlling his rage by writing for the El Clarín, feeding his despair by too often visiting the camposantos where too many of his children—victims of World War II, Korea, and Vietnam—were buried; Rodey McQueen lay awake at night, fearful of Joseph Bonatelli, and worried also that if his daughter continued to search for the real motives behind Pueblo electrification, sooner or later she would discover the secret—and then her well-being might pass out of his hands into the realm of an impersonal judiciary determined to shut her up in any way possible before she blew the whistle; and Icarus Suazo, hardened now into a loneliness as rigid as petrified wood, maintained his immediate surroundings cleansed of mortal companions so that he would be emotionally strong and invulnerable when dealing with white men on the convoluted and frightening electricity scam.

But April Delaney was born again. At 10:00 P.M., the sunroof of her Beetle open and the moon so bright she could extinguish her headlights, clanking along the white highway in natural nocturnal light, April sailed with a happy heart toward another rendezvous. George met her at the car even before the motor had died, embracing her as she got out. Pressing hard, kissing urgently, they plucked at clothes. April unzipped his fly and dropped to her knees: George pulled her up roughly by the hair, spun her around, folded her onto the front hood, and entered her from behind. April laughed, shouted, cursed at the top of her lungs. If the sex was joyous, let the world beware! "Come on, god dammit!" she hollered. "Stuff it up me, bang me, screw me! Hey, I love that cock! It's so hard! It's so BIG! *I can feel it all the way up in my throat!*"

"It's only an average American cock," he protested.

"It's wonderful," she laughed giddily, digging her own

silly hyperbole. "I love it. It must be at least ten slimy roaring raw red inches long!"

"Actually, I measured it once and it's only six inches long." George bent over, nibbling the nape of her neck, puzzled by the triple-branched scar he had noticed for the first time. "And I read somewhere that the average length of the American penis is about six and a quarter inches, erect. So I'm about fully a quarter-inch under the national average."

"It's not the size of the cock in the fight, it's the size of the fight in the cock!" April shouted dizzily. Her words rippled through the mesa blackness like technicolor hurricane bunting.

George whispered into her ear, his lips brushing the small lump April refused to think about: "Hey I love you so much, April Delaney. This affair is suddenly so *easy*. It's so much fun. What a miracle. We're so lucky. I feel like I'm sixteen years old again. I walk around all day with a sensual contraction in my gut, anticipating you. This is the most wonderful time I've had in fifteen years."

"It's good, George, it really is. Let's take care of it; let's cherish it."

"We must have been made for each other."

They chuckled, proud of themselves, cocky, jubilant.

Halfway seriously, George said, "I wish we had gotten together when we were seventeen, eighteen, twenty."

"No you don't. It wouldn't have been like this."

"But maybe . . ."

"No. This could only have happened now."

Inside, April fixed tacos on the hot plate. They ate ravenously, drank beer, ate again, drank more beer, and made love once more. How good it was to. be insatiable! April sat in his chair at the simple desk, smoking Mexican cigarettes—Delicados; George reclined on his mattress, staring at her in the dark. They gleamed faintly, lavishly naked. The smell of her perfume, her body, the black tobacco was wonderful and mysterious. George fingered his own muscles and pubic hair, amazed by how good he felt all over—shiveringly clean and spare and strong. For years, despite frantic efforts to keep physically fit, his body, unloved and unloving, had always been sluggish, in shape but not in tune. And April's flesh had awakened after a long novocained time. Unfeeling heavy appendages yesterday, suddenly her breasts felt pretty and youthful, effective weapons in an erotic arsenal. The slightly swollen curve of

293

her abdomen deserved seven transparent veils; the contours of her buttocks against a hardwood chair sent delicious slivers of shapeliness up her own spine. April's shoulders prickled from an awareness of her attractiveness and special sexuality.

Hours grew muffled and indistinct. A subdued and amorous drone nestled inconspicuously around their quiet talking. About literature and art; old days, old ways, old haunts, old taunts. History, politics; the Future. He described playing football, being the best; she analyzed ramifications of the fifties art scene in New York, and described the sham and the tinsel, yes—also the immaculate excitement of being the star of a big show. Trout fishing, in small Chamisaville streams, was his forte; Mediterranean sardine fishing (Enrique! Enrique?) could be one of hers: triangular globes at night—orange blossoms in Valencia, Costa Brava pine trees—on the fabled sea. George had once trained for cross-country on autumn evenings, high in the Mosquito Valley when yellow aspen leaves mingled with light snow falling; she talked about the Collioure autumn harbor when okra-green and white boats were inverted on the rocky beaches, and mellow-yellow slabs of light extended from snug, deserted cafés onto damp cobbled streets—espresso machines sputtered and hissed. George described his first glimpse of his newborn children; April recounted the births of Duane and Tina, Lamaze all the way, Matthew beside her bed counting contractions, holding her hand, shrieking when blood from the episiotomy dazzled the antiseptic air. On his mind, George had ripe red apples in leafless October trees, a tiny snowcone on each apple; April remembered the marronniers blooming in a Paris spring, and yellow ginkgo leaves on Morton Street in Manhattan on rainy Sunday afternoons. He read from the poetry of Carl Sandburg, Edgar Lee Masters, e. e. cummings; she responded by reading García Lorca, Pablo Neruda, Dylan Thomas. "The People, Yes"—on his roof, by flashlight, under summer garden stars; "In Just Spring" and "Buffalo Bill"—between tacos and beer and violent fornications; "Verde, que te quiero verde"—whispered into his ears during a drowsy lull; "Fern Hill"—they both knew it by heart. They felt like Princes of Apple Towns, like Horses in Whinnying Green Stables. My God, but life could be rich, though they sang in their chains like the sea. Unabashedly sentimental, and happy, and satiated.

And they made love. It was something George had never

experienced before. And, despite her intimate connection with a multitude of men and a few women, April had only shared such an intensity a handful of times. Tears, laughter, teasing; they were silly and playful, slow and gentle, violent, almost brutal, rolling off the mattress and around the floor, upturning his table and chair, bumping books from the cases, spewing the contents of his cardboard files. They watched themselves in a mirror, observed their lampcast silhouettes on the wall, screwed on the roof, in the back seats of their respective cars, on pine needles under a spruce tree during a fishing trip on Magpie Creek. They shouted, cursed, and laughed while rolling and banging around, clawing each other bloody with fingernails, dramatically spitting out pubic hairs; and they slithered like snakes, grappled like happy wrestlers, in and out of all shapes and all possibilities and all rhythms; until finally they lay sprawled and inert, covered with sexual grease smelling like sweat and blood, panting heavily, amazed and happy and not really hurt, although bruised and aching, and astonished by the sensations driving them through this happy sexual fiesta. "Oh joy!" April hollered. *"Oh such sweet joy!"*

Her heels gently drummed against his buttocks as he lay on his stomach, breathing stertorously, unable to slacken up. "Whited out" inside, contented and numb, April groaned, "I feel resurrected, I really do. Such *correct* loving."

Slumped over his desk with his forehead resting against folded arms, George said, "Sometimes when we're making love like that, so violently—sometimes when it's like that I want to haul off and slug you with all my might. Other times when I'm gripping your throat I want to strangle you—"

"I know. But don't let it come to that. Let's be kinky and rough and tough, but within all the bounds of a compassionate loving. No S and M, George, not that crap."

"All my life," George sighed sleepily, toying with her beautiful thick hair, "I've had fantasies of being a sex maniac. Ever since I hit my teens. But this is the first time I've ever had maniacal sex."

"It's perfect. We are so lucky."

"You're so big and wet and supple. God, I love your tits and your shoulders and your fingers and your throat—"

April sucked noisily on his thumb. George probed into her with his big toe. April sat on his calves, spread his

295

buttocks, and swished her hair against his anus—he giggled, wriggled. She moved up his body, giving tiny nips to his shins, kneecaps, thighs—George twitched with each nip. She licked around his penis, tongued his balls, nibbled on his abdomen, snuffled in his armpits, then probed her tongue-tip in a nostril, making him sneeze.

They popped open beers and swallowed hungrily. April lit up a Delicado, and the black tobacco scent prickled against their tenderized flesh.

While he drowsed, smiling, April played her guitar, crooning "Yesterday," or "Bridge over Troubled Waters," or things that she had written herself—political tunes, mournful and biting; and lazy ballads, all slur and a hominy accent, casting them both in a shadow of Dixie-drawling blues:

> In my honky-tonk castle
> You were my sweet rascal,
> We drank together 'til dawn;
> I played sweet melodies,
> On wornout piano keys,
> Then I lost you when you traveled on.

"Oh wow." Such gratification made him timid. "This is so perfect. I'm frightened of what might happen—of how it will turn sour—"

"Don't be that way, George. It isn't fair. Just leave it alone, don't think about it, enjoy it while we can. If you start worrying about it you'll create a problem where none exists. You'll kill it in the end simply by being afraid that it might end."

"I've never been so happy. I never believed that anything like this could happen, not in a million years."

"I never thought I would find a love like this, at this stage," April admitted. "Life is bizarre, bewitched."

"The things we say are incredibly banal."

"Banal is beautiful."

"Let's go for a walk down to the gorge."

Wearing tennis shoes and no clothes, they zigzagged through the midnight summer, April leading, George a few steps behind, fascinated by her bluntly chugging buttocks: her moonlit hair rustled against rounded pearly highlights on her shoulders.

"You're limping a little."

"Don't fret, George. I banged my leg making love."

Near the edge of the gorge they surprised four mule deer: the delicate, graceful animals bounded away in several directions. Incredibly, one doe leaped twice, blindly, the second arc carrying her beyond the cliff—she fell from sight without a sound; several seconds later they heard the velvet animal thud against talus boulders one hundred feet below.

*"I don't believe it!"*

From the edge they could see a faint nacreous shape among dark volcanic matter. Eight hundred feet farther down, the Rio Grande was a sensuously winding silver line. Behind April, his arms wrapped around her, George nuzzled in her hair. His elbows flattened her breasts, his fingertips curled into her furry crotch. April's palms, behind her, pressed against his thighs, her buttocks faintly pinched his penis fitted down between them. After a minute he nudged her gently down and April kneeled on all fours while George entered her from behind. As if a magic juice had been freed by its shattered bones, the dead deer on the cold boulders quivered in a soft phosphorescent outline. And the bright silver Rio Grande trickled through sinister pitch-black ferrous velveteen.

*Oh Lord*, April thought. *I wish I could stay on this earth forever!*

## Soap Operas

A BUSINESSMEN'S CABAL, including Rodey McQueen, Bob Moose, Moe Stryzpk, and Randolph Bonney, appeared early one evening for a confab in Mayor J. B. LeDoux's construction company office. With this group were Junior Leyba and Joseph Bonatelli. Icarus Suazo rounded out the gathering.

Leaning back, J. B. casually folded his hands. And, pretending nonchalance by tapping his lips with his thumbs, he attempted to assess the power structure paying him the honor of this visit. Except for Bonatelli, he knew everyone present: in both a construction and a political capacity,

J. B. had been involved intimately with much of their profit-oriented skullduggery. Yet at this moment J. B. wondered if he had ever really understood their schemes, or how they planned for things to happen. He felt totally ignorant of a future already mapped out, for himself, personally, and for others cooperating in the Betterment of Chamisaville.

Despite his supposed success in life, J. B. knew he was akin to those early black men allowed to break baseball's color barrier because they could guarantee the owners a World Series payday, or at least a run for the pennant. Those ballplayers, never truly a part of the organization, were expected to sleep and chow down in separate hotels, they were ordered to endure racial taunts from the fans, opposing players, and their own teammates—"for the good of their race." Talented individuals all, they were traded immediately—too quickly—when age, injury, or psychological pressures impaired their talents.

Despite his apparently lofty political position, J. B. had no clear overall view of how things were coming down. Buffeted in one direction or another by meetings like this, or through advice given by men like Junior Leyba, J. B. had intuited more than once that the Junior Leybas themselves were intermediaries for higher-ups, taking and transmitting orders from Moe Stryzpk and his ilk, people who also lacked an overall conception, being more conduits for orders, ideas, and opinions they had received from their bosses, the Bonneys, McQueens, and elder Mooses. And no doubt even those honchos atop Chamisaville's festering heap received crucial input from higher-ups gazing down at the valley from Hija Negrita Mountain, or from enormous, almost empty airplanes drifting overhead at thirty thousand feet en route from New York or Chicago to Phoenix or Los Angeles.

Occasionally, J. B. suspected a rational plan was guiding all their overt and covert actions. But damned if he had the energy, these days, to try and figure it out. Swamped in shame and his flagging lust for a revenge he feared his cowardice would never let him carry out, J. B.'s only gambit had become survival. Puzzling, how everybody else seemed to know exactly what they were doing. Rodey McQueen, a no-nonsense tyrant responsible for creating a town so muddled it couldn't tell its municipal ass from a pit in the ground, never wavered, he always understood exactly all the processes going on. And even if his plans, due to some human miscalculation or bizarre aspect of weather, crumpled like a brand-new automobile diving a thousand feet into the Rio Grande Gorge, McQueen never balked or blinked an eye. He simply swept the pieces under various rugs or locked them up in a shadowy tax shelter, and proceeded to work his progressive magic just as cool and confident as a peacock, with never a moment's uncertainty or chill reflection. Because McQueen's mind was made up; he believed in himself; he knew all the next steps to take; and he was eminently convinced it was worth it.

J. B. hated Rodey McQueen; he also admired the man. He envied anyone with faith in himself. The mayor always acted according to somebody else's orders. He always did what he thought they wanted him to do. He always waited for a sign from the Anglo Axis to guide him—and despised everybody, especially himself, involved.

Joseph Bonatelli lit a cigar. McQueen said, "J. B., I want you to meet part of the executive committee of the Northland Grazing Association."

Everyone nodded cordially and shook hands. J. B. was so tired of acting civilized—why didn't he have the guts to tell everyone to go screw themselves? Then McQueen said, "We are going to build three five-hundred-unit motels on land I'll sell to this corporation. And we have decided to finance them with two and a half million dollars worth of tax-exempt municipal industrial revenue bonds, which you and your erstwhile council members are going to vote for at your next regularly scheduled meeting. Naturally, the usual construction plums for you can be taken for granted."

Something snapped. "You want the town to help finance a *private* business venture?" J. B. blurted, astonished at their brass balls. "Who are you trying to kid? That's so illegal it even makes me blanch. Local businessmen will scream so loudly about municipal involvement in a private, competitive enterprise that either the feds will finally decide to bust up this village, or else I'll find myself at every other council meeting being asked to support some new tax-exempt bonds enabling the El Gaucho to start serving champagne, or so that any second-rate promoter within a hundred miles bearing a pipe dream in his pocket and a voice loud enough to scream 'foul!' can build anything from a chicken coop to a château under the good auspices of our wonderful tax-free municipal industrial revenue bonds! Not only that, but if you try to hook up three new

299

five-hundred-unit motels to our current sewage plant, the damn thing will explode and there'll be nothing but shit in all our potholes. Besides, this town is already moteled and hoteled to death. There's no *need* for what you propose!"

Recovering from his shock, Rodey McQueen bellowed: *"Don't you try and tell me how to suck eggs, J. B.!"*

The mayor had actually considered bolting clear of his chair in a fury, when Joseph Bonatelli gave a soft little grunt, at the same time making a slight, lifting gesture with his right, sapphire-clad pinkie, and the mayor—indeed, the entire room—froze as if suddenly hit by a space-age ray gun's beam.

"Gentlemen," Bonatelli said sadly. "Puh-lease."

J. B. sank back, expelling a long, terrified sigh, and whispered, "Sorry."

Bonatelli nodded slightly toward McQueen: "As you were saying."

"I finished what I was saying. Let J. B. talk."

Bonatelli's eyes flicked over and stared with deadened impassivity at the mayor.

J. B.'s throat felt dry, he cleared it; his heart felt worse. But what could he lose at this point?

"All right," he began apologetically. "Please excuse my intemperance. You took me by surprise, that's all. Like I mentioned, sewage hookups are a problem. Already the FHA won't finance some homes the LULACs are trying to build because we can't give them legal sewer hookups. Operation Breakthrough is stalling because they're nervous about lack of hookups—but you know that. Every week we get a dozen complaints about sewage catastrophes. Right now we're paying out eight hundred bucks for two backups that destroyed a living room with a real Persian rug on the floor, and a garage housing a '52 Chevy pickup. Half the motels and restaurants in town don't carry grease traps on their sewer lines, in violation of state health codes galore, so we get all kinds of garbage you wouldn't believe rotting in the pipes and clogging them long before whatever survives the underground gauntlet zooms through our useless plant and gives trout fishermen hepatitis.

"Of course, if the outdated sewage plant was our only problem, I wouldn't object that strongly to the three new five-hundred-unit motels you're talking about. I mean—what the hell? I don't like cutting off my construction nose to spite my contractor's face. But I doubt also that we could ever deliver water to them, making any consideration even of sewer hookups superfluous. Our four water-pumping stations are so outdated that only two work, none have effective chlorinators, and water service, as well you know, is constantly being halted due to breakdowns, or due to breaks in the antiquated lines. About once a week there's a little flood somewhere, and only yesterday Junior here received notification of a suit filed by that waitress in the Prince of Whales, Gloria Armijo, who claims water from an exploding city pipe flooded her basement and the entire house—it's one of those Mutual Help–Turnkey deathtraps you and I prefabbed, Mr. McQueen—and then the house collapsed into the water and partially dissolved. Naturally, we believe we could update our water system to pay for what they use. However, a third of our meters seem to be constantly broken, and half the houses and business establishments hooked into municipal water aren't even metered, including, of course, the Shalako, the Chamisaville Inn, the Don Quijote, and the Bluebird, a situation I presume I needn't go into here.

"So if you want to build three new five-hundred-unit motels, for whatever reason—and maybe you know something I'm not aware of—then you have to get me a new sewage plant before I'll give you the hookups, whether I'm contracting one of the jobs or not. And you must acquire enough active water rights to cover what those establishments will use. Garbage service I won't even mention, except to note that we've got pretty much the same statistics there as with the water meters. Jim Bob Popper, head of city sanitation, told me yesterday we've got about fifty percent bill-payment delinquencies, and we run about a thousand in the red every month. Our solitary truck broke down again three days ago, and, as I suppose you've noticed, garbage has been building up since that time. The DA, Damacio Mares, claims his brother could buy us a new used truck cheap, but there are so many state departmental flatfoots in town already that we're gonna have to put the replacement truck out to bid, which will take at least thirty days. Damacio's brother says if we can't let him sell us a truck, how about at least letting him import a thousand vultures, which he says he can get from a Peace Corps volunteer in Guatemala for two bits apiece. My personal opinion about the problem is, if the garbage really stacks up and becomes menacing, the town could ask Mr. Suazo here to hire a group of unemployed caciques from the Pueblo to walk around sprinkling powdered bat wings onto the refuse and ordering it to go away. If that didn't work, they could execute the garbage with deer rifles."

During an awkward silence, nobody cracked a smile. Icarus Suazo shifted. Joseph Bonatelli closed his eyes: his plump, impassive frame seemed to shift, slouching, going to sleep.

Embarrassment circled the room. A mayor was off his rocker, perhaps indicating a temporary hitch in plans.

Placing his palms flat on his desk, J. B. scrutinized the backs of his hands, large-veined, scarred, the sides of his fingers callused, a fingernail split, another—struck by a hammer—black and blue.

He was sweating, and felt cold; his mind was a blank. J. B. wished it were snowing outside. Faintly, he heard recorded church bells playing "My Country 'tis of Thee." Genoveva Bachicha was hexing Texans, trying to dissolve them in greasy, chicken-fried poofs. Malaquias C. de Baca hung around the old courthouse, now Junior's Picadilly Circus, discussing the 1936 presidential election with his friends J. F. Valdez, Esquipula Gallegos, and Joe Archuleta. His own wife, Teresa, was manning—or was it personning?—the plaza information booth, no doubt trading the Dynamite Shrine origins with a pilgrim from Canton, Ohio, for a description of the Pro Football Hall of Fame. The tattered plaza flag flapped listlessly. And, being Wednesday, the Garden Club, the Daughters of the Eastern Star, and the DAR had placed fresh-cut flowers on the World War I memorial. Chamisaville was uneventful, placid, timeless. As if, now that he seemed assured of finally losing everything, the violence and confusion which had belabored his life since childhood was only a dream.

McQueen said, "Ah-hem." On that note the men got up. They nodded at one another, at the mayor; and everyone except Junior Leyba walked out, heads bowed pensively.

Junior approached the window: bumper-to-bumper dusty automobiles crawled along the narrow highway outside.

"What the hell is the matter with you, J. B.?"

The mayor rubbed his eyes. "I'm tired. It's been a long life, already."

"What are you going to do now?"

"Quién sabe? The work day is finished. Think I'll drive over to that carwash the cute little girls from Alamito run and have my car laundered. Then I'll go home, kill a martini, eat dinner, do a little paperwork, watch TV—

whatever's relevant. I don't know. Suddenly, these days, I'm tired. My son is dying and I can't stop him."

"Let's drop by the La Tortuga for a fría."

"Too many Anglos. Too many poodles. I don't want to drink with a bunch of gabachos wearing softball jerseys and a bunch of miniature canines flaunting little pink hard-ons. Not tonight."

His face ugly, sarcastic, Junior suggested, "How about the El Gaucho, then?"

"Fine."

"Hey, cut it out. Christ."

"Let's go, I'll buy. I haven't been in there for thirty years."

"You gone crazy? What kind of a place is that to be seen in?"

"What kind of town is this to be seen in . . . ?"

Junior said, "Suit yourself," and, like a good rat, without so much as an adiós, he left that sinking ship.

J. B. LeDoux wished he could be Celestino Lucero, trapped in a trailer park, still farming in a fifteen-foot-square plot, shoveling manure from a tiny corral every day, with his only companion a foul-mouthed pet magpie called Tierra o Muerte the Twelfth, nothing—except his dignity —left intact. Instead, growing progressively richer, more unstable, and spiritually ineffectual, J. B. seemed even to be losing a grip on his rage, so enfeebled from hate-filled inactivity that he was finally petering out, accepting what he had not the strength or courage to reject, a pitiable puppet with a fat bank account, caught in all the hack-neyed contradictions, rendered impotent. Demoralized, friendless, increasingly docile—a fucking doormat he had become. In the last *El Clarín*, that cocky little Pueblo son of a bitch Anthony Martínez had published a grotesque cartoon of J. B. kissing a donkey (an ass!) with the face of Rodey McQueen. No slouch with words, having studied hard to get where he was at, J. B. grumbled, "I've become a rudderless, fatuous, neurasthenic, disheartened, sterile lambe. My life has become enmeshed in trivial considera-tions. I'm a vendido, a coconut, the equivalent of an apple, an Oreo cookie, an Uncle Tom."

Oh Lord . . .

THEORETICALLY, April Delaney was in the capital attend-ing a three-day U.S. Civil Rights Commission hearing.

Actually, after leaving Duane and Tina with their grandparents, she had journeyed south to see a doctor.

Virgil Leyba's old drinking buddy, Abe Gallegos, a plump, constantly sweating little man, had frizzy white hair and a neatly trimmed white moustache. He wore thick rimless glasses: a Phi Beta Kappa chain decorated his vest. Although he resembled a tottering, scatterbrained dreamer out of Dickens or Cervantes, there was no better cancer specialist to be found. After scanning her records and analyzing a biopsy and several other preliminary tests, he sat down with April in his cluttered hospital office, poured them both a jelly jar of whiskey, and, after swishing around the bitter liquid for a second, swallowed the stuff, gasped, and removed his glasses, peering at her tiredly.

"It's the same problem, of course—you probably knew that. And it goes without saying you should have contacted me when that lump at your ear was the size of half a dime instead of a whole nickel—but no matter. Aside from being infested with a fatal disease, you're the healthiest woman your age, or even twenty years younger, that I've looked at in decades. Naturally I'll attribute it to your nonstop smoking and unparalleled consumption of alcoholic beverages."

Abe winked, licked his plump lips, and fiddled with his glasses, smearing fingerprints across both lenses.

"The tumor ought to be a fairly routine operation. From the way it feels I doubt seriously the roots go deep; we should be able to remove it clean. The hip I don't know about—"

Abe unbuttoned his vest, loosened his tie, tugged free a shirttail and clumsily, plump fingers fumbling, polished his glasses.

"It could be an arthritic condition, I don't know. When you come back for the operation we'll have to do a bone scan. Given your history, I've got to look for diseased cells in the hip giving you the pain in your left leg. If we get a positive scan, we'll treat with radiation."

"I don't want that kind of poison in my body."

"Who does? I hope it isn't necessary. We'll wait to read the scan. I'm just telling you how I'll treat if we've got the sarcoma down there. You should be aware of all the possibilities."

"I know. I appreciate that."

His glasses back on, Abe sipped the whiskey. Within a few minutes—his tie loosened, his vest askew, his shirttail out, his belt undone—the doctor had seemed to disintegrate, unravel, come apart at the seams. Neat when April first said hello, now he was totally disheveled and comical, an absurd and sorrowful-looking little fat man resembling more a buffoon than a man of his high position and extensive training and skill.

Abe glanced sideways, out the window. "Oh, aren't we the grown-up people, though?" He squinted as if trying to distinguish some detail far beyond the window. "I hate cancer, you know. It also fascinates me. But sometimes I like it better when everybody involved weeps and tears out their hair, beats their breasts and accuses me of being the devil in disguise for hand-delivering such discomforting news."

"I don't know what to say, Abe. I already did my melodrama trip in New York. Most of my life has been traumatic, theatrical. Now, time is a little more precious, I guess. I'm making efforts to control my energy. I'm trying hard not to be a totally undisciplined person. But you have to be straight with me; you have to lay it on the line."

"Of course." He faced her, drenched in sweat. Despite the efforts to clean them, his glasses were still smudged with greasy fingerprints. "So if the bone scan is positive, we'll probably put you through radiation. I'd imagine for about a week, six days, once a day for a few minutes each time ought to do the trick. Depending on the success of the operation, we may have to zap you around the ear also, just to make sure we got everything. You should be prepared to lose some hair around the ear, your sideburn, maybe a touch of eyebrow. There's an outside chance they'll hit a lachrymal gland also, which would severely reduce tearing and necessitate drops in the eye so that you won't damage the cornea."

"How often would I have to put in the drops?"

"Maybe four or five times every hour at the beginning."

"Oh . . ."

"It depends. Who knows if it will hapen like that? I can't even say at this stage if we're going to use radiation or not." As he talked, Abe rummaged through the mess on his desk, searching for cigarettes. After locating a pack, he began foraging around for matches, probing among envelopes, pieces of paper, and professional journals, and then he ransacked his jacket, vest, shirt, and finally his pants pockets, where he located a crumpled matchbook, lit his cigarette, shook out the match and flicked it onto the floor, mumbling, "Three cheers for these cancer sticks," and continued.

"Sometimes patients, especially women, get a little upset by the cosmetic effects of radiation. I don't want to scare you, but just keep it in the back of your mind that you might be losing a little hair. I imagine, also, if we pop the hip joint, you'll probably also lose maybe half your pubic hair. If you're still married, if you've got a boyfriend, you might discuss these things beforehand, so that if anything like that actually happens he won't be totally unprepared."

"And after the operation? After the radiation, if it's necessary?"

"We'll go to the chemotherapy again. I don't like the IVs every week, and anyway, it's a long trip down from Chamisaville. What we'll do, I think, is put you on a program of one shot a month—Oncovin. Then for five days, back home, you can take pills—Cytoxan and Prednisone. They'll make you sick, but we can buffer that with various antinausea agents. Shouldn't be much of a problem."

April said, "In your opinion, Abe, how long have I got to live?"

He frowned; his eyes flitted into the disorder on his desk. With one hand, Abe tried sweeping ashes off some papers; instead he swept the papers onto the floor. Somehow, while they had been talking, his clothes had become so rumpled it seemed as if he'd just been tumbled in sand by a desert twister. A line of sweat droplets crossed his brow, a stench literally crashed from his damp armpits like a big bass drum of odor.

"Hell, I dunno," Abe said quietly. "If you got to have cancer, this is the best kind. In many cases we can hold it at bay indefinitely—five years, ten years. Of course, if we have to radiate, you should know there can be adverse effects in the future, maybe ten years hence—leukemia might develop. Basically, what we are doing is buying time. Your case, with these lumps cropping up at irregular intervals in irregular places, is fairly rare. Hard to tell how it will develop."

"So how long, Abe?"

"I promise—in fact, I'll guarantee, that you will be alive one year from now."

"That's it?"

"I think you're going to lick it entirely. I'm fairly con-

306

vinced you have at least five, maybe seven, and very likely ten to twelve years, depending. But if you want me to nail down something *exactly,* all I'll guarantee is that you'll still be alive and kicking, chain-smoking and chain-boozing, one year from now."

"If I cut out the cigarettes, if I cut out the booze—that'd help, wouldn't it?"

He shrugged. "As a cancer specialist, I'm obviously not about to recommend you smoke two packs of cigarettes a day. I won't tell you to cease smoking altogether, either. Right now your lungs are healthy enough, and the cigarettes aren't causing any fatal damage in your lymphatic system. If you can quit, you should quit. If you can't, try some moderation. If you can't moderate, at least enjoy. What the hell, life's too short. I'm betting you'll outlive us all."

"Thanks, Abe." Standing, April reached across the desk, clasping his hands. "You're aces in my book."

He joshed: "How often does a dirty old man like me get to pinch, probe, and fondle a body as voluptuous as yours? The thanks are all mine."

April tweaked his bulbous nose. "You're the most charming male chauvinist piglet I know, Abe." And, trailing behind a radiant smile that brightened his office shambles for a while, April strode buoyantly out of the room, relieved that she had finally faced the thing, made the arrangements, and replaced imagined horrors with real facts.

In the parking lot, however, she collapsed. She had just brushed her hair, refreshed her mascara, and touched up her mouth with pale pink lipstick, when suddenly tears erupted. Bone scans, radiation, chemotherapy, lachrymal glands, shedding pubic hairs—what right had her life to skirt even the edges of such dreary and humiliating adventures? I'm too beautiful for this banal evil, she thought bitterly. I have too much energy and love of life. I have so many important things to do, projects that count on historical scales, ambitions that mean something good for humanity. What will George say if I shed my eyebrows, if my pubic hairs disappear? Why must I undergo those embarrassments on top of everything else? In the middle of balling, swimming, eating, will I have to stop and put drops in my eyes? It isn't fair! This isn't my destiny! It has nothing to do with *me!*

"Ah, go screw yourself, you poor little rich girl! You

spoiled brat!" How often, during the past week, had she seen photographs—in the newspapers, in magazines, on TV—of Vietnamese mothers cradling napalmed children, of old Asian men and women squatting over plastic body-bags, wailing for their dead, trapped in an unrelenting slaughter. Butterfly bombs and plastic CBU pellets maimed beautiful, innocent, important people. Entire societies were starving to death in the Sahara, in India. Amazonian tribes were exterminated wholesale by government settlers in Brazil. Closer to home, Juan GeeGee was dead, and his wife Amaranta was half crazy in the hospital, apparently slated to lose her home. Benny LeDoux fabricated a sense-less doom with senseless flair. Four impoverished good men had spent forty years in the state pen for snatching a rich bastard's daughter in hopes of extorting their families' survival. Virgil Leyba was drowning in the pathetic trou-bles of little people that had plagued his existence from childhood on. Even among the enemy, physical and spiri-tual pain ran berserk. Moe Stryzpk brooded among the ashes of phenomenal success; Miranda drank to kill bore-dom and unhappily screwed April's father. J. B. LeDoux seemed headed for a head-on collision. Junior Leyba was trapped in the eye of a venomous storm. Consumed by anger, bitterness, and frustration, Juan Ortega pedaled his rusty bicycle around the valley, ashamed that he had never written a novel: half his family had died uselessly in wars that never changed anything for people like the Ortegas. The long flapping ghosts of his children trailed back from the base of the old newspaperman's brain like college scarves on a losing autumn weekend.

How selfish to mourn, even for a minute, the pampered, well-fed little tragedy of a single American girl ten thou-sand miles away from tiger cages in Saigon and trailer-park farms in Chamisaville.

April blew her nose, stuck her tongue at the mirror, dried her cheeks with a Kleenex, and hit the road. Dark-ness fell as she entered the gorge, singing along with Spanish songs playing on a Capital City radio station. Static interfered as the russet cliffs closed over, and she turned the radio off, clicking on her lights. Topped a thou-sand feet above by an aluminum blue sky, the black gorge walls echoed no gleaming: she couldn't distinguish the river. The air was cold; she put on Charley's old bomber jacket and felt snug under its heavy fleece. April gunned her little Beetle, going fifty-five on the twisting roads, then

308

sixty, tires squealing as she cornered sharply five hundred feet above the invisible water, comfortable in her speed. As wind buffeted her through the open sunroof, April felt like a racing driver churning for an abstract record, ". . . winding sinuously, also pell-mell, but *never* out of control, through L-I-F-E!" she chortled out loud. And shouted the *William Tell* Overture.

At the top of the gorge, a faint light remained. Sagebrush glittered in an eerie brittle glow that seemed crisp and cool, almost an arctic landscape even though the temperature must have been seventy. Halfway toward Mota Llano, April zipped onto the dirt road leading to the old Martínez shack. When she spotted a light and George's car parked outside the front door, April braked, and sat still for a moment, thinking about George, herself, their affair. Getting out, April shut the door carefully, without a sound, and leaned against the roof, arms crossed, calming herself, cherishing a quiet moment before they met. Nighthawks beeped, chopping quiet plateau airwaves with their white-striped falcon-shaped wings. Up north, lights shimmered at the foot of the mountains. A warm dry pine scent undulated past her nostrils. The universe rustled amicably.

April lit a cigarette, allowing the smoke from her first exhale to drool luxuriously upward over her cooling lips. "Ay, the wonder of it all—!"

At the heart of the slaughterhouse—always—enough room to nourish awe.

UNABLE TO SLEEP ALL NIGHT, Charlotte Leyba sat up against several pillows, smoking a cigarette as dawn light touched the windows. Beside her, Junior was sleeping, or at least drowsing fitfully, muttering taut unintelligible sentences, rasping when he breathed. Charlotte loved their bedroom, the white brocaded bedspread, the baby-blue blankets, the thick pink wall-to-wall rug, the green and gauzy curtains. It was a sweet, luminous space: clean, quiet, and peaceful. White bedside lamps, cream-colored walls—nothing cluttered the room. A single light-blue bureau occupied one corner; several quiet drawings decorated the walls. A true sanctuary, refuge, retreat. Junior had wanted the color TV in there; she had refused. This beautiful spareness, undisturbed, was what Charlotte wanted; simple and full of airy light.

*A peaceable kingdom,* she thought. Now where did that expression come from?

Junior uttered a cry and his eyes flew open abruptly, staring straight at her. "What are you doing?" he asked.

"I'm just sitting here, smoking a cigarette, watching you dream."

"I don't like you to do that."

"I'm sorry, I couldn't sleep."

"Well, what are you doing, are you trying to pry into my life?"

She shook her head, letting her eyes glaze against the softly glowing windows: dawn light was entering like slow flowing cream.

"I just couldn't sleep, Junior."

"Why?" Sitting up, he fumbled for a cigarette, and swung his feet out of bed, his back to her.

"Who knows why? You know why. I wish we could talk. The only time you try and say anything to me is in your sleep."

His body stiffened. "What did I say in my sleep?"

"I don't know, I couldn't make it out. You twitch; you're so restless; you look so unhappy."

"What are you doing, staying awake just to spy on me?"

"Please, darling, don't start that. I just couldn't sleep."

Junior crushed out his cigarette and turned around. His face scared her; so much emotion, crowded into it, she did not understand—bleakness, hatred, fear. Too, self-pity weakened his features. Although handsome, classic and strong, they were contorted by the man underneath, who was running more than scared.

Reaching, Junior grabbed her arm. Charlotte said, "Don't, please."

He yanked her roughly over sideways, grabbing her hair with his other hand. "Shut up. I do what I please."

Charlotte closed her eyes, waiting for his next move. He put just enough pressure on her hair so that it hurt, not badly—yet the threat of a yank was there, and she knew he would do it eventually. Or perhaps he only wanted to tease her this time. And his fingers dug painfully into her arm.

For a minute, neither moved. Then Junior yanked her hair so hard there was an audible snap in her neck, and Charlotte cried out. He slapped her off the bed, then flopped atop her, apologizing, whispering, "What am I doing? Why am I doing this? What's the matter with me?" while she smoothed his hair and whimpered, "I don't know. I really don't know. I just don't know."

310

They were trapped in it, doomed, sinking. Junior calmed down after a while and went into the bathroom, showered and shaved. Charlotte lay on the soft rug in the pale morning light, wondering how to survive the day, let alone the week. When Junior came back, he paused, looking down at her, seeing the most beautiful woman he had ever known, a pale, exquisitely formed creature with a wonderful and timid face, and a love for him he could no more understand than could she. Charlotte floated against the pink rug like an angel, a pearl, an apparition of feminine peace. Junior dropped to all fours and kissed her belly, her thighs, her breasts. He straddled his frightened woman and confronted her openly sorrowful face, beautiful lips, delicate nose, liquid eyes. Charlotte's dark hair spilled against the vague pink rug like ink, glossy and thick. Run away from me, leave me, I hate you, I love you, I'll kill you, I'm no good, they'll kill me, I'm so bored I can't see straight, I wish it were over, I want to commit suicide, why do you do it to me, why do you stay, why don't you go away and save yourself were some of the thoughts in Junior's head, but he said nothing.

Southwestern summer light made a pastel cathedral of their wide room, a light, Charlotte thought, as if from heaven.

"Someday I'll really hurt you," Junior warned. "Someday I'm going to kill you. I'll break your neck. I'll crack all the bones in your arms and legs."

Junior lowered his face and they kissed tenderly, Charlotte's eyes brim-full of tears she would not release.

"We could move," she said. "We could go somewhere else and begin again."

"This is my home. These are my roots. If we went now, they'd find me."

Soap operas, Charlotte thought. How she loved and hated this man!

Junior cupped her cheek, solicitously; but his fingers trembled. He circled them around her throat and held the caressing posture. But she could tell it was an effort for him not to choke her. Bird songs entered through the window; church bells pealed. An aroma, a faint aroma of coffee and baking bread intruded, circling their bright and beautiful room.

"When will you be home tonight?"

"Who the hell knows?" Abruptly, Junior stood up, went to their walk-in closet, and began dressing.

311

"What do you want for dinner?"

"I don't care."

"Will you be home for dinner?"

"That's up for grabs."

"Are you bringing anyone home for dinner?"

"Listen, baby—" Junior buttoned up a shirt so white it hurt her eyes. "I'll call you when I call you, I'll let you know. Right now, everything is uncertain. I'll have to see."

Charlotte remained quiet while he finished dressing. Before Junior left, he hovered over her again, his face going through such emotions she wanted to weep for him. He really is going to commit suicide or murder, she thought. I don't know anything about his personality. How did we get so estranged?

"Are you just going to lie there like that all day?" he asked coldly, placing one foot on her belly, the chill leather of his sole making the skin crinkle.

She stared at him.

Junior changed completely, his face going hard and nearly powerful, almost confident. Firmly, he said, "You are so beautiful."

And turned heel, then, walking out—he was gone. Junior ate a businessman's breakfast at the Prince of Whales or some other town café, with Damacio Mares, or J. B. LeDoux—those men.

Alone, Charlotte relaxed a little. No hurry now, half the day lay before her, she had no appointments before opening up the hospital auxiliary thrift shop at 1:00 P.M. She would read, watch TV maybe, call someone for lunch, wash her hair, do her nails, go for a walk before driving over to the hospital.

Charlotte tried to meditate, washing away the morning's bad aftertaste, centering down into her pained body, ridding herself of a fear of Junior which always kept her on edge until he went to work. She breathed deeply, heavily, and then quietly. The rug soothed her back; she spread her arms and legs, and smiled at the wide, white ceiling. A peace came; sunlight landed on her skin like a good friend. Charlotte grew drowsy, fell asleep, dreamed for a little while, and then, for no reason she could think of, awoke, determined to do something she had never done before.

Downstairs, a soft gray terrycloth robe drawn about her, she entered Junior's den. He had a thousand times threatened to kill her if she ever pried into his affairs,

312

but now she was determined to pry. All her life Charlotte had believed in the sanctity of a person's privacy; she had never read letters on the sly, nor rustled through Junior's drawers, nor in any way attempted to invade anything he might choose to keep secret. But now she was fed up. Her man had become an unintelligible monster, they were estranged beyond hope, and she had no insights into their relationship or into her husband. His shell simply limped around their house, berating her, hating her, exhausting her, using her, discarding her. Charlotte needed some communication; why worry at this late date how she got it?

His desk drawers and filing cabinet were locked; the little safe was locked. So where to begin? How to begin? Seated in Junior's desk chair, Charlotte smoked another cigarette. Then she opened the thin middle desk drawer, the only unlocked drawer in the room, and the keys for the rest of the desk and for the filing cabinet were just sitting there in a compartment of a thin wooden tray.

Charlotte held them for a moment, feeling slightly queasy, her heart beating quickly. "Calm down," she said firmly. "Don't be stupid."

Then she began opening drawers.

APRIL INFORMED NOBODY of her operation. Instead, she fabricated an elaborate lie about visiting New York City. Having family, friends, anyone but herself aware of the disease could only cause irreparable damage, she knew. Damned if her relationships would be strangled by the emotional sloppiness of sympathetic, commiserating, slightly frightened onlookers. And anyway: having made it alone through her New York operation and chemotherapy, she believed in that approach. Solitude, isolation from a lover's sentimental consolation or a friend's distress, made her less vulnerable. With George on tap, she would have to deal with his reactions, their love affair, the future, the past. She would worry about how her appearance affected him. His vivid presence and vitality might cause her to lose control, feeling jealous, cheated, ripped off. Better to deal only with her own temperament: keep it simple. And at all costs avoid any maudlin scenes related to the fact that she might be dying.

Again, April dumped the kids on her parents, threatening to disown Rodey and Cynthia if they spoiled the children rotten. A champagne and enchilada dinner at the Martínez shack, followed by a two-hour debauch, concluded her activities with George. And, early next morning, tires squealing along the rollercoaster gorge road through one violent little cloudburst after another, April zoomed south.

The hospital brought her down. Instead of a ward, she was assigned a room with an old Chicano woman who had just lost a leg and both arms. The woman's husband, José Duran, a meek weather-beaten man with cloudy, old-dog eyes, sat in a chair beside his Angelita's bed with his hat in his lap, saying little. Occasionally, he reached out and pathetically touched his wife's thigh: her bandages were black with blood. After signing in, April dressed herself in a sky-blue provocative nightgown and a burgundy-colored lounging robe, making sure—with skin creams, mascara, lipstick—that she looked extra beautiful. Shuffling reading material across her lap—Lukács on art, novels by Thomas Mann, Bernard Malamud, and Saul Bellow, and magazines ranging from the *Guardian* to *Vogue*—she soon discovered her attention span could only handle a half-dozen *New Yorker*s filched from her parents. Doctors came, introduced themselves, reviewed her case, measured the lump with tiny metric rulers, probed and prodded. Friendly and straightforward, everybody joked a lot. Exceptionally considerate and personable, they repeatedly explained in detail tomorrow's operation procedures, encouraging questions about any aspect of the process she did not understand. April learned that an intern sang opera; the anesthetist was a student from Costa Rica. Abe Gallegos ducked in once, his hair and clothing horribly askew: even standing still in the stagnant air he had the appearance of a man buffeted by a gale. Seated beside April, he held her hand, smiled kindly, and reexplained, in minute detail, the events to come on the following day, from the time she would receive her first tranquilizer until they wheeled her down to OR. "Don't eat after midnight, don't smoke, don't fornicate," he cautioned.

"Fornicate? With whom, pray tell?"

"Listen, all those doctors and interns, med students and anesthesiologists who've been visiting all day are downstairs in a lecture room right now drawing straws for who gets first crack at the movie star in room 1202," he joked quietly.

"You're the movie star, Abe—I love you. Don't worry —I'm cool. Just keep your fingers crossed that there's no complications, okay?"

"I always keep my fingers crossed."

"I don't envy you, I really don't. I'm gonna make myself really strong tonight, though, thinking about you, sucking up your courage."

He touched one pudgy finger to the simple ring on her finger. "This has got to go—no jewelry in the operating room. Maybe you should ask a nurse to put it in the safe tonight."

"Oh no you don't. This travels with me, I'm sorry. You tell them I don't want it removed under any circumstances."

Abe looked out the window and sighed. "What is it so precious you want me to tell them to break all the rules?"

"A Vietnamese woman gave it to me in Cuba. It's made from the metal of an American bomber shot down over North Vietnam. It reminds me that struggle is worth it, with guts you can overcome any adversity, and the underdog can win."

"I see."

"So you just tell them that I don't go anywhere, I don't do anything—and that includes being cut open—without this ring on my finger. If they insist on taking it off, I'll pick up my stuff and walk out of here, to hell with the operation."

"I guess we can wrap it in tape," Abe grumbled, getting up, irritated by yet another patient's crazy whim. So far this day he had comforted the parents and young husband of a nineteen-year-old girl bleeding to death from leukemia; he had held the hand of a bitter blind woman while her husband died watching moronic TV quiz shows right to the end; he had spent an hour in a lecture room, reviewing six patients and their slides with the hospital's entire cancer-oriented staff; he had spent frustrating hours in conference with hospital administrators, formulating requests for government research grants; and he had seen three patients into and out of the operating room.

"You're beautiful, Abe. I'm sorry you got such a lousy job."

"I love this job. I'd just like to save more people deliberately, instead of always having to thank a miracle for getting results."

He bustled away with five more patients to see before quitting for the night.

April refused a sleeping pill, taking two shots from a smuggled-in bottle instead, fell asleep quickly, and dreamed. Virgil Leyba on a white horse rode through the sage—he resembled Abraham Lincoln. George Parker in his football uniform jumped through a paper picture of a Panther stretched across a hoop held by shrieking cheerleaders. Her father sailed gracefully into their heated swimming pool—snow covered the lawn and hung heavy in evergreen branches. Amaranta GeeGee slowly entered the picture carrying an empty birdcage. Tim Lanahan poured them each champagne and, arms linked, they drank to each other's health. Black powder smoke from Jesus Etcetera's pistol eddied suddenly when a meadowlark song bounced through it like a happy jumper launched from a trampoline. Rain spattered against the gray rocks on the Collioure harbor beach, and Enrique, wearing a tiny black bikini, stood in a foot of water, laughing and pounding his breast, yodeling an earsplitting Tarzan noise. Charley Epstein sat in his barnstorming airplane with an old-fashioned aviator's helmet on his head, smoking a cigarette, gazing at her sadly while she stood a short distance away wearing his bomber jacket, lazily waving goodbye. It was sad. The corpse she and George Parker and Rebecca Valerio had propped against Al Lamont's door a million Halloweens ago, fell forward, with a big *BOO!* on its forehead, into *her* arms. Pat GeeGee served a glass of beer, bent down, and impishly blew some foam into her face—they both laughed; April hugged him lovingly. And Gloria Armijo set down coffee and a silce of apple pie at the Prince of Whales counter, then ruffled her friendly fingers in April's hair; the smell of that coffee was so *sweet—!*

In the morning a nurse gave her a first shot. Cast back nearly into dreams again, April drifted, only dimly aware of being rolled toward a different location. She went under. And awoke much later in pain, profoundly depressed, alone in the world and unprotected, aching in every joint, sick to her stomach, dehydrated, dismayed, and fragile as hell. What had happened to her false teeth? April's tongue-tip probed the gaps—how had she lost those dentures? Alarmed, she pinched her finger, the ring was still there —thank you, Abe!—heavily wrapped in masking tape. An IV dripped fluid into her left hand. Her nipples felt chalky and weird. Why hadn't she told anybody?—Virgil, George, her folks. A friendly voice could have done wonders, performed miracles, uplifted her spirit. "I want to hold somebody's hand," she whispered. But nobody cared, nobody gave a damn. If they had been on their toes they would have seen through her lies and trickery. If they had really loved her they would have found out and been here. "Oh, hey, I'm drowning! I can't *breathe!* I want to *hold* somebody. I want to be *held*—" In the recovery-room twilight Enrique was running around hitting himself with rocks. Juan GeeGee smiled from his hospital bed, waved, could not speak. Tina stared at her bug-eyed, somber, remote. Duane had run away to join a circus. Nobody was left. Her life was a field full of tombstones. All dead, all gone, loving others—nobody cared. April started to cry. A nurse's voice broke through: after a while, when April could make sense of the questions, they transported her back upstairs, shifted her to the bed, and let her lie.

"Where's my false teeth?" she asked. "I want my false teeth. I want them back in my mouth right now!"

But they had all bustled away again: nobody heard.

"I'm thirsty," she said angrily. "Somebody give me a goddam drink!"

But they were unconcerned. She was abandoned, humiliated, scorned. With her free hand, April patted gingerly around on the bedside table, searching for water. The sudden smell of flowers stopped her: another person's fingers landed on her hand.

"Who's that?" April opened one eye, but everything was blurry.

"It's me—Virgil."

"You don't mean it, love!" April was so happy she didn't know what to say. "How in hell did you find out?"

"Abe told me."

"Gallegos?"

"Sure. We know each other from way back. Sometimes, when I came down to print up the old *El Clarín* years ago, we drank together and sowed a few oats."

"He told you? That son of a bitch!"

"Don't be quite so tough," Virgil advised. "You look like you could use a friend."

"Please don't tell anyone else."

"Of course not."

"I'm gonna be all right, Virgil. Have you seen anybody? Does Abe have any results from the operation?"

"He said it came out pretty clean, it's apparently malignant, all right, and he thinks they got the entire growth."

April wanted to smile. "Virgil, I need my false teeth

317

back in my mouth so I can give a big grin, okay? Be a darling, would you, and hunt them up?"

Virgil located the bridge in a nightstand drawer: April clicked it into place, pressed the plate against the roof of her mouth with her tongue, and opened both eyes.

"Man, excuse me for crying, but am I glad to see *you!*" she blurted happily.


JUNIOR LEYBA was in the La Tortuga getting drunk. He had worked late at the office, dined at the Dynamite Shrine with Damacio Mares, and then decided that instead of going home he would stop by the bar to hear a new folk-singer Solomon Teel had just hired. But he couldn't stand the songs that bearded creep was singing. Only a few years ago, if you sang solely in English, you couldn't earn a living in any Chamisaville nightspot. Now, half the patrons guzzling Harvey Wallbangers at the bar, drinking Coors—despite the boycott—at round, ebony tables, or stuffing their fat faces in the nearby dining room were from out of town, out of state, out of this world. Mixed in among the affluent transient crowd were a bunch of locals, however: Junior eyed them venomously as drink increased his anger and his guilt. He hadn't called Charlotte either from work or from the Dynamite Shrine Dining Salon; he wouldn't call her now. He rarely did, of course, but that was small consolation. Impossible to fathom why she would not flee from the coming conflagration, leaving him in the lurch and with a reason to hunt her down and kill her. But maybe one day he could hurt her so badly she would murder him, ending their mutual misery. Junior couldn't think very straight these days, especially when drunk. And he was getting plastered more often as they came closer to electrifying the Pueblo.

What exactly he had in mind for himself, Junior rarely articulated. His personal ambition was a mystery. He possessed a driving force to be rich, but not for the sake of wealth. Junior had little interest in accumulating money per se. He also understood clearly that no matter how great a personal fortune he amassed, nothing would change his status in the eyes of the Anglo Axis. They used him—Junior knew that. One of their token Chicano "success" stories, proof that democracy, capitalism, the free-enterprise system worked for all races, colors, creeds. And Junior tolerated the situation because he was also using it to achieve his own revenge.

Money generated power, an old and simplistic axiom. And Junior wanted that power desperately enough to keep his mouth shut, play tennis regularly with Al Lamont, screw his own father legally at every possible turn, and consolidate the ample holdings of men—Mooses, McQueens, Bonneys, Stryzpks—he despised. The only point was to stockpile land and cash, improving his own position, weaving himself indelibly through the complex patterns of their schemes. In the process, Junior was packing his files with any secret available, insinuating himself onto every board of directors, advancing himself as the invaluable mouthpiece for every businessmen's group or economic or social organization that played a key role in governing society. Junior was working his way right up there alongside Moe Stryzpk and Rodey McQueen and Bob Moose, keeping his cynical mouth shut, studying their methods, picking their brains and their files, so that when the time came he could double-cross them at will, using the methods they had taught him. As the McQueens and Bonneys grew older they would slow down, losing their mental edge, and Junior would be in a position to take over the town, wresting the main controls from their grasp. And in the process he would kill two birds with one stone.

By working for the Betterment of Chamisaville, Junior knew he was little by little strangling his father. The process made perfect sense to the slick, sullen lawyer, even though he had seldom dared analyze why. Perhaps the roots of his hatred for Virgil traveled back beyond his own birth, into the savage porridge of history, race, peasant Indian origins. In any case, Junior wished to destroy his father, he owed him that. Owed it to Virgil for his pathetically bloody role in the useless Mexican revolution; owed it to Virgil for not continuing his self-righteous militant politics in the United States; owed it to him for co-opting his American roots right from the start. He owed it to Virgil for shaming Loretta Shimkus with a hundred extramarital affairs; and he owed it to his dad for marrying a white woman in the first place, ensuring that Junior would be confused, twisted, tormented, his body harboring chromosomes that had been locked in mortal combat ever since the sword of Cortez lathered itself in Aztec blood. He owed it to Virgil for being so busy all his life that he had rarely played with his suffering child; and he owed it to Virgil for a childhood of economic deprivation. They could have been rich; instead, the old lawyer had defended a bunch of pathetic peasants having no money. Their family had existed enveloped in the tensions generated by a life lived at the embarrassing edge of financial ruin. Junior owed it to Virgil for giving him such a weird and aloof gringa for a mother: and for abandoning him, Junior, to that woman's custody when he deserted the family and they were divorced. And he owed it to Virgil for siring an only child when Junior had wanted a dozen boisterous brothers and sisters for company, making his experience like that of his neighbors. And he owed it to Virgil for being stiff, formal, uncommunicative with his son, unable—or unwilling—to give abrazos. And he owed it to Virgil for being a close friend (and long-ago lover) of April Delaney, a bitch who had once murdered his— Junior's—child up north in a Wyoming hotel room. And he owed it to Virgil for being the sort of courageous human being that from an early age Junior had realized he would never be, though he had no inkling why. A darkness, a weakness of character had been present at birth. His destiny? To be a man without honor despite a first-class brain; a son who could never measure up to the old man. That quality in Virgil, making him almost noble, which had allowed him to be trusted and loved despite all his failings—his pigheadedness, his gloomy demeanor, his infidelities—had been denied the son. Why? Because of the woman Virgil chose; because of the moon phase in which they screwed; because of the loving emotions (or lack of them) that the father had put into the conceptional act—because of all the choices made, the chances taken, and the luck involved, Junior hated his father. "I'll wear him down, tire him out, punish him slowly and mercilessly for his sins." He would chastise Virgil for fathering that brooding out-of-kilter quality in the son which could never achieve the sorrowful dignified mien of his dad. Working on him like a boxer out to humiliate rather than KO an opponent, carrying him for the full fifteen rounds in order to hurt him badly—that's the revenge Junior wanted on his father.

When Junior had achieved the necessary power, he would also rub out the Anglo Axis. Having helped create, for them, a valley in bondage to their selfish interests, he would collapse the governing structure. Having consolidated a majority control over the social, legal, and economic apparatus, he would scuttle the works just when everyone involved believed they were home free. That meant developing a more encompassing overall view than Moe Stryzpk. It meant insinuating flaws into every structure he had helped formulate, so that when the time arrived and he pulled a string, everything would collapse into a jumble of lawsuits, bankruptcies, foreclosures—financial, political, and social anarchy. In every case he built and concluded, in every organization incorporated through, and guided by, his brilliance, there had to be a carefully disguised fatal weakness. He stockpiled positive evidence of blackmail, extortion, and all other financial and political skullduggery firing the corruption and fueling the power plays directing Betterment. So that when Junior decided to knock down the cards, blowing the whistle to federal or state investigators, he could place reams of evidence in their hands, leaving nothing to chance. "So long Moe, Rodey, Bob, Randolph, Solomon, and Irving, J. B. and Damacio—we're gonna wipe the ledger *clean!*"

And then he and Charlotte—

Junior tinkered with the overall plot as if it were a toy globe of the world, rolling it around in his head, inspecting it from all angles, redefining the territory he already knew by heart, sending little boats across oceans and up tiny rivers, charting new terrain, fantasizing about crucial discoveries and their consequences. Government funds he had recently won for the partial subsidization of a municipal swimming pool, whose operation and maintenance would further undermine a shaky town budget, could eventually blow up into a major scandal toppling the likes of Damacio Mares and J. B. LeDoux. Many incorporation papers, licenses, plats, grids, and complicated bond issues all had marvelous secretly documented kickbacks and payoffs and bribes camouflaged by their elaborate foliage. Proceedings involving the proposed new sewage plant, the route of its pipes, whose land got condemned and why, were a veritable gold mine of compromising he might expose at a future date. How the Catholic church disbursed its moneys in land purchases and renovation contracts (and even in a Capital City massage parlor) contained enough inherent irregularities to cause more than a mild uproar in heaven. Standard, illegal bidding procedures on road contracts had the county commissioners in Junior's pocket: he could slit their throats whenever doing so might tickle his fancy. The style in which recent "improvement districts" for raising road-paving taxes had been railroaded into being, contained enough illegal snafus to send a half-dozen important men to jail. And forty years' documentation of the conservancy district—from Wayne Tupalo's suppressed hydrological report on the Cañoncito Dam to the use of conservancy taxes for private Mosquito Valley development—could put several dozen bigwigs behind bars, and maybe even break the governing structure of the First State Bank.

And now electrification of the Pueblo. As the Electric Co-op's chief counsel, Junior already had enough on Randolph Bonney to demolish him. Hadn't Junior himself personally siphoned off and laundered co-op funds for the Bonney Trailer Towne in Vallecitos, next door to the Dynamite Shrine complex? And weren't co-op funds fronting a new hardware enterprise theoretically under J. B. LeDoux's tutelage? But the big deal—this final deal at the Pueblo—could topple the whole shooting match if Junior played his cards correctly. He was funneling co-op payoffs to the outside, he knew all the Pueblo recipients and BIA flunkies on the take and Forest Service personnel in on the action. Junior himself handed envelopes to local legislature representatives, and a few state and federal politicos and Interior administrators governing the play. He had more goods on Joe Bonatelli than the *El Clarín* could learn in a hundred years. He owned thick dossiers on the Bonatelli henchmen, business partners, financiers, and enforcers who would be involved in everything out there. And he had extensive goods on all the government hydrologists, engineers, surveyors, and bagmen involved. Talk about a complicated—fecund—soup! So complicated almost nobody—aside from Joe Bonatelli and aging Moe Stryzpk (and Junior)—could trace all the individual lines. Right now it was so opaque, everybody was protected. The deal resembled a canvas on which all colors had been mixed so that only a mud remained. But he wasn't going to pull his string, not for a while. Not until after the structure had been imposed on the Pueblo, on the Indian people, on Chamisaville and its surrounding communities, and on the entire valley, quashing the last vestiges of two venerable civilizations while consummating the final stages of the Betterment of Chamisaville.

*Then* he would attack the foundation laid by Rodey McQueen and his Anglo Axis these past forty years. *Then* his files would be complete, truly organized. Duplicate files hidden in different secret places would keep him alive. One day, he would contact those thieves—the politically ambitious, the economically greedy—outside Chamisaville proper who might have a stake in blowing the lid off the whole mess. Those government investigators and police agents and congressmen would converge and make real hay of all the local principals involved. Chamisaville would collapse, half its big cheeses in prison! And if Junior went down also?—what the hell. "Adiós muchachos, compañeros, de mi vida. . . ."

While Junior drank, people circulated around the lounge. Benny LeDoux, son of the pimp, a wasted life himself, wearing sunglasses despite the gloom, and on the nod, spoke not a word to his girlfriend, Ramona, or to his crippled pal, Alfredo GeeGee, or to the pot plane pilot, Skeezix McHorse. Next door, the FBI—Chet Fulton, Len Goodwin—was drinking with Father Molé, Judson Babbitt, Irving Newkirk, and Denzil Spivey. Nearby sat Anthony Martínez and two Pueblo members of the Anti-Electricity Coalition, young toughs named Charley Gomez and Aurelio Duran, half blasted already and talking loudly in their own tongue. Junior could have throttled the smart-aleck *El Clarín* reporter for a cartoon he had published two newspapers ago—of Junior as a high-flying vulture, his enormous black wings spread threateningly, a frightened little Chicano farmer labeled *Chamisa County* in his brutal claws.

Espeedie Cisneros, Celestino Lucero (and Tierra o Muerte the Twelfth), and Perfecto Torres had abandoned their trailers, Operation Turnkey deathtraps, and Dynamite Shrine Motor Court cubicles for a night on the town. Three old troublemakers, soulmates of Juan Ortega, Virgil Leyba, Pat GeeGee, and "that crowd," they quietly consumed bottles of Dos Equis, and so far had caused only two minor disturbances: the first, when Celestino had been asked to check his magpie at the door; the second, when waitress Margie Martínez had brought cans of boycotted Coors to their table when they ordered beers.

Standing, Junior surveyed the scene, wobbly on his legs but feeling so all-powerful that a combination of sheer elation, arrogance, and cynicism kept him aloft. He pitied their prosaic brains and eagerly anticipated hearing their dolorous cries from underneath the rubble of their various empires when he pulled the string, reducing all their contaminated hopes, felonious trysts, and Mephistophelian deviltry to a nonsensical hodgepodge.

Suddenly, everything stopped. The folksinger was between songs; all conversations had arrived at a point of lull. Air quivered, smoke stood still, a single clank carried from the kitchen. All the La Tortuga's customers froze in attitudes of puzzled urgency. Outside, the entire valley seemed captured by instant mummification. As if out of some Bunyanesque fable, nighttime dynamite booms from the Mosquito Valley atrophied halfway down the canyon and settled harmlessly—soundlessly—into treetops like a spent fallout of big-city cinders or settling dawn crows. Accenting the eeriness, the Custer Electric Co-op suffered a brief blackout: all Chamisaville went dark; car headlights angled dreamily through the gloom like tropical fish in cooling midnight water.

Lights flickered on. Junior touched Fernando Popper's arm. "Have you noticed these lulls before?" he asked dramatically. "They happen all the time. Even during a busy day. It's as if suddenly the entire valley has a little heart attack, blood gets cut off in a crucial artery, the muscle driving the whole enchilada halts. And everybody —you, me, Moe Stryzpk, Judson Babbitt, my pop—we're all plunged into a five-second death with no air to breathe, no shadows, no sounds, no nothing. It's like a deaf-mute thunderclap has hit. And something enormous happens, something characterized by the total lack of anything worthwhile happening—"

"Goodnight, Junior. You be careful driving home now, hear?"

"There's a ghost in our music, Fernando . . ."

In his car, Junior slowly circled the plaza, almost striking arthritic old Nicanor Casados and Genovivo Arrellano as they galloped strickenly out of the El Gaucho, pathetically reliving their horse race up Chamisaville Canyon almost forty years ago. He paused at the signal light, then remembered it was broken, and, angered by that nonfunctioning traffic control apparatus, he floored the gas pedal, lurching recklessly across the North-South Highway and along the Plains Road at a great speed.

Perhaps a hundred yards beyond the last art gallery in a strip of jewelry, curio, and other tourist-oriented clip joints, Junior saw a roadside figure hitchhiking in his direction. With no intention of stopping, Junior accelerated, going almost sixty when he realized the hitchhiker was April Delaney, nude, asking for a ride.

With a cry, Junior twisted the wheel, skidding off the

macadam. He plowed right through her, glanced off a cottonwood tree, knocked down a flimsy shack, and, catching the bank of an irrigation ditch, flipped over and rolled down a grassy slope into an alfalfa field, thinking, as a fantastic cocoon of crumpling metallic violence roared around his stock-still, peacefully floating body: *Well, this is all right after all, this is really what I wanted, this is what should have happened long ago. I'm sorry, Dad. I love you, Papá. Forgive me for everything, Virgil Leyba. Please forgive me. And I know you will because you are the most beautiful human being on earth!*

ON THE NIGHT APRIL RETURNED home from the capital, George Parker was seated on the edge of her portal. He did not rise when she opened her door. April walked over and tousled his hair. "Hello, love. Long time no see." Comfortably arranged beside him, she lit a cigarette. With his finger, George drew aimless circles on her thigh, feeling awkward and constrained.

"Hey April, I missed you so much. I was going crazy without you. I never got a letter, I didn't know where you were, you never called—"

"I'm not about to phone your house, love—thanks anyway, but do spare me that maladroitness. And there's no phone on the mesa. So how did it go while I was gone? How's by the novel?"

"You never wrote when you might return—"

"I didn't know, really. I only got in right this minute."

"But I don't understand. . . ."

April stiffened. "Listen, my friend. You don't own me, George, get that out of your head. This is an affair. I didn't sign any legal papers offering myself to your bondage. I move at the command of my own personal will, not yours. I refuse to give up one iota of my independence, and if you start whining and bitching when I move according to my own rhythm, it's over—justlikethat!—you and me."

He quit drawing on her thigh, buried his face in his hands. April smoked, so weary she could barely think, let alone deal with a heavy confrontation. Yet she knew what was coming and couldn't stop it.

A long time passed. Troubled, dark, uneasy, George said, "I don't understand."

Well, what the hell? Slipping her arm through his, April snuggled against him. "I never visited New York, love. I'm sorry. Lord knows I've told a million fibs in my time, but I'm not inherently a liar, it's not my style. Leastways, not now, not these days."

"You were with somebody else?"

"Would that I had been, querido. No, I was down in our mundane capital, in a hospital. Later, I stayed at a motel for a few days. I had an operation. Afterwards I underwent some treatment. I'm still popping pills—part of the treatment—and they make me feel nauseous and generally lousy, so I'm sorry this confession lacks pizzazz. I guess I had myself convinced that somehow I could avoid this confrontation. But that's stupid. It's just that for a moment, even if it wasn't perfect, everything did seem . . . oh, remember that word we used to say a lot as kids? It seemed really *swell*. We've had some lovely moments together, George."

"What are you saying? What do you mean—operation? sickness? treatment?"

"Believe it or not, sweetness, I've got cancer. Don't be shocked because all the instruments agree: I'm tough and I can live to be a hundred. But every now and then they cut me open and exorcise a couple of devils."

"*That's* why you were limping."

"I wasn't limping, dammit. You *never* saw me limping!"

"No, once when we walked through the sage to the gorge, remember? When the doe fell over the cliff and we made love on the edge. Going down, when I walked behind you, I thought I detected a limp. Remember? Didn't you tell me that you had bumped it making love?"

"Well, there you have it—see?" April threw up her hands, wondering whether to cry or vomit. "Turns out April Delaney, the Living Legend of Chamisaville, is fallible just like everybody else after all."

"Why didn't you tell me?"

"Oh, who knows, man—who the hell knows? Maybe I'm still a little girl, a spoiled brat. I can't stand the idea of being flawed. I've always been so vital, sexy, healthy. Also proud, pigheaded, arrogant, blind. So it just gives me the creeps, that's all, to have this rotten thing in my body—is that against the law? I guess I had hoped not to disrupt our little idyll by injecting a crass note of mortality—who knows? Maybe I merely figured if I kept my mouth shut the problem would split of its own accord. Cancer, cancer, go away, come again some other day, little April wants to play."

"Don't be like that."

"Yeah, you're right. Pardonnez-moi, je vous en prie." April fumbled for another cigarette. "I'm not myself, this isn't like me."

"Where did they operate?"

"It wasn't one of my tits, darling, so don't shit a brick. I've still got the best bosom this side of Sophia Loren, bar none."

"Do me a favor and shelve the sarcasm, would you?"

"Maybe I'm a little defensive about the whole situation. I'm sorry." *Apologies again, Jesus Christ!* "Nobody ever gave me a crash course in how to tell friends you've got a slight touch of a fatal disease."

"April, please stop. Please just shut up, okay?"

Self-pity blossomed inside like wild morning-glory weed, its prolific tendrils reaching for all her internal organs, from the heart to the spleen. April cut it off sharply and smoked fiercely, fighting back tears, dismayed that she had told him, feeling cheated, tricked, double-crossed—by herself, by life, and angry at George already for however he might react. Now that he knew, her condition was bound to affect their relationship, their lovemaking, the whole damn thing.

Staring straight ahead, April vowed tightly, "I'm just not going to be any fucking character in any shithouse *Love Story*, do you understand? You'd better get that straight. I wasn't born to die with some kind of glamorous semi—Walt Disney whimper."

"Look . . . I understand." George placed a hand on her shoulder. At his touch her tears almost broke. But she caught herself in time.

"For the record, George, it's called lymphoma. That's cancer of the lymphatic system. I had one operation in New York. That's this fine triple-pronged scar on my neck, throat, shoulder. I did six months of chemotherapy after that. It subsided, and I really believed that I was cured. Then a lump developed in front of my ear, just below the temple—maybe you felt it, maybe you didn't— I dunno. You never mentioned. I should have treated it sooner but we were having such a wonderful time. The bone scan they did after the operation showed there's disease in my hip joint, so last week they cooked that spot and believe it or not, finally, it's beginning to feel better— the pain is almost gone. Now, if you've got any questions, you'd better ask them right now—I'll discuss any aspect you want to discuss. Only this is the last time, savvy? I won't live with this thing hanging over my head. Nobody's making me cater to any asshole disease. So speak now or forever hold your peace."

Elbows resting on his knees, forehead laid against his palms, George stayed dead silent.

"I might lose part of one eyebrow because of the radiation. There's also a good chance I'm going to lose some pubic hair: already the skin down there is pretty burnt-looking."

"It's because you've got such a hot twat," he joked feebly. "That's nothing new."

"Just so you have the complete picture, there's another thing. Once a month I get shot full of periwinkle juice, and then I spend five days taking Cytoxan and Prednisone pills. In New York I didn't lose any hair off my head, but that may have been because I was receiving different stuff, and in weekly, one-shot IV increments. My doctor now says that thanks to the current combination of shots and pills, I might lose the hair on my head."

"All of it?"

"He wouldn't put it past me to wind up balder than a bowling ball. Telling you ahead of time like this is called 'psychological preparation for the worst.'"

"Wow."

"Yeah . . . wow. And in case you're wondering why I've never gotten a period, that ended with the New York treatments. I think it's officially called a premature menopause. Induced by the chemotherapy."

April smoked, George didn't move. Her body felt icy, the muscles constricted, aching.

"If you feel sorry for me, George, then our romance has got to end right now. I'm not gonna screw anybody with an aroma of pity—or fear—hanging over me."

"You don't have to be so defensive, do you?"

"I have to be what I have to be."

"What I'd like to do is make love," he said. "I've been walking around with a hard-on for ten days, sticking it into cantaloupes, into sheep, into hot cow patties—"

"You don't have to. I told you, whenever you want it to end, all you have to do is just say so."

"Lighten up, April. I want you very much, this minute—" But his head was still buried in his hands.

"All right. I wanted to be sure we understood each other, though." April slipped her hand under his arm again, and snuggled her head against his shoulder. They were quiet, attentions held vaguely by Duane's upturned bicycle lying nearby.

"Shall we go inside?" George asked.

"Whatever. The kids are still over at the mansion." And then she cupped his face, forcing him to look at her. "I'm sorry, sweet. I'm sorry that the honeymoon is over. But I'm gonna make it up to you, I really am. Don't worry, please. The only purpose of any of these tribulations is to overcome them, growing stronger in the process. I really believe that, and you have to also—okay?"

He faced her, looking hurt, a little confused, slightly ashamed. April cocked her head, squinting quizzically.

"What's the matter, George?"

"Nothing's the matter," he replied.

THOSE TWO OLD DENVER LAWYERS, Joe Brady and Win Potter, had materialized in his dreams again. They were seated in an anonymous and empty café, drinking coffee, when Icarus Suazo entered and sat down across from them. Each old lawyer took a cigar out of his breast pocket, and then set fire to a thousand-dollar bill and lit the cigar with that bill—

At the precise moment of dawn, Icarus Suazo swung out of bed and dressed in the dark in a single fluid movement, lit the kitchen stove and put on coffee, and, while the water heated, by the light of his kerosene lamp he combed his long gray hair and braided it. After that, he sat in the dark at his table drinking coffee while a dim light began trickling down through the minuscule skylight above his head. When he finished, Icarus wiped the coffee cup clean with a dish towel and went outside: a gray velvet pall from the smoke of a hundred fires hung over the two ancient compounds, gods gallivanted, people hauled water from the river, climbing laboriously up and down ladders; they swept their stoops, and called out greetings. Pickups and second-hand cars started and coughed about in the bright, early days of summer sunlight that were a wet gold tamping down the dust of the wide plaza area.

He would feed two enormous white workhorses that he kept in a pasture slightly north of the Pueblo. Icarus had bought the horses long ago, and although he rarely if ever used the team himself, he loaned it to friends and neighbors and he loved the animals dearly. A saddle horse he kept in another, smaller pasture; his cattle, about ten head in all, were mixed with a relative's herd. And he checked them all, every morning, before heading to an office in the large pink BIA building a mile south of the compounds.

Slowly, pampering the early morning stiffness of his old bones, Icarus climbed two ladders down to the earth, circled some beehive mud ovens and drying racks, stopped for a moment at his outhouse, then swung around a wooden corral to the space where he parked his truck.

Unlocking the vehicle, he lifted himself in, inserted his ignition key, and was about to turn over the motor when Marshall Kickingbird appeared in front of the truck, shaking his head, somberly warning Icarus with feeble, almost effeminate hand signals, and the Pueblo secretary stayed his hand. Immediately, a breeze blew apart the apparition of the one-time Indian lawyer; his mistlike tatters evaporated into the morning air the way surprised snakes silently evaporate into long grass.

Gingerly lowering himself from the cab, Icarus circled to the front and lifted the hood, reached inside, and, working very carefully, removed a crude dynamite bomb, defused it, and placed the two tightly wired sticks in the bed of his truck. Pulling himself back into the cab, he drove out to feed his workhorses, realizing that they were dead even before he got there.

They lay not far apart on the close-cropped, dusty grass, each shot once in the head, almost directly between the eyes, by a small-bore gun, no doubt a .22 rifle. A few ravens and several magpies scattered as he approached. Icarus kicked one of the horses in the belly, knelt, grabbed a few blades of grass, and sprinkled them across the carcass. Blood streaked the white hide where birds had already pecked.

"All right," he said quietly, sneering at the far-from-impartial mountains. "So be it. But I will not waver."

# THE
# LAST
# BEAUTIFUL
# DAYS OF
# AUTUMN

# IV

# Where Will It
# All End?

ONE DAY AFTER J. B. LeDoux and his town council voted
to back Rodey McQueen's tax-exempt municipal industrial
revenue bonds, the *El Clarín* headline screamed: NORTH-
LAND GRAZING ASSOCIATION???? A subhead added MOB
$$$ IN CHAMISAVILLE? over a story sketchily running down
the Bonatelli-McQueen-Suazo axis and intimating those
three comprised a corporate board which might have ties
to gangland money aimed at constructing three new five-
hundred-unit motels and also connected with a monster
scam tied to the return of Pueblo Albino Pine land in ex-
change for an electrical monopoly opening reservation
territory to the sort of development Pueblo folks had al-
ways feared.

Forces were at play in Chamisaville, Juan Ortega spec-
ulated, that would make the past forty years' exploitation
appear like so much bush-league tinkering.

A front-page Anthony Martínez cartoon depicted J. B.
LeDoux and Icarus Suazo as moronic puppets. Manip-
ulated by a large, furry monster labeled *McQueen and
Moose, Inc.*, they were handing Chamisaville, on a silver
platter, over to sinister fedoraed gangster types. In the
background, monolithic bulldozers razed Hija Negrita
Mountain, in the process burying the last of the old-time
farmers and native peoples in a pit labeled *Our Own Babi-
Yar*.

On page two, the *El Clarín* asked: WHO IS JOSEPH
BONATELLI? Accompanied by a lousy Anthony Martínez
photograph of a shadowy plump figure regally ensconced
in the back seat of a bulletproof limousine, the article
briefly detailed everything April and her friends had been
able to uncover about Bonatelli's past and current connec-
tions.

From time to time, over the years, Joseph "Coffin Kid"
Bonatelli had cropped up in the state's tabloids. He had
a few fingers in the Capital City Downs racetrack: the

Bonatelli name always circulated vaguely around yearly scandals rocking the racing industry. Once, a Bonatelli "in-law," Franklin P. Mazurka, had been stopped for speeding, after a particularly lucrative Saturday quiniela payoff, with a trunkful of horse urine samples stolen from track security offices an hour earlier.

The *Capital City Reporter* also had once mentioned that Bonatelli had been investigated by the federal government sixteen times, by Nevada gaming authorities five years in a row, and was currently the subject of three federal grand jury probes. Too, the federal government's Los Angeles–based U.S. Organized Crime Strike Force had been investigating a Bonatelli fly-by-night Nevada land development. But the *Reporter* noted that Coffin Kid had retaliated by asking the Nevada attorney general to investigate the strike force and the gaming authorities, whom the attorney general subsequently severely chastised for "unnecessary allegations of bribery, extortion, and kickbacks," accusing them both of "distorting the true facts regarding Joe B.'s stellar enterprises." Then the AG committed suicide by shooting himself in the left temple and chucking his pistol out through a locked window (without breaking the glass) into some shrubbery (from which it was never recovered) before expiring, leaving behind in a safe-deposit box twenty thousand crisp clean dollars in alleged payoff money that could never be traced to anyone.

Bonatelli was also involved with a subsidiary of monolithic ITT, the Moosurelli Commercial Corporation, headquartered in Moose Jaw, Saskatchewan, a prime source of land sales contracts for several Sunshine Community System Corporation land developments in such diverse locations as Portal, Arizona, and Valdez, Alaska. Moosurelli also financed Industrial Latrines and airplane building equipment and underwater diving paraphernalia, managed an art-gallery string running from Madison Avenue through Chamisaville to Scottsdale, and represented four Japanese vertical corporations which logged southwestern timber, trucked it to San Diego in semis jointly owned by the Asians and Moosurelli, shipped the trees—in Dutch boats manned by Jamaican sailors, skippered by American captains, and leased to Moosurelli by a Greek—to Japan, where the trees were transformed into lightweight pulpboard units shipped back to America for the sort of low-cost prefabricated housing that Rodey McQueen and J. B. LeDoux, in conjunction with the federal government's Department of Housing and Urban Development's Mutual Help–Turnkey Program, had recently "constructed" in Chamisaville, among them the house, purchased by Prince of Whales waitress Gloria Armijo, which had capsized and dissolved in a flood caused by a burst city water pipe.

J. B. LeDoux was in his office, lethargically downing a beer and rereading the *El Clarín*'s brief Joseph Bonatelli exposé for the third time, when Junior Leyba limped in and dropped a thick sheaf of papers on his desk.

"What's that?" J. B. grumbled.

"Applications from various so-called businesses to the Town of Chamisaville, asking us to float a whole slew of tax-free municipal industrial revenue bonds so that they too can make a million bucks."

J. B. leaned back, squinting his eyes narrowly, wondering how Junior had escaped from his terrible car accident with nothing worse than a slightly turned ankle. "Like from who, for example?"

"Oh, it runs a gamut." Junior plunked onto the frayed couch, lighting a cigarette. "The El Gaucho wants to install a pay pool table in that back room where the drunks sleep, and hang Tiffany lamps from the ceiling."

"Come on, they're joking. That's your insane old man and Pat GeeGee, April Delaney, and the *El Clarín* crowd."

"Sure, but they can raise a stink."

"Yeah, yeah—what else?"

"Well, there's another from Flakey Jake Martínez and his kid Anthony. They want to build their own dynamite-fetish factory to be wholly owned by Indians, and they also want to construct a three-hundred-unit motor hotel on Pueblo land to serve Indians from other reservations when they come on their vacations to gawk at the curious honkies and vendidos of Chamisaville."

" 'Honkies and vendidos'?"

"That's their phrasing. It's in the proposal."

J. B. closed his eyes. "What else?"

"Oh, little bit of this, little bit of that. The *El Clarín* you got there would like us to float about fifty Gs worth of bonds so they can build their own office, buy a press, and compete with the *Chamisaville News.*"

"Jesus Christ." J. B. smiled forlornly. "Now, how the hell are we going to humor them?"

"Humor the *El Clarín,* the El Gaucho, and Flakey Jake?

We'll tell them if they don't like it they can go suck green meat."

"Sure," J. B. said. "Who reads that rag anyway?"

"I noticed you were reading it."

"Of course I'm reading it. It's the only place I can get any information about what's going on in my town right underneath my nose that neither you nor McQueen nor your Mr. Bonatelli there have had the common decency to let me in on, that's why I'm reading this piece of bumwad!"

"Calm down, cousin. We got a long road to hoe."

"Row, Junior. Row."

"Row?"

"A long *row* to hoe. Weren't you ever a migrant worker?"

"What—and ruin my manicure?"

"Hah hah."

"Also among these papers are requests from the Dingle Lodge to build an addition, and from Irving Newkirk, who wants to build three five-hundred-unit motels right across the highway from each of the Northland Grazing Association's new structures. Just to keep everything honest and aboveboard, I've applied myself to upgrade the Dynamite Shrine Motor Court, like with a swimming pool out back. Other than that it's mostly small potatoes: Claude Parker would like us to float just enough paper to buy him a new hearse, an atomic trocar, and some newfangled contraption called a cadaver detoxifier. And the Catholic church, of course, would be pleased if we'd float some tax-free scrip on their behalf, enabling them to buy new tapes of bells chiming out patriotic songs."

"Is that all?"

"That's the bill of particulars as of this moment."

"What do we do?"

"As town attorney, my advice to you and the council would be to give me my renovated motor court, humor the Catholic church, and explain to anyone else that because that bonds us out to our legal capacity, they'll have to tap other sources for their capital improvements."

J. B. fished forth a handkerchief and mopped his soaking brow.

"Oye," he said, dropping into Spanish. "Yo me escuché un nuevo 'knock knock' chiste ayer. Vaya. Empiezemelo."

"Pos bueno," Junior said. "Knock knock."

"Quién es—?"

Junior looked befuddled for a moment, then snapped: "Christ, J. B., I'm not supposed to begin. You're supposed to say 'Knock knock.'"

"Carai!" exclaimed the mayor. "Debe estar el calor. Bueno: Knock knock."

"Quién es?"

"Boo."

"Boo quién?"

They mayor looked puzzled this time around; he stared at the floor, mouth agape, wondering why the damn thing hadn't worked.

"So what's the joke?" Junior said. "I don't get it."

"I guess it doesn't work in Spanish. You're not supposed to say 'Boo quién?' you're supposed to say 'Boo who?'"

"Why are *you* crying?" Junior cackled lethargically, slapping his thigh and spilling ashes all over the couch.

"Oh go fuck yourself." J. B. heaved up and slouched over to the window. It offered the usual view of bumper-to-bumper automobiles, nearly obliterated by a poisonous haze of their own making, creeping through the sizzling town. A water main beneath the recently retarred surface had broken, and rust-colored liquid was bubbling slowly up through the fresh tar.

"Why are so many people still afraid of electrifying the Pueblo?" the mayor asked after a moment spent regarding this destined-to-be-unalleviated mess.

"Who can say? Perhaps instinctively they know what we're going to do once it's in there."

"What *are* we going to do?" J. B. asked.

"That remains to be seen."

J. B. said, "Did you hear Cipi Fernández died last week? For fifty years he made the best chokecherry wine in the valley. J. F. Valdez croaked too. Twenty years as a miner in Colorado. He worked in the smelters up there, also. Nobody around here ever played a better accordion. All the old geezers are dying."

Junior said, "Time marches on."

J. B. made a fist of his right hand, stared at the fist for a long, drawn-out moment, then delicately kissed one knuckle, after which, with a sudden desolate cry, he punched out the window.

THE MAYOR WENT MOMENTARILY BLIND, adjusting his eyes to the gloom, then discovered he was almost alone in the El Gaucho, with only Virgil Leyba and Pat GeeGee, and perhaps something—Gabe Suazo, Nicanor Casados—off in a dark corner, buried under a blanket exhaling stertorously, for company. Nodding tersely at the old revolutionary, J. B. located himself several stools north of the lawyer, feeling more out of place than he had felt in a decade, and twice the fool.

On the defensive, in English, he ordered a martini. On the offensive, in Spanish, Pat GeeGee growled, "Does this look like a bar that serves martinis?" On the offensive, in Spanish this time around, J. B. said, "Listen, you liverspotted old cadaver, give me a six-pack of Coors, and have a little respect for once in your life."

"No Coors, I don't handle it. There's a Chicano boycott."

Deflated, the mayor gave up. "Give me six cold ones of whatever you've got." He dropped a five-dollar bill on the bar. "Keep the change."

"To go? I'll even throw in a bag, free."

"No such luck. Save your bag and your wisecracks. I'll drink it here."

Pat clunked six before the mayor, took the five bucks, made change, and set the money on the counter in front of J. B.

"I said keep the change, Pat. What the hell, you need it more than me. There's plenty more where that came from."

"*You* keep the change, J. B."

"Listen, god dammit! If I tell you to keep the change, you goddam well better keep it, you understand? I don't want any of your self-righteous airs, Pat, I know you're poor as hell, struggling to make it, and I got money to burn! So keep the change, dammit, before I shove your rotten teeth down your throat!"

"You earned it, J. B., you keep it." Insolently, Pat turned his back on the mayor: J. B. almost burst into tears.

Then he pried loose a beer, popped the top, and emptied the can in three gulps. Wrenching open another can, he demolished half. Then, breathing heavily, he reconnoitered the bulletin board through tearing eyeballs, wandering disconsolately through that discolored history of the town and the people he supposedly governed. The Cipi García funeral postcards; Claude Parker's whale; a local team-roping duo that had once won a rodeo championship; the relatively unyellowed, if toothless face of Juan GeeGee atop a shore news article in which he no doubt explained his six-million-gallon water bill last year, the result of a town computer error; and hundreds of faces—of politicos who had ruled for a while and died; of a championship slowpitch softball team. Other photographs recounted the annual summer fiestas . . . folk dancers in old costumes, fiddlers and accordion players, a shot of the Balena Park floating bandstand, children on the hundred-year-old merry-go-round. And there was the plaza ages ago, populated by wagons with iron-rimmed wheels parked around a dirt square with wooden sidewalks. Later on, a gazebo appeared, precursor to the current pillbox-bandstand. Then automobiles entered the scene. In other areas of the montage fuzzy-faced men bent over sheep, about to shear them. Young couples, getting married, wore new hats, held flowers, smiled nervously. Teen-agers in military uniforms scowled importantly. Ancient men and women, posed formally for Karl Mudd's camera on their golden wedding anniversaries, looked proud and disdainful—"We made it." There were fires and other disasters. And a photograph of the Balena Park skating pond the year it opened, with grown-up folks in strangely formal clothing, wearing suits and top hats and ankle-length dresses, looking terribly wooden upon the ice. Finally, J. B. lit upon that picture of himself, on his knees in front of the Dynamite Shrine, surrounded by tourists, newspaper reporters, and the Anglo Axis.

"Hey," he growled. "Take that picture down."

"Which one?" Pat asked.

"You know which one. The one of me on my knees in front of the shrine."

"I don't tell you how to run your town, J. B. So don't you tell me how to run my bar."

"I don't like that picture, Pat. Get rid of it," J. B. insisted dispiritedly, immediately wishing he had never called attention to the photograph.

Pat latched onto the telephone, saying, "Who'll it be if you give me trouble, J. B.—Fernando Popper? Big Bill Baca? Or Gray von Brockdorff?"

"Aw, the hell with it," J. B. said sheepishly. "Forget I ever opened my big mouth. I was only joking." The mayor was sick of alienating people he wished would love him. Or at least respect him, if only just a little.

. He finished the six-pack. Eyesight blurry, booze mixed with tears of self-pity, he couldn't take his attention off that historical montage, and in particular off himself on his knees during the Bataan thanksgiving demonstration. Finally, without looking at Virgil, his heart beating too quickly,

J. B. said, "Virgil, old enemy, what is going to happen? Where will it all end?"

Virgil spat a tobacco flake onto the floor. "When I was very young, J. B., I fought ten years in a revolution that I and my people believed in. At the end it was difficult to say whether we had won or lost, or whether the great cost was worth it. Later, it was easy to understand that we had lost, and some of us made a suicidal gesture from which, for unknown reasons, I escaped. Many years have elapsed since I was a young idealist with five bullet holes in me, traveling by night on a journey of two thousand miles ending in this lovely valley now rapidly going to pot. As to where it will end with me, personally, or with you, or with all of us—that's no problem. It ends in death, of that be assured. But as to where, in the larger sense, our society will wind up, I'm afraid I can't tell you. Someday, of course, a billion years from now, the sun will sputter and die. Maybe tomorrow a hundred hydrogen bombs will take care of this curious business we have dubbed the Affairs of Humankind. As for myself, I am grateful that, in a not very wise old age, I am still an idealist clothed in shreds of hope, who wakes up every morning wanting to kick the living shit out of you and out of all those vultures touching their cattle prods to your buttocks and testicles making you hop around this town like a grasshopper off of which little children have pinched the wings."

With a drunken roar, J. B. skidded from his stool, and, amid a phenomenal clatter of empty beer cans, he hurled himself at Virgil, but missed, falling about two feet short, doing a resounding bellyflop against the rancid floorboards.

Incredulous, first because he had leaped at such a frail old man, secondly because he had missed his target by such a wide margin, the mayor found himself not only unable to move, but with all the rage knocked out of him by that single, painful pratfall.

He just lay there, gasping. And then breathing heavily. And then breathing quite evenly. Until after a while, like a man who has finally returned from a long and exhausting voyage, J. B. fell asleep.

"WHAT IS GOING TO HAPPEN?" Virgil mused ironically. "Where will it all end? Or, to open a page on Lenin: 'What is to be done?' "

That was more properly and pragmatically the question

to ask. Leave the big, self-pitying questions to the ghosts of a nineteenth-century bourgeoisie.

Telling Pat to tote up the damage and add it to his tab, Virgil slipped off his stool, stepped over the mayor, and entered the muffling night. Stretching, he yawned and gazed upward at aluminum-colored tree leaves and at a limp phosphorescent flag Filiberto García had forgotten to retire. Chamisaville, quiet as a weedy grave, baked sourly in the ruthless darkness. A few cheerless crickets sawed away: a faraway jester's cackle of copulating coyotes drifted sluggishly over the town. For too long a sere, baked odor had stagnated in the motionless valley air.

Virgil headed for his pickup, a tired angular ghost jerking through the plaza's mercury vapor glare. Stopping once, he pressed his nose against his office window on the ground floor of the Plaza Hotel, experiencing momentary guilt pangs on viewing the chaotic disarray characterizing his workday hovel. Ears, tongues, flaps, tidbits, and snippets of legal documents dripped, spewed, or flowered from his filing cabinets and partially opened desk drawers. Each morning, on entering that scene, Virgil was briefly overwhelmed by sensations of unfinished business. Often, head in his hands, he released a few desperate sobs over the cruel 9:00–A.M. realization that life itself is an unfinished business. After all these years, Virgil had enough ego going for him to resent the fact that life would continue after he dropped dead. It gave him great and continuous sorrow to understand that when he died, his work would not be completed: two dozen cases would be hanging fire on court dockets; all his land grant and ejido research would be inconclusive. To make matters worse, a young jackanape from some future Legal Aid office might take over, idealistically bent on continuing his work. *His work*, not just a job to Virgil, *an extension of his soul!* To which some bumbler might have the audacity to believe he or she could do justice.

Bumbler? Virgil thought with poignant and heartbreaking chagrin. I have been a first-class pendejo in my time, including the present. And he wasn't helping matters by spending half of all his days pickling aches and pains in the El Gaucho, the real, physical hurts, and the more frightening, utterly savage despondencies which daily tossed his heart like hurricanes, fracturing a lifetime's structures, structures Virgil painfully rebuilt each morning with coffee and cigarettes and the daily paper, reconstruct-

ing the universe until he took heart again and commenced work with renewed vengeance, determined to
make a son of a bitch squirm that day, or to score a small
triumph for some infinitely patient and doomed little
family needing a tiny victory even more than they required
air to breathe.

A state police siren boiled several miles away. Alarmed,
the plaza crickets ceased their fidgety racket. Virgil quit
contemplating his soul's unfinished business and plodded to
his truck parked in a vacant lot behind the Moose and
McQueen Insurance Company just off the plaza.

A gangster had slashed all four tires and smashed the
windshield with a brick.

Kneeling, Virgil gingerly pinched wrinkled rubber. Then
he unlocked the driverside door and spent a minute brushing tiny glass shards off the seat—but that felt silly; he
stopped. For a second he looked all around suspiciously;
maybe the culprit, a gleeful sadist, was still hanging
around, loving his discomfort.

After that Virgil rustled in the glove compartment for
the registration and a box of ammunition, fished his fifteen-
dollar plumber's wrench from among the tools under the
front seat, wedging it in his belt like a pistol, and, astonished the vandal had not lifted his gun, he removed the
deer rifle from a rear window rack, relocked the vehicle,
returned to the El Gaucho, and telephoned April Delaney.
She came in to pick him up.

The old lawyer folded himself uncomfortably into her
Bug. They drove quietly out to Alamito and up Virgil's
dusty driveway to his small adobe house. When April
turned off the engine, they sat for a moment, listening to
the motor crackle, gathering enough strength to open the
doors.

Virgil started drifting off: April turned his head so that
he was facing her. "Hey," she said. "Hey, Virgil Leyba."

He opened his eyes.

"You're working yourself into an early grave."

"Who isn't? So are you."

"Maybe you've got to take it easier," April said.

"Bullshit."

Over the years, Virgil's eyes, once dark, hard, and unforgiving, had assumed a more gentle look intimately related to the decent but bitched souls whose skinny buttocks
had rubbed through the blue paint on a wooden bench set

against one wall in his office. April said, "Your eyes are so sad, old man. They look worried and dog-tired."

Virgil gave her a sardonic grin. "When a man puts down the revolutionary life, attempting to elicit redress for the mighty sins of a completely haywire political system by means of persuading the hand-picked judiciary of that system that it is in their best interest to act against their own best interest by allowing their downtrodden masses to live like human beings, then he deserves such weakened eyes."

"I wasn't putting you down."

"It's all right. Let's go in. I'll make you a coffee."

Inside, his house was a mess. The living room, enclosed by wall-to-wall bookcases, had a wooden table in the middle. On the table a typewriter was surrounded by a holocaust of legal documents and several opened books and magazines. Fist-sized balls of crumpled paper overflowed the lone wastebasket and littered the rugless floor, inundating more books and magazines, a cassette tape recorder and a cardboard box holding jumbled tapes, plates piled high with cigarette butts, half-filled coffee cups, and an empty liquor bottle.

"Why are our houses such a mess?" April moaned.

Virgil rummaged in a kitchen cupboard for something to lace the coffee with. He located a bottle, and brought two steaming cups into the living room. April carefully moved aside some correspondence to clear a chair for him; folding her legs, she sat on the floor nearby.

Cheap Diego Rivera reproductions decorated the walls, and Virgil often sat back, as he did now, recharging his batteries with Mother Earth, warlords, social chaos, naked bodies swimming through fantastic tunnels of light, a clenched fist arisen from mountain peaks, and revolutionaries with crossed bandoliers engaged in the only struggle and on the correct side, holding absolute confidence in the emergence of a positive universe from these countless centuries of madness and blood.

"J. B. LeDoux asked me tonight where it would all end," Virgil said after they had been seated quietly for a while.

"And what did you tell him?"

"I sort of told him to go jump in a lake."

April laughed. "And where *will* it all end?"

"I don't know. To tell the truth, the thought rarely enters my mind. Life, history, they are an unending process: struggles never cease. So it will never end, and there's no point in worrying about how it will end."

A large gray cat sailed onto Virgil's lap. Without realizing it had arrived, he began lazily to stroke the animal.

"The important thing, of course, is to have at least one finger on the world's pulse," Virgil said sleepily. "I think my lone virtue is that I have an insatiable curiosity about the course of my times. And, having taken sides, I feel a stake in all outcomes, big or small. When I win a case, I congratulate the world. If I lose, I apologize to Fidel, George Jackson, Emiliano Zapata, Pablo Neruda, Fidel, I. F. Stone, and Malcolm X."

April said, "You're such a pompous old man. Give you an inch and you'll take a soapbox."

"So be it."

"You're insignificant, Virgil my love. You're just a little speck on the flypaper of life."

"Don't try to tell me *I'm* insignificant," he snapped. "Don't try to tell me *I'm* powerless to change things. Don't ever say to me 'What can you do?' or 'What's the use?' "

Fatigue making her slightly giddy, April changed the subject. "Virgil, teach me not to be afraid of dying."

The lawyer looked at her for a second, puzzled. Then he said: "I'm not afraid of dying. But as death approaches, life grows sharper, more complex, and sweeter. My beer I enjoy much more at my advanced age than I did at twenty. My twilight years are ten times more fascinated than my youth was by the banal choreographies of everyday people hanging out laundry, riding horses, talking on the courthouse steps, staring at geese. Worldly wonders multiply as my time nears a conclusion."

And with bittersweet self-mockery he added: "Sometimes—and I must sincerely apologize for this—but sometimes I wish I was immortal."

He faced her—tired, dreamy, momentarily playful, also sad. Then suddenly, thoroughly exhausted, Virgil slumped and began sliding off the chair.

On her feet, April grabbed his shoulders; the cat floated lightly onto the floor.

"Hey, Virgil. You're a demented old man who's so tired he can't see straight. Time for bed."

The lawyer placed a hand on her shoulder and blinked, struggling to keep his eyes open.

"You can't work this hard anymore, love. You're going to kill yourself."

"It's the only way to kill myself," he mumbled. "Single-handedly, I am going to halt the Betterment of Chamisa-ville."

"No, sweet. I'll keep you into bed."

April dug her hands under his arms, guiding him out of the chair; she supported him into the bedroom. The double bed was unmade, a chair beside it held an empty glass and an ashtray filled with old cigarette butts. Another cat stirred from the blankets as April eased him down: Virgil flopped backward and, closing his eyes, sighed.

"Do you have pajamas?"

Opening one bleary eye, he mustered the strength for a wan grimace. "I sleep in the nude."

Over him, April undid his tie—and stopped. Virgil's eyes were wide open, alert. They stared at each other for a second; then she cupped his face with one hand. April loved this man more than she had loved anyone in Chamisaville, perhaps more than she had loved anyone in her lifetime. She believed in him, respected him, and had wanted to take better care of him, but could not because he wouldn't allow it. Virgil gave her more strength than she wanted to admit; she depended on him more than was healthy.

"Virgil, I love you."

"I know that. I love you, too. It's okay."

Leaning over, April kissed him on the lips. Lifting one hand, the old man placed his palm against her breast.

"There's such a deep and terrible sadness in things," April said.

"No. It's okay."

"Oh shit," she blurted. "All this loneliness . . ."

"It's okay."

April brushed back the folds of his suitcoat and carefully unbuttoned his shirt. He smelled of sweat, and yet sometimes he seemed so lanky there could barely be room for liquid in his body. His chest was cold, nearly hairless. His skin was tightly layered against bone, thinly but tautly muscled. An ugly pair of purple scars flowered in his visible skin, livid, and seemingly alive. April touched them with her fingertips, she bent over to kiss them. Virgil slid fingers tentatively into her hair.

"Virgil, I love you."

"You can love me, it's all right, we understand each other. More isn't necessary."

344

"I know, but I really love you. You're a battered old letch, but you're beautiful."

"Of course I'm beautiful. What other way is there to be?"

"You've also got a hard-on."

"That goes without saying. Excuse me for my impoliteness."

"You're excused."

A cat, ignoring them, landed, weightlessly on the bed and curled up against her thigh. With one hand resting against his scarred neck, Virgil fell asleep. Kneeling beside him, April smoothed his chest with her hand while he snored, twitching with dreams.

SUCH DREAMS.

Every night, incandescent ghosts with spurs clanking, chain-smoking cigarettes, backs broken from hoe wielding, flaunting machetes and machine guns, with glistening breasts or tousled dusty hair, dancing, groveling, herding sheep, singing songs, playing guitars, saying rosaries, tossing dirt into sunny holes, faces smudged from teardrops— every night Virgil's dreams liberated those specters from his skull's tiny cubicle. And the house reverberated with their noise, stench, and rhetoric, terrifying his cats, whom Virgil located anew every morning, tugging them out, hissing, from beneath the refrigerator, bureau, or stove; fishing them from trampled nests in his filing cabinet drawers; or pulling them by their bushy tails out of his irrigation boots, their protesting claws slashing holes in the rubber, so that the boots immediately filled with water whenever he irrigated.

They smoked, these fantasy characters, filling his ashtrays with gray flaky heaps that he emptied at dawn. Knocking about restlessly, they tipped over lamps and chairs, and brushed against paintings, tilting the frames at lopsided, irritating angles Virgil corrected when he awoke. Mud-covered generals abounded, as did multiple ghosts of Loretta Shimkus, and two Cipi Garcías (before and after his brain was retired by Onofre García's revolver of erudite lineage). Too, there were several wispy manifestations of Virgil himself at different ages: the wide-eyed sullen peasant child; the arrogant revolutionary; the gaunt and often physically cruel young man unable to comprehend his attraction to Loretta Shimkus; the concerned young

345

father posing in the mouth of Claude Parker's embalmed whale with Junior in his arms—

Juan Bautista Godoy y Godoy emerged to wreak havoc in Virgil's lonely little house, escaping hand in hand with his wife, Amaranta, and accompanied by a hundred old-fashioned types like themselves. And these ancient people —Espeedie Cisneros, Celestino Lucero, Ursula and Perfecto Torres, Ikie Trujillo, Max Jaramillo—these ancient people, whom he had tried to protect against the Betterment of Chamisaville for so many years, gathered around his bed, often squatting and drawing on his floor with twigs or with their arthritic fingers as if in dirt, giving him all the sordid details again—and again—of their sad and frustrating adventures. They piled imaginary old documents on Virgil's bed until he broke into a sweat—the covers were too heavy.

All night, every night; a thousand people, orchestrated by waltzes, polkas, and inditas, the roar of Pat GeeGee's airplane, the murder-and-madness mariachis of Mexico. Cuachitlán old-timers—Emiliano Tafoya!—rambled about hugging precious boxes against their breasts, the keepers of the legal rights to what was legally being robbed. They burped, opened their boxes, and traded stories—always the same story. Their bare feet raised gobs of dust; Virgil spent half his nights sneezing. Scuffles occurred: the ghostly manifestation of his own son knifed the ghostly manifestation of a Palafox in the back. Fernando Popper had a knock-down, drag-out with Flakey Jake Martínez while Irving Newkirk made book on the side. Pink, erotic women oozed through the crowd flaunting themselves, then clambered through legal documents weighing down his blankets and caressed Virgil's deteriorating flesh, arousing terrible, murderous longings, desires so strong that, when gratefully he awoke, the smoky household air contained within it the last weak echoes of his all-night whimpering.

Seated on his bed in 6:00–A.M. sunlight forging rainbows among filaments of ghost-smoke choking his rooms, Virgil might weep, amazed and grateful for tear ducts still able to function (though all his life only in private) after so many years. Then he would wiggle his feet into shabby slippers and shuffle about locating the cats, opening doors and windows to air the place, ridding it of smoke, perking fresh coffee before heading into town for breakfast, hoping the coffee smell might erase the scent of those women and

346

tired sheepherders and unwashed revolutionaries—an odor which never entirely dissipated with the smoke.

Virgil awoke suddenly, expecting to catch the menagerie in full tilt. Instead, the house was quiet. Kneeling beside him, April was smoking a Mexican cigarette, gazing out his window. Virgil said, "I know I'm crazy, but so what?" and fell asleep again.

At dawn, when he awoke for good, April was still seated on the bed, holding a half-empty tequila bottle, chain-smoking Delicados.

"I want to go for a swim," she said sleepily. "How about it, old man?"

"Give me a drink, first."

Half an hour later, with a buzz-on, they piled into April's VW and drove to the Rio Grande. Virgil sat on the rocks while April stripped and eased into the murky green river. The lawyer feared water, never having learned to swim. With her old bomber jacket over his shoulders, he watched the woman, her big white body afloat in the heavy currents, wanting to call out, "Be careful!" Yet he had never uttered the warning. April did as she pleased, and if the river killed her, that would be another human being to mourn for the rest of his days. Virgil was not complacent, nor fatalistic, but, trusting neither a drunk April nor the river, he nevertheless had a feel and a respect for certain reckless rhythms.

Swallows twittered between the high walls of the gorge; the river was deep, slow, and green; April white and lush. Virgil burned. He wanted to leap up, cry, kill somebody, rape that unselfconscious woman who was his best friend.

Instead he sat on a rock, lanky and old, clothed in a wrinkled suit, his neck scrawny in a collar that had been designed for a stem covered with more flesh, his teeth aching because he hadn't seen a dentist in years. Old, coverd with dust, damp from unrequited longings and a madman's dreams—a foolish, idealistic idiot.

Though still—thank God!—on fire.

*On fire.* Virgil closed his eyes. Flames sprang up. Smoke twisted and billowed and twirled back to earth, the vapor assuming a variety of foggy human shapes, coalescing into a mysterious drama of ghostlike personalities, a crowd of dignified, wraithlike pelados—the immortal salt of the earth. I'm going crazy, Virgil thought: the strain has taken its toll. Yet what better vision to prove my love, giving the beautiful history of all anonymous diffident seraphim the stature they deserve? Decrepit Eloy Romo, chewing a cigar, dreaming of the afternoon he knocked out eleven and was decked sixteen times, scared lizards and sent ants scurrying as he impishly imitated the Ali shuffle. Sparks snapped, a burning branch sizzled, then puffed up and exploded into fiery cinders. A bittersweet nostalgic ectoplasm seethed among the flames. Imagination? Illusion? Hallucinatory daydreams? The pain of a discontinued people? Joe Archuleta, composed of rarefied ether, slit the throat of a fleecy pig—an effervescent crimson lather danced from the wound. Inessential J. F. Valdez, locked into celestial poetry, played a cumulus accordion and laughed. Virgil rubbed his eyes, roasting in this spook-filled dream.

A momentary funereal darkness shrouded the inner landscape. His mind dived into abstract reveries. Another age, disquieting echoes, ran a fever in his blood. A rush of something, perhaps danger, the Angel of Death, uncontrollable events whispered through supernatural regions. Kittens mewed unhappily, crickets and peepers employed hesitant nervous rhythms; bats left frantic, leathery trails in the air. A stick snapped, a hot skull popped, uneasy lovers enveloped in cracking emotional crusts wept without knowing exactly why. Sheep bells tinkled forlornly; tiny stars no bigger than snowflakes fell into summery meadows and twinkled like diamond pepper. A teen-age April Delaney, breasts so full they pranced like eager puppies on a leash, came crashing down through his body like an enormous ponderosa pine tree, snapping the branches of his heart; the broken limbs bled tears.

Oh there had always been a vital severity to life that had birthed incredible, unrequited yearnings!

"When I know it's time for me to die," Virgil mumbled vaguely, "I'm gonna walk out to the mesa and expire. The coyotes and buzzards, the rattlesnakes and the ants will eat me as they should, and they'll shit me out in varioussized little turds onto this lonely, beautiful land, and that will be that. My bones will burrow lazily into the sand. I believe in the earth and in its wild creatures. I don't want Claude Parker to drain my blood and fill me full of combustibles, fiddle with my eyes, my nose and my cheeks, and then dress me up in a paper suit and nail me to rest in an elaborate pompous cajoncito that they would then cover with rocks and surround by a white iron crib in the La Ciénega camposanto where the ravens, the vultures, the magpies, coyotes, ants, and flies couldn't get at me.

The shit would rot in my intestines and the liquid in my eyeballs would turn sour, breeding mosquitoes."

Flames died. Virgil squirmed uneasily and opened his eyes. Violet green swallows set the air overhead atwitter with colorful, frenetic motion. And April Delaney still floated in the river with her eyes closed like a lazy, erotic trout.

# Memories

CYNTHIA EGGINGTON McQUEEN had seldom paused to reflect on the nature of things.

A busy woman with a hectic schedule, she ran the show at the McQueen mansion, entertained according to her husband's whims and his business and their social requirements, and usually spent at least six weeks of the year out of town, with or without McQueen, cruising the Caribbean, in Acapulco, or somewhere in Europe. While in residence, she was the most active woman around, a past Worthy Matron of the Order of the Eastern Star, a current chairman of the Hospital Auxiliary, a big wheel in the Chamisaville Garden Club and the County Historical Society, an active member of the women's division of the chamber of commerce, and a trustee of the Cipi García Miracle Memorial Museum.

In her capacity as a powerful member of these various civic and Masonic organizations, she did work for Boy Scouts and Girl Scouts, local 4-H Clubs, and the Association for Retarded Children. She organized Garden Club house tours, set up hospital bazaars, arranged benefit teas and silver teas, planned food booths for raising money during the annual Cipi García fiestas, arranged benefit concerts and Harvest Fiesta Balls and raffles of everything from turkeys to automobiles, was instrumental in putting together the annual Chamisaville iris shows and flower shows, had a steering hand in the Balena Park beautification gardens and in the town plaza landscaping and war memorial floral displays, made sure the plaza's tourist information booth was running smoothly and staffed by competent volunteers, and was always an important organizer of the Heart Association's annual Circus of Hearts Ball and of the Easter Seal, Hope Chest, and March of Dimes campaigns.

From Cynthia's vantage point, Chamisaville was an embodiment of the American dream. If she moved in circles which precluded almost all contact with the native populations, that lack did not disturb her. She bought eggs and tomatoes from Celestino Lucero, goat cheese and apples from Canuto Tafoya, and labor from Amaranta GeeGee, to name a few—what more could they possibly want?

And then April had to come home and start embarrassing them with her social-studies course, her moratorium demonstrations, and that horrible little newspaper.

On several occasions, Cynthia had almost admitted to herself that she hated her daughter. But she suppressed the feeling, never really articulating it; she merely laid her ears back, smiled frostily, and followed her husband's lead.

Yet with April back in town, Cynthia had come to be unhappy in a new way. All the resentments, all the old bitternesses were present, of course, also the anger. But April's return had conjured in Cynthia something she would not have predicted; suddenly the woman experienced a sense of irreconcilable loss. And Cynthia found herself yearning for confidential talks with April. She wanted to call up her wayward daughter, arrange a clandestine get-together, and beg April for details of the outside world as she had lived in it. Yet such a meeting was closed off to the mother: Cynthia could never make that uncharacteristic a move.

Then Cynthia was also perturbed to discover that in a life which had previously been unrelentingly busy all day, occasional lulls were occurring. A noon in which she had no luncheon date would roll around; Cynthia wound up eating a sandwich alone on the patio, remarking almost with wonder at the silence governing her walled-in world. Or again, fresh from an hour of morning telephone calls, she would dress for the next appointment, only to discover when she checked her calendar that she had no next appointment. And she would sit down in her expansive living room, feeling petulant, a trifle surprised and upset, wondering how *that* had come about. Was she growing absentminded, or just slowing down? What was the process taking place here, uncomfortably nudging her soul?

Cynthia's rhythm, in subtle ways, was coming apart. A faint longing for unknown appetites lodged unobtrusively in her breast; April halfway occupied her mind. And on two or three disconcerting occasions, she had caught herself viewing McQueen with a critical eye. Little stirrings inside belonged to a sexual urge that had been repressed for ages. Cynthia considered approaching him again; but their arrangement was all too defined and accepted to admit change: impossible to broach the subject; ridiculous, at her age, if she did. McQueen got his satisfaction; Cynthia knew where but made no attempt to stop him.

Still, sometimes Cynthia found herself wanting to escape from Chamisaville, have an adventure, make love with a tall dark stranger before it was too late.

Then all at once the estate's four walls, instead of giving her a feeling of snugness and magic, became prison walls, barring her from an outside life.

Cynthia's body was coming alive with intangible yearnings and vague, discomforting desires. Occasionally the unsettled feeling inside had identified itself as loneliness, and it enveloped her, begging the aging woman to act on her own behalf, escaping into life before death ended the drama. At those moments, she really wanted to approach McQueen, touching him gently, asking for a caress in return. What had happened in their lives to create the suave ice between them? They liked each other: but why now feel cheated that their early passionate loving, so entangled with her father's—and then her own—fortune, was gone? "All my life I thought I had everything I ever wanted," she told the mirror. "But lately I seem to be losing it all. I wish I could begin again."

Outwardly, nothing changed: not in her visible attitude, nor in the lives they led. Nor would their cadences ever change, Cynthia surmised. She and McQueen were molded in the way they were; their lives—defined by the social scene, the business world, and community doings—would allow no eccentricity to force a deviation from time-tried norms.

And yet once admitting to shortcomings in her life, how Cynthia could ache: for a lover, for an emotional explosion, for some peace of mind. Looking at herself in the mirror, Cynthia prodded and probed her bulky flesh: standing naked, truly facing that nakedness for the first time in decades, blushing from head to toe at being so revealed, she was ashamed of her body, repulsed by its blotches, folds, and heavy sags, misshapen breasts, wrinkled belly, and ponderous shapeless thighs. Who could desire me? she wondered fitfully. Another voice replied, But I'm only human, I have my intimate rights—

Dressing carefully, Cynthia spent ages putting on a face, dabbed herself with an expensive cologne, and, despite the heat, drew on gloves. Carefully adjusting her hat and veil, she assessed the mirror again, facing a big, elegantly coiffed, very neat and powerful-looking woman. A high-class, imposing matron—imperial, arrogant, wealthy. Her position in life and attendant activities beamed from her haughty demeanor, expensive clothes, and chic, sexless odor.

The woman wished she could cry.

During one of those inexplicable lulls in her life, Cynthia drove across town to the Cipi García Miracle Memorial Museum, a solid brick structure beside the Balena Park graveyard where Cipi himself was buried beneath an enormous stone column draped in roses and topped by a granite angel plucking a lyre.

A cool, serene building, the museum always rendered to Cynthia a certain amount of comfort. A sense of history dwelled there, reaffirming the magic origins of magnificent events. The matron could pause for long enraptured minutes, gazing through glass at the tiny canvas tent her husband and Cipi García and the rest of that ambitious young crew had pitched on the floor of the Cow Palace, Madison Square Garden, and the Gare St.-Lazare. A nearby case contained many pairs of Cipi García's shoes; the tops of the toes, worn through by pilgrims' kissing lips, gave Cynthia a sense of sorrowful well-being; it excited her into remembering the rapturous turmoil of those hectic times, of McQueen's burgeoning hopes and his fledgling expectations, when legal, personal, and spiritual snarls had to be ironed out during that difficult struggle to consolidate early gains, making the Cipi García Miracle really grow beyond the limits of its own possibilities.

Cynthia had never been able to fix Chamisaville as a place in her mind before the miracle. To her, the histrionic destruction of Vallecitos began it all: previous to that emphatic moment the valley simply had not existed. Thus she believed herself to have gotten in on the ground floor, falling in love with, and eventually bankrolling, a marvelous and dynamic man who had pulled history out of the earth, originating a real society where none had gone before.

Her identity was bolstered by the museum: her origins with Chamisaville, and with McQueen, justified. A framed copy of McQueen's original contract with Cipi García, Icarus Suazo, and R. J. García decorated one wall: around it, numerous Karl Mudd photographs hung—of Cipi García, her husband, and the troupe; of workers constructing the original baths complex, the Dynamite Shrine Motor Court, the Shalako Lodge . . . and tarring the North-South Highway. Another case harbored the two pistols— belonging to R. J. and Onofre García—which had played such a significant role in the infamous boardroom meeting many years ago.

The thrill of history lay everywhere evident: the entire half of another wall was occupied by photographs of influential town citizens—Cynthia and her husband, Randolph Bonney, Moe Stryzpk, Al Lamont and others— posing in the mouth of Claude Parker's whale.

Oh Lord, Cynthia thought. Those were the days! Life was straightforward then; people were more honest. And Dale had shared his hopes and frustrations, all his plans with her; and she had given him, as well as money, good sound advice in return.

Now her husband rarely discussed business; it had become too complicated for a lady. Cynthia felt seduced and abandoned . . . though of course he had really abandoned her a long time ago. McQueen's wealth had outstripped her personal fortune, and the higher he rose the more his wife had been relegated to a spectator's role, supporting him, finally, without questioning his motives, his decisions, or his outcomes. "I have given you all this!" he took to crowing expansively: and it became understood she was not to mention that her father, and the fortune he had bequeathed to Cynthia, had enabled the Muleshoe rake to succeed. "I'm a self-made man!" McQueen often bragged to cohorts, business associates, or interested strangers. "I parlayed two hot springs, a tiny chapel, and a mentally retarded blacksmith into one of the biggest fortunes in the Southwest. I literally carved a city of fifteen thousand from a festering mound of sheep dung!"

So be it. For Cynthia, the museum gave focus to a past full of fonder memories; it was a simplistic haven in the confusion of modern times.

Seating herself in a dark corner on the old stool Cipi

García had used while shoeing horses, Cynthia had a slight urge to cry. But before she could properly release a tear, a strange, vacant-looking boy, wearing a gunbelt with an old .44 revolver lodged in the finely tooled holster, entered the museum. He was soaking wet, and some kind of limp plant—*seaweed?*— was draped over his ears. *Oh my God,* Cynthia thought incredulously: *Ralphito García?* With that, the apparition outed his pistol and, turning rapidly while pulling the trigger, he emptied the cylinder, shooting a hole through the old miracle tent, blasting away a pair of Cipi García's kissed-apart shoes, shattering several picture frames on the wall, and knocking over the display case holding R. J. and Onofre García's guns. And then, realizing—when she screamed—that Cynthia had witnessed his entire performance, this oddball resurrection from the old days pointed the pistol at her and pulled the trigger, but the weapon was out of bullets. So, holstering the gun, Ralphito shouted, "Qué viva La Raza!" and scurried dementedly away.

Cynthia tumbled to the floor in a faint, the past forever behind her now.

GEORGE PARKER couldn't believe it.

Before him, the most beautiful woman he'd ever seen squatted in front of his hot plate, preparing a meal. She wore a one-piece skintight floor-length lime-green jersey evening dress, French suede shoes, simple gold hoop earrings, and Chanel No. 5. In a frying pan, snails sizzled. On a tray, some caviar and rye toast, two glasses, and a bottle of Mumm's champagne. Why this party, and why now? he had asked her. "Because it's the twenty-sixth of July and I love you," April had replied.

George sat back, watching her in disbelief, holding his groin. They had already killed one bottle, and April felt high and mighty gorgeous. Another *El Clarín* had gone to the printers that morning. She had spent all afternoon at a farm team Little League game in Balena Park, watching Duane proudly strike out and make errors: hamburgers and root-beer floats at the A&W had followed. Back home, she had played a moronic chess game with Duane, washed Tina's hair in a foamy bath they took together, sung her kids to sleep with the guitar, then luxuriated over a drink in their quiet house, relishing the silence as she lackadaisically—enjoying each step—prepared herself for the evening, choosing a dress she had not worn in ages, applying

354

cosmetics and perfume in a way she had abandoned for many years, putting together an evening with nothing on the line except food and drink, and being beautiful and seductive.

"This is too nice. What's going to happen to us?" George asked lazily.

"Who knows? Me, I don't worry about it."

"I worry about it a lot."

"That's your prerogative. But I'm just taking it one encounter at a time, sucking out all the nourishment I can get."

She poked steaming snails into their shells, opened another Mumm's, and they ate by candlelight, savoring each bite, delightedly exaggerating their murmurs of satisfaction, playing footsie and giggling over how unbelievably good it was to be alive and trysting and engorged with greedy anticipation of sex.

"You give me such a dreamy contentment, April. I wish I could explain to you the loveliness of your features. Of course, I know you must be tired of having had so many people drool over your good looks—"

"Don't say that. You're special, George; I love to hear it from you. Your words are fresh, and they break territory nobody else ever broke before. I don't compare you with anybody, nor do I ever even remotely think of anyone else when I'm with you."

"In moments like this, and in moments when we're making love, your face changes from being old-young, it softens and blurs and becomes so youthful, it loses all the sharply defined features of age, and it hardens such an ache in me . . ."

"I feel like a little girl. It's weird, it's fun. I'm so grateful for this happy loving."

"Where did it come from?"

"I don't know. We're just lucky."

"I want to discover you, April Delaney. I want to know everything about you. I want to know the story of your life because you're the most exciting person I've ever met. Go ahead, please tell me—start at the very beginning."

"Oh, what's the point, sugar? I've never been much of a glutton for the past. It's so crowded, and convoluted. So much happened and I've forgotten most of the details. If I remembered it all there'd be no space for the present, I'd smother in historical claustrophobia. I'm not a sentimental person, you know. I've never had much truck with nostalgia. Adventures, people, ideas—they were good or bad, and I always moved on."

They clinked glasses, hook-linked arms, and drank champagne.

"But you know so much," George insisted, his eyes smiling out of an iridescent languor, coaxing her to fess up. "You've had such variegated times, been with so many people. Tell me about Charley, and about Delaney—what kind of men were they? I want to know. Have you ever attended an orgy? What is it like when a marriage collapses? Or to be widowed?"

April held a champagne-drenched finger over the candle-flame. He slipped his hand into her dress, cupping one breast.

"Is that a pickle in your pocket, George—or are you just glad to see me?"

"Hey . . . Tell me about your life, April Delaney. I'm always spilling my heart out. You know all about me, my incredible high-school athletic career, my thrilling life of monogamous conjugality and kiddie-raising. And now that the troglodytes have said their piece, it's time for the Icaruses around here to pony up."

April was hypnotized by the candleflame, their party, her nice-feeling outfit—a way she had never thought she could be again. Relaxed, woozy and off guard, April almost wept for joy.

"Oh I loved everyone, I guess. Indiscriminately. I trusted too easily and abandoned situations too carelessly. I was always involved in a very complicated personal theater. I got in way over my head often, and somehow always got out in time. A lot of people hurt me; I hurt a lot of people back, I suppose. It was exciting and full—I don't think I ever really made a bad mistake. Things just worked out for me in certain ways. I wouldn't change any of it for all the cane in Cuba.

Lighthearted and loving, April told about meeting Delaney in the storm at sea, looking for whales. She outlined the marriage with Enrique, explaining why it could never work, and assessed her guilt following his death; her rough dreams—especially after the relationship with Matthew crumbled and the cancer began—when Enrique beckoned from beyond the grave. She relived those marvelous days traveling around with Charley Epstein, and remembered blissfully the sensation of being snug in his bomber jacket watching that forlorn man risk death from icy wings to perform for a gaping Nebraska crowd. Once begun, the stories tumbled. A frigid woman at a New York party had begged April to have sex with her husband: he had turned out to be a wonderful, jolly lover: "The only man who outright guffawed when we were screwing—I'll never forget that." She had briefly dated an all-around RCA rodeo cowboy during those restless crazy years. She remembered the fifties art scene in New York and famous painters she had known: Clyfford Still, de Kooning, Franz Kline. And described some crazy parties, East Hampton summers, her memories clicking into place and then shifting like kaleidoscope patterns. April rambled easily and at will, conjuring up a rich and boisterous, comic and tragic carnival of experience, while George listened, prompted, smiled, his eyes glittering provocatively from champagne. In the worst way, April wanted to tackle and grope, but it could wait —this was fun. Most often, in her life, lovers had suppressed her history, ordering her to shut up whenever recollection of a good man or a loving time arose. Defensive, jealous of her lavish and teeming yesterdays, they had queered any happy reminiscences—threatened by such a prolific background. Now she had met a man who allowed her the enormous gift of speaking freely without fear of physical or emotional reprisals.

April told of her affair with a movie star, of writing that novel alone in Collioure, of free-for-alls among the beatnik poets and East Side artists during storefront happenings, of the vigil in Union Square when the Rosenbergs died, of a bloody welfare demonstration on Forty-second Street. Graphically, she described the 1967 Pentagon march. Some of her holocaustic battles passed in review; they laughed over antics of other boyfriends. One, a mad painter, had torn out her telephone and waited below on the street for almost a week, threatening to beat up any person who approached her building. There was a never-ending struggle to write, paint. Close friends had died— so many of them alcoholics, sloppily and stupidly and self-pityingly boozing themselves into the grave, among them her second husband, who, right up until he died in Provincetown, used to telephone at least once a year, threatening suicide if she didn't return to him. And the Venceremos Brigade Cuban experience almost brought nostalgic tears: she twisted her American bomber ring. "Everybody was so together, so united for the revolution. A communal

357

feeling of worth and sacrifice and purpose dominated the people."

Getting drunker, laughing a lot, April chain-smoked Delicados; she had not felt this animated and carefree in years. In scintillating, technicolor detail, April shamelessly romanticized a harrowing motor-scooter trip through Italy —ay, the wonders of Florence, Rome, Naples, Ischia! What a breezy, crazy, wonderful community in Paris, Madrid, Ibiza, Marbella! Contessas, counts, bastard kings, matadors, Communists, Fascists, movie stars, beautiful no-bodies—hundreds upon thousands of them in her life! "Just call me Anaïs Nin!"

George marveled, hiding pain, and gently caressed her hand. His smile came across slightly wounded, but friend-ly. Though profoundly moved by the prodigal disorderly woman loving him, a turmoil he had neither expected nor prepared himself for when he demanded her life story had sprung up inside. Exhilarating sensations competed with presentiments of doom; a powerful jealousy of the promis-cuous bedlam of her days spawned an immediate anger that churned in the same cauldron containing immense feelings of love. Bitterness and tenderness confused his motives for urging her on. Cruel thoughts of revenge were released by a single flicking mention of adventures with another man, other people, contact with a famous person. He struggled to disguise the helter-skelter emotions. The heart of this night held an immense relief and excitement at being able to tolerate such frank revelations from such a quixotic woman. Yet the relief was belied by the puri-tanical square inside himself castigating her for her reck-less and slipshod life—for being wishy-washy, careless, a madcap nymphomaniac, a superficial and harebrained pros-titute, an unbearably loose and incompetent woman. How could April call herself a Communist after such an impru-dent, squalid, and checkered career? What gave April a right to speak for humanity after her botched existence? Although it wasn't botched, George knew: tumultuous and messy, perhaps, but done with style and gusto. Alternately agitated, amazed, hurt, and charmed by April's drunken assault on her own past, George absorbed her magic dare-devil story, and when finally she ran out of gas, falling silent and reflective with a sexy lax smile, her giddy essence glowed in his bones, and he was inspired, he wanted to be an adventure that would compare favorably with all other adventures crowding her impetuous heart.

And April lay quietly, eyes closed, wonderfully plastered, feeling terrific. A magical buoyancy lightened her flesh, creating an eagerness in her body, a lust to fulfill something—work, loving, her own idealism—before it was too late; before this generous season ended. The same feeling she'd often experienced in her younger days, during the final October or November weeks of indescribably beautiful Indian summers, when the miracle of hot autumn sunshine and blue skies were extended illogically beyond its cutoff point of winter, and each morning she would awaken disbelievingly—the entire valley would awaken—to yet one more golden and dreamy day, knowing that the sweet extension into winter's territory was precious beyond any measuring, a stolen gift that would be murdered tomorrow by long-overdue fierce winds, overcast skies, snowstorms, and freezing weather.

God how she had loved those last beautiful days of autumn! And would take them, metaphorically—and enjoy them right now—any way she could.

"You look decadent," April said happily. "I love you to look like that, George. You're so pretty—I love your biceps, your clean blue eyes. You're a regular Robert Redford."

"Decadent?"

"I don't mean real decadence—that doesn't turn me on. Not the heart of it, the cigarette part, the poison part; but the smoke that comes from that cigarette, a whiff of that is the sort of decadence I mean. And love."

Stumbling to his feet, George dropped his tight, powder blue corduroys. And, wearing only a black T-shirt and Jockey shorts, he strutted around the room, playfully assuming he-man body poses while chanting:

"Ladies and gentlemen. For the main event tonight, in this corner, wearing a black Fruit-of-the-Loom T-shirt and size thirty-two Jockey shorts, weighing in at approximately one hundred and seventy pounds, a man of superlative strength and lasting power, with a pile-driving style which earned him a first place in World Cup competition only last week—Mr. George . . . 'Super Stud' . . . *Parker!*"

"And in this corner?"

"And in that corner, coming—literally!—to us after an extended tour of Europe, wearing a green eye-grabber, no undergarments, and three-inch heels, and weighing in at approximately one hundred and twenty-five pounds, the noted longtime professional fornicator and two-time holder of the Woman's Middleweight Bang of the Year Award, a female Jimmy Brown who has not slowed down despite one of the heaviest schedules of recorded memory, a woman with perhaps *the* most outstanding and distinguished career of international coitus, copulation, fellatio, sodomy, and other assorted kinky contortions that we have yet observed in this ring—Mizzzzzz *April Delaney!*"

Standing, April took a dramatic bow. Kneeling before her, George lifted her dress, dropping it over his head, and nibbled at her crotch: "Lip-smacking *good!*" April pulled the dress over her head—"Don't take off your shoes, love," he begged. "Promise me you won't take off your shoes." April tugged him upright by his ears, lifted off his T-shirt, and backed away.

Grinning stupidly, they faced each other. "I feel utterly wonderful," April crowed. "I also feel incredibly silly."

"Me too." George stepped clear of his underwear, and, suddenly inspired, began to do jumping jacks. April kicked off her shoes and joined in. And for a moment they did that exercise, howling and sputtering because her breasts and his penis flopping all over the place looked ridiculous. Then they collided and danced together, just barely tilting from side to side like starstricken teen-agers . . . while out on the mesa scrawny coyotes howled.

WHEN SHE WAS RELEASED from the hospital, Amaranta GeeGee, who stood four-foot-eleven, and now weighed only sixty-three pounds, headed straight for Virgil Leyba.

He was asleep at his desk when she walked in, and, not wishing to disturb him, Amaranta sat down on one of his blue benches, with her enormous hand-embroidered purse on her lap, waiting for him to awake.

Virgil snored erratically. After a while, tilting her glasses and squinting pronouncedly, Amaranta thought she detected wisps of smoke trickling from the lawyer's ears; and for a moment she wondered what gruesome thoughts influenced that man's imaginative noggin. Shortly thereafter, as the wisps enlarged alarmingly, she realized that Virgil himself was on fire. He had tipped over and gone to sleep with his tie and various crumpled portions of his shirt and jacket resting against an ashtray in which a cigarette still burned.

Amaranta limped over, tapped Virgil on the shoulder, and, as he straightened groggily, she whopped him in the chest with her satchel, striking him hard enough not only to extinguish the fire, but also to almost kill him.

"Hey!" Virgil cried. Immediately he launched a tremendous coughing fit which Amaranta cured by lambasting him again with the satchel, this time on the back, so hard Virgil sprawled atop his desk, knocking half the papers, several ashtrays, two books, and a water glass onto the floor.

"Stop! Por favor, señora—*don't kill me!*"

"I got very bad troubles," Amaranta said, eyeing Virgil suspiciously as he straightened up. "They are going to take away everything I own."

"Sit down, please." Virgil sank gingerly into his own chair. "Let me collect my thoughts for a minute."

Amaranta kneeled on the floor and began gathering all his papers.

"Please, don't do that, señora. I'll get all that stuff in a minute, as soon as I catch my breath. Just sit down on the bench and quit moving for a minute until my head clears."

"You know what they say, Mr. Leyba, don't you?"

"No, I'm not sure that I do, señora."

"They say if you stop moving around it's because you are probably dead."

"Well, that may be, but you are making me pretty damn dizzy with all this bustling."

No matter. Virgil sat there, quasi-stunned, watching Amaranta scramble around collecting all his papers, which she arranged in neat stacks on his desk. Then she asked for a broom.

"I don't have a broom. Now if you will just—"

"This place is a pigsty, you'll excuse my saying so, Mr. Leyba. Doesn't anybody ever come in to clean up?"

"Sometimes." Virgil sighed. "Every now and then I push a button on the floor under my desk here, and two little duendes materialize out of the walls and put everything in order."

Amaranta tilted her glasses again, peering at him. When he grinned and shrugged, she grinned back, picked up as many glass fragments as she could locate, and dropped them daintily into the wastebasket.

Realizing, finally, that he had been on fire, Virgil removed his tie and suitcoat, bunched them up, and dumped them into the wastebasket.

"Now," he said slowly, nervously eyeing the tiny woman.

She burst into tears. "They are going to take away everything I own. What will I do? Where will I go? All my brothers and sisters are broke, living in tiny trailers off welfare and food stamps—nobody wants another mouth to feed!"

"Which bank holds the mortgage, señora?"

"The El Conquistador People's Jug."

"And who is the officer who swung the mortgage and signed all the papers?"

"Mr. Leyba—your jito. The son of a bitch. Of course, I was sorry to hear about his car accident. Naturally, I'm glad he escaped without even a little scratch, thank God."

Virgil swiveled slightly in order to look out the window. Sooner or later, asking these questions, the people always rammed into a brick wall. Jake Martínez was passing by. The ancient gadfly stopped, pressing his nose against the window, peering in. Virgil waved, Jake waved back and wandered on. The old lawyer lifted his eyes to the treetops, seeking no answers, only a momentarily neutral vision while he composed himself.

"Mr. Leyba?"

"Here's what I'll do." Virgil swung around to face her. He shuffled through the mess on his desk, looking for a pen or a pencil. Amaranta reached into her satchel, rustled for a second, and found one. She gave it to him and returned to her seat. Virgil began scribbling on a yellow legal pad.

"First, you have to give me all your papers. You have a grace period, we'll make sure you're getting it. Then we'll appeal to the bank personally for an extension: that probably means I'll have to talk with my son, so there's not too much hope there. Still, we have to try everything. Give me time, I'll think of at least a dozen angles to tie them up for a while as we search for a way to beat them."

"Is there really any hope?" Amaranta asked timidly.

"Who knows? The odds aren't so good. But we'll dig down to the bottom of the legal barrel, I promise."

"What will it cost me?"

"I can't tell for sure," Virgil deadpanned. "But estimating conservatively, Sra. GeeGee, I would say in the neighborhood of a hundred thousand dollars."

Amaranta uncorked a blissfully uninhibited cackle, and Virgil had to chuckle along with her. Then she reached into her satchel and rummaged again for a moment, locating a pair of crimson knitted socks decorated with blue angels and white crosses. She tossed the socks over to Virgil, who managed to catch them in spite of himself.

"I made those socks for Juanito. Try them on. If they fit, they are for you."

"I will," Virgil assured her. "I certainly will."

"Right now, would you mind?"

Virgil grimaced discreetly, bent over, and laboriously untied his shoes, took off his socks, and tried on Amaranta's pair: they were much too big.

"How do they fit? she asked anxiously, craning her neck to peer around the cluttered desk.

"Perfect. They're just perfect." Virgil put his shoes on quickly so that she wouldn't be able to tell.

"In that case . . ." Amaranta reached into her satchel and began taking out knitted socks, some of them argyle, others with various designs—the head of Jesus, little lambs, crosses galore, shining stars, holy grails, crossed tennis rackets, and little kittens. She dumped a pile of about two dozen socks on the table, blurted, "God bless you, Virgil Leyba!" and fled.

Virgil glowered sleepily at those dead man's socks sitting atop his afternoon's labor. Then he carried his metal wastebasket across the room and set it against the wall, returned to his desk chair, and, one by one, fired the lovely socks basketball-style across his office into the big tin can.

After the last pair had landed atop the others for a perfect score, Virgil sat with his head in his hands, not moving. He broke the pose suddenly, reached for the telephone, dialed a number and asked for Junior.

"Junior? This is Virgil."

"If it's about the double-Godoy place, Dad, don't bother. We'll give her the grace period, of course, but once that's over she's a dead duck."

"*What came out of my body that could create you?*" the old lawyer hollered in anguish, slamming down the phone.

# All That Is
# Solid Melts
# into Air

LABORIOUSLY, April worked through the *El Clarín*'s town-dump documents file, separating the wheat from the chaff, and in the process developing a less sketchy view of the connecting lines between all those people and businesses consummating the Betterment of Chamisaville.

A scribbled message on notepad paper said: *Bob, Jr. suggests the M. should get a kicker of, say, 1,000 F. & Co., in return for urging the TC to cooperate in that matter we discussed.* A week later she came across the following on similar paper, same handwriting: *Bob, the loan would be sub. only to customer accts. and/or any bank loans, obviously. Equity, of course, to be underneath. I'll put back from me to myself, also from J., P., and L., who won't balk. Substantial premium to you, I need hardly emphasize.* And later she discovered another note in the series: *Bob: Wonderful. Promissory exactly what we wanted: option to sell is perfect. Check with the M. first, though, to soothe any ruffled feathers.*

At first, April could not interpret such terse communications. They figured in the general picture, and would, if she pursued her files, make more sense as information accumulated. And there was so much information, openly, almost derisively painting a picture of the no-holds-barred wheeling and dealing coming down. A subculture of businesses, corporations, and exotic letterheads, which a year ago April had never heard of, were doing business in Chamisaville. No doubt registered and on file with the proper agencies, they had never been mentioned publicly, and certainly not in the *Chamisaville News*. Some, no doubt, were harmless concerns; yet when she tried tracking down others, April immediately became snarled in webs of impossibly obtuse connections designed deliberately to create chaos, obliterating all evidence; their original intentions had disappeared without a trace.

Yet with perseverance, April believed she had a chance. If the architects constructing the overall development picture could understand and manipulate it to their personal gain, why couldn't April also decipher the occult inner workings of her hometown, eventually learning enough to map the Betterment of Chamisaville, patching together all the lines of power and the people involved so that there would be a chance to strike back?

April sifted through the cardboard boxes, salvaging whatever seemed even remotely tied into that specialized chaos bullying the town. She selected information and built up files, putting it together piece by piece, a great jigsaw puzzle made from garbage, a crazy and seemingly anarchic structure of disparate shenanigans that gradually formed a haphazard picture of Chamisaville's entire land and banking and commercial nature. The picture first acquired focus on the outer edges, among satellite scans and expectations where negotiations were almost simple-minded, the stakes small, where the little leather shops, local bars, and tiny food stores dwelled, revolving around the dense center of activity like subservient asteroids, accumulating innumerable heartaches though not many dollars. Yet, as cells on the outer, visible skin, they were kept alive by the Powers That Be as examples of time-honored, democratic, competitive tradition.

Closer to the core, however, things fused, overlapping in peculiar ways, becoming lost in a foggy network of implicit understandings, friendly agreements, and mutual desires. The closer April got to the center, the less clear everything became. Connections between banks and housing developments, law firms and civic organizations, town and county and state and federal governments, distributors and politicos and licensees and manipulators—they all blurred, merged, consolidated. The "state of free competition" essential to a democratic society did not exist. An overpowering force manipulated the entire shebang with as tight a control, despite the surface chaos, as any authoritarian government ever wielded. And when April pieced it together like that, gaining moments of objective lucidity, the extent and the nature of that control frightened her.

By and large, nothing fell neatly into place; not toward the core. It was impossible to forge satisfactory constructs of each molecule functioning within the larger scheme.

April had files full of telephone bills: from the mayor's phone to Rodey McQueen, to Junior Leyba and Bob Moose; from the First State Bank to Irving Newkirk's empire, to the Shalako Lodge, where Joseph Bonatelli hung out. But to decipher it all, drawing the bills together into the revealing connections she knew existed, would have been a Herculean task: she had not the time nor the strength for it.

Yet she and Anthony and Juan Ortega had done enough legwork through their files to realize inordinate numbers of long-distance phone calls from key Chamisaville offices and people in the past six months had gone to Phoenix and Detroit; and their files had further confirmed associations between one Rainbow Mountain Water Company in Arizona, Sunshine Community Systems Corporation, Futz and Company, Moosurelli, and a dozen local merchants. And they also understood, again thanks to wrinkled Sierra Bell chits stained with coffee grounds and tomato sauce, that Randolph Bonney and the electric co-op were intimately connected with Joseph Bonatelli's financial empire.

Despite all these clues and leads, however, a blank place existed at the center into which April had been able to fit no pieces. No phone records or scribbled notes, no letters, no portions of deeds or records of oblique financial transactions. Nor had she ferreted out a single letterhead of, or official reference to, the company she knew occupied the heart of Chamisaville's picture. Yet that company was the key to the final extermination of the people and the way of life April knew, loved, and was fighting for, it was the genocidal machine that would—after the last small valley farmer had been uprooted, sent packing, or buried —then be turned upon the area's last whole community, where the native American people survived, if just barely, under a blanket of so-called federal protection. And April knew that the blank space at the heart of the design covered the Pueblo area, and that it was called the Northland Grazing Association.

She couldn't prove it, not yet. April did not even know its real nature. The thing was enormous, and very touchy, and no doubt fraught with high-powered, complex illegitimacy; and it was totally absent from all the script floating about town, casually alighting in her files. An entity conspicuous by its elusivity, it was the one thing that somehow eluded all the *El Clarín*'s probing. Anthony Martínez, his ear to the Pueblo grapevine, could discover nothing, although an unease permeated the native air, a sense of doom had everyone irascible. But the secret apparently resided in a small group of elders who were not talking. Perhaps only Icarus Suazo, still dealing for fifty thousand acres of sacred forest land, was privy to the exact nature of the beast, its demands, and what it offered in return.

One morning April awakened as tired as if she had not been to bed at all. Something was wrong—with her, inside her body. And, even before fully alert, she touched a tiny bump on her forehead above the eyebrow—her heart sank. Barely three weeks had passed since her operation, five days of radiation, and the first chemotherapy treatment, yet the disease was back!

Still, all that day she worked feverishly on a special History in Perspective edition of the *El Clarín*, writing articles and editorials helping to explain the growth of today's seemingly anarchical development, the culmination of the Betterment of Chamisaville. Just below the masthead, in bold letters surrounded by plenty of white space, she had planned to print a quotation from the Communist Manifesto:

> Constant revolutionizing of production, uninterrupted disturbance of all social conditions, everlasting uncertainty and agitation distinguish the bourgeois epoch from all earlier ones. All fixed, fast-frozen relations, with their train of ancient and venerable prejudices and opinions, are swept away, all newly formed ones become antiquated before they can ossify. All that is solid melts into air, all that is holy is profaned . . .

But then, deciding it might be politically tactless to thumb Marxism at her readers that prominently, April yanked the quotation and remade the entire front page, trying to fill in the space with certain articles, various pictures. But nothing worked. The phone rang constantly, all day. Juan Ortega, "out in the field," as he liked to put it, kept calling in the latest atrocities: Espeedie Cisneros's cow had been arrested by the Forest Service; Father Molé had finally convinced J. B. LeDoux to fire Filiberto García for raising an upside-down flag; Malaquias C. de Baca had dropped dead in front of Junior Leyba's Picadilly Circus; Judson Babbitt was calling for a federal grand jury investigation of the Pueblo's Anti-Electricity Coalition.

Other niggling problems had hounded her all day. An

update on Junior Leyba's landholdings and legal and financial involvements was slated to run underneath a picture of the car he had totaled recently—but Anthony's photograph was terrible, the negative almost completely washed out. Then Perfecto Torres and Celestino Lucero dropped by to talk about the school board's attempt to close the Ranchitos Abajo elementary. If the board succeeded, local kids would be driven out of the community, further weakening the social fabric of that picturesque aldea. Deciding the story ought to be told immediately, April grabbed a camera, drove eight miles to the little village, and traveled from house to house gathering the men, women, and children of the RA Elementary Defense Fund for a snapshot on the front stoop of the two-room schoolhouse. Then she photographed the decay of the school, a deterioration caused by deliberate official neglect as the school board sought to build its case.

Back home, April developed the film, answered the phone a dozen times (including an obscene caller and one more anonymous threat on her life), fed the kids and Juan Ortega and Anthony Martínez, and spent another hour typing up *El Clarín* subscription renewals while Anthony and Juan addressed mailing stickers. Finally, throwing everybody out of the house, April poured a stiff shot of Jack Daniels, heaved an enormous sigh, raised her hand to her head, and probed that tiny lump again.

Still there—not her imagination. "God *dammit!*"

In the bathroom April combed her hair forward and cut it into bangs obscuring the bump on her forehead. Absentmindedly plucking strands of hair from the brush, she bunched them up and dropped the soft ball into a wastebasket. And groomed her hair awhile longer. But when next April looked at the brush, she stopped: twice as many hairs as there had been a moment ago were trapped in the stiff bristles.

Seated on the toilet lid, April fashioned a tiny hairball, and stared at it incredulously.

"Well, if it ain't one thing, folks, it's another." She started crying. For a minute April let the tears fall. Then, standing up again, she brushed her beautiful hair, using hard downstrokes, confirming the obvious—her hair was falling out by the handful. "Autumn in your body, kid, and you've got a deciduous cranium."

In the kitchen, pouring another stiff belt, April decided to get good and drunk. And she had polished off half that drink when George Parker's Blazer jounced up the driveway.

"When it rains, it pours!"

Outside, the night smelled sour, stagnant; mosquitoes clustered. Cutting the motor, George sat behind the wheel as April approached his open window. Brushing fingers against his cheek, she said, "Hello, darling. Long time, no see," and gave him a butterfly peck on the lips.

"Wow, you're really shoveling that liquor in, aren't you?"

"Been a long day, hon. No recriminations. For a variety of reasons I've decided to play Polonius to the honky-tonk in me. So don't mess with my head, daddy-o, I ain't in the mood."

George said, "I love you, April. And I'm sorry if this sounds stupid but I want to marry you."

"Oh NO!" But what else, given her day, their unscrupulous love affair, and life in general, was there to say? "I knew today wasn't quite over. I realized I had to be drinking for some reason. Well, now I know."

"Don't make fun of me, I'm serious."

April touched his shoulder. "Of course you're serious, love. Life is a serious proposition. Asking somebody to marry you isn't just your average run-of-the-mill daily occurrence."

"Hey, what's the matter with you?"

"I'm a little tiddly, George. Bit pooped, too. Tack on discouraged also, if you want. I'm sorry if I can't react more nobly, but, as they say in the local vernacular—la vida es sometimes puro pedo."

"You think I'm a real asshole, don't you?"

"Yes, occasionally; but in general, no. God, I hope I'm not that cynical." April smiled, trying to make it warm, gentle, compassionate. "Actually, I think you're a tad touched. In fact," and here, pinching his chin between her thumb and forefinger, she turned his head to face her, "if you don't mind my saying so I think you're out of your skull."

Brusquely, he jerked away and looked down into his lap. "Great. I knew this would happen. Forget I ever said anything. I was only kidding."

"Oh come on!" April cupped his crotch, probing for the lie of his penis. "Is this a pickle—"

"Why do you make jokes? I don't understand at all. I mean, it's not like I haven't been thinking about this for

369

a while. Maybe you couldn't care less, but I had to resolve to get divorced, lose all three kids and my house, maybe even my job—I mean, this isn't some whimsical fantasy that just popped out of my mouth ten seconds ago."

"What do you want to do, George? Do you want to nurse me while I die, does that feed some sort of romantic tapeworm inside of you, is that it? Maybe my dramatic demise would give you some good stuff for that novel you're writing, huh? Get your feet wet in death, hold my hand just like Ryan O'Neal, pump me about my glamorous past, take my kids out for ice cream cones and a Frisbee game in the park during those poignant breaks from the around-the-clock hospital vigil and martyrdom? Marrying good old fabulous immoral harum-scarum full-tilt April Etcetera is some kind of rite you've devised for finally terminating your small-town innocence? George, it makes no sense. Another lump sprouted over my right eye, and I just discovered that all my hair is falling out. Not only that, but I'm a halfway—even if half-assed—radical lady whose politics are a millennium to the left of your insipid bourgeois liberalism. At least I'd like to think I'm a quasi-Communist gringa with some kind of political justification for my mediocre life and for the suffering of all those people I love going down fast and hard around me, and I don't have any time for domestic bliss, George, I really don't! Furthermore, I don't need the added stigma in my legend of snatching you out of the bosom of your dear, sweet, all-American family; I really don't need that rap, I'm taking a big enough chance as it is just seeing you—"

"I don't believe what you're saying!"

"Oh I love you, George, I'll admit that. At least I love our sex—boy, do I ever! But I'm fairly equivocal about us, too. And I certainly don't want any more from you than I'm already getting. Our arrangement is as perfect as something this impetuous and foolhardy can be. I'll admit, all my life I've sort of hunted this kind of flagrant affair and good sex with your kind of man, all muscle and good looks and athletic energy. But Jesus Christ, love, have a heart. I've been in so many untidy traps, the shadows of their bars are etched indelibly across my heart. So lighten up lover, I mean it. You don't owe me; you have no obligation to shoulder that heavy a load."

"One of these days Susan will find out."

"I should think so. You'd have to be a real moron, in a town like this, to stay in the dark forever."

"What are you trying to make me do, hate you?"

"Oh come on, come on. Don't take it all so personal. You're right, of course she'll find out, that's inevitable. Obviously, I deliberately haven't thought about the consequences, which is irresponsible on my part. Alongside my desire to forge a right-on political being I'm balancing a very inconsiderate and careless person, George. We all know that. My personal history is written on the wind. I also drink too much, didja ever notice?"

"Sometimes I practically have to choke myself to avoid telling her."

"Aw . . . I can even see the bruise marks on your throat."

"You laugh. But it's shit, it really is, to screw somebody you don't love! And I can't pretend with her anymore. Hell, I haven't been able to pretend for years. After we're together—you and me—I'm high, happy, full of pep. When I go home I have to make myself deliberately morose so that she won't suspect. But it's crazy because I feel so wonderful. I mean, she must be able to see that my skin is sparkling."

April finished her drink. "For what it's worth, sugar, I've only been through the nonloving balling bit about a couple dozen times."

"Well, aren't you just about the world's most popular cunt!"

"Oh Lord—" April backed away, shaking her head. "Here we go. In this corner—"

"I don't want to fight," he mumbled, appalled by the nastiness of his own cut, which had caught him completely by surprise.

April meant to let it ride, forgive and forget, but instead she replied contemptuously: "Don't worry, sweetie. That wasn't even BBs, and I can fend for myself quite well, thank you, even against cannons. I wasn't born yesterday. And I didn't grow older two thousand miles from civilization in this pathetic little tank town, either."

George clammed up, horrified.

April caught a heel against the cement portal step and sat down abruptly, dropping her glass—it shattered at her feet; she ignored it.

"I'll tell you something else, man, for your information. Just because I happen to like a good lay every now and then doesn't mean you can start calling the shots, is that clear? Just because I may occasionally enjoy catering to

371

your chauvinistic fantasies, doesn't mean I'm simply another piece of ass panting to be the groupie of somebody who was a high-school jockstrap twenty years ago."

George started quietly crying. April taunted: "What's the matter, can't you take it? Come on, this is peanuts, love. A bagatelle. This isn't even the first grade of insulting each other. Still want to get married?" she coughed triumphantly. "Where's a stinking cigarette?"

April fumbled in pockets, got up, almost fell off the step, retreated into the kitchen, and was thrashing about in a counter drawer looking for matches when he roared: *"You wouldn't believe how happy I was driving over here! You wouldn't believe how excited!"*

"Don't shout, you'll wake up the kids! Do me a favor, pick up the glass out there, would you?"

April gestured at the ceiling. What was it with men, they always wound up apoplectic. In a minute, no doubt, he would start punching her around. They got you pregnant against your wishes and then screamed when you had an abortion—God forbid you should kill *their* kid. One night several years ago a dear New York friend had been raped and knocked up by a black teen-ager holding a gun to her head: later she had an abortion. When April told Matthew about it, he had said: "What right did that white bitch have to kill a black baby?" Astounded, April grabbed a pot full of day-old cold beans and brained him with it, and that had resulted in their "all you honkies are just trying to commit genocide on us blacks" free-for-all. Brilliant! And then when you *wanted* a baby, they threatened to walk out if you didn't have an abortion. If you desired a free-and-easy time, they insisted on marriage. If you had a lust for tying the knot, they insisted on having a good time. Wow, I must really be discouraged and exhausted, because after those two drinks I'm really blasted, April thought. I haven't been this soused in a coon's age.

Bending over a gas burner, April lit her cigarette. Then she collapsed at the kitchen table with a fresh drink, lifted it to the empty chairs, and said. "Here's lookin' at you, kids." Outside, George sat behind the wheel, fuming, fearful, confused. Excited moths fluttered around the porch light bulb, they pinged against her screen door. The impasse continued until finally George started his motor, tarrying a while longer, hoping the engine noise would lure her back outside, effecting a reconciliation. When April stayed pat, he backed up angrily, smashing into the basketball pole near her woodpile, knocking it over backward, then gunned the car so hard bolting convulsively down her potholed driveway that one epileptic faena of jolts jackhammered his head against the ceiling, almost knocking him out. At the end of the driveway, woozy and nauseous, George stumbled out of the car and threw up.

Back in the kitchen, tears in her eyes again, April presented her liquor glass to the empty chairs and with derisive cheerfulness toasted them:

"Chin-chin."

Then she waited, wrapped in an almost blithe stupor, for the phone to ring. When it did, April said, "Hello, George, what's happening at the PDQ phone booth?"

"I'm not at the PDQ. I'm in the booth at Salazar's Exxon, and you're not even funny."

"Sometimes I think I'm a howl."

"Well . . . I'm sorry for all the things I said."

"I guess ditto."

"Huh?"

"I guess I'm sorry too, love, even though it really felt good to tear into you a little. I haven't been snotty in a long time, and you're a regular setup. But what the hell, in the end it's lousy. Forgive me for being facetious, but I'm drunk, I had a bad day, you know? All the standard excuses apply. I'm not whining, but once in a while when I go through a real lowdown mean redeye jerk of a day I get tanked and I become very sarcastic and ironical and cynical and disparaging, and you caught me at the end of one of those days. It was ugly of me to react like that to your proposal. You should also understand that sometimes I dislike you, I dislike both of us, the assumptions underlying the affair. I get bitter about your lack of radical politics and my own equivocal political temperament. Also, you're healthy and I'm not, and that makes me jealous, bitter, ugly. Defensive. I can't help it, I've never learned how to curtail these savage moods."

"Let's forget I ever said anything about marriage, okay?"

"Believe me, I already forgot."

During a strained pause, April could hear him struggling with crucial thoughts. His vibrations literally blistered her ear—embarrassment, anger, longing.

"George—you still there?"

"Of course I'm here."

"Can I say something?"

"*I'm* certainly not stopping you."

"I think you better be careful about me. I'm no light-weight pretty piece of fluff. I'm a fairly headstrong, difficult, and independent person, and I have been that way for a long time. I'm a real street fighter and I've been in the ring with some people that make you look like a marshmallow in petticoats. I know how to hurt, slit, chop, use every dirty trick in the book, and get instant revenge. I can take it, I can also dish it out. And although I don't wish to hurt you, I think you'd better ponder long and hard about me, and about our relationship, and about the risks involved. I mean, I'm not easy—really, I'm not."

"I guess I know that."

"Is that unbridled enthusiasm I detect on your part?"

"I don't know—I guess it's okay."

"George, do me a favor. No petulant martyr or *ex post facto* jealousy role, okay? I'm not capable of, nor willing to do, that scene."

"I wasn't . . . I didn't . . ."

"Why did you call back?"

"I wanted to be friendly. I wanted to be loving. . . ."

"I accept, then—I really do. Believe me, I know how you feel, and I feel positively rotten myself. But let's do ourselves a favor and not talk anymore. Go to bed, get drunk, whatever—mañana's another day. I wasn't kidding you, love, when I said my day was atrocious. I wasn't kidding you, either, when I said I'm probably gonna lose all my hair in the next few days. I'm not one to go around crucifying my pals with my own self-pity, but you must understand that tonight I figured I owed myself one, and you happened by at an unpropitious time, that's all. And now I'm sitting here getting stewed to the gills, and believe me, lover, really, it's very *very* difficult to keep from lashing out, not so much at you personally, as at just somebody, because I feel real blue and raped and cheated and double-crossed, comprendes?"

"All right, okay, I'm hanging up."

*"Don't hang up!* George?"

"What?"

"I want you should come back over here. I wanna screw in some really kinky, lascivious, nasty way. Because I think we'd better get in our romantic all-out hair-pulling licks while the getting is good. I want you to remember me with a tawny mane and a bushy cunt. And then I wanna bawl like a baby in your arms."

"You don't mean it. I don't understand the game you're playing. . . ."

"Jesus Christ! Spinoza no less. Good-bye, sweet. Everything will look better in the morning."

April hung up, killed her drink, poured another, stared at herself in the bathroom mirror again, sadly primping her hair, then walked to the end of her driveway, waiting in a clump of cottonwoods until she recognized his headlights turning onto Upper Ranchitos Road. Stepping into the driveway, April hurriedly lifted off her shirt and unsnapped her bra, and was standing half naked with her thumb out like a hitchhiker when he veered into the driveway and slammed on his brakes.

"I don't believe you," George grinned out his window. "Why don't you start acting like a grown-up, April Delaney?"

"Who are you, stranger?" she remarked with playful, drunken tartness: "the local beaver man?"

A PHYSICAL-FITNESS BUFF, Randolph Bonney was out jogging through the deserted streets of Chamisaville before breakfast. There was a freshness to the morning, a zip that would be gone within the hour. Exhilarated, breathing deeply, the co-op executive wanted to laugh, his lungs bulged strong and full. The squeegee sound of his new white Converse All-Star sneakers sent pleasant, almost sensual shocks up his sweat-suited spindly legs. At sixty-eight he could hold his own with the best of them. "I'll live to be a hundred if only I survive until we jam electricity into that goddam Pueblo!" he puffed aloud.

Bonney jogged across the North-South Highway, circled the plaza, taking the finger from Nicanor Casados as that pathetic drunk stumbled from the hotel—liquor store alley, nodded a perfunctory good morning to a vaguely disquieting and lost-looking teen-ager with seaweed draped over his ears, exited west onto Guadalupe Street, cursed a couple of lacklusterly snarling dogs, and trotted slowly up a dusty rise past the old Catholic elementary and the Chamisaville middle school. And, as his long shadow, caused by the rising sun, blipped across old lime stripes on a nearby football field, he noticed, in the immediate distance, a bright orange bauble jerking nervously about on the concrete junior-high tennis court near the specialed building and one of the co-op's windowless electric routing stations. Drawing slightly closer, he realized that

Al Lamont and Junior Leyba were engaged in a heated game of tennis.

Bonney swerved off the road, crossed a dusty softball field, jogged up to the court, nodded hello to the two combatants, and collapsed into a sitting position, his back against the fence, panting heavily, glad for the rest, and interested in the game.

Al Lamont fascinated the co-op chief. The way that uncoordinated, loudmouthed dandy handled an oxygen tank on his back and a tennis racket at the same time belied the inept surgeon's notorious reputation. For Lamont stumbled with a weird yet effective agility all over the court, his face purple as he sucked in the ozone, defying death, the fluorescent tank slapping noisily against his back, the hose flapping like a trapped Slinky, the stitches in his oft-lacerated heart straining to burst—

Some guts, Randolph Bonney thought, not unaffectionately. Al Lamont was one of *them:* they had grown up together and old together—this was their town. Junior Leyba, on the other hand, he did not trust at all. Aside from a natural-born prejudice against Spanish-speaking people, Bonney disliked Junior for other, darker reasons. The instability of Junior's origins and his personal outlook, he suspected, might one day land them all in a peck of trouble. Yet, in all important dealings you had to have one or two, like Junior or Damacio Mares or J. B. LeDoux— they greased the local wheels, they kept up appearances.

As usual, Lamont had goaded Junior into a black mood in which the lawyer, upset at himself, ashamed at being inferior to a prattling old man, could do nothing right. If Lamont tripped and fell diving to bloop a return, Junior, wishing to slam the ball down the prostrate doctor's throat, wound up bashing it into the net instead. If, on his own serve, he led the encumbered autocrat forty-love, inevitably—unnerved by the sight of Lamont's purple puffed visage behind that rosy mask glass suckling in pure oxygen as if each gasp were his last—Junior double-faulted four straight times. And occasionally, getting set to stroke the ball easily into the opposite corner from where the stumbling Lamont fumbled to adjust his mask, a sudden sharp report—half hiss, half fart—from Lamont's compression apparatus caused Junior to miss the ball entirely.

The doctor was moving handily toward set point; and Randolph Bonney felt at peace with the world, his face beet red, his body drenched with healthy sweat. A flotilla of dandelion seeds drifted over some nearby Lomita Street rooftops and languorously weaved through the silent tennis match. Neither contestant spoke: the ringing *thwock* of racket meeting ball, the squeak of tennis shoes were all that could be heard.

Suddenly, from where the dandelion seeds had come, an object flew. Small, round, bumpy, and dark, it sailed through the air, landed at Al Lamont's feet, bounced across the concrete into the net, and stopped.

It lay there, smoking a little.

Lifting his visor, Lamont sauntered toward the object, bent over, and squinted at it. Small yellow letters stamped on its side said: *Love, from the anti-electricity coalition.* Junior stood by the base line, irritatedly bouncing a bright green ball as he asked, "What is it?"

*"Jesus Christ it's a hand grenade!"* the doctor shouted. As he spun away, his oxygen tank's safety chain swung free, caught in the net, and tripped him up: one tennis shoe snagged in the rope webbing, and Lamont went down, landing on his back with an explosive clang.

Even as the surgeon cried *"Help!"* Randolph Bonney scrambled to save his own ass, rolling over, heaving upright, and running smack into the chain-link fence. He squealed, spun away with his face crisscrossed by red lines, and plunged out the open doorway, nose-diving into the pebbly bare turf of the elementary-school baseball outfield.

Junior, on the other hand, sprinted for the net, his hands flailing, grabbing at the doctor's shoe and at the snap on his oxygen tank's safety chain. He ripped Lamont's foot out of the sneaker, breaking his ankle, tore apart the safety chain's latch, grabbed the dazed septuagenarian under the armpits, and, paddling frantically backward, dragged him beyond the base line in two seconds, shoved aside the oxygen tank, flopped atop him, and squeezed shut his eyes.

Nothing exploded.

Still, they waited, panting heavily.

But nothing happened.

Lamont whimpered in pain. Junior opened one eye, peering across the concrete at ground level to where a last trickle of smoke left the grenade and dispersed, and the thing lay inert.

"It might still blow," Lamont cautioned. "Don't move!"

"It's a dud," Junior whispered. "It's somebody's idea of a joke."

"It still might explode, and something is wrong with my ankle, I can't run, so for God's sake, Leyba, don't move."

"No, I really think it's a dud." Junior's fear left him almost as rapidly as it had launched him into this puzzling frenzy of Boy Scoutism. Distastefully, he got off the old son of a bitch, dusted his trousers, and looked about for his racket. Outside the court Randolph Bonney remained spread-eagled on the dirt, eyes closed, his hands protecting his ears.

"It's all right everybody," Junior said, pleased at being the noncoward in the group. He approached the grenade, nudging it with his toe. "Just a toy, looks like to me. Some cabroncito over there in those houses, in cahoots with the Anti-Electricity Coalition, is getting his rocks off on the spectacle we made of ourselves."

Bonney sat up, hating Junior with a passion. The lawyer helped up Al Lamont and gave him a shoulder to lean on as they hobbled over to Junior's car. Lamont, aided by Junior, eased into the front seat, groaning, "Who is going to set this ankle? Who can do it in this town? I don't trust any of the new quacks around here, they're all bumblefingered sadists, they'll *kill* me!"

The co-op executive creaked onto his feet after they had zoomed off. He stood there bitterly eating their dust—ashamed, ashamed, ashamed. "I'll kill you, Junior Leyba!"

That night, Judson Babbitt's prize-winning basset hound, Michelangelo, slipped out of his doggie door, trotted down Guadalupe Street, crossed the elementary-school baseball field, entered the tennis court, and paused, en route to the exit door on the other side, to pee on the grenade.

It exploded, instantly etherizing the classy pup and digging a hole through the concrete three feet deep and ten yards wide, pulverizing a main Custer Electric cable leading into the nearby routing station, and plunging all of Chamisaville into darkness.

The telephone started ringing at Randolph Bonney's home: and it didn't stop ringing until he floundered out of there at dawn, taking to the streets in his sweat suit once more so that he wouldn't have to hear all those complaints.

* * *

CHARLOTTE LEYBA telephoned her father-in-law, asking to meet him someplace where nobody would see them together: she wanted to talk.

"How about on top of Nobody Mountain," Virgil joked. "I need the exercise, and I haven't been up there in ages."

To his surprise, Charlotte agreed immediately. And so on his lunch hour he drove to the mouth of the canyon: her car was already parked at the bottom of the hill. When Virgil tapped on her rolled-up window—the motor was idling, the air conditioning going full tilt—Charlotte jumped, her face drained.

"You took me by surprise," she apologized, stepping out, a manila envelope in her white-gloved hand, wearing an outfit that stopped Virgil for a second—a soft pink cashmere sweater, a charcoal gray skirt, stockings, and pink suede slingbacks.

"I thought we were going to climb the mountain," Virgil said.

"Of course we're going to climb the mountain. Do you know, I've never even been up this hill."

"That's your hiking outfit?"

"Oh." Charlotte appeared startled, then she giggled. "I guess I wasn't thinking. Well, it'll have to do."

"This is a strange way to meet," Virgil said, as they began to climb the trail. Immediately, he was breathing hard and had to stop, catching his breath before pushing on.

Charlotte nodded: yes, it was strange. But she said nothing more, picking her way carefully and a little awkwardly up the trail, her ankles turning whenever she stepped on small stones, her hand constantly plucking at Virgil's sleeve to steady herself.

On top, no breeze was blowing. The air, the sky, the surrounding piñon trees were very still. Folding his jacket and tie over one arm, Virgil wiped his forehead with a handkerchief and sat down on a large volcanic rock. Charlotte found a seat nearby, looking prim, feminine, and terribly uncomfortable. Her lipstick, an apricot color, made Virgil ache. What a fantastic, totally misplaced woman.

"So . . ." he said finally.

Charlotte would not face him. Instead, her eyes traveled around the valley; she seemed in a kind of daze. Prompting, Virgil cleared his throat; but when she failed to respond, he calmed down and waited. It was peaceful on

Nobody Mountain, and Virgil thought: I'm glad I made the effort. The valley pleased him even though it appeared hot, dusty, agitated. Too much construction was evident: everywhere large yellow earth-moving machines chopped at the land. Backed up along the North-South Highway, a long line of cars glittered. A mood of great flux prevailed around Chamisaville. Trees were lying down, splintered; gouged earth indicated development scars. Yet, farther out from the center, green fields emerged from the dust. And beyond, the mesa lay tranquil, ribboned by the dark streak of Rio Grande Gorge, backdropped by the soft western mesas where the eye finally settled into a compassionate landscape able to nourish the soul.

"I don't know if I should be doing this," Charlotte said. "Maybe it's stupid. I know it's a betrayal of trust. But we haven't really had that in ages, Junior and I. He doesn't trust me, I don't trust him, I don't even know what it is we live for. Not each other, not anymore, that's for certain."

Charlotte fell silent again; her eyes locked so intently on the valley that she could have been hypnotized, immobilized.

Virgil could be a patient man. Eventually, fiddling nervously with the manila envelope in her hands, Charlotte said, "I think Junior is in some terrible trouble. I don't know what it is, but I'm so afraid, I'm so worried. This—" And she made a motion with the envelope to indicate its contents: "these things in here, I don't really understand them—"

Charlotte stopped.

"What is it?" Virgil asked. "What's the matter?"

"I shouldn't be doing this. It isn't right. It's so private. Maybe it isn't anything."

"That's for you to decide."

"Maybe I should think about it a little more. Maybe the things I feel, my fear, maybe all that isn't valid. Junior and I are so rotten together—I don't know. Suddenly, right now, it felt as if I was doing this just because he has been a son of a bitch to me. I shouldn't have gotten you here, I shouldn't have brought these papers."

Virgil sighed. How could he help this woman, a captive of his son?

"He'd kill me if he knew I was here with you."

"I doubt it. He's a bully, but not a murderer."

Charlotte said, "Oh Lord, I'm sorry, Dad. I shouldn't

380

have gotten you here. I don't want you to see these things. I was wrong. You hate Junior. I doubt you could ever give him a fair shake."

Smiling wanly, Virgil said, "Nobody should be asked to betray a person they love. Whatever you have there, about Junior, maybe there's no reason to expose him. I would like to know what he is up to because I hate his guts for poisoning this valley and I'm trying to stop him from doing any more damage. But if you love him, I don't think there's a crying need to betray him."

Charlotte started crying. "I don't think I want you to see these things, Dad. I'm sorry I asked. I need help, we both need help. I've talked to him about psychiatrists, he laughs in my face. But this, these things, maybe they're just irrelevant. Suddenly I don't like my motives at all for coming to you. I don't know if I'm worried about Junior, about things he might do, or whether I just want revenge."

"It's your decision." A slight ruffling breeze cooled the old man's forehead. Coughing, he reached for his tobacco and papers and busied himself slowly rolling a cigarette.

Charlotte stood with her back to him, her chin high, neck taut, a weary and beautiful woman who might have just been snatched off a downtown metropolitan street and planted atop this woozy little hill.

"I'm not going to show you this stuff, Dad. I'm sorry. I made a mistake."

"All right."

"I'm heading back down, is that all right?"

"Sure. I'm gonna stay up here a minute, though, rest awhile, watch the valley."

"Dad, I'm really sorry."

"It's okay, don't be sorry. I wish you had a better life."

"I'm okay. Sometimes I feel sorry for myself, that's all. I wanted things to be so different. But that's just a little girl in me. Maybe despair is part of growing up."

"Don't be foolish," Virgil snapped. "There is no way to rationalize despair."

"Good-bye, Dad. . . ."

She kissed him lightly on top of his head and departed, dropping out of sight down through the piñon and juniper, leaving behind a slight scent, of Chanel or Arpege.

And as for Junior? thought Virgil. Junior was like a cancer in that woman's body, a dark carnivore eating outward from her bones.

For a moment, closing his eyes, Virgil felt terribly sad.

Already, this week, two more old friends had died. Joe Archuleta had raised pigs: every year he had brought Virgil a big bag of chicharrones. And Eloy Romo, the infamous boxer, had had a fatal heart attack two days ago when he tried to lift up a drunken Pueblo bum who had collapsed on the magazine emporium's doorstep.

Not only that, but people were being metaphorically rubbed out right and left, and Virgil seemed almost unable to help them.

A hundred innovative lethal programs were afoot in the valley. Pressured by a well-meaning but politically naïve ecology-oriented group of middle-class Anglo citizens known as the Amigos of Chamisa Valley, the town council had recently passed an ordinance barring outhouses within Chamisaville limits. Meaning approximately one hundred impoverished families, unable to afford indoor toilets and a sewer hookup, would either have to sell out or mortgage their homes in order to make improvements, incurring debts impossible to meet and only forestalling for a year or two the ultimate loss of their homes. Of course, the ordinance should have been unenforceable because a district court injunction forbade new hookups to the old sewage plant, which merely tipped its hat to the waste matter entering its algal lagoons en route to the Midnight River.

Still, all families using an outhouse within town limits had been issued warnings. Next, they were fined exorbitantly for not complying with the new ordinance. And when they could not pay the penalty, Junior Leyba took them to court, where Virgil tried to defend them.

"How can I install plumbing, a septic tank, a toilet?" Amaranta GeeGee had complained angrily, waving her condemnation notice in Virgil's face. "I got no cash, Juan is dead, the roof leaks, I had them shut off the gas already —and now *this!* Do plumbers take food stamps?"

Then the well-meaning Amigos of Chamisa Valley had decided all junk cars desecrating every indigenous family's front and backyards were a tremendous aesthetic eyesore necessitating immediate correction. So an ordinance had been passed providing for the immediate evacuation of all nonfunctional automotive heaps from town and county yards. Anybody loath to comply with the new ordinance paid through the nose. Randolph Bonney's junk yard was set up to receive the shells; and the Amigos had gladly dumped their treasury into Bonney's lap, enabling him to dispatch cranes and flatbeds for hauling in the eyesores.

Junk-automobile owners had protested vehemently. Cried Espeedie Cisneros: "My car hulks, they are a price-less source of spare parts for every home gadget and farm machine imaginable; they also doubled as dormitories for many years! This is outright *murder!*"

But what could be done? Armed with a dozen ordi-nances, subpoenas, papelitos, and legal jargon, the wreck-ers, cranes, and flatbeds arrived, and if the people refused cooperation, they were fined. If they threw punches or threatened to shoot, they wound up in the county jail, facing fines and/or court costs capable of demolishing in a week resources it had taken years to accumulate.

So valley yards were in the process of beautification: and a few more farmers, one-cow ranchers, and subsistence hustlers were going bankrupt, losing more land to Moe Stryzpk, Rodey McQueen, and Bob Moose.

The noon marijuana plane, a single-engine Cessna—piloted by Skeezix McHorse—flying bush in from Mexico under the watchful eye of local police authorities, droned over the western mesa, heading for the Chamisaville air-port. Virgil made a gun of his hand and, cursing as he aimed, shot it.

A noise, a slight cough; Virgil turned. Joseph Bonatelli, a pair of binoculars around his neck, a camera with a tele-photo lens slung over one shoulder, was about ten yards away, stock-still, staring at Virgil through dark sunglasses, a cigar in his mouth emitting faint rivulets of smoke that wriggled past his glasses and disappeared like tiny snakes into his curly blank hair.

The two men faced each other for a moment. Then Virgil creaked onto his feet, and, without so much as a nod, headed down the trail toward his truck.


BENNY LEDOUX and his girlfriend, Ramona, were lying in the dark on the bed in his Dynamite Shrine motel room, when Junior Leyba rapped once on the screen door and burst in.

"Hey man—!" Benny sat upright, blinking his eyes, try-ing to focus and make out, against the sunlit doorway, the dark shadow of a man who might have come to kill him, arrest him, score, collect a debt, or thump him for having been burned in a deal. "Who the hell is that?"

"It's me, Junior Leyba. What do you say, Benny? Cómo te has ido, cousin?"

"What are you doing here? I'm clean, I got no junk, no acid, no mary jane, no nothing. I'm so clean I smell like Flash Gordon."

"I'm not a cop, Benny, I'm a lawyer, remember?"

"Big deal—cops, lawyers."

"I don't want him to be here," Ramona whined. "Tell him to go away."

"Let's not beat around the bush," Junior said quickly. "I'm on my lunch hour, my time is valuable."

"What's it worth?" Benny sauntered over to the sink, turning on a spigot, and doused his face. "Ten cents an hour? Twenty cents an hour?"

"Be nice to me, Benny, or I'll sic a hundred people on you who'll eat you like zopilotes eat garbage."

"I don't like him," Ramona said wistfully. "Tell him to go away."

Benny scoffed, "Shee-it!" grabbed a dirty towel, and rubbed his face dry.

Junior said, "You can do something for me, and I can pay you for it. Two hundred dollars."

"What do I have to do, Junior—let you fuck me or just give you a blowjob?"

"Don't talk to him like that!" Ramona covered her eyes with her hands. "Don't talk to him like that Benny, he'll hurt you."

Junior held his composure. Benny sat down on the edge of the bed, probed for a cigarette in a wrinkled package, set the last weed between his lips, and, crumpling up the package, fired it across the room. The wad bounced off Junior's thigh and into a wastebasket.

"All right already," Benny said at last. "What kind of job you talking about?"

"It's very simple. You walk into Pat GeeGee's place and turn on. I'll tell you what day to do it and at what time. You'll get busted immediately, of course, but I'll bail you out within the hour, and you'll never go to trial. You'll never even smell a jail—I'll have the whole thing quashed, no problem. It's free money, Benny."

The junkie squinted, trying to make out Junior's face in the dark. First it was Jesus Etcetera; now it was Virgil Leyba's gabacho kid—everybody was out recruiting. Junior's suit sparkled faintly; a gold tiepin shone clearly like a tiny electric light.

His sluggish mind fumbling for the catch, Benny said, "I don't get it. What's the point?"

"Do it, don't ask questions." Junior reached for his wallet and selected two bills.

Ramona whimpered, "It's a trap, they're going to kill you."

"Hey man, hold on a second." Benny stood up. "What's the, like, you know, man, what's the gimmick? What do you mean 'free bread'? Who ever tapped in on free bread? What am I doing in the El Gaucho smoking a joint in the first place?"

"That's my business."

Ramona gripped one of Benny's shoulders: "It's his business," she whispered, scared stiff.

"So take your business and shove it."

Junior was across the room in two steps. He grabbed Benny by the collar and slammed him back up against the wall. "Here we go again," Benny said. "Fun time at the Dynamite Shrine: mug a tecato for luck . . . and a buck."

"You don't do it, you pathetic son of a bitch, and Big Bill Baca will break in here at four o'clock tomorrow morning, beat the guts out of you for resisting arrest, maybe blast you for armed resistance, and, if he hasn't killed you he'll take what's left of your ruined body down to the county jail, dump you in solitary, cut off your supply, and let you rot."

"All right, Jesus Christ. Leggo, will you?"

Junior released him and backed away, into the shadows, where his features became indistinguishable again.

"Do it," Ramona pleaded. "Please, Benny, just do it. You always do it. Just do it and then they won't kill you."

"Superfly wants to know why, that's all. Dig it, Junior —I got to have a reason."

"You don't *got* to have anything, Benny." Junior laid the two bills from his wallet on the sideboard. "Here's your money."

"Not me, man. Not unless I know why I'm doing it."

Junior thought for a minute, scaring the mayor's son half to death because he was so quiet. Benny wanted to sit down again, but he was afraid to move for fear the motion would trigger another outburst from Junior.

"What you don't know can't hurt you," Junior said.

"Bullshit." And then his brain cleared up for a second and it hit him. "It's the liquor license!"

"You're very intelligent. You got a mind like a steel trap."

"What are you gonna do? Bust me, cite Pat, take him to court, knock his teeth out, grab the license—and lay it on one of those new motels they're planning? Hey man, that's pretty slick."

"Like I said, you got a mind that's a steel trap."

Ramona was curled halfway into a fetal position on the bed, shaking her head. "Don't talk back," she whined. "Don't talk back, Benny, please."

"Get out of here, Junior. Go fuck a maricón."

"I told you what would happen—"

"Split, man. Make tracks. Beat it before I break your face. I'll mop the floor with your asshole, scumbag."

"I walk out of here without a deal, Benny, and your life isn't worth a ten-cent tip."

"I'll rip your balls out!" Benny raged. "I may be fly-shit, man, but I'm not gonna help bust Pat GeeGee or your old man or any of those other poor dudes trying to keep you honkies from ripping off everything in sight! That ain't my trip. Take your bread and split, I can support my habit in other coin. Go try Little Kid Lujan next door—used to be he'd fuck a snake if somebody gave him a quarter! Whew, what a *bummer!*"

Junior returned the money to his wallet. "I walk out of here without a deal, Benny, and it's good-bye. That's it. Finished."

"Don't let him go!" Ramona cried. "It doesn't matter, Benny. None of it matters."

"Take a walk. Screw you. Go bug the upside-down flag-man, Filiberto García—I hear he's looking for scratch. Maybe Celestino Lucero's magpie could dig a little Panama Red in the El Gaucho, and it'd only cost you a bag of sunflower seeds!"

Junior went straight out the screen door, letting it bang shut behind him. Gratefully, Benny moved, collapsing onto the bed again, rubbing his itching face. His fingertips felt numb. Ramona was sobbing quietly. And Benny sat there in the hot gloom, listening to the summertime lunch-hour bustle, to the repetitious dynamite blasts rumbling across town, dislodging boulders on the new Mosquito Valley ski runs. So what if his days were numbered—good riddance. Orale, carnalito: the scene around here was beginning to get real heavy.

Ramona complained, "You shouldn't have done that. You're not even brave, you're just crazy."

"What the hell do you know about it?"

"I know you're crazy. He'll kill you for sure."

"Shut up," Benny said gently, laying a hand on her blouse. "You don't know nothing."

"I know," she whimpered, settling her hands over his, pressing his palm against one breast. "I know, that's all."

Tiredly, Benny leaned over her. They kissed, barely moving; then he unbuttoned her blouse and touched his lips absentmindedly to her flesh. After a while they made love, awkwardly. "I love you," Ramona said fearfully. "I'll always be with you, Benny, I want you to live. You make me happy, you're my man."

They finished, and the whole thing unnerved him: he was getting tense, jumpy, all strung out. In the bathroom he took a hit, then dressed up clean and polished his shoes and went out. From the public telephone booth at the Dynamite Shrine office he called Junior Leyba.

"What the hell," Benny said unhappily. "I might as well do what it is you want me to do."

"Thanks," Junior said. "It won't be necessary, now. Plans have changed, keep your mouth shut. But thanks all the same. Maybe another time."

Benny hung up, wondering: Did he mean it, or are they going to kill me?

When he left the booth, Benny walked right past a vaporous golden skeleton sporting enormous white wings without giving it so much as a second glance.

GEORGE PARKER arrived at April Delaney's house shortly after midnight at the end of a dreary day for both, and they salvaged a magic time.

A wind came out of nowhere, cleaning the stagnant night with a single mighty whoosh: cottonwood leaves clattered into the driveway, the chicken coop, the back field. High with a peculiarly wonderful weariness after his plodding day, George felt unaccountably heady, cocky, "happy as a buzzard in guts!" he laughed, and pranced away from her into the back field.

"Wipe that idiotic grin off your face!" April hugged herself against the sudden wonderful crispness of the air, against the almost stinging clarity of stellar brightness.

"My body is so cool and coordinated," George crowed, going through a few muscle-building contortions, spinning on tiptoes. "All one hundred and seventy power-packed pounds of me can float through the air daffy as a feather. Look at me. There isn't an ounce of fat anywhere. I'm so beautiful I ought to be declared against the law!"

He flashed his teeth, made another muscle, hit his stomach. April, with her arms folded, regarded him somewhat dazedly, feeling good from being boozed up, feeling sad and apprehensive also.

"You're a buffoon," she said gently, loving his enjoyment of himself. Life was a series of such incredibly mercurial changes—

"I don't understand why you don't leap at me, tear off my shirt, rip my belt apart with your teeth, yank off my pants, and gobble me up, I really don't. I'm a certified menace to society, I'm so gorgeous. Every time I walk into the plaza it's like Elvis Presley walking onstage—a riot begins. Last week I broke all my fingers trying to fight off a multitude of lovely little teenyboppers. I tell you, I oughtta be against the law!"

Grabbing his shirt, George ripped it open, popping off the buttons. "How can you resist me?" He wrenched off the garment, rolled it into a ball, and heaved it skyward. The shirt unfolded and undulated off into the night like a gentle ray-shaped moth flapping through heavy ocean currents.

Naked to the waist, he gleamed, his muscles silvery, his eyes bristling with mischievous, loving humor. Enthusiasm richocheted off his wide grin. George stretched his arms toward the stars, digging himself and the cornball shapes of his posturing.

"I'm gonna *kill* you with my vitality!" he exclaimed.

"You and whose army?"

He strutted in the field. "I'll dance for you, would you like that? Do you think you could stand it without fainting from oversensuous stimulation?"

When she failed to answer, he danced anyway, twisting himself slowly and deliberately, extending his arms in a serpentine way, curling them up slowly like flowers retracting from darkness. And he was right, he *was* beautiful. George made up a chant and started to dance a little in an Indian manner, then laughed, his laughter somehow constrained, a joyous chuckle.

"Take off your pants," April jeered affectionately. "Let's see the cash goods."

He complied, tossing them gaily over his shoulder: the

trousers headed off into the Midnight Mountains flapping like an enormous raven.

George approached her and halted. "Hey, hit me in the stomach!" He grinned at her, pleased as punch, very much in love. "Go ahead, you can't hurt me, hit me in the stomach. Hit me with all your might."

Expelling a little grunt, April hit him with her fist, in the stomach, as hard as she could.

"*Ow!*" George doubled over so fast he lost his balance, tumbled at her feet, and writhed, truly hurt, his wind knocked out. He stared up at her pop-eyed, gagging, his mouth and chest working to suck in air as April cried, "Oh no, what did I *do?*" She fell beside him, shaking her head, fluttering hands over him as George rocked in frightened agony until he latched onto a breath and labored toward less hysterical breathing. Finally, gasping, he wailed, "What . . . did you do . . . *that* for?"

"But you said—"

"I know . . . what I said. But *Jesus* . . ." Tears had been forced from his eyes.

"Are you gonna be all right?"

"Sure I'm . . . gonna be all right. Wipe . . . the grin off your face!"

"I can't help it, George. You're such an idiot. You make me laugh sometimes. Occasionally I have such unadulterated fun with you."

"This is *fun?*" He sat up, still breathing hard, gingerly massaging his stomach.

"You ain't as tough as you thought you were, are you?"

"Well, when some crazy broad comes up and without warning belts you one in the stomach, what are you supposed to do?"

April gave his nose a friendly flick.

"I had a vision of you last night," George said, abruptly serious. "I was out at the shack, and I lay down on the mattress and couldn't really go to sleep, but went fairly drowsy, though, and my mind began wandering all over the place. Then at one point I looked up and I thought you were sitting in my desk chair."

"Perhaps I was. I do a lot of astral traveling, you know —I project myself all over the world. Was there a little silver thread trickling down from my fanny out from under my trouser cuff and across the floor, out the door, and up ten miles of highway and out Ranchitos Road, turning right on Upper Ranchitos Road and right again at my driveway leading up to my flesh seated in the lotus position in the center of my grubby little lawn?"

"No, you were stained with mimeo ink, smoking a cigarette and sipping wine from a plastic yogurt cup. Your eyes looked kind of pouchy and bruised, you were coughing a little like you always do, there was a blanket draped over your shoulders, and you were wearing a baggy sweat shirt and your short shorts. You looked numb and defeated for the moment, all played out, and exquisitely beautiful."

"You say things nicely, love." Apirl brushed moonlight off his icy clean shoulder, ran her fingernail down across his torso onto his thigh. "You're going to write a good book, I know it."

"At home I lie in bed thinking of you naked, thinking of your wide shoulders, and your breasts, and your belly, and your long legs. And I want you very much."

"Of course." April rested her hand on his groin. "I'm a very wantable person . . ."

"Hey, don't cry."

"I don't think I can help it. This is all-American tear week or something, I'm sorry. Dunno what's wrong with me. Believe it or don't, but I used to be an almost semi-self-controlled person when it came to tears, I really did. I never cried very much at all."

"It's okay." George gave her shoulder a reassuring little pump. "Really, everything is going to be all right."

"I know that. Don't you think I know that?" April blurted. "When do you think I was born—yesterday?"

George shifted, facing the Pueblo's sacred mountain. A silver peace hung over the mountains, radiating light like old bones, exuding an odor of memories dulled by time, the bitterness softened away.

"Oi vey," April sputtered, unable to stem the tears. "Vey iz mir, everybody. *Vey iz fucking mir!*"

"Hey, April—You know how much I love you? Guess. Know what I'm gonna do? How far would you say it is, once around this field, huh? How far?"

"How would I know, George?"

"I'm guessing, oh, let's say just about an eighth of a mile, okay? Well, here's what I'm going to do, just to prove my love is really something. I'm going to run around this here field, in the nude, three miles' worth—that's twenty-four times. And after that, when I'm all hot and covered from head to toe with sweat, I'm gonna grab you right here in the grass, and if the earth doesn't move for you, you get a refund."

"Cut it out. You're crazy."

"I'll show you who's crazy."

Jumping up, George took off at a steady jog, cutting to the barbed wire and beginning to circle the fence line, leaping once over the ditch bisecting the field. Through her tears, April watched him go. He turned right by the three skinny chinese elms at the eastern fence, and caused two of her neighbor's horses to bolt away snorting when he changed direction at the next corner. Veering once more on reaching the chicken coop fence, George ran easily, a man who for a long time had stayed in shape. "You're crazy," April said again, not even loud enough for him to hear. After that she held her tongue as he made good on his promise and actually ran twenty-four laps, taking about twenty minutes to do it, running strongly and rarely changing his pace, his penis flopping about, his breathing strong and—after a while—heavy enough to hear.

April just sat there quietly with this strange man running laps around her in the middle of the night, and—totally absorbed by the tragic, silly sweetness of the ephemeral moment—she found it impossible to check her weeping.

# Dreams
# and
# Hallucinations

MORNING LIGHT, filtered through venetian blinds, landed in thin stripes across Moe Stryzpk's face; it sparkled in the thick lenses of his glasses. He was sleeping on his office couch, in the heart of his command module. At the touch of sunlight, Moe lurched awake. For a second his lids twittered, eyes jumping around—lost and wondering, as always, where he was. Strange dreams lingered—wet, complex, childish. Fantasies had occurred under a Maxfield Parrish sky; naked girls with ringlet hair cavorted through Victorian woodlands; crimson ribbons settled and disappeared among enormous boulders. Pretty and desolate, the dreams carved delirious aches into his brittle bones. No solace for Moe in sleep; no freedom from tormented desires, stifled flesh.

When the ceiling focused, when wall maps, bookcases, and filing cabinets materialized, Moe calmed down, his heart recommenced a regular beating. Lifting his hands, Moe inspected them: wrinkled, liver spotted, ink stained, nicotine stained—but not trembling. Then Moe relaxed, listening to things; a digital electric clock on his desk hummed; a refrigerator built into a bookcase cupboard droned comfortably. The rest of the house slumbered, Miranda still recuperating from last night's trysting. Outside, roosters were crowing; the recorded church bells already banged away. Moe lay very quiet, staring up at lovely vigas and aspen latias. "Another day, another dollar." God bless America. Time for a cancer stick.

Moe heaved into a sitting position, snagged an arm of his wheelchair, set the brake, and, grumbling softly, pulled himself into the vehicle. The job took several minutes; sweat bubbles covered his forehead by the time he made it. Using a breast-pocket handkerchief, Moe mopped his brow. After his heart had slowed down again, he fitted a wrinkled weed between his lips and, fumbling with a lighter on a chain around his neck, lit it, exhaled smoke, and surveyed his domain.

Survey maps, hydrological maps, development plats and grids on every wall, a dozen filing cabinets, his enormous and cluttered desk, bookcases crammed with legal tomes, state statutes, planning reports, duplicate county tax records, conservancy district books, ski-valley plan reports, environmental impact statements, stockholders reports, investment portfolios, preliminary studies of the Pueblo electrification scheme, Forest Service multiple-use planning volumes, and so forth—the whole schmeer. What Moe Stryzpk didn't know about the convoluted machinations of Chamisaville's economic and sociological structure hadn't yet transpired. Still, Moe derived no great satisfaction from his power anymore. To be at the controls, in this engine room, gave him little sense of accomplishment. Moe was a burnt-out case, traveling on leftover echoes of the ambition he had possessed forty years ago, before Onofre García's blunderbuss of erudite lineage crippled him for life and delivered Miranda over to the sexual whims of Rodey McQueen.

With the butt of his first weed Moe lit a fresh cigarette. As he did so, his telephone gave a lyrical jingle: Moe checked his watch. Christ, it was only six-fifteen! What was the matter with people these days? Losing their ability to control all the various strands, they became addled by the confusion, lost all sense of time, couldn't sleep at night, were running scared. Everybody except Joe Bonatelli, that is. Moe wheeled over to the desk, clamped the receiver against his shoulder, selected a pencil from a felt-lined leather dice cup, poised it over a clean sheet of yellow legal paper, said "Stryzpk," and punched a button activating a tape recorder in his top right-hand drawer.

"Moe, this is McQueen—you up?"

"I'm up." Moe brushed ashes off the legal paper. "But it's only six-fifteen in the morning."

"Who gives a pig's dork what time it is? I just fell downstairs—can you believe it?"

Grunting, Moe resisted an impulse to doodle on the pad, and waited for the point of the call.

"I could've been killed," McQueen said angrily. What does he think I did, Moe thought—greased his fucking stair? "I don't know what's the matter with me, I'm getting so abstracted lately. Maybe the combination of dealing at the same time with Icarus Suazo and Joe Bonatelli has gotten my brain a tad mushy, I don't know. I had a dream two nights ago that was crazier than a magpie going after wheat kernels in horseshit. If I didn't know better I'd think my nerves were shot."

Moe said, "Mmmph."

"You remember that time, back when April was a little tacker, that she fell off the roof?" McQueen said. "That's what I dreamed about, Moe. And it was as real as if it was actually happening, dammit! She was wearing one of those little pink chiffon dresses and she was barefoot, and had her blond hair in ringlets. Me, I was sitting on the side lawn in the chaise, reading the paper, when I heard a tiny noise, like a pebble dislodging, or maybe it was just an itty-bitty little squeak, I dunno. But anyway, I turned, and there she was—already in the air . . . as if she had suddenly fallen from the sky. Before I could move, she hit the lawn on her stomach, bounced onto her back, jumped up, dusted herself off, and shouted, 'Hey, Daddy, I can fly!' That's what she said in the dream, Moe, just

393

exactly like she said it in real life over thirty-five years ago: 'Hey, Daddy, I can fly!' "

Moe held still and kept quiet, listening to the faint whirr of his tape recorder.

"April was always getting hurt," McQueen rambled on. "But nothing ever fazed her. Once she pulled the marble lamp in the game room onto her head—it required thirteen stitches. When she was three she drank a whole bottle of codeine cough syrup and I had to run with her piggyback to the doctor because Cynthia had the car. And I couldn't count the goddam times she broke her nose and her bones falling out of trees, off horses. Hell—you know what? Cynthia saved all her casts. Yep, she did that, Moe. They're up in the attic in trunks. And I went up there just a few days ago and looked at them."

Moe grunted.

"Sure, I actually went up and looked at them and read all the inscriptions. There's four or five arm casts and a couple from her leg. Shit, you know something? I can't hardly remember a time in childhood when April didn't have a cast on one limb or another. She always looked like a goddam racehorse that had tried to gallop blindfolded through a prairie-dog town!"

Moe said, "Oh."

"So you know what happens after that dream about her falling off the roof, Moe? I'm not even awake enough to distinguish a tit from a lemon, but Randolph called me. And you know why? To tell me *he* had a lousy dream that night, can you beat it? What I want to know is— what's going on around here? What's happening to everybody? There's more confusion in this town than a bunch of tomcats fighting for bones in a garbage can! This is the biggest thing any of us ever pulled off, there's more money in it than there is pawpaws in the Deep South, and it ought to be *fun*. But instead of being fun, everybody's so nervous they don't know whether to shit or get off the pot, pump gas or kick tires. What's the matter with everybody anyway? Far as I'm concerned, there's no point to any of this Old Crap Game if it ain't fun. All my life I had more damn fun than a fat fox in a chicken coop, Moe, and god dammit, if it wasn't fun—the hell with it, I backed out, I dropped it like a four-card flush. Now we've got this deal with more fine points, finagling, and financial farting than a wind twister in a west Texas cathouse, and instead of it being fun everybody's walking around with long faces and assholes so tight their turds come out in quarter-inch-thick ribbons ten feet long! Me included, I'm sorry to say, I must have caught the disease from everybody else. What do you think about that?"

"How come you called?" Moe asked. *You thought maybe Miranda would answer?*

"I dunno." McQueen seemed genuinely surprised by the question. "Know something, Moe—I really can't figure why I called. I just had an impulse, I guess. I'll be damned. Like a year-old heifer, I reckon I just woke up with a hankering for mama's titty."

"Well—?" Moe said brusquely.

"Well, good morning," McQueen said gruesomely. "Shit on a hazel stick." And hung up.

Pensively, Moe cradled the phone and punched off his tape recorder. Opening the drawer, he rewound the tape, and was sitting there, head in his hands while coffee percolated nearby, listening for the fourth time to McQueen's call, when an automobile crunched across the driveway gravel, somebody knocked on his door.

"It isn't locked." Moe stopped the machine and shut the drawer as Junior Leyba entered the room. Wearing a rumpled suit, a tie more than a little askew, Junior hadn't yet shaved, and looked tired, his hair was uncombed, his normally shiny shoes were dusty. Hyped up and flying after obviously staying up all night, Junior had liquor on his breath, too. Moe gave the lawyer a look that said he was scum, but Junior didn't see it: he never looked Moe in the eye.

"It's six-thirty in the morning, Junior. What have you been out doing all night long, shooting hippies?"

"Hey, so it is. That's strange. I thought it was around nine o'clock. Sorry, Moe, I'll come back later."

"Stay, now that you're here. What's up?"

"I had an idea." Junior perched nervously on the edge of the couch, lighting one of his own cigarettes, then leaning forward to light Moe's as the cripple set another weed between his lips. "Remember those two old Denver lawyers used to work for the Pueblo, back around the time I was born, Joe Brady and Win Potter—remember them?"

"What about them?"

"Where are they? I want to look at their file."

"What for?"

"I just had an idea." Junior jumped up, pacing while he spoke, glancing everywhere but at Moe. "Icarus Suazo fired them, right? when he discovered something—they were doing what . . . passing information to you people, as I understand it? He nailed them for a conflict of interest, and they were fired, and disappeared next day. And were never heard from again, I assume on your advice, or Bob's advice—am I correct?"

Moe smoked, neither acknowledging nor denying the truth of Junior's statements.

"But as I understand it, they were never paid. Not by Suazo, or anybody else out there. On the grounds that they had tried to sabotage Pueblo legal operations, isn't that right?"

Moe grumbled, perhaps affirmatively.

"All right. I think we should find those two old bastards, haul them out of mothballs wherever they may be if they are living, or get hold of their heirs if they aren't alive, prep them a little, and bus them down here, prepare to file suit against the Pueblo for the legal fees they never received, and use them to bargain with Icarus Suazo, forcing his hand."

"I already thought of that a long time ago."

"You what?"

"They are both still alive and residing in Denver. I've kept in touch. If we can use them we'll bring them down. But I don't think right now, not yet. It isn't the time for it. It's a card we don't play until almost everything else is worked out."

Junior looked Moe straight in the eye for a second, asking, "Mind if I look at their file anyway?"

"Help yourself." Moe flipped him the keys. And while Junior sat on the couch riffling through the papers, jotting notes, Moe poured himself coffee, mixed in Pream, and never asked his fellow conspirator if he would like a cup.

When he had finished, without looking up, Junior said, "So we've got five out of six Pueblo council members—everybody except whatshisname . . . Lujan—we've got that many lined up. Any more word on when the old bastard will fall?"

Moe shrugged.

Junior said, "Do you think Suazo has told them? Do you think any of them *really* know? I mean the *real* reasons?"

"I doubt he's come right out and said it. But instinctively, they know. It has no shape or name for them, but instinctively I believe they understand precisely the nature of what's in the works. Those people are like that."

After Junior had left, Moe wheeled to a window, pulled up the venetian blind, and raised the lower pane. An elaborate garden patio, planted with numerous hollyhocks, irises, and marigolds and shaded by several apricot trees, glimmered prettily in the bright morning light. In the shallow pool surrounding the base of a little satyr fountain, several goldfish lolled. Hummingbird feeders dangled from tree limbs, as did a suet ball and a glass-paneled seed tray full of hen scratch.

Moe selected one of three BB guns from a rack beside the window, and settled it across his lap. He enjoyed sitting at this station, plinking at butterflies, hummingbirds, or sparrows and finches. Right now a magpie in the apricot tree boldly stared at him; for some reason it had not fled as birds usually did whenever he pulled the blinds. Slowly, Moe raised the BB gun, drew a careful bead on the large black-and-white bird ten yards away, and squeezed the trigger. Chest-feathers fluffed as the pellet hit; with a startled yawp the bird fell over backward, wings wildly flailing to maintain its perch, then it slipped off the branch, scrawking, and began falling to earth. But after a few feet its large wings caught air, and the raucous bird aimed toward Moe, never once taking its bright, angry eyes off the cripple's impassive face. The magpie flew straight through the window into his hands; Moe grabbed it just inches from his nose, wincing as wing-feathers beat against his cheeks. Blood spattered, and the bird cursed him in a vile, foreign invective: "Chinga tu madre, mamá tu padre, chupa la puta—!" Moe fumbled, enclosing the wings in his grasp, and then held the magpie in his lap, astonished by the event. Furiously, the bird gasped for air and continued cursing; blood covered Moe's clothes. *"Tierra o muerte!"* the bird screamed. "Cuando vino el alambre, vino el hambre!" it croaked.

Then Moe came to his senses, and, giving the magpie a terrific squeeze with his powerful hands, he made its eyes goggle. The bird unleashed a final hoarse insult— *"Gabacho maricón!"*—and died.

For a moment, Moe held the hot damp carcass in his hands. Then he tossed it out the window into some flowers, wheeled over to his desk, and lit up another Lucky. Shaken by the incident, and seeking to take his mind off its implications, Moe opened the tape recorder drawer, pushed a rewind button on his machine, and watched tape thicken onto the takeup spool for a moment, then stopped it, and played the section he thought would contain Rodey McQueen's phone call.

Instead, a strange voice, hollow as if coming from a mysterious historical echo chamber, said, "Hello, Moe, remember me? Del árbol caído todos hacen leña—?"

And then the ghostly voice jumped at him in an angry shout: *"Up against the wall, you crippled honky mother-fucker! Brown Power's gonna get your mama!"*

AT THE CRACK OF DAWN, four old men opened their eyes. It always surprised Pat GeeGee a little to find himself alive. And he lay very still for a moment in his narrow bed in the almost empty room above the bar, adjusting his ears to the town's early morning frequencies: last dog barks died away, plates began rattling in the Prince of Whales, a magpie clatter traveled the length of the valley. For a brief, disquieting moment, he thought he heard strains from "The Handkerchief Waltz," faint echoes of Espeedie's violin, his late brother's guitar, Juan Ortega's accordion, and Loretta's piano on the Balena Park floating bandstand. Then Pat rolled his aching bones out of bed and sat quietly adjusting his heart, thinking with a bitter sadness of his friends who had died recently. Jacobal Mondragón from Mota Llano: years ago he had herded goats in the Mosquito Valley before McQueen ran him out. And Esquipula Gallegos of Borregas Negras: a lover, an artist, a thief . . . also the best gravedigger Pat had ever known. Bob Moose and Moe Stryzpk had bought his land for a song when the insurance policy Esquipula had bought from them wouldn't pay off the year he spent in the hospital with cancer.

A mile away Juan Ortega awoke with a start, immediately uneasy and impatient, his veins, arteries, and nerves humming. He had innumerable things to do; an article he had been working on until 3:00 A.M. was still in his head. Bones and weary muscles creaking loudly, Juan hustled out of bed, sat down at a desk, and typed another sentence, paragraph, page. Then he scribbled some ideas in one of a thousand notebooks. Finally, he pulled a volume from his enormous bookcase to check something out, running down a specific reference.

Opening his red-rimmed eyes, Virgil Leyba was greeted by the smoky remains of all the ghosts who had spilled

398

out of his brain during the night. A powerful stench attacked his nostrils. Virgil sat up; his head ached; his heart was heavy with morbid sensations of desolation and doom. His world was a mess, his life incomplete, his body useless, his brain a lackluster, ineffective organ. Six recent court defeats weighed heavily on his mind, and he was especially afraid that Amaranta GeeGee was doomed to lose her old home unless a miracle happened. The valley, the world, and Virgil Leyba were going to hell, one-way ticketed: Sorry folks, no reprieves. I should commit suicide, he thought, get it over with. And, his shoulders stooped from an unendurable weight, he slouched about the small house searching for his cats, opening windows, righting the pictures on his walls.

Flakey Jake Martínez had anticipated the sun by an hour. He was already dressed and outside in his field irrigating when it rimed the mountain peaks with a thin golden lining. While he tromped around wielding his shovel, guiding water into his bean plants, corn, and squash hills, Jake hummed a vigorous chant, feeling good, powerful, indiscreet, sly, and horny. He burst out laughing for no other reason than that he felt like laughing. And as the sun finally hove into sight he shook a fist at it, shouting, "It's about time, lazybones!" Buzzing hummingbirds suddenly appeared at the sunflowers growing in clumps all over the place. Jake laid down his hoe and began walking into town.

Pat GeeGee dressed, gargled, fitted in his teeth, and started negotiating the stairs leading down to the bar and out to the street. Juan Ortega stuffed pencils, pens, notebooks and paper into his knapsack, and, on his bicycle, he pedaled comfortably toward town a mile away. Virgil Leyba fumbled into a shirt, a tie, and his suit, tinkered with his truck for ten minutes before it started, and blearily jounced down his driveway, dying with each jolt, headed in the same direction as Juan Ortega.

In fact, Virgil overtook Juan on the way. The lawyer was locked into such a dismal mood, however, that he failed to see the writer, ran him off the road, and kept on going, oblivious to the pudgy septuagenarian on his knees in the roadside ditch, screaming obscenities and shaking a fist at the receding pickup.

Virgil parked in the lot behind Moose and McQueen Insurance, absentmindedly left the truck in gear and running, took his foot off the clutch as he opened the door to descend, and the vehicle leaped forward with a crunch, hitting the back wall of the insurance building as Virgil sprawled on the ground. He got up, dusted himself off, reached for his keys, slammed the door, and, leaving the truck's front bumper embedded in the adobe wall, he tottered around the corner and sleepwalked across the plaza toward the Prince of Whales Café.

Pat GeeGee already had their table. Denzil Spivey and Al Lamont were at another table dunking glazed doughnuts into steaming cups of Pero. Virgil plopped disjointedly into a chair, upturned his coffee cup with a loud, demanding clunk, sank his head into his hands, and groaned. Pat said, "Good morning, Virgil," and Virgil replied, "What's good about it?" Gloria Armijo popped up, a regular ball of pudgy sunshine, tousled Virgil's hair, chirruped, "Muy buenos días, Virgil Leyba, you're looking like Mr. Wonderful today," and, leaning over to pour his coffee, she nudged his shoulder with her hefty bosom. That nudge, coupled with the smell of her starched uniform, the perfume on her neck and underarms, and the gauzy sheen along her bare brown arms, gave Virgil a small kick. His ears and nostrils quivered; a sensation, perhaps of life itself, maybe hope, did a faint flounce in his groin; and the strong coffee aroma caused his sallow, sagging cheeks to twitch.

Juan Ortega bought a *Capital City Reporter* from Little Kid Lujan, stormed into the café, dropped his knapsack on the floor, and grabbed Virgil's arm, shaking him angrily. "You son of a bitch! You demented old coot! You senile paraplegic! You ran me off the road this morning! I'll sue you, I'll have you put in a rest home! I'll make them disbar you! I'll force them to revoke your license!"

Virgil confronted Juan curiously, a faint light trickling into his bloodshot eyes. His universe, the pieces of his broken world, were coming together again as they did every morning. "Where's the newspaper, Juan?" he demanded sullenly. "Did you pick up the newspaper on your way?"

"You're a menace to society," Juan grumbled lovingly, slapping down the *Reporter*. "If you weren't such a helpless old bastard, I'd stick you a fat one right in your arrogant Mexican snoot."

Flakey Jake stomped through the door, loaded for bear. He plunked down at the table, demolished Virgil's coffee

400

in three gulps, snapped his fingers for Gloria Armijo, and ordered a breakfast fit for a king:

"Bring me a roast pheasant under glass lacquered in marmalade, three French croissants buttered with real butter, a piece of apple pie à la mode, two porkchops done well and smothered in parsley, one baked potato, a vanilla milkshake, and another cup of coffee, Gloria, would you please, dear?"

She brought him the coffee, a nondairy creamer, and half a grapefruit.

When Virgil opened the newspaper a tide arose in him, commencing in his toes, making them tingle. Moving swiftly up his legs it restored feeling to his calves, knees, and thighs. It circled quickly through his penis, giving him a slight erection, and spread out from there, filling his body, giving definition to his heart and his lungs, his biceps and his fingertips, and at last to his brain. Virgil's ears turned red as he scanned the news about Vietnam, Azerbaijan, and Toledo, Ohio—murder, wars, recipes—the stuff of history, day-to-day living, humanity and life.

Every morning, these four fragile bulwarks met. They settled like smoke around each other's vitality, restoring each other to the literal pink, bolstering their aging frames with an implacable camaraderie.

Tired already from the early morning rush, Gloria Armijo sighed and poured herself a fresh coffee and planked gratefully down at the counter, waiting for the next customer to put her back on her aching feet and varicosing legs. After loosening shoelaces to let her feet breathe, she lit a cigarette, and had just released a glorious exhale when the air changed remarkably, growing clear and almost totally cleansed—of smells, of noise—as if suddenly depressurized toward a vacuum. A strange lull settled on the Prince of Whales Café. A soporific hush descended; even flies quit their frantic thrashing against the plate-glass windows and stayed still, awed by the quietude, ashamed of their noisy hopeless antics. And the smoke from Gloria's cigarette, instead of rising toward laxly swirling currents, stopped in the dead air almost as it left her throat, failing to dissipate, hanging by her nose in a thick bluish cloud that seemed to sink slowly instead of climbing—heavier than air.

Without the customary bang and jangle, the café's screen door swung open and Atiliano Montoya, deceased vendor of the La Ciénega grant, entered. The valley's original

401

traitor advanced two steps and halted, gazing pale eyed, almost blindly, at the surroundings. Nobody else in the café looked up. Afterward, had she dared report the incident, Gloria would have been hard pressed to explain the way she visualized the old man, as if filtered through a gauzy web of mystifying filaments that made his figure shimmer, almost—but not quite—sparkling in an enchanted manner, as if the space he occupied had just been purified with aerosol champagne.

Cautiously, balancing himself by touching chairbacks between tables as he approached the counter, Atiliano selected a stool near Gloria, and, while she circled behind the counter to take his order, the old man produced the necessary accoutrements and commenced rolling a cigarette.

Cheerfully, Gloria said, "Hello, Atiliano—cómo le ha ido? Haven't seen you around these parts in many a moon."

"Gimme the burrito plate, green chile, couple of sopaipillas and coffee," the plump turncoat said in Spanish, surly as ever. Gloria replied, kiddingly: "Check, Roger, Wilco, Tory, George, Mary, over, under and out, Sr. Montoya."

On her way back to the kitchen to slap the order ticket on Henry's wheel, however, Gloria suddenly felt faint. Her knees buckled; and, in order to remain upright, she slumped against the refrigerator, grabbing onto the handle for support. Because it had just hit her:

*Atiliano Montoya?*

IT HAD BEEN ANOTHER ONE of those days. Having worked until 3:00 A.M. the night before, April awoke at 7:00— exhausted, sore-throated—when Tina crawled into bed and wriggled persistently against the tired curve of her body. When she sat up, her pillow was covered with hair; the entire top half of the bed was lousy with beautiful blond filaments. April felt bloated, ugly, puffing up again, veins constipated; the lump over her eyebrow had expanded. Jumping out of bed, she charged into the bathroom, dousing herself awake with cold water. April put on coffee water and returned to the bathroom, cautiously brushing her hair: already it was only half as thick as it had been several days ago. While fixing the kids french toast, she made several phone calls, solidifying the day's arrangements, lining up people to attend an evening town meeting about the new juvenile crime problem—teen-age hoodlums were going berserk. Then, deciding to wash away the headache and her blues with a bath, April turned on the tub: there was no hot water. Angrily, she checked out the heater in the utility room off the kitchen, discovering what she had feared was true: the ramshackle thing—it had been leaking now for years—had cracked, spilling water over its own burners, a lost cause.

"Hallelujah!"

At the kitchen table, over coffee and a cigarette, she wondered: What next? The house reeked of lethal fumes —Duane going ape in his room building airplanes, trying to murder them all with model glue. Tina staggered in screaming, a piece of glass in her foot—vicious residue from that jelly jar April had broken a while ago on the night George proposed. While Tina shrieked, April probed and poked with needles and tweezers, located and extricated the shard, and bandaged the kid up, ordering her to wear sneakers. Getting dressed then, April decided she was sick and tired of being at the mercy of servicemen— "To hell with my other commitments, I'll buy a new hot-water heater and install the thing myself!"

Accompanied by his dad and Juan Ortega, Anthony Martínez showed up. After she had laid down the day's *El Clarín* schedule, April commandeered their pickup and raced into town, purchased a new hot-water heater, brought it home, asked Anthony for help carting it inside, unpacked it, and, shooing them all away, she manhandled the thirty-gallon tank into the utility room and went to work disconnecting the old heater. Most of the fixtures had rusted together; April battled for hours simply to crack the connections with a plumber's wrench. As she struggled mightily, water and grime collected all over the place; soot fell from the vent pipe into her hair and eyes, black and greasy smudges soon decorated her face. April cursed, grunted, and screamed, ordering Anthony and Juan to beat it each time they offered aid or suggestions. "I'm sick of being at the mercy of you male chauvinist bastards whenever this kind of problem comes down!" Then she yelled for help moving the old tank after spending a fruitless hour trying to drain the heater—it was clogged by sand and pulverized insulation.

Drenched for years by slowly leaking hot water, the sagging floor was dangerously rotten. April hunted up a saw and stray pieces of lumber, measured out a new section, banged the old one apart with an ax, a hammer and a chisel, nailed in new boards, and scrambled into the crawl space, turning on the cold water for Anthony—he needed it for developing a roll of film. April wrestled the new heater into place, and commenced bending old copper tubing to fit the new apertures. She made a list of the elbows and nipples required, measured out sections of pipe needed to run an escape line from the pressure relief valve through the floor, spent twenty minutes knocking a small hole through the floor, made a sketch of the apparatus and each fitting, and returned to town, buying the accoutrements, having pipe cut and threaded. Back home, just starting to smear pipe dope on her first male connection, April read a label on her new hot-water tank, and learned that it was a natural-gas heater: her house ran on propane.

April shuddered, polished off a beer in six gulps, heaved the heater into its box, dragged it to the pickup, and drove back to the appliance store with her sad story. Fortunately, they could exchange it for a propane heater that had arrived that morning, same make and style but for a pressure relief valve located on the side instead of the top of the thing, invalidating her previous pipe-length calculations. At home, April set the new heater in place, remeasured escape pipes, and roared back into town before the plumbers closed to have new pipe cut and threaded. Home again, working feverishly, one fingernail turning blue, a Band-Aid covering a deep gash on another finger she'd cut on a rusted length of old flue pipe, April smeared threads with pipe dope, bent copper tubing to line up with nipples, and slowly hooked up the cold water, the hot water, then the relief valve, and finally the gas.

Triumphantly, she cut in water and gathered the *El Clarín*eros to witness her craftsmanship. As the tank filled, a hissing noise developed at the hot-water outlet elbow. And pressurized water suddenly gushed noisily from a tiny fissure in the elbow threads, spraying them all.

"Oh *shit!*" April scrambled through the trapdoor, dropped into the spiderwebbed crawl space, and attacked the cutoff valves. "I don't believe it!" she cried. "It isn't *fair!*"

Sitting in the hole looking up at their amused faces, she threatened: "Don't any of you say a word. Not one single word."

"I'm hungry," Duane hollered. "What's for dinner?"

"Me too," Tina whined. "Who's cooking supper?"

Supper already!

Anthony tackled the tank with April's wrenches; Juan cooked hash for dinner; April retired to the bathroom, cleaning up before the town meeting. Lacking hot water, she couldn't wash her sooty hair. No great loss, April figured, because if she did shampoo it the rest of her tresses would probably shed themselves, leaving her bald. April patted her head with a damp washcloth, washed her face, hands, and arms, thought she looked ghastly, splashed on more makeup than she had used in a decade, kissed her comrades good-bye, and raced off, late, as usual, to the meeting, where juvenile-probation officers argued with town councilmen and local realtors about teen-age criminals. Business people like Irving Newkirk wanted to form vigilante groups. Randolph Bonney, Lurleen Spivey, and Moe Stryzpk blamed crime on the freaks trickling into town. A few counterculturists representing some of the local communes complained that they were victims of the local rednecks' incipient fascism. Ben Updike, Chamisaville Inn bartender and anthropology Ph.D. from Massachusetts, accused the local "Spanish" of being racist. Everybody was uptight, nasty, petulant, off-balance, angry, ashamed, shrewd, stupid. Espeedie Cisneros and Canuto Tafoya expressed puzzlement about the helter-skelter urbanization of Chamisaville. In the middle of a heated speech castigating lily-livered Milquetoasts like Espeedie and Canuto for being against Progress, Al Lamont suddenly clutched his chest, turned purple, and, with a garbled apology, staggered out the door. Postmaster Onecimo Herrera angrily denounced outside Commie agitators and ordered them to go back where they came from. Judge Panky Santistevan called for relegalization of the death penalty. Alfredo GeeGee cried, "If God had meant for Texans to ski, he would of given them mountains!" Charley Gomez, Anthony Martínez's Anti-Electricity Coalition pal, threw in, "Custer died for your sins!" Some lawyers spoke—Bob Moose, Junior Leyba, DA Damacio Mares; also the police chiefs, Fernando Popper and Big Bill Baca. Nobody really knew why the juvenile crime problem existed, nor what to do about it. There were no funds. There was no desire. Amusing kids cost money and cut into profits. Town bureaucracy was understaffed and underpaid; it couldn't take care of regular services like garbage disposal, let alone develop programs to keep youngsters off the street. "I don't think our juvenile crime is out of hand," said Rodey McQueen. "It's just the normal result of the usual growing pains associated with economic progress."

Flakey Jake Martínez said, "Our children are dissatisfied, their lives have been cheated of traditional meanings. Ashamed of their aimless foundations, they mostly destroy the property of our own people, lashing out against their mothers and fathers and themselves as losers because they are afraid to attack the real enemies, the rich and powerful members of the Anglo Axis who have deliberately created this mess that suffocates communal initiative and makes enormous profits from the inarticulate situation."

April listened, teeth gritted, for two hours, keeping her mouth shut for once, too tired for a fuss, totally dispirited by the ease with which people could be driven apart, led astray, their energy wasted, duped into becoming ineffective political morons. What had George Jackson written? *Why do we make it so easy for them to kill us?*

When it was inconclusively terminated, and the right-wing faction of the meeting ordered everyone else to pledge allegiance to the flag, April just barely managed to stagger out of there.

In the car, she rubbed her eyes for a minute, then said, "All right, let's go, move it or lose it," and, snug in her old bomber jacket, sped down the highway to the old Martínez shack.

"George, I know we didn't make a date. If you're working, I won't bother you. I just feel slightly insane. I think I'd like to walk on the mesa, okay?"

"Come on—it's great to see you. But what's the matter? You look terrible."

"I'm not exactly feeling in the pink."

He opened the jacket and held her; she felt nothing. They kissed, April responding sluggishly, offering no resistance. George wanted to be rough. April could have used some gentle love—but what was the use? "I love you so much," he murmured passionately—trying to convince himself more than he meant to convince her? On her stomach, April accepted his loving from behind, wincing when he grabbed her hair. She started to murmur "Don't—" then slumped as he gave a startled cry: a big clump of strands had come loose in his hands.

"Wow." George stopped everything. "You weren't just kidding the other day, were you?"

April lay there, liking him inside her, feeling terribly

406

sad that all this was happening—but what could she do about it? Nothing at all.

George became gentle, cautious; his hands squeezed her breasts self-consciously, as if afraid of feeling a lump. Now he's making love with a corpse, April thought wearily. It has finally hit home that his glamour girl is in real trouble. Passionate, alluring, decadent, right-on politically, no-holds-barred April Delaney does not come free. As usual, there's a price tag. And all of a sudden he's getting a glimpse of what that price tag might be.

George came, then settled on top of her. But not heavily, rather diffidently, propping himself on elbows and one leg so as not to squash her. Previously, he would just flop and crush, and April had loved it that way.

Deferential his body; hesitant his breathing; cautious his hands. Sensing all that, April grew defensive and pissed off.

When without a word he got up, she rolled over, lit a cigarette, and sat on the mattress, her back against the wall. George left for the outhouse and stayed away a long time. Returning, finally, voice strained, he said, "It's a lovely night."

"I'll bet it is."

"Why are you hostile all of a sudden?"

"I'm not hostile, sweet. I just made a comment on your comment."

"Well, it was a huffy comment. The tone of your voice—"

"You know what I'm sick of, George? I'm sick of your self-pity. And I'm sick of your chickenshit—"

"And I'm sick of your self-righteousness!" he interrupted. "I'm sick of your goddam left-wing bullshit big-cheese I've-been-everywhere-I've-done-everything arrogance!"

"Okay. Entendu."

"French, no less. You're so cosmopolitan."

"Oh George, grow up." April went outside and stood shivering among the old bones, listening to the faint jingle of wind chimes. If she weren't losing her hair, if the hot-water heater hadn't been such a pain in the ass, if her eyebrow lump hadn't gotten bigger, if the meeting hadn't been so hopeless, if she weren't dying, none of this would have happened.

"If, if, if . . ." How could life be so suddenly transformed from magic realms to deranged banalities? She recalled Matthew Delaney on the deck of that boat in the storm, remembered herself asking how he expected to spot a whale in such a tempest, and clearly heard his retort: "If I want to *see* a fucking whale, I got to *look* for a fucking whale, no matter *what* the fucking weather. N'est-ce pas?"

"N'est-ce pas," she told him now, and went back inside, about to collapse from fatigue.

Considerately, George said, "I heard of some new people in town, some healers—you know? Maybe they could help."

"Oh screw that, sweet. No mumbo jumbo. The only person who can deal with this garbage is me. I don't want anybody else pulling their stupid psychic strings, not for thirty bucks an hour; not even for free. I'm not that undisciplined. I can get rid of this by myself."

"I wonder. Maybe someday you ought to accept help."

April stroked the guitar she had left there last time around, and sang hoarsely:

> *One fifth of whiskey, one fifth of rye,*
> *I don't need any help I can drink it all by—*
> *All by myself!*

Then she lay flat on the mattress, crossing hands on her belly, and murmured, "Cover me up, love, and do me a favor, don't talk anymore. Just let me sleep. And set the alarm at four A.M. so that I can fly home before the kiddies open their eyes and realize I ain't in our happy little nest."

AMONG THE NUMEROUS MOURNERS stood (or sat) the surviving founding fathers. Rodey McQueen, Bob Moose, Moe Stryzpk, Randolph Bonney, Claude Parker, and Karl Mudd were gathered around the grave in somber homage to Al Lamont—"One of our own."

Although bright sunshine made the event seem like a kind of toy death, ominous dark blue clouds were slouching off the Midnight Mountains, acetylene bolts of lightning flickered. In the valley and toward the western plateau, a limp calm prevailed. And for the first time all summer a rare humidity plied the normally arid atmosphere. Mourners sweated: the Episcopal minister Dagwood Whipple droned on cautiously; the day was so quiet they could almost hear the wingbeats of a maroon-and-gold butterfly as it flip-flopped gaily over their heads. A kind of fluff occupied the air, not from cottonwoods this late in summer, more likely from a species of dandelion. It drifted about like hallucinogenic snow, attaching itself to some sweaty faces, floating lazily into the grave. Children were delighted; their pudgy hands surreptitiously sought to capture any weightless puffs drifting near.

To the south, a kingfisher, rattling like a machine gun, flew by, looking for water full of fish.

Deference for the dead?—not Moe Stryzpk. He kept on smoking. Al Lamont's final hole in the ground was no more than a final hole in the ground. Moe had no fear of death—it was just another appointment. He had no plans, dreams, love affairs, or life lusts that death could interrupt. Thoughts about the existence or nonexistence of an afterlife bothered him not a whit. No sanguine reflections from Moe Stryzpk on the occasion of Al's planting. For Moe, funerals were a nonevent. His chest ached, his eyes throbbed—he wasn't used to the sunshine—that's all.

Next to Moe stood Claude Parker. In his seventh decade and suffering from bursitis, arthritis, bleeding gums, a weak heart—he had a pacemaker—and a colostomy, Claude was tired. He chain-smoked cigarettes, killed a third of a bourbon fifth every evening, and had recently confirmed, through X rays, that there were more spots on his lungs than on a leopard. His days, in short, were numbered. Whatever he had aspired to forty years ago was over. Relatively well-off, with a large house and various real-estate holdings, stocks and bonds . . . when he kicked the bucket Rachel would be sitting pretty. And his kid—no, he wouldn't disown George . . . what was the use?—would inherit, after taxes and after Susan and the kids were taken care of, almost fifty thousand dollars. Not bad, Claude sometimes mused, not that bad at all for a tank-town undertaker.

Despite a life preparing the dead, Claude had no special affinity for his own mortality. Although he had long since ceased to reason why, he wanted to live a much longer life than was apparently in his cards. He wanted to work, drink, and chain-smoke for another ten, fifteen, twenty years. If his body constantly ached, if the youthful idealism which had embalmed that whale and trucked it to Chamisaville was gone, still, a curiosity survived: he wanted to see what would happen next. Society he found terribly interesting. Weather, too, was stimulating. Claude also enjoyed being high on booze and he loved especially the early morning zap of a first weed. Little things, but they could make his world go round.

Claude enjoyed polishing up the corpses of his old friends as they were carted in. Nothing devious or perverse darkened his interest in their bodies. Somehow he just felt calm in the lab with old and scrawny, misshapen, pot-bellied cadavers, stretched out so quietly in the aluminum bright light. He often paused during his labor, clicked off whatever KKCV program was keeping him company, and, seated on an aluminum bar stool, smoking a cigarette despite the danger of blowing up his prep room, he reflected on this deceased's or that deceased's life. Maybe only yesterday he and Rachel had shared drinks at the Shalako with today's body. "Here today, gone tomorrow," Claude chuckled while blood drained, or the trocar gurgled, pickling an abdomen. From time to time he directed ridiculous little monologues toward the dead person, such as one he had directed at his old pal only yesterday:

"Well, Al, so it goes. I saw your kid Melissa in Safeway not an hour ago, eyes swollen, buying canapes for the guests. No more golf, my friend—you've checked into that Big Country Club up in the Sky." Claude loved to throw those clichés around when alone with a body. He'd get into the silliest moods and wind up chortling over some great, syrupy cliché: "Yessir, Al, it's the old Immortal Nineteenth Green for you, a pair of Pro-Flite wings, and an Adidas halo, the works, kid—you always deserved the best."

As the man at the finish of a hundred lives he had followed with interest, Claude enjoyed conducting a quiet summing-up during the private hours he enjoyed with an individual between the Fatal Blow and the Grave. Funny, how everybody shied away from his banal métier. Fearing its mystery, calling it morbid, always skittish about walking through a mortician's shadow—as if he possessed knowledge they feared to know, or performed grotesque feats of almost mystical derring-do in a forbidding Frankensteinian atmosphere. Cynthia McQueen had once asked him, sincerely, "Don't you ever worry about going insane?"

Insane? Claude laughed. He made sensational money performing moronic tasks on chunks of meat no more frightening than puppy dogs. Many *alive* people scared Claude, or at least made him very uncomfortable. But just let them die and he felt indiscriminately altruistic toward all. He patted their tummies, tweaked their noses, and good-naturedly chided them for driving a hundred miles an hour down the North-South Highway after thirteen highballs at the Los Amigos Supper Club as he sewed them back together again. Sometimes, for a laugh, when taking a cigarette break, Claude lit up two weeds, fixing one between the body's lips for company. Rachel was always catching him at it, though, bursting into the prep room to ask if he wanted to have dinner with the Mudds, or attend a movie with the Stryzpks. She would snatch the cadaver's cigarette, grind it out on the body's sternum, and flip it into the blood bucket, saying grumpily: "Claude, you're still a little boy, do you know that? When in God's name are you ever going to grow up?"

Grow up? *Please.* Even now, at his ripe old age, when a mature dignity should have tempered his bent for shenanigans, Claude nevertheless committed some acts going beyond the bounds of propriety. For example, he derived kinky pleasure from lipsticking messages on a cadaver's belly or buttocks, much as air force pilots and crew members were apt to crayon cheerful greetings on the noses of their atomic bombs: *Hi there, worms—Go to it!* Or: *Danger—Formaldehyde: If ingested, induce vomiting.* Or again: *Beat 'em, Panthers.* It had gotten to be a trademark with him, the Claude Parker seal of approval, his ongoing message to the underground. They might be as different as *God bless Barry Goldwater* or *A stiff in time saves nine,* but it gave Claude a little lift to put one over on the family, the mourners, society at large. The slogans hurt nobody; and, especially with deceased friends, it made him feel friendlier toward them, as if they too, in death, would appreciate the joke and enter the earth chuckling.

Claude felt bad about Al. He had enjoyed playing golf, and always liked shooting the political breeze on Sunday mornings at the plaza drugstore when he walked or bicycled in for the paper. With their wives they had played a million bridge games. And over the years Al had removed Claude's appendix, portions of his stomach, a large piece of colon, and had even stitched him up on occasion, especially one memorable time when a fishhook tore apart the undertaker's earlobe. He would miss Al, his raucous humor, his intrepid sporting. Claude also figured that once the old boys commenced keeling over, there was likely to be a rash of dying—a little hole in the dike made by Al

Lamont's departure, and pretty soon death might come boiling through. When it rains it pours, Claude thought, glancing at the premonitory clouds shading the mountains. Would Dagwood Whipple notice the approaching tempest, or, failing to glance up even once, would the oafish preacher keep them all sweating at their posts until the shit hit the fan?

The performance by Randolph and Helen Bonney, and Bob and Letitia Moose, would have drawn raves from Emily Post. Heads humbly bowed, eyes propitiously lowered, hands crossed in front of their crotches—contrite, reverent, stylishly grief stricken. Yet Bonney was aware only of a slight ache in his chest—angina?—and a gurgle in his stomach. The mind of Bob Moose was back at the office, flitting among briefs, suits, cases, wheels and deals, wondering how much time (and money) would be forfeited by this lumbering adiós to an old friend. A seed fluff settled against his nose. Before Bob could raise a liver-spotted hand to dab it off, the cheerful little thing made him sneeze, and the sneeze defrosted his business preoccupation, granting a sudden clear vision of the morning Prince of Whales coffee klatches where henceforward there would be an empty chair. With that, the old lawyer grew momentarily dour and sad. Half remembering a bit of schooldays' doggerel, Moose tried to put it together in his head: a poem, about kings and beggars . . . someday they all must . . . return to dust—blah blah blah. His crotch itched but he dared not scratch it, not here.

And Rodey McQueen, his head held high, gazed beyond the grave and the droning Whipple, across the mesa and the gorge to the friendly buttes and hills beyond. All his life a visionary, a man of strength and action, McQueen had no time for reflections on mortality. Too much to do: too many fascinating endeavors occupied his mind. Only that morning he had bragged to Cynthia: "I feel good, powerful, healthy, diabolical, Machiavellian, Gettyish. I'm more powerful than a million-dollar stud horse in a barnful of dripping mares!" He was a bit irritated at Al for forcing this pause in their daily routine; and for copping out early, as it were, when all of them still had much tread to wear down. McQueen had always figured he could live to be a hundred. Occasionally—and this was one of those occasions—he pictured himself still controlling the valley at that age, an old and venerated patriarch, a regular Moses on the mount who would take no crap from anybody, his brain as sharp as ever, a golf score somewhere in the high seventies, and a young filly for a mistress whom the robust white-haired old man—out-Russelling Bertrand Russell, out-Chaplining Charlie Chaplin, and out-Younging old Brigham Young himself—would plunder with his usual youthful abandon. Convinced he had almost a third of his life left to live, McQueen saw no point in preparing for his immediate future by reflecting in tranquility upon the immortality of the soul. So he kept his head high and pretty much blanked out the fact that his old pal lay in that ornate box about to go under for the first and final time.

After a while McQueen turned slightly, facing south where the hang-gliding people were "doing their thing," as the youngsters put it these days. Their colorful kites rippled off the nearby foothills like quicksilver-smooth silken birds.

Fascinated, despite his hatred of the sport and its aimless participants, the old man's attention was held by one apparatus locked in a particularly graceful flight, spiraling dramatically in a sort of updraft, soaring upwind until its buttery yellow shadow actually entered the graveyard and McQueen, to his abrupt horror, could see the sallow, slightly puffy features of the unhelmeted pilot who wore a soaking-wet Beethoven T-shirt, cutoff bleached dungarees, and blue-and-white Adidas sneakers. The moment McQueen caught his eye up there, Ralphito García took one hand off his guide bar and waved at the Muleshoe tyrant. As he did, a puff of air punched up under his tail, almost tipping him over in a somersault. The youth struggled frantically with his machine, seeming to lose all control; he started a dive toward the ground, wobbled, attempted to adjust his kite, and, heading straight for the mourners, finally managed to get his nose up slightly just as McQueen lurched free of his daze, shouting, "Look out!" as he stumbled over backward, throwing his arms up over his head to ward off the runaway kite that seemed intent upon ramming its sharp nose right through his heart.

But nothing happened.

After a few seconds of utter silence had gone by, McQueen lifted his arm and opened one eye. Astonished by his weird antics, all the mourners were staring at him, wondering why on earth he had toppled over like that.

"Excuse me," McQueen mumbled confusedly. "I guess the sunshine made me faint."

THAT SAME NIGHT, clad only in his underwear, Rodey McQueen loped slowly across his lawn, stumbling clumsily to a halt by the edge of his own swimming pool. A lasciviously plump nude woman, her white skin rippling like gelatined milk, floated in the emerald water. On the other side of the pool, smoking a cigar and wearing obscenely tight pink bathing trunks, Joseph Bonatelli sat in a black Naugahyde armchair, his flesh, his features, his spirit immobile. Never had McQueen encountered such a sexually attractive woman. Her odor alone was so hot it could have dented a fender. Wetting her ruby lips, she leered at him, then smiled provocatively. Kneeling by the pool edge, McQueen beckoned her to swim over. Her laugh, a cute little bitchy tinkle, mocked him as she paddled away, the water slopping over her enormous breasts like pornographic silk. He moaned. Across the swimming pool Bonatelli never stirred, registered no expression. McQueen circled to the end of the pool to catch her, but she paddled into the middle and, cupping her opulent breasts —floating on her back—offered them tantalizingly to him. McQueen hurried to the far poolside, but again, barely fluttering her lovely legs, the woman propelled herself out of reach. On his knees again, McQueen pleaded for gratification, so sexually aroused he could not stand the sight of her for another minute. But the woman turned her head very slightly, and, although she did not mean for him to catch it, McQueen saw the gesture anyway—she winked coyly at Joseph Bonatelli: *in cahoots the two of them!*

In his sleep Rodey McQueen stirred uneasily, disturbed by his dreams . . . and then by alien sounds, soft tampings of iron-shod hooves, ancient leather squeaking, the puttering breath of large animals, the slight rattle and vague clanking of bits shifting in equine mouths. McQueen's lips twitched; behind the lids his eyeballs jumped, bulging the fine wrinkled skin. A troubled moan came from his throat as he switched from his back onto one side. The vapors of a dangerous dream huffed along a slick subconscious surface like mist above a calm lake, never evaporating long enough for McQueen to view the reflection in his own not-so-placid depths. Was that indistinct human muttering in a foreign tongue Spanish? He cupped his privates, feeling abused, ridiculed, incensed by his own ignorance of the language. Somebody was talking, as people had always talked, behind his back, smiling when he caught their eye, innocent as Hades. Though it was night, he heard flies buzzing, and a swish-slap of rasping fibers. Odors, carried on dew-heavy breezes ruffling the second-story white curtains, were of drying sweat, dribbles of green foam, and horse manure; of clean flanks recently rubbed shiny by loving hands after a summertime drizzle. Human sweat, also: old armpits and unwashed crotches; dungarees so dirty they were caked shiny, torn at the knees. Bacon grease; tobacco spit; old leather. It was almost as if the puffs fluffing his curtains were bewhiskered and grimy. He sniffed muddy boots, bony buttocks hardly protruding beyond saddle-sore bones. A sulfuric spurt, and the troubled monarch's nostrils dilated; a moment later curlicues of cheap Mexican black tobacco wafted up from the lawn. Skin all aprickle, Rodey McQueen awoke, sat up, and looked at his wristwatch.

Head cocked, he listened . . . breath held . . . mouth open. Beyond his window, the summer night unfolded, rippled only by the sound of swimming-pool water lapping. Otherwise, framing the immediate silence, were dogs barking, a late-night car honking, the whoosh of souls leaving the hospital on the first stage of their journey toward heaven.

His heart, which had been beating rapidly, slowed down; his throat muscles relaxed. "Only a dream, McQueen." He checked his glowing wristwatch against the alarm clock's dial, set his timepiece so the two were synchronized, settled back, and for a moment adjusted his powerful aged flesh. Then, one licked lip and scratched earlobe later, his head clear and his fears flown, Rodey McQueen recaptured a gracious, well-fed slumber.

In the morning, Cynthia shook him awake before the alarm rang. "Dale, you won't believe what happened last night! We were invaded! Somebody entered the yard!"

"Don't be ridiculous. The gate was locked. How could they?"

"Come and see. I don't know how, but it's a mess, it's a scandal! I've already called Fernando Popper, Big Bill, and Gray von Brockdorff."

"Jesus Christ, why the cops? None of those men could pull a greasy string out of a cat's ear!"

"I thought it might be in their bailiwick. Hurry, put on a robe, here's your slippers—"

Frowning, McQueen covered himself and followed her downstairs, across the living room, out the french doors, onto the lawn.

"You've got to be kidding!" the astonished conman exclaimed.

Chewed up, trampled, shat upon by horses, his beautiful lawn was ruined. Puddles of urine on the tiles indicated where irreverent men had pissed into his swimming pool. And several calling cards glittered golden on the battered turf. McQueen stooped, gathered them up, and bounced them incredulously in his palm—three old-fashioned, black-powder, .45 cartridges with hand-molded lead bullets, the sort that were normally used in the hallowed, if relatively clumsy, Peacemakers of yore.

# The Most
# All-American
# Snowjob on Earth

ABE GALLEGOS WAS as disheveled as ever, his fingers nicotine stained, his glasses smudged, his shirt and tie askew, his shoes untied, his desk a mess, his personal life collapsing just around the corner in an unseen background. Abe nibbled on the tiny black cap of a ballpoint pen, prying the cap out and sticking it by suction to his tongue, then poking it back into the pen. Finally, he said:

"I'm sorry, April—I guess it's the Cytoxan. For what it's worth, the hair will grow back, maybe even better than before, probably in about six months."

He snapped off the arm tourniquet, and neither of them spoke while the Oncovin shot entered her vein. When it was over, April blinked a few times, took in a bunch of deep breaths, and said, "Abe, cancer is a pain in the ass."

"God is testing you," he said wryly.

"God, shmod."

They laughed together. Abe chucked the injection kit toward a gray metal wastebasket, but missed: the plastic hypodermic skidded across the floor.

"Maybe you been guzzling Coors, eating scab lettuce and drinking Gallo wine despite the boycotts," he said. "That's why you got in all this trouble."

"Qué no me chivas, cabrón!"

"Well, I dunno." Absentmindedly, Abe doodled on the back of his hand, drawing an Aztec symbol while April rubbed her sore arm. "I'm no philosopher, believe me. God don't mean beans to me. I watch a lot of people die, of course, and I manage to keep fairly removed from the whole thing—but it's not much fun. I never figured another way to be than to tell people straight what is going to happen, if that's what they want to hear. If they don't, I keep my mouth shut. There's no pie in the sky, that's for certain. And in the end what can you say anyway? Fuck it. You look tired, you need more rest, cut down on the booze and the cigarettes, conserve more energy, you're killing yourself. The cancer's no problem, we can lick that or stall it, we can buy you lots of time. But you should try stacking the odds more in your favor, I think. Lighten up a little."

"That's not the way I live, Abe."

"I know, I know. Rarely do I get people in here with your kind of vitality. But from the looks of you, compared to last time down here, I think you're squandering a little. Perhaps it's time to treat experience with a trifle more deference."

"You're beginning to sound like a little old lady."

"In the rotten and devious corazón of every cancer specialist there dwells a little old lady," he joked feebly.

April said, "You were going to give me the name of a wigmaker."

"Sure, of course. . . ." He tore paper off a notepad, wrote down the name and the address, and handed it over. "Just ask for Shirley, she's my man; the best in the business. You'll like each other. She's handled a million patients of mine. Gives me kickbacks all the time."

"Abe, this whole thing gives me the creeps."

"Join the crowd."

"What about another operation?" April asked, touching the lump on her eyebrow.

"Not right now—it isn't crucial yet. The growth seems stabilized. Let's wait until the chemotherapy is finished, then see what happens. Measure it regularly, of course, and call me if it suddenly gets much bigger."

They stood up together, giving each other strong abrazos, April squeezing him until he grunted. Then she turned and fled, heading straight for the wigmaker.

A buxom lady in her early sixties, covered with pancake makeup and wearing a teased peroxide blond creation of her own making, Shirley chattered good-naturedly while she combed and fussed over the wigs April tried on, putting her client at ease immediately by chortling irreverently: "Honey, I love you, I really do, 'cause you cancer patients are making me rich. Abe, that old devil, he'll probably stop by 'round closing time to cash in on another customer sent my way by trying to cop a pinch of my pretty buttocks—honestly, that man! I swear, child, he's a real honest-to-goodness flirt, he certainly is. Don't know where ever he could have come from. Lord, sweetie, in *this* one you look purty as a pistol!"

Afterward, April walked through several museums and an art gallery, browsed for an hour in a large bookstore, bought a copy of last Sunday's *New York Times* at the La Fonda Hotel, and sat in the lobby reading for a while. Then she went downtown to an old Mexican café and dined on an enormous enchilada, several sopaipillas, and three Dos Equis beers. As darkness gathered, she drove north of town to the outdoor opera, purchasing a standing-room-only ticket for that night's performance of *Salome*. And for three hours April stood in the crisp, late summer air, sick to her stomach from the shot, and feeling weird in her new wig, watching the melodramatic fare and loving every minute even though the production stunk.

On the road home at midnight, April flung off the wig and drove like a madwoman, stopping three times in the gorge to throw up. But in between the vomit calls she sang Spanish and Mexican songs at the top of her voice along with a Capital City radio station, at once exhausted and high, the journey north to Chamisaville her favorite drive on earth.

Pulling out of the gorge onto the high flat mesa aiming north toward town, April steered into a roadside rest area and got out of her car. The plain was bathed in light; the sky dead-clear and overloaded with stars. Chamisaville twinkled beautifully beneath the enchanted mountains. And, isolated in that dark expanse south of Mota Llano and Borregas Negras, she could just make out a tiny light in the old Martínez shack.

Suddenly, the wig stirred an excitement inside April. It looked good, she could get used to anything, it was possible to go bald and actually survive! Amazing, how quickly she could adjust! I'll get two or three different styles, she thought. Long hair, short hair, Texas beehive, and braids to my waist! Out of my way, all you tonsorial fetishists, I don't drive with my horn!

A shooting star streaked over the mountains. Jesus Etcetera was alive and well and mobilizing an army. Each day, hope sprang eternal in Virgil Leyba's chest. There were no excuses, ever, for any protracted moping. And the lights of the tiny communities up north were like phosphorous in a mystical ocean wave forever frozen halfway toward glory.

AROUND FIVE O'CLOCK the next day, FBI agents Chet Fulton and Len Goodwin sauntered up to April Delaney's portal. She met them at the screen door, her heart pounding—an infuriating lack of control. Len Goodwin said, "Howdy." Chet Fulton touched two fingers against his hat brim, nodding slightly. And April just stood behind the screen door, arms folded, confronting them with what she hoped would pass for relaxed, if slightly hostile, indifference.

"Mind if we ask a couple questions?" Len Goodwin said. Appalled by being so downright scared of these bullies, April snapped back, "Yes, I'm afraid I mind very much. I have nothing to say. Sorry for being impolite, but I really don't want to talk with you."

"Well now," Chet Fulton drawled, "you realize that just makes our job a little bit harder?"

"Not hard enough," April said quietly, ashamed by her quavering voice. "I'm sorry." Oh, how despicable that apology sounded! But it had been a reflex—automatic—that she seemed unable to control.

"Actually," she amended meekly, "I'm not sorry at all."

"Well—" Len Goodwin shrugged good-naturedly, making a so-be-it gesture with one hand. And then, turning sideways to appraise her apple trees and the small pasture beyond, Chet Fulton made a slight, offhand comment: "Nice place you got here." And that statement profoundly chilled April because she sensed more threat in it—of murder, harassment, and heavy politics—than if they had both pointed revolvers, flashed badges, and growled, "You're under arrest."

Chet Fulton's cheery observation carried within it, implicitly, a menace to her place, her friends, her children.

419

And as she watched them strolling laconically back to their nondescript Pontiac, April almost panicked, wondering: What happens to my kids if I'm arrested? How would I go underground in a town this size if I had to? How could I escape, obtain false papers, cross borders, reach a foreign sanctuary if those pleasant relaxed bastards with their casual airs and sunny dispositions really wanted to bring my ineffectual activities to a halt?

Jesus, she really must have been physically fragile, or worn out, to get this paranoid over a single brief visit from those two morons!

A thousand friends would care for Duane and Tina. April had always stressed to the kids that they had a hundred mothers and fathers, sisters and brothers; the only true family was universal, uncircumscribed by the limited loyalties and jealousies encouraged by insular, alienating America. Yet if a catastrophe befell her, she would fear terribly for their futures, mistrusting the ability of close friends to love them well, even while understanding, intellectually, that many friends might be able to give them better homes, a less confusing love. Although the truth of the matter was that her parents would take the kids, and raise them to be good little Fascists within the corporate American state.

That cavalier, low-key federal pair had made her sick to her stomach. April sat down, lit a cigarette, and took a drink, calming herself. Then she drew a hot bath, soaking for ten minutes, letting the tension drain.

They were a reminder that somebody worried about her activities, somebody was watching, keeping track. However insignificantly, she counted; files in cabinet drawers somewhere no doubt contained a profile of her life, photographs for identification, and a list of people to whom she was close, worked with, and loved. They probably had every copy of the *El Clarín*.

Their mere arrival and departure had made her feel so vulnerable. Suppose they planted dope in the garage, or threw it out a window into the front field, returning later with local law-enforcement officers to frame her on a narcotics charge?

Of course, if they really wanted to do that, she could not combat them. They could simply pick her up, produce a quantity of one "controlled substance" or another in a courtroom, claiming to have found it on her property, and that would be that.

All the same, after the bath she ought to walk around the place, searching for . . . who knew exactly? Marijuana plants, probably, that might have been seeded months ago by agents stopping by while she was out.

The paranoia their brief visit nourished would linger: she had confronted the FBI before, in New York, and knew the feeling. It would be impossible to wash her life of their vibes. Now, even after only an hour in town, on her return she would always sniff for their scent in the air, and make a nervous little swing through the house, flicking her eyes over everything, checking loosely to see if some article had been rearranged, taken, disturbed.

If I'm ever arrested, I'll call Virgil, she thought, slouching deeper into the tub. He's my hope, he would gather my friends, he would take care of the kids, he would make sure the chickens were fed and that Duane's tropical fish didn't die. And he would make sure Juan Ortega or Anthony Martínez read the Hardy Boys or the Babar stories to the children before bed, he would tell them to brush their teeth, he would see that their clothes were mended for school and that Duane put mothballs in his butterfly mounting boxes.

"This fucking slaughterhouse!" she shouted angrily: those two agents had ruined her day.

Out of the tub, wrapped in an enormous crimson towel, April gingerly brushed her remaining real hair. Abruptly, something about the process of prolonging the inevitable made her furious, and she slashed hard on the downstrokes, deliberately jerking out strands: within minutes, gasping from the effort and from the shock of seeing herself bald, she had brutally completed the job.

It was so awful April lost her breath and plunked down on the toilet lid. Immediately, she jumped up and locked the bathroom door so that the kids wouldn't barge in and see her like this.

She sat on the seat horrifiedly touching her scalp, muttering, "I really don't believe all this is actually happening to *me.*"

After ten minutes, calmed down a little, April approached the mirror again. Fearing to hasten the hair loss, she hadn't washed her head in two weeks. Her scalp itched, it was filthy. Gratefully, April bent over the sink, soaped hard and rinsed off, and then faced her gleaming self, relieved to have made the final plunge. She adjusted her wig, then gathered all her old hair in a paper bag and stashed the bag in the top of her bedroom closet. But a moment later she angrily retrieved the bag, shoved it into the wood-burning half of the kitchen combination-stove, set it on fire, and went outside to avoid the smell as her hair went up in smoke.

Thank God it was over: time to get on with more important aspects of her daily existence.

CHARLOTTE LEYBA was trapped in a nightmare impossible to escape. For hours she faced the bedroom mirror confronting her ineffectual beauty. Entire mornings she wasted putting on different outfits, and she would stare at them interminably; herself, her image, her life. The colors she chose were soft, radiant pastels, blues which seemed to have been aged by centuries and a master's hand, greens that deferred to her body like a shy spring, grays that encircled her like summer mist, oranges softening into faint dawn-golds. Her body was perfectly proportioned, her skin youthful, her face as delicate and beautiful as a Balinese dream. Her tangled raven hair was abundant, voluptuous. Imprisoned within this fragile and classic beauty, Charlotte was also a captive within Chamisaville, her home. No strengths she possessed could deal with the shackles. Shedding her clothes, she lay naked on her bed in the pastel airy room among her robes and blouses and scarves like a sorrowful city girl flung from the twentieth floor who had crash-landed gently and died in a rainbow of mute, deferential color, without a noise.

Charlotte smoked, but did not drink. She had a dozen books from the library—Mary Renault, R. F. Delderfield, Taylor Caldwell—but only read snatches, unable to concentrate. She paced around the house, dressed in her bra and panties, noiseless on thick wall-to-wall carpets. Lying in summer sunshine she tried to relax and believe that the torment would end, that one day Junior would come home with a sudden compassion in his fingertips and his eyes, sink to his knees and tenderly kiss the swell above her pubic hair, begging forgiveness and outlining plans for a new life.

Trapped in a situation she did not understand, Charlotte awaited a different tide. She had no idea how to change things herself, believing that destiny, like weather, was something she could affect, although sooner or later it was bound to change. She asked God to purge the lethargy in her bones: she asked Him to deliver her from this evil; she begged for Junior's return.

Once, twice, three times weekly she opened the left-hand bottom drawer in Junior's desk, removed the manila envelope, carried it upstairs, and spread the contents across their bed, noting if new items had been added to the tormented file. She tried puzzling out the disparate pieces of information, but could never forge connections that would make it entirely meaningful. And hated herself for prying on her husband, a man whom she began to see as a figure in a Greek tragedy.

She thought about suicide, convinced that her life juices were steadily draining, aiming her body toward a dreary and uneventful finish. And her beauty arose with her each morning, a mocking apparition in the mirror. Charlotte faced her body, honestly awed, knowing her flesh to be special and almost otherworldly. So why had there been no prince charming in her life, no Monaco, no nothing?

This was it.

Spread out on their bed were the contents of that manila envelope: several passionate letters Junior had written to April Delaney—April McQueen—many years ago, and a few that April had penned in reply—lurid, arrogant, joyful —oh Lord, the energy they had shared! A few of Junior's letters—dismayed, disoriented—had been returned marked *Address Unknown*—in April's own hand. There were a few dance cards from high-school proms, and a packet of amateur photographs, developed in a home darkroom, of teen-age April McQueen in the nude, or in glamour-girl poses in silk underwear, in a bathing suit. A blue horse-show ribbon she had obviously given him, along with some pressed flowers, a lock of blond hair, a lipstick imprint on a handkerchief, a newspaper clipping about April as homecoming queen. Other photographs had been taken more recently. Grainy, shot from a distance and blown up, they caught April in her own yard, unaware of the camera, on her lawn in an abstract moment, or getting out of her car with grocery bags in each arm. A few had her on the plaza, among crowds; obviously, the pictures had been taken by a secret observer. Every issue of the *El Clarín* was present in the file. And a series of almost mystical letters, riddled with incomprehensible terms, discussed April and the *El Clarín* and the Northland Grazing Association and vague projects and unnamed people, and they were signed by somebody named Chet Fulton, a person

Charlotte had never heard of. Finally, carbon copies of letters from Junior to that Chet Fulton mentioned April Delaney, her patterns and background. Yet they too were so vague, and couched in such specialized innuendos, that Charlotte could make no sense of them at all.

Of course, the whole thing was evil. Charlotte didn't understand, nor did she want to understand. Drawn to the material, she refused to add up the implications, choosing, at the same time she was afraid, to be lazy. After all, the nightmare had to end, her inertia would dissolve and disappear, her loneliness would recapture Junior's heart, and she would save them both from "a fate worse than death."

Charlotte had nobody to turn to. The world was imploding, she couldn't breathe; her loveliness was wasted; she wondered if she would ever be able to think straight again.

APRIL COULD FEEL IT going wrong even before she arrived at the old Martínez shack around sunset time of a real dog day. Yet, needing the contact and badly wanting sex, April wished to exist in an isolated situation out there for a while, away from town, home, the *El Clarín*. A few beers, a hike across the mesa to the gorge, a dozen deep breaths would cleanse her soul, setting her up for another go-round. Better yet, they might simply make love and then she could lie on the mattress while George worked at his desk, drowsing as he shuffled papers and tapped his toes against the floor, and the coyotes barked outside. But April had presentiments of disaster even before leaving her own house, kissing the kids good-bye, giving Anthony a big hug for staying with them—she'd had presentiments, but ignored them. After all, hadn't she ignored them all her life?

Cool when she came through the door, George swiveled in his chair—but didn't rise. Kneeling beside him, she smiled and joked, "Don't get up love, don't stop working, I'll just give you a blowjob and fly back home, you mustn't say a word."

He softened, holding her face in both hands, looking down, soberly confronting her bloodshot eyes, slightly puffed skin, graying face—"You're working too hard, April. You ought to quit for a while. Take it easier."

"I'm okay. But I really have no desire to talk now— that's the honest truth. I just came by for a bit of your luscious bod. Then I might take a nap while you create great art. Ultimately, I'll disappear without a sound, leaving no traces."

"That's dumb." George smiled. "You know something? —you're a real oddball."

"I'm the most mercurial event that ever hamstrung your existence." April unzipped his fly and fluttered her tongue against the tip of his penis. "Hmm, such an enormous cock. . . ."

"I keep telling you it's a quarter-inch under the American average."

"Big deal."

George held her head gingerly, afraid of dislodging the wig and embarrassing them both. Eyes closed, April sucked gently, caressing his balls. An easy quietude captured the moment. When she felt him on the verge, April said, "Don't come, I want to make love." She led him to the mattress and they began. It felt awkward though, their bodies bulky and cumbersome, their moves graceless. Out of sync with each other, locked into uncomplementary rhythms, they fumbled disconcertedly, vaguely annoyed and unnatural, trying too hard. The wig bothered George— their sex act seemed perverse, a little grotesque. April immediately picked up on his phony ardor. Too strenuously he pretended.

They struggled for a minute, hoping to get it right. On her back, April wanted to hold him close; instead, embarrassed by eye contact, George turned her over, entering from behind; he stuck his thumb in her anus. "Not there, not tonight," April whimpered. "I'm sore, love, I ache all over." Ignoring her, George bumped roughly, shoving her around, and when she raised one hand to steady her wig, he pushed the hand away. "Why don't you take that thing off, April? I hate it."

"Oh no you don't. Not on your life. Nobody sees me bald while we're making love—no way."

"But it's stupid. I'm afraid to touch you or knock you around. I'd rather you were bald."

"No you don't. I'd disgust you, I know. Frankly, already it feels as if I do. So, I'm sorry, but that's the way it's gonna be. Maybe someday in the future when we're both used to the idea, I'll take it off when we screw. Not right now, though, I can't bear the thought."

George yanked off the wig and tossed it across the room.

They stopped. "Oh shit," April muttered in a small voice. "What was the point of that?"

"I'm not going to watch you keeping one hand on your head all the time, that's all."

"You just killed any enjoyment I could possibly get out of this."

"Too bad." Hostility really flooded his voice. "I don't care."

"Okay, time's up, I'm going home." April started to rise, but he pinned her arms and sat on the backs of her thighs, refusing to let her move.

"George, don't be cute, let me up."

Instead, he thrust into her.

"You *bastard!*" April bucked hard, throwing him sideways, turned over quickly, and had half scrambled off the mattress when he tackled her, knocking her back against the wall, and held her so tightly she thought for sure he would crush her ribs.

"What the fuck has got into you?" April asked warily.

"Just shut up. Don't talk for a minute," he threatened quietly, panting and sniffling a little, beginning to cry.

For about five minutes they held that position in silence, until his grip relaxed, his breathing evened out. Cautiously, April slipped her hand behind his head, asking, "George, are you okay? What's the matter, man? What's going on here?"

"I don't know. Everything is a mess."

"So what else is new? But not between us, sweet. We have a thing that can be lovely—even without hair. It exists apart, it's wrapped up in this safe cocoon on the mesa—"

"Oh shut up!" He pushed off, lunging to his desk and opening a drawer, and returned with six photographs, blown up into eight-by-tens, which he slapped into her hands—of naked April, age sixteen, the pictures she had taken of herself in the mansion basement . . . and sent to Charley . . . and given to who else?

"Where did you get these, George?"

He slumped into his desk chair. "An FBI agent named Chet Fulton gave them to Susan yesterday. He told her about our affair—you wouldn't believe all the details he gave. I don't believe them myself. I don't believe that something like this could really happen. In Chamisaville, no less! They must really want to break your ass. What are you people doing over there at the newspaper, making bombs? Are you responsible for burning those Forest Service signs? Susan wants me out of the house, of course, right away. And for good. She wants a divorce—"

Speaking fast, April said, "You can't let them do it, George. You can't let them be successful. You can't get scared and let everything fall apart and believe their version of everything and just play into their hands out of your own fright—you can't do that, love, don't let it happen, that would be too awful if they actually hurt you and Susan and your kids and you and me just exactly the way they want to hurt us all."

"What about those pictures?"

"What pictures?"

"The pictures you're holding in your hand!"

"These?" April glanced at them dopily. "I don't know where they got them, I really don't. I took them of myself when I was sixteen, I sent a few to that guy, Charley, the first man I married, when we were writing to each other."

"What do you mean, you took them yourself?"

"With a camera. Down in the mansion basement. You know how it works—there's a time device on the camera and I'd set it and then run over and strike a pose and ten seconds later the shutter clicked. I had my own darkroom, everything—hey! Wait a minute, what is this? What am I on—some kind of witness stand?"

"How did the FBI know about *us*? That's what I'd like to know. And how did they come across these photographs?"

"How do I know? It's the American way, George. I'm sorry. Believe me, I didn't send them a letter."

"It's because of what you do—your politics, the *El Clarín*—that they entered our affair this way!"

"Let's not shout at each other, okay? Let's try to keep cool, otherwise we'll come to blows, and they will have gotten us to act exactly as they want us to act."

"It's gonna cost me my marriage, you son of a bitch!"

"Well isn't that just tough tits, Lord Byron!"

"You sound so sympathetic."

"For the past three months I've only listened to you run down how pathetic that marriage has been for the last fifteen years. I've only held your hand and your head and your cock and commiserated at every turn, and given you the best loving you ever had, and kept my mouth shut while you told me about having kids with darling Susan, and about hiking up in the wilderness areas with darling

Susan, and about how wonderful the lovemaking was in the beginning with darling Susan—"

"What about you, April? You rub my nose in Charley Epstein and you still wear his fucking bomber jacket, you flaunt it in my face! I know all about you screwing Junior Leyba and J. B. LeDoux and who knows how many other millions of assholes in this town before you ran away—people say Judson Babbitt and Staughton van Peebles and a half-dozen other old faggots also got in their licks! Then there was how many millions in New York City? Let's see —Tim Lanahan, the distinguished poet, hubby number two! Not to mention the famous painter, and the actor, a dozen one-night stands, the musician, the art critic—I'm gonna have to take off my shoes in a minute and start counting on my toes! Then off to Europe with—who was it fucked you on the boat? A famous sculptor, a big businessman, a notorious critic? I don't remember, I wonder if you do either, there were so many! Then there were a half-dozen bohunks in Paris, followed by a brain-damaged Spanish refugee, followed by a Hungarian freedom fighter, an Italian count, a couple of bulls in Madrid, a nigger in New York City—"

*"Shut up god damn you!"*

George halted, staring out the widow, horrified by his own explosion, the whole situation.

"You're not gonna blame me for your divorce," April said slowly. "That just isn't my fault, Charley, I'm not responsible."

"What do you mean, 'Charley'? Who's 'Charley'? My name isn't 'Charley.' That's your *first* husband's name. Or your *third* husband's name. Or the *tenth*, who can remember?"

"You don't have to be this ugly, George. It isn't necessary."

"You called me 'Charley.' *My name ain't Charley!*"

"Well, then, excuse me please, it must have been a slip of the tongue!"

"Why don't you put your wig on? I can't *stand* that bald head!"

"Who took it off in the first place? Who threw it across the room?"

"I don't care who did what, just put it back on would you please before I kill you or something!"

"Oh wow!" April retrieved the wig, settled it on her head, dressed, and lit a cigarette, ashamed, humiliated,

428

furious. They stewed, alternately ejecting muffled exclamations, trying to quell anger in order to face each other more temperately before everything was ruined.

"I don't want to be with you anymore," George said eventually.

"Looking for an easy out? Terrified of responsibility? Scared of cancer, are you? Suddenly the wonderful alluring April McQueen is a bald bitch with a lump in her eyebrow and the FBI on her ass, and it's time for all Godfearing cowards to beat a hasty retreat."

"I never believed you could be so ugly."

"I was just thinking the same thing about you."

"You yourself said I was too innocent. You yourself said any time I wanted it to stop, all I had to do was say 'stop.' Okay, now I'm saying it."

"Saying what?"

"You know."

"Yeah, but I want to hear you say it."

"All right. Stop."

"That's it? You didn't leave anything out? You didn't forget to say, 'Thanks for being a great lay,' or anything like that?"

"Come on April. Don't be so cruel."

"*Me* cruel?"

"Yeah, you."

"Oh, I'm sorry. Excuse me, George. I didn't mean to be nasty. Please forgive me, sweetie. It was so wonderful while it lasted. I'll always be in debt to you for the lovely time you gave me while we were together."

"Jesus Christ you're some bitch! You get first prize hands down!"

"If you can't stand the heat, George, stay out of the kitchen!"

"All right, I'm out of it!"

"Thank God!"

She smoked. His back to her, he sat at the table. April finished the cigarette, immediately lit another one, located a bottle of cream sherry she had brought down a week ago, wiped a jelly glass clean with her shirttail, and poured a drink. When she had finished the drink, April took a deep breath, saying as gently as possible:

"Lovebird, you can't let them just ruin everything."

"I'm sorry but I don't want to deal with you anymore," he whispered. "It's too complicated. I didn't bargain for all this emotional and political complexity."

"I can understand that, I guess—nobody ever does bargain for what they get. But we have a good thing, love, and I don't think good things should end so suddenly, not because of cancer, or the FBI, or anything else. We've shared a nifty vitality, George, and believe it or not I cherish our affair, I really do. I love the giddy fun we've had, and it's been sheer pleasure to make love with you. Believe me, I don't know where you got it from, but you have a rare sexual intensity, and I don't want to lose access to it, not right now, not because I'm sick or because you're scared of my politics, or because you are afraid of some government flatfoot, or because you are afraid of breaking up a marriage that has made you miserable for fifteen years. I'm a fighter, I don't give in easy. And I know when you have something of value, like we have had, something that special and erotic and just filled with joy, that you don't kill it simply because the going gets tough."

"I've got a school job. They'll probably fire me."

"Not Claude Parker's son—who are you trying to kid?"

"If the FBI gave Susan those pictures they must have duplicates ad infinitum. They can hand them to anybody in town. I can't stand the thought of that. I hate you for allowing it to happen, I really do. It's incredible. I don't believe you actually spread around naked pictures of yourself."

"I can't claim that wasn't a stupid thing to do. But it happened long ago. What else can I say? Now they'll use them to hurt you, and to try and destroy me, wreck all my credibility, drive me away from this miserable town, solve all their problems with any cheap shot they can deliver. But I won't let it happen, George. I really won't. I'm tougher than that. I came home to make my stand, and come hell or high water I'm gonna make it."

"No doubt you will. You don't know when to quit, you really don't."

Standing behind him, April kneaded his shoulders.

"I love you, George. Not too much, though—I'm not going to trap you. I for sure don't want to marry you. I just want to protect this intimacy that we have for a while because it's one of the few cherishable things in both our current lives."

"It doesn't matter if I say 'stop' or not, does it? You really didn't mean that when you said it, did you?"

"I meant it. But things always change."

"One of the things I can't stand is thinking about all the

adventures you had, all the men you were with when you were beautiful and healthy and full of energy. And now, when finally we are together, suddenly all your hair falls out, you got lumps galore, you got that fucking fatal disease inside."

"It isn't fatal, dammit! And with just one eye, one leg, no hair, one tit, and a naked twat, I'd still be more of a pistol, love, than anybody else you ever met in your life!"

George reached back and squeezed her breasts, and they both looked at their reflections in the window beyond his desk.

"I suppose the real problem is I'm scared stiff," he said.

"Who isn't?"

"I feel so queasy. I've never been frightened like this before."

"I haven't either."

"What's going to happen?"

"I don't know."

"See, the trouble with me," George said quietly, "is for some reason when I was a kid growing up in this rustic little haven I felt very safe because I really believed somebody had their finger on the right thing, you know? A few adults, or brilliant persons, they were guiding it all in the right way, seeing that it went smoothly, and they were the guardians, too, of a really moral way of living. So all you had to do was comply with this moral way of living in order to always have your foot on a base of absolute safety. And life would never be at all ambiguous, or dangerous, or contradictory. . . ."

"That's the most basic—and most all-American—snow-job on earth."

"Christ. You're certainly a fighter."

"When the going gets tough, the tough get going."

"Oh fuck off!" he blurted, squeezing her breasts so hard she yelped—and, startled by the sound, they both laughed.

LEN GOODWIN AND CHET FULTON, aided by Big Bill Baca and Fernando Popper, broke into Benny LeDoux's Dynamite Shrine cubicle, grabbed the edge of the junkie's bed, and tipped it over, dumping him onto the floor. Before Benny could shriek or raise an arm to defend himself, Len Goodwin yanked him upright by the hair and Chet Fulton grabbed one ankle: together, the two cops swung Benny into the wall, where he hit with a rough thud that knocked down a plastic landscape. "Hey—!" Benny blurted, even as the two FBIs grabbed for him again, Len Goodwin slapping his lips with the back of one hand, Chet Fulton kicking him in the butt. Furiously, Big Bill grabbed the skinny mattress, flipping it away from the bed, then he spilled drawers from the bureau and flung them across the room at the sink, up against the cupboards, and through a window. Glasses and plates in the dish rack shattered, a chair tipped over, its legs splatting apart. Chet Fulton and Len Goodwin jerked Benny onto his feet and shoved him over the bed into a plywood closet door, which buckled. In shock, gasping, Benny tumbled to the floor just as Big Bill slammed the bureau on top of him. Amazed by his fellow lawmen going berserk, Fernando Popper held back, slightly sick to his stomach. Len Goodwin heaved the bureau off Benny, grabbed the junkie's skinny arm, and wrenched him half erect as Big Bill kicked him in the stomach. *"I don't got no shit!"* Benny screamed, gagging, vomiting. *"I'm clean!"* "Bullshit!" they replied. Chet Fulton knocked the cheap closet door off its hinges, and grabbed Benny's clothes, ripping them off hangers, flinging them willy-nilly about the room. Big Bill crashed the bedsprings into the mess made by jumbled bureau drawers. Then he flung open the kitchenette cupboards, scooping the contents off shelves onto the floor. Glass jars busted; he stomped apart boxes of cereal, powdered milk, and crackers and booted them all over the destroyed room. Len Goodwin had Benny by the throat with one hand; grabbing a tennis shoe, he jammed the toe into the junkie's mouth. Benny's eyes bulged; he tried squirming free, but on either side Big Bill and Chet Fulton held him down, twisting his arms and legs, everybody panting as Chet Fulton snarled: "We'll kill you, Benny . . . unnerstand? This ain't nothing compared . . . to what we *could* do . . . you got that? This is peanuts. This ain't even for starters. This is just a calling card, see? In case we decide some day to hurt you. Is that . . . fucking clear?" Big Bill banged the heel of the tennis shoe and Benny arched, unleashing a muffled scream. Chet kneed him, not too hard, in the groin. "No more dope off the pot plane, Benny, you got that? We already talked with Skeezix McHorse, and he understands perfectly— you dig? This is it, no more, never again. No cutesy little drops out on the mesa, no nothing, no extra . . . no extra cuts, no skimming, no more cheating. Got that?" Big Bill cuffed him alongside the ear. "Everything clear? Everything hunky-dory? Do we make ourselves understood? No more double-cross, no more funny business, no more nothing—you savvy you little piece of despicable birdshit? All right—" They slammed his head against the wall, gave him final painful digs, then all arose in unison, dusting off their hands against their pants, tucking in shirttails. Big Bill's foot kicked against an object, he retrieved it—the .25 automatic Benny had purchased at Irving Newkirk's pawnshop with money Irving had paid for the engagement ring Benny found in his wall. Big Bill aimed it right at Benny's chest, shouting, "What's this, a fucking *gun*? A fucking *illegal* gun? *What are you doing with a fucking illegal gun, LeDoux, you planning to shoot somebody?*" And, as Benny lifted one hand to ward off the bullets, Big Bill emptied the clip into the wall two feet over his head. Then he leaned down until his face was inches away from Benny's nose and snarled, "One other thing, dumbbell. If it turns out we want to use you for something in the future, I expect you to say 'Yes sir,' and hop to it, unnerstand? Cross us again like you already crossed Junior Leyba that time and I'll come in here and stab needles in your eyeballs, Benny! I'll tie a rope to your cock and a brick to the other end of the rope and I'll throw the fucking brick through the window—*is that clear?*"

With that the four cops dashed out to their unmarked car, spun around in the courtyard and peeled away, nearly running down Little Kid Lujan. The entire operation had taken less than three minutes.

AND ICARUS SUAZO AWOKE again from a nebulous but menacing dream about Joe Brady and Win Potter, instantly aware of murder afoot. A slight scraping sound in his chimney, the creak of misplaced toes overhead, warned him at once of the danger: but nothing plopped into the fireplace.

Then he realized they were lowering an object, and, from the sound, he judged it to be glass—a large bottle, some kind of jug.

A smell followed, one he recognized instantly, of damp raw lime, fulminating, and all at once he could hear it as the jug lowered into the room, fizzing and bubbling as the wetted lime generated gas within the tightly capped gallon bottle. A second before it blew the old man gripped the edge of his thin mattress and yanked it up against himself as he slid into the wall. The jug popped with a loud, strangely empty bang, and jagged pieces of lethal glass sprayed into his ceiling, walls, and floor; they ripped into the mattress, tearing out large, cottony chunks; and one small shard sliced a half-inch off his middle fingertip.

Icarus howled, flopped out of bed and rushed to the door, cutting his feet on the jagged crystal embedded in his dirt floor, and hobbled onto the roof, his hand, with the severed fingertip, held aloft, calling down upon their heads the wrath of all their mutual gods.

Sarcastically, the Pueblo echoed his challenge: nothing in the shadows changed, nobody scurried guiltily away. If everyone was asleep or awake, it did not matter. Icarus wavered slightly, his arm held high to halt the bleeding, his heart beating dangerously fast. The sky was peppered by stars so brilliant they seemed a hallucination. Coyotes barked, quick and cynical—out hunting mice. To the south, Chamisaville lights twinkled against the silently booming backdrop of midnight velvet, more mountains. And a bobcat trotted nonchalantly along the Midnight River, a dead cuckoo in its jaws.

Naked, with his scarlet arm upraised, Icarus held fast. A deathly peace prevailed, his people wrapped in centuries-old dreams and chicanery. They all had tired hearts. What would happen, he wondered lightheadedly, if electricity came and mercury vapor lamps garished the compounds? Their rich adobe tint, renewed each day by each night, would grow pale and sickly, the color of overwatered corn. The people would be doomed to eternal insomnia because night would never fall. Stars having died, drunks would no longer be beaten to bloody pulps in mysterious alleyways by other drunks gripping rocks in their fierce fists; and Midnight River water, no longer bruised by illicit blood, would sicken, hampering irrigation. At last, the moon, off-balance, would tumble into the mountains, necessitating once-a-month efforts to relocate it. But the search parties would quarrel among themselves, initiating half-assed, undignified murders. And barbecued bones, scattered all over the forest, would twinkle like cheap prostitutes.

"Wake up," the old man told himself in a measured, conversational tone. "Don't faint, you can't afford it. They will cut out your heart if you fall."

Yet he was riveted upon the rooftop with his arm upheld, offering it for a cure to the sky, the mountains, the mysterious emanations of moon. The night loneliness pulsed gently. He could feel the tension of gravity holding things firm, keeping the atmosphere in place. In the heart of a billion-year-old explosion, Icarus could barely breathe: nature itself was suffocating.

The sky quivered, readjusting slightly. A horse, in a corral somewhere close-by, peed. And the sky shifted again, exuding a threatening odorless scent which caused Icarus Suazo's skin to prickle.

The bleeding stopped: his head cleared. He went inside and was careful this time to tiptoe between shards embedded in the floor. Standing on the kitchen chair, Icarus scooped spiderwebs from a ceiling corner and packed them around his fingertip.

Building a fire, he made coffee, and smoked a cigarette, assessing his position on the electricity problem, adding up what he hoped to gain, for himself and for his people, and what it would cost him—even including his life—to achieve his objectives.

When he had it added up and back in place again, Icarus lowered his head onto the table and fell asleep. In the morning he would pick the glass out of his floor and out of the mattress and the walls and the ceiling, and meet with Bonatelli and McQueen and Bonney and all the rest of those gangsters, trying to manipulate them a little closer to his goals before his own people learned how to kill him.

The screen door he had forgotten to lock rattled slightly in faint, early morning breezes.

# Bourgeois
# Blues

THE WORLD WAS COMING to an end. Chamisaville was populated by creatures who must have migrated from outer space. And Amaranta GeeGee had to vacate her old house and the tiny patch of prolific earth around it by the end of the month.

Nothing made sense anymore.

Tired of the fight, Amaranta drowsed away much of her

afternoons, or at least that portion of them during which sunshine warmed her portal. And while she drowsed, the past tiptoed with a thoughtful concern into her fogging brain. That in old age a woman, whose total expectation in her youth had been to be surrounded by an enfeebled but dignified husband, many children, and twice as many grandchildren, plus acres of productive land and a general all-around physical and spiritual bounty harvested from a lifetime of decent human endeavors . . . that this woman should wind up encaged by a half-acre fence and a loneliness she would never have believed possible forty years ago—well, it wasn't fair.

Her children visited her melancholy slumber, apologies in their eyes. A young April McQueen touched Amaranta's lips with her sensitive fingers while Amaranta told stories, recited poems, and sang songs, teaching the gifted child Spanish. Weak fingers, appendages of a joyless old age, an imperfect and crudely exploited finish, plucked at the unresonant strings of an old guitar. Memories faded, were jaded. Put down, laid down, inoculated with the blues, Spanish-, Mexican-, Chicano-style—stripped and whipped, all our young people co-opted, stolen, embalmed with smack and cocaine and just plain booze, the earth riddled with cheap houses, chopped and stolen, the pastureland upon which our childhoods grazed to make us fat for the winter of our old age robbed long ago. All the cultural strains that had been so strong now going faint. And the survivors suspicious of each other, everybody out for themselves in a desperate survival play, yet terminally fatigued from decades of nothing better than a holding action, going down with a whimper, or in a senseless disorganized rage—the best men, the best women, the best children.

Amaranta drowsed, trying to fit together the pieces of what went wrong, but forgetting who exactly to blame, or how, exactly, it had all happened. She frowned in the sunshine and clutched her embroidery, twisting it in her lap. Magpies landed in the dusty yard, fighting over a caterpillar —she hardly heard them. Her children, the soldiers who had died in all those wars, leaned over to kiss her, hiding their guns in their pantlegs, in their sleeves, ashamed and embarrassed about being claimed so young. A church choir was singing. On Christmas morning the kids came around, tramping through knee-high snow—"Mis Crismas, mis Crismas"—trick or treating:

*Oremos, oremos,*
*Angelitos somos*
*del Cielo venimos*
*y si no nos dan regalitos,*
*puertas y ventanas*
*quebraremos!*

Bread baked; they mudded up the orno with the chicos inside; they made ristras of red chile and heated and peeled the green chile. Espeedie Cisneros came by with his horse-drawn rig to rake the hay: Amaranta stood in the doorway watching the men and the boys pitching it onto the hay wagon: the moon was up high in the limpid aqua sky; the two horses pulling the wagon were white; afterward a calico cat sat in the middle of the field, unmoving, waiting to catch mice. Violins played at the wedding dance; late snowfalls meant better irrigation come summertime; they dried apricots, having cursed, once more, the late freeze that killed the apple blossoms; and paid the midwife in corn and frijolitos. Hiding behind bushes, they watched the Penitentes whip themselves while pulling along la muerte in a wooden cart. And rode horses bareback across hundred-acre vegas; and patted down adobes into wooden frames by hand; and made the tortilla; and once a month, for a special treat, maybe, brought each of the chavalitos a Coca-Cola.

A rosary in her fingers, sound asleep, Amaranta nevertheless whispered the incantation: "María, madre de Diós, ruega para nosotros pecadores . . ."

And in the snow the Navidad luminarias flickered all around town. You could walk up to the top of Nobody Mountain and see them everywhere, candles fixed into sand in paper bags, lining rooftops and driveways and walkways with the albino freckles of a sweet Noël storm, giving to the memory the heart-wrenching quality of an aged photograph taken at a happier time: todo el pasado fue mejor. And maybe that was the truth after all . . . Amaranta dreamed.

Hoofbeats awakened her. Galloping up the driveway, three horsemen reined in not ten yards away from her portal, and for a moment her sticky eyes couldn't focus. The horses panted heavily after a hard run.

"We've come to requisition supplies, señora," Jesus Etcetera said, doffing his hat politely. "Our people are hungry, and the ones of us composed of flesh and bone

437

have need of more substantial foodstuffs than others among us require. Your husband told me that perhaps we could prevail upon you to help meet our needs—we'll pay of course."

In a single fine leap he was off his horse with a flourish: but the roly-poly little man was so weighed down by his thick rope vest and lethal hardware that when he struck the ground, slightly off-balance, his short legs crumpled, and he fell with a great clatter into the dust. He was up immediately, however, dusting himself off with dignity, and, assuming his comic, bowlegged gait, proceeded up to Amaranta and laid twenty dollars in her pink and wrinkled palms.

"If you can harvest what's left of that garden, I'd be most grateful," Amaranta sniffed.

And the old lady sat on her porch while three weird bewhiskered dervishes rooted about in her squashes, beans, and turnips, filling old feed sacks with the vegetables, gathering grist for the machine that might one day run the revolutionary mill; and she sighed—

"Heaven help us all."

Then Amaranta fell to dreaming about the town she had lived in all her life.

An immense confusion prevailed; the traditional forces of Chamisaville reeled. Land was being shaken so loose that fields had begun a capricious pattern of shifting, overlapping, or simply drifting off. An old-timer awakened to find his beanfield had slipped a few degrees westward overnight, crushing a neighbor's alfalfa. Wind, catching in bushy cottonwood tree-breaks bordering some fields, powered those rectangular pieces of land like sailboats through neighboring vegetation, slicing down corn plants, occasionally chopping the legs off cattle and horses unable to outrun the thin, ruglike lots. From time to time, a one-acre field, after trembling for days, suddenly lifted off with a great rooty tearing and floated like a magic carpet to the east or west, spilling snakes, prairie dogs, and rabbits over its sides until crumpling with a great earthen hullabaloo of dirt, alfalfa blossoms, and grasshoppers into a mountainside. Or it settled gently onto deserted mesaland, an incongruous green patch decorating that misty purple expanse for a few days until the alfalfa died or Moe Stryzpk's bulldozers arrived to drag it back for sale. And once in a great while a small brome field or a pretty little orchard sailed absentmindedly into the Rio Grande Gorge, descending between the lonely, deserted walls, catching swallows the way a seine gathers minnows on the way down, drowning a thousand little birds as the thin earthen blanket touched tumultuous waters and was instantly torn to shreds.

A noise interrupted the dream; Amaranta's eyes flew open; her heart had stopped.

AMARANTA GEEGEE WAS DEAD, interred that afternoon with only Virgil and April, Juan Ortega, Espeedie Cisneros, Perfecto and Ursula Torres, her longtime employers Cynthia and Rodey McQueen, and a handful of other old-timers attending. Sorrow, such as she had rarely experienced, landed upon April's shoulders. With each death the pain intensified, as did the sense of loss. A wonderful, complex, and valuable epoch was being wiped out by a future of pathetically lesser stature and sensibilities. The process was more ruthless—despite all the evidence she had accumulated over the years—than April could have possibly imagined.

She drove to the old Martínez shack, openly looking for succor. But found George at loose ends—he hadn't shaved in several days. They embraced, but afterward he couldn't face her. "Why are you avoiding my eyes?" April asked. "What's wrong now? What did I do bad? What did I forget? Who's been talking to you? How many times did the FBI visit in the past five days?"

"It isn't that. . . ." George fixed his gaze beyond the window: Steller's jays hopped in the piñon and juniper trees. He had built a table outdoors, spreading hen scratch across it; small birds pecked up the grain.

"Well, then, what is it?"

"I don't know. . . ."

"Bullshit. That's the world's most chicken answer. We've come this far, you can at least be honest."

He blurted, "You should look at yourself in a mirror sometime! You've aged ten years in the past month. I don't know how it happened, but you're getting heavy! In the spring you were beautiful, you looked eighteen. Now your eyes are swollen, red-rimmed, your legs and ankles—oh, hell. I dunno. I can't stand that vicious little lump over your eye and that fucking wig—"

"It's still me, George. My head and my heart haven't changed."

"So I'm a male chauvinist pig," he said miserably. "I

know all the reasons you're supposed to love somebody; I've tried them for twenty years. I know how the relationships between men and women are supposed to be. I know it's not cool anymore to be a macho asshole with a broad on his arm, a sexy dame who wears stockings, high heels, peekaboo bras, and looks like Jayne Mansfield. I know I'm supposed to be above all that, but I'm not. I want you to look good. I want you—on top of everything else—to be a sex object. I want you to look young—"

George buried his face in his hands, a gesture that was beginning to bore even himself.

"Hey, come on. It's okay, love, really. I understand. But I told you, it's the drug, the Prednisone. Abe said while I've got that gunk in my system it'll be tough to lose weight."

"Sometimes I sit here and I can't stand it. I sit here and I think of all this shit—cancer, wigs, operations, the FBI—and I hate you. I hate you for letting it all happen *now* even if it wasn't your fault. I hate you for the politics that made them give Susan those nude photographs. I hate the fact that you took them in the first place, shared them with another man, and were so indiscreet and careless, or maybe egotistical, that they got into the hands of the FBI. I hate all the times you were married and all the stories you've told me of how traumatic those marriages were. I feel like shit, like just another asshole on your scorecard, and maybe the final one, at that. I feel like I've been duped, tricked, sucked in under false pretenses. Why does all this have to happen *now*? I know it's wrong, but I sit here adding up all your past affairs and adventures, and I feel like the world's greatest patsy. If I have to accept all your husbands, your countless lovers, even your kids, why can't I at least have you *the way you used to be*—?"

"Is that it? Is that *all* of it?"

"Oh who the hell knows?—I'm tired. Susan and I are getting divorced for sure. That's unavoidable. Suddenly— I don't know how it happened so suddenly. And I'm giving up that particular agony for *this* one? It's ludicrous. For fifteen years I dreamed of freedom, but I couldn't even muster the guts for an affair. Now—what kind of freedom is this? I'm jumping right out of the frying pan into the fire."

"Hold on a minute, love. You don't owe me anything. Nobody's talking about marriage. This is an affair, nothing more."

440

"I told you 'stop' once, and you told me to fuck off."

"All right, maybe I shouldn't have. But it was because this thing has also been good, George. You told me yourself that our relationship, our sex, our ability to *talk straight* to one another gave you such hope for the future. You said—"

"Even a fish wouldn't get caught if he kept his mouth shut!"

". . . I see."

"I don't think you do."

"I see perfectly."

"I'm not gonna teach school in the fall, either."

"Why not?"

"For one thing, I quit. For another thing, I'm going to be fired. My own father, a member of the school board, he told me."

"Okay, I'm sorry. But you can fight them, they can't just fire you for nothing. Virgil will take them to court."

"No he won't. Don't be so sorry. I don't care about it. I wanted out. It would have happened anyway. I probably would have quit. I guess the thing that hurts most is losing the kids: sometimes I can't stand it. It's funny, for years they've just seemed like spoiled American brats to me. I got sick of them so easily. I hated their guts for being selfish, racist—I don't know how it happened with them. They bored me stiff. And of course I was ashamed of not being a better father, of not being able to mold them into a more respectable image. Now that it looks like I'm gonna be gone, they seem vulnerable, unsure of themselves— what will they do without a father? I was taking a bath the other night, suddenly I burst into tears. All summer long it seems I've been bawling at the drop of a hat—now it's worse than ever. I see kids on a family TV program, tears well into my eyes. I see children around town with their folks, I can't stand it. I pass by the Balena Park Little League field during a game and this despair grips me, I cry again."

"Where are you going, George?"

"I don't know. But if everything is doomed to collapse I think I'll really leave this town."

"And go where?" she repeated.

"Would you believe New York? Maybe San Francisco. Where do people go when they decide to start over?"

"Well, I guess that's fairly heavy news." April sat down

441

in the doorway, her back against one side of the jamb, her feet against the other side, and lit a cigarette.

"I know what you're thinking."

"What am I thinking?"

"Plus ça change, plus c'est la même chose."

"Not really."

"What are you thinking, then?"

"I'm thinking you've got a rough road ahead. I'm thinking it's awful what you're going through—I'm not heartless, believe me. I'm thinking I'm partially guilty for the state you're in, and I'm sick and tired of being guilty for the states men get themselves into."

"Nobody's blaming you."

"Thanks, darling, that's really good to know."

"Do you have to be sarcastic?"

"No, I don't. And I'll try not to. I always think, Someday you're going to grow up, April Delaney, and you're not going to take cheap shots when people hurt you. But I always wind up taking cheap shots. Forgive me, please."

"You know what I want to do?"

"You want to escape from the environment that gave you claustrophobia for half of your life. You want to see the world. You want to have adventures. You want to discover a way to be that is more exciting than anything you've ever known before it's too late. Big deal—join the club."

"You make it sound mundane."

"It's both exciting and terribly mundane, sweet. I have heard a thousand variations on that same theme. I left Chamisaville playing that tune. It's a pretty standard dream arising out of pretty standard complaints—but don't get me wrong, it's valid. It's one of the most valid cries on earth, and I wouldn't deny you it, not under any conditions. Obviously, it makes me sad, that's all."

"Would you tell me why?"

"I know this sounds contemptible, love, but I've been there, that's all. I've been there a lot."

"But I have a curiosity. I want to know other women, I want to know their bodies, I'm curious about being intimate with them, I'm curious about their lives and how they make love. I've taken life so seriously up until now, I don't want that anymore. I don't want to just live this life . . . this, this moronic small-town life, this sheltered, isolated existence, this small-time English-teacher role, faithful hubby, good and dedicated father—I want a life like you've lived, I really do—before it's too late. I've got to know what it's like."

"It's not that great—" she started.

"Don't tell me, I haven't been there yet. People who've done it all are always telling people who yearn to do it all that it's really not so hot—that stinks."

"Have it your way, then. But for the record, I finally came home trying to find something solid, trying to find a way that would make it all add up."

"That's you."

"Of course."

April smoked, George doodled on a piece of paper.

"If it hadn't been for you—"

"Don't say it, George. I don't want to hear it. Not right now."

"Don't say what?"

"Don't say if it hadn't been for me you'd never have had the courage to break ties and strike out on your own. Don't say if it hadn't been for me liberating all your sexual prowess and drive and intensity you'd never have had the courage to go to New York and start banging every teenybopper that twitches her butt at you as she saunters by. Don't tell me about how I was the catalyst that enabled you to break the chains of your marriage at last, reject your kids, and flee from this bitched little town into the adventurous world beyond. That's just not something I'm in the mood to hear right now."

"It's true."

"George, don't turn into a total bore."

"You're the most vicious person I've ever met."

"You're not bad yourself, kid. You learn fast."

"Do we have to start one of these?"

"No, what the hell—I guess not." April stubbed out her cigarette, flicking it up at the wind chime, then inspected her fingernails—she had been chewing them lately: times were tough.

"When do you expect to leave?"

"I don't know—maybe soon. School will begin, and I don't want to hang around town during the divorce. I guess pretty soon, then—but I really don't know. Everything is up for grabs. It's so strange. I feel as if . . . as if . . ."

"As if a great weight had been lifted off your shoulders?"

"Man, you're cruel."

"I work at it, love. You better work at it, too. You're going to need a lot of weapons out there, I assure you. New York City will see you coming a thousand miles away. They'll pluck you and fuck you back there, George; they'll hold all your dreams and expectations up to ridicule."

"You say."

"Yeah, I say."

"You're crying?"

"So what else is new."

"Why are you crying?"

April's jaw dropped. "Did I hear you correctly? Did you really ask that question? Did you really ask me why I was *crying?* I don't believe it—"

"I'm sorry, I wasn't thinking."

*"Well start fucking thinking you big boob!"* she yelled, and, scrambling to her feet, April plunged for her car, started it, backed around hysterically, and gunned out the rutted road, pebbles and an enormous dust cloud flying.

RODEY MCQUEEN, a powerful old man standing before a full-length mirror, slowly removed his clothes, unbuttoning his shirt and tossing it to the foot of Cynthia's bed, letting his slacks fall and kicking them over there also. He dropped his shorts and stepped out of them. For his age, McQueen looked strong and felt that way. His body had retained its shape, his muscles were prominent and not too loose, his belly was several inches larger than at age thirty, but he weighed the same. McQueen made a muscle, inspecting it, and himself, critically. "I look good," he said quietly. "I'm gonna live to be a hundred."

Not smoking had done it; and he had never been a booze-hound. He played tennis every Saturday morning with players much younger than himself: J. B. LeDoux, Junior Leyba, and Bob Moose, Jr. On Sunday he golfed with Randolph Bonney, Bob Moose (the elder), and Claude Parker. And after work every day he came home, changed into his swimsuit, went out to the pool and swam laps, or did careful dives off the board. Once a week a Swedish masseuse, an enormous powerful woman named Annie Sverdka, drove up from the capital to give him a pounding, after which he went through the bathhouse sauna—in summertime, in the winter, too.

He felt vigorous, healthy, as powerful physically as he was economically in this town: "I've led a good life."

444

McQueen squinched his toes into the thick golden rug, squiggling them deep into that lush rich cover, and touched himself admiringly with his hands.

Cynthia stopped behind him, assessing his body. He smiled at her, arrogantly. No love was lost between them, yet they understood one another, had made it together, their love was embodied in the routine of their public life. And if an intimacy had died, if they had become very private persons, that was not a major cause for worry. At their age, this active, so much a part of Chamisaville's past, current, and future history, they had only the stars to bless.

"You're still a good-looking man, Dale," Cynthia said, catching McQueen by surprise. The tone of her voice, almost gentle, vaguely sentimental, was quasi-loving.

"I took care of myself. We lived the good life. We don't have to bow down to anyone. I make no apologies. I have no regrets."

"Junior and Charlotte are already downstairs." Cynthia's mauve dressing gown swished against the heels of her silver slippers as she brushed past him into her changing room.

But McQueen tarried a moment before the mirror. Not for a long time had he actually contemplated his physical self, the outward appearance of the inner being, and it stacked up all right. He was a powerful, useful man with —Lord, who knows?—maybe another twenty, twenty-five years ahead of him if he was careful.

What happened to his mirrored image in the next few seconds, McQueen could not say: perhaps nothing at all occurred. But there was a flutter in his body, an alien sensation that caught at his breath, just for the length of a heartbeat—then it was gone. Leaving behind a thin icy streak from his groin to his Adam's apple.

McQueen gulped, disbelieving it, immediately wondering if it had actually taken place. And he forgot about it almost at once, turning away from the mirror, his mind momentarily, and uncomfortably, blank as he strode over to his bed, where a maid had laid out his clothes—white suede loafers, black socks and garter belts, plum-colored pants, tailored western shirt, and a double-breasted cream dinner jacket. Dressing quickly, he did a swift trim on his moustache, brushed his long Buffalo Bill hair, and went downstairs.

In the living room, Junior Leyba stood beside the fireplace mantel with a vodka and tonic in one hand, and a framed photograph, taken from the mantel, in his other hand. Through the french doors, McQueen could see Charlotte, dressed in a white jersey pants suit, sitting in the rich grass near the pool, a drink held absentmindedly at her lips as she gazed at the shimmering blue water. A hummingbird buzzed over her head just as McQueen entered the living room: and a slight breeze ruffled the yellowing aspen leaves out by the pool, their clear quivering reflection obliterated by the cat's-paw that accompanied the breeze. Autumn was almost upon them: a sugary sprinkle of snow had capped the mountains last night.

It was a beautiful life; just perfect. The complicated Pueblo deal was nearly consummated: apparently Icarus Suazo had finally almost manipulated their last council member out there into voting for electricity. McQueen was strong and talcum powdered, freshly laundered, rubbed down, and healthy—yet he felt that catch again, that almost indistinguishable rustle deep inside his body, as of something crucial shifting an inch, out of place.

As usual, Junior did not look up. McQueen was unthreatened by Junior's sullen personality, however. A fairly keen judge of people, he had Junior figured for the weaknesses that the lawyer did, in fact, possess. Hence, Junior worried him less than might a more jovial, less obviously hostile person.

The patriarch aimed toward the porta-bar, intending only to glance at the picture Junior was scrutinizing as he went by. Yet halfway to Junior he realized what picture the lawyer held in his hands, and again that catch occurred, this time in his throat. And, as he passed behind Junior, McQueen avoided the photograph, not wishing, at this moment, to see it.

But Junior looked at the picture longer than necessary. Other guests, among them Joseph Bonatelli, Icarus Suazo, and Randolph Bonney, would arrive soon. Mixing himself a drink, McQueen offhandedly remarked, "Whatcha got there, Junior—something interesting?"

Junior neither looked up nor in any way acknowledged McQueen's seniority. "It's this picture of April," he said.

Pretending a certain disinterest, McQueen sidled over, letting his eyes fall on the picture, which had been on his mantel for decades. Only this time, when he looked at it, a pain jolted his heart.

"She had just turned eight in that picture. Or maybe nine."

April was standing on the lawn, seemingly demure and very pretty in long pigtails that came to her waist. She wore a white party dress with a half-dozen petticoats underneath, white kneesocks, and a pair of Oxfords. Around her waist was a double holster set, a sixgun on each hip.

For years McQueen had thought of the photograph as the most adorable picture ever taken of his wonderful, wayward daughter. Now, under scrutiny by Junior Leyba, the picture jumped out at McQueen, crying either for help or for revenge.

Gently but firmly, he coaxed the photograph from Junior's hands, walking with it over to the open french doors. The summer evening was growing crisp: a dusty sagebrush and juniper smell lingered across the lawn. Charlotte had not moved. She was pretty there, that demure, sexy little woman who would never fit in—Junior's folly.

A queer light struck the frame in McQueen's hand. April's eyes were so big, her dress so white. With age, a slight glint on the handle of one cap gun had grown a diffuse sparkle.

McQueen felt hopelessly lost for a few seconds. Then Junior came up beside him, ice rattling warningly in his glass:

"A prophetic photograph."

The old man cocked his head, trying to think of a retort, but found nothing to say. Turning on his heel, he strode back across the living room, setting the picture not on the mantel this time, but in the liquor cabinet beside the fireplace.

Yet around eleven that same evening, McQueen came downstairs in a yellow terrycloth bathrobe and sought out the photograph. Over at the french doors, he looked at it in bright moonlight. Outside, a scent of dying hollyhocks and rotting apples mingled with sage and juniper. Preliminary titillations of snow were carried on the early September breezes. McQueen pushed open the door and walked onto the lawn, stopping midway between the house and the softly lighted swimming pool.

Suddenly, that familiar photograph had a capacity to break his heart. He held up the picture, catching the light. And gasped—and shuddered. Music, from a rock band off

447

at some remote bar, floated over the wall; mariachi singing came from elsewhere. The rustle of first-fallen dry leaves filled him with a nameless regret. McQueen was cushioned at the secure heart of his estate like a precious jewel in a perfectly balanced setting.

An unhappiness—powerful, unrelenting, downright scary—took his breath away, making him so vulnerable that he quickly looked around to see if anyone, off in the luxurious shadows, had caught him naked.

Cynthia called down from a window: "Dale, it's eleven-thirty."

McQueen walked over to his swimming pool, quietly stripped off his robe, and, slipping without a splash into the water, started doing laps. But his leaden limbs did not respond. Irritating leaves ticked nervously off his forehead. He ceased fighting and floated around in the tepid water, paddling erratically, drifting from side to side. Sudden wind puffs clattered in cottonwoods; the big leaves floated down and settled invisibly around him on the water. A night bird—he had never learned its name—called. The stars were enormous directly overhead.

Something formed in the sky directly above. It was at once both very far away and terribly near. McQueen squinted, trying to focus. It was a vague cloud, some final emanation of summer steam, and then it almost formed a shape. And for a second McQueen saw Cipi García's grinning yellow skull framed in great white wings. But before he could ascertain that the thing was really there, it dissolved.

A cold wind swept across the lawn; a gust from the upcoming season.

McQueen shivered, covered with goosebumps, scared half to death.

Autumn . . .

AUTUMN, WITH ITS SAD and mystifying alchemy of death; autumn, that colorful deciduous time of year when leaves tumble off cottonwoods, elms, and aspens in great clattering sheaves, skittering among chickens and dry papery cornstalks, gathering in crisp drifts against the firewalls of dirt roofs. A southern sun, dead leaves, and smoke heralded the end of another brief season. A marvelous stench of apples, apricots, and pears permeated the air. Yellowjackets fed on rotting fruit. Squash proliferated in the Chamisa Valley; there was an almost grotesque plethora of zucchini. Tiny trees rife with greengage plums were bent over double, touching the ground, groaning from abundance. Fat cattle broke through flimsy fences and wandered along the roadways, cutting their hooves on broken glass. Horses grew shaggy winter coats, and broke free, looking for sex; their manes and tails soon became impossibly caked with burrs. After the last alfalfa cutting, hundreds of sparrow hawks stationed themselves on telephone wires above the stubble, committing genocide on mice. Suddenly flotillas of southbound ruddy ducks, mallards, goldeneye, and coots landed on Chamisaville's tiny ponds, marshlands, and stock tanks. They rested for a few days, dodged shotgun pellets, then disappeared abruptly on misty mornings. Lilac bushes shivered with bursts of Audubon and yellow-throated warblers, flitting and twittering: great flights of pine siskins cavorted among stands of wild sunflowers. The roads were lined by bright flowers; blue asters blossomed everywhere like pieces of fallen sky. In salt cedars along the clear-flowing streams, an explosion of azabache and gold caterpillars occurred. Russet and jet woolly bears, curled up into fuzzy nubs, floated atop the sensuous currents and were nudged, but not gulped, by inquisitive trout. Cranes came down the Rio Grande flyway, soaring steadily and unemotionally in high Vs—or were they only geese heading south . . . hard to tell from the ground.

A restless bustle of wood gathering occupied the valley's rural survivors. Trucks heaped with piñon logs, ponderosa, and lumber-mill slab ends rattled about on the back roads. And the Chamisaville High School Panthers started playing football games. One morning Espeedie Cisneros quit chopping wood and listened to the high-school band playing as it marched down the North-South Highway on a Friday morning before the homecoming game, and there was a sweetness to that pause in his sunny, hard-working day that left Espeedie more content than he had felt in years. Meanwhile, hunting rifles were sighted in at various gravel pits. Men rode horses into the mountains, looking for signs of elk and bear; they quartered the western mesa trying to determine where antelope herds would be when the season opened. Pigs were shot, scalded, and butchered on frosty mornings; little kids got sick on chicharrones. Sheep were tied up by one leg and their throats slit; women held pots beneath them, capturing the blood. Steers, dropped with a single .22 bullet

449

between the eyes, were gutted. Fatted chickens, turkeys, and geese met cursory dooms. Enormous haybale piles grew up overnight. Denzil Spivey ordered Tranky Martínez to bring his sheep down from the mountains two weeks early; Tranky sold the underweight lambs at auction up in Colorado, but lost hundreds of dollars because of the early deadline that had denied his animals important, fattening grazing time. Doves flocked in Rio Grande willows; big fat brown trout gobbled hellgrammites in the deep marshmallow-green waters of that artery. Robins and meadowlarks and killdeer disappeared: chickens molted, grew better feathers, and stopped laying eggs. People sprinkled chile powder in the poultry water, trying to stimulate their chickens into producing throughout the brumal season. Monarch butterflies laid eggs on milkweed plants, then fled to Brazil and Ecuador. Celestino Lucero filled a wheelbarrow with yellow pumpkins; then he wrapped his dry bean plants in a blanket and smashed them out of their husks with a two-by-four bat; and his tiny plot yielded fifteen pounds of the frijoles. Already he was training a new pet magpie to talk: Tierra o Muerte the Thirteenth.

J. B. LeDoux got into his pickup and went for a drive around town. Hospital Auxiliary ladies selling Buddy Poppies floated past his windows; jovial Lions hawking brooms for the blind waved; and Juan Beaubien was hosing down the PDQ parking lot. J. B. recalled that Juan had been the best hurdler in the state. And he remembered when Chamisaville had won the state triple-A basketball title the year Juan captained the team just about the prettiest little guard anybody had ever seen. J. B. remembered the fans cheering them on, and he remembered the jubilant homecoming parade around the plaza, horns honking wildly, the team seated in two old convertibles, a late spring snow falling. Such a feeling of triumph they had shared: *"Christ,* we were good!"

The mayor parked in the First State lot beside the Catholic church. Walking gingerly, he entered the plaza. Pat GeeGee was behind the bar in the El Gaucho, and merely nodded, offering no condolences for his mood.

At a table Eloy Romo, Malaquias C. de Baca, and Filiberto García were nursing beers: they nodded morosely when J. B. raised a perfunctory finger in greeting. At another table Benny's crippled friend, Alfredo GeeGee, was playing chess with a dripping-wet Ralphito García. Pat served the beer J. B. asked for and melted back into the gloom. The mayor scanned the yellowed bulletin-board collage until he found photographs hailing that old championship basketball team—three newspaper action shots, and a glossy print of the boys with their trophy. He picked out his own face, Juan Beaubien, Fidel Mondragón, J. J. Valerio, and Gunner García, and gazed at them while sipping the beer.

Later, his eyes drifted across the board, flicking ashamedly away from himself on his knees at the Dynamite Shrine. Other faces, personages, events swam in discolored melancholy nostalgia. The Horse Without Shit; skaters on the Balena Park pond; the Sunday-afternoon floating bandstand; Espeedie Cisneros playing his violin; Pat's airplane; Junior Leyba as a Korean hero; his father, Virgil, displaying a three-pound brown trout, caught in the Rio Grande, winning the *Chamisaville News* fishing contest in July 1949.

Finally J. B. located the old photograph taken by Karl Mudd atop Nobody Mountain on the morning of Cipi García's funeral. Squinting, he tried to make out the features of a young boy, himself, standing beside his poor father, the doomed mayor, on that historic day. What was I thinking, what were my hopes back then, did I comprehend it all? the mayor wondered. Then so much bitterness touched his heart and his head that he had to leave before doing something really stupid, like throwing a beer bottle at Pat GeeGee, who irritated the mayor no end, clothed—as that derelict always seemed to be—in a self-righteous fog, having grown up and grown old in the Chamisa Valley toeing only his own, and nobody else's, line. He paid, took his change without comment, and got out of there.

J. B. drove along the road a hundred yards, pulling onto a shoulder near the municipal swimming pool. A bunch of immigrants were playing soccer on the junior-high football field. Mostly blond and blue eyed, many spoke in foreign languages: French, German, Scandinavian—English. By and large people from the ski valley brought in to manage condominiums and chalets up there, they were powerful, always grinning, relaxed and healthy. An ease complemented their motions. J. B.'s grief readjusted into a sense of universal loss. The air was so dry it crackled. Booms—his dynamite, his construction business, his rising fortune—echoed down from the mountains.

A little kid, a smart-aleck hippie child with a bathing suit rolled up in a towel under one arm, his eyes blood-shot from chlorine said, "Hello." J. B. failed to respond. The kid took a step back, placed the towel on his head, recited

> Popeye the sailor man,
> Lived in a frying pan,
> Turned on the gas,
> And *blew off his ass!*

and ran away.

J. B. recalled reading somewhere, recently, a quote by Woodrow Wilson: "We are all caught in a great economic system which is heartless." The soccer players, with their bright smiles and white teeth, made him so nervous that he drove elsewhere, just cruising.

Caught against his wishes in the traffic flow, the mayor was carried down Chamisaville's main artery. Past Safe-way and Foodway and a new Gibson's Discount Store, an Aaronson's, a double-dozen gas stations—self-serve, tiny aluminum–plate-glass boxes set on expansive carpets of macadam, their neon, even in daylight, sputtering. Then two new PDQs, a couple of Speedways, Lota-Burgers, a Pizza Hut, A&W, Tastee-Freez, Big Boy, used cars, new cars, rent-a-cars, appliance stores, ski shops, sporting goods, Wacker's, TG&Y, Piggly Wiggly, curios, art gal-leries, low-cost housing developments, trailer parks, three branches of Irving Newkirk's pawnshop, and a new court-house on the highway, inconducive to loafers. But that was only for starters—there followed an Army-Navy, Monkey Ward, Sears, hardware and lumber companies, restaurants and cafés—and dusty denuded cottonwoods poisoned by exhaust . . . his car crawled. Tranky Martínez waved and disappeared into a greasy blue billow. So many fields were out of production, harboring tumbleweeds, goat's heads, broken glass, beer cans. Cipi Fernández materialized, nodded, and was sucked down a prairie-dog hole. Local bums and hippies patrolled the roadsides, gathering re-cyclable waste—they waded ankle-deep through pretty yellow leaves. Was there really a package store every fifty yards? The Jehovah's Witnesses had built two Kingdom Halls. Amaranta GeeGee whooshed across his windshield —no, it was only a tiny dust devil, a puff of autumn smoke. He heard acid-rock music: Benny? There was a juvenile pool hall next door to a new Honda motorcycle shop—one of Bob Moose's nephews rented trail bikes to tourists, whose buzzing could be heard summerlong in the wilderness country. Two auto-parts stores had already commenced selling snowmobiles beside their Rototillers; you could even rent typewriters nowadays in Chamisaville. Jacobal Mondragón was hitching a ride, but when J. B. braked, his essence broke apart with a *poof!* A cinderblock addition was going onto the Our Lady of the Sorrows Hospital. Teen-age punks played football and air hockey in a café beside the Alfred Gracie Lamont Bowl-A-Drome; Eagles were getting loaded at the bar in back. Marina LeDoux lounged in a doorway, swinging her pocketbook—Mother? No! No! Several record stores sold music by Albuquerque ranchera mafiosos Al Hurricane, Tiny Morrie, Baby Gaby—whatever happened to Pedro Infante?—and other insane maniacs with names like Sly and the Family Stone, Humble Pie, Alice Cooper, David Bowie, Cream. Hang-gliders in Cañoncito. A new gospel tent. A go-cart track. Big-O Tires. Miniature golf. And talk of businessmen's vigilante groups to curb crime. Tools had been "ripped off" from his pickup twice already this summer. Brought up in an unlocked world, J. B. still couldn't get used to all the larceny afoot, to the idea that his worldly goods, if left unprotected for a moment, would be filched. Counterfeit ten-dollar bills had just flooded town. A tennis ranch was going up. Pancho Ortiz y Pino gave him the finger. Yesterday, the electronic gate on the new municipal parking lot had clobbered a tourist on a motorcycle, an accident that would cost the town a hundred grand for whiplash, no doubt. Next weekend was the Chamber of Commerce Balloon Days—a plane would release a thousand colorful globes, some carrying "Shop Chamisaville First" gift certificates. Four days ago J. B. had tried to have coffee with Junior Leyba and Damacio Mares in the new Cosmic Banana Café. Some weird goons had been playing zithers and flutes. The waitress had smelled like incense. Suddenly, a six-foot-tall blond lady carrying a female chimpanzee named Irving had sat down at an outdoor table. They didn't have coffee on the menu, only a substitute called Pero. Like Hitler, J. B. had wanted to stuff the whole joint into an oven. None of the junior-high girls wore bras anymore. They smoked dope and got laid too early. Their boyfriends, hair down to their navels, clomping around in stupid platform shoes and flared denims and chartreuse muscle shirts, drove brand-new crimson automobiles with wide mag wheels or racing slicks, and shaggy purple angel hair on the dashboard, and Day-Glo rainbow stripping around the windshield, and violent flames darting against the front-hood curves. What was happening to values? Rhythm? Conscience? J. B. turned right and left the strip, heading west before he suffocated. But Chamisaville was not in the business of offering solace.

Something caught the mayor's eye. In a field belonging to the late Johnny Cisneros, where only last week two chestnut horses and a small roan colt with a white blaze on its forehead had been grazing, a tall blond stranger wearing a pair of gray lederhosen was strolling around plucking a banjo. Nearby, a barefoot girl wearing a long billowy skirt and a hazy purple blouse dreamily assumed a variety of ballet-like poses, graceful and poetic against that field of green.

Lovely, perhaps. But a rage in the mayor combined with such a sense of loss that for a moment the desire to murder these strangers was so strong in him he almost reached into his glove compartment for a gun.

"This used to be a rare and beautiful valley!" he cried.

# DEADLY
# CONCLUSIONS

# V

# Ditch Boss—
# Gimme Water!

APRIL DELANEY BABIED another paste-up of another *El Clarín* onto the Capital City bus, proceeded wearily over to the El Gaucho, and reclused in a corner for an hour, feeling played out, at the end of her rope. A cutworm moth Icarused into her beer; stirring it absentmindedly with a finger, she daydreamed of sleeping for twenty-four hours under a thick crazy quilt in a room with wide-open windows and a blizzard raging outside.

Virgil slouched in, a sheaf of problems under one arm. Failing to notice April committing spiritual suicide back there in the gloom, he slumped against the bar, grunted for a beer, and commenced shuffling through the papers, his head bowed, eyes squinting in the bad light, nose almost touching the briefs. Christ, he looks horrible, April thought; just like a man on the verge. Emaciated, bone-weary, his face was puffy from overdrinking, from fatigue, from loneliness.

"Hey Virgil," she called. "Don't you ever say hello?"

The lawyer gathered up his papers and joined her. "I dunno," he said gloomily. "Maybe I'm getting old, maybe I'm not the one to defend these people anymore. It used to be I lost about half my cases, but now it begins to feel like a miracle if I win, or even fight them to a draw. All my clients wind up in the carcel or in the camposanto. Last week I got an injunction against the town prohibiting them from bulldozing down Sofio Medina's orchard to make way for their proposed new sewage line, and Sofio was so happy he had a heart attack and died, and now his son-in-law, a cousin of Damacio Mares and in the construction business himself, says he'll donate that orchard if the town will only pay him to drive the bulldozer that knocks it down."

"Vey iz mir."

"Whatever."

They grumbled incoherently about life in general until Juan Ortega limped in mopping his brow, a sportcoat slung over one shoulder, his white shirt drenched with sweat from pedaling his bicycle. Ignoring April and Virgil, he wobbled onto a bar stool, ordered a beer, and, when it came, downed it at once, then launched a brutal coughing jag. April jumped up and slammed his back. When he had calmed down, Juan ordered another beer and sagged into a free chair at their table.

"Well," he said masochistically, "the news out there is just great. Believe it or not, two old coots up in Denver, lawyers by the name of Joe Brady and Win Potter, just filed suit against the Pueblo for eight million dollars in legal fees they claim Icarus Suazo and company owe them for work done forty years ago before they were fired for conflict of interest when Icarus Suazo caught them turning over confidential material to Bob Moose and Rodey McQueen. If they win, the government may have to turn that Albino Pine land over to them instead of to the Pueblo. Which should take away any hole cards Icarus Suazo might be playing. Other than that, it's the same old story. Irving Newkirk is going to show X-rated movies on closed-circuit TV in that new motel he's building. Happy days are here again. Excuse me for using bathroom language, but I say fuck this goddam Betterment of Chamisaville."

They stayed silent for a while.

"You know what I would like to do?" Juan said abruptly. "I would like to bed down under a great big crazy quilt and sleep for twenty-four hours straight with the windows open and a blizzard raging outside."

Anthony Martínez stumbled into the El Gaucho, his shirt torn and dirty, his face smudged, one cheek inflamed as if somebody had punched him. He bumped into the bar, asked Pat for a beer, downed it all at once, and began to cough uncontrollably. April and Juan jumped up, blamming his back while he clung to the bar wracked with pain, his eyes watering. When he had calmed down, they asked, "What happened?"

"I went over to the Shalako where those two lawyers, Joe Brady and Win Potter—who just filed suit against us for eight million dollars—are staying, and I was standing in front of their doorway ready to knock when a gang of hoodlums I never saw before jumped on my back and beat me up."

Virgil asked, "Why did you want to see those lawyers?"

"Oh, I wanted to tan their unscrupulous hides, and possibly kill them into the bargain."

April, Virgil, and Juan ordered fresh beers, and the little group sat there, staring at their glasses, at a loss for words and plumb tuckered out, until Anthony said:

"You know what I dream about every night?"

"I can guess," April said.

"Go ahead, then."

"You dream about going to bed and sleeping for twenty-four hours straight, all wrapped up in a buffalo robe in a room with the windows wide open and a blizzard raging outside."

Anthony threw up his hands so hard he fell over backward.

MOE STRYZPK SAT IN his wheelchair in the dark, smoking a cigarette. Miranda had left for the evening. Alone as always, facing a sacred mountain that glowed dimly in the starlit darkness, Moe numbly calculated the score. He wasn't in it any longer for the fun or because he needed the money: Moe had played out his emotional involvement in Chamisaville long ago. Now his work was just logistics to keep him occupied until he died. And, doing business without a soul, treating the enormous, history-shattering Pueblo project as simply another problem to be solved with memorized equations, it suddenly struck him now—finally—after a lifetime at his nefarious helm, that it really did not matter if he won or lost. The world, an empty, vacuous place, bothered him not at all. He had never found a key making the adventure worthwhile. Maybe the only thing that had kept him alive this long was a hatred of his wife and of Rodey McQueen. Yet how—alive as he was, crippled and impotent—how could he ever hope to avenge himself?

A strange rustling occurred in the dark room. Somebody else was present. The air stirred faintly. While Moe hadn't been paying attention, vaporous beings had melted through the walls into his command module. Breath held, Moe cocked his head: whoever had joined him stopped moving. Moe waited, holding smoke in his lungs until they started to burn, and then he let the smoke out slowly. Something stirred: springs in couch cushions squeaked faintly—

Frowning, Moe wheeled over to his desk and snapped on a lamp. Seated on the Castro convertible, facing him, were Jesus Etcetera, Rudy LeDoux, and the burnished golden skeleton—with enormous white wings—of Cipi García.

"Time for you to make out a new will, old man," Jesus Etcetera rasped.

And Moe shrugged: what the hell? "Let's do it," he muttered drearily.


RODEY McQUEEN AWOKE SUDDENLY, in the dark, alert, listening. Something was wrong—a burglar? In her bed beside him, Cynthia was also awake.

"What's that?" she whispered.

"I don't know, I just woke up."

"There's somebody downstairs?"

"I don't know—"

They listened, able to hear nothing.

"Did you hear something?" McQueen asked.

"No. I woke up because you woke up."

"Maybe it was a dream. Maybe it was something uncomfortable in a dream."

"But it's still around here. There's something wrong. I can feel it."

"I can feel it, too."

"Get the gun."

Carefully, making no noise, McQueen opened a drawer in his bedside table and lifted out a loaded .45 automatic. He released the safety.

"Are you going downstairs?" she asked.

"I don't know, let's wait a minute."

"What *is* it, Dale? There's no draft, I can't hear anything. But something is definitely wrong."

McQueen swung out of bed and went to the window. The dry, faintly frost-sprinkled lawn and the empty pool, the trees and the dead flower beds were lit up by the moon; naked trees cast shadows that probed everywhere, angular, sharp, impressive.

"I'm going downstairs."

"Be careful, Dale."

McQueen tiptoed on his bare feet down the carpeted stairs. At the bottom, he waited, listening. The hums of various heating and refrigerating units were all he heard.

McQueen concentrated on his bare ankles, straining to detect the draft he would undoubtedly feel if a door had been ajar, a window jimmied open—but there was nothing.

The old man entered his living room; it was empty, calm, at rest. He tried the french doors, but they were locked. Opening them, careful to make no noise, he stepped outside and halted, probing all the shadows. Assured that nobody threatened, he canvassed the lawn, and checked the empty swimming pool.

Beside the pool, he listened once more for a dissonant sound within the usual night noises. Dead leaves rustled—that was all.

Back inside, McQueen carefully locked the doors behind him and checked all the other downstairs doors and windows; without exception, they were tightly shut. Nobody was now, or had been, in his house.

Upstairs, Cynthia asked, "Where did you go? I was frightened to death. Why didn't you call up to me?"

"It's all right, nothing's the matter."

The telephone rang. In a dither, Randolph Bonney blurted, "Dale, you'll never guess what's happened!"

"I don't even want to try."

"Miranda Stryzpk just found Moe, and he's dead!"

"He's *what?* How can that be? Only yesterday we had coffee!"

"He hung himself from a viga with an electrical extension cord!"

"No!"

"I'm not kidding. I figure he had to have stood up for the first time in forty years to accomplish it, and medically that should have been impossible. It's a miracle!"

"I don't believe it," McQueen said, his dry throat causing his voice to crack. "He was one of *us*. We're minutes away from getting electricity into the Pueblo. We were almost home free!"

"That's not all. Listen to this—"

"There's more?"

"He left a will. But not the will everybody thought he was going to leave. He redrew the entire thing, probably just tonight, and left it on the seat of his wheelchair."

"He left it with a good-bye note?"

"What good-bye note? The will *is* his good-bye note. Wait'll you hear what it says."

"I'm waiting, already."

"He cut off Miranda, the kids, the grandchildren, the hospital, the library, the Cipi García Museum—he cut off everybody!"

"And?"

"And he divided all his assets equally between the Anti-Electricity Coalition and the Albino Pine Defense Fund!"

J. B. LEDOUX WAS SO TIRED he couldn't see straight. His father had returned, back from the dead on the day Moe Stryzpk committed suicide, and he had moved into their house, planning to torment them into eternity.

At first J. B. blamed Teresa for moving things on the mantel, eating his liverwurst before he could get to it, polishing off the liquor almost overnight. But when he complained to her, Teresa confronted him so queerly he understood immediately she was innocent.

Rudy LeDoux hid J. B's car keys in strange places making his son constantly late for work; J. B. was always searching for those keys, frantically turning the house upside down, berating Teresa as they flung cushions off chairs, scrambled through trouser pockets in the laundry, sifted insanely through driveway gravel bits. The keys finally appeared in his closet, in a shoe, or in the refrigerator on a plate, or on a bathroom shelf in the glass containing J. B.'s extra false teeth.

One morning he could locate neither pair of false teeth: Teresa found them two days later on the bird feeder outside their bedroom window.

On another morning, when J. B. raced out the door late for work again, he almost killed himself tripping over some bones on the doorstep. Teresa said they were animal bones, probably discarded by a stray dog. At first, J. B. agreed with her. But when he picked them up they were hot to the touch, a sign from his old man; perhaps they were actually Rudy's misshapen femurs, tibias, ribs. J. B. hurled them into a field next door. Later that evening, however, ostensibly out for a walk, he searched for the bones, finding them easily because they glowed with a phosphorescent light in the dead grass. J. B. stored them in a plastic garbage bag in the garage: but next day they were gone.

Teresa went to bed early, but sleep eluded J. B. Camped in the den watching television, he could not concentrate on the programs; an invisible hand kept changing the channels, so frightening J. B. he did not dare get up and switch back to the program he had been watching. Instead, closing his eyes tightly, he tried to ignore the diversions. The flesh on the back of his neck prickled.

Or, sitting alone in the dark with a drink, J. B. simply

waited for a grotesque occurrence. He heard footsteps downstairs: the refrigerator opened and closed: there were strange squeaks: the radio suddenly went on and clicked off: somebody chuckled: someone else whispered words he failed to catch. There were scratching noises.

J. B. said, "Papá? Is that you—?"

All the sounds stopped: the house became terribly still. "Papá, is that you?"

That was his litany these days. He was always cocking his head, hearing things. J. B. took time out to visit the grave: but it looked undisturbed. "Please, stay there," he begged nervously. "That is your place. I'm sorry. I can't take no more, leave us alone." And tears came, but he refused to cry.

That night Rudy LeDoux left mud on the kitchen floor. Dollars from J. B.'s wallet were scattered on the living-room rug. Several piano keys clinked during the night. Somebody cried, "Mayordomo—dame agua!"—*Ditch boss —gimme water!* And the front door, carefully locked by the mayor before going to bed, was wide open when he staggered downstairs at 4:00 A.M. to fix hot chocolate and fumble in a cabinet for Valiums to give himself rest.

LORD, how Anthony Martínez danced!

He felt superfine—young, husky, reeling with good blood, good food, good vibes. Winter turned him on, set his blood to racing: snow was the most marvelous stuff on earth! Traditionally, when the mountains turned white, Anthony awoke, startled to discover himself so alive! And he was learning so much so quickly that his brain might kick off on an overload one of these days! The action involved in reporting stories, taking photographs, putting the rag together, meeting a dozen crises a minute was heady stuff that often left him feeling ecstatic. There was nothing he could not now handle.

I'm so strong I'm dangerous, he felt. My mind is so alert that if I touch it with a metaphorical thumb I'll cut myself on the clarity. Everything, but *everything*, lay before him. When not at April's or doing *El Clarín* legwork, Anthony stayed at home devouring library books, anything he could get his hands on—fiction, poetry, history, rebellion, sex, philosophy, psychic phenomena, mountaineering. In one day he galloped through *From Here to Eternity,* on another, *Annapurna.* Recklessly, he mixed Vladimir Nabokov with Wilhelm Reich, downed them

462

with a chaser of Damon Runyon, and topped off the concoction with some William Shirer sprinkled over a potion of Jerzy Kosinski, *Rabbit Boss, Shaking the Pumpkin,* Jean Genêt, Henry Miller, Vine Deloria, Jr., and Piri Thomas. The world, a dangerous place indeed, flowered with lush, criminal vitality through which Anthony rampaged like a hairy, spittle-festooned wild child.

What luck to discover things! I'll sail around the world in a tiny skiff and climb Mt. Everest, go to Hollywood and tame tawny movie stars, wrestle with my own sacred mountain, save my people and give interviews to awestruck news reporters, then steal home by back routes and watch myself on the family's new tube!

Unafraid—his ample muscles bulged. He paced restlessly, begging those around him to move faster, and ached from his own vigor and sexuality. And he was convinced that the mean little genocide manipulating gears driving the Chamisa Valley toward the last quarter of the twentieth century could not hurt him. A swashbuckler supreme! Something—some intangible force of freedom, goodness, and cultural self-righteousness—had merely to say the word, and like a maniac, like a potentate of devastation, he would slay with a biblical fury, splashing the clouds with blood, smiting all the town's assholes dead in their purloined tracks (what the hell did *purloined* mean?)— he could do that because a liquid mountain-chain coursed through his native (you bet your sweet ass!) American (right on!) blood.

Suddenly Anthony felt so good it was downright scary.

He was sculpting a lot these days. His fingers tingled with creativity, his hands always itched to handle the knife. His body was not quite coordinated enough to meet the demands of his imagination, it would have to be trained, but train it he knew he could. His miraculously clear vision could inspect the woodpile and suddenly, like a dowser's branch, dive toward the correct piece to carve— what was it, in his body, that gave him the correct selection so easily? Often he did not have to articulate in his head the shape of the thing to come, the wood carved itself, a form emerging as if the piñon had a separate life: birds, rabbits, sinuous abstractions, sensuous limbs, stiff, traditional faces, secretive attitudes, smooth and liquid twistings. The wood emerged from his touch so transformed that sometimes he gazed at it in astonishment, giggling at his talent.

Anthony had a spot, a favorite retreat, an old adobe ruin which had at one time belonged to his father, an ancient summer home located at a point where irrigated valley land touched the first ripple of foothills. It was close to a Midnight River feeder stream, and had a view of the entire western United States. Anthony often retired to that house, carrying a book, a carving, and, propped against its crumbling outside walls, or slumped into a comfortable corner inside the ruin, he rushed through words or shaped wood or simply sat and meditated, or smoked dope, or slept soundly as turquoise bluebirds rustled among the sagging vigas. It was his place, his inspiration, his hideout, a ball-bearing upon which his world turned.

While inside this place one wintry afternoon, smoking a joint and reflecting on the catastrophic nature of the wonderful universe, Anthony heard voices outside. At first he figured they were a simple manifestation of past history, his ancestors come by for a chat, planning to drop a revelation or two for his benefit and edification. But after a spell he realized the voices were speaking English; and from the general tone of things, they seemed to be discussing something banal, complex, and down-to-earth—like a business venture.

Sighing, Anthony ordered his mind to cease drifting and concentrate on matters closer at hand. It cost him some minutes' hard labor, but he began to decipher various syllables being articulated outside his retreat; and in due course he could make sense of the conversation taking place between several individuals out there.

Sitting up sharply, Anthony slapped his cheeks, blinked, and really forced himself to listen. Because Joseph Bonatelli was out there, with Rodey McQueen, both Bob Mooses, Junior Leyba, and the two old Denver lawyers, Joe Brady and Win Potter. And their concern over the site had nothing to do with its being a good spot for picnics, Kiwanis meetings, or a wild-mustang roundup.

The hair on the back of Anthony's neck prickled; his balls shriveled.

They were going to put a dog track on this spot, right on top of his grandfather's ruined adobe house; and they were wondering where exactly the parking lots should go, and how many motels could line the river over there; and they were running down loopholes through which a gambling enterprise could circumvent state laws by being on

Indian land; and they were discussing the possible terms of leases to be negotiated for the track and the motel-hotel development; and they were talking about damming the river just north of here to form a recreation lake; and they were speculating about building a housing development for upper-middle-class outsiders on the lake's shores, providing jobs for the Indian people—they would all become fabulously rich.

They laid that down during the fifteen minutes Anthony listened, growing cold . . . and old. What an innocent useless parasite he had been all his life, especially of late during his euphoric coming-to-grips with the wondrous nature of This Savage Life!

His throat became so dry he could barely breathe. His body, indestructible moments ago, now felt as frail as a crisp autumn leaf that would disintegrate if anyone stepped on it.

Anthony's ears rang. He was foolish, inane, insane, cut adrift. It had been going on under their noses all this time, and although they had sniffed all around it they had failed to smell it out.

Appropriately, his fear eventually turned into a young man's rage. Inappropriately, this rage got the better of his instinct for survival. Anthony suddenly showed himself at a hollow window, and, even before his eyes registered the group gathered ten yards away, he shouted:

"What the hell are you people talking about? You're out of your skulls! *Get off my land!*"

Their reaction he would remember afterward, remember it for as long as he lived, if he lived that long. The group as a whole, like a cocktail gathering blandly looking up to slightly acknowledge a newcomer's arrival, assessed him with unperturbed emotion, gazing at him blankly as he bellowed; and they continued fixed on him, slightly puzzled but not at all disturbed, for the ten seconds it took the echo of his shouting to die; then Joseph Bonatelli moved, including them all in a swift, casual glance as he said, "Gentlemen." On that signal, they turned, all except Icarus Suazo, whose presence Anthony had not known of because the old man had said nothing during the discussion. Icarus stared blatantly at Anthony while the others, their camel's-hair and tweed greatcoats flapping softly against their legs, moseyed thoughtfully down a slight incline toward two Land-Rovers.

They faced each other, the elder and the younger man,

until Icarus Suazo's features fell apart for a second, his imperturbable set going haywire, cracking like the face of a father witnessing the death by drowning of his son, unable to save him. Anthony caught a fleeting glimpse of that disintegration, and then the Pueblo secretary cut it off, and, walking steadily, without hurrying to catch up, he retreated to the vehicles, a bitter wind flicking a few loose strands of his white, carefully braided hair . . . of his white, carefully braided composure.

As the tiny figures entered the Land-Rovers, Anthony began to tremble. He would outline the scam to April, and in the next *El Clarín* they would fit all the pieces together, blowing the lid off this rotten thing.

But it wasn't going to be as easy as that, Anthony knew. It took no genius to figure that out.

Nothing would ever again be as easy as in the past.

Ever again.

Leaving the ruin, Anthony glanced at the threatening sky, shifted his eyes toward the westward panorama, then looked behind him at the forest, the sacred mountain. Hunching his head down, feeling as vulnerable as if a dozen telescopic sights were tracking each step, he gingerly headed for home, convinced that he would not make it.

But nothing happened.

Yet that night he could not tell April about it. By doing so, he would transfer to her a piece of the new doom measuring his days, and he loved her too much for that, he wanted to protect her from the news, he wanted to protect them all. None of those men out there had spoken, or in any way given him to understand anything had changed, but they did not have to. It was all clear, all incontrovertible.

Suppose, however, that they assumed he had gone directly to April and spilled the beans? That made sense. Of course they would think it.

Anthony made plans to approach Joseph Bonatelli, explaining that he had kept his mouth shut.

But would they listen to him now?

Anthony shuddered.

A raven tumbled awkwardly out of his dreams and apprehensions and landed at his feet, disheveled and panting . . . then it was dead as a doornail. Marshall Kickingbird unleashed a weird, soft wail, centuries old, pitifully obsessed. Doom, and a continuity of bleak centuries, caressed the valley's picturesque corazón.

Suddenly, before autumn had barely begun, winter came: it started snowing.

THE SNOW FALLING past her lace-curtained window had so lulled Charlotte Leyba that she never heard Junior enter the house, on his lunch break, the first time he had been home at that hour in ages. Nor did she hear him ascend the stairs and halt in their bedroom doorway, taking her in, and then noticing the contents of his April Delaney file scattered across the bed. In her hand she held a letter, from Junior to April McQueen, a letter she had literally memorized, one of the most vituperative and heartbroken statements she had ever read: his reaction to April's abortion when they had been lovers.

Junior made no move. Charlotte, stationary in her chair by the window, gazed stupidly at the laxly falling snow, mesmerized, thinking of nothing. She was wearing a beige-colored nightgown, silken, trimmed with white lace. Her thick hair, in dual ponytails just for "fun," was tied with pink ribbons.

"What are you doing?" Junior said finally. "Why are these things on the bed?"

Although it took Charlotte completely by surprise, his voice did not startle her. It was to be expected. Secretly, she had been praying for this to happen, she had known it was going to occur . . . sooner or later.

"You're home."

"It looks that way."

"You never telephoned to tell me."

Still, Junior was unable to enter the room. He could not believe that she had actually gone into his private papers, and he could not believe she had located this, of all files, and spread it out, in public view as she had, openly admitting that a certain ugly aspect of his existence had become her secret also.

A panic arose: Charlotte should not have seen those papers. Junior's eyes flitted about the documents and photographs, trying to assess what she knew, trying to remember what was written down or photographed there for her to learn—his darkest secrets, his obsessions, his debilitating weaknesses, his love and hatred, his insidious vague plans for the future. And he felt trapped, like a little boy with his hand in a cookie jar, just that stupidly caught in some naughty act. Flushing hot all over his body, Junior had no idea what to say or how to proceed. It was so incongruous for Charlotte to delve into his private affairs: Junior had thought they were secluded in an inertia precluding that. And he was amazed by her courage, or her curiosity, or whatever it had been—anger, jealousy, love—that had spurred her to discover the file.

"You shouldn't—" Junior began. But his voice cracked. Instead of summoning his anger to deal with her brutally, he found himself wanting to cry, to go down on his knees, begging her to understand and soothe his hurt, to assure him it was all right, she loved him anyway, she did not mind.

Junior stood in the doorway, having caught his wife in a terrible act, and all he could think was that he loved her and wanted her to love him back. And a sensation, almost of relief, spread through him because he was no longer carrying the entire thing alone. It did not occur to him that she might not realize what "the entire thing" was.

The phone rang in another room, and they let it ring. Charlotte felt at peace, glad that it was over. The snow fell outside, onto their lawn, onto the birdbath, onto the bird feeders; it gathered in spruce branches and in the twisted Vs of large cottonwoods. Cars going by slowly on the street beyond had their lights on. In the corner of each windowpane a slight, scalloped condensation moon was growing.

Junior crossed the room, placing his hands on her shoulders. Ready for anything, Charlotte did not flinch. Let him kill me now, she thought, and end this terrible emotional impasse. Junior's hands felt tentative—almost gentle. In a moment they would deal hurt, and that was all right. She expected real horror; she desired it with all her heart. This time his attack would be for good, because the transgression was, as she had known and hoped it would be, unpardonable.

Slipping his hands down off her shoulders, Junior cupped her breasts: lips touched her head, his breath warmed the skull. It would begin with his hands, when suddenly he gripped her hard, twisting until she cried out. Or he might bite into her hair and jerk his head, tearing out black strands.

But nothing happened. He fondled her breasts, almost delicately. Charlotte was very serene and grateful—she smiled. The snow was lovely, her skin was lovely. Junior let go of one breast and removed the letter from her hand, dropping it onto the floor. Circling a bit, he sank to his knees and embraced her, pressing his face against her chest, then lowered it into her lap, snuggling his nose between her thighs. He stayed quiet, breathing deeply, slowly. Charlotte slipped fingers into his hair and held him, massaging his scalp a little, faint puzzlement touching the back of her brain. A sun somewhere above the thinning storm cast a calm light, and faint snowflake shadows trembled against her arms, his head, her bare legs.

In a moment, Junior stirred. Carefully, solicitously, he prodded her from the chair, onto her back on the rug. His face he kept lowered, turned away from her. Charlotte did not now understand what was happening, it was nothing she had expected or emotionally planned for, nothing their past experience together could decipher.

Kissing his wife tenderly, Junior seemed to melt into her, handling her body with gentle restraint, whispering that he loved her; and they made love with such a profound intimacy and complete lack of hurting that Charlotte cried out in pain, as an orgasm, something she had not experienced for a long time, mellowed through her body like a magic spring day in the heart of a savage winter season.

"Thank you," Junior whispered over and over again. "Thank you, thank you, thank you. . . ."

They lay in each other's arms. The snow stopped falling and a gray light infused their pastel room, making them drowsy. Junior and Charlotte drifted, breathing quietly, into sleep.

# A Beautiful
# Danger

ALTHOUGH MUCH SNOW had already fallen, and the Mosquito Valley winter season would soon begin, the blasting on the new ski runs continued.

Two days after Anthony Martínez learned about the electricity scam, Rodey McQueen called J. B. LeDoux, laying down some ground rules concerning Len Goodwin and Chet Fulton.

Apparently, these two had received a tip somebody intended to steal dynamite from several of the mayor's ski-valley blasting sheds. Therefore they wanted J. B. to leave a shed unlocked during several specific evenings when they planned a stakeout, hoping to trap the guilty parties. J. B. started to balk, wondering why they couldn't operate their stakeout just as well with the sheds locked. But then he philosophized that if he had a nickel for every time he had been involved in something fishy these past twenty-five years, he would be a rich man—which he was. Hence, it would be foolish to stand on principle at this stage of the game. So J. B. met the federal dicks, listened to their plan, and agreed to leave a shed unlocked on a certain night. And sure enough, someone extremely clever stole two dynamite crates from directly under the stakeout's noses. Len Goodwin scratched his head in good-natured puzzlement, telling the *Chamisaville News* it must have been invisible thugs who crept in there Under Cover of Darkest Night to make off, undetected, with such a formidable payload.

In a small one-paragraph article, the *News* reported the theft, letting it go at that. April Delaney read the tiny item, puzzled over it a moment, then pushed it to the back of her mind, where it would not stay. She mentioned the article to Virgil: but he was so harried it went in one ear and out the other. "This is a blast-happy town," he said. "And there's enough dynamite up in those sheds to level the entire Rocky Mountains. These people have used that stuff all their lives, for removing boulders, knocking down unwanted trees, pulling out stumps. It's as if those ski-valley shacks are practically bulging at the seams with free candy. Anybody could want it."

The dynamite job also sat poorly with J. B. LeDoux. Why, he could not easily understand. After all, in a society run by thieves, with him right in there at the heart of things, why quibble over one more robbery? Yet the dynamite theft, under the very noses of the two FBI agents, had exacerbated the normal tensions inherent in J. B.'s everyday operations. That simple, little-noted deed had perhaps upped the ante beyond his willingness to pay. A new ingredient had entered the play—menacing, and unforgiving. Forces with which he was involved and had been involved for ages had decided upon deadly conclusions, ending the charade.

One afternoon J. B. visited the ski valley to view proceedings while a foreman delivered a progress report. Hiking above the new chairlift toward the wilderness area, J. B. arrived at a cleared promontory offering an open view of the blasting on slopes across the ravine. The explosions, muffled by four feet of snow, were unearthly, frightening, beautiful, seeming to take place in an invisible, pristine molasses, the snow heaving up slowly, an icy, mushrooming monstrosity, unfolding a powdery cloud of blinding-white ice that seemed of a single piece until a blowout at the core scattered violent spray over the surrounding forest, settling slowly atop bending evergreens in a limp fallout for several minutes.

Impressed, the mayor watched the dynamiting. Ultimately, something terrible caught at J.B.'s throat and he fled. But that night, in his dreams, the casual eruption of snowy slopes, the remote, muffled blasting that caused it, had him in a frantic sweat. Although he drowsed, he logged no rest. Ghosts—his dad, Atiliano Montoya—kept rustling around clumsily in the house, shifting and breaking things. He thought he heard his father talking quietly on the telephone with his whacked-out son, Benny. The natural order of a familiar chicanery had evolved toward foreign, murderous conclusions.

J. B. awoke at 4:00 A.M. and sat up, awaiting a sound. Almost immediately he heard it—the distant *whump!* of a small dynamite explosion. But not at the ski valley . . . out toward the Pueblo. Seconds later the town was so quiet he wondered if he had actually heard that sound or imagined it.

An angel, a golden Cipi García skeleton with big white wings and a pet magpie on its shoulder, formed at the foot of J. B.'s bed. Frozen with fear, he thought he heard it whisper something—"Del árbol caído, todos hacen leña"—then it disappeared.

In the morning, while shaving, J. B. learned from KKCV that the explosion had been real, destroying a small, prefab BIA storage shed on Pueblo land. Fortunately, the shed, used to store elementary-school materials, was almost empty, so the loss was negligible.

ANTHONY MARTÍNEZ HAD NOT specifically planned a meeting, no arrangements had been made, yet he understood that it would happen, and where. On horseback, progressing slowly across rolling pastureland above the Pueblo's buffalo herd, he spotted another horseman approaching from some distance away and reined in, waiting for Icarus Suazo to catch up. It was a gray neutral day, no wind stirred; the air was too warm, almost but not quite melting a few inches of hard old snow on the ground. Behind him the mountains were sullen, immobile; the western panorama was hazy and limp—he could barely make out the buttes and soft round mountains beyond the Rio Grande Gorge. A black-and-white morning, devoid of color. Ravens drifted lazily overhead, calmly scrawking.

Icarus Suazo took awhile, keeping his horse at a deliberate walk. Drawing near, he gave Anthony a slight nod, and guided his horse so that the men were side by side, both facing west. A moment of absolute silence ensued. Magpie calls sounded clearly in the becalmed morning.

Icarus said, "You have a knowledge that can cause you great harm."

Anthony nodded and held his tongue.

"Have you told others?"

"Nobody."

"That is just as well."

"Meaning—?"

Icarus did not answer. His horse shifted, snorting comfortably, gobs of steamy breath bubbling out its enormous, velvet nostrils. With his hands crossed over the saddle horn, the old man raised himself slightly forward, old leather creaking, and settled back again, more comfortable. He removed cigarette paraphernalia and rolled two cigarettes, handing one to Anthony. The young man scratched a kitchen match on his fly zipper, giving a light to them both.

They smoked while the morning grew even quieter, settling into a dead calm. Faintly, horns tooted in Chamisaville; church bells rang.

"All my life I worked toward the return of our sacred land," Icarus began. "I was very young when the president, Theodore Roosevelt, declared that this land, that all this sacred Albino Pine territory no longer belonged to our tribe, but was to be considered public forest land thenceforward. At an early age, through a series of political accidents, I became, as you know, a spokesman for our people, especially in dealing with outside interests. I have been in Washington, D.C. and Albuquerque, New Mexico, Dallas,

Texas, and a great many other places more times than I care to remember. Always I have tried to make our points and listen to what the other side was saying and to read between their lines, assessing whether they were correctly reading between my lines. I understood immediately that it was a cutthroat business, and that we did not hold many cards. I have told a thousand lies to men who were telling me a thousand lies and I have tried very hard to stand fast. Perhaps I became so obsessed with securing the return of this sacred land that it blinded me to the realities of the situation, I don't know. I never believed we would get something for nothing, but I believed that if I could study the problem until I dominated it completely I could eventually effectuate a fair trade, or even one that tipped the balance in our favor. You must understand that I was never dealing from a position of tribal strength, always from a position of overwhelming weakness—politically, economically, though not, of course, spiritually. And I believe that we are, to a certain extent, still a whole people —exploited and confused as we may seem to be—partially because I was able to strike a hard bargain, giving the appearance of dignity and strength way beyond what I actually felt or believed in. Of course, I ask no one to consider me noble. I have sucked some bitter cocks in my time, and had my own shit shoveled back into my own mouth as fast as the other side could shovel it there. I have made deals, bribed people and accepted bribes, stolen from the Pueblo treasury to pay thugs in very high government places a great deal of protection money. I have done this with income from the tourists, with income from the land, even with income from the foster-children programs, denying our kids clothes, books, candy. I have done it, swallowed my shame, fouled my bed again with that shame, and swallowed it again. I made compromises which seemed necessary to our survival as a people. Perhaps you could argue today that they were not necessary, I don't know. I have never been a prophet, I have no mystical powers, my native spirit is as tired and as strained and confused as anyone else's. You do not rub elbows with sharks and bastards all your life without becoming a shark and a bastard yourself. Fair enough. There is nothing inviolate, and I have violated everything in my time, believing only that if I became a bigger shark and a bigger bastard I might someday be able to beat them at their own game without totally befouling my nest. So I sold out, cheated, lied, bluffed, stole, finagled, threatened, retreated, attacked, cajoled, farted, shat, and vomited whenever it seemed prudent to do so, whenever it seemed that I might gain an inch of irrevocable ground by doing so. And I always gave up that ground whenever it seemed prudent to give it up. In this way I never really won anything, but I never really lost it either. You may laugh, but an equilibrium of sorts has been maintained over these past fifty years of dealing with the white man for nothing less than our right, as a people, to survive.

"More recently, finally, I knew that I was close to my goal. I had something to give, at last, which demanded some enormous concessions in return. For two years I have conducted innumerable high-level consultations and court cases, which as you know finally have us on the brink of winning back our sacred land, in conjunction with introducing electricity into our community. I have for years thought this a fair trade. All my instincts told me it was the best I could hope to do, and that the time was now ripe to drive the bargain, since I am an old man and do not know how much longer I will live, and I felt I was best qualified to complete the negotiations. So I went ahead and I have all but done it. I have signed most of the contracts: I expect to give the announcement within two weeks. Then we'll have our land, they'll have their electricity in our ancestral homes. Our people, no doubt, will argue for many years over the outcome, they will weigh and complain, accuse and vilify. Myself, believing that there could never be a clear-cut victory, I scrambled to attain as much as I could. When Joseph Bonatelli turned up in the negotiations, I realized that we were in trouble. He was a man whose bluff I found difficult to decipher. Reading between his lines and through his resumé, I understood he would be involved in the race-track project, for I knew about that. But I came to the conclusion that things would stop there. And I assured myself that the development around it would be centered in Chamisaville, starting with the Northland Grazing Association's three new motels, which turned out to be fictitious smokescreens, and the municipal industrial bonds, which they have no intention of selling, it seems. Still, I felt that the track could be isolated from the rest of the Pueblo, a new road leading directly to it off the highway bypassing by six or seven miles all our settlements, and I had plans to cut off the tourist trade at our apartment buildings, since the objective financed by those tourist funds, the return of our sacred land, would have been attained. I also had high hopes that state and federal regulations combined with the recalcitrance of our own Pueblo council once the Albino Pine land was returned, would eliminate the dog track, and, double-crossing those sharks and bastards, we would come out of it home free. I had a sound and logical basis for believing all this, and I lied like hell to Bonatelli and McQueen and all the others to bring it about, thinking I was leading them into a trap, and that I could perhaps dispense with them all as the Sioux and the Cheyenne did at the Little Big Horn long ago. It was a gamble, granted, but well worth the risk, especially since I don't believe that in the long run electricity will be that bad. It is an aspect of nature that we can learn to control with time."

The secretary stopped speaking, dragged deeply, and exhaled into air so limp that the smoke hung about his head in a gray-blue cloud, scarcely moving.

"And all the rest?" Anthony asked.

"That is what I failed to read between the lines. Their hole card. Those two tottering idiots from Denver that our people once employed years before you were born. Where or how Bonatelli and his crew dug them up I'll never know. But, insane as it may seem, they can win in court. I won't go into the details, except to state what you already must understand all too clearly, and that is that the white man's laws are, and always have been, stacked against us. And all these negotiations, everything, have taken place within that legal system. But enough: if you wish to study it, I can let you see fifty years of files concerning this single struggle to win back the land. It is enough to say that this came up suddenly at the heart of the deal after I had already already affixed my signature to a hundred documents, and I realized that they not only had me by the balls, but that they had stabbed me in the back. If the track falls through, they have the lake, the development, the motels and hotels, the resort. And they probably have all that anyway, such is the nature of the thing. Even before we have finally won back our land, its future rests in the hands of those gangsters. And, as a people, we most surely are threatened worse than before. An incredible mistake on my part, the reason for which is simply that after a fifty-year education in the ways and the laws of these relentless people, I still could not defeat them on their own turf. The government, as you know, has never been on our side. And, once giving up proprietorship of the sacred land, they will offer us no more protection than as always, which is inefficient at worst, genocidal at best.

"Still, at this point it is a very touchy process for them. However much they control us, they must still work with us. And, because of the national political climate, because of ecologists and conservationists and a thousand other mixed-up but quasi-viable forces, they have got to tiptoe until the thing is assured. As long as the lid is not blown, I still have much to bargain with, and may yet salvage a more equitable settlement, I don't know. I will tell you also that I have contingency plans to murder the two old lawyers from Denver, which would definitely put a crimp into their blackmail, throwing a dozen of the more constricting documents up for grabs. Admittedly, I am afraid the entire snarl has become too complex for my understanding at this point. So much is at stake, so many tentacles; and I trust no one, not even among our own people. Too many shadows roam the alleyways at night, too many covert and whispered discussions take place, too much unattached money and motives are floating around, unanchored, disloyal, piratous. I have always held that the confusion is intelligible and decipherable, largely because it is so expertly manipulated by those who must, perforce, understand it. Yet I often find myself treading water in a sort of unintelligible anarchy, and at those moments I wonder if it is because I am a native that I lack some refinement of mind or heart or character which prohibits me from seeing the logical patterns at the center of that universe of confusion. Believe me, I am no native American who fears that if he does not genuflect to the stars they will kill his corn, or that the astronauts will strangle to death in strands of long white hair growing from their own armpits for having desecrated the sacred spirit of the moon, though I sincerely wish such a thing could happen. I do not muck about in gardens of mysticism, I have had no time for that. I have studied the big-bang theory of the universe, understand what is in the makeup of stars and why they twinkle; I could recite to you the composition of the sun, quote to you the exact distance to the moon and how its gravity affects our tides. Yet I also believe in the spirit and culture of our people. I believe that my entire life has been a struggle to preserve and fortify our sacred origins, because they *are* sacred, they have a place, and we have much to give in return. But perhaps there is an inherent contradiction in entering their arena to achieve this other thing. Perhaps it would have been better, avoiding all compromise, to commit suicide like heroes by taking an all-or-nothing stance. Yet I could never feel at peace with the idea of becoming a trenchant historical footnote in some white man's best-selling collection of atrocity stories and noble-red-surrender speeches. If that rhetoric is unquestionably beautiful and poignant, it also makes me sick. Flowery defeatism has no place in my personal lexicon."

Another raven, enormous and pitch-black, floated by overhead, flapping steadily through the motionless air. It scrawked once, laconically . . . scrawked again. Anthony snapped his cigarette butt to earth, and shifted uncomfortably.

The old man continued. "What I am saying is that if you or the *El Clarín* crowd blow the whistle, I might lose whatever bargaining position that remains to me. You reveal the racetrack and development scheme before the agreements are finalized, and the council may veto the last few moves making it all possible; we might even have a riot out here at the Pueblo; most certainly *I* will not get the votes I need to give us back the land in return for the electricity. Never mind how connections link up from a tank-town electric co-op, through Joseph Bonatelli, to the Congress of the United States: on such bastardized circuits the world turns. Of course, I am willing to admit that I am tired, and it might be a welcome relief to have the thing out in the open, the cards laid upon the table, the fight occurring before the public—which would take some pressure off me because, despite my power, our people could probably generate the force to strip me of everything. Perhaps I would be murdered. On the other hand, if you blow the whistle, I feel that the next song I sing will be over your grave. In fact, it goes without saying that even if they understand you'll keep quiet, you are already practically a dead man. Still, this country is not quite yet at the point where they can dispatch enemies brazenly, with complete impunity. If you wish, I can tell them you heard nothing and have spoken to no one about it. That would greatly relieve McQueen and his people, who have no taste for lethal shenanigans. But Joseph Bonatelli—how can I speak for him? He is a stone."

Half a mile away, below them, a beige two-door sedan jolted to a stop at the end of a dirt track, and two figures got out. Both Anthony and Icarus Suazo could tell at once that they carried rifles and that they were white men. The figures left the road, ducked through a barbed-wire fence, and walked up the rolling pastureland toward the two horsemen, in no hurry, their guns held vertically, barrels pointed toward the sky. They had proceeded about thirty yards when their posture and stride revealed to Anthony that they were cops, not town or county fuzz, but outside police. Neither he nor Icarus Suazo made a move to meet the men halfway. The elderly man rolled another pair of cigarettes and Anthony again lit them. Sitting straight in their saddles, they awaited the inevitable as the small figures carefully and deliberately neared them. At a half-mile, both natives understood the men were FBI. Their feet crunched in the old, crusted snow. A raven floated over the two horsemen, scrawking, and passed over the armed men, scrawking again. Distance diminished, clothes took on colors, features became apparent. The men—Len Goodwin and Chet Fulton—arrived. Their rifles still held casually pointed at the sky, they halted ten yards before the horses, grinned good-naturedly, and said, "Howdy."

Icarus Suazo tilted his head slightly at them. His heart beating wildly because he knew they had come for him, Anthony nodded.

"You, Martínez," Chet Fulton said, tilting his gun barrel an inch toward Anthony. "I'm sorry, but we have been instructed to take you in on a federal warrant of conspiracy to dynamite BIA installations."

Why protest? Anthony understood the process at work here, had given up hope, felt it was useless.

He said, "All right."

The four faced each other a moment longer, absolutely without sound or motion, until Chet Fulton said, "Follow us." Turning, he began walking back toward their minuscule vehicle.

Anthony nudged his horse and, keeping a short distance behind the two men, who never once glanced back, he followed. Expressionless, his features filmed in limp smoke, Icarus Suazo did not move.

He remained there, chiseled into place, scarcely breathing, as the two men on foot and the horseman diminished, becoming tiny toylike figures almost swallowed up by the expansive white range. At the far fence, Anthony dismounted, led his horse south to a gate, and walked up to their car. He attached a rope to the halter, tied it around the rear bumper, and all three figures entered the car, one in front, two in back. Cautiously, the automobile retired along the bumpy track, the horse following at a trot. Icarus kept his stern eye on the vehicle until it had disappeared.

Another lone raven glided by overhead, emitting an occasional froglike sound. The old man did not look up. His eyes were fixed upon those faint, far buttes almost whitewashed in milky, dead pollution. The day remained weatherless, banal, nondescript. No life, no motion—becalmed. Cigarette smoke, which had hovered about the old man's face for minutes, seeped into his eyes, lean cheeks, tight lips, gray hair—an extension of that gray hair. Like a lizard, stiff and alert, he did not move.

The faint dingdong of church bells sounded; and a far-away horn beeped, crossing the airwaves from a distant country.

APRIL, VIRGIL, FLAKEY JAKE and Gloria Martínez, and Juan Ortega showed up at the Chamisa county jail to free Anthony.

Contrary to the usual lethargic scene, the entire state and county police force seemed to be on duty—the foyer bristled with weapons. When April and company banged through the door, Gray von Brockdorff, two deputy sheriffs, and Big Bill Baca blocked them off, Big Bill holding a rifle crosswise, the two deputies' hands resting nervously atop their pistol butts.

"No further, folks," von Brockdorff said politely. "Sorry."

"What the hell are you talking about?" Virgil exploded. "I've come to spring a client. Who's the sergeant on desk duty in this mess?"

"Nobody's springing anybody, Virgil," Big Bill said.

Flakey Jake blew his top. "I got a son in this cesspool, and I intend to get him out before you rats kill him or poison his food with botulism! Since when does the American system of injustice deny a person the right to bail? Move aside, you thugs, before we sue you for breach of the American system of democratic principles, inalienable even to us uneducated savages, believe it or not!"

The four cops advanced a menacing step, bumping lightly against Jake and Virgil. "No trouble, please," Gray von Brockdorff said evenly. "Everybody hold their temper, we don't want any problems here. As of this moment, no bail has been set. You want to file for a hearing, go over to the

479

courthouse and I'm sure the judge will be only too glad too oblige. But right now we don't want anybody in here. And until bail is set and he's released, that's the way it is going to be."

"What are you doing to my boy?" Gloria shrieked. "Where is he? Why is the entire United States army occupying our jail? Is he alive? *You killed him, you murderers!* Let me in, I want to talk to my Anthony! Out of the way, you—"

Big Bill gave the woman a shove that almost propelled her backward through the plate-glass door.

"Listen, you idiots, we're *serious!*" von Brockdorff said. "No more fun and games! You people get out of here and get out fast before there's trouble, understand?"

"We'll go," Virgil said apologetically. "Please excuse us. Come, everyone." And, his arms around them, he herded the flustered crew outside onto a sagging patio. A stranger, obviously federal, seated in a nearby parked car, watched them from behind dark glasses.

"Okay," April said. "This isn't funny."

Gloria wailed, "Where is my son? What are they doing to him? He's innocent, my son! How can they jail an innocent boy and not even set his—"

"Shut up!" Jake snapped. "Let the lawyer talk."

Virgil looked up at the sky, closing his eyes. He sensed what was in the works, sensed the danger to all of them gathered here, remembered the *News* article about stolen dynamite, and, understanding that Anthony was innocent, nevertheless wondered what the boy had discovered and why he had not told the rest of them, or at least April. And although he had always known it would come down to this, for it always did, Virgil was ashamed to admit that because of his age, because of being an old man who had grown lazy and tired, he had made no preparations, he had simply hoped it would never happen.

Leading them across the cracked and buckling courtyard toward the courthouse building, Virgil expected to find no judge in any chambers or any office—not today, not for a while. But he went anyway, knocked and waited, and knocked again, going through the motions. Then he returned to the jail, asking the judge's whereabouts, receiving a chorus of shrugs. Outside again, Virgil sighed. "Well, I'll get on the telephone. I'll call the capital, I'll call everybody affiliated with the district that I can locate. I'll notify the *Capital City Reporter* so they at least get a

480

hound up here sniffing around, asking questions. And if I can't get a bail hearing by tomorrow afternoon, I'll go as far as Washington, D.C., if I have to, in search of one. I don't know. In the meantime, I'll try to see Anthony, I'll stick a needle into Damacio Mares, I'll do whatever it takes."

"And what about us?" April asked.

"Sit tight, sweat it out. We're probably going to need money, can you raise it? As much as two, three, five thousand in cash? Or maybe a lot more in property?"

"Sure . . . of course. I can try—"

"Juan, Jake, you have a camera; I'd stay here. Just sit tight and watch who goes into the jail and who comes out of it. Make sure they all know you're here. Keep any kind of vigil you can until they tell you to move out. Even then, wait in the car, in the parking lot—be stubborn, although not to the point of getting arrested. Or, perhaps, one of you *should* get arrested, for loitering, for disobeying a police officer, just to get inside, make sure he's okay. Although I suspect they're not that stupid. Apparently, this is a tight-assed operation, and we had better get moving."

They dispersed, April racing home, Virgil walking up to his Plaza office. As he went, a few snowflakes started falling. Virgil raised one hand, dreamily watching them touch against his palm, melting immediately, gone—like people . . . peasants, revolutionaries, soldiers, sweethearts . . . back during his young manhood. The sidewalk was warm; all the snowflakes melted; and Virgil had a crazy daydream, plodding slowly uphill toward the broken plaza traffic light. A million tiny people floated serenely out of the sky, disappearing in minuscule smears of blood when they struck earth, every snowflake a life, a human being, a rich, melodramatic, and sorrowful story, eradicated without a sound. Afterward the sky, a bright blue, exhibited no traces of the humanity it had dropped into death. Limpid, unscarred, beautiful—as clear as a bottomless lake was the sky, without compassion or love.

For a second, stopped in his tracks, Virgil wavered, the victim of a slight dizzy spell. Immediately, he was surrounded by a crowd of pathetic hopeless souls. Emiliano Tafoya, false light glinting off the single lens in his spectacles, shook a fistful of documents. Abe Gallegos, disheveled and beautiful, offered him a drink from a silver flask. Amaranta GeeGee moaned softly, searching for her man. Others appeared: Filiberto García, Vidal and Eduardo

481

Mondragón, Rudy LeDoux and Atiliano Montoya, Alberto GeeGee and Pancho Ortiz y Pino, Celestino Lucero and Marshall Kickingbird, Jesus Etcetera and Andrés Ortega and Jacobal Mondragón—ghosts, living bodies—the specters of his lifetime, clients and old pals and a few ex-lovers, milling around his battered body and even more dilapidated soul, sucking out his life-force, smothering it even with the memory of their vital misery. Loretta Shimkus eyed him quietly, a loving poison inherently destructive in her sad accusations. "So what?" the old lawyer mumbled tiredly. "Go away, vanish . . . qué no me hinches los cojones . . . I have not yet begun to fight!"

Before initiating the hectic motions that would keep him occupied into the night, Virgil stopped by the Prince of Whales, easing himself carefully onto a counter stool. Gloria Armijo leaned forward, and, as she thoughtfully brushed snowflakes off his head and shoulders, Virgil copped a nice glimpse into the unbuttoned top of her blouse, into the posh northern swell of her bosom.

He reached up, touching her considerate hand and smiling gratefully before ordering coffee.

ENRAGED, APRIL TELEPHONED Damacio Mares. "What the hell is going on?" she shouted. "How come there's no judge to be found within ten thousand miles? Who set this thing up anyway? Where's the evidence you've got to hold him on in the first place? Or do you even know one goddam thing about what is supposedly occurring under your jurisdiction, *Mr.* Mares?"

"I'm not at liberty," the DA said. "I'm just not at liberty, right now—"

"Bullshit! You don't know your ass from a hole in the ground! You're a puppet, Damacio! You're a wishy-washy toy bigwig, that's exactly what you are! You sit behind that big desk sucking your thumb while thieves and murderers go berserk, compliments of the Chamisa County DA!"

"April, I'm just not at liberty—"

"There's no evidence! Are you going to call for a grand jury, isn't that what's supposed to happen under these circumstances? Or are you just going to suck FBI cocks and take orders from my father and sign whatever they stick under your nose without even bothering to read it?"

"I'm sorry, but I'm just not at liberty to say anything right now. It will all be cleared up in the morning—"

482

"The hell you say! What kind of a naïve asshole are you, anyway? The FBI doesn't pick up somebody for no reason at all unless they've got a pretty good reason, or there's some kind of fishy setup going on! Like, why isn't he a federal prisoner if the FBI picked him up in the first place? Do you have any guarantee, they're not going to kill him in that jail tonight?"

"Oh, come on, please, grow up. This isn't the Middle Ages. Nobody's—"

"Don't you tell me nobody's going to do anything! What do you take me for, a perfect idiot?"

"Nobody's perfect," he joked lamely.

"Oh, you're funny, man. You're really funny. You're a fucking laugh and a half. Dammit, this thing is taking place under your auspices! And I want to know what justification any of you people have for holding him, that's all I want to know, and I want to know it right now!"

"I'm just not at liberty, April."

"You're so chickenshit!" April howled. "I don't believe that you're all so chickenshit!"

"All right. I don't have to take your insults—"

"I just want to know *why*," April reiterated. "That's all. I simply want to know why. Because if this is some kind of bag job you helped concoct, Damacio, I won't rest until you are busted right back to the meek little cowardly law-books you were before my father set you up on the DA's throne, I really will. I'll call in every kind of investigation that's ever been invented—"

"It's legitimate, I assure you," Damacio said. "But I'm just not at liberty—"

"Who taught you to say that?"

"What?"

"That fucking 'I'm just not at liberty.' "

"What do you mean, who taught me?"

"Who was it—my father? Joe Bonatelli? Chet Fulton? Which one of those thugs coached you on what to say when this came down?"

"Your father is not a thug."

"My father is the *chief* thug!"

"Shit, April, you've gone bananas. What's the matter with you anyway?"

"They can't hold him! So you get him out of there right *now!*"

"You can't bully me, April."

"Why not? Everybody else does."

"Call me back when you're rational," he said tightly, and hung up.

April tried to go to sleep, but she felt very weird, more than frightened: doomed. After a while she had trouble breathing and opened her eyes. Even in the dark, funny spots were dancing. Then, on the right side of her vision, curious electric squiggles. April blinked, rubbed, they stayed. She sat up, shaking her head, but was so tired she flopped back down. Her head felt light and woozy—she was terrified. April got out of bed, turned on lights, put on Charley's old bomber jacket for warmth, stumbled on her way to the bathroom, bumped into a door jamb. Her hands were cold. She sat on the toilet, reading an old *Time* magazine. The words in an article about a new play made no sense, she couldn't adjust them into correct patterns in her brain, and, after trying for about a minute to read a single sentence, she let the magazine drop, really petrified now. With an enormous effort she got up, went into the kitchen, poured a drink and lit a cigarette and sat at the table in the dark. Something was going on outside, a flitting of people, ghosts, brief apparitions: had Amaranta Gee-Gee's face just floated past a window? Was that Eloy Romo's cigar she smelled? And Jesus Etcetera's horses? The phone rang—Matthew Delaney?—she answered . . . a buzzing filled her ears: had it actually been ringing? Filiberto García raced through the night, carrying an upside-down flag, crying "Auxilio! Auxilio!" Her right hand went numb, and, whimpering, April flexed the fingers to bring back feeling; she slapped the hand against her thigh; banged her fist against the table, stood up and circled the kitchen, whimpering, grunting, whispering, nonsensically to herself. Her teeth began chattering. After a few minutes the numbness in her hand departed, a soft tingle remained. She opened the refrigerator, peered into the gloom of its frosty innards, which had been dark ever since the bulb burned out a year ago, and closed the door. Feeling slightly nauseous, trembling, she padded back to the bedroom, sat down, and suddenly started to cry, at first soundlessly, trying to stop herself, and finally loudly, shouting out her sobs and rocking on the edge of the bed, cupping her groin, for maybe ten minutes. The sorrow of her existence seemed overwhelming. All her losses had finally torn her to shreds. Whatever had happened to all her loves?—gone, lost, damaged beyond repair. Matthew never called anymore, not even to speak with the kids. Charley had died anonymously—where, when? She would never know. Tim Lanahan had perished in booze; Enrique's soul swam like a crazy green fish in hostile, eternal seas. So much intimacy and good life-forces had become dust, and been blown away. So much passion had settled into dark closets of old age. Her children had a lifetime of suffering to go. George Parker was a lost cause, one more vital experience with a bitched finale. She felt abandoned. "I've lost so much," she groaned. "The hell with it all, I wish I could die. I can't stand any more losses, I'm not strong enough, it isn't fair. I can't care so much about people, places, language, politics, art. I'm tired of all these tragedies! I'm sick of broken hearts! Loving is a cruel trap; responsibility is a thug; life is a joke. *Oh shit I can't take any more losses, I really can't.* I'm tired. I'm getting old. I'm not beautiful anymore. I'm not glamorous. My mind is battered, I'm not even that bright these days, I've become a wishy-washy thinker. . . ."

And then, run-down and worse than exhausted, April got dressed, checked on her kids to make sure they were covered, went out to the car, cranked open the sunroof despite the bitter night weather, and gunned her Beetle down the highway toward George Parker's isolated little shack.

Halfway there she slammed on the brakes, turned around, and, cursing her own weaknesses, drove—like a madwoman—back home.

AROUND MIDNIGHT, Pat GeeGee entered Virgil's office carrying a six-pack. The lawyer had done everything he could, and he had accomplished nothing. Phones were busy, nobody was home, people with influence did not wish to interfere in an internal problem. Virgil had threatened, cajoled, pleaded, cursed, and burned bridges. The case was bigger than he had suspected, because the lid was on everybody: in the voices of the people with whom he had spoken there had been a cool professionalism he seldom encountered. Anthony Martínez was being handled in part, yet not officially, by the feds, so nobody wanted to become involved, and anyway—"What could I honestly do to help?" they crowed innocently.

This one was not up for sale.

Disgusted, Virgil popped open a beer and thirstily upended it. Slumped in the lone armchair over by the bookcase, Juan Ortega glared at him with a pouchy, jaundiced eye. Pat decided to rest his weary bones for a minute—screw the bar. He sat down on the blue bench opposite Virgil's desk and treated himself to a beer.

They remained silent for a spell, three old men shaking their heads, mumbling incoherently, scratching their nuts, wondering what might happen.

Juan said, "All these dead-ends. I don't understand all these dead-ends. What the hell is going on?"

Virgil shuffled over to his window: scattered snowflakes swirled through the icy plaza. It all seemed very dead and quiet, and Virgil, chilled clean through, was short of breath; he felt beaten.

"Better I should have died weighed down by bullets," he murmured fitfully. "Instead I spent fifty years learning how to digest shit."

Juan grunted and cleared his throat: "Don't let me hear you speak like that, my friend. You did what you could."

Pat GeeGee said, "I remember when you first came to town, Virgil, and entered my bar. Your lips were as compressed as death, there were stones in your eyes. Your hardness frightened me. I think you said nothing to me for a year. Yet I thought you had been sent by a deity to save our people. And I was correct. Right from the start I trusted you and I believed in you. Nothing has occurred these past years to change my assessment."

"That's right," Juan said. "He speaks the truth."

"What is this, a eulogy?" Virgil complained. "I'm still alive, qué no?"

Juan and Pat actually blushed.

Wearily, Virgil said, "Political power should come from the barrel of a gun. Our gun or their gun. That's the way life stacks up. It's inevitable."

"I don't know," Pat said. "Myself, I could never pull a trigger."

Juan agreed. "Though I've always wanted to shoot people, I have really never wanted to. I've hated Rodey McQueen and that bunch for all these years, I have dreamed about killing them, but I don't really want to kill them. I always hoped that somehow, in spite of their rapaciousness, things would change."

"Rapaciousness," Pat scoffed. "Listen to the Einstein."

"I knew right from the start that they should have been killed," Virgil said. "But by the time I reached twenty-five I was tired of killing. I had done enough and seen enough, I was pooped clean through. I also discovered, when I woke up after being executed to find myself still alive, that life was inordinately precious. A very strange transformation occurred. I wanted so much to live that I couldn't kill anymore. And they have stepped all over me ever since. Just look at us now."

"What's the matter with us now?" Juan said.

"Well, just look at us. Ineffective, doddering, impotent. They laugh at us."

Juan protested. "They don't laugh at *me*. And anyway, they're afraid of us. The United States government, Rodey McQueen, the Electric Co-op—they're terrified of us."

"Bullshit." Virgil returned to his desk, grabbed the telephone, cradled it on his shoulder, and dialed a number.

"Mr. McQueen? Virgil Leyba. Sorry to disturb you, but—"

"Virgil?" What the hell are you doing, calling at this hour? Do you know what time it is, man? It's twelve-thirty at night, dammit!"

"I know, I realize that, but we've got a problem. See—"

"I don't give a damn about your problem, Virgil. You call me at my office in the morning, my secretary will put you through when I'm good and ready—"

"No, you misunderstand. I'm choosing to talk to you right now, because there are certain problems here which have not been resolved."

"In the morning, Virgil, for God's sake." And he hung up.

Virgil dialed his own son: Charlotte answered sleepily. "I'm sorry to bother you," the lawyer said. "Let me speak to Junior."

"I can't, Dad, he's not here. He hasn't been back since this morning."

Virgil sat with the phone in his hand, wondering what to do next. The three old men faced each other, weary as if in mourning.

Juan said, "I remember, before McQueen came, what it was like in this valley. I also remember the day he arrived, and the explosion. I was making love with my wife and suddenly the mattress stood straight on end and flew across the room with us against it and slammed into the wall. I had a bent pecker for six months."

The men chuckled.

"I was playing cards with McQueen himself," Virgil said quietly. "Before the explosion I started to take a pot with aces and eights. After the explosion I was beaten by three kings."

"I was in the El Gaucho with my wife Lucinda," Pat remembered. "Anyway, I think Lucinda was there. Maybe she wasn't. I had no front window then, so the blast did not level my front window. Or maybe that was after I had the window installed, maybe the glass was shattered. But I remember very clearly. I had just drawn a beer for my brother, Juan, and I was handing it to him when the miracle occurred. A strange thin cone of something, not air, but rather the lack of air, barged into the bar with a loud bang and zipped between us. The glass in my hand shattered; a fist-sized hole appeared in the back door—and that's all. It was as if an invisible cannonball had passed through the joint."

"It's time for bed," Juan said gently. "It's time to give up for tonight, my friends. We need to sleep."

Pat said, "It's been a long day."

"You boys go, get out of here, leave me alone."

"I can't ride my bike or walk in this weather," Juan said. "You promised to drive me home."

"Take the truck. I'm going to stay at the office."

"What for?"

"I've got a hundred calls out. Maybe some of them will come back in."

Virgil gave Juan the keys, and, yawning prodigiously, the writer left.

"So," Virgil said to Pat GeeGee.

"These are difficult times. They were not made for old men like us. I wish there was more young blood in this valley. Jesus Christ."

Virgil dialed a number again: Rodey McQueen answered angrily. "Hello—? Hello—?"

"Hello, Mr. McQueen. Virgil Leyba here."

"Virgil? God dammit man, I'm trying to get some sleep!"

"Just wanted to say hello," Virgil said.

"You *what?*"

"Just wanted to say hello, Mr. McQueen."

"You're kidding."

"Not me," Virgil said, and hung up.

His telephone rang. "Virgil!" McQueen roared, "What kind of a game are you playing? What is the meaning of this harassment?"

"Just killing time instead of people," Virgil said, hanging up on him again.

Pat got up, saying, "It's late, Juan is right. We should all go to bed."

"Go. Sleep with the angels. Get back to your bar before they steal your liquor license."

"Take care of yourself," Pat said, heading for the door. "I'll see you tomorrow, God willing."

And Pat was gone. Virgil rolled a cigarette, pried off his shoes, placed his stockinged feet on the desk, and closed his eyes. He was so tired. Ashes toppled off the cigarette onto his heaving chest—that breathing trouble again. The lawyer's head swam for a moment, then he conked out, too tired even to dream. But he awoke abruptly two hours later, the dead cigarette butt in his fingers, a large red welt where he had been burned. Loretta Shimkus had been sitting on his visitors' bench; she dissolved as his eyes focused. Virgil dialed Rodey McQueen's number and let it ring five times before hanging up. He lit another cigarette and promptly passed out again, allowing this cigarette to burn his fingers once more.

When Virgil awoke around four, Cipi García, dressed as the Angel of Death, was sitting across the room on the blue bench, patiently biding his time. Virgil sighed, fluttered his hand weakly, and returned to his snoring. He slept in a clammy hinterland devoid of noise and action and personalities, like a drugged being at the powerfully sterile mile-deep floor of an ocean.

Around five, Virgil came to once more, dialed Rodey McQueen's mansion, and hung up. Fecundo Lavadie, Bonifacio Herrera, Max Jaramillo, and Ikie Trujillo, inundated in weaponry, smoked thoughtfully on the visitors' bench. Virgil rolled his own cigarette and lit it and went to sleep immediately, and did not awaken when the cigarette again burned down to his fingers.

No DOPE, Anthony Martínez figured he had better ditch the Chamisa county jail, but fast, or else he was a dead man. In a trance almost from the moment those two FBIs began walking across the wide white expanse toward him, Anthony had snapped out of it after ten minutes in his cell, spending the next half-hour cursing his own ineptitude, banging the walls for allowing himself to be taken so easily, given all the warning he'd had.

With any smarts at all, he could have been atop Hija

Negrita right now, cooking up a mess of venison, safe at least until next June, which was about the earliest any white man would dare enter the wilderness. Instead, thanks to his own fear and the indecision induced by it, here he was, wrapped up, signed, sealed, and all but delivered to the state penitentiary. And, judging from the amount of hardware congregated out there, they had no plans for allowing his escape.

Anthony picked at the soft masonry with a fingernail, wondering if he could scratch his way out, or, possibly, eat a hole in the wall.

Some pickle. When he finished gnashing his teeth, Anthony quartered the cell, back and forth, searching for alternatives. The air ducts had been cemented over, the concrete floor had been reinforced with a steel blasting mat; the toilet had been bolted to the floor. When he screamed for a lawyer, who might smuggle in a pistol or a hacksaw or—miracle of miracles—a bail bond, which he would, of course, jump immediately, they told him to drop dead. When he told Big Bill Baca that denying him a conversation with Virgil was against the law, Big Bill replied, "So is blowing up BIA installations."

Anthony sulked all afternoon, all evening, waiting for his brain to awaken and ease him out of the joint. He barely noticed when Benny LeDoux and Alfredo GeeGee joined him, landing in separate corners like rag dolls. Let them stew in their own misspent youths, he had enough troubles. After cursing his jailers for a minute, Alfredo folded up his artificial leg, laid his one arm across his stomach, and went on the nod. Benny muttered and fluttered, mumbling about his lack of cigarettes, casting venal glances at Anthony. Two glue-sniffing, hopheaded, juicing, mainlining tecato dudes, Anthony grumbled disconsolately. And then he screamed aloud: *"Dig these beautiful accommodations!"*

Benny LeDoux grumbled, "Hey man, cool down, like my ears, huh?" And then he started whimpering petulantly: "I think I'm dying. Nobody realizes it, but I'm scared shitless of dying. I really don't want to die, not like this, man. See, I had it all figured out. Like, when I felt really finger-popping good I was gonna do an OD on STP. Do my celestial chorus number when life was a bowl of cherries, join all my old pals. Crazy Dave and Cheryl Berry, Shaggy Mike and Fargo, the Kilo Kid and Debbie Delight. They ain't heavy 'cause they're my brothers. Home free, no more doggin', deep-six in the bosom of bosom buddies. I was eighty-sixed from life and I ain't talking about a magazine. The Kilo Kid sells five thousand hits of mescaline to a federal narc, that's okay by me. No tears. Suerte, Chamaco! Richie's in the pigpen and Danny's dead, but four hits of up and two of down, couple reds, like coke, and a button, and I'm off like an eagle, sailing into the rainbow gorge. Dig it. When we went to Texas, Sam the Spider taught us how to change drivers at seventy miles an hour."

At a loss, Anthony suffered this drivel in silence, arms folded, eyes fixed on a distant hunting ground—his stoical, inscrutable redskin role. Huddled in a corner, Benny continued to twitch and whimper, doing a half-baked withdrawal. Alfredo GeeGee snored for a while, woke up and vomited, then returned to his corner and rubbed his single icy blue foot. Anthony himself was damn near frozen—where the hell was the heat? His brain was so cold all his thoughts had congealed.

Benny started to cry. It seemed as if he had not wept in years. Touching fingertips to his cheeks, he stared at them, then licked the salty liquid.

"Sam the Spider, he's the invisible one, you know. Oh, did we ever eat a lot of medicine. This Native A. Sam knows, he gave us a bunch of dead moth wings, also this stick that all we had to do was poke it in the ground and look around and pretty soon there's Big P everywhere. Four hours we gathered and then Lucky Linda almost stepped on a vipora—but that's cool. Only the field telling us: 'Enough, brothers and sisters. You got what you came for, leave something for others.' We could dig it. Good old Sam the Spider. Play taps, Charley. We get it past the BPs down south, then he flies it to New York. That's where the prices are. New York, New York. Big Apple, Gotham, rotten to the core. Never went. Shoulda gone. Outtasight. Far fucking out. Aspen, too. Lot of rich druggies up there—"

Suddenly, his eyes closed and he passed out. Anthony breathed a relieved sigh. All the commotion out there died down as the federal, state, county, and deputized law-enforcement personnel drifted off to cozier confines offering booze, warmth, and women.

Around 1:00 A.M. Benny's eyelids snapped up like runaway window shades. And, in perfectly normal tones he said, "Hey, man, let's split."

Anthony ignored the lunatic junkie.

"I said, 'Hey, man, let's split.' "

Anthony was tired of being inscrutable. And anyway, maybe the disheveled punk had an idea. Any old port in a storm. He deigned to reply:

"Sure, I'll lay my finger beside my nose and bust a hole in the roof on my way out."

"Cut the shit, I got a key."

"Oh sure."

"I ain't kidding. Check on this." Benny held up a big, iron key. "It was lying on the desk when those pigs booked us. So after they frisked me and took all my crap, I picked it up and put it in my pocket."

"It can't be for this cell."

Benny flipped it into Anthony's lap. "What can we lose, man, huh?"

Anthony unfolded, spent a minute straightening his back, jogged in place to get his blood circulating, then crossed the cell, poked the key in the lock, gave it a twist, and opened the door a few inches.

Benny said, "Don't thank me, cousin, just throw bread."

Carefully, Anthony pulled shut the cell door and re-locked it. For a moment he listened for lobby sounds, hearing nothing except the faint crackle of the dispatcher's radio; nobody seemed to be answering.

"There's got to be some jerk on duty," he whispered. "They had chotas out there like gnats on fresh horseshit when they brought me in."

"It's okay," Alfredo GeeGee said, "I got a gun."

"Aw, cut it out."

"No, serious, look." He reached into his pocket and produced a little .22.

Anthony whistled. "How in God's name did they let you in here with that?"

"I dunno." Alfredo gazed stupidly at his gun. "They took my boots, my belt, my wallet, my money, my keys, my switchblade, my matches, my comb, my hard dope, my deck of cards, my rabbit's foot, my gum, my pens, my Saint Christopher's medal, my watch, and my ID bracelet, but they forgot to take my gun, my artificial leg, and these two joints of Acapulco Gold I had behind each ear."

Benny lit the joints. Anthony sucked, held it dramatically, and got hit by a flash that left him feeling rubbery-loose and so friendly he almost kissed his roommates. After the second toke, Anthony's mouth dropped open, he couldn't close it, and he figured he could dissolve himself like smoke through the walls, simply drifting off into some unendangered anonymity sparkling with goodwill and pixie dust. Acting on the fantasy, he slammed into the immobile wall, losing one tooth. Spitting into his palm, he shrugged, giggling, "I guess we got to leave by the front door."

Benny turned the key; Alfredo, the gun held uselessly at his side, led the way. They rounded a corner into the brightly lit and totally deserted foyer. Anthony went behind the west counter, located the belongings file, found his envelope and tore it open, slipping his wallet in a back pocket, threading on his belt. They tiptoed—all giggling—out the front door, and melted, unmolested, into shadows.

"Let's get drunk," Benny suggested.

"Yeah, yeah. Right on, brother. Dig it."

Benny led them across the highway to a liquor store, scouted around the building for a rock, chucked it through the plate-glass window, and, burglar alarms shrieking, he reached through the jagged opening and pilfered some scotch, bourbon, and tequila. Anthony and Alfredo accepted their fair share; the escapees retreated behind the bus station, plunked down among garbage cans, opened the booze and lazily lit into it as the town came alive, police sirens wailing up and down the North-South Highway thirty yards away.

After two drinks, Benny's eyes went glassy and he started babbling again.

"Jesus this stuff tastes good! I feel so parched. Oh man oh man. It's crazy out there. None of the structures of this fucking town relate to people anymore. Ay qué hoyo es esta aldea!"

Alfredo said, "Yeah yeah, I know what you mean."

"Horseshit! Nobody knows what I mean. My abuelito choked to death on his own balls. Puro pedo! Celestino Lucero offed a mountain lion barehanded, but Moe Stryzpk squashed him with a teeny pinky. Jota Eme Jota! Juan GeeGee whacked his ax while they rammed a real redeeming red-hot radiantly rotating railroad ramrod up his asshole. Pinche pendejo! Cojon de conejo! We die with giddy smiles, while Rodey McQueen twists piano wire around our scrawny Chicano throats. Fuck it, fregame, chinga el mundo! Staughton van Pebbles made a U.S. mint paying destitute Injuns nicklitos to sit still and be noble. Dig, cuate! Figurale, compadre! The ghost of Atiliano Montoya crawls through the hotel alley busting bottles and licking sticky liquor off the insides. Qué kilombo! And April Delaney has tough tits, good gams, and a target for their big bullet on her ass. Orale, primo, orale! Her pop boffed Miranda Stryzpk—kiss 'em and kill 'em!—while uptight do-gooders shoved toilets down Amaranta GeeGee's throat. Toda madre! La vida es un gran crudo! Don't jive me, motherfucker! All my friends are camposanto cuties: the last six chicks I balled were dead meat, smack Patties, strung-out putas—no, what's the gabacho word? Poontang! Up against the paredón vato, carnalito homeboy! Ram bam thank you Uncle Sam! Mira tú! Lowriders of the world, unite! Oh where did they went to, all them old Vidals and Filibertos, Jacobals and Josés? I used to care, man. Float like a mariposa, sting like hell. Cuando vino el alambre, vine el hambre. La vida es una sopa! For a hundred years my stomach grumbled. Pa'ondesta mi lonche? Pa'ondesta mi troca? No tengo brekes! Mayordomo—dame agua!"

"What's the matter with him?" Anthony asked Alfredo.

"Ain't nothing the matter," Alfredo replied. "He just gets like this."

Benny's hard sleepy strung-out eyes fixed goofily on Anthony. "Gabacho! Juero! Gringo!" he hissed. "Chota! Mota! Marrano! Borracho! Tell Jesus Etcetera I'm sorry. Viva Atzlán! Don't mourn for me boys, organize. M-16s, bazookas, Saturday Night Specials. Mayordomo—dame agua! Oh oh oh. Speedy Gonzales told me 'This won't hurt—did it?' And Chamisa V. is like a fresh pile of steaming pig guts on a frosty morning—"

They drank for an hour, heaved two empty bottles onto the bus station roof, scrambled up a dirt bank behind the library, circled around another liquor store and two art galleries, crossed the street into the PDQ parking lot, entered the alleyway between the Plaza Hotel and Vigil's Liquors, lay down among a half-dozen drunks lightly powdered with snow and sawing away, and grabbed some shut-eye.

Close to dawn Anthony awoke, Benny over him lightly shaking one shoulder. "Come on, man. Time to split. It's too heavy around here. Let's get out to some fields and trees where we got room to maneuver."

Trying to move, Anthony discovered that his joints had rusted overnight. And his pals were coming on a little too bright-eyed and bushy-tailed considering last night's fling.

Alfredo labored beside Benny, urging him onto his feet at last.

"I'd like to brush my teeth," Anthony said.

"Cut the bromas, man. C'mon. Let's get moving."

Hunched over, they scuttled through the icy blue pre-dawn, trailing clouds of steam. An overcast, leaden sky weighed against Anthony's shoulders, pressing him toward the earth. Alfredo GeeGee, with only one arm and a wooden leg, was a graceful ballerina compared to him. Several times, unable to focus his eyes or hear things correctly, drugged by that strong bush and hard booze, the Pueblo teen-ager took awkward spills, striking hard against the concrete earth, cursing loudly as his fellow escapees fumbled clumsily to lift him upright and flee again.

They stumbled down an embankment, leaped a narrow, iced-over irrigation ditch, and hacked into a willow stand, emerging on the other side with scratched and bleeding faces, nicked ears, and clothes torn half to bits.

"They'll have that Forest Service bird up in another half-hour," Benny said. "Let's go."

"Where are we going?"

"I got an uncle lives out by the Middle Road camposanto. He built this little house down by the Rio Chiquito years ago, it's just a ruin now. But it's on the edge of willows, cottonwoods, elms, this real thick stand—they couldn't find us in there without dogs, which they ain't got. We'll hole up there for a day until they get tired of hunting, then rip off a car and blow this burg."

The plan sounded stupid. But Anthony's head was so loused up he had decided to let the others do the thinking. At least until the hangover subsided. Then he would drop these two dingbats and haul ass to where he belonged, namely Pueblo land.

Dumbly, Anthony trudged along behind them, slopping through ditches, creeping on hands and knees past small herds of disinterested cattle, elbowing clumsily through willows. They had progressed in this manner for about fifteen minutes, when Benny held up one hand and they stopped.

"Well, that's the house over there."

They were standing among chokecherry trees with naked vines, about a quarter-mile from the two-room ruin. Between them and that shelter lay five narrow fields, the grass grazed short. A dry ditch, about twenty inches deep, starting almost at their feet, ran straight through all the fields, curving toward the river just in front of the house.

"Vamonos," Benny said.

"Uh, wait a minute," Anthony protested. "One of us should go first."

"What for?"

"Well, maybe there's a bunch of chotas or something sitting in that shack waiting for us to fall into their laps."

"Stow the paranoid, man. Do you see any signs?"

"No, I don't see any signs, but I haven't seen much of anything for the past half-hour, you want to know the truth. Every time I lift one foot I'm having a hell of a time finding the ground with it again, that's where I'm at right about now."

"Okay. We'll wait a minute, case the joint, make sure nobody's hanging around in there, if you want."

"That'd be just fine. By the way, where's the gun?"

"I dunno," Alfredo grunted. "I guess I dropped it. . . ."

They hung out, stamping their frozen feet, jiggling frozen hands in their groins, keeping an eye on the house and nearby surroundings. Nothing moved, nothing changed, nothing happened.

"Christ, man, I'm going," Benny said.

"Me too," Alfredo chimed in.

"I think I'll wait here and see if you guys make it okay," Anthony stammered through chattering teeth.

"Why you chickenshit fuckin' Injun."

That's what I need, just what I need right about now— a fight, Anthony mumbled to himself. "Uh, hey pal, no offense. I mean, I'm really grateful, no kidding. It's just, well, the three of us walking up to that ruin, if they did have somebody crouched in there, let's say just on a hunch, why, they'd nab us all for nothing. I think just one should go, give us an all-clear, then the rest follow."

Benny said, "Screw you, freeze to death, I'm going."

"Me too," said Alfredo.

"You guys get there okay, gimme a sign and I'll follow," Anthony said, lying through his teeth because it had suddenly occurred to him a guy could get killed hanging out with these inept birdbrains.

"Bueno, screw you, adiós." They pushed into the open. Walking upright, casually, they ducked through one barbed-wire fence after another, reaching the house in five minutes, disappearing inside. Immediately, in reverse, Benny stumbled out the doorway, landing on his back, and

496

a tall blond man wearing a goosedown ski parka jumped after him, a rifle in his hands.

The morning was dead quiet, threatening more snow: Anthony could hear their voices.

"Hey man—!" Benny yelled.

"Shut up and get up, Martínez!"

"Take it easy, cuate—"

"Get up with your hands on your head or you're a dead man! Right now!"

Benny raised himself deliberately, lazily, flaunting his lack of concern at the flustered cop. What the hell is he *doing*, Anthony wondered. Did he tell that son of a bitch he was *me*?

"On your *head*, Martínez!"

Backing up laconically to the edge of the ditch, Benny put his hands on his head. "Go fuck yourself, pig!" he giggled. "You're a moron!"

The agent raised his rifle, swinging it up until it was at point-blank range, six inches from Benny's face. Anthony first saw the little irregular-shaped splatter emerge from the back of Benny's head, and then, as the body collapsed sideways into the ditch, he heard the gunshot. And even though the junkie had to be instantly dead, he heard Benny scream:

*"Orale Diós, Mamá, Papá—lo siento mucho! Mayordomo—cabrón—DAME AGUA!"*

Two other men, herding Alfredo GeeGee at riflepoint, emerged from the small ruin. In shock, doomed anyway for the role he had played in this botched setup—what had gotten into Benny anyway?—Alfredo had his hands over his ears. He couldn't look toward the body, or tell them they hadn't killed anyone, they had just helped a lost soul commit suicide. Quickly, those two men, neither of whom Anthony recognized, though both were obviously federal cops, marched Alfredo along a fence line up to a dirt road and down the road out of sight. The man who had killed Benny disappeared into the ruin, and reappeared carrying a rotten fence post three feet long, which he arranged carefully beside the body. Next, moving along the ditch toward Anthony, he removed a glass pop bottle from his jacket pocket, smashed it on a small rock, and, returning to the body, dropped the jagged bottle neck beside the junkie's hand. Then, unzipping his parka, he got a walkie-talkie, calling in to somebody. And afterward stood there quietly, looking up at the sky, waiting for his people.

Anthony heard sirens blaring; they jolted him awake. Backing carefully into the naked bushes, he waded the icy Rio Chiquito and headed for April Delaney's.

GEORGE PARKER'S DREAM took place on a placid winter afternoon toward dusk; a casual snow was falling. On the concrete court in Balena Park, he was shooting a basketball. A warm bread odor from somebody baking in a house beyond the graveyard and the Cipi García Miracle Museum mingled with crisp snowflakes. At the start of this dream the court was barely damp, the storm having begun only a few moments earlier. In T-shirt, shorts, white socks, and sneakers, George was very aware of his body, the graceful way it performed. Totally into himself, he was also removed, an onlooker twenty-odd years old. Viewed in slow motion, his arm muscles, taut shivering ribbons, slowly bunched and then luxuriously snapped, rippling backward with almost erotic undulations on each delicate shot, his fingers fluttering for a tantalizing instant against the ball's hard rubber skin before it floated unerringly toward the basket. And, as it sank through with a snap, the net backlashed lazily away from the sphere: shot perfectly, one of sports' arrogant gestures as pure as the most buried intentions of all life.

Virgil Leyba, an onlooker, with the collar of his tattered suit drawn up against the snow, clapped his gloved hands a couple of times; beside him Celestino Lucero looked on morosely, saying nothing.

George took long strides, or stuttered his pace heading for a rebound, eyes automatically calculating distance, controlling the timing involved. As his weight settled on first one, then the other leg, his bad knees holding up, he admired the various shapes patterning his muscular thighs, calves contracting, going rubbery and loose, a universe of strain and shifting energy with each realignment of weight or change of direction. Oh, he was excited, watching himself move in slow motion as snow continued falling—he was awed by every tone and striation, by every visible and invisible evidence of tendons and ligaments perfectly controlling bones, effortlessly awarding this great gift of coordination.

His heart was beating, muffled; he felt avalanches of blood tumbling through arteries and veins, feeding lung

498

nodules so that he never lacked for air. His ankles bent with impossible limberness, his sneakers squeaked against the softening concrete. And the snow kept falling as darkness emerged across George's shoulders in a puffy explosion.

Violin music began. A careful hand struck a quiet guitar chord. Espeedie Cisneros and Juan GeeGee had joined Virgil and Celestino on the sidelines. Espeedie, his old violin tucked under his chin, was covered with blood from killing sheep: Juan's guitar hanging by an old leather strap around his neck almost touched the ground because his legs had been blown off at the knees.

Playing this game against an imaginary adversary, George scored nicely on a fading jumpshot, then tied himself on a long set, went ahead with a careful free throw, laughing as the bright orange ball whispered against threads, not even touching the rim. Their muffled clapping reached his ears. Waltz music floated liltingly, a pretty and parched echo from the Good Old Days. Then, his observer's eyes focused exactly on that split instant when the slightly off-shaped sphere rising from pavement met a halt against his spread fingers, each finger separately absorbing different stress and yet acting in remarkable unison, controlling the ball as his limbs guided the whole athlete through impossibly intricate maneuvers—then he scored against himself on an opposite-hand lay-up, coming off it looking back over his shoulder as the ball, an orange whirlpool, spun around the rim, gradually screwing itself clockwise into the net, which bulged up as he pranced serenely off again.

The snow was still falling. The park was beginning to fill up with people, old-timers, men and women strolling as if on a Sunday afternoon, old-fashioned and impressionistic under umbrellas, the wretched of the earth in a Monet mood. Amaranta GeeGee, Eloy Romo—in his cape and gloves—and Jacobal Mondragón. Soundlessly, they drifted together, choosing partners, and began to dance gracefully the waltz of the brooms, and then the waltz of the handkerchiefs.

Darkness accumulated, mobilizing like the white stuff encroaching on that area in which he played. It expanded like a gentle threat, like his mother's not-forgotten voice traveling through a childhood evening, calling him home, killing his playing time, ending another day.

Reluctant to end this feeling of being good, George did

not stop. He wanted to play and practice, dribble and shoot, experiencing all the languid and dynamic rhythms he controlled, a master of the simple, crucial forces involved with being alive. He wanted to prove to the spectators, the dancers, the silent admiring cripples, the war victims, and the people like Ursula and Perfecto Torres— he wanted to prove that his world was insulated from the kind of misfortune that had so savagely clipped their wings. By now, dozens of them floated languorously around the park, lightfooted waltzers, greeting each other, black silhouettes under graceful umbrellas, nostalgic shadows, beautiful though ruined, supremely and serenely tolerant of misfortune, enduring despite it all. They smiled whenever he caught an eye, and gave little waves. April was there, dancing ring-around-the-rosy with her children, her chin jutted defiantly. Alfredo GeeGee and Benny LeDoux slouched past her, smoking joints, angelic and lost and cynical, powdered with white stuff, grotesquely beautiful. The guitar and the violin were off-key, the accordion wheezed asthmatically, several piano keys gave tinny plinks. But the music—"Adelita," "Adiós, Mariquita Linda"—could break your heart.

The darkness and falling snow persisted. Time to call it quits, yet George couldn't admit the session was over. Vaguely disquieted, still enraptured by the sight and sensation of himself angling through the hushing storm to score, George leaped gracefully, with the syncopated move of a good loose shooter, up for another jumper, and, as he settled down laughing, rigorously shook out snow from his hair, a little exploded bunch of it momentarily hovering like a ghostly talisman above the spot where he had been and would never exactly be again, so infinite were the eloquent variations his limbs and muscles could afford.

Wet, the ball slipped off his fingertips. Lunging, George's first awkward move, he recaptured it, but one foot skidded slightly. A thin film was building on the playing area, and George could see his footsteps, shining with varying intensity, at different levels in the powder. The key, the free-throw lines, the boundaries had disappeared, taking from him something crucial to confidence and orientation.

A panic entered the strenuous exercise. Muscles ebbed and bunched nervously; it was harder to maintain balance and control his ball in the uncertain footing created by the storm. Shots which had fallen true only minutes ago, now missed by inches. George staggered while driving, but recovered, the ball starting to bounce away . . . he snatched it back, scored. Who was leading this imaginary struggle between himself and the anonymous competitor within?— he had forgotten, was forced to begin again.

Now George saw himself fading, his white outfit merging with blackness and the snowfall. The pallid spectators grew faint as the storm intensified, melting into its thickness.

Then the scene took on a lovely desperation, as if George believed that by hustling every second he could somehow keep the snow and the engulfing darkness off his playing area, and the game, his praiseworthy coordination, might continue forever.

During a moment when George had his right knee raised, his torso twisted, his head turned leftward, looking back at the basket, his right arm extended high and slightly forward, fingertips guiding the ball off his hand in a hook shot, the snow so thick it gave to the entire surroundings and to the action within the setting an air of impressionistic pointillism—during that split second all motion froze.

Waking at dawn, George would forever remember himself like that, helplessly captured in a beautiful danger he refused to acknowledge, his passion for a permanent definition and security at the immediate heart of life ridiculed by the icy, obliterating weather, by the slowly turning world, and by a faintly snow-spreckled lawyer, a couple of dim junkies, and a fat old man stroking his violin.

# Cry of the Peacock

WRAPPED IN A faded purple robe, smoking a cigarette and working on a cup of lukewarm coffee, her eyes bruised from sleeplessness, April sat at her kitchen table as dawn formed behind the mountains, while Anthony ran it down: the dog track, the hotels, the lake, the housing development, his talk with Icarus Suazo, the jail escape, the death of Benny LeDoux. As he spoke, she felt herself withering, shrinking into fear, her normal paranoia becoming too heavy to bear—overwhelming, terrifyingly concrete. Her fingertips tingled, her head buzzed; perhaps she would vomit. She was struggling to control her breathing, sucking in slow, wheezing breaths.

April had thought about this situation for almost a decade. Everything she had read and experienced confirmed that the time would eventually come. And yet she had never believed it would arrive when she was so unprepared, so vulnerable, such easy pickings. And she was unprepared because, she thought, her own work had not pushed them far enough. The *El Clarín* was so ineffective. They couldn't possibly care: Their Side was winning by such a large margin they could afford to be magnanimous, altruistic, tolerant. And besides, being blood kin to so many sharks cruising these specific waters meant that a built-in immunity would protect her, the kids, their future.

Anthony paced, tapping cupboards, craning his neck looking out the window, suspicious of every car that cruised slowly through the blue gloom of rising dawn.

"You should stay away from windows," April whispered, afraid to speak naturally for fear her obvious terror would make him more skittish.

"Oh Christ, why bother? They probably got five guys out in the chicken coop with tape recorders. There's probably a pig in your crawl space monitoring something connected to a loudspeaker in the DA's office. There's probably some son of a bitch squatting in your back ditch taking telephoto movies of my mouth moving that an expert lip-reader flown into town especially for the occasion transcribes every stinking afternoon. They could kill me by remote control from down in the capital just by pushing a button—"

"Hush, please. I'm sorry. Let the kids sleep a little longer."

Anthony put more water on for coffee, sat down, got up, paced for a moment, sat down again, got up immediately, spooned instant coffee into two cups, filled them with hot water, and sat down again, drumming his fingers on the table.

"If I could just get across this valley to Pueblo land and into those mountains," he whined tightly. "If I could just do that—"

"I can drive you there."

"You?" Anthony banged the table. "Come on, April. It's light now. We walk out that door together we wouldn't even be halfway to your car before somebody with a pair of binoculars on a neighbor's roof or up in a tree would click on his walkie-talkie and alert a couple hundred trigger-happy goons that we're on our way. We'd die like Bonnie and Clyde."

"It might not be that way."

"Maybe I didn't see a kid who was supposed to be me get blown away an hour ago, either."

April said, "I don't know what's wrong with me, I can't think what to do. I should call Virgil."

"Brilliant. You're asking me to believe that Virgil gets up, gets dressed, hops into that dilapidated pickup, and toddles over to April Delaney's house at seven A.M. and nobody who might be interested in that particular little chain of events happens to notice? This roof would cave in from all the attention landing on it if Virgil did that."

"So." April warmed her hands around the cup. "We wait here, just like this, helplessly, at this table. We wait for them to do whatever it is they're going to do?"

Anthony was up again, tightening his belt, loosening it, opening the refrigerator and staring blindly at the contents, closing it.

Poking in a cupboard, locating some piñon nuts, starting to crack them between his teeth, he said, "How come we're so helpless? I don't understand it. I thought we were smarter than that. How come, with all the talk we did about what can come down, we still never prepared for it to happen?"

"I don't know. I'm sorry."

"Maybe we're blowing it up out of proportion. Maybe they mean to murder us in cold blood, but perhaps they're also as stupid and clumsy and bumbling as ourselves. I mean, they deliberately offed the wrong banana by mistake. Maybe I could simply walk down to the road, hitchhike across town in broad daylight, stop by the house for some things, saddle up one of my dad's horses, and trot off into the mountains with my saddlebags full of taco chips and bean dip, and nobody would notice. Maybe you could drive me into town and we could stop by Virgil's office for some advice, and all three of us could chow down in the Prince of Whales, then cross the plaza to Pat GeeGee's, celebrate the fact that I'm going underground for a while with a couple rounds of prime rotgut, and finally drive on out to the foothills, completely invisible all this time to the two hundred and fifty rabid, trigger-happy clods flooding the valley looking to blast my ass."

April giggled nervously, lit another cigarette, coughed, and pulled her robe tighter.

Tina appeared in the kitchen doorway. "Hey, what's the matter with you guys?"

"Nothing, darling. Come and give Mommy a kiss good morning."

The sight of her rosy-cheeked daughter in a pink frilly nightgown and fuzzy blue bunny slippers advancing sleepily into her arms almost caused April to burst out crying. But then Duane stumbled groggily into the kitchen, staggered over to the refrigerator, and struggled with his pajama fly to release his penis so that he could take a leak. "Stop!" April cried, grabbing her son, whom she propelled into the bathroom, throwing up the toilet lid just in the nick of time as her sleepwalking babe cut loose.

Anthony said, "I know those SOBs, they'll grab the kids at school and grill them about me, I know they will."

"You really think so?"

"Doesn't that make sense?"

"None of this makes sense."

It was surreal, crazy. Outside, the land was so quiet, the naked tree branches serene, the mountains—fused with a ripening violet light—untroubled. Inside, at the kitchen table, the children gobbled raisin bran smothered in apple and banana slices and slurped up hot chocolate, oblivious to rumblings of murder. It was so normal April's fear subsided. In the next room, Anthony stood at a window, watching magpies cavort in bare branches. The kitchen radio played country-and-western music.

To hell with them all! Anthony went onto the porch, gathering chopped piñon for the kitchen stove. He fed small logs into the dying fire and went outside again. Crossing the driveway to April's woodpile, he grabbed an ax, and, for about fifteen minutes, while April fed her kids, Anthony split wood to replenish the porch bin, working himself into a lather that felt good, while his brain, unable to fabricate a way out, took a temporary vacation.

Wearing a long red stocking cap, an Aztec ski mask and wind goggles, old-fashioned driving gloves, a red ski parka, knickers, and hiking boots, Juan Ortega pedaled up the driveway.

Dismounting at the woodpile, he said, "When did you get here, Anthony?"

"You say that as if you expected I'd be here."

"Where else?"

"Hey, wait a minute, Juan. It's not supposed to be that easy to know where I'm hiding."

"Oh stop it. Any moron capable of putting two and two together could figure it out. Where are you going?"

"Inside. Up the chimney. Who knows?"

"But wait a minute." Juan fetched an enormous brown paper bag from the bicycle's grocery basket. "I've got a plan for saving you—"

"You're crazy!" April and Anthony cried in unison as Juan upturned the paper bag on the kitchen table, dumping out an Aztec ski mask and goggles, binoculars with a leather neck-strap, a long, cheap cigar, a pair of Levi's knickers, and black motorcycle gloves. And as he shed his bright red ski parka in order to remove the bright yellow ski parka beneath it, Juan said, "Of course it's crazy. But we have to get you back onto Indian land and up into those hills until the heat cools off. So I've only concerned myself with the problem of getting you from here to there. Which might be simple enough, providing there's no basic flaw in my analysis of the situation. I mean, we all know they're out hunting you; and they realize you know the wrong person was killed this morning. Therefore, they are expecting your every move to be surreptitious as all get out. For that reason, are they looking for you in the middle of the highway, in the center of open fields, or behind the wheel of a car stopping at one of their roadblocks for a routine inspection? Not at all. They're searching for you in the shadows, in the alleyways, among the garbage cans, atop the roofs, in the thickets, in all the dark corners and protected places of Chamisaville. They're out there shining flashlights down into prairie-dog holes, looking for Anthony Martínez. They're knocking apart every conceivable hiding place they can imagine, conjure up, or bump into. The logical way for you to elude them, then, is by not trying to elude them at all. If they see you out in the open, flaunting Anthony Martínez to the world, pedaling April's three-speed bike behind my own bike down the center line of each road leading to the Pueblo, jauntily smoking that cigar, attired in this ski mask, goggles, parka, binoculars, knickers, and sneakers, with a

505

Roger Tory Peterson *Field Guide to the Western Birds* in your basket, how could they possibly suspect a thing?"

April said, "Juan, I think it's time we got serious."

"I *am* serious. How much longer do you think they are going to keep away from this house? Maybe an hour, maybe a half-hour, maybe even less time until somebody puts this place back under surveillance. Meanwhile, you should see the fields and highways and byways of this town: they're bristling with cops, agents, deputies, squad cars, district attorneys, and armed bounty hunters. You try to *creep* out to the Pueblo, and this time around you won't have a double to accept your medicine for you."

"You're trembling."

"Of course I'm trembling. I'm scared stiff."

April said, "All right, let's at least consider the alternatives. I could carry him in the trunk of my car when I take Tina into daycare."

"They'll stop you ten times between here and town; ten more times between town and the Pueblo."

"I'll call Virgil, he can drive over in his pickup. We'll hide Anthony in a load of wood."

"With Virgil at the wheel? They'll yank him out of the truck, pour kerosene on the wood, and set it on fire."

"We'll hide him out here until dark—"

"Where?"

"In the crawl space."

"If you were an agent searching for a fugitive you thought might be hiding in this house, what would your first question be?"

" 'Where's the trapdoor to the crawl space?' "

"Precisely."

"He can lie up on the roof, protected by the firewall."

"They already have the Forest Service helicopter searching around Mota Llano, Cañoncito, and La Lomita."

April said, "Maybe they won't come to the house."

"Maybe Duane has two noses."

"All right, I give up. This is a nightmare."

Anthony put on the outfit, lit the cigar, gave April a brief, haunted glance, and said abruptly, "Let's go."

April and the children watched them pedal down the driveway, as ridiculous an ensemble as they'd ever seen —but invisible because of their blatant visibility? They allowed a school bus to pass, turned left, and, cruising nonchalantly, headed for their destination.

"Ai, you missed the bus!"

April pushed her kids up from the table, in motion at last, determined to prevail. Business as usual until they decreed otherwise, she decided, ordering the kids to find their shoes, brush their teeth, comb their hair—"But not with water—it'll freeze, you'll catch pneumonia and drop dead!"

When she herded them out the door, each child looked sparkling, clean, and happy, though as usual neither Duane's gloves nor Tina's socks that she was using in place of her misplaced mittens, matched.

April sat behind the wheel of her Bug as it warmed up, lit a cigarette, and then buried her face in her hands: Anthony was gone. George, too.

"God *damn* this slaughterhouse," she murmured, and put the car into reverse, beginning her day.

J. B. LeDoux phoned Junior Leyba. "*Junior!*" he cried. "*How did it happen?*"

"I don't know, J. B. Apparently those three escaped from jail last night, and Benny was accidentally shot to death early this morning. They captured Alfredo. Anthony Martínez is still at large. There's a manhunt going on, and I imagine they'll have him in custody within the hour, unless he took a pill to make himself invisible. I can't tell you how sorry I am, J. B."

"How did a six-foot-two-inch-tall, two-hundred-and-ten pound FBI agent armed to the teeth manage to kill my unarmed five-foot-eight-inch, hundred-and-thirty-pound kid, Junior, answer me that!"

"Benny took him by surprise. And he wasn't unarmed, he had a board and a broken bottle. He was hiding in the ditch, he jumped out, and when Robinson swung his gun around to parry the blow it went off by mistake. I'm sorry, J. B. I don't know what to say. It's awful."

"Bullshit, Junior! You couldn't care less! Nobody gives a damn! He was set up to be murdered, anyway. I just talked to Claude Parker and he told me the bullet was fired from less than a foot away entering his face just below the upper lip, smashing his front teeth, and exiting from the top rear portion of the skull. And listen to this! He says Benny's little finger on his right hand was blown clean off, suggesting to him my son had his hands on top of his head when he was killed. How do you like them manzanas, Junior? You assassin! And not only that. From police photographs of how the body fell, backwards into the ditch, Claude deduced that far from leaping forward in an attacking position when shot, my kid was either standing upright quietly on the edge of the ditch, or backing up when that trigger-happy slob let him have it! Who decided to kill him—Joseph Bonatelli? And what was the reason, Junior? *I want to know your reason!"*

"Claude Parker doesn't know his ass from a hole in the ground. What's the matter with you anyway, J. B.? It was a horrible accident! I can't tell you how sorry—"

"Sorry? Listen to this, Junior! How come Claude isn't going to issue the real report? Explain to me why he's going to give Damacio Mares a piece of paper totally unrelated to the facts, would you? Claude's gonna lie through his teeth just to corroborate Damacio's statement about a 'purely accidental death.' So what I want to know is who set this thing up? I want to know who decided to start deliberately murdering my sons in my town, because this is still my town, I'm still the mayor, believe it or not!"

"Pipe down, J. B. Hysteria won't get us anywhere. Everybody's on edge, of course. Don't make this worse than it is. Somebody got confused, your boy was drunk, he attacked an officer, he was shot—"

"He saw the whole thing, didn't he?"

"Who did?"

"The *real* Anthony Martínez."

"I don't know, I wasn't there. I didn't even know they broke out of jail."

"The hell you say! *I'm* the only one didn't know they broke out of jail. *I'm* the only one who didn't even know they were *going* to break out of jail. *I'm* the only one who doesn't know shit around here! My boy must have known something pretty big to get killed like that! What did he know, Junior? What had he found out?"

"Dammit, what is that supposed to mean, J. B.? Obviously, you're upset. I can sympathize. But—"

"Who else is manipulating this sack of garbage? What is happening out at the Pueblo? Where does Bonatelli's interest really lie? What is the Northland Grazing Association—an affiliate of Murder, Incorporated?"

"J. B., all I can say is I'm sorry."

"Big deal. You're in on it, aren't you, Junior? You and old man McQueen and every Moose in town, Randolph Bonney, Big Bill, the FBI—you're all in it together, aren't you? Claude, too, Damacio, Irving Newkirk—everybody except me."

"Cousin, you are as much a part of this town as the rest of us," Junior said quietly. "We're all in it together. These things happen, and they affect all of us."

"*How* do they happen? Like for instance, assuming the entire charade was preplanned, how is it that three strange cops who couldn't identify one prisoner from another wound up in that ruin? And how is it that somebody who saw the whole thing is still free as a bird and capable of relating the whole chain of events to the world at large—is he gonna be killed by accident too? And why was all this necessary in the first place? Because you know what gets me, Junior? I know that dynamite theft was no accident, I don't even think it was stolen by your average run-of-the-mill thief. I think it was taken by the same crew running that stakeout on my shed. And I think they did it to frame Anthony Martínez and maybe others, especially the *El Clarín* crowd, getting them under wraps because of what they had uncovered or were about to uncover, and my Benny was just a fall guy, a jerk who was supposed to finger Martínez. And if somebody doesn't tell me, cuate, what really happened, I'm gonna raise a fucking stink you won't believe about the autopsy, whether Claude denies it or not! I'll have your ass, Junior! I won't rest until everybody from McQueen down to Cipi García's ghost is hanging from the goddam rafters!"

"What's bothering you, friend?" Junior suddenly snapped. "You afraid you're not going to be included in a big enough piece of the action, J. B.? What the hell do you or any of us want an insider's view of the structure for, if the benefits keep on accruing? Listen to me, J. B., I'm sorry Benny's dead, it's awful, but don't you try and rub my nose in his corpse, you son of a bitch. You both hated each other's guts!"

"But what am I gonna *do*, Junior? Read all about what's been happening under my nose for the past year in the next issue of the *El Clarín*? Are they gonna give me the real scoop on how Benny was murdered? Or am I finally going to figure it all out when some idealistic state or federal district attorney decides to poke a stick into our ant pile? I didn't risk what I've risked all my life, giving up what I've given up, sacrificing what I've sacrificed, just to be used for a doormat by a group of outside tycoons who see me as just another spic piece of toilet paper handy for wiping their fat asses! *That's my boy whose head they blew apart this morning!*"

*"Get off it, you idiot!"* Junior yelled, slamming down his telephone.

J. B. dialed Rodey McQueen. When he came on, the mayor said, "What are you going to do now, McQueen, are you going to put out a contract on your own daughter, is that the way these things work?"

"Who is this?"

"Does it matter?"

The old man hung up.

J. B. sat there, tapping the phone with an index finger, trying to think. His body, alive with rage and fear, felt very queer. His nerves were shot, his skin was so tight it hurt to touch. Murder was in his heart. When he stood up, a ringing in his ears caused him to stagger; immediately he sat down again. Things were falling apart, disappearing into an opaque mire. Wires were snarled, water meters broken, cars stalled in traffic, potholes growing, roads insufficient, sewage backing up, drunks getting drunker, embezzlement causing problems, federal and state programs going haywire, his teeth full of cavities, and soon worms would be excavating in the rotting flesh of his murdered son.

Dazed, J. B. wandered outside, found his car, and drove to the site of the killing. Parking on a dirt road, he ducked through barbed-wire strands and crossed a field. Walking along the dry ditch from which Benny had supposedly leaped, he was struck by how shallow the acequia seemed; it was impossible to be surprised by anyone crouched in this ditch—you could see them from a mile away.

J. B. tried it himself, curling into a tight little ball on the ground—exposed, totally vulnerable.

Nearer the house, he discovered pop-bottle fragments around a small rock. Farther along, bending over a spot of blood-soaked earth, he discovered where his boy had lain.

Scattered snowflakes were falling. J. B. woozily confronted the dark brown circle at his feet. Hugging his knees he rocked slightly, teeth chattering, unable to think of what to do. The fields around him were deserted but for a few animals, quiet and pastoral. By this time next year they would be under construction, another housing development, more money in his pocket.

With a fingertip he touched the splotch. Already the ground was frozen; his finger came away clean. When he looked up Teresa was seated on the dry ditch bank, dressed only in a ruffly diaphanous nightgown, breast-feeding little Benny. Her shy melancholy smile tunked savagely into his heart. In the background, the wrathful angel Cipi García wandered dazedly, frothing unintelligibly at the mouth, orchestrating catastrophes. Like a dirigible, Claude Parker's whale loomed through the storm high overhead, and then retreated. Farther away, riders galloped noiselessly past—Jesus Etcetera and the four kidnappers, Atiliano Montoya and Vidal Mondragón and Ralphito García, Amaranta and legless Juan GeeGee; and even his own father, Rudy LeDoux. They raced by without touching the ground, figments of his dying imagination grown momentarily bold, ghost riders from his befuddled mind, passing in review like fragments of some almost extinct corrido or nearly forgotten poetry, revived by the nostalgia that tragedy breeds. The hell with them, those ineffectual omens from a less incomprehensible era! They were only a leftover confetti dirge blown from a fiesta season that had ineffectually petered out long ago. Still: an old cowboy hat at the mercy of the wind tumbled across the close-cropped grass; sheep bells tinkled; strains of a waltz from the violin of Espeedie Cisneros wept through the quiet snowfall. J. B. envisioned all the ladies under their parasols, and the dogs and children romping about while Karl Mudd took photographs. And the gay carnival tinkle of the fiesta merry-go-round, the halcyon cumulus buzz of Pat GeeGee's airplane— It was lost, that heyday of gallant criminals and plump ladies, wild horses and cottonwood springtimes, aspen autumns and hayrakes and childhood sunshine, and piñon smoke at dawn! J. B. dreamed of ripping open his chest with his own two hands and liberating his heart, shaped like a withered leaf—it would flit off into brutal historical currents, tumbling away through this lament of weather, leaving him cold and imperial and finally immune.

Snow started falling in earnest; J. B. didn't move. In a few minutes the ground was completely white. His teeth stopped chattering, he felt numb. It was as if he no longer possessed the right to grief—had sold that too over the years. And no fatigue that J. B. had ever experienced prior to that morning could compare with what now besieged his limbs. His eyes went out of focus, blurring the snowfall, filtering it through a kind of shimmer—as if viewed from underwater—through his bloodshot eyes, into his bloodshot brain.

An alabaster glimmer caught his eye; an out-of-place white sparkle despite the overcast day and the snow. J. B. raised himself wearily, and progressed painfully to a nearby fence. One post glittered eerily, so white it hurt his eyes. A bleached bone, J. B. suddenly realized; a relic from the days of Claude Parker's whale. Kneeling, he kissed it. Then, working feverishly, tearing his flesh against the barbed wire, he tore free that hollow, surprisingly light and beautiful bone, held it for a second, experiencing a frightening thrill, and then, with all his might, J. B. hurled it up toward the origin of snow. Zooming away it sparkled for a second like a magic thing, and then disappeared, as had yesteryear, into the vast and muffling atmosphere.

The air quivered—a whispering, old-fashioned embroidery. It was all terribly serene. J. B.'s heart stopped beating, but he kept on living anyway.

JUAN AND ANTHONY REACHED TOWN, circled the plaza, waited patiently in line for five minutes at the broken traffic light, pedaled north on the North-South Highway practically hemmed in by police cars, stopped at a drugstore for cigarettes, bore right on the Pueblo road fork, and, up ahead, faced the blinking lights of a roadblock.

"Just act casual," Juan said. "Act as if we own the road, give them a friendly little wave, and pedal on through. Oh by the way, are you carrying a wallet?"

"Yes."

"Throw it in the ditch by the corner of this field in case they frisk us. I'll pick it up on my way out."

Anthony removed eight dollar bills from his wallet, kissed it goodbye, and did as Juan suggested.

They were slowing down, about twenty yards short of the roadblock, when a flea-bitten mongrel lunged from a chokecherry thicket, charged Anthony, and sank its teeth into his ankle, tipping over the bicycle. Anthony landed on his back all tangled up, with the dog, clamped tightly onto his leg, growling ferociously. Juan braked, hopped off, then tackled the dog. All five officers manning the roadblock—one state cop, a county undersheriff, two FBIs (including Chet Fulton), and a deputized posse member —raced to the rescue. Anthony was beating the dog's head, Juan was tugging a leg, when Chet Fulton interceded.

"Get back!" the agent shouted, shoving Juan off with one arm. Drawing a revolver, he stuck the muzzle into the dog's ribs and fired. The animal, half its internal organs immediately scrambled by the hollow-point bullet, gave a tremendous lurch, eyes going rigid; but the mouth stayed clamped tightly around Anthony's ankle.

Chet Fulton squatted atop the dog, trying to pry open its jaws, but they were shut as tightly as the steel jaws of a bear trap.

"Hey!" Anthony wailed. "Somebody *do* something!"

Everybody gathered around, looking on uselessly for a few seconds, smothering laughter as they wracked their brains for a solution.

Anthony howled, *"I don't believe this is happening!"*

"Take it easy," Chet Fulton cautioned. "We'll think of something."

"You pigs are all alike!" Anthony shrieked. "You can run around the goddam country like a bunch of blood-thirsty Boy Scouts blasting the shit out of innocent no-bodies, filling the morgues full of helpless bums, busting decent American citizens for smoking dope while you subsidize the hard-drug pushers, shaking down honest lit-tle neighborhood businessmen while acting as thugs for the big corporations, but when some poor little person like myself gets bitten by a goddam raving lunatical dog and a *real* emergency exists, you ain't worth shit, spit, or Coca-Cola for all the assistance you're able to give!"

"He's hysterical," Juan explained. "He doesn't know what he's saying."

"The hell I don't know what I'm saying! Fuck these use-less pigs! Go to hell, all of you! I've had it with pigs! I've had it with the American system! Go kill a Commie for Christ, you blazing trigger-happy chotas, I'll get rid of this goddam dog by my goddam self, thanks all the same! *Give me that gun!"*

"What are you going to do with it?"

*"I'm gonna shoot this goddam dog in its goddam head until I manage to blow its goddam brains and jaws apart, that's what I'm gonna do!"*

"You might miss and hit your foot," Chet Fulton said.

*"That's a chance I'll take! Now gimme that goddam gun!"*

"You hurt yourself, I'm not responsible."

*"What do you want it in, do you want it in writing?"* Anthony screamed, apoplectic.

Chet Fulton gave Juan a significant glance, shrugged his shoulders, and, addressing Anthony, said, "Yeah, I'd like it in writing."

*"Oh Jesus Christ!"*

On the back of an arrest sheet, the agent wrote a paragraph absolving himself and all the other officers from any blame if Anthony amputated his own foot. After the fugitive furiously scrawled his signature on the document —*Anthony R. Martínez*—the FBI agent handed over his gun, and, without a glance at it, folded the release and tucked it into his wallet. Everybody stepped away. Steadying the weapon with two hands, Anthony thumbed back the hammer, touched the barrel to bone directly between the dog's eyes, and fired.

The jaws, no longer attached to anything, popped open.

Anthony handed the weapon, butt first, over to Chet Fulton, righted his bike in a huff, mounted up, snarled, "Let's get away from these Fascist creeps," and pushed off. Barely able to function for the terror Anthony's outburst had fired in him, Juan nevertheless managed—wobbling precariously—to follow after the steaming escapee.

"Wow," one cop exclaimed as they sauntered back to their roadblock. "I don't think I ever saw anything quite like that." Guffawing loudly, he added: "Who *was* that masked man, anyway?"

AN HOUR LATER, dark blobs grew steadily larger within the luxurious storm. J. B. LeDoux got hold of himself, forcing his eyes to focus on April Delaney and Juan Ortega. About fifteen yards away Juan raised his right hand in a slow, not unfriendly greeting:

"Hello, cousin."

"Hello Juan. April."

"What are you doing out here without a coat on?" April said gently. "You should be inside, J. B. This is no place—"

"What better place?" J. B. said vaguely, ashamed of his tears. "But what brings you people to this neck of the woods?"

April walked up to the shallow ditch. "We came to view the scene. I apologize for how you feel, J. B., but somebody did a terrible number on Benny." Turning angrily to Juan, she said: "I don't *believe* they've got the brass balls to say he jumped out of concealment from this thing! Tina couldn't hide in this ditch. In fact, we'll put that on the cover, on the front page. Hear that, J. B.? Go tell that to those thugs. We'll put Tina in the ditch, because she's about one-third Benny's size, and we'll photograph her from various distances, from all different angles,

514

to show how impossible it would be not to see somebody from pretty damn far away. Jesus, they have gall! Where exactly is the spot?"

"Over here," J. B. said wearily. "I'm practically sitting on it."

Painfully, he backed off a little way, and stood there, one hand pressed against his temple, swaying.

Squatting, brushing snow off the frozen bloody earth, April directed Juan to take photographs from different angles, making sure they had the exact location when they returned to snap pictures for the paper. Juan also photographed the pop-bottle rock; they fingered small, remaining shards. J. B. said nothing as they moved along the ditch, checked out the ruin, and quartered the field a bit on both sides of the ditch, looking for nothing in particular, but hoping to stumble across something. After April had gathered a handful of small stones and arranged them loosely but in a pattern she would later recognize as the spot where the body had lain, she told J. B.:

"Again, I'm sorry. It's a terribly rotten thing. Can we give you a ride?"

"No, I just came. I just want to stay a while."

"Is Teresa all right?"

"I don't know. I guess so."

April and Juan looked at him. He gazed back with a weary, perplexed expression.

"What are you going to do about this?" he asked.

"As best we can figure it out, we're going to write what really happened."

"That won't do you any good," J. B. said. "It won't do anybody any good. People don't even blink when the *El Clarín* comes out. They buy it because it's cheaper than toilet paper. You people are a laughingstock. You're so impotent it's pathetic."

"What about you, J. B.? What about Benny?"

"At least I admit it."

April said, "Give us the body, J. B. Let us take it down to the capital for an honest autopsy. Virgil has a friend down there, Abe Gallegos, who could arrange it. You can fight them, you can put people like my old man and Junior, Randolph Bonney and those FBIs behind bars if you want. You know as well as we do that it was a setup, they intended to kill Anthony, and Benny was supposed to lead him into a trap. Instead, he chose to commit suicide."

"He's been committing suicide for years. I killed him in

515

the cradle. It was all inevitable. It's the American dream—"

"Give us the body, J. B., and I'm almost positive we can prove what really happened."

"So what? Five minutes of sunshine can't melt Mount Everest."

"Help us, please. They're going to wipe out the Pueblo. They're going to destroy whatever's left of Chamisaville."

"Talk to Teresa," he said faintly. "I don't care anymore. I'm not viable any longer. I don't want to be a part of events. I give up. Nothing I ever did makes any sense."

"Come with us. Tell Teresa it's all right by you."

"Tell her yourself, you bunch of ghouls."

"I'm sorry, J. B., I know this is all incredibly ugly— but you have to fight back."

"You, maybe. Not me. I been deluding myself for years that I had the guts to seek revenge. Now, finally, I admit for once and for all that I don't. They win. I quit.

"Hey," J. B. called as they left. "Take my picture. 'The Honorable Mayor of Chamisaville, visiting the picturesque scene of the crime several hours afterwards.' You want a quote to go along with it?—I'll give you a quote. He said: 'This is not the end of the killing, the killing has only just begun.' How will that grab them—good copy?"

April stopped, Juan just beyond her. The snow fell steadily, a white buildup powdered J. B.'s head and shoulders.

"All right, Juan. Why not? Let's take the picture."

"That would be heartless—"

"Take it anyway."

Juan took it.

Again, April asked: "Are you okay, J. B.? Can you make it back to your car?"

"I'm all right. I forgot to eat my Cheerios this morning, that's all. Got that? *I forgot to eat my Cheerios.*"

"We'll help you up to your car—"

"Help yourselves, please. You're the ones who will need it."

"Fine. Let's get out of here, Juan."

"Don't hate me!" J. B. called after them. "It was my own son who got killed!"

They receded, dissolving into the storm, becoming blobs again, adrift in that thick ghostly weather.

\* \* \*

516

FLANKED BY TWO SUITCASES, George Parker stood on the highway shoulder in the snow. The eastern foothills were almost completely obliterated; up north he could see nothing of Hija Negrita or the taller Midnight Mountains beyond Chamisaville. Behind him, the sagebrush mesa dissolved into the unfocused, pulsating whiteness. He was leaving Chamisaville, escaping from this dog-eared, surreal little town—finally launched. A terrible future might lie in store. The past had given no foundation, the present was a mess. Never had he been this disoriented, indecisive, puzzled. It was too late to retreat; he had not imagined it this way at all. Wanting adventures, a new life, something —anything!—different, George wondered if it was all, inevitably, grasping at straws. Too many loose ends—the discomforts would forever grow stronger. He seriously doubted his ability to cope outside the safe, known confines of banal and ordinary Chamisaville. Yet hypocrisy, at least one kind of hypocrisy, *his* particular situation, had to end.

A conventional being long enough, George was about to quest for all those immortal things he longed for. A bus to the capital, a train to New York City—simple, direct. He had money. Deliberately, George forced himself not to think of Susan or the children, or the incredibly ruined life left behind. But what a joke in the end, no? Smashing apart a firmly rooted life and family had hardly caused a ripple. Susan and the indifferent kids smiled wanly, relieved to have him go; his father and mother thought it was high time. George had expected to be crucified, ostracized, and raved at for causing the family's walls to tumble down, driven with his guilty tail between his legs into a melodramatic pariahdom. Instead, the unsavory business had resolved itself with a tolerant whimper. What had happened to George—his life-change, his need to quest for a different existence—was taken for granted by everybody from his mother to the *Parade* magazine that arrived with the Sunday paper spouting theories about male menopause. Ha ha, Chicken Little—go screw yourself! One million divorces a day are granted in the U.S.A. We're *all* doomed to a prosaic destiny. What he had feared (and hoped) would cause an earthquake had barely caused a belch. Of course, Susan would always be his friend—what had he done not to deserve *that*?

Soft yellow yolks became visible in the thick storm, the headlights of the Trailways bus. George stepped onto the roadway to make sure the driver could see him, and vigorously waved the bus down. Air brakes hissed, tires skidded slightly on new slush. The door sighed open, and, awkwardly lugging his suitcases, George climbed aboard, paid for his ride, and staggered back through the nearly empty bus to a seat midway between the driver and the rear bathroom. After wrestling his bags into the overhead rack, he sat down.

And was startled to find himself beside one of the three other passengers on the bus, a fat and familiar old farmer, as broad as he was tall, sitting almost formally with a battered cardboard box on his lap, a violin case under one arm, a frayed straw cowboy hat on his head.

George said, "I'm sorry, I don't know what's wrong with me—I didn't even realize this seat was occupied."

"What's to be sorry for? I'm glad of the company. You're Claude Parker's kid, qué no?"

"Sure. And I recognize your face, but the name escapes—"

"Espeedie Cisneros. Until today, I lived in Chamisaville all my life. Now—my house gone, my land long disgraced by developers—because I got a son who lives in Phoenix I'm going to die in Phoenix."

George noticed an animal nose sniffing through a crack on top of the box. Nodding toward it, he said, "What have you got in there?"

"Two rabbits."

"Aren't they illegal on a bus?"

"Everything is illegal. Breathing is illegal in this country. Earning a living is illegal. Dying in your own house on your own land is illegal. Did I ever tell you the fable of the trout and the gabacho baby? No? Pos entonces, I'll tell you right now—"

It seems that one day a baby gabacho wandered away from his family and fell into the river. He couldn't swim and immediately sank to the bottom. A bunch of hungry Chicano trout, hearing the splash, came to investigate and commenced nibbling on the baby with the intention of devouring him posthaste. However, a Wise Old Trout said, "No, we will not eat this gabacho chavalito, for that would be against the compassionate laws of the Great Trucha." Instead, they gathered the baby gabacho on their backs, lifted him up to the surface, and dumped him into some cattails. Then they raced up and down the river collecting crayfish, hellgrammites, and various and sundry larvae to feed the baby gabacho, because he was very hungry. They spit the goodies out of their mouths into the baby gabacho's nest among the cattails. For weeks and months he ate ravenously, thanks to the efforts of all those hard-working Chicano truchas. But after a while, the big pink monster outgrew the efforts of all those trout to feed him. So the baby gabacho found a stick and a piece of string and a hook, and he baited the hook with the crayfish and hellgrammites the trout were spitting his way, and began catching the fish and eating them. In fact, the baby gabacho had such a voracious appetite that he soon grew to enormous proportions, and also cleaned out the river of Chicano trout. Finally, the baby gabacho landed the last fish in the stream, the Wise Old Trout responsible for saving his life. "Wait!" cried the wise old fish as the baby gabacho was about to bash his head. "If you kill me, you'll have no more food supply. Put me back in the river and I'll collect hellgrammites and crayfish and caddis-fly larvae for you." But the baby gabacho was hungry right that minute for fish, so he bashed dead the Wise Old Trout, and swallowed him whole. But then, because he couldn't swim, and because he hadn't even left a couple of trout for breeding purposes, his food supply dried up. For days he crawled along the banks of the river staring down at the happy crayfish and snails and hellgrammites, unable to arrest them for his palate. Finally, weakened by starvation, the baby gabacho fell into the river and drowned.

"So I don't give a shit if these rabbits are illegal—you understand?"

George said, "Of course . . . of course."

And after a moment he asked nervously, "Where are you taking the rabbits? What are you going to do with them?"

"I got a job with a magician."

"You're kidding!"

"Yeah, I'm kidding. These here rabbits?—I dunno. I guess I will eat them by and by. For now, though, I just need the company. All my life I had rabbits."

"I see. . . ."

The bus went off the lip of the mesa, dropping into the gorge, proceeding cautiously through the fast-melting snow. George wanted very much to cry, but he couldn't, of course, not in front of this old man. And for some reason, he couldn't just rise and select another seat. Yet he cursed whatever had made him blind to the fact that this seat was occupied in the first place.

Espeedie clicked open his violin case, tightened his bow strings, did a quick tuning, and then hit the strings, playing a waltz, a snappy sentimental tune that recalled the old days of the Balena Park floating bandstand, those dreamy Sundays of a golden yore.


WHEN APRIL DELANEY, Virgil Leyba, and Juan Ortega arrived at the funeral home to claim the body of Benny LeDoux, Claude Parker figured he was in trouble. Rachel admitted them; they were seated in the office when he entered, sat down at the desk, smiled disarmingly, and asked: "What can I do for you?"

April explained that they had come for the body. She gave him a paper signed by Teresa LeDoux. "He wasn't our child anymore anyway," she had intoned hollowly. "Do whatever you want with the poor thing."

"You mean to make the funeral arrangements," Claude said.

"No, we're going to take the body down to the capital, where a friend has arranged for somebody who will do an honest autopsy," April said. "We've got a truck outside and there's a coffin in the back of it, and we'd like to know the procedure for getting the body into the coffin."

"What are you talking about? You can't do that. This is completely irregular."

"Why can't we do this?"

"Damacio Mares hasn't issued a release yet. The boy's already in a coffin. And you simply can't go around switching bodies from one coffin to another, just like that. And what kind of a coffin are you talking about anyway? There are laws—"

"We know the laws," Virgil said, dropping the rest of their papers on Claude's desk. "There's a release in there, signed over to the family, documents for transporting a body, the works."

"Where did you get a coffin in this town, if not from me?" Claude said, angered now, his dander up.

"We built it."

"You can't just build a coffin. It's against regulations."

"Check your regulations, Claude. Come on now, quit holding us up. Things are ugly enough."

"Hold on, Virgil, not so fast. I've handled that body,

my hearse brought it here, I was just going to embalm it—"

"I'll pay whatever it costs," April said.

"When I see all this in writing, from them, from Teresa and J. B., I'll release the body."

"It's in these papers. You make out a bill right now," April said, digging in her purse for a checkbook, "and I'll pay it right now."

"I . . . um . . . well—"

"God dammit, Claude, how much?" April gasped. "Everybody has been through enough shit for one morning without having some two-bit alcoholic vampire with a turd-bag strapped to his ribs rubbing their noses in it some more!"

Virgil put a hand on April's shoulder. "Take it easy, hija," he cautioned. "Calm down—"

"Oh screw it, take the body, get it the hell out of here!" Claude blurted, pushing away from the desk and staring hard out the window at the snowfall, his moist lips trembling.

"Give us the real autopsy report," April urged. "Save us a trip, Claude. And time. And money."

"Damacio has the real autopsy report."

Virgil said, "You're going to look real bad when we publish the findings of an honest coroner. This whole thing already stinks to high heaven. Why multiply useless complicities? We'll get them to flush every license you have down a toilet."

"So do it. I should live so long. What are you going to do, publish your findings in the *El Clarín?* In that joke?"

"Let's get the body," Virgil said.

"Back your truck into the driveway. Does this wonderful coffin, perchance, have a lid?"

"And a tarp," Virgil said.

"I'll need help. Both you men."

Claude went back through the home: Virgil and Juan left by the front door, turned the truck around, and backed past the window. April was alone in the office for a moment, gazing out the window, hypnotized by the falling snow. Already half a foot had accumulated, and although the plows were out, they would probably have trouble making the capital. The whole affair was too strange and ominous. They were being trapped, cut off, their cries muffled, things being buried by the storm, all motion and movement compromised, facts covered over by the smothering whiteness slowing everything down to a crawl so that quadruple the effort would be required to drive this investigation home.

The truck passed the window: April arose, heading outside.

Caught by an impulse, she asked, "Is it open? The coffin?"

"Yes."

"Is it wrong if I take a look?"

"We've got to get moving—"

"It'll only take a second."

April climbed into the bed, folded back the tarp, fiddled with the two latches Juan had installed, and lifted the lid. The eyes were wide open, the hair clotted with blood, the mouth smashed, the skin dead-gray, crusted with black blood in spots, Claude's rough stitches everywhere, the clothes torn, dirty, and damp. April locked into the dead junkie's eyes for a second, snowflakes hitting against his face and not melting. A dizziness entered her head and traveled like electricity through all her limbs. Enrique splashed in shallow Mediterranean water, laughing, beating his own head with a rock. Carlito, in the enchanted airplane, leaned over to kiss her. April pulled up the dirty sheepskin collar of his precious old bomber jacket that had kept her warm now for twenty years. Mandolin, guitar, and violin music wove through the storm like a weird and pretty breed of prehistoric arctic fishes, mutants of some gaudier tropical strain. Whatever had happened to all the Amarantas and Teresitas, to all the Jacobals and Josés? Benny LeDoux, brought up safe in material Yanqui abundance, had lost focus in a world of dead gooks, acid rock, and smack. The snow was fleece from long-departed flocks. A heavy, sorrowful voice, accompanied only by a homemade wooden flute, carried through the storm, and through the obliterating tempests of memory, singing a mournful penitente alabado, "On This New Day";

> *Because of God the flowers bloom,*
> *And the fields turn green;*
> *And the trees bear pretty fruit,*
> *And the sun spreads its golden sheen—*
>
> *Warbling praises from the boughs*
> *Are all the cheerful birds.*
> *And all the fish in crystal waters,*
> *Sing out the holy words. . . .*

April reached down, placing her palm against Benny's folded hands, and removing it quickly. "All right."

She closed the coffin, gave Juan a hug good-bye, and entered the cab with Virgil. They pulled into the street. Plows had been down the highway once, but already a fresh inch had accumulated. Beyond Cañoncito cars disappeared; they were alone, chugging along at twenty-five miles an hour in poor visibility. And although barely noon, the day was vested with an evening darkness. Virgil turned on his lights. The heater whizzed noisily, flooding the cab with so much warmth April had to roll down her window a little. The noisy wipers clunked away, sweeping great flaky chunks off at every beat.

Up ahead three deer, a buck and two does, occupied the middle of the highway, observing their approach with detached interest. Virgil blinked his lights and beeped, but the animals, majestic beige creatures, did not move. He slowed, skidding a little, and pumped the brakes carefully, jerking to a halt about ten feet from the grouping.

The motionless deer gazed at them, intrigued and curious, vaguely indolent, then trotted unhurriedly off the highway, disappearing into the softly raging twilight.

Five minutes later they dipped out of the storm into the Rio Grande Gorge, where the sun shone brightly and the road was perfectly dry.


IN THE EVENING, April and Virgil returned to Chamisaville, their mission accomplished, a pathologist slated to examine Benny's body the next day. But it had been an exhausting, emotional afternoon: endless, traumatic, morbid. When they arrived at April's house, Juan Ortega was there, baby-sitting the kids. He had developed the morning's film and drawn up a rough outline of their case and how the El Clarín might play it. While they sat around the kitchen table, April rustled up some dinner, and they discussed their next moves.

"First of all, we've got Anthony's story on what he overheard out at the Pueblo," April said wearily, puttering over a frying pan. "We have his account of that long statement Icarus Suazo made to him just before he was arrested, and we've got a hundred documents in the files which are all drawn together by his testimony about the racetrack, lake, and development. Tomorrow, Juan, you and I should go through the files, yank some of the most pertinent material related to Moosurelli, the Northland Grazing Association, and Joseph Bonatelli and all his in-house and outside cohorts, and decide which documents to reproduce in the paper."

"I'll be here at eight A.M."

"Good. Now the snowfall is really going to hang us up taking sequence photographs at the ditch, but I think somebody should go out to the Pueblo, to Anthony's ruin, and take a snapshot of the area where the dog track, the lake, all of that is slated to go."

"I could also do that," Juan said.

April said, "What about the killing? If possible, we'll get a snapshot of Benny tomorrow from Teresa; I would also like somehow to get a picture of Robinson, the one who did the shooting. Naturally, we'll publish both Claude Parker's doctored autopsy and the report from down in the capital. Again, we have Anthony's eyewitness account of the killing, which certainly ties into the evidence we've got, which ties into the entire Pueblo scam. I would like to bring up the dynamite theft. In fact, it wouldn't hurt us to find that dynamite itself. I've got a suspicion that if we leaned hard on what's left of J. B. we might learn the true story of that stakeout, tie it all together with a lot of circumstantial innuendo, and make a very strong case. It seems to me if we handle it correctly, the state is going to have to come up here and start excavating the skeletons. But we have to work very fast, because . . . well, you know."

They ate silently, contemplating the task ahead, each piecing the thing together mentally, figuring out the best way to get it across, wondering what the effect would be, and aware that a man had died barely twelve hours ago for what they knew and were planning to reveal.

After supper, Virgil drove Juan home in his truck, and, leaving Duane as the baby-sitter, April tagged along for the ride. They dropped off Juan and stopped by the El Gaucho for a nightcap. A lone person was sitting at the bar, a blue-eyed boy with strange, golden skin, wearing a Levi's jacket that had a pair of elaborate white wings embroidered on the back in beautiful silken thread. April and Virgil sat close by, ordered beers, and sipped on them wearily.

The Levi's jacket moved onto the stool beside April. "Hello," he said, "my name is Jim Stetson, and I'm the ding-banginest holy-hell-bent-for-leatherest rock star you probably ever ran across, higher than Mount Everest, man,

524

with more zippety-doo-dah than a brace of fifty-caliber genuine U.S. Army–issue gas-operated machine guns— what's yours?"

"What's my what?"

"Name, babe. Moniker, tag, Joanna Hancock."

April gave him a queer, intense look.

"Hey, no offense, man. I mean, it's a free country. Like, dig, know what I mean? I mean, I like people, that's all, I like to talk with dudes and chicks and find out where they are at. I gotta learn about life, and about other people's heads. I mean, you don't do that and it's all over, right?"

Under her breath, April muttered, "Oh Jesus Christ."

"Hey, listen, don't put me down. I'm not just anybody's nobody, man. I play in a band. I just did sixty-eight thousand people in a rock concert in Muleshoe, Texas. Talk about tripping. Boy, they're beautiful people down there, I had to cry, I really did. Like, you know, you're just sitting backstage before it all begins, smoking dope, snorting a few lines, and, like, rapping with these little lizardy wizards who put it all together, right? I mean not pretentious people, nothing like that, man, they were just plain dudes —like you and me. And then there's that big electric hum and we're out there, and I sang ten songs and they roared, they loved it so much it made me cry, it really did. Wow, but those were beautiful cats down there. They liked it so much the National Guard had to come in and fly us out of there in Jolly Green Giants, they really did. It was beautiful. I felt so humbled by it all I actually got down on my knees, I really did, and thanked God for making me what I am, and for making me a citizen of this far-out country, I really did."

"What are you doing in Chamisaville?" April asked weakly.

"We're gonna make a picture, I mean this really heavy flick, man. I wrote the script and the score and it's, like, well, you wouldn't believe how beautiful. It'll be about this area, we'll shoot it all around here, this is such gorgeous terrain—I mean, wow, know what I mean? In this film, see, what it's about, is there's this group of freaks, they're known as the Hippy Bandidos, and they get in a tangle with the Penitentes around here—you know anything about the Penitente sects around here? See, it's this bunch of weird Mexicans, man, they got this real medieval religious trip coming down, like, where they flagellate each other and really groove on these flippy rituals. So the Hippy Bandidos, man, they try to set up this peace-love trip, dig? Out on some land somewhere, but the Penitentes can't feature it, see, because they're these incredibly uptight screwballs, and in the end they snatch the leader of the Hippy Bandidos, who's this beautiful dude with long wavy hair to his shoulders looks just like Jesus Christ, and they crucify him."

"Oh," April muttered.

"Well, what the hell." Jim Stetson drained his glass. "I mean, I can picture some of the scenes in this thing. Like, you know, contrasting the beautiful countryside against these uptight, middle-age Mexican rituals. And then, before the heavy shit comes down, you know, these Hippy Bandidos will do a peyote ritual with some Indians—that'll be beautiful. And I wrote this theme song, can you dig it? Runs all the way through the movie. It's called 'Dyin' Ain't Easy, But It's Fun.' And what it treats is the fact that if you're like me, this big-time rock singer, or if you're like the leader of those Hippy Bandidos, which they are a metaphor of course for, like, the dudes in life who've got it on, know what I mean? For the dudes and chicks who've reached this higher consciousness and have really got their shit together and are doing it—well, it can't last. There's always some mean cats strung out on, like, that middle-age mumbo jumbo, like this whole society, gunning for you. *Easy Rider,* man. Like the *real* America just has to come at you from the barrel of a shotgun, right? So just getting it on like that is self-destructive, you can't survive it, there's not even any point to trying. Like Janis or Jimi or Lenny. Like if you really get it on, that's gonna happen, you just turn on and ball chicks and there's nothing you can do about it. It's the price of fame and adulation."

While talking he had edged off his stool and was standing practically over April, pressing his groin against her leg, breathing heavily toward her ear.

April said, "Would you please get your cock off my thigh?"

"Oh, Jesus, excuse me. Wow. Hey, that's *beautiful.* Oh wow, I really dig chicks, like, who don't take any shit, know what I mean? Fantastic. You're beautiful, you know? I bet we could make it, I really do. What's your sign? I mean, you're not like any ordinary chick, I can really see that, I'm not shitting you. I respect you, I really do. You don't know how rare it is for a chick to, like, be frank like that. No kidding, I really do respect you, you're beautiful —Hey, why are you crying?"

"Virgil, please," April whispered. "Get me out of here. Take me home."

She slumped, almost falling off the stool. Virgil put an arm around her, guiding her out the door and around the corner to his pickup. Head buried in her hands, April wept while Virgil started it up and, allowing the motor to idle, he reached over awkwardly, touching her face, gently cupping the back of her head, saying nothing.

"Oh shit, Virgil, what is going to happen?" April sobbed. "Where does everybody come from, what are their body love anybody? Is there any human material left to expectations, why are they like that? How can we make a dent? Am I crazy? Why is it so impossible? Does anybring about a change?"

Virgil stroked her neck lightly, giving no reply. The night was quiet, snow glimmering. The taped church bells rang, playing "The Star-Spangled Banner." A crystal darkness echoed through the stilled town, adrift in the standstill anarchy produced by snow, the snug comforting halt to blithering confusion brought about by an act of weather. As if awed by the beauty, almost nobody was out drinking, bars were empty, and couples, made lazy by the muffle, had retired early, their skins softened from firelight glows. Virgil clicked on the radio to KKCV's nighttime classical music program, and continued to hold April while she cried, feeling an utter doom which he himself had lived with all his life and could do nothing about.

"I'm sorry, excuse me, I'm so tired," April said. "Let's go home. I need rest. Tomorrow there's so much work to do."

They were halfway out to Ranchitos Arriba when Virgil spoke. "I wish it were not this hard. I know it will get much worse. We have to be strong. If you wish, I'll stay all night in the house with you."

"No, it's all right. I want to be alone. I'm not frightened, really. Not deep down."

They traveled a little farther. April wiped a hole in the windshield condensation. "Virgil, I really love you," she said quietly.

He reached over and held her arm for a moment, squeezing gently, then placed his hand back on the wheel.

At home, April bundled up well and walked into her

back field. Smoking a cigarette, she gazed at the tiny lights, some too bright, some very warm, twinkling in town. The enormous mountains towered above them all: somewhere, deeply dug into the safety of that wilderness, Anthony was safe for the time being. There was a peace and beauty afoot to set even the most hardened heart at ease. The sensation of well-being felt universal. A pause had occurred in the hectic affairs of human beings; a vacuum had settled onto the cacophony, gentling troubled waters. Despite her day and the El Gaucho incident, April suddenly felt infused with a sense of security: she felt strong, she was so glad Anthony had made it. If the universe was willing to bestow the gift of a moment like this, there could be no irrevocable plunder afoot. Her heart swelled; she laughed softly. A peacock cried twice and fell silent—the air trembled. And although it was close to eleven, she could distinguish dark pines on the mountainsides—tiny, sharply etched shadows. A few night clouds, reflecting a silver glow, hung above the peaks, motionless cottony apparitions.

April tramped around in the unbroken snow. After a minute she broke into a trot, and very shortly was running, zigzagging everywhere, writing her name in the snow with her feet, stretching it diagonally across the half-acre field, high and eager and happy and strong once more.

Gasping for air, she stopped, lay down, and made a snow angel, and then quit moving her arms and simply confronted the clear sky, the stars. Aching for George, for simple physical relief, she wanted to celebrate the moment by making love. But he was gone—and good riddance! Yet a sudden image of that powerful, chickenshit, shining, confused man caused her to squirm in the snow. April slid a hand into her crotch and gently masturbated, her fingertips considerate, moaning gratefully when she came, feeling small and abandoned, lucky and resolute, determined never to let the sorrow of existence subvert her love of life.

Rising, April made a snowball and chucked it at a tree. She rubbed snow into her face, gasping at the refreshing, icy pain. Wandering back to the house, she paused at the clothesline to take off some tattered plastic bread sacks Duane had filled with water, hung on the lines, and shot with his BB gun. Then, instead of entering the kitchen, she climbed up an old ladder onto the roof, lit a cigarette, and took a look at her back field, at the neighboring fields and communities, at the town and at the solid, looming mountains. Only after that did she descend and happily enter her house, where Chet Fulton, Len Goodwin, and two other FBI agents were seated at the kitchen table, awaiting her return.

In front of Chet Fulton was a pile of letters, documents, clippings and photographs, which April recognized immediately; they had come from *El Clarín* files. Nearby sat a medium-sized, unmarked, cardboard box.

As soon as she entered, all four of them stood up.

"What are you doing here?"

"We have a warrant for your arrest," Chet Fulton said, flashing something.

"What for? Let me read it."

"You can read it later. Let's go. Quietly."

"I'm going to call my lawyer," April said, reaching for the wall phone.

Len Goodwin pointed a snub-nosed revolver at her, saying, "Don't do it. Please don't resist arrest, ma'am. We don't want to hurt you. You have to come in with us, though—immediately."

"What about my children? Who's going to take care of my children?"

"When we get there, you'll be allowed to call somebody."

"I'll call somebody right now. You have no right."

One of the other agents made a quick movement, grabbing her arm. He touched a gun barrel to her temple, saying, "You must understand, Miss Delaney, that this isn't a game. This has to do with felonies, destruction of public and federal properties, violation of local, state, and federal firearms and explosives acts, and if you don't do exactly as we say, it could go badly for you. Now—outside. *Please.*"

"What are you doing with our files?"

"Evidence," Chet Fulton said, bumping against her firmly as the other agent prodded her outside.

"Where are you taking me? Where is your car?"

"We'll take yours. Quick now, in back."

Len Goodwin put on some gloves and got behind the wheel. Chet Fulton and another agent carrying the cardboard box slipped in back on either side of April. Len Goodwin started the vehicle, backed up, and jounced cautiously down the driveway. Turning left, he headed for town.

"I really must call somebody about my children," April

said. "I really don't want to leave them alone in that house. You have to give me a phone call immediately, please. You have to do that. I can't leave my children alone, don't you understand?"

"They'll be taken care of," Chet Fulton said. "Nothing to worry about. Now just relax."

April sat stiffly between them, terrified, faint from premonitions. The men were silent as they reached town, circled the deserted plaza, waited for a beat at the broken traffic light, turned north onto the highway, and then right onto the Pueblo road.

"Where are you taking me?" April asked. "Where are we going? How come we're not going to the courthouse? This isn't right—"

"We have to pick up somebody," Chet Fulton explained.

"Who? Who are you going to pick up at this hour?"

Nobody answered. They were still about a mile from the Pueblo when Len Goodwin braked to a stop at the edge of the deserted road, about twenty feet from a National Forest sign marking the Pueblo-Floresta boundary. He shifted the car into neutral, set the emergency brake, left the motor running, opened his door and got out. The other agent in front and the one in back whom April did not recognize got out also. April said "What—?" and was starting to turn toward Chet Fulton when he raised Benny LeDoux's tiny .25 automatic, touched it to her temple, and fired a shot, the slug entering April's brain and killing her instantly.

Chet Fulton pocketed the gun, opened the cardboard box on the floor, fiddled with something, placed the box on April's lap, and hurriedly backed out of his door. A large quiet automobile, coming from the direction of the Pueblo, stopped just short of April's car, picked up the four agents, and sped into town, where it made two stops, dropping Chet Fulton and Len Goodwin off at the Shalako Lodge, and depositing the two other agents at the county jail, where they immediately integrated themselves with the ongoing search for Anthony Martínez.

In his bed above the El Gaucho, Pat GeeGee heard the explosion; and, halfway across the valley, Juan Ortega and Virgil Leyba heard it. Back the other way, in La Ciénega, J. B. LeDoux heard it. The few people listening for it, expecting it, they all heard it, too. And Icarus Suazo heard it. And Anthony Martínez, in a warm bedroll among thick pine trees, heard it. A thousand other people in Chamisaville, and in the valley surrounding the town, heard it, and they would go on hearing that explosion for the rest of their lives. It was permanently forged in their memories, whichever side they supported, a lesson and a warning to all, a great lie which many understood to be a lie, a murderous distortion, a definitive end—or a beginning.

Depending.

Bits and pieces of the automobile landed on the highway and in surrounding fields as far as seventy and eighty yards away from the explosion. And much of April Delaney's body was never found, only random chunks and indistinguishable pieces of flesh and bone and parts of limbs were ever scraped together into a plastic bodybag. The rest sank into the snow and disappeared, or was eaten by tiny rodents, a stray dog or cat, and ravens.

# Now We
# Are Ever.

WHEN VIRGIL LEYBA HEARD the explosion, he knew something was terribly wrong. He had been lying in bed, tired and queasy, hoping to sleep, when the muffled roar sounded from the Pueblo, and instinctively he thought of April. Virgil telephoned her house, sitting on the edge of his bed in the dark little room, gazing out his window at the winter scene. Close to his window a small crab-apple tree had lost its leaves long ago, but not its fruit, and a thousand tiny withered apples, each with a delicate white cone atop it, gleamed in the spectral moonlight, a weird tree of jewels. Police sirens sounded, moving toward the Pueblo; and April's telephone rang.

On the twentieth ring, a fumble, clatter, and sleepy grunting occurred on the other end as Duane bobbled the phone off the hook. He said "Hello?" into the earpiece. Virgil shouted, "Duane, where is your mother, let me speak to April, put her on the phone!"

"Huh? I can't hear you—oh." He reversed the phone. "Hello? Who is this?"

"Duane, listen—"

"Virgil?"

"Duane, this is important, where's your mom? I have got to speak to her."

Duane shouted, "Mom, it's Virgil! Mom?" He opened the kitchen door and shouted, "Mom, telephone! It's Virgil!" And explained to Virgil: "Maybe she's in the outhouse. The toilet won't flush—"

"Check, please, quickly. See if she's sleeping, see if she's out there, all right?"

"Sure. I'm gonna hafta put the phone down, though, okay?"

"Yes, you look for her now. I'll wait."

He waited while Duane puttered sleepily into the bedroom, checked out the utility room, put on a coat, some socks and sneakers, and crossed the driveway to the outhouse, and returned to the telephone.

"She isn't anywhere. The car isn't even here. I guess she went into town."

"I'm going to come over, Duane. I'll be right over. And Duane, do me a favor, leave the phone off the hook when I hang up, all right? If the phone rings again you don't want it to wake up Tina. So just leave it off the hook and I'll come over because there are a couple of papers in the files I need—"

"Okay, Virgil."

Duane set the phone on the window ledge. Virgil dressed quickly, threw on an overcoat and galoshes, and went outside. From town, there was a hubbub of sirens. Virgil started the pickup, allowed it to warm only a minute, and swung out of the driveway, flooring it for April's. He arrived in two minutes, and hastily entered the kitchen. Duane had returned to bed; the house was very quiet. Virgil settled the kitchen wall phone back in its cradle; immediately it rang; Virgil answered.

"Who's this?" a voice on the other end barked.

"Who are you?" Virgil shot back.

"Is this the April Delaney residence?"

"Yes."

"Well, who the hell are *you?*"

"I asked you that same question."

The caller hung up; the phone jangled immediately when

Virgil set it down. This time Juan Ortega was on the other end.

"She's dead," he said quickly. "They killed her."

"I heard an explosion—?"

"Yes."

Virgil tried to think.

"Virgil? You there?"

"Yes, I . . . yes, of course."

"I'll come over," Juan said.

"I don't think this is any place to be, right now."

"Excuse me for saying this at a time like this, but we should maybe save the pertinent things in the files," Juan said slowly, having trouble shaping his words. "I'm sorry, but maybe you better check. We can mourn later."

"Yes," Virgil said vaguely. "Hold the phone."

He wandered into the living room, bumping against the walls, stumbling, and sat down on the foot of Tina's bed for a moment, catching his breath. The children were sleeping and the only sound was the muted bubbling of Duane's tropical fish tank on a stool beside his bed. Virgil gathered himself together, snapped on a lamp, and pulled out a file drawer, realizing immediately that it had been ransacked, most information relating to the Pueblo projects and the death of Benny LeDoux removed.

It took forever to regain the kitchen. Once there, he sat at the table, staring at his hands. Then arose, opened the refrigerator, and blankly regarded its innards for a moment before closing the door. Over at the sink he tried to see out the window, but only confronted a reflection of himself. He clicked on the radio—a late-night jazz program crackled in from a thousand miles away; he turned it off.

Suddenly, Virgil remembered that Juan was on the phone.

"Juan, you still there?"

"Yes."

"As was to be expected, apparently they took everything."

Juan said, "Virgil, are you all right?"

"No. Of course not."

"Forgive me for bringing this up," Juan said quietly, "but we don't have much time. It stands to reason we are going to be arrested, indicted. It also stands to reason that, to make it look good, they'll raid the house there and discover whatever is left of that dynamite, which I assume they have planted somewhere. Maybe we could help ourselves if we found it, before they 'discover' it, and get rid of it."

"Where?" Virgil said.

"The most obvious place is the crawl space."

"Just a minute . . ."

Virgil went to the utility room, snapped on the light, kneeled and lifted the trapdoor, and, simple as pie, there it was, a cardboard box next to the water pump. Virgil lowered himself gingerly into the hole, lifted out the carton, climbed up again, and set the carton on the kitchen table, unfolding the flaps. There were about twelve sticks inside.

"Yes," he said into the telephone. "You were right. It's just as you guessed. I've got a box full of high explosives here."

"Can you get out of there and dump it someplace? I think you'd better move quickly, because their logical next step is to arrive out there, make the find, and arrest at least you and me, and perhaps everybody even peripherally connected to the *El Clarín* for conspiracy, et cetera—you know."

"What about the children?" Virgil asked.

"They are asleep?"

"Yes."

Juan said, "I don't know what we can do about the chidren, friend. Leave them alone, perhaps. For our good, you've got to get the dynamite out of there."

"Yes," Virgil said. "Well . . . I don't know."

"I'm going to hang up," Juan said. "Better leave as fast as you can."

Virgil replaced the telephone, carried the dynamite out to his truck, started the truck and allowed it to idle, and returned to the house.

"Duane?" He shook the boy's shoulder. "Duane, wake up, we're going someplace."

Startled, Duane sat up. "Huh? What? Where's Mom?"

"Get dressed in something," Virgil ordered. "We're going someplace. Right now, quickly."

While Duane dressed himself, Virgil carried Tina, wrapped in a blanket, out to his truck.

Duane appeared at the door while Virgil was still adjusting the blanket around Tina. The boy climbed in, and Virgil slammed the door and drove away, leaving the house with its lights blazing.

Halfway to his own house, Virgil stopped the truck, got out, and buried the box of dynamite in a snowbank—that would have to do for the time being. Back in the truck, Duane was wide awake. "What's the matter?" he asked. "Where's Mom?"

"She's dead," Virgil said. "They have killed her. I'm sorry."

Duane continued staring out the windshield at the snowy road. "What do you mean? Who killed her?"

Virgil's head buzzed, his thoughts were terribly scrambled. Yet he figured that perhaps all he had left with these children was a half-hour, maybe less, maybe only this ride from one house to another, in which to give them the story from April's point of view, from his own point of view. He was the last person who might not lie to them, and therefore he had a tremendous obligation, to the children, to April, and to the future. He must make an impression on this child, soft-pedaling nothing, glossing over nothing. He must give him something clean and correct at the edge of his memory to carry, nurture, and protect into a distant time.

Virgil said, "We were working on a story about some things happening out at the Pueblo, you know a little about it—" And he explained the racetrack, motel, lake, and housing developments, attempting to simplify the structure and people involved, even as he tried to be accurate, forgetting nothing, running it down in terms Duane might understand, leading him by the hand through Anthony Martínez's arrest, the shooting that morning, and everything else they had done during this endless day. Finally, he told how the dynamite had been stolen from the ski valley, used by provocateurs, and finally planted in the crawl space, and, he assumed, in April's car, killing her. And he tried to explain why they would now say his mother had killed herself while trying to blow up a Forest Service sign.

Duane listened, eyes trained out the windshield at the snowy road. Virgil went over it all again, extra careful and thorough with details. But finally he had exhausted speech and fell silent, able to talk no more. Immediately his heart felt broken and he became so dizzy he feared they would never make it home.

But they did. Virgil entered the driveway, coasting to a

535

stop, pausing to knuckle an eye, rub his forehead, and clear his brain for the last forty yards.

"Are we going to live with you now, Virgil?" Duane asked.

"No. Legally, there's no way I could have custody. I don't know where you will live, although I'd guess you will be with your grandparents, I don't know. There's a chance your father might try for custody, that is, to have you go live with him, but I think your grandpa would say no. Whatever happens, your lives are going to be very different. What you must do is accept it, and grow up to be strong, and take great care to remember your mother because she is a wonderful person, among the best I have ever known, and no matter what anybody tells you, you must remember that she was on the correct side."

The boy was not crying, but Virgil, feeling like an old, abused imbecile, had begun to shed tears. He popped the clutch, stalling, and, rushing to start the truck again, he flooded it.

"We'll have to get out here."

Duane led the way: Virgil followed, carrying Tina. He tucked them both into his wide bed, and then sat on the bedside staring out the window at his strangely beautiful crab-apple tree. Duane lay stiffly, facing the cobwebby rafters. A cat came and snuggled on the bed. Virgil placed a hand on the boy's forehead, saying, "I'm very sorry, this is a terrible thing to happen. But you must remember that millions of people die every day. It is a sad, but normal occurrence. If you want to cry, you should cry."

"I want to but I can't."

"I'm sorry."

They sat. The sirens had stopped. After a moment, Virgil heard a tiny twinkle of music in the night, and puzzled about its origin until realizing that he had left the truck's radio on. But he did not move. The old lawyer sat on the bed, his hand touching Duane, aware that all he could give was a rigid, dusty comfort, a foreign compassion, feeble with old age.

But after a while Duane reached up and held his hand. Then he sobbed, quietly, and afterward he drifted off to sleep. About that same time the tinkle of music from the truck radio grew fainter as the battery died, and then those melodies winked out altogether.

Virgil continued sitting there, afraid to take his hand out of the boy's grasp, even when the phone rang and continued to ring for almost two minutes before it quit. Over in a corner Emiliano Tafoya stood quietly, in mourning, saying nothing. Loretta Shimkus materialized and sat down stiffly on the edge of the bed: she was crying. Amaranta GeeGee floated through the window, and curled once about the room, then settled onto a chair and closed her eyes, whispering an old-fashioned cradle song:

> Hush, hush my little child,
> At end of day don't weep;
> Hush, hush, pretty girl
> When night falls we sleep.
>
> Birds are gathered on their branches,
> Lambs are snuggled safe in hay,
> Even piglets now are snoring,
> Waiting for another day.

A BARRAGE OF COPS, fortuitously accompanied by *Chamisaville News* and Capital City reporters and cameramen and the police photographer, Karl Mudd, landed on April Delaney's home about an hour after she died, playing a role to the hilt. Parking squad cars and unmarked cruisers on the paved road, some officers circled through fields to the north side; others scrambled up the driveway and planted themselves in the small orchard; a last group kept to the west, taking up stations beside a large cottonwood near the front irrigation ditch. Through a bullhorn, Chet Fulton announced their presence.

"All right, whoever is in there, this is the police. Now, we have the house surrounded and we don't want anybody to get hurt. So will you please come out carefully, with your hands raised, one at a time. I repeat, this is the police—"

He kept it up for an appropriate time. Then, communicating by walkie-talkie, Chet Fulton announced that he was going to enter the house with Len Goodwin.

It surprised the agents to find the children's beds empty. Quickly, they checked the house, and, calling in other cops and the press waiting outside, they set about to play out the final act. While the reporters gawked uneasily, and

Karl Mudd snapped photographs, they began searching the beds, slitting open mattresses. They splintered bureaus, looking for hollow bottoms, smashed the mimeo machine apart to get at the ink drum, chopped open typewriters kept in locked cases on the suspicion that weapons or dynamite might be in those cases, and slit apart cushions, stuffed chairbacks, and the underside of a couch. After fifteen minutes of waging methodical war on the house, somebody—not Chet Fulton, not Len Goodwin—discovered the utility room trapdoor to the crawl space, opened it, and dropped down.

The FBI agents stopped hacking things apart and waited for a triumphant shout, which never came.

A county undersheriff and a recently deputized man gathered expectantly around the trapdoor, while a third man, nervous about spiders, crawled under the house flashing a bright beam into every corner.

"What'd you find down there?" Chet Fulton prompted impatiently.

"Not a damn thing."

"What?"

"Not a damn thing. Bunch of dead spiders, is all."

"You're kidding!" The agent pushed his way to the trapdoor. "Nothing at all?"

"You better believe it. Dry as a bone, down here. Oh, there's a mouse skeleton. And here is somebody's shoe looks like it was manufactured in 1820."

The two FBI agents exchanged glances.

At the same time that Chet Fulton and his partner discovered they were not going to locate any dynamite for the benefit of the press, other officers, in separate maneuvers, were arresting Virgil Leyba and Juan Ortega as members of a conspiracy by *El Clarín* workers to dynamite Pueblo installations, Forest Service signs. Each man was informed that a cache of explosives remaining from the ski-valley theft had been found in the crawl space of April Delaney's house, and—while a deputy ferried Duane and Tina to the Rodey McQueen mansion—both Juan and Virgil were manacled and driven to the Chamisa county jail. There, the arresting officers issued statements to another *Chamisaville News* reporter and a stringer for the *Capital City Reporter,* declaring that since both men had close connections with the dead woman, and since a cache of stolen dynamite had been found in the crawl space of a house both men had often frequented, they were being arrested on suspicion of conspiracy to dynamite national forest and BIA installations, also for other radical, revolutionary activities as yet unspecified.

The call ordering everyone concerned not to mention a dynamite cache arrived at the jail approximately five minutes after the *Reporter* stringer had phoned in the story, not only to his own paper, but to a Capital City television station as well.

IT DIDN'T MATTER, however. None of the discrepancies mattered: and nothing Virgil or Juan or anybody else did or said or revealed could change what had occurred, or— for the time being—avert what was destined to happen.

When the telephone rang and he learned of his daughter's death, Rodey McQueen listened to the telephone even after the caller had hung up. He listened to the faint electronic buzzes and crackles, the remote static, trying to push what he had heard back through the line, back into the caller's mouth, back into oblivion, into a space where history was no longer valid and events were the easily malleable material of dreams. Then his heart did a lurching flip-flop that made him gasp, and, queasy all over for a second, he dropped the phone and sat down. Inside his head there was a crash, like a crystal glass breaking. Dizzy, unable to breathe very well, he wanted to call Cynthia for help, but, opening his mouth to squeeze out a sound, nothing happened. Then his heart calmed a little, and the dizzy spell subsided. McQueen got up, slowly crossed the living room, poured himself a scotch and clunked in two ice cubes, and swayed out the french doors into the snow.

Understanding, of course, that something terrible might happen, he had not really believed it could happen, not to April, not to his beautiful daughter. McQueen's brain was in such a muddle he could think of no way to govern his reaction, focusing it on something tangible, getting a grip on himself so that he might carry out the next grisly, appropriate moves.

McQueen stood on his side lawn in fresh snow, with the scotch in his hand, feeling weak and helpless. That phone call had done something terrible to him; he would not have believed that any blow could ever be so devastating.

An enormous squeezing sensation in his stomach made him gag, and he sank slowly to his knees. McQueen coughed, gasping for air, and felt tears being driven up through his eyes like stone splinters pounded by a hammer. He kept moving his mouth, trying to speak, shout a curse, unleash a cry—anything, but no sound issued from his constricted throat. Snow fell: the town beyond his high walls was quiet.

For five minutes the patriarch strained to utter some protest, and when at last he realized he could force no noise between his lips into the world, with his finger Rodey McQueen wrote in the snow a single word:

### Please!

JUNIOR LEYBA HAD HEARD about it before he arrived home. Parking the car carefully, he went inside. It was nine o'clock in the morning, and he had been out all night: his suit was slightly rumpled, his tie loosened in the button-down collar. Charlotte was in the kitchen, wearing a robe over her nightgown, drinking coffee, reading a recent *New Yorker*.

Junior sat down across from her at the table.

She asked, "Do you want some coffee?"

"All night I've been drinking coffee."

"I can make you some breakfast."

"I'm not hungry."

"I don't know what to do for you, then."

Junior nodded. He couldn't face her: he just sat there. After a long time he located a cigarette in his jacket pocket and lit it. Charlotte lit one of her own and smoked with him and waited. The radio was on, playing country music. Junior got up and turned it off and sat back down at the table. He fiddled with a couple of matches on the orange plastic tabletop while he smoked.

Charlotte said, "Something awful happened."

"Yeah."

"What?"

He didn't answer. Instead, Junior got up and went outside, crossed to the center of the front lawn, and wiped a capping of snow off the frozen birdbath. And he stood there, listening to the town waking up, to the cars moving about, to the faint tinkle of winter tourism. He felt sick to his stomach, lightheaded. The death in his heart was so calm he thought he might lose his mind. He remembered a time with April McQueen when they were both teen-agers, up on the western mesa between Ranchitos Abajo and Borregas Negras, parked on the old dirt airport runway, drinking beer. Since he had no money for a car in those days, it had been her vehicle, a Chevrolet convertible. The top was down, the radio tuned to late-night dance music, the stars overhead as they should have been—so crystal they were spooky. After they made love quickly, more or less clothed, and in the front seat, April climbed in back and, standing on the folded roof, joyously took off her clothes, piece by piece, flinging them into the dark sageland. And from the front seat he looked at her, seated atop the back seat, nude, drinking a beer and singing along with the radio, and he thought: *My heart will break forever if this girl doesn't marry me.* So he proposed. But she replied: "Although I love you in certain ways, Junior, I really want a bigger adventure." With that, April stretched her arms to the sky, giggling at her cornball gesture, and bellowed lustily, a cry Junior had heard in his heart ever since:

*"I want it all!"*

Okay, Junior thought, beginning to cry for that night so terribly long ago: Now we are even.

AND ANTHONY MARTÍNEZ QUIETLY walked several yards away from his tired father, plodding through knee-deep snow away from the edge of a high-country tree line. When he stopped, in the clear, the young man folded his arms and gazed three thousand feet down into the Chamisa Valley, sneering belligerently in order to hold back tears.

"I'm going to return with you tonight," he said. "I'm coming home."

"No you aren't. Not until the heat subsides."

"I am going to return, Father, and one by one I am going to get revenge. I'll cut their fucking hearts out."

"No you won't. Nothing would be accomplished."

"My revenge is all I care about."

"Then you are neither a warrior, a revolutionary, nor a human being."

Anthony closed his eyes and held them closed: the lashes froze together.

"Eye for an eye," he whispered. "I'll start with Rodey McQueen."

"To what avail?" Individual assassinations are pointless. It's a novel way to commit suicide, that's all."

His lips trembling, Anthony did not reply. He pressed hot fingertips against his eyeballs, melting the ice, and opened the lids once more.

"You will wait until you have a calm heart, and until it's safe, then you can return. And all of us will begin anew."

"I loved that woman," Anthony said.

"I know. I am sorry for you. Many people loved her."

"I want to die. I want to take a bath in their blood. I want to tear their balls off with my bare hands and take scalps. I want to rape their wives and daughters and shotgun their business associates and set fire to their buildings. I want to split open their skulls with hatchets and watch their eyeballs bulge as their brains slop out. I want to slit open their stomachs, shove in my fist, and rip out guts. I want to—I want—"

He clammed up tightly.

"I don't care what you want, you need to learn theory," Jake said evenly. "That first. And history. You need to understand what you are fighting for and why, and then you need to study much more in order to learn how to fight. You're too emotional right now, you would be totally ineffective."

"I want to kill them. I don't care about anything else. I want to see them die."

"You talk like a moron."

"I *feel* like a moron."

"This is only a first sorrow," Jake said. "It's nothing. This kind of sadness will multiply a hundredfold before you die."

"I can't take it, then. I'm not strong enough. I'm sorry."

"Don't dribble like an idiot. You can be a useful human being someday. Stay quiet now for a minute: let your heart calm down."

Anthony stood there with his arms folded, gazing into the valley, waiting for his head to clear, for his heartbeat to become regular. But it all seemed impossible. Behind him, Jake gazed past his son's shoulder, also into the valley. Sunshine patterned snow at the lower elevations: their higher altitude was canopied by clouds.

Jake said, "I will sing a grieving song."

Anthony again closed his eyes. And after a while he was lifted, by his ancient father's cracked and courageous voice, into a more peaceful realm.

# IN MEMORIAM

# VI

# As We Hammer
# Out Iron We Shall
# Hammer Out
# New Days

THE MESSAGE OF April Delaney's death was not lost on those who read about it, heard about it, dreamed about it, and together talked it into myth.

Yet April's constituency was all but gone by the time she died. Old men and women who had trusted in her, approaching Virgil and Juan and the *El Clarín* for a platform from which to be heard, were gone, dead, displaced, elsewhere . . . ghosts in the childlike graveyards.

Each day, Pat GeeGee visited the Chamisa county jail right after a bus dropped off the *Capital City Reporters*, bringing Virgil and Juan the news, some cigarettes, a rundown of local scandals. The bartender also smuggled in liquor and did not know what to say. Five days after April's death, Pat had tacked a new photograph on the bar's collage board, of April sitting on her porch smoking a cigarette, cupping her bare knees, a drink in hand, her hair in double ponytails, laughing at the photographer, her all-American face bruised-looking and lovely. The picture stayed there for three weeks, until Pat lost his liquor license, which passed from the El Gaucho to the Northland Grazing Association.

Flakey Jake Martínez came often to the jail, always trailed by a plainclothes FBI agent or BIA flunky hoping that sooner or later the father would lead them to the son.

"Anthony is okay," Jake told Virgil and Juan loud enough for the cops to hear. "He is hiding in a forest cave eating nothing but bear meat so that come springtime, when he emerges from his hiding place, he will be strong enough to string Rodey McQueen up by the balls and cut out his heart and sauté it in mushrooms and Blue Bonnet margarine."

Others came by, wishing to be kind, speaking in hushed voices because they were frightened. Ursula and Perfecto Torres; a grave and silent Celestino Lucero. J. B. LeDoux even brought food, cigarettes, and books to read, but Virgil and Juan sat there quietly, eyes fixed on a spot above J. B.'s head, unwilling to accept the offerings, refusing to speak to the mayor when spoken to. "Say something!" J. B. shouted. "God damn you, you self-righteous old farts —*please speak to me!*" But Virgil and Juan remained silent, not even blinking an eye, until J. B. was gone and the other prisoners had divvied up that loot.

From Gloria Armijo they accepted cigarettes, candy, magazines—whatever she thought to bring. Virgil touched her hand through the bars and, once, reached into her provocative blouse, pressing his old man's fingertips to her ripe bosom for just a second, when nobody else was looking.

To pay for their legal fees, Virgil put his small house on the market, and in due course he was informed that the house had been sold.

So he had joined the rest of them. For so many years he had taken their cases, fighting to stall the takeover, saving their houses and their land, and in the end he had wound up in the same pickle.

J. B. returned to their cell. In a tired voice the mayor told Virgil, "I bought your house."

"Well, more power to you."

"You don't understand," J. B. said nervously. "When you get out, you can have it back. I'll turn the title over to you. The word is that they are simply going to do pretrial maneuvers, refusing to grant bail, until you are broke, and then drop all the charges, which they could never substantiate anyway. But they won't drop them until you and Juan are broken men."

Virgil said, "I need no favors from a person like you."

"If it will make you feel any better, you can buy it back. I'll even charge you interest, if that would help. But you can arrange your own terms. All I'm saying is that I bought it, and I don't want to do anything with it except give it back to you if you'll take it."

"I am not going to help you feel less guilty, thanks all the same."

"There are no strings attached. If you like, don't ever speak to me again."

"But you don't understand," Virgil said, and J. B. left the jail weeping.

The mayor wept a lot these days, at any old drop of a hat. There were rumors of impeachment.

On the same day that a heavy midwinter snowstorm landed on Chamisaville, the United States government reached a landmark decision, deeding the Pueblo's fifty thousand acres of sacred Albino Pine land back to the Indian people. In conjunction with this move, Randolph Bonney also announced that the tribe's ruling cabal had signed an agreement with the Custer Electric Co-op, admitting electricity into the Pueblo. These dual pronouncements had barely landed on the public's frostbitten ears, than a flotilla of backhoes thundered across the reservation boundary, chopping trenches running in every direction, while another division of red co-op trucks began to lay thick, insulated cable. Almost before a week had passed, the Chamisaville Pueblo, an institution that for many centuries had balked against the corrupting logic of modern times, was up to its ass in electricity, poised on the brink of a great leap forward—perhaps into oblivion.

One day, on Virgil Leyba's request, Abe Gallegos came up from the capital and put the old lawyer through a rigorous physical. Accompanied by a guard, they spent several days over in the Our Lady of the Sorrows Hospital, where Abe saw Virgil through a battery of tests. When it was over, Abe sat down, uncorked a half-pint whiskey bottle, took a big slug, and offered Virgil a drink, saying, "Well, Virgilio, old friend, revolutionary bastard, unconscionable womanizer, and champion of the poor—it looks like Big C." They killed the liquor and embraced, Virgil sneering grimly, Abe unabashedly crying as he cursed, quoted maudlin philosophers and sickly-sweet poets, and in general carried on childishly because he loved Virgil Leyba as he loved most courageous human beings, and wished he could dish up a pill making his old pal immortal.

And the ghost of Amaranta GeeGee often stopped by the jail cell to reminisce about the fabulous Horse Without Shit and other phenomena from the good old days. Her withered inessential form hovered against the wall like a memory of taciturn grandparents, autumn, the smell of cracked saddle leather, fresh butter, and old wooden beams. And her essence awoke in both Juan and Virgil an ardent nostalgia, an almost crippling, certainly passionate, desire for youth.

IN A TINY SOUTH VILLAGE APARTMENT furnished with a single bed, a simple desk, one typewriter, and many books in piles on the floor, George Parker lived the big-city cliché, more alone than his heart could fathom, inflamed by the excitement and fever of New York. He worked, but never for very long. Howls and clangs and sirens repeatedly drew him down to the street. He stumbled about the noisy avenues feeling like Thomas Wolfe, Walt Whitman, Dylan Thomas, overawed by the criminal vitality, the majesty of indifferent skyscrapers, the Babelian ruckus among cultures on the filthy sidewalks. Massive vistas boggled his mind; women turned his head every second. Such plumage! Enormous black men in ankle-length greatcoats, golf hats, and platform heels scared him shitless. He envied young people, felt sorry for himself, stared impolitely at the street life, experienced moments of savage excitement. How utterly ridiculous, and also sublime, to have such a marvelously innocent catharsis. What crippling and frightening joy to enter any of a thousand bars, unknown, and simply down an *anonymous* beer! His small-town connections were severed. George paced restlessly, occasionally breaking into a trot, traveling everywhere and going nowhere, adrift, happy, scared stiff. Pigeons launched off rooftops dazzled his eyes. Taxis were wonderful. Times Square appeared so evil that his heart murmured each time he was attracted back there again. Everything ugly, hostile, cynical, and above all *massive* triggered in him sensations of adulation, and nervous creativity. He went to hockey games and boxing matches, pornographic movies, art galleries, museums, Coney Island, Central Park. Sea gulls, jackhammers, muggings, radical-chic. He walked up Fifth Avenue from Washington Square to the Plaza Hotel, and down Sixth Avenue to Canal Street, and up Hudson Street and then Eighth Avenue and through the Central Park Zoo and east to Second Avenue and downtown to St. Marks, then west to his apartment—all in one day! Such a beautiful danger! Bums, a crazy in a gorilla costume, secretaries in mini- and maxi-skirts, hardhats enveloped in steam, subway passengers, graffiti, skateboards—George gasped and meandered, trying not to think of home, and he felt foolish and irresponsible attempting to be—actually feeling—so young again, optimistic, thrilled! He wanted to work out, stop smoking, cut off the booze, and watch his muscles and his stamina grow. He played volleyball with blacks, Puerto Ricans, and N.Y.U. students in Washington Square; met a girl and screwed her; read three newspapers every day; and then wept for April Delaney.

When he heard, in a letter from his dad, George wanted to grab rocks, bricks, whatever was handy, and bang his head with them as had that fisherman husband of hers. Unable to believe it at first, later he decided it had been inevitable. But murder? Or revolutionary suicide? Or an incomprehensible accident? *How could it have happened?* Not to April! Invisible stones battered open the bones protecting his chest, and true terror entered. An enormous pain constricted his rib cage—he could barely breathe. George sat at his desk, facing a clean sheet of paper, wanting to say something, compose a requiem. But what? What could he write to make something of it, to explain his role, his feelings, to give her life, or to formalize her death so that he might believe and accept it and not be tormented by a hideous guilt the rest of his days?

Finally, he began typing. A letter to a jailed man with whom he'd rarely spoken—Virgil Leyba. George wanted to write a powerful memorial, a passionate eulogy; instead it was a banal and weeping letter, short and awkward and despairing. Suicide occupied his mind during the entire process of writing it. Breaking down, he called for help. "Tell me something about it that will make it possible to understand!" he pleaded. "Don't let it just happen two thousand miles away, unrecorded by New York City. She had a million friends in this town—"

Of course, the second his letter disappeared into the corner mailbox, George wanted it back, destroyed, eradicated without a trace. Why couldn't he be more of a man? Pathetic, his inability to control his fatuous, childish impulses. When would he ever grow up?

Virgil had plenty of time and wrote back immediately, a straightforward letter, not at all condescending—grateful, perhaps, for an opportunity to articulate the event in both historical and political frameworks for her former lover, and for himself. He included in his package the simple ring made from the metal of an American bomber that a Vietnamese woman had given to April in Cuba: Celestino Lucero's pet magpie, Tierra o Muerte the Thirteenth, had brought it home one day.

And at the end, he wrote:

Each person leaves a legacy, and many people receive a piece, a single small portion of that legacy, to carry on the memory, the words and the deeds, to make richer each individual life and the collective life of humanity as a whole. Despair is an indulgent and despicable bourgeois affectation; you must not allow it. Self-pity because a loved-one died is senseless. As for what happens next, there is only one answer. The Cuban poet, Regino Pedroso, once said: "Cómo forjamos el hierro forjaremos días nuevos." "As we hammer out iron we shall hammer out new days." Take heed. En Amistad—

Virgil Leyba

CYNTHIA McQUEEN WANDERED into April's old room and sat on the bed, gazing dreamily out a window a maid had recently opened to let in the fresh air. At first, her mind wandered from one upcoming obligation to another; in fact, she did not even realize that this was April's room. Of late, during the strange periods of inactivity encroaching on her life, she had begun wandering through her house, rather aimlessly inspecting things, a habit she had never indulged in before. After all, maids cleaned and made sure all was in order: she inspected rooms and beds only when guests were expected. Cynthia had rarely cataloged her life or her possessions without some definite purpose in mind.

Yet now she was seated on a bed in April's room, drawn there for no reason, and with nothing specific in mind.

After a while Cynthia sniffed, smelling something—a fragile scent. It aroused in her much emotion—anguish, perplexity. Growing alert, she cocked her head, trying to pinpoint that scent's origins—the open window? And then she guessed certainly it must be a fantasy, nothing real, for it was as if her daughter, aged fifteen, was hiding in the room, under a bed, in a closet, wearing a cheap teen-age perfume or one of those bright lipsticks that had made her pink mouth float through the house, the town, and her school like a wounding angel.

Cynthia enacted a most absurd charade. Slipping off the bed, and after first checking at the door to make sure no maid patrolled the hall, she got down on her knees, raised the spread, and checked to see if anybody was under the bed.

Nobody was.

Heading for a closet, she slid open the door, facing April's teen-age wardrobe. The rhythmic colors flowed out of the closet like a released stream of colorful sunny water, rippling over Cynthia, flooding the room with nostalgic radiance. The mother selected a dress, holding it up for critical inspection, a light blue and fading emerald shirt-waist: she pressed it against her big body, crinkled the fabric against her nose, and believed that she could smell that provocative perfume.

Gingerly, hoping not to disturb her strange and almost lightheaded mood, Cynthia began taking clothes out of the closet and laying them across the white bedspread. Lovely chiffon blouses floated like clouds, their sweet blues and ambers resolved softly into gaudy feathers and flower gardens. Mexican blouses were low cut, black and white and snappy with silver spangles; other outrageous blouses were as naughty as Mardi Gras, loud and profane. There was a tight-knitted, bright red dress, and formal gowns so white they cried out for sainthood, a suede skirt from Paris, and wide-brimmed straw hats to which April had pinned shockingly purple and pink and yellow paper flowers. Cynthia removed a satin T-shirt, a red velvet dress, and a black velvet jumpsuit. And a hanger of ribbons: Mexican ribbons and Ukrainian ribbons and dime-store ribbons—April had always used them for tying up her ponytails. And wild Spanish rebozos, and cashmere sweaters—lime green, mocha colored, childlike pink . . . so pliable they felt like an unbearable extension of teen-age breasts. Cynthia carried the clothes from the closet and laid them on the bed, fluffed them, tossed them, and let them float gracefully into a profusion of gay color antithetical to the physical appearance of this house and her life.

A breeze ruffled that gorgeous display. A perfume odor hovered in the room, either a residue from clothing, or simply a remembered scent, a redolence in the old woman's mind. Cynthia stood over the bed, lightly touching material with one hand, one finger turning the folds of a scarf, describing a collar, sweeping thoughtfully across the adolescent fuzz of a sweater. Colors merged; it was a noisy, also delicate ensemble. And for a moment April was more precious to her mother than she had ever been. I missed her, the woman was thinking. I missed everything. Now it's much too late. There were no gifts to be given now. And she had not felt this sad, or this lonely, ever.

ON HORSEBACK, proceeding slowly through old snow, Icarus Suazo reached the high, vast meadow of the sacred Albino Pine Tree. Late afternoon sun gilded the tree's thick branches; they gleamed as if golden. The smoothly crusted and unbroken meadow snow shone as if plated with a copper-colored leaf. In the background rose naked rocky slopes, wind-plastered and icy white; enormous boulders seemed involved in an explosion, bursting frozenly without motion toward the sky, caught in a fantastic apocalyptic upheaval intimately connected to the creation of all universes, all legends, all myths badgering the tiny brains of human beings.

Icarus had never seen this meadow and the mountains towering above it so beautiful. No warriors guarded the sacred tree; no need for that anymore. The land had been returned to the tribe for safekeeping; the tree stood at the heart of a vast and lonesome area whose secret soul had reverted to the native people. An invisible magic wall now protected the source of their spiritual well-being; he believed that despite electrification of the Pueblo, their survival as a viable nation within imperial America was assured. To hell with the racetrack, the development, the motels and hotels, the artificial lake; if the Pueblo had lost in the end, it had also gained. The bones, mysteries, and rituals of their forefathers had sanctified this forest land, these mountains, and this simple tree at the sacred river's source. And no matter how exploited the natives might be in a future already permeated by capital despair, each man, woman, and child could now strip naked and melt back into the earth. And the souls of all the drunks and all the wasted lives could be reenergized in this land that outsiders would never control again. With such profoundly rooted claims, the people would somehow survive.

His horse plodded through the snow, approaching the sacred pine. About fifty yards from the tree, Icarus reined in, dismounted, and withdrew an old rifle from his saddle scabbard. Forty years earlier he had aimed that same gun at Rodey McQueen standing atop Nobody Mountain during Cipi García's funeral. Calmly, the former Pueblo secretary chambered a shell, muttered a quick apology and a prayer, and shot his horse between the eyes. The animal crunched into the snow, twitched once, and lay perfectly still, faintly steaming, while blood bubbled out the hole in its skull.

Icarus assessed the sky, squinting his eyes. A moment ago that chilly blue expanse, growing mauve and rosy with dusk, had been deserted. Now he located the eagle, a tiny dot, circling way on high, and nodded, making a slight reverent motion with his hand.

Removing his sheepskin jacket, a flannel shirt, his undershirt, his boots, socks, and Levi's, Icarus stood naked in the snow, with only a single feather in his hair. The old man was so small, light, and dusty that his weight did not break through the solid white crust. From the saddlebags, he removed a small cosmetics jar of natural tincture, dipped in his fingertips, and put four short crimson streaks down either cheek, then pressed a handprint of red against either breast. Walking a slight distance away from his dead horse, Icarus lay down on top of the snow, just beyond the lengthening shadow of the Albino Pine. His arms rested at his sides, his ankles touched. His wrinkled skin was spreckled with age, ghastly pale; almost immediately it turned blue from the cold.

Eyes wide open, Icarus stared at the sky, willing the eagle to earth, bringing it down toward his shriveled little body, forcing it to become the caretaker of his soul. The bird circled earthward, growing larger as the sky—infused with sunset colors—took on characteristics of muffling, suffocating velvet, lowering to the tips of surrounding mountain peaks. The enormous golden eagle alighted with a great clatter of feathers only a few feet away, settled its wings with a haughty commotion, and, for a second, as Icarus turned his head, stared cruelly into the Pueblo secretary's eyes. Then the bird hopped onto Icarus Suazo's chest, and with short, deadly chops of its beak and talons dug swiftly past the old man's brittle sternum, grasped his heart in its claws while he was still alive staring at the bloody sky and muttering prayers in his native tongue, tore the organ clear of his chest with a scrawk, and, smashing the stiff snowcrust with the powerful downthrust of its wings, took off again, rising over the Albino Pine Tree, spattering its beautiful branches with Icarus Suazo's blood as it soared back into the tumultuous heavens, and shortly disappeared.

"*So be it!*" the old man cried, joyful at last. And, closing his eyes, he entered another world.

On a sunny February day when the valley was decorated in fresh snow, J. B. LeDoux, Junior Leyba, and Damacio Mares climbed Nobody Mountain to survey their expanding domain. Puffing hard to catch their breaths, they allowed their eyes to roam over the land below, experiencing certain proprietary guilts and feelings of pride, a trifle awed by the changes which had occurred, a bit winded by the way in which their pastoral valley had been transformed into a quasi-urban environment. A strip of motels, hotels, pizza parlors, cafés, radio shacks, laundromats and the like now flanked the highway from Cañoncito to the Chamisaville traffic light, and most of the land on either side of the highway, reaching to the mountains in the east, to the mesa on the west, had been developed. Buildings such as the new junior high and elementary school, three large shopping centers, several trailer parks, and an even dozen low-income and high-income housing developments were in various stages of completion. There were two pool halls, two bowling alleys, a representative from every chain drive-in restaurant in America, a half-dozen used-car lots, a half-dozen new-car lots, sixteen gas stations, a tattoo parlor, forty-six art galleries, twenty-one gift and curio shops, several condominiums, four beauty shops, lumber yards and hardware stores galore, and a glittering junk pile of other commercial establishments, cheap homes, and newfangled estates. Everywhere construction met the eye, running from La Ciénega to the Cañoncito Dam Golf Course. Construction had taken over the Mota Llano ridge; it extended west to Ranchitos Abajo, where a new sewage plant, located in the heart of that reeling community, was nearing completion. The haphazard building spread north over the entire valley between highway and mesa to Ranchitos Arriba and into the Vallecitos Dynamite Shrine and Baths area, and it was beginning to trickle beyond. A moccasin factory and three small-time weaving and garment operations now augmented the Dynamite Fetish plant, and three other national companies—one making rugs, another radio parts, a third oral contraceptives—had plans to locate either in the new industrial park or out at the Pueblo.

And, though legal problems were delaying the racetrack, groundbreaking for something large, nobody knew exactly what, had already occurred at the site of Anthony Martínez's adobe-ruin retreat.

Despite the fresh snowfall, the valley looked chopped

up, scarred, and confused: ugly dirt mounds rose everywhere, as if enormous prairie dogs had been excavating. The skeletal frame structures of new buildings abounded; a thousand trees were down, a like number of driveways paved over. Fluorescent red No Trespassing and Keep Out and Private Property signs winked like hostile stars.

But it looked vital to that trio. Or, to each other, they pretended it did, anyway. The incapacitating roots of the old days had been extracted; an impoverished way of life, and all the language, culture, tradition, and lore that had gone with it had been expunged from the valley in favor of more technological dreams. "You can't stand in the way of progress," the mythical "They" had said. And a new environment had been created—crude, active, ugly. The town, as always, was embroiled in a massive traffic jam.

J. B. wandered away from the others for a moment. And, while gazing at the overall scene, the camposantos caught his eye, tiny squares near the heart of where individual communities with unique personalities had merged with Chamisaville, annexed or soon to be annexed neighborhoods in a city of fifteen thousand. J. B. noticed the camposantos because they reflected the only color down there, and strange indeed they appeared, sparkling disconcertingly in the drab landscape, reflecting rainbow colorations from blankets of plastic, no-fade flowers placed on the graves of the ancient dead, on the graves of the more recently deceased.

They made him nervous. J. B. averted his eyes from the colorful cemeteries and returned to the others.

To the west, over the mesa, the noon marijuana flight, glinting like a cute toy, buzzed toward the Chamisaville airport, whose runway was being lengthened to accommodate small, executive jets.

"Well, boys—" Thoughtfully, Junior licked his lips. "I guess that's it, I guess we have done it. For once and for all. The whole enchilada."

"What's that?" Damacio asked.

"The Betterment of Chamisaville."

Junior excused himself and walked about twenty-five yards into some trees in order to take a leak. While he urinated, Junior was thinking: All right, now that I have got it in the palm of my hand, I can pull the string and watch it collapse, drowning McQueen and Bonney and J. B. LeDoux and everybody else, even Joseph Bonatelli. If he played his cards correctly. And that catastrophe, that scandal, that revenge would be a sight indeed for his sore eyes. He had waited and planned and plotted and finagled for a long, long time.

Junior had just tucked himself into his pants, when Jesus Etcetera and two dozen members of his army rode out from all sides of the piñon-juniper cover and reined in their horses: Junior was completely surrounded. Jesus Etcetera himself led a saddled but riderless animal. With the barrel of his old rifle he made a motion for the lawyer to mount up. And, coolly urging them all to stay calm with a gesture of patting the air away from his chest, Junior readily complied.

"Hey, take it easy now, comprendes? I don't know what you want but be careful with all those popguns. If they go off they're liable to hurt somebody—where the hell are you taking me?"

But nobody would talk. Stone faced, they circled north of La Ciénega and trotted through Indian land barely a half-mile south of the Pueblo. Crossing the North-South Highway just beyond Vallecitos and the shrine complex, they continued silently toward the gorge, the riders completely encircling Junior, giving him no room for escape. At the gorge rim the small party aimed north, traveling for another half-hour until they reached the bridge. Without hesitation, Jesus Etcetera motioned Junior to nudge his horse onto the highway, and thence onto the bridge. The roly-poly little man and his comrades followed behind the lawyer's mount, until, in the center of the span, Jesus Etcetera said, "Stop."

No car approached from either direction; the macadam seemed permanently deserted. A few swallows twittered underneath the bridge. In the unseasonably hot sun, metal railings, macadam, and nearby sagebrush sizzled. A thousand feet below the milky green Rio Grande flowed.

"Get off the horse," Ikie Trujillo said.

"Now hold on just a minute. If you filthy old bats think you can order me around, intimidating me by—"

Fecundo Lavadie spurred his horse up behind Junior's mount, and with an abrupt chop-swing of his carbine knocked the lawyer to the ground.

"Now, jump off the bridge," Max Jaramillo said quietly. "It's high time you committed suicide."

"You're kidding!" But when Junior quickly checked all their faces he realized they weren't kidding.

"Aw come on, you guys, you can't be serious. Who *are*

you anyway? Come on, cool it. I mean, I can understand where your jollies are coming from, but, like, it isn't funny anymore, saben? I went along with the gag until now, see, but—"

"Jump off the bridge."

"You mean it? You honest to Christ Almighty are actually telling me to jump off this bridge? It's a thousand feet to the bottom. I'll be dead before I even hit water. You people are crazy. Do you know who I am? Do you know who you are trying to push around here? I mean, you aren't too smart, you know that? I mean, you ought to have your heads examined. I'm not just nobody, I have connections—"

"Jump off the bridge."

Junior shook his head incredulously. "I *really* have to do it?"

A dozen rifles and pistols leveled down at him: cylinders clicked as hammers were thumbed back.

Junior took two steps over to the four-foot-high metal guardrail. "Hey listen—"

"I'm counting to ten," Benny LeDoux said wearily. "One . . . two . . ."

At that, with a weak exclamation—"Oh shit . . ."— Junior set both hands on the top of the railing and hopped over it as nonchalantly as he might have hopped over the low wall of some outdoor municipal parking lot. For an instant, curious swallows engulfed him, then he was gone, planing slightly in the air, his dark hair streaming, his jacket and then his shirt tearing and releasing shreds that popped off like feathers and left a wake behind, graceful tatters of lovely cloth flowing off his body in pretty Victorian loops, almost like a curiously ornate, and also comic calligraphy saying *That's All Folks*.

DEPLORING THE INDOLENCE, Rodey McQueen had rarely accompanied Cynthia on her trips; he'd always been too busy. But now, feeling somehow prematurely retired, listless and almost submissive, the old man stood at the railing of a cruise ship advancing quietly through a becalmed sea beneath the blue Caribbean sky. Terns and sea gulls coasted nonchalantly over their foamy wake. Nearby, Cynthia was playing shuffleboard with an acquaintance. Behind her, on the starboard side, several men of McQueen's vintage, wearing hunting vests stocked with shotgun shells, were popping at clay pigeons with .410 shotguns.

A steward approached McQueen, offering a tray of saltines and beef bouillon, but the old tyrant never acknowledged his presence. The steward tipped his head and pattered away. McQueen was barely eating on this voyage. Indifferent, trapped in an unrelenting lassitude, he refused to don trunks and swim laps in the pool, have a massage, or take a sauna. Most days Cynthia alone showed up at their dining table. Lost in forlorn and anesthetizing thought, McQueen kept to the deck, almost in panic breathing the fresh warm winter air. For long hours he stood immobile at the railing, or lay on a deck chair wrapped loosely in a light blanket, a magazine or book unopened and unread on his lap, drowsy eyes fixed blurredly on the flat sea, the neutral sky, the lemonade-green horizon. Few words had passed between the man and his wife. At night in their stateroom, occupying a separate bed, McQueen lay sleepless despite soporific sea swells beneath him; during the day he dozed, took a dozen naps, and wandered about unable to concentrate, his mind a turbulent blank. The dullness and lull of this recuperation cruise seemed a prelude to some totally unheroic demise. And it was as if the fire inside McQueen that had adrenalinized him all his adult life had depended for its oxygen supply on the vitality of his swaggering daughter.

Now that he had helped lay a foundation for April's death, McQueen had abruptly lost the will to consolidate a lifetime of brawny, imaginative chicanery. His productive vision floundered. Electricity had entered the Pueblo at last, all systems were Go on their magnificent scam—so what else was new? Dollar bills in his hand were textured like little green corpses. Money had always pulsed in McQueen's grip, alive and exciting . . . but no more. What the hell? Cynthia was handling their cash, paying tips, pacifying the purser—McQueen couldn't have cared less. The lovely, vacuous sky, the pretty, stagnant ocean, the passionless rocking of the luxury liner should have rested his aching bones, swaddling his heart in mollifying cotton, but no such relief had occurred. In a painful limbo, devoid of sensation yet suffering profoundly, McQueen confronted the dull weather and moronic tourist situation with a level apathetic gaze, observing little or nothing.

The torpor was lethal.

Mesmerized by that last dynamite blast in his life, ending his vital connection to the Old Crap Game even as the first dynamite blast had liberated his undisciplined imag-

559

ination, accumulating for him immense power and wealth, at this moment the former Muleshoe conman found it impossible to recall with even a little fondness any details of his past four decades. Instead, his memory unleashed vivid recollections that had lain dormant for forty years. Of a skinny hobo tacker wild as a corncrib rat riding boxcars, hunting cigarette butts in gutters, pitching hay on west Texas prairieland until his back was almost broken, curled up under tattered blankets in snow-sprinkled winter arroyos half starving to death, grappling with big-breasted farm girls ugly as homemade soap in horseshit-smelling three-room shotgun shacks, and getting drunk in disaster alleys with other tow-headed buck-toothed big-eared scrawny redneck good ol' boys on Saturday nights in small cowboy towns with names like Lampasas, Tulip, Ropesville, Tokio, Turkey, Matador, Rankin, and Iraan. McQueen had strung barbed wire, milked cows, played $6.98 Sears Roebuck guitars, shot horses for meat (and rustled them, too), hunted rattlesnakes in annual roundups, stolen cars, spent a year in jail and another six months in the workhouse and on a road gang, managed a traveling carnival, and ridden broncos and bulls bareback in a hundred rodeos. He had failed in a dozen occupations before arriving in Chamisaville: logger, cowboy, trainman, wetback runner and farm contractor, oil rigger, all-around conman, poacher, Bible salesman, semipro football player, whatever had come his way. For years he had traveled always with the law right on his tail, it seemed. Only by inches had he avoided the daring violent escapades of a Bonnie and Clyde. Instead of attending church he had patronized brothels. Cooties, bedbugs, crab, lice—you name 'em, he'd had 'em. McQueen had witnessed one lynching of a black man, and he had been in two poker games where men died as a result of gunplay. In fact, he had once sat down to cards with Pretty Boy Floyd. And he had picked cotton and pecans. During the Mexican revolution he had twice run guns across the border. A short stint in the U. S. Army had ended in desertion before he could be sent to fight. Twice married in childless teen-age unions that had barely lasted an entire year, McQueen had simply walked away from them, never bothering with a divorce. He had killed one man—a nameless bum—in a Sweetwater flophouse in a stupid argument over a pair of boots. His travels had gone as far east as New Orleans, where he trapped alligators in bayou country. Down near Brownsville, his farthest southern exposure, he'd run a still for a while. Later, McQueen's bootlegger talents had involved selling illegal jake in Oklahoma, operating out of towns as far north as Mobeetie. And McQueen had journeyed as far west as Navajo Indian country in New Mexico and Arizona, buying up rugs that he had sold for disappointing profits in Dallas.

Dale Rodey McQueen had been born before the age of automobiles and airplanes and supermarkets. He had lived through two world wars, a depression, Lindbergh's Atlantic flight and his baby's kidnapping, Prohibition, the Atomic Bomb, and the Jazz Age. The violent lives and deaths of men and women like John Dillinger, Al Capone, and Ma Barker had occurred in his lifetime. Presidents from William McKinley to Richard Nixon had ruled the nation—thirteen men in all, two of them assassinated. A king had abdicated for a commoner in England: Babe Ruth had hit sixty homers: bronc riders and calf ropers had gotten so rich they now flew from one rodeo to the next in their own private planes: Hofheinz had built the Astrodome: the Korean and Vietnam wars had been disasters: boys could let their hair grow down to their shoulders and get away with it: college girls fucked like geese in heat and walked around without enough clothes on to wad a shotgun, their nipples showing through their blouses: and Americans had landed on the moon. All that had happened between McQueen's birth and the time his daughter went violently to her grave.

At the railing, eyes glazed, without an appetite for life, McQueen made no moves to fight his spreading coma. Much had happened in his lifetime and it was all almost over. A few months ago his life-experience, politics, social attitudes had rested on a granite foundation: when he looked at the stars they had made perfect sense. But today only an insignificant, ridiculous scrabble existed up there. Perhaps a powerful and invisible life-giving thread had always been stretched between McQueen and his daughter; in any case, numbness had entered his body, spreading like painless venom, a novocaine leaving him languid, unfeeling. "Null and void," McQueen said weakly. Life was a poor player, full of sound and fury—a tale told by a real idiot. Christ, what a terrible, almost evil sky: the sea was so obnoxiously tranquil and blue. Finding it impossible to talk with McQueen, Cynthia couldn't stop crying. Barely five words had passed between them since April's funeral

—or did the lack of communication travel as far back as twenty or thirty years? The ocean was so damnably placid. The universe was as clear and as unruffled and as blank as a pretty postcard. McQueen felt close enough to hell to smell the smoke.

Just like that, all the fun had gone out of the Old Crap Game.

It had gone out of trips like this, out of money, out of golf, out of cigars, out of friends.

The fun had gone out of the Betterment of Chamisaville. It had gone out of everything.

IN THE EARLY SPRINGTIME the case against Virgil Leyba and Juan Ortega dissolved, simply disappearing into the Chamisaville ether: a jailer opened their cell door one misty April morning and told them to beat it, all charges had been dropped. They were not considered dangerous anymore, the Pueblo deal had been consolidated, the public acclimated, and two feeble old geezers, one of whom —guilty or not—had been disbarred in the interim, the other of whom no longer had a paper to write for, could not harm the established order of things. And Virgil had been diagnosed as a terminal cancer patient while in prison. Of the lungs—Where else? thought Virgil, lighting his first cigarette in freedom, confronting with bitter wonder the slew of mammoth earth-moving machines lumbering along the highway.

Yet you could hear meadowlarks in the fields, in the tiny, inviolate community graveyards. Their melodious songs could slide like liquid mercury around or through or over all obstacles.

Virgil and Juan crossed the highway to Irving Newkirk's café, ordered one-hundred-percent pure beef horsemeatburgers, and sat there quietly, relishing each adulterated mouthful.

"Well Juan," Virgil said. "So we begin again from scratch."

Juan said, "Yup."

After another thoughtful pause, Virgil added, "Well, if I only got three months to live, we'd best get cracking."

The old reporter said, "I'm with you, Virgil, what the hell."

But they tarried a moment longer, savoring freedom, two old men in their seventies, vestigial entities in this savage environment, discarded philosophers, gadflies, keepers of the flame. Virgil's five bullet-hole scars had pulsed bitterly ever since he had learned of Junior's death; and his chest ached, too. But through chinks in the pain he could feel a singing inside; and he felt light on his feet and eager and angry, ready to begin again.

During a particularly busy moment, when the cashier's attention was absorbed by a busload of Texas Baptists, Virgil and Juan walked out without paying.

They made straight for the El Gaucho, but it was closed, boarded up. Crossing the plaza, they found Pat GeeGee slumped on a stool in the La Tortuga Bar. They embraced, shared a round, and reminisced, first about the distant past, then about the most recent past, and finally about the less recent past, about April Delaney's death.

"We should bury her," Virgil said. "That will be the first thing on our agenda."

"What are you talking about?" Pat stirred his drink with one finger. "She's buried out there on McQueen land in McQueen's private graveyard."

"No matter. She belongs to us and we'll bury her for the people."

That night, Juan and Virgil slept on the floor of Pat Gee-Gee's room above the old El Gaucho. Next morning, just at dawn, carrying a mayonnaise jar filled with normal fire-place ashes, a small group climbed to the top of Nobody Mountain: Juan and Virgil, Flakey Jake and Gloria Martínez, Gloria Armijo and Pat GeeGee and a handful of stray old-timers, among them Ursula and Perfecto Torres and Celestino Lucero with Tierra o Muerte the Thirteenth on his shoulder. As they climbed, the ghosts of a thousand departed valley dwellers became a sticky mist clinging to their limbs and clothing. Jesus Etcetera led his fiery band out of the piñon trees and the junipers, joining the silent procession. Fecundo Lavadie, Bonifacio Herrera, Max Jaramillo, and Ikie Trujillo; Atiliano Montoya, Rudy LeDoux and his grandson Benny; Juan and Amaranta GeeGee, and the whale-bewitched teen-ager who had mysteriously drowned himself in the Pacific Ocean, Ralphito García; the cigar-smoking boxer, Eloy Romo; a half-dozen Casados and Arrellano brothers, who remembered how defiantly April had galloped horses as a child; Pat GeeGee's wife, Lucinda, and Pancha Cisneros and her sons; the fabulous Horse Without Shit crowd, Bernardo C. de Baca, Pancho Ortiz y Pino, and his little brother, the oversexed deaf-mute they had called Pedro Cabrón y Puto; the courthouse loafer Malaquias C. de Baca, and the bruja, Genoveva Bachicha; Filiberto García carrying his upside-down flag and still murmuring sibilantly, "Auxilio, auxilio—"; Gabe Suazo and enormous, pathetic Marshall Kickingbird; and a host of other old-timers, among them José Archuleta, Cipi Fernández, Jacobal Mondragón, and Vidal Mondragón. In tatters they arrived, wearing sweat-stained straw cowboy hats, carrying cheap battered guitars, weighed down by ammunition belts and clumsy holsters, hand-rolled cigarettes between their lips, lovely old mantillas on the heads of some women, pretty rebozos around their shoulders. . . . They joined the procession to the top of Nobody Mountain, reined in, gathered around, and fell silent, eddying slightly in spring breezes.

At the summit, Virgil kept it simple. "This is for the spirit of our friend," he said. "I hope we will get strength from affirming that we loved her and believed in her beliefs, and will miss her. By making this formal good-bye we also affirm that nobody here is gonna die of a broken heart, much less give up hope because of last winter's tragedy. These things happen, fuck death, it is time to get on with the show. I love April Delaney, I consider that she lives in our hearts as we lived in hers, and in the name of that woman of whom we are all a part I would like to commemorate these ashes into the valley of her birth."

With that, he unscrewed the lid, and with a short, thrusting motion, flung the ashes into a spring breeze. They burst apart in a small puff, minute gray rivulets whisking away in different directions, floating into the springtime activities below.

A high-powered rifle shot echoed out of a mysterious canyon deep on sacred Albino Pine land, and the gunshot rattled loudly down the entire length of the Chamisa Valley.

Virgil coughed, lit a cigarette, and focused on the dreamlike western skyline of buttes, mesa tops, and softly curved mountains. He felt no bitterness, although he hated the idea that before the aspens and cottonwoods turned yellow he was going to be dead.

Then, No, he thought: to hell with the prognosis. What did Abe Gallegos know anyway, that old womanizing rumpot? I'll live at least long enough to see the cottonwoods turn yellow, and after that happens, I think I'll take an extension until the first snow. And after I've seen the first snow, I plan to go ice-skating at least one more time on the natural ice rink in Balena Park, gracefully gliding around among all those plump, beautiful high-school girls in their long scarves and fluffy rabbit-fur collars and tight pants and snow-white figure skates with little bells or cottontail pom-poms on the laces. . . .

In the meantime, they would resurrect the *El Clarín*. They would do that, beginning today. They would locate somebody with a mimeograph machine, and between himself and Juan Ortega and Pat GeeGee and anybody else willing to volunteer, they would tell how April Delaney truly died and why, giving her an epitaph to fix her role within a historical context, keeping the sparks alive, at least, until all the fractured, disparate molecules across the nation could join into some unified, single connection able to affect the course of things.

Early morning sun suffused the valley, giving a golden glint to still-naked trees, lighting up the remaining irrigation ditches and rivers, sparkling off the steep tin roofs of the older houses.

Virgil remembered that tiny group of old men and women from his burnt-out hometown of Cuachitlán with their box full of precious documents. He remembered in vivid detail every one of their faces as they crossed the plaza to meet him on that day fifty-odd years ago, when they had gathered around him, opening the box, and had taken out the first of the invaluable records. And thinking of that he remembered other situations not personally experienced, historical moments which all his life had enabled him to have courage in the present and hope for the future. Mao Tse-tung in a tiny room somewhere, founding —with how many . . . ten? twelve? comrades—the Chinese Communist party. Young Eugene Debs in a Terre Haute meeting room waiting alone for union recruits to arrive—recruits who never came. And Fidel Castro high in the Cuban sierra with only twelve survivors from the disastrous Granma landing, arrogantly announcing over a battered radio that the days of the Batista dictatorship were numbered.

And Virgil felt confident, cancer or no cancer, because he knew he was on the correct historical side.

The old lawyer picked up a small stone and flung it as far off the hill as his feeble arm could project it. And as Virgil and the living people turned to leave, there was a gentle sigh in the air, a strange hot breath of wind that came from an antique place, and the misshapen, gritty

565

ghosts of all the dead gathered on that hilltop seemed at once to dissolve together, becoming a rich spiritual smoke that merged and swirled for a second. And then, suddenly, poignant streams of ethereal filaments seemed to flow directly into the wan bodies of Virgil and Juan Ortega and Pat GeeGee, and the others gathered in April's name. For a second, a wonderful foamy glow hovered at their stooped shoulders. Then only stray wisps of a mysterious mist played lightly against their necks and thinned-out hair. And the air around the summit sparkled invisibly with sensational clarity: Jesus Etcetera and his army had been absorbed.

Virgil said, "All right. Amen. Let us descend."

They had work to do.

# The best
# in modern fiction from
# BALLANTINE